STEPHANIE FLYNN

Small Fish Publishing
USA

Also By Stephanie Flynn

Find my catalog at StephanieFlynn.com

Immortal Protector series

0.5 Vampire's Distraction

1 Vampire's Deception

2 Vampire's Secret

3 Vampire's Promise

3.5 Elf Bound

4 Vampire's Demand

5 Vampire's Destruction

6 Vampire's Conquest

Immortal Protector Side Tales

Deer Holiday

Love Claws

Depths of the Heart

Matchmaker in Time series

0.5 Minutes to Live

1 Seconds to Act

2 Hours to Arrive

3 Days to Hide

4 Years to Savor

Pirates in Time series

1 Pirate's Prize

2 Pirate's Treasure

3 Pirate's Plunder

Time Travel Romance Shorts

Fateful Time

One Crazy Time

If you like your urban fantasy without the romance, too, check out
Stephanie Flynn's other name, Marie Flynn!

This is a work of fiction. Names, characters, places, and incidents either are the products of the author's imagination or are used fictitiously. Any resemblance to actual persons, living or dead, businesses, companies, events, or locales is entirely coincidental.

Copyright © 2021 Stephanie Flynn

All rights reserved. This book or parts thereof may not be reproduced in any form, stored in any retrieval system, or transmitted in any form by any means—electronic, mechanical, photocopy, recording, or otherwise—without prior written permission of the author, except as provided by United States of America copyright law.

First edition

Cover design by Stephanie Flynn
ISBN eBook: 9781952372520
ISBN paperback: 9781952372537

PIRATE'S PRIZE

STEPHANIE FLYNN

Small Fish Publishing
USA

Special Note

While the events of this novel are fiction, the pirate raid on the Spanish divers recovering the gold from the Plate Fleet Wreck of 1715 was real. To this day, millions of dollars in gold remain below the sea off the coast of Florida.

Chapter 1

At thirty-eight years old, Emily Porter had spent years scraping by to squirrel away some savings to change her life. She'd done the app coupons, gig jobs, careful budgeting, and apartment hopping when rents increased. And all this time, she'd never loosened the reins. She'd never 'lived' a little. Growing up in poverty, it was all she knew, and she vowed to never be there again.

When she'd met starry-eyed, ambitious Tyler, she was swept away with his big dreams. He'd convinced her to invest her savings in their new joint business venture. Their relationship was young for such a commitment, but at Emily's age, she didn't want to waste time.

She should've.

All the red flags were there, but her rose-colored glasses shrouded them in plain sight. And still, the business had yet to open. Emily hadn't signed any documents. All the while, Tyler spent much of his day lounging at home in pajamas, "working" from his phone, and Emily's day job hours had been cut. She needed a few bucks back to tide her over until the next payday. Text after text was met with excuses.

So she knocked on his door.

Confrontation was rarely a great idea, but Emily was beyond betrayed; she was furious. Her fist connected with his apartment door, likely angering the neighbors, but they hadn't lost five figures in life savings. A muted shuffling came from the other side of the hollow door. Emily stopped and waited.

The door opened to Tyler's surprised face. His hair was dishevelled, like she'd woken him up, and sweatpants hung low on his hips. A wrinkled T-shirt covered his smooth upper body. "Em? What brings you here?"

Normally, he'd move aside. "Are you going to invite me in?"

Tyler glanced over his shoulder as if Emily hadn't seen the mess before. "Now's not a good time."

Emily leaned in close for privacy's sake. "I need my money back. I've texted you many times."

"I saw," he said, but Emily waited a beat for an excuse that didn't come.

"And?" Emily prompted.

"And what?"

She was done being polite. "Give me my money back."

Tyler rubbed the nape of his neck in a dismissive gesture. "No can do. Sorry."

Finally, she got an answer, but it wasn't the one she wanted. "Excuse me?"

"I don't have it."

"Where is my money, Tyler?"

"It's invested." The casualness of the tone wasn't reassuring.

"This is the first I'm hearing about it. Do you have paperwork for me to sign?" Perhaps she'd been too impatient. Getting a business going did take some time. If Tyler was following through with his promises, she could scrape together a few more gig jobs.

"Why would I have paperwork for you?"

The fury zipped along her body, tensing her. "Partners need to sign paperwork to make the business official both for the city and the IRS. I know that much, Tyler. Don't patronize me."

"Partners?" Tyler said with a chuckle of disbelief. "Partners have to trust each other."

"I gave you all my money. Isn't that enough proof for you?"

A nearby door opened, and a cranky woman scowled at them before closing it again.

In a lower voice, Emily asked, "Can we finish this inside?"

"That's not the problem," Tyler said, ignoring her request for privacy again. "It's that I don't trust *you*. Every time I needed something, you failed to deliver. I can't go into business with someone who's flakey like that."

Emily couldn't believe what she was hearing. How could he consider her to be unreliable? How was that an excuse for the plans they'd made? "I sacrificed for years to save up that money, and I handed it to you up front...for this partnership. I don't understand why you think I'm flakey at all."

Tyler shook his head, but he hardly met her gaze. It was the same discomfort Emily had seen right before her father left her mother. That same crushing pile of guilt was written all over Tyler, and a rock settled in Emily's gut. Rather than own his choice head on, he was trying to avoid the confrontation, the pain.

"Tyler." Her voice lowered. The anger had already drained. The familiar, scary feeling of abandonment creeped under her skin. "Are you telling me there is no 'business' at all?"

His disinterested gaze swung back to her. "There's no business between us."

Emily had done everything right, everything he'd asked. All she wanted was to be loved and cherished by a partner who was committed to her and respectful. Tyler was slipping through her fingers like melted chocolate, the sweetest thing in her life slowly gliding away, and there was nothing she could do to stop it.

"Then what do you need from me? I want this to succeed. I believe in us." Emily reached out to touch his face, but he pulled back.

"Em, the bottom line is when I need you to do something immediately, I can't trust you to listen. Always questioning and so skeptical. We don't have the proper foundation to succeed. It's simply not there."

Emily dropped her hand. Each sentence was like a hammer's swing on her crumbling heart. Emily exhaled a deep breath. He was breaking up with her. "If that's how you feel, then I want my money back."

Tyler shook his head. "I told you the funds are invested."

Emily didn't see how that was an excuse. Sell the stock? Sell the equipment? "Cut me a check. Post-date it if you have to."

"Sorry, babe. Can't do that either."

She lifted her voice. Apartment walls be damned. "I want my money back now."

"That's not how this works." Tyler looked at the floor and smoothed the mop on his head. Emily finally saw the real man—a coward.

"You refuse to start a business with me, after you promised we would. I gave you my money to invest in said business, but now you won't return it. Am I getting this right?"

Tyler's mouth opened, but Emily held out a hand to stop him. "You're a lying, despicable thief."

For the first time since she'd met him, Tyler was speechless.

"Return my money or I'm taking you to court." Emily turned on her heels and left, marching down the apartment building hallway, head held high but tears on the verge of spilling.

From a partner sharing his big dreams to a cold thief in one conversation. Emily had a feeling the small claims division of the district court had too low of limits. She'd never had a reason to check, and she couldn't afford to retain an attorney.

He might've stolen her money, but he really stole her life.

And now the tears fell.

Chapter 2

EMILY HAD MANAGED A last-minute shopping gig on an app and pocketed enough coin to tide her over. But months passed, and after one sharply written letter from an attorney, Tyler still hadn't paid her. Shockingly, Emily didn't have the funds to hire additional services, and unshockingly, Tyler hadn't volunteered to return her money. Men who walked away from the women they loved, leaving them destitute, were absolute scum—unworthy of respect or another second of her time. Tyler joined that growing list alongside her father.

She never thought she would have to make a list in the first place, but she'd keep her eye out next time. No one else was going on that list.

Emily had one thing she was looking forward to—the Tall Ships festival. Since Tyler had no reason to use his ticket anymore and she didn't want to go alone, Emily asked her best friends, Robin Hall and Angela Foxe, to keep her company. Neither of them were fans of the idea, but since the festival would never come around Green Bay, Wisconsin, again, Emily couldn't miss this.

"Any word from Robin yet?" Angela asked from the driver's seat of her car. Emily and Angela worked for the same big-box retail store. Emily was usually assigned to stock shelves or to the supervision of the self-checkouts. She also volunteered to be on the first responders' team in case of a medical emergency. Angela was a tough chick who ran circles around the men in the warehouse. Unlike Emily, Angela was disgruntled by the boring khakis and the store's branded polo, so when Emily dangled the promise of a cute dress, Angela was in. Emily was grateful for a strong arm to lean on. Angela had survived heartbreak—worse than Emily's—and the woman was tough as nails about it.

After a few pints of ice cream and a haircut.

Emily rode shotgun, her body tingling with excitement and anticipation. The international Tall Ships festival had journeyed up the Great Lakes for a weekend visit. People all around gathered to explore maritime history—including both privateers and pirates. Others, weirdos like Emily, would dress in pirate cosplay, showing their fascination with an antique world only seen in movies and books. She checked her screen, and apparently in her single-track focus today, she'd forgotten to unmute her phone. "Oh, yeah. She says she'll meet us there."

"Think she'll show?" Angela asked.

Robin was reserved. A new police officer to the force, she had something to prove while being careful. Robin Hall had a public image to maintain, but after much more begging, Robin reluctantly agreed, too. "I hope so."

"Me, too," Angela said, navigating the car into the lot of the downtown riverside park. Down the hill, naked masts reached for the sky, their sails furled for safety. The moment the shifter moved into park, Emily sprung from the vehicle.

Since it was the middle of summer, and the Halloween stores weren't open yet, Emily urged her friends to order bagged costumes online to join her in spirit. Emily had spent years handcrafting her outfit of brown leather boots, knee breeches, and a leather jerkin over a white tunic, which hid a tank top with a built-in bra. She wore it to every Halloween party and afterward adjusted it as needed for durability, flexibility, and comfort. Last year's party at the University of Wisconsin Green Bay left her with a splash of beer on her tunic. Angela had said it made her shirt more authentic, but Emily explained pirates at sea didn't drink beer, and she still wanted to wear the tunic she'd sewed. Emily spent far too long carefully cleaning the fabric before the stain set in and ruined all her hard work. To finish out her look, Emily's shoulder-length blonde hair was covered under a red kerchief, leaving only a loose lock on the side of her face. A dress couldn't give her feminine curves, not that she'd wear one, anyway.

Angela climbed out of the car and smoothed her dress. "I don't know," she said with pleasant surprise. "This feels a little sexy." Angela chose a ruffled high-low dress, off-the-shoulder black blouse, and a decorative corset on top—the typical pirate wench outfit. Angela twirled the material. "I could get into this."

"You look amazing. Come here." Emily hooked her arm around Angela's and pulled her close for a selfie. Angela's car was in the background, but it didn't matter. Emily didn't want to forget anything about this day. After a few different angles and faces, Emily pulled her best friend through the parking lot and down to the admissions tent.

The excitement put a spring in her step, and while waiting for the line to shorten, she beamed at the ships docked behind them. Emily had purchased tickets months ago, but to board a ship, she needed the stamp on her hand. She pulled out her phone, opened the email confirmation, and brought up the barcoded ticket that granted her access to the ship and a sail tour. She and Tyler were supposed to have a romantic sail on the bay this afternoon, but instead, Robin and Angela were her plus-ones, and she wouldn't trade their company for anything, certainly not a despicable thief who shall not be named again.

"Thanks. I think I like it. When you told me about this stuff, I was thinking of Captain Jack Sparrow, and drunks with too much rum." Angela wriggled her fingers at a guy walking by, and his eyes raked her curvy body. "But I can see why you like this stuff."

Emily's hobby involved pretending to be something she wasn't, daydreaming of a world that no longer existed. She'd been born and raised in Wisconsin, and she'd always dreamed of taking to the seas and sailing away. But her parents weren't interested, if they could afford it, and after Dad ran off, it wasn't in the cards—not even a commercial cruise based out of Florida. When winter came around each year, Emily spent her time reading research materials with contradicting information. And she'd maintain or add to her outfit. Slowly she'd built her savings to change her life—school, a business, or even a round-the-world cruise.

Frankly, she wanted the cruise, but since it was an irresponsible use of funds, she'd held back. And now that wasn't even an option anymore. So this ride on a historical recreation of a seventeenth century ship was the best she was ever getting, and thinking of how close she was brought tears to her eyes.

"There's a few hot guys here, Em. I bet we can find a sexy captain for you."

The idea should be appealing, someone with the same interest as her, but Emily wasn't done with the long-reaching effects of Tyler's betrayal. "I'm not ready to dive back into the dating pool."

"In that case, let's get drinks."

The line shifted closer. "There's no alcohol served."

After a flash of disappointment, Angela said, "Maybe I was talking about the slushies."

"A slushy sounds great." Emily smiled and glanced longingly over her shoulder, trying to convince herself she was finally here. A light breeze sent gentle waves lapping at the dock, and seagulls drifted in the sky, sleek white and gray against the shining sun.

Emily never wanted to forget this. She had been at the festival for a few minutes already, and she hadn't thought to document this momentous day. She pulled her cell phone out of her pouch and nudged Angela. "Say cheese."

Making sure the ships were in the background, Emily snapped a few goofy-faced pictures and several sweet ones. "Robin better get here soon. I need pics with her too."

"Did she send you an update?" Angela craned her neck through the thickening crowd.

Emily checked her phone. "Nothing yet." She took a step closer and skimmed too. About half the festival attendees were decked out like Emily, and she smiled at the plush parrot stitched to a man's shoulder. A woman strolling by wore envious boots with her hair in long red ringlets, reminding Emily of the famous pirate Anne Bonny. Yep, these were her people.

Finally reaching the booth, Emily flashed her digital ticket. The festival worker squinted at the screen. Oh, no. She could not be denied entrance now. Setting down the phone, Emily said, "I have the paper ones in here." In a hurry, she dug in her pouch tied around her waist, fishing for the folded paper she'd printed ahead of time.

"I can see them well enough. Hold out your hand." The worker reached for the ink pad. Emily and Angela held out the backs of their hands and received a cold, wet stamp each. "Have a good time."

Emily beamed. "We will. Thanks!"

Emily slipped the phone back into her pouch, next to her emergency sewing kit, travel sized bottle of ibuprofen, a few first aid items, and some individually wrapped chocolates as a pick-me-up. She expected the vendor food to be a little out of her budget. Emily had thought of everything, and nothing was going to interrupt this awesome day. They headed down the hill toward the water, but Angela tugged her in the wrong direction. Emily protested. "The ships are that way."

"We have to wait for Robin, so let's go shopping! Look at all those vendors just waiting for money. My treat?"

After toeing the line of homelessness too many times, shopping had never appealed to Emily. But she'd set aside funds in case a fellow enthusiast was selling anything that tickled her inner pirate. And Emily was thrilled to see Angela enjoy herself. For that, she could wait to board the ship just a little longer. "I can cover my own. Don't worry about it."

Rows of yellow tents with folding tables bisected the festival grounds. Angela pulled her past several vendors with wares that didn't interest her. "Who wants to buy a fake sword, anyway?"

"I do prefer real ones," Emily said, half joking. The closest thing to a sword she'd ever wielded was a honking, serrated bread knife. But when she regularly cut herself, she could rock a sewing kit like a beast.

"Maybe I can knock one of these hot guys over the head with one, and you can play Emergency Response Team. He might need CPR. You brought your sewing kit, right?" Angela teased with a wicked grin.

"Never leave home without it, but Robin's going to be here soon. I don't need either of us arrested for assault, no matter how hot the guy is."

"Eh, you're no fun."

Emily chuckled and kept moving at Angela's insistence. In the back corner, slightly away from the other vendors, was a withered old woman, sitting in front of glass display cases. Angela leaned closer and gasped.

"What is it?" Emily asked, gazing back at the dock. She patiently waited to hear the creak of the ancient wood beneath her feet as they glided across the calm bay and wished it was the aquamarine blues of the Caribbean Sea.

"How beautiful! Oh, Em, check these out. They'd go great with almost anything."

Emily leaned in. Necklaces and bracelets hung on clear hooks. They were pretty, and they looked expensive—sparkly colors, shiny metals, and ornate patterns. "You could have one for each outfit."

"Good morning, ladies." The old woman stood from her squeaky chair, her raspy voice not much above a whisper. "See anything you like?"

"Everything is beautiful!" Angela pressed a fit to her chest, enamored.

"I can certainly wrap up everything." The old woman chuckled. "But I sense something in the two of you. Especially you." The woman stared at Emily.

"Me?" Emily asked, now paying attention.

"You'd rather be somewhere else. Somewhere far from here." Her crooked finger tapped her knowing temple. She was a little creepy.

Sure, Emily would love to be in the tropics on a sailing cruise, but that was a dream, and this was reality. Glancing at the tall ships anchored at the dock, there was literally nowhere else on earth she'd rather be. Emily smiled. The slightly strange woman was way off. "Not at all. I've been dreaming of seeing ships like these my entire life, and I can't believe they're here. I never want them to go."

"I suspected some wistful thinking there. I have just the thing for you. Come here." The frail vendor urged them to come around to the side of the tent, and she bent down, crooked fingers unlocking a small wooden chest. Emily smiled at its authentic look—like an ancient treasure chest. Now that was something she'd like to have in her collection.

The woman lifted something sparkly, and in the palm of her hand, she held a pair of necklaces. "These powerful gems have been known to grant your truest desire while protecting you from bad humors, so be careful how you use them."

The necklaces sounded cursed, and now Emily was fascinated. Why buy a purple amethyst when you could have one that was haunted with stories of the past? Emily and Angela each took one. The pretty purple gemstones hung on a copper chain, and the ends of them were dipped in melted copper. Not too flashy, a little rustic, and somewhat antique. She loved it.

"How much?" Emily asked immediately.

"Yeah," Angela added. "I'll take this one too."

"Five dollars each." The old woman smiled again.

Emily hated to take advantage. "Come again?"

Angela said, "We'll take these both, but do you have more? We have a friend we're waiting for. She'd just die for one, too."

The old woman chuckled. "If I sense they need them, your friend will get one as well. Let me bag those for you." She held out her hand, and both Emily and Angela returned them for packaging.

While the woman bent to bag them up, Angela dug in her purse and whispered, "This lady's crazy! Five bucks? Can't even get a sandwich for that."

Emily freed a pair of fives, intent on paying a little more to ease the guilt. "They're worth way more than that."

The old woman stood and refused to accept anything beyond the five she'd asked for. With a shrug, Emily and Angela completed the transaction and accepted small brown paper bags with handles.

"Thanks, lady!" Angela said, waving, and they strolled toward the ships. "I still can't believe something this beautiful was so cheap."

"We offered, and she refused," Emily said. "Come on. The barque is open." This time, Emily dragged Angela to the ship, flashed their hand stamps, and walked up the gangway. Emily grinned like a loon and marveled at each step, memorizing it forever.

"What about Robin?" Angela followed.

Emily rubbed the wood rail with her palm, and giddiness rushed through her. Her cheeks hurt already, but still, she couldn't stop smiling. "She'll be here. I'm just going to absorb this whole ship while I can." There were plaques mounted in different areas of the ship, explaining what happened in the past and what the living conditions were like. A vendor sold T-shirts and mugs in the corner, branded with the ship's name. The boards underfoot shifted with each step. The scent of the bay was so much stronger here, and the gentle movements under the lapping of the water were a relaxing sway. She would never be able to sleep on a ship like this. She wondered how the crew did it. Not because of the motion, but because this was a ship from history. Emily lifted out her phone and started snapping pictures.

"You sound like a sponge." Angela said, scanning the faces climbing aboard. "We should've dragged a few hot guys on this tour."

Emily gazed up at the crow's nest, wondering if she could take a trip up the ratlines for a view.

She'd never come down.

"Ladies, for safety packages are not allowed." A member of the ship's crew, wearing neat and clean ship-branded clothing, appeared out of nowhere. He had a sexy accent. "There's a basket on land to store your belongings." Without waiting for a response, he moved on to the next offender.

"There's your hot guy for the tour," Emily said.

Angela snorted. "I am a sucker for an accent."

Emily too.

Just off the ship was a large crate guarded by the man checking stamps.

"I'm not leaving this behind to get stolen," Angela whispered.

"Me neither. He didn't say we couldn't wear them." Emily shrugged.

"True." Angela and Emily dug their necklaces out of their bags and slipped them over their heads.

In the blink of an eye, something went wrong.

Very wrong.

Chapter 3

"Stowaway!" A barrel-chested man with an English accent pointed at her accusingly. He wasn't wearing the branded polo like the staff member had been. This guy was rough and dirty—very authentic, and a little scary.

Emily's cheeks flushed at the embarrassment of being singled out. She still held the vendor bag in her hand. She sheepishly smiled and waved it. "It's empty. No rules broken here."

"Sweep the hold for others!" he commanded, in character at a level even Emily admired.

Threadbare cosplayers dashed around the deck to obey orders. None of these people looked like fellow tourists—no cameras, no sunglasses, no sandals, no silly Hawaiian shirts or costumes from a bag. No plush parrots sewed to their shoulders. Perhaps these men were the real crew, who'd come from below deck for the sailing tour.

Emily looked down. The color of the wood was different. Scanning the ship's details, the plaques were gone, and underfoot was a galleon. She swore she'd boarded a barque. The vendor selling T-shirts and mugs in the corner was gone.

Had Emily blacked out? She hadn't been drinking. She didn't take anything unusual.

Emily turned. Where was Angela? Did she find someone to take below deck?

Did Emily hit her head, and now she was dreaming? Or in all her excitement to experience the ships of history, a lifelong dream turned reality, did she concoct a believable fantasy? A true hallucination? She'd built up this moment so much, she'd finally snapped. Emily lifted her hand and touched the copper chain holding the amethyst pendant she'd tucked under her tunic. So her mental break began after their trip to the withered old lady.

If Emily was trapped in her head, she was going to damn well enjoy it.

The large pungent man gripped her arm with a squeeze of a constrictor snake preparing its next meal.

The smile fell from her face. Maybe not so much. Why would she include someone like this in her fantasy?

"Nobody swindles a ride on this vessel." His breath was unfortunate—stale and yeasty.

Going with the flow of her unusual choice to include this guy in her fantasy, Emily twisted her arm from his crushing grasp. "I'm not a stowaway! I bought a ticket, and I can prove it. It's right here." Emily ruffled into the leather pouch tied around her waist and produced the backup paper ticket she'd printed at home. She held it out in offering and the wind rustled it. But the meaty man glared at her, refusing to look at it.

In a lightning-quick strike, he backhanded her cheek, sending stings like dozens of rubber bands snapping across her face. Tears involuntarily filled her eyes. The ticket flitted to the deck and blew through the bulwark and into the water.

Emily cupped her cheek, and her mouth popped open. She wasn't one to demand a manager, since she'd dealt with those kinds of complaints at work frequently, but assault was justified. Emily didn't think this guy would hand over his manager's digits, though. Besides, this was a fantasy. Although it was becoming a little too twisted, even for her tastes.

"Hold your disobedient tongue in the presence of one Captain Donald Sinclair." The captain sneered and ran his beady eyes over her. "You'll earn your unlawful boarding. Scrub the deck." While glaring at her with unwarranted hatred, he shouted, "Fergus! Bring the scoundrel a bucket of water and a brush."

"Aye, sir," Fergus answered, a Scottish man by accent and thin as a twig with bushy red hair. He appeared no older than twenty years of age as he dashed below deck.

The captain leaned in close, as if searching her for a hidden truth, and Emily leaned back. "You're not of King George's country. Where are you from?"

The tall ships traveled the world, visiting groups of ports at a time, and right now, they were sailing the Great Lakes, ergo, the USA. But his grip and his slap hurt, even in her fantasy. She needed to be careful, and she wanted to know what year her hallucination brought her to. There were several King Georges throughout history. "Which King George?"

Apparently, that was the wrong answer. The captain bristled, leaning back to spew his next angry accusation. "The one and only! His majesty took over the Crown just over a year ago. Are you illiterate? Where are you from?"

King George the first began his rule in 1714, so a year later put her in the year 1715. A century not known for being kind to women on ships. Emily felt herself shrink down. What would make the captain less suspicious? "An island off the coast of the colonies," she answered with a slight question, hoping to avoid another slap.

The captain's sharp eye zeroed in on her copper chain. Before she could twist away, the captain's meaty hand squeezed her shoulder, holding her in place, and the other tore the necklace from around her throat. He scrutinized his ill-gotten gains, face darkening as he wound up for the next lashing.

Escape. All she could think of was escaping. Emily looked for the gangway, but it was gone. She spun. Nothing but glinting bright blue waters stretched on the horizon. Where were Michigan's shores? Wisconsin's? Her fantasy really filled out the details. Even the air felt...salty. Emily faced the captain again. Unfortunately, too many details.

"Thief! You dare steal from my ship? From the Sea Trading Company?" The captain shook her necklace and growled his words in pure rage. "You know what the punishment is for theft."

Anything she might tell him would end with another slap. Emily shook her head, breath caught in her throat. The captain slipped the purple gem into a pocket in his breeches just as the twiggy redhead returned with the bucket and a brush.

"Sir, as ye requested." Fergus set them down and scurried back to work without delay.

Ignoring Fergus's interruption, the captain said, "The cat. Ever heard of it?"

Emily nodded, so she didn't anger him further. She'd read about the cat-o'-nine-tails, a whip with nine lengths and nine knots at the ends. Was this some form of self-punishment? Was she conjuring this physical pain as punishment for her stupidity in falling for Tyler's thievery? If that was the case, she was over it. She was over Tyler's betrayal, and this whipping was unnecessary.

"Swab this deck clean enough to eat from, while I determine how many lashes I'll be personally delivering." The captain smirked and shoved her bodily to the deck. She landed with a sharp pain to her knee, and the captain hawked a loogie right by her leg.

Gross. Emily's face curled with disgust. The filthy captain, a greedy, selfish brute, strolled away with her necklace, but he had the audacity to accuse her of thievery and punish her with a whipping for it. Emily wasn't waiting around for it. She needed to find Angela and get the hell off this ship…

…or out of her own head.

She hated to go there, but she did—would the whipping wake her out of this twisted version of the history she adored? And if this was her fantasy, she would've included her best friend. So where was Angela? Emily craned her neck but couldn't see her. She couldn't hear her either.

"Angela?" she called carefully, so the captain wouldn't return with more excuses to punish her.

No response from anyone. The crew moved around on deck, attending their duties.

"Angela?"

No laughter, no screams of ecstasy or shrieks of terror. Was she unconscious?

Emily's knee ached, and if the slap on the cheek and the squeeze of the shoulders were indicators, Emily would rather figure out something else than endure a whipping. Emily grimaced at the condition of the deck, stood up, and craned her neck around. Blue-green waters of the Caribbean. Salty air. A small rocky projection was within swimming distance, but that would be a different sort of punishment.

Her fantasy really did the details well.

Some could've been left out.

The twig Fergus rushed up to her and pointed at the deck. In a low voice, he said, "Return tae work right noo. If th'captain sees ye shirking orders, he'll add many more lashes. Trust me when I say ye dinny want them."

"But—"

"Dinny argue. Jus' dae." Fergus set his jaw firmly and glared at her in warning.

Emily folded down on her aching knees. Expecting the redhead to stand by to make sure she followed orders, she lifted the wire brush and dunk it into the water. She started brushing and looked up for approval, but Fergus was gone.

Emily sighed. The deck was covered in bird droppings, smears of blood, and liquids of unknown origin. She stroked the bristles across the wood planks. Overhead, sails flapped as they lost the wind. She shielded her eyes against the sun to watch the meager crew climb the ratlines and adjust the yardarms. Wood groaned its protest. There was no joy in their dirty faces, nor pride in their work, and no downtime. They were machines, not men happy to be at sea.

Emily herself struggled to find the enjoyment she expected to find on a ship. She continued lazily scrubbing, determined to never complain about public toilets again. She worked her way around barrels of whatever goods the ship traded, careful not to get stepped on. Her arm was tired already. She swiped a sweaty forearm across her forehead, wishing for a shower.

Loud boots approached across the hardwood, alerting Emily to the captain's return. A pit formed in her stomach. She exhaled a shaky breath and stood.

Captain Donald Sinclair carried the famous whip in his hand and an unnervingly friendly demeanor. "You'll be pleased to discover I've sentenced you to only ten lashes. The entire crew shall be watching—as a warning to them, as much as to you."

At the terrible news, Emily's eyes darted over the rail. The desolate spit of land was long gone. How else was she going to get out of this? Men were treated worse than dogs on this ship, and a woman would be so much worse, Emily didn't want to imagine it. But if the captain meant to whip her, there were two things the crew was bound to notice.

The captain gripped her forearm—as if she'd planned to escape. "Secure the stowaway for punishment!"

A pair of grimy men captured her arms and pulled her face forward to the mainmast. This was going to happen, and she was out of ideas.

Emily struggled against their grip and cried out, "Please don't! I beg of you. I didn't stowaway, and I didn't steal anything. The necklace is mine, I swear!"

The men strapped her wrists, forcing her to hug the mast.

Fergus leaned in close and tugged on the binds. He whispered, "Dinny fight it. Captain won't quit 'til it's done. Th'more ye struggle, th'worse it feels."

Hot tears stung her cheeks while the two men wrenched the biting rope. "Please. Make him stop."

"I canny. Nae one can," he said softly. "But I wish I could."

The men and Fergus left her, and time stretched as Emily awaited the first searing strike. She squeezed her eyelids shut and wished she'd taken a chance swimming with the sharks.

From behind her, the captain said, "This is what befalls any of you for stealing passage or merchandise from the Sea Trading Company. Fergus, cut away the jerkin."

Emily's heart punched up her throat. She sucked in a desperate breath, and yanked and twisted her wrists, rope biting into her flesh. They couldn't find out her secret. This couldn't be happening. When was she going to wake up?

Chapter 4

"Sails!" a voice called from above her. Emily craned her neck the best she could. In the crow's nest, a man pointed south. She followed his finger. Sails at a distance were approaching.

"What colors does she fly?" Captain Donald Sinclair responded with an unusual edge to his voice, almost a hint of fear. The captain lifted a spyglass from his pocket and held it to his eye as he surveyed the horizon.

Thrilled for a delay in her unfit punishment, Emily frantically attempted to escape her binds. And then what? She didn't know, but staying here and doing nothing was not in her nature. How did she go from the happiest day of her life to prepared for a whipping that was infamously cruel?

She remembered boarding the barque, certain it was a barque. Then an employee of the Tall Ships organization told her no merchandise was allowed. So, she and Angela had put on their matching necklaces rather than leave them ashore and risk their theft. The irony only frustrated Emily more.

The withered old lady had said, 'These powerful gems have been known to grant your true desire...' Emily had wished for an adventure on the sea since she was young, and here she was, but she didn't care what anyone said—magic wasn't real. The possibility of time travel was ludicrous, scientifically impossible.

But the condition of this galleon and its crew was far too real to be cosplay alone. The soft blue-green waves and gentle salty breeze of tropical air were damned convincing. Had the necklace transported her through time by some mystical means? Then Emily's only way home was to put on the magic necklace again. But how was she going to find it? And where was Angela?

"She's flying the French colors!" the crewman above shouted back.

Captain Sinclair dropped the spyglass and grunted. He collapsed the tool and lowered it to his side.

"Shall we attempt communications, captain?" Fergus asked carefully.

"All hands bring her to!" the captain shouted, and the crew sprang into action, leaving Emily stranded and helpless.

The captain approached and sniveled in her ear, "Expect to receive your punishment after my dealings with the French. Refrain from attempting to escape. There's nowhere for you to go." He chuckled.

A glint of light came from his pocket—her necklace poked out of his breeches. He still had it! If she could free herself and rush him, she could steal it back and put it on before anyone could catch her. It was the best plan she had. It was the only plan.

The captain returned to the rail with the spyglass, keeping tabs on the incoming ship.

Emily worked at the ropes binding her hands while the crew slowed the behemoth ship. She had learned passing ships frequently shared information on the seas, so Captain Sinclair's decision to slow wasn't alarming, and Emily was grateful for the extended reprieve.

"Th'vessel's approaching rapidly." Fergus stood at his shoulder. "She'll be wit'in firing distance soon. Is she a man-o'-war?"

"Barque." The captain's eye flashed, and the color drained from his face. Something was wrong. "Jorgenson!"

A bulky crew member rushed to the captain's side, ready for orders.

"Gather all available hands and hide the provisions in the carpenter's walk."

Jorgenson nodded, and men scurried below deck with fear on their brows. They knew what was happening, but Emily didn't. She could guess it wasn't good. She twisted, pulling at her ropes, trying to stretch the length just enough to slip free.

"To the rest of you, brace round forward, and set the courses. Flank speed immediately!" The captain slipped the spyglass into his pocket and paced the deck, ignoring Emily. The crew adjusted the sails to catch the ocean breeze. Instead of slowing, he was metaphorically running. What caused the sudden change in plans?

Emily's wrists ached as she pulled at the ropes holding her prisoner, and the roughness cut through her skin.

The boom of a cannon echoed across the water, and the shot splashed alarmingly close by—a warning even Emily understood. The captain raised the spyglass to his eye once again. "Belay those orders!" he shouted with a quiver in his voice.

Fergus returned to the captain's side while keeping an eye on the crew's work. "Sir, have the French signaled us?"

Emily strained around the mast. The other ship was close enough to see. The French flag lowered with jerky movements, and a black flag with a skull and crossbones took its place. "You got to be kidding me." For a second, she chuckled at the ludicrousness of it all. Pirates? Actual pirates? The real ones were nothing like the movies. If she thought Captain Donald Sinclair was an animal, pirates were the things animals feared. Snapping herself back to this unbelievable reality, she struggled harder, heart pumping, ears ringing. She had to get that necklace from Sinclair's pocket and disappear.

"Strike the colors," the captain ordered, all the wind his in proverbial sails gone.

"Sir?" Fergus asked, confused, and turned to see for himself.

The captain's intimidating posture slid away. This was one of defeat. "She's flying the black, and she's too fast to outrun. We're surrendering."

"But captain," Fergus protested. "Th'owners forbid such an act."

Another cannon boomed from the pirate ship, but this one crunched wood on impact.

"Would you prefer death to being discharged? Now do as you're told!"

Refusing to surrender to pirates was the equivalent of consenting to fight. Pirates chose nimble ships for their speed, and they carried many men and plenty of guns. Merchant ships were the exact opposite—under-crewed, under-protected, and cumbersome to maneuver. Neither side wanted to fight. Pirates didn't want to take damage, and merchants didn't want to lose their trade goods. No one wanted a ship to repair either.

The smartest choice was to surrender, allow the pirates to take what they wanted and leave, but some weren't so amicable. The most ruthless would slaughter the crew for sport or spite. If Captain Sinclair's orders weren't followed quickly enough, the pirates just might make an example out of them.

Wild-eyed, Fergus rushed to lower the English flag. While the helmsman held the wheel steady with the wind, the rest of the crew joined the captain. Everyone huddled at the starboard side, watching their impending fate unfold.

Emily was helplessly forgotten at the mast.

The merchant crew numbered about a dozen and a half. As the pirate ship approached, their opponents lining the rail numbered over seventy, maybe eighty. Dirty, sweaty, leather-tanned faces snarled at them as the barque closed the distance.

Emily's heart pounded harder. Sweat beaded on her forehead and chest, and she fought her scratching binds like her life depended on it.

"Dear, god," Captain Sinclair whispered. "Lemoine's coming."

He and the crew scrambled away from the rail as grappling hooks soared through the sky, landing like a string of muffled gunshots. A charge was shouted, and dozens of pirates lowered gangplanks and crossed over. Some jumped on the rigging with cutlasses and pistols at the ready. The pirates swarmed the deck like locusts, encapsulating the merchant crew, ready to devour their prey.

Emily shivered, arms aching, wrists burning and bleeding, not wanting to believe any of this was real.

From the sea of filthy testosterone, a single pirate stepped forward and approached the merchant captain. He was dazzling and completely handsome. A friendly smile lit up his brown eyes, and sunlight glinted off a gold earring. A sexy, neatly trimmed beard gave him a ruggedness Emily hadn't seen outside of the movies. He stood a few inches taller than her five-foot-nine height, and while his hands were empty, a cutlass and pistol hung from a belt. This contrast to the rest of the crew led Emily to believe this man, wearing a dark cocked hat over wavy brown locks tied at the nape of his neck, was their captain. He oozed confidence, as if he owned all these men, and they'd run into the line of fire for him. Judging by their rough appearances, that was likely true.

Captain Donald Sinclair paled, and the pirate captain strutted over to him. The merchant captain displayed a gruesome personality on his sleeve. But the cheerfulness of the pirate captain made him more dangerous. He enjoyed stealing from others, inciting fear in their hearts, and terrifying their minds.

Emily had made too many mistakes in the man department. She would no longer be swayed by a pretty face. This one was a despicable thief and proud of it.

"Let me be first to thank you for surrendering, good sir. You have made the wise decision to save us bloodshed. I'm Captain Lemoine of the *Sea Lion*. While my crew searches your hold, I'll be the judge of your trial." His voice was smooth, charismatic, and lilted with a swoon-worthy French accent—a trifecta of danger.

The other crew members quickly relieved Sinclair of his goods, carrying the barrels from below deck across to the pirate ship. The quartermaster recorded the ill-gotten goods on paper.

"Trial?" the merchant captain repeated with raised brows. "I did nothing wrong. We surrendered. Take what you must and leave us in peace!"

Captain Lemoine shook his head with amusement. "That's not how this works." He signaled with a nod, and a handful of pirates captured Sinclair and dragged him toward Emily at the mast, but they paused and traded looks of confusion.

The brutish merchant captain stared Emily down with wild eyes. But he didn't apologize. She had nothing to say to him except, "Give me my necklace."

The anger returned to his features, and any sympathy Emily carried vanished.

"Captain?" one of Sinclair's captors prompted.

Pirate Captain Lemoine swaggered toward her and scratched as the scruff on his chin. Despite her much better judgment, Emily's heart sped up as he assessed her appearance, deep brown eyes raking her from head to toe and back. Heat sizzled—did he like what he saw? Because Captain Lemoine was very easy on the eyes, and if she had half of Angela's mind, she'd take him...

Captain Sinclair uttered a soft noise of terror, snapping her out of the ridiculous fantasy. The horrible brute was terrified of this handsome, charismatic pirate, so Emily's fear surged as Captain Lemoine reached her. Was he simply excited to decide on a new punishment for her?

"You, sailor, what have you done?" Captain Lemoine demanded with playful curiosity, while both merchant and pirate crews watched her.

But all Emily could see was Captain Lemoine. Up close, Emily guessed he was around forty years old and far too attractive for this vile life he lived. She glanced at Sinclair again for a reminder. Attractive or not, this pirate was not a knight in shining armor here to rescue her.

She had to stick to the plan—retrieve her necklace and find Angela. Then go home.

Captain Eric Lemoine needed a win today. So far, things were looking better than average without any loss or damage to his ship. The crew secured their prize, and that meant he could keep his hide intact for one more account. Most of the time, Captain Lemoine dreaded the standard trial and torture of the rival captain, but not this time. Captain Donald Sinclair was a nasty fellow, and he deserved the darkest pain Lemoine could conjure from the bowels of the seas.

And he'd take pleasure in it.

But Captain Lemoine hadn't expected to interrupt a punishment in progress. The promise of disparaging Sinclair to his face lifted Lemoine's spirits beyond what he'd thought possible lately. He didn't need to don a facade at all for this. But when he'd laid eyes on the prisoner in question, Lemoine was taken aback. His focus shifted.

The prisoner's clothes looked proper, but there was something off about them. They were too clean. The materials were too new. The cut was custom-made. He appeared weaker than his counterparts, but yet well-nourished. And the prisoner's face was...stunning. There was a fire behind those smart eyes warring with terror. A spark of life unheard of among these seadogs. And mid-thirties in age, if he had to guess—not at all the usual range for sailors. This prisoner didn't seem to be a merchant sailor at all.

Lemoine didn't typically find himself fancying men, but there was something about this one that left him both puzzled and fascinated. He needed to know everything about him.

Scratching at his beard in amusement, Captain Lemoine repeated his demand, unsatisfied until it was answered, "Why are you tied to the mast?"

"The captain stole my necklace, but claimed I was the thief." The prisoner's voice was lighter than he'd expected, with almost a feminine lilt, and that excited Lemoine even more. This prisoner was certainly not like the others.

"Preposterous," the nasty fellow declared. "He's a stowaway and a thief!"

Ah, the heart of the accusation. One clearly punishable by whipping, but rather than dole out the earned punishment, Captain Lemoine's curiosity only grew. Instead of booking proper passage, this man stowed away, which could only lead Lemoine to believe this prisoner was on the run. He didn't want to be found. But why was a man running with a necklace, of all things?

"What does this necklace look like?" Captain Lemoine asked as a test of his powers of deduction. A liar wouldn't have specifics at the ready, and he hoped, for the prisoner's sake, the accusations were false. Not just because he wanted to slight the captain. Lemoine couldn't see himself harming this prisoner.

"It's amethyst on a copper chain, and it's still in his right pocket."

That was perfect. With a satisfactory grin, Captain Lemoine approached his rival and searched his pocket, revealing the gem matching the description.

"This the one?" Captain Lemoine asked, holding it for him to see.

"It is. Please give it back." His words were a gentle plea.

Captain Lemoine lifted up the symbol of innocence, and a noise of admiration followed. It wasn't for Lemoine's efforts to prove Sinclair's disturbing countenance. No, that was well known. The noise was for the appeared value of the gem. Likely stolen, and that was the reason the prisoner ran. Lemoine would free this prisoner, but he still wasn't satisfied.

Captain Lemoine tucked the necklace into his own breast pocket. Now the prisoner would not leave until Captain Lemoine was finished with him.

Chapter 5

Captain Lemoine was a pirate, so Emily shouldn't have been surprised by his actions. But since she'd asked nicely, she thought he'd be a decent person and hand it over. Instead, all the terror she might've entertained was smothered by fury. "That's mine! You can't take it," Emily shouted at his back.

Captain Lemoine turned and smiled. "You'll do well to thank me."

Emily flinched. "What? For what?"

Captain Lemoine gestured, and a pair of other men, not currently securing Captain Donald Sinclair, moved to the back of the mast and freed her. All the wind in her proverbial sails stalled out. At his shocking kindness, she was no longer irate, but she couldn't stomach gratitude. Emily rubbed her cracked and bleeding wrists.

Captain Lemoine closed the distance between them, and the scent of leather, salty sweat, and a splash of rum filled her nose. As she'd guessed, he stood a few inches taller than her, the perfect kissing height. "You're welcome," he said softly.

There was an intimacy in his tone, and Emily was speechless. She should've been afraid. She should've hated him. Logically, she should assault his person and forcibly take her necklace back, but she didn't. Emily stood inches from this man, his eyes memorizing every inch of her, while dozens of men watched. Captain Lemoine was no knight in shining armor, but he did save her.

Before Emily could ask for the necklace again, the captain casually gestured. This time, Captain Sinclair was tied to the mast, face outward, reminding Emily of this sexy man's incredible danger. With Captain's Lemoine's attention shifted, Emily melted into the remaining merchant crew, finding a small safety in Fergus's presence.

"What's going to happen?" she whispered.

Fergus bent down to her ear. "They're gunna give th'crew a chance tae make a case against th'captain, and if the pirate chooses, he'll kill him."

Emily was disgusted by the brute who intended to strip her half naked, whip her to within an inch of her life, and then...do whatever he wanted with a helpless woman. She couldn't watch, but she couldn't look away either. As much as she didn't condone this type of public display, she wanted to know what kind of person Captain Lemoine was. When he'd freed her, there was a spark between them. She was sure of it. But why did Captain Sinclair mumble his name in terror when the pirates approached?

Both crews formed a thick circle around the mast, but the pirates kept the merchant crew collected in a nervous group. Captain Lemoine paced and began his trial. "Merchant sailors! Has this man done you any wrongs?" The crew twitched and fidgeted, as if afraid of punishment for speaking out. Emily would've added her voice if her dilemma wasn't already known. "Has this captain been fair to you all? Rations plenty? Wages satisfactory?"

Fergus stepped forward. "When a storm hit, th'ship rocked tumultuously, an' I dropped a ration in th'mess, purely oan accident. But I ate it wi'out complaint. None was wasted at all. The captain declared me an inept, blundering fool, and I begged fur mercy under th'cat."

Fergus had implied he'd experienced the whip, but the irrational and excessive use of force still shocked her. The captain really was going to whip her just for possessing a necklace.

"Anyone else?" Captain Lemoine prompted.

Another man, more like a boy, stepped forward and cleared his throat. "Captain Sinclair docked my wages and removed my rations for two days, because I fell asleep on the night watch. I did mean to!"

"Fair enough," Captain Lemoine said as a means of accepting his testimony, not agreeing with the punishment given. "Any others? I want the full truth. And I promise no consequences shall befall any of you."

When the pirates swarmed over, cutlasses and pistols at the ready, she'd expected a bloodbath, not a fair trial. Emily was baffled at the kindness shown to the merchant crew.

"Aye, sir," a deeper voice came from the crowd, and a hefty man stepped forward. "I was repairing a hole in the hull, but the hammer smarted my thumb, and I shouted, disturbing the captain's rest. He took a cane to the back of my head." The crewman swiped the wound, and brown matted blood crusted on his fingers, proving his tale, and showing it happened very recently.

"I never...!" Captain Sinclair shouted.

At the cowardly protest, Captain Lemoine gripped the pistol from his waist belt and fired a single shot into Sinclair's gut. The brute moaned in agony.

Emily startled at the noise and covered her open mouth with her hand, but the crew around her remained calm, even Fergus. Captain Lemoine just...he just...shot the man, and no one seemed to care. That shot wouldn't kill Sinclair for a while. It wasn't meant to be a quick execution.

Captain Lemoine tucked his expended weapon back in his belt where he stored it. "Gentlemen, an easy choice awaits you. Stay here and secure your fate with this wicked captain, or join us aboard the *Sea Lion*." The captain made eye contact with each man as if everyone's decision was important, but when it was Emily's turn, he lingered. Her heart leaped into her throat.

His voice carried. "If you want nothing to do with our crew, we will happily deposit you in Nassau to find your own way home."

The merchant crew mumbled among themselves. Fergus stayed silent, as did Emily.

"But, if you choose to sign the articles of agreement, you'll find yourself bestowed with more riches than any merchant crewman could dream of. We may have declared war against the world, but on our ship, all men are equals. One vote each, no matter his station. What say you?"

The merchant crew huddled together as if making the choice as one. They quietly argued, debating both sides. Some readily wanted to join the crew, while others wanted to go home. Fergus still remained silent.

Emily would not stay and die like the animal shot and tied to the mast. She had a necklace to retrieve, a friend to find, and a festival to get back to. That meant she had to follow Captain Lemoine, but men didn't treat women kindly aboard ships. And every passing minute had her worrying more for Angela. So Emily had to assert herself as one of them.

Emily broke from the murmurs of the merchant group and approached Lemoine, head held high, but her heart pounded in her chest the closer she got. The last person who argued with this handsome man received a fatal wound in the gut. "I'm Porter. Emile Porter, and I choose to accept your gracious offer to board the *Sea Lion*. But my companion, Angela, is missing. Can I search for her before we leave?"

Captain Lemoine smiled and scratched at his beard again. Emily wanted to run her fingers through it. Catching herself staring at his hands, she focused on his dark eyes. That wasn't much better. "Price?"

Emily was lost. She thought the offer was free, and the only thing of value she had, he'd already stolen. "Pardon?"

"Sir?" A man approached with a clipboard. The quartermaster. He wore his hair in a long braid down his back, and his clothing was almost as fancy as the captain's—a long dark coat with gold buttons over his breeches and tunic.

"Has anyone found a woman below deck?"

Price scowled. "I would've heard of it." He had a charming British accent, but his clear distaste for women turned her off, even though she expected such a response.

"Angela isn't here? You're certain?"

Price swung his eyes to her. "We would never leave behind a prize such as that."

No kidding. Emily nodded, accepting his answer, and Captain Lemoine gestured for her to cross a gangplank to his ship. "Wise choice, sailor."

Emily approached the plank, not realizing until this moment she was slightly afraid of heights. Hugging a crow's nest with the safety of modern equipment was different to traipsing on a rocking, unsecured slab of wood between two moving ships over two dozen feet in the air.

If she fell, she could swim, but that wouldn't do her much good if the hulls crushed her.

Emily shivered and held out her arms for balance as she crossed the unstable plank. After her feet landed on pirate territory, Emily exhaled in relief. Fergus hopped down behind her. Then more continued until all the dozen or so men climbed over. Pirates returned, filling the deck and beginning the slow process of setting sail once again.

"Will ye be signing?" Fergus asked in private.

Emily wasn't remotely attracted to the lanky younger man, but she could listen to him speak forever. "I'm going to do whatever it takes to get my necklace back."

"It's that important tae ye?"

"It's all I know." Emily didn't realize how much she appreciated the mundane of home until now.

A handful of remaining pirates carried barrels on their shoulders and settled them around Captain Donald Sinclair. Cries of mercy floated over from the merchant ship.

"Are they doing what I think they're doing?" Emily asked her new friend, nerves spearing through her. She'd trusted Quartermaster Price when he said Angela wasn't there. But there's a finality in what was happening. No more chances to be sure. But if she and Angela put on the necklaces together, and Angela wasn't here, where did her best friend go?

"Appears tae be so. Canny say I'll miss it."

One final barrel was unsealed and spilled in a long trail around the deck.

Captain Lemoine returned to his ship and shouted gleefully, "Weigh anchor, and we'll continue the account as planned."

While the crew set to work, knowing what to do, the man with the barrel tossed the empty away and lit the black path of gunpowder. The grappling hooks were cut free, and the ship drifted with the tug of the wind.

Captain Donald Sinclair's cries for mercy were carried away by the breeze. After a short distance, flames hungry for the gunpowder engulfed the deck. A thunderous explosion sent debris and splinters of wood soaring through the clear sky. Emily ducked below the bulwark, eyes wide, and checked the other men for their reactions. No one cared.

Except Captain Lemoine watched with his hands clasped behind his back, grinning.

The brutish captain went down with the two halves of his ship.

Chapter 6

In the mess below deck, candlelight flickered on long tables while high-spirited men told tall tales. Their peals of laughter and sloshing drinks lifted Emily's lips. She and the merchant crew were perched at the end of a table, a place for guests, while the pirate crew spread out. The atmosphere reminded her of a dingy neighborhood bar filled with old friends, but in desperate need of ventilation.

Surprisingly, the pirates were hospitable, offering biscuit and drinks. But this…This required a strong stomach and weak tongue to swallow without gagging. The smell alone was enough to make her want to dive into the ocean and hope for the best. She would've felt slighted, but everyone ate and drank alike. The captain had been truthful, thus far.

Her thoughts drifted back to the brutish captain, whose end was violent and abrupt. Angela had accompanied her on the replica ship, but her date was supposed to be Tyler. Skipping the part where her ex-boyfriend wouldn't buy or wear a necklace, Emily mused if Tyler had been on that ship with her, he'd have wet his pants facing Sinclair.

Like Captain Lemoine, Tyler was a smooth-talker, but unlike the captain, Tyler was all talk, a chicken under those pretty feathers. Picturing it literally, Emily chuckled. Now she wished he had joined her, if only so she could give him an ultimatum—return all her money and apologize until she was satisfied, or stay here forever.

"What could possibly amuse ye at a time like this?" Fergus whispered. He hadn't been amused by the camaraderie down here. If he hadn't told his tale of being whipped, Emily would've believed Fergus preferred to stay with the merchant ship.

"Personal thoughts, that's all."

Fergus swallowed a draft from his cup while staring at her in thought. Emily shifted uncomfortably in her seat, wishing he'd look anywhere else. So far, no one questioned her being Emile, and she couldn't afford suspicion.

"How did a merchant sailor come tae possess a necklace o' such rare beauty?"

Emily blinked. She hadn't expected to explain herself, so she concocted a memorable fib. "My sister gifted it to me, so I could sustain myself once I reached the mainland. I couldn't find a buyer willing to offer a fair price, and I wasn't going to cut it into pieces. So I hid aboard the merchant ship for a trip to Florida."

Fergus smiled. "Ye did stowaway."

Heat crept up her cheeks once again. "Were you really going to cut off my jerkin?"

Fergus bit off a crunchy piece of biscuit and spoke with his mouth full. "Nae one deliberately defies the captain. But I've bin sailing th'seas aboard a merchant ship since I was but a wee lad, so I can assure ye, whatever these scoundrels would dae is much worse than Captain Sinclair."

Emily had observed just the opposite—fairness and a chance to defend oneself. "If that's the case, then why had Captain Lemoine treated your crew so well? Why didn't he just kill us all after taking what he wanted?"

Fergus's lips thinned, and Emily had no idea why she was defending them—the pirate captain shot the merchant captain for no reason and taken her necklace. She chewed her hard biscuit, avoiding Fergus's judgmental gaze.

A loud banging at the head of the table, like a sword's hilt against the hardwood, silenced the room. Captain Lemoine addressed all hands. "To our new friends, welcome aboard." He lifted a cup and drank to his short toast, and the pirate crew followed suit with cheery hollers.

Listening to his lilting French accent, Emily bit back a smile. There was something about him. Every time Captain Lemoine spoke, he commanded the room, and no one else existed but him.

When the crew settled, Captain Lemoine continued his grand speech. "We have been accused of being dirty thieves, but the hypocrisy is right in front of you. The Crown itself takes and takes and gives nothing in return. Merchant ship captains treat you no better than slaves in their hold—shorting wages, withholding rations, the constant threat of the cat."

Murmurs of agreement came from the merchant sailors, and Emily was enthralled with his defense of being a thief. Tyler denied what he'd done and played stupid. Captain Lemoine was admitting it and explaining his actions. She might not approve of what he'd done, but she could respect his stance.

"But as you sit before me, you're free from those chains. Now I offer you something more. Aboard the *Sea Lion*, all men have an equal vote and a fair share in rations and prizes. Tired of being hungry? Tired of being broke? The right prize can award more dollars than a year's salary!"

The men murmured again, dazzled by the promises of riches. Emily wasn't on board. What good was living a life of luxury when all you did was take someone else's? There was no honor in that. And since it involved taking other ships by force and risking one's life, Emily was definitely not interested. And on top of that, injuries and deaths were so common, Captain Lemoine thanked the merchant crew for sparing the pirates that usual fate. There was her final 'no thanks'.

"You'd be foolish to turn your back on this opportunity. With that in mind, you can decide on your future right now. Remain merchant sailors, where your careers shall be tarnished when word returns of your surrender to pirates. You'll be begging for a new assignment, and if you find one, suffer with pitiful wages." The captain paused for effect and the pirates jeered and pounded their cups on the tables.

The captain flashed his radiant smile, and his gaze lingered on Emily. Was he trying to tell her which option he wanted her to choose? Her heart skipped a beat at the decision she'd already made.

His gaze moved away. "Or sign the accords and be rich and free, because aboard the *Sea Lion*, we are all free men!"

The pirates cried out in celebration, rattling their cups, and drumming palms on the tables like a marching band. Their excitement was contagious. Emily smiled.

"Ye no' seriously considering this hogwash?" Fergus asked. The scowl on his face made it clear the captain hadn't won him over.

"It's pretty convincing to me."

Fergus scoffed. "How could ye? Look at them—a pack o' animals—brutes, thieves, murderers, enemies tae th'Crown. Ye want th'threat o' a noose over yer head every day? Th'worry about th'next sails ye see being th'Royal Navy's? Th'fear yer next battle ends in miserable bloodshed and prolonged agony o' mortal wounds? I'm staying oan th'good side o' the law, an' I advise ye tae refuse."

His arguments didn't make sense to her. "As a merchant sailor in pirate-infested waters, aren't you exposed to all those same concerns, except for the noose?"

Fergus studied his cup. "Ma conscious is clear."

Unsatisfied with his answer, Emily pressed, "You'd rather endure abuse and starvation from a merchant captain than live the freedoms of a pirate?" Captain Lemoine explained they weren't simply thieves. They were taking back what the Crown had taken from them. And that Emily could understand—as she gazed longingly at the captain and wondered which pocket her necklace rested in. The pirates took what they needed and freed men from worse situations. They didn't want to hurt anyone.

They weren't the monsters depicted in the books. They were angry men without hope.

Of course she had to sign. She'd do whatever it took to get that necklace back. Besides, if she chose to disembark at Nassau, what kind of life could she make for herself? As a retail worker used to electronic inventory systems and monitoring the self-checkouts, she had no relevant job skills here. She had friends and family to return to, and an ex-boyfriend to hound for her money back. The only way back to her life was to join these pirates.

Fergus didn't answer her question before a rhythmic pounding on the long table reached an excited commotion, drowning out all other sounds. Captain Lemoine beamed from the support and gestured at a small table with a parchment, quill, and inkwell lit with candles. The quartermaster stood next to him, holding a clipboard.

The pirate crew stood with ceremony and lined up against the wall. The defeated crew was urged to sign with continued vocalizations in support.

The merchant crew stood one by one and in pairs, and lined up at the table.

Emily joined them, hanging at the back of the line, wanting to watch the others first. With each signature, the captain smiled, patted the recruit on the back, and said something to him, inaudible over the cheers. The line progressed smoothly until Fergus, who was ahead of her. Rather than take up the quill, he approached the captain and said, "I mean nae insult, but I canny, in good conscience, sign. I'll disembark safely at Nassau, as promised."

The quartermaster made notes on his paperwork, unflinching at the refusal. But Emily focused on the captain as firelight danced across his strong features. He showed no signs of insult. He didn't try to sway him further. The captain respected Fergus's decision.

"As you wish," the captain replied.

Emily pressed a finger to her lips to stifle a chuckle at the captain's use of Westley's declaration of love for his dearest Buttercup.

Captain Lemoine turned his attention to her and raised a brow, but he wasn't upset with her. He was curious. "Is something the matter, Porter?"

There was so much the matter, Emily didn't know where to begin.

Chapter 7

THE ENTIRE COMPANY OF pirates stared at Emily, but the only one whose scrutinizing gaze sent waves of nerves through her stomach was Captain Lemoine himself. Or maybe the biscuit didn't agree with her. Could be that, too.

"No. Nothing's the matter at all. Please continue." Emily said, face burning hot. Sweat trickled down her back.

The captain returned to Fergus and said, "Your needs shall be met until port, and until then, no harm to your person shall transpire."

With a quiet audience, her friend nodded and stepped aside, satisfied with the promises. Two more men declined to sign, and Emily stepped up to the table next to the captain, staring her down. Her heart thundered in her chest, and blood wooshed in her ears. He stared back, but there was a softness in his eyes—not the hard angles of a dominant male asserting his position. This was a man silently pleading with her to sign.

Had he figured out she was a woman?

The pirates remained quiet while Emily made her choice. She bent over the parchment and the cursive handwriting flickering by candlelight was beautiful. Had the captain penned this himself? A real life article of agreement, the pirate code, right in front of her. This belonged in a museum. She was afraid of touching it and having the delicate paper crumble—but it was new, not an antique.

If she signed, would her name appear in history?

Emily blinked. Everyone was watching. She couldn't take the time for an existential crisis. Down to business.

The first articles were expected—*equal vote in all affairs, and a fair turn in all prizes. No gambling or theft amongst the crew. Extinguish lights and drinking at night.* And *pistols and cutlasses in working and ready order at all times.* Surprisingly civil.

After that, Emily grew concerned. *No one breaks up the account until each man has earned 1,000.* Her face pinched in confusion. A thousand days of service? A thousand dollars? Emily wasn't familiar with their standards, but she had no intention of sticking around that long. She wanted complete clarification before signing a contract—she'd learned the hard way to protect herself—but she didn't think the captain would like her questioning. And Emily couldn't draw attention to herself more than necessary.

A quarrel on the ship is settled on shore by sword or pistol. Emily made a note to avoid all confrontation.

Refraining from battle is punished by death. So if the captain chose battle, she could die, and if she chose not to partake, she'd be killed. That was...not fair. How much worse could this get?

"Something the matter?" Captain Lemoine asked.

Emily straightened, quill in her hand. "I'm just reading it first. The handwriting is beautiful."

The captain grinned, sending her heart fluttering. "How are you not familiar with the articles? Everyone at sea knows them."

"I'm new," Emily said, and bent back down. Faster. She needed to go faster. She skimmed ahead and immediately regretted it. Emily re-read the passage, disbelieving her own eyes. *No fornication or women on board, and any caught are to suffer death.*

She'd known women weren't treated well, but *death*? This was an oppressive world, far removed from what she was familiar with. No amount of reading passages in books, translated and pieced together over centuries, could prepare someone to experience it. And even though her country had many social issues, she was thankful something this brutal wasn't one of them.

If Emily didn't sign, she'd be removed from the ship at Nassau, leaving her with a very narrow window to coax her necklace back. Otherwise, she'd remain trapped here forever. She truly had no choice. She just had to not get caught. Surely the captain didn't already know her secret and was allowing her to sign her own death sentence, right?

Emily peeked up at the captain.

A bell chimed above deck, and Emily whipped her head around in alarm. Another ship? Another battle? Good thing she hadn't signed yet. She silently searched the captain's reaction, hoping for reassurance.

He tilted his head at her quizzically.

"Seven bells. You know your places," a man said.

Emily turned. Several men quietly left the mess, disappointment on their faces. That man must've been the boatswain, in charge of the hull, rigging, cables, and deck crew. A few of the shift-change men mumbled about Karl interrupting their fun. And still, these witnesses waited for her. Emily swallowed a thick lump in her throat.

IN ALL HIS YEARS freeing sailors from their wretched fates, Captain Eric Lemoine had never once encountered a man so unsure of this decision. So unfamiliar with the rules before him.

Who was Emile Porter?

Why did the shift change bells alarm him so? Why did he still hesitate to sign? Either he went with the rest of the crew who refused, or he joined us. The choice wasn't *that* difficult.

Emile bent down toward the parchment again, and a different possibility struck him. Could this man not read? Pity filled him at once. Captain Lemoine had been raised in privilege with the best education available, but he'd chosen this life.

It wasn't forced upon him.

And he, along with the original crew he'd rounded up, drafted these articles together. And yes, he'd written this—and re-written it with each new crew turnover.

"Shall I read it to you?" Captain Lemoine asked quietly.

Emile straightened, red burning on his smooth cheeks. The man was a master at shaving so close to the skin. His bright blond hair wouldn't have been enough to disguise it. No, this unusual and perplexing man was a master with a blade. Someone not to trifle with; someone Lemoine wanted close.

Captain Lemoine cared not what lied beneath Emile's breeches and tunic. He cared what lied inside that fascinating mind, and that desire led him to Emile's lips. Captain Lemoine wanted to kiss him.

Emile's gaze lingered on his lips as well, but then they tracked low and remained for long enough to tell Lemoine what he wanted to know. The captain's interest was reciprocated.

"See something you like?" he asked quietly.

Emile flustered, tipping his face away, bitting his lips. And that amusing blush returned to his cheeks. Emile wiped his palms on his breeches and smiled. His teeth were beautifully white and perfectly straight. He came from money too. "I was just thinking, but I'm ready now."

With a trembling hand, Emile lifted the quill and dipped it in the inkwell. He moved very slowly over to the parchment, and a drop of ink landed spilled.

"Oh, shit." Emile swiped at the stain, but it was going anywhere.

Captain Lemoine hid his amusement. This man had never used a quill before. How strange!

Finally, the signature scratched onto the parchment. Emile straightened, set down the quill, and squared his shoulders, lips pressed thin and cheeks burning bright.

He was staying.

The captain beamed and clapped the man on the back. "Congratulations, Emile. Nothing to fear, no? If you need any assistance in understanding the contract you signed, please do ask. My door is always open." The captain let that statement hang for a beat.

Emile blinked silently, as if not understanding.

Captain Lemoine needed to be more straightforward with this one. He leaned in close enough to feel his body heat, and the scent of this man puzzled him further. What sailor smelled like...flowers? "Welcome aboard, Emile Porter. You made the right choice."

Emile smiled, capturing the captain's full attention as he addressed the whole room, "Rum all around. Allow us to celebrate the new arrivals properly!"

A violin played an upbeat tune, and the men cheered and danced. A handful rushed to the cask and pried it open, and many swarmed it, scooping out the sloshing rum. Emile stayed behind. Captain Lemoine was thrilled for a chance to talk in private.

The quartermaster, always so serious, crossed the room and said in confidence, "Eric, we don't have enough rum for a full round."

The man needed to lighten up. For someone who knew the ins and outs of the ship and its finances, one would expect he could assuredly enjoy himself from time to time. The situation on the ship wasn't *that* dire. "How can you say we don't have enough? We raided a merchant ship, Price! What was the take?"

"Slops for half the men. Twenty barrels of sugar...."

"Sugar has considerable value."

Price wasn't convinced. "When sold at port, I agree, but we're far from port now." The man flipped pages and referenced his paperwork. "And we gained enough leather Monmouth caps for the whole crew."

That sounded like the entirety of the list, and that was terrible news. Lemoine grimly looked at his elated crew. "No more rum?"

"It pains me to say, but no. The sooner we make port, the sooner we can replenish our stores and our pockets. You have to keep them together until then."

No easy feat. "Can you dilute the remaining supply?"

"Do you think you can fool these men? Be careful, Eric." Price shook his head and retreated from the celebration.

Suddenly, Lemoine was no longer in the mood to celebrate.

Emile approached, and Lemoine could sense the man everywhere he stood. His presence alone pulled him from the melancholy problem before him.

"May I have a word with you, sir, privately?" Emile asked.

Captain Lemoine smiled. He needed a pleasant distraction, and he could think of none better. He hooked his arm behind the handsome man and walked him toward the deck. "Tonight is your night."

EMILY WAS KEENLY AWARE of the captain's presence at her side, the feel of his arm behind her. She was worried he'd accidentally touch something that gave her away. But she didn't want distance between them.

They climbed the ladder to the main deck, and Emily gasped at the clear sky, spinning in place with her head tilted back. She'd never seen an unimpeded view of the stars, free from untold numbers of satellites, rocket debris, and airplanes. With a smile on her face, she rushed to the rail and leaned over. Moonlight glinted and shimmered off the gently lapping ocean waters. And the quiet. She'd never experienced a relaxing peace like this. Nature just as nature intended.

The world seemed endless from here, blackness in every direction. No cruise liners, no speedboats, no flashing lights from lighthouses. It was more beautiful than she'd ever imagined.

"It's as if you've never seen the sky before," the captain mused.

Emily spun at his words. The captain was leaning against the rail, intently watching her.

"This is beautiful," she said without thinking.

"It is, isn't it?" The captain straightened and strolled toward her. "When the crew enjoys their drink, I step out here. I prefer the fresh air over the pungent lower deck."

Emily laughed. "Pungent is accurate."

The captain smiled, intense gaze assessing her. Emily covered her arms over her chest, pretending to be chilled. She definitely wasn't.

"An extra pair of eyes watching the horizon doesn't hurt. Not all ships move with light shining through their portholes." He leaned in close, and for a flash, Emily worried he was going to confront her over her grave mistake—signing as a woman. He said, "Don't tell the others, but I know the crow's nest sometimes dozes off."

Emily relaxed and joked, "Since you have a healthy-sized crew, I'm guessing you don't kill them as a punishment for it." She covered her mouth with her hand. That was distasteful and rude. But she was curious about the truth of her assumption.

Captain Lemoine tapped his nose with a spark in his eye. He seemed like a decent guy, but then why shoot another captain and burn him alive before blowing his ship to smithereens?

Needing an explanation, she asked, "Why did you do it?"

The captain folded his arms across his chest, smile fading away. "To what do you refer?"

Emily rubbed the gentle night breeze from her arms. This time, the chill reached her skin. "Captain Sinclair was immobilized on a ship doomed to be destroyed. Why did you bother to shoot him first? Doesn't it seem...I don't know...barbaric?"

Captain Lemoine squinted at her. "I understand the concern you carry for your captain. Being free can be hard to adjust to. What do you do now? Where do you go? How will you sustain yourself?"

"It's not that."

"But you signed, so you have no worries about any of that. On my crew, you'll be taken care of. The code we agreed to is binding for all and strictly enforced."

Emily dropped her eyes. She figured as much.

"That was supposed to bring consolation, but I sense it hasn't." Captain Lemoine touched her shoulder, exploring the handiwork of her jerkin. Her stomach tightened with unease. "Your clothing is familiar, but the fabrics and stitches are not. In all my years exploring this vast globe, your speech patterns are completely unrecognizable. I found you on a merchant ship, yet you behave like you've never seen the ocean. Your smooth skin tells me you're a master of the blade, but your nervousness tonight makes no sense. Please tell me, satisfy this deep yearning to understand, where are you from, Emile Porter?"

Emily backed toward the rail. He was too close, his suspicions too high. She couldn't fail already, so she spun his questions back at him while offering a taste of satisfaction. "Sinclair wasn't my captain, but you figured that much. Now, Captain Lemoine, satisfy my deep yearning to understand." She playfully used his words against him. "Your crew steals from honest merchants, destroying the livelihood of the sailors. As judge, jury, and executioner, you have no qualms about killing people. That tells me the stories of pirates are true." The captain closed the distance again, slowly, like a stalker in the night. He didn't like what she was saying. "But you freed the crews from tyrannical captains. And you offer them safe passage or a chance to join as equals with no questions asked. That altruism…that generous regard for others doesn't fit the profile. I cannot make sense of you."

The captain smiled under the moonlight and leaned in close. "If that was your attempt to quell my curiosity, you failed."

Emily had to be more blunt. "If I don't fit in here, then teach me, starting with explaining why you shot the captain, so I understand exactly what I signed up for."

Captain Lemoine scratched at his beard. Emily wanted to run her fingers through the short scruff, but she would never risk it. Not even if the captain had a good explanation for such a monstrous, tasteless, unnecessary act. "Trust is a valuable commodity aboard this ship."

Emily had already given her trust to the wrong people. Every little girl trusted her father to be loving, and always there. He had been the first to break it. She'd tried again as an adult, capable of choosing who she wanted to trust, and Tyler was a bust too. They appeared decent people on the outside.

Regardless of his benevolent intentions, how could she trust someone who proudly proclaimed to be a murderer and a thief?

Angry men wearing frowns and shouting incoherently spilled onto the deck, interrupting their conversation. As if she'd been discovered, Emily stepped away, trembling like a leaf in the breeze, but the mob closed in around them both.

Chapter 8

Within moments of the captain telling her he'd take care of her, Emily and Captain Lemoine were surrounded. Shouts demanded answers that Emily believed wouldn't be appeased with simple words of encouragement. Emily also didn't believe the captain would protect her, because she was just another one of the crew. Seeing a narrow opportunity, she sidled closer to the captain, anyway. If any of these angry pirates caused a shoving match, Emily planned to be close enough to dig in the captain's pockets without him realizing.

It was a terrible plan, but the only one she had.

"Captain," a filthy man said with a scowl. "Price says no more rum. Can I wager why he cut us off after *you* told the whole crew to indulge?"

"Simply my mistake," the captain placed a fist over his heart in solidarity. "I believed the stores to be in fine order, but Price's documents show otherwise."

Unsatisfied, he leaned closer. "According to the articles, we can vote on a retrenchment."

"You are within your rights to do so, but the outcome doesn't change the quantity left. You can drink it all down tonight and hope we don't suffer a thirst, or you can ration it out until we reach port."

The pirate thought on it for a beat. Others around murmured their opinions. "How long until we restock? Are we talking weeks or months?"

Wait, months? Emily needed enough time for her escape, but to be stuck here with these unstable cretins for months was...terrifying.

"Worry not. We must unload the sugar in Nassau to make room in the hold, and our guests who chose not to sign shall disembark. Soon we shall make landfall."

The explanation sounded reasonable to Emily, but she was curious what they needed room for.

"It's just like you to make promises, but failure after failure is all we see," the pirate continued, and others nodded and mumbled in agreement.

"I understand your disappointment—all of you." The captain turned, addressing glaring pairs of eyes. "But this afternoon's prize was unscheduled and came at no cost but time. I want to celebrate our unexpected good fortune, but the situation at hand requires patience."

"Patience!" another man hollered. "We don't want none of your patience. We want drinks!"

Emily made a mental note to never anger a half-drunk crowd.

"I bet the captain's keeping it all to himself!" another voice shouted. "Supposed to be equals, yet look at his clothes, and look at ours. He's got a cabin. We sleep in hammocks, shoulder to shoulder. He gets two shares of the prize, while we get one. What's fair about that?"

Emily understood higher pay for higher skilled positions with more responsibility, and it wasn't like the captain and his officers received a hundred shares over the workers. With their pay, they could spend on their choice of clothing, but she had nothing to defend the cabin. With the whole ship ganging up on him, a thread of pity wove through her. Despite not knowing the man and having witnessed him shooting a man for suffering's sake, she believed his words were sincere. Emily didn't want to see the captain harmed, but what could she do against all of them?

A hand gripped Emily's arm and tugged. She allowed herself to be pulled from the mob and was surprised to see Fergus. "What are you doing?" she asked sharply, having lost her chance to frisk the captain.

"Getting ye out o' there. An angry crew ainlie leads tae one thing."

Emily stared, assuming he was going to finish. She prompted him, "Well, what? What is it?"

Fergus cocked his head as if puzzled why she wouldn't know and said, "Mutiny. An' if they succeed, th'captain's previous orders be nullified."

"Meaning, your safe passage is at stake?"

Fergus nodded. "An' ma two friends, who also declined th'crew's offer."

Emily couldn't afford to lose the captain. From what she'd heard, they could simply tip him overboard. It was an extreme solution, but Emily didn't know these people, and the captain seemed nervous and unsuccessful in placating the mob. She needed something, anything, that would calm them down. The crew suspected the captain had a spare barrel for his private use. Could Price be wrong about his count? It was the only idea she had, and she needed muscles to help. Fergus wouldn't be her first choice for the job, but she'd take what she could get. "Fergus, you need the captain to stay in charge for a little while longer, just as I do. Come help me before we're too late."

Emily headed down the ladder below deck.

Fergus followed curiously. "Wi' what?"

Emily remembered schematics of ships in her research. The hold was always below deck, and this ship wasn't that big. Inside, she found all the barrels taken from the merchant captain, as well as the pirates' meager stores.

"Find some liquor, any liquor. There's got to be a discrepancy here."

"An' if we're caught?"

"Act crazy, and I'll tell them I followed you for your safety." Emily systematically opened barrels and checked their contents.

Fergus folded his arms across his narrow chest. "Ye want me tae cover for ye? Ye know how this looks? Stealing from pirates is the worst offense. It was in the articles ye signed."

"The more you balk instead of help, the longer this takes."

Fergus sighed and opened barrels. Emily moved from one to the next. After clearing most of the hold, Emily found one barrel that might work. She leaned down for a quick whiff, and her eyes watered—not from the strength, but from the stink. This was the stuff.

She shouted louder than she'd planned, "I found one!"

Emily replaced the lid carefully, and Fergus fished his way over. She assessed her friend's strength. "Can you carry it?"

Fergus frowned. "Why? Canny ye?"

Uh, no. She couldn't. Emily stared, pleading with her friend.

Fergus scrutinized her appearance again, and Emily wished he wouldn't be suspicious. "Then why are ye insulting ma person?" he asked playfully and picked it up with ease. "Of course I can."

On their way back up to the main deck, Emily kept watch for Price, but the lower decks were vacant. Emily urged Fergus to hurry. "You first. You're carrying the precious cargo." Emily climbed up behind him, and Fergus set the barrel down on the main deck. The pirates shouted among themselves, as if the crew had split their loyalty. She wasn't too late.

Fergus backed away. Clearly, he didn't want credit for helping the crew.

"Hey! Anyone want a drink?" Emily shouted and slapped her hand on the wooden lid for their attention.

All the men ignored her, unable to hear over their own noise. Frustrated, Emily waved her arms like a cheerleader and shouted again. Still nothing. Emily marched up to the first pirate and pulled on his arm. "I have liquor over there!" She pointed and quickly, more heads turned.

The bickering quieted down, and with last glares and pats on the back, the men surrounded the barrel, many with empty cups still in their hands. They lifted the barrel and carried it down to the mess, song returning to their lips and cheerfulness returning to their countenances.

Fergus followed them with a last glance over his shoulder at her. He wasn't grateful, but he wasn't angry. There was a sadness on his features. Why on earth would he be sad his protection was no longer threatened?

The captain waited until they were alone. This time, his playfulness was gone. His features were darkened by the shadows cast by the moon. "Where did you find that rum?"

Emily shivered at the menace in his tone.

CAPTAIN ERIC LEMOINE HAD been as careful as possible with the crew lately. He knew the prizes hadn't been satisfactory, and the last one was pure happenstance. If they'd taken damage, he feared he wouldn't be captain at all right now. He never thought he'd want to thank old Captain Sinclair for his cowardice.

The rum situation was, as they'd said, more akin to a straw that broke a camel's back. But Emile Porter blew that straw away before the irreparable damage had been done. The question was, how? Emile already filled Lemoine's thoughts with the unanswered puzzle, and now Emile went and did this. But the man didn't carry confidence in his decision as he should have. It was reckless and impulsive.

Emile Porter was afraid.

"The hold," he said softly.

Lemoine dragged a hand down his face. "Quartermaster Price is going to have your head."

Emile gasped and covered his mouth with his hand. He truly knew nothing of our seafaring ways. Captain Lemoine bit back a chuckle at the perceived literal sense of his statement. Because of Emile's imbecilic decision, Lemoine lived another day, and that gratitude needed to be expressed. A simple 'thank you' would do nothing to prevent the due punishment. Considering Quartermaster Price was as rigid as a charred rabbit over a spit, that was no easy feat at all. Lemoine said gently, "But you saved mine."

"You're not mad?" Emile asked.

Lemoine tilted his head at her. "Do I appear unhinged? I thought my arguments were plain. And now I'm reminded of your strangeness. Can you offer me one answer?"

Emile's breath caught. "Sure."

Captain Lemoine grinned hungrily, as if a treasure of his own, dangling beyond reach, at last had been offered. He closed the distance between them until the man stood within inches of his chest. Lemoine wanted to reach out and capture the man's smooth jaw between his hands, and he wanted to taste the curve of Emile's upper lip. Which truthfully surprised him, but when Lemoine wanted something, he didn't abstain...

...except the articles forbade such actions.

"Where are you from, Emile?" he asked in almost a whisper. He thought it was a simple question, one easily answered, and one that would satisfy a miniscule piece of the puzzle.

Emile hesitated. "I'm not from around here."

Captain Lemoine tried to hide his disappointment. A captain and his crew needed trust to operate smoothly and safely. But having his newest recruit choose a lie by omission was more than just a chink in the chain. It stung. And that reminded him of the problem Emile had caused. "Indeed. Well, Porter, despite your benevolent efforts, I find myself in an unsatisfactory situation."

"What do you mean?"

Lemoine crossed his arms over his chest, the desire to retaliate for the personal slight taking over. "You subverted my authority in front of the crew."

Emile stepped back, and as the words sank into that pretty blond head of his, he frowned. His words came out unsure at first, then grew with assertiveness. "I...I did what I had to. I heard the crew was going to mutiny. Without me, you'd have no authority left to defend."

Lemoine admitted to himself he had a point. But Emile's actions left him with different problems. And yet the puzzle remained. "All actions have consequences."

Emile's boldness washed away, and the fear returned. He rubbed his arms as if chilled. "Am I going to be punished?"

"The crew, no doubt, shall delight in telling the story, and the quartermaster shall catch wind of it. He alone decides the punishments as set forth in the articles, but Price is not well liked by the crew. He's a decent man, it's simply the requirements of the job. I may be able to negotiate a mercy."

"I don't know how to thank you enough."

"Don't thank me yet."

"I'm sorry for what happened. I didn't know." Emile swiped his forehead.

"I believe you," Captain Lemoine said. "I wish I knew how it was possible."

Emile's drawn face shifted away. He gazed at the sea once again, lost in thought. Lemoine didn't guarantee a stay of punishment, because he couldn't. But the perplexing man only tried to help. To ease the burden of waiting for news, Captain Lemoine could offer him a small peace. "If the time comes, I owe you a personal favor."

Captain Lemoine hoped that wasn't another mistake. He turned and headed for his cabin across the deck before another word was spoken. Convincing the quartermaster of anything was a difficult task.

Chapter 9

In the small morning hours, Emily opened her eyes. Despite all the worries on her mind, the soft movement of the ship and its rhythmic clicks and groans had lulled her to sleep. Overhead, thick wood beams ran from port to starboard. She was on the gun deck, in a sea of canvas hammocks swaying as one. She rubbed the sleep from her eyes. Her wild adventure had not been a hallucination.

Which was both exciting and incredibly terrifying.

Emily had wanted to cash in on the favor immediately, but the captain had marched away and disappeared behind a door before she could ask. He had a lot on his mind, and she didn't blame him. Emily had read the articles clearly before signing, but she didn't know what Price would charge her with.

Marooning was a death sentence—being left on an uninhabited island to die of thirst. That was three days of torture with an end in sight. She couldn't risk getting the cat. The whip alone was horrific but survivable. She was more afraid of being stripped half naked, of being exposed to several dozen men starved for something that wasn't food. That was a torture with no end.

While the pirates snored soundly, now was her best chance of escaping. Placing her feet on the deck, Emily carefully slipped out of the moving bed and tip-toed down the narrow space. She found a quick path across the gun deck and moved swiftly. Climbing the ladder to the main deck, she craned her neck, seeking the night watch. She hoped they'd fallen asleep tonight. With the moon behind a cotton cloud, she couldn't see anyone patrolling the main decks. And her vision wasn't strong enough to discern any movement in the crow's nest.

Emily exhaled a deep breath and climbed out, keeping herself low as she crossed to the mainmast. She ducked between the longboats and listened. Near-calm waters softly lapped against the hull and nothing more, not a snore, nor a footstep. She crossed the open space and reached the door to the navigation room, once again waiting, watching. Emily scanned the area for witnesses, and her heart punched into her throat as she turned the knob slowly to avoid squeaks. It opened enough for her to slip inside.

The room was dark, and Emily wanted to use her cell phone for the flashlight feature, but that would be stupid. Her hands slipped along the wall, stopping when she reached the door to the captain's quarters. Emily pressed an ear on the battered surface, but no sounds came from the other side.

Emily placed her hand on the final knob.

If she went inside, she would be violating Captain Lemoine's personal space, and whatever grain of trust she'd earned would blow away in the breeze, never to be recovered. The captain had driven home how important trust was on this ship, and after the crew threatened him, did he have anyone he could trust?

Emily didn't want to hurt anyone. But she had friends, a simple job, a cute apartment, and a plant. What she'd considered a fairly successful life, ignoring the fact that she was broke and the most important men in her life had betrayed her. It was what she knew. Emily was confident in her world and her choices. She could be who she was. Here she had to hide, pretend, deceive. It was exhausting, and she couldn't wait to get home.

Emily had to find her necklace and put it on. Failure was not an option, because no number of favors from the captain would save her from the articles she'd signed.

Exhaling a deep breath, she turned the knob.

Emily closed herself in the cabin with only a tiny dot of a flame at the bottom of a melted candle. Blood swished in her ears, and her heart pounded in her chest. She exhaled deep breaths to slow it down. She needed to hear. Focusing herself, she listened for a stirring or footsteps. Coughs or snores. Creaks of wood underfoot or a gasp of surprise.

All she could pick up were the soft sounds of deep slumber. She jutted her arms around to prevent herself from smacking into anything and causing a disruptive noise, but only a few steps in, her knee knocked the captain's bed post. Emily strained to bite back a grunt of pain just as moonlight broke free and filtered in through the row of windows. She frowned, keeping her swears at Mother Nature to herself and took advantage of the light provided.

The extravagant interior stole her breath. Underfoot was a woven rug. His bed was small, perhaps full size, with curving shapes carved into the frame. Numerous shelves and cabinets lined the room. He clearly liked to read. Then again, with no electronics, what else would a person do?

The captain's desk was solid wood with a quill and inkpot next to an hourglass. Curiosity pulled her toward it, and an open book sat on the surface. She tried to read the antique cursive, but a combination of the lighting and archaic language left Emily following the beautiful curves without understanding anything but dates and times.

Emily moved toward the book, many of which appeared to be older captain's logs—details of everything the captain had done, had taken, and had explored. Nothing would be more exciting to read, but her time was limited.

The captain shifted in bed, and Emily froze, focusing on the pattern of breaths and seeking changes. He was still asleep. He may have been used to sleeping through noise and movement, but she couldn't take any chances. Where would the captain keep a valuable necklace?

Emily tapped her chin and turned, reassessing everything over again. In front of the desk, the captain's jerkin was draped over a chairback. Emily tiptoed across the room, keeping the creaks to a minimum.

The captain turned over in bed, a startling rustle, and Emily gasped and slapped a hand over her mouth. The swishing returned to her ears, and Emily found to calm herself. Seconds stretched and her breathing strained, Emily released the spent air from her burning lungs and listened. He was still asleep.

Emily closed the distance and patted the fabric, seeking the telltale lump of her amethyst pendant. She heard a metallic jostle, and she gasped with excitement. It was here! Emily scrambled to find the pocket.

"You there! Halt!" a scratchy voice said from the door.

A lantern shined from behind her, and in desperation, Emily's trembling fingers moved faster. She was too close to give up now. She couldn't get caught. Breaths pumped in and out of her chest. More and more, she scrambled, metal jingling. Emily gripped the material and scraped at it with her nails, trying to find an opening to reach the gem.

"I said halt!" Loud boot steps pounded on the floor, closing the distance rapidly. "Captain!"

Shuffling and clattering came from the bed.

Faster, faster. She needed to pull the amethyst over her head, and this would all be over. There, an opening. Emily squeezed a hand inside, and her fingertips brushed against cold metal. A powerful fist gripped her wrist, locking her movements in place. She fought him. She had to fight. The consequences were too much to bear. Tears pressed against her eyes.

She couldn't give up, but the night watchman was too strong. Picturing for a flash, all the men with their hungry grins prowling toward her, Emily sniffled. How could she have failed? She was so careful.

"Captain!" the night watchman repeated, squeezing harder. Bedding flung aside, and the captain sat upright, eyes meeting the man holding her. "I saw the bootless bugger sneaking inside, and I came at once."

Emily knew little of the era's slang, but that descriptor couldn't be nice. She faced her captor. The bearded waif of a man with a yellow glowing face from the lantern stared her down, refusing to release her.

The captain stood from his bed, tugging up his baggy breeches. Emily exhaled a deep, shaky breath while giving him the once over. His chest was broad, taut, and streaked with short dark hair like dabbled brush strokes. Without them fastened, his breeches slipped low, showing off sculpted hips. And Emily wanted nothing more at that moment than to run her hands over his body and feel the movement of his muscles under her touch. She wanted his thick arms to wrap around her body and pull her close. He was painfully handsome. Looking at him truthfully hurt, because she could never have a man like that. The minute she decided she wanted him, the timer on a betrayal began, and Emily couldn't survive another.

"Why the urgency, Hyde? Is something of concern with Porter here?" Emily noticed his use of her last name. He was still upset with her. But rather than speak directly to his guard, Captain Lemoine looked at Emily, and his face wasn't friendly. A sinking feeling in her chest told her that grain of trust had blown away.

Chapter 10

At Captain Eric Lemoine's question, the night watchman released his grip on Emile. There was nowhere for the man to go anyhow, and Lemoine didn't want anyone's hands on Emile but his own. He expected, with Emile's lengthy study of the articles, he understood section two. Robbery between two men aboard resulted in the guilty having his ears and nose slit before abandonment on a harsh shore. Emile Porter would risk mutilation and desertion for a necklace? It must've been far more valuable than he'd imagined, and he was right to keep it on his person. But had Lemoine been sitting on a vast treasure all this while? Could this simple jewel solve all his problems?

And the puzzle grew.

"He...he smiled, sir," Hyde said nervously.

Once again, Lemoine had to cover for the strange man who didn't understand their seafaring ways. The last thing he needed was more trouble for Emile—which meant, for himself.

"Smiling is cause for disruption to my sleep?" Lemoine crossed his arms over his bare chest to flex his thick biceps. He'd certainly noticed Emile's not-so-subtle gaze, and Lemoine like it.

"I thought he was a larcener, sir. Or he meant you harm." Hyde's confidence slipped.

"No one is a threat to anyone else on this ship. Must I remind you to keep your eyes on the sea?" Lemoine kept his tone firm, but he wasn't upset. Hyde had prevented Emile from retrieving the necklace. Since

Lemoine, too, withheld its value from the crew, he was just as guilty of defrauding the company of its fair share. "You are dismissed."

Hyde took one last look at Emile before following orders. There was a flicker of suspicion there. Keeping Emile safe was growing more difficult by the day. When the door closed, the captain was left alone with Emile, bathed only in faded moonlight.

Lemoine released his flex and approached his newest recruit. "Larceny is a severe offense."

"I didn't steal anything from anyone."

"Then how did you come into possession of that necklace you're so desperate to retrieve?"

A fury pinched Emile's gentle face. "Are you accusing me of stealing from Captain Sinclair?"

"Tell me the truth." All he wanted was answers.

The fascinating man shifted his gaze aside at the question. What was he hiding? The secrets and unanswered questions drove Lemoine mad! Captain Lemoine moved, his body so close to Emile's he could feel the heat radiating off him. The smell of flowers had faded away, but there was something else. Something deeper, more luxurious, even more puzzling.

"I can't." Emile met his gaze, sure of his answer. "I can't tell you. You wouldn't believe me, anyway."

It was an answer, just not one Lemoine wanted, and it satisfied nothing. He searched the dashing man's smooth face, as if he could find the answers buried behind those hazel eyes or resting on those soft, curving lips. The longer he lingered, the more Emile's breathing picked up. This fascinating stranger wanted him just as much. If only it weren't forbidden! His lips were so close. One little touch wouldn't be discovered.

But Lemoine couldn't stop at one, and he couldn't stay quiet enough, either. Giving in to temptation would lead them both down a path of ruin. Lemoine couldn't do it. He was too close to having what he needed, and he couldn't further endanger Emile.

The beautiful man was proficient at that on his own.

Finally, Lemoine identified the scent, and he lifted his brows. "Chocolate."

Emile laughed, and he covered his forehead with his hand, blocking his beautiful eyes from Lemoine's view. Shoulders shook from peals of laughter.

"I hardly understand what could cause such amusement." For a moment, he worried Emile was laughing at his reaction to the man.

Emile opened the leather pouch on his belt. A rustle of paper followed in the darkness. "Open your mouth," he whispered.

Oh, how he yearned to! But Lemoine couldn't. He had to fight these clear signs Emile wanted him to. It had to be enough. The mutual attraction alone had to satisfy until they landed at port. "I cannot."

Emile laughed. "Is chocolate forbidden on this ship? I didn't see it specified in the articles."

"Rarely is anything ever just chocolate." The captain closed his eyes, wishing Emile would open up to him. They may not have physical relations, but they could be friends, and Lemoine wanted that connection. He wanted to trust someone. He felt like Emile was that someone, but the handsome stranger refused at every turn.

"Well, this is, and it's melting in my fingers. Just take it. No strings attached."

Lemoine looked at the soft hand. A small square of chocolate was pinched between his fingers. Could he have one taste? Could he stop at one?

EMILY HAD TO STOP herself from laughing at the absurdity. The captain acted like a piece of chocolate was devilry sent to trick him into burning in hell. But the longer he delayed, the longer she got to memorize his naked torso, and did she ever enjoy the view. She was so close, the smallest wave could tilt the hull in her favor, and she could reach out and grab him for balance.

A girl could only hope.

The captain still hesitated. It was a risk to offer a modern treat, but she could explain that away. "It's not stolen. It's mine. I brought it along, and I'm offering it to you."

The captain closed his eyes. "I insist I cannot."

So damned strange. Emily popped the chocolate into her mouth and licked her fingers clean. She appreciated the flavor after the tasteless crunchy biscuit she'd dined on. The captain was into her. That much was obvious. Under different circumstances, she wouldn't turn him down, either. But this wasn't the twenty-first century, and these weren't her rules. The moment he discovered what lied beneath her handcrafted clothing, he'd kill her—regardless of whether he'd want to. The betrayal would destroy him, and the articles were clear.

"I know I don't belong here, and I know I've caused you a great deal of trouble. For what it's worth, I'm sorry. If you'll return my necklace, I'll be on my way."

The captain opened his eyes, gazing at her with a trickle of anger. "The articles you signed clearly describe all prizes are to be divided per the shares agreement. That means the necklace belongs to the crew now. At Nassau, I will have the appraiser document its value, and I'll sell it. Each man will get his due."

Emily refrained from jutting a finger at his bare chest. "That necklace is not from Sinclair's ship. It's not part of the prize. It's my personal belonging and, according to section two of the articles, your withholding of my personal belonging is robbing me."

The captain's lips twitched, as if he were fighting back a grin of amusement. Emily hated when he did that—treating her arguments as invalid. She wasn't stupid. She signed carefully.

Soft yellows and oranges of dawn stretched along the smooth horizon through the cabin windows. It was a breathtaking sight of beauty she never could have imagined. A sudden and stupid urge had her reaching for her pouch again to take a photo with her cell phone camera, but she quickly reminded herself that would mean death. She smoothed her sweaty palms against her breeches.

"It's a beautiful sight, isn't it?"

"I didn't think anything could top the night sky."

"Tell me," the captain whispered. "If I were to return the necklace to your possession, where would you go?"

Emily gazed back at the horizon. "Home."

"And where is such a place?"

The captain was always fishing for information. Was she that weird? "Far from here."

"As I suspected," he said with a tinge of disappointment. But he wasn't wrong to realize Emily didn't belong. Wisconsin was a long way off from the Caribbean Sea of 1715.

"Then why do you keep asking?" She turned on him, curious herself why she, of all the newest members of the crew, kept getting singled out for questioning.

The captain studied her as the dawn light shined in her face. "Because I'm struck by a fatal case of curiosity, but I'm grateful you continue to reject me."

Emily blinked. He hounded her for answers, but appreciated she didn't give them. Now, who was the strange one? Emily could tell where she wasn't wanted. Emily turned and strolled toward the cabin door. If she left, he'd be turning her back on the necklace. Glancing over her shoulder, she said, "I've already told you. Return my necklace, and I'll cause you no more trouble."

The captain didn't move. Not a word passed between his lips. Emily walked out.

EMILY LEANED AGAINST THE port rail, watching the morning light dance on the surface of the sea, wishing for coffee. Sailors around her manned their positions. She didn't have one, and no one assigned her to anything, so she absorbed the breathtaking view and tampered down the guilt creeping in. She wasn't a freeloader, but she didn't know the first thing about sailing. She wished she did, if only to take her mind off the captain and give her hands something to do.

Captain Lemoine didn't want her, but he wouldn't let her go, either, and Emily couldn't figure out why. If he would've given her the necklace, she would've been home by now, laughing with Angela at the absurdity of this adventure. And telling Robin she was lucky to have avoided it entirely.

But she also knew Captain Lemoine would haunt her dreams.

"Porter!" a stern man's voice commanded behind her, and it wasn't the captain's.

Emily turned, stomach clenching, and found the quartermaster with a clipboard in hand and a frown on his brow. "I assigned you hammock seventy-two, correct?"

Emily had snuck out of bed to slip into the captain's cabin with no intention of returning to her hammock tonight. Since she was trying to be stealthy, she hadn't packed it up at that hour. She'd since forgotten.

Without waiting for her excuse, Quartermaster Price continued, "Leaving hammocks hanging on the gun deck impedes movement in the event of an attack. Secure your bedding in the net over the rail."

Since he was the man in charge of her still-yet unknown punishment, Emily thought it wise to be kind. "I'm sorry. It won't happen again."

Quartermaster Price nodded, and Emily rushed below deck to correct her oversight. She found her lone hammock swaying with the ship's movement, but she couldn't reach the hooks attaching it to the ceiling. Searching around, she found a wood crate and moved it over. Emily stepped up and worked the fastenings, freeing her hammock. Wiping the sweat from her brow, a man cleared his throat.

Now what?

Emily spun and lost her balance with the heavy sack in her arms and a sway of the ship. The rotund man with a grease all over his apron caught her and gently set her on her feet. He wore a friendly smile. "I'm Giles, the cook. We haven't met formally, but since I didn't see you at breakfast, I thought I'd bring you sustenance." He held out a biscuit, and Emily accepted it. "You're not a sailor, I'd wager."

"No, not at all." Emily bit off a dry bite, but since she was hungry, she wasn't complaining.

Giles beamed. "I expected as much. Well, a piece of advice for you. Tend to your duties and keep to yourself. Some of these men are not friendly to new faces."

"And you're not one of them."

Giles winked.

"Thanks you for the tip." Emily swallowed down her biscuit, throat dry like a Wisconsin wintry morning. The ship's stale air didn't help, and with the sweat beading on her body and the salty, sticky air, Emily would welcome snow.

Giles offered her a cup of mystery liquid, and Emily downed it without a second thought.

"Good luck to you." Giles took the cup back from her and climbed down to the galley. In a sea of seventy or more men, she had two friends she could count on. Emily lugged her heavy pack up the ladder and leaned it against the rail. After sticking her head over the edge, she found the netting Price had mentioned. With a great struggle, she forced the pack into position neatly along the row of others. Emily panted with exhaustion, tired from a brief night's sleep.

A loud yawn came from behind her, and Emily stood upright and turned, ready to defend herself against further scrutiny. But Fergus's friendly face relaxed her.

"Yer hammock was empty half th'night."

"Couldn't sleep."

Fergus leaned against the rail next to her elbow, and Emily copied his posture, both staring off at the rising dawn. "Any family awaiting ye?" he asked.

"Do I have kids of my own?" she clarified. "No, but I have a houseplant and an ex…" Emily trailed off. She could give Fergus some truth, but spun for her safety. "A woman I courted recently, but I lost her." Emily hoped wherever Angela was, she was safe and happy.

Fergus lightheartedly patted Emily's shoulder. "Yer Angela? It's a man's veritable nightmare."

Loud footsteps captured Emily's attention. She turned to find the captain, and his intense gaze met hers. He'd dressed fully in a cocked hat, breeches up where they belonged, and a tunic under his long coat. He looked hot as hell, but she preferred the half naked version. "We land in Nassau in three days hence."

The crew cheered at the captain's announcement, and, eager to reach port, the men suddenly had more bounce in their steps. The masts swiveled in harmony, and a breeze caught the sails with a sharp snap. Emily grinned at the beauty of it. She watched, enamored, as the boatswain hollered commands to help the men coordinate their movements with chants. The helmsman, who wasn't the captain, took to the wheel and turned the rudder. The force pushed Emily against the rail, and her cheeks hurt from smiling so hard.

"Ye hear that?" Fergus said, voice bubbling with excitement. "Three days! Th'captain shall retain his command long enough fur us tae depart this wretched vessel, thanks tae ye."

Wretched vessel sounded accurate to her. She watched the captain on the quarterdeck, shoulders squared, hands clasped behind his back, and chin lifted as he gazed at the horizon. She'd never left the country, so a chance to visit a historical site on a tropical island sounded very appealing. Even better if she could shower and find real food. "I'm looking forward to exploring."

Fergus lit up. "Join me. I know of some exciting places."

Emily wanted a day of debauchery on shore with the captain, but she'd rather have Fergus than no one. "I can do that, sure."

Fergus grinned. "Time tae get tae work. Ye signed and now ye're expected tae sail this ship," Fergus said. "Since I canny wait tae disembark, I'll assist. Are ye coming along, then?"

Emily rubbed her forearm sheepishly. "I don't know how to sail."

Fergus smiled and patted her shoulder. "I thought no', but ye must learn sometime, pirate. Come along."

Emily followed her friend and smiled at his back, happy he was understanding rather than judgmental. As they crossed amidships, she glanced up at the captain next to the helmsman. He looked like a leader, strong, brave, and sexy as hell. She wanted him to notice not only was she cooperating, but she also wasn't attempting to break into his cabin again. Mostly, she just wanted him to notice her.

Emily's research left her dreaming of what life was like beyond the worn documents—how the men experienced all the wonders of the sea's power. And now here she was—an actual pirate, signed articles and all. But if she had to do any real pirating, Emily just knew she'd be the worst, because Emily wasn't a thief, and she didn't hurt people. The closest thing to a weapon she'd touched was a replica sword hanging in her bedroom.

Captain Lemoine's eyes followed her.

Chapter 11

Not much time passed before the glitz and glamour of living on a ship had waned. When Emily was young, her mother couldn't afford lavish trips. Instead, they went camping in the upper peninsula of Michigan—only a few hours' drive from home—with her mother's friends and their children. Emily's favorite site was Wells State Park on Lake Michigan. It had a beautiful beige sandy beach, fresh water for swimming, and hiking trails through the woods—an adventure so close to home.

And in the evenings, they'd roast marshmallows over an open firepit. When Emily was in her teen years, she was allowed to drink beer with the adults. And when she was an adult herself, she continued the tradition with her friends. She, Angela, and Robin swapped scandalous stories from their community college years. The three of them would lounge on the beach at sunrise, watching the pinks and purples dance in the sky and the sun shimmering on the lake's surface. Loons sang their eerie yodel.

At the end of each trip, she'd be exhausted, dirty, and sore from an air mattress, wishing for a hot meal. A short drive would get her all the modern luxuries she needed, including a hot shower.

This was so much worse than camping.

The physically demanding shifts in the salty sea air and penetrating sun left her needing a nap. One more day of this and she'd beg for rat duty below deck, except Emily didn't have the heart to kill the little dudes. They just wanted food and shelter like everyone else.

Emily pulled the line while Fergus expertly tied it, and Emily swiped a dirty arm across her sweaty brow and frowned. Because of a nightly chorus of snoring and thoughts of the captain on replay, Emily hadn't slept well. A poor diet of watered-down wine and stale crunchy biscuit, which resembled bread that had been left to harden in the sun for weeks, didn't help any. She'd known a pirate's diet was less than ideal, since scurvy and dysentery were major problems. All she could do was daydream about a cheeseburger and fries. A sizzle of grease from her favorite eatery filled her ears, and Emily turned her head to see if she had, in fact, lost her mind. They'd reach Nassau soon, but she wouldn't find a cheeseburger there.

With each passing hour, the quartermaster still hadn't called upon her for punishment. Emily began to believe it wouldn't happen. Maybe all those threats, all that excessive punishment in writing, had just been to scare people. No one really cut off someone's ears and nose for stealing, and no one really dropped someone off on a deserted island to die of thirst and exposure. The reality was, they were nice people—dirty, starved, and a little perverted—but nice in general.

"Porter, come with me," a familiar voice said behind her. The quartermaster had arrived.

Emily swallowed a thick lump, but it was caught in her dry throat.

Fergus wove the line around a belaying pin and stood straight beside her, as if he wanted to challenge Price for her attention. The quartermaster gestured with his head for her to follow. Emily met Fergus's concerned face, but he said nothing, only watched as she tilted her chin up, and walked off to whatever fate the quartermaster had in mind.

Below the main deck, in the aft of the gun deck, was Price's office, filled with rows and rows of old leather-bound books. These were not captain's logs. Of all the things she'd expected in a pirate's office—gold and jewels, namely—pleasure books were not it, since literacy rates were so low. The more she learned of the real pirates behind the legendary stories, the more she was intrigued. They weren't savage animals. They weren't greedy monsters slaughtering people for money. Pirates were just people, a product of their time and harsh circumstance. As much as she missed her modern amenities and well-rounded diet, this wasn't such a bad life.

Price closed the door on the two of them and sat behind his desk. He invited her to take a chair across from him, and Emily did. The quartermaster always held a seriousness to him, like someone who didn't know how to have fun. Perhaps he was allergic to it, but right now, he looked downright disgusted. That didn't bode well for Emily. "Do you know why I requested a meeting?"

"Is this about the rum?" It concerned her greatly that he'd needed days to settle this issue.

"Clearly, you're new to the world of free men. And you mustn't have been a merchant sailor at all. We have an understanding, a rank, that shall not be broken, no matter the issue at hand."

"I—" Emily tried to defend herself, but she gassed out. What excuse could she give that would satisfy him?

Price leaned forward, brow darkening. "Taking what isn't yours is stealing, no matter how noble the cause."

"But I'm one of the crew. The first section of the articles states all men have an equal claim to the provision and liquors and may use them at pleasure. I can't steal from myself."

Price's lips thinned. "Unless a scarcity makes it necessary to vote on the decision, but Lemoine convinced the men that wasn't needed."

Emily sat back. She had no right to freely give what wasn't hers to give, even if it solved the problem at the time. She'd jumped the proverbial gun to save an ass that didn't need saving.

"And even worse, you made a liar out of me." The anger festered, shifting the muscle in his jaw and twitching his eyelid.

"I didn't mean to undermine your authority. I was only trying to help the captain. They were so angry with him. I'm sorry." She hoped a sincere apology would be enough.

"The crew would agree with you, but there's a reason they aren't in charge. Both Lemoine and I have a right to settle a quarrel with you, which would take place on shore with swords and pistols. But after your embarrassing display out there, I'm of the esteem you know nothing of either weapons."

Price and the captain wanted to kill her? Emily couldn't even believe it. They *were* animals—filthy, disgusting, soulless monsters. "Well, you're right. I don't, so I guess it'll be an easy kill for you. Not so satisfying though, right?" Emily was pissed, but she didn't have the guts to stand up and march out of there. Something about how he paused led her to believe there was more, perhaps a lesser sentence. So she waited.

Price glared. The anger remained. "Lemoine declined to punish you, but since we have to follow the articles to keep authority, trust, and order in place, I'm not."

A string of swears poured through Emily's mind, but she kept her mouth shut. When the quartermaster deposited her on Nassau for their duel, she'd run like hell. She had a feeling Fergus wouldn't turn her in. He'd go with her.

"To spare your life, I'm sentencing you to ten lashes."

Hearing what was to come drained her anger away, and the fear of exposure returned once again. Instead of facing a dozen or so starved merchant sailors, now there were several dozen pirates. "How exactly do you go about giving those lashes?"

Price squinted at her. "Our lashes are doled the same as any other. We found you tied to the mast on the verge of the same punishment, so I don't understand where the confusion stems from. Regardless, your sentencing will commence momentarily. Refrain from defying orders in the future."

Emily's eyes widened, and she nodded, not knowing what to say without angering him further. Getting the hint he was finished, she launched out of his office in a state of imbalance and terror like a chain shot from a cannon.

There was no pirate ship to rescue her from the pirates.

QUARTERMASTER PRICE HAD STATED his case. The man was right in his decision, but Captain Eric Lemoine couldn't do it. He couldn't choose to duel the beautiful young man and take his life, but he also understood a punishment had to happen for the crew to maintain its order.

Lemoine could never have done the quartermaster's job. He couldn't take a life or make anyone suffer.

Captain Donald Sinclair had been the one exception.

Price had scheduled Emile Porter's punishment for nine bells. While Captain Lemoine braided his hair, a flurry of activity had already begun on the deck—barrels moved out of the way, lines pushed aside. Price needed enough distance to apply the proper force.

Lemoine shucked his coat and folded it before resting it over his chairback. He removed his tunic and draped it carefully over the coat. He exhaled a few deep breaths. Ready to fulfill his promise, he squared his shoulders and marched out of his cabin.

All but the essential crew surrounded the mainmast. Price was speaking to the men, holding a modified rope—their cat-o'-nine-tails. Rope stung a little less than leather at first, but it took longer to heal. The rough surface and frayed ends left several more scrapes and burns than sharp leather did.

The men parted for him to pass, and most of them didn't object.

How strange. Lemoine snorted softly to himself.

He entered the circle and faced his crew, meeting them eye to eye. He nodded once to acknowledge their thoughts and his decision, and Lemoine faced the mast. Karl Dillon, their boatswain, did the honors of tying Lemoine to the mast, exposing his back to Price. Karl was an honorable man. He might appear round, but he was sharp as a knife. He kept this ship functional, kept the wind in the sails, and kept the men flowing as one.

Karl offered Lemoine a knotted fabric bite block. "Take this. It helps."

Without a word, Lemoine opened his mouth, and Karl inserted it just right. Lemoine bit down, the sun making him sweat, but the breeze helped keep him cool. The ties at his wrists were to help keep him steady. After all, he'd volunteered, and he wasn't afraid. He'd experienced the cat before, had the scars to prove it. It wasn't pleasant, but he'd be fine...eventually.

When he was a boy, on the verge of adulthood, he'd been in this same position. Back then, he'd been terrified. He didn't know how much it would hurt, and the grim faces around him scared him worse. Those adults were afraid for him. But now he was grown, a man experienced with the harsh realities of his lifestyle. One thing never changed: Lemoine kept his word.

Karl patted Lemoine's back in solidarity and stepped away.

A man broke from the crowd and rushed to his side. It was Emile, and Lemoine didn't want to face him. He knew the man would object, and Lemoine wasn't changing his mind.

Emile whispered in urgent tones, "What's going on? What are you doing?"

Lemoine couldn't answer. Emile figured it out and tugged at his bite block.

Lemoine didn't let go. There was nothing he could say that would appease the beautiful man. And causing a scene when this punishment should've been his would only add to the crew's disgruntlement.

They appreciated Emile giving them their rum.

They hated Lemoine for allowing it and taking it away.

They hated Price for lying about it.

This had to happen, just as it was.

But as expected, Emile wouldn't give up. "Talk to me, please."

Price continued to answer questions from the crowd. The quartermaster was allowing Emile to get his answers, so on the next tug, Lemoine relaxed his grip on the bite block.

"Why are you tied up?" Emile whispered in a panic. "You didn't do anything wrong. Is this the mutiny?"

Captain Lemoine turned his head to meet those hazel eyes, now filled with fear. "I owed you a favor. Consider it repaid."

"Repaid? Are you saying…?" Tears glistened on Emile's lids. "No, you can't. This isn't right. I screwed up. It's my fault. Not yours. Please, don't do this, please."

Lemoine hadn't seen such guilt in a long time, but doing this would placate the crew and keep Lemoine's word honorable. Mostly, his choice kept Emile from facing this pain, because Lemoine couldn't handle if the roles were reversed. "Return my bite block," he said and opened his mouth.

Emile wiped his nose on the back of his hand and shoved the block forcibly into his mouth. "You're a selfish ass."

Emile ran off into the crowd, and Lemoine's brows lifted as he adjusted the bite block's position. Why would Emile assume such colorful things about him for this selfless act? With the cat about to hit, Lemoine couldn't let his thoughts wander. He focused on breathing deeply.

Price appeared and touched his shoulder. "Are we ready?"

Lemoine mumbled, and Price removed the block. "Push my braid aside." He held his mouth open again, and Price returned the block and swept his braid off his back.

The quartermaster lifted the whip. "And we begin."

The whip hit a second before each count, preventing Lemoine from tensing before the strike. Price wasn't going gently on the whip. Sometimes Lemoine wondered about him. Strike after strike lashed his bare skin. Blood ran down to his breeches. Each cut was like a hot knife searing through skin, and it burned, but for Emile's sake, he kept his face as blank as he could.

But he met the man's worried gaze.

Lemoine wanted to show him ten lashes were nothing. He didn't want the man to worry more. Emile was already on the verge of hysterics, such an uncommon thing for a man his age, but that only added to the mysterious puzzle. Where would someone find a man so beautiful with such strange mannerisms and clothing? Focusing on Emile lessened the pain, but by the final few strikes, Lemoine's face showed the burning agony.

"Ten."

Lemoine bit the block and pinched his face, trying to keep his eyes on Emile, but this last one, he couldn't. The whip came down hard, and Lemoine held his breath. The searing heat tore through damaged flesh, and more blood poured down his fiery flesh.

But it was over.

Lemoine dropped the bite block and panted. While Karl untied his wrists, Price coiled his cat. His face showed sorrow and regret, but Lemoine knew, deep down, Price had wanted to do that for a while. He'd jest with him later.

Lemoine cast Emile a comforting look before trying to stand and failing.

"Doctor!" a man shouted.

Emily's instincts were to run to his side. This was a medical emergency, and she was equipped to respond, but the captain's gaze told her not to. It would be too suspicious for her to attend to the needs of the man who'd already taken her punishment for her. And damn him for it. She was so angry he'd hurt himself for her sake.

But he saved her life.

Just as she'd saved his.

They were even, but that didn't stop her from wanting to help him. She couldn't imagine the indescribable pain, and he'd held himself together, stoic, brave, taking the licks without a cry of pain. It wasn't the first time. Captain Lemoine's muscular, broad back was crisscrossed with raised scars—previous whippings.

Emily would've been screaming and pleading for mercy—if they'd decided to go forward with the cat after they stripped her top naked. She still would've screamed and pleaded for mercy.

A stout man with a long white beard pushed through the crew and assessed the captain's wounds. At least there was a real doctor on the ship. Emily's relief was palpable.

"Take 'em down to the infirmary." The heavy medic climbed down the ladder ahead of his patient, and in moments, the injured captain was assisted down into the bowels of the ship.

No one had ever sacrificed themselves for her like that, favor owed or not, and Emily didn't know what to do with that. She wished she could be in the infirmary with him. Taking the lashes was the deal he'd made without her consent, but healing from the wounds was something else.

The crew mumbled to each other, and Boatswain Karl commanded everyone to return to their stations. Emily struggled through the day, doing whatever Fergus directed her to do, planning how she could help the stubborn captain.

Chapter 12

EMILY HAD SPENT THAT night tossing and turning in her hammock, covering her ears against the barrage of snores, creaks, and night shift orders. All she could think about was the agony the captain must've been suffering on her account. She wished she could sneak into his cabin and tend his wounds. It was the least she could do, but that was too risky. Even a wind of favoritism would be enough for the crew to uphold the last of the articles: *no boy or woman to be allowed amongst them.* They didn't need to prove any bedtime activities to punish her with death. The assumption was enough. Emily wasn't going to risk her life just to scold the captain, and she wasn't going to send away a perfectly qualified doctor from his duty.

All day, the crew hadn't gossiped one peep about the captain's punishment. Price had answered all their questions to their satisfaction, and that was that. Unlike them, Emily couldn't forget it, but she didn't know what to do about it.

Emily finished tying her line and rose to take a break and stretch her back. Her eyes immediately moved to the navigation room, through which the captain's cabin rested. And as if her wishes simply came true, Captain Lemoine emerged. He wasn't wearing his coat, just breeches and a tunic. But he was alive, and a flush of relief eased the ache in her bones. That was the only news she'd received on his condition since the whipping. He was alive.

Captain Lemoine moved with the stiffness of fresh wounds, climbing up the quarterdeck, steady on his feet, and he spoke with the helmsman, Hodgens. Emily had a small chat with the man the other day. He had the personality of bread—ordinary, bland, but with a little warming up, delightful. They were too far away for Emily to hear them.

"Sails!" the man in the crow's nest shouted.

Their heads turned, and Emily copied them. She skimmed the horizon, but seeing nothing discernible with the naked eye, she watched a man rush below deck and quickly retrieve the quartermaster. Price joined the captain and Hodgens on the quarterdeck, and both Price and Lemoine took turns observing from the spyglass. Neither of them looked pleased. Before she realized what she was doing, Emily's feet brought her within earshot of the men just as Boatswain Karl joined them. Master gunner, McKee, followed, but she hadn't met him, only caught his name in passing.

"Royal Navy," Captain Lemoine said with a grim set to his jaw.

"Are you certain?" Price asked with a shocking tremble in his voice. Emily hadn't believed the man capable of feeling anything but grumpiness.

Captain Lemoine returned the spyglass to his eye and flinched. Emily assumed it was from soreness, not worry. His voice was light, almost joyful, just like when she's first met him. "Three gun decks, English flag. Perhaps I'm mistaken?" Emily smiled. The captain was back to his old self.

Then she processed the words. That size ship could be nothing but a man-o'-war.

Price accepted the offered spyglass and peered through it. The crew, without critical tasks, filled in around her, awaiting news and orders, and Fergus appeared at her shoulder. She noticed the lithe man frequently stayed by her side; this time he was grinning like a fool.

"What part of a man-o'-war makes you happy?" Emily asked.

"I, fur one, am grateful tae have skipped signing th'articles. When we're caught, I'll be spared th'noose."

Emily frowned. "And you don't care that I won't be?"

Fergus looked at her with a softness she hadn't expected. "I dae care, but if ye'd heeded ma advice, ye wouldn't be worried noo. Th'three o' us, who refrained, shall be free, ainlie noo we dinny have tae wait fur Nassau."

Emily's voice grew louder. "Do you hear yourself? Have you ever considered no one deserves the noose?"

Heads turned to her while waiting for the captain's news and orders.

Fergus raked a hand through his red, bushy hair and caught glances of the crew around him. His voice quieted, "Aye. I dae." He gazed at her as if the words were meant for Emily only. "If ye swear ye were pressed, th'Crown shall be lenient. Extra steps fur ye, since ye signed, but still th'same outcome."

Emily folded her arms over her chest, not satisfied with his confidence. "You think if I lie in court, they'll free me? Have you read the hist—?" Emily cut herself off before earning herself more questions. Many pirates claimed to be pressed for the sole purpose of not being sentenced. It didn't work much of the time.

"When th'*Sea Lion* is captured, consider ma advice this time?"

"Your advice was not to sign because these people are worse than Sinclair, but you're clearly wrong."

Fergus flustered. "I'm noo wrong about them." He nodded toward the ship approaching.

She wasn't going to give him the satisfaction of an answer to that. If the Royal Navy arrested her, she was as good as dead, like all the others. The Royal Navy didn't conscript pirates into their ranks, so the only other option was to flee their custody. But since they were surrounded by ocean and sharks, there was nowhere to flee toward.

Emily focused on the captain. He was their leader. He knew what to do. The quartermaster returned the spyglass to the captain, and Boatswain Karl asked, "Your orders, captain?"

Captain Lemoine kept his eye on the man-o'-war. The grim set to his jaw returned. "The barque can outpace her if we dump the cargo."

Because of their size and heavy artillery, and carrying hundreds of trained soldiers, man-o'-war ships were cumbersome, gliding castles. If the *Sea Lion* was within the warship's range, the damage would be fast, efficient, and catastrophic. If instead the soldiers boarded the *Sea Lion*, the discrepancy in the number of soldiers versus pirates meant a slaughter was inevitable. She glanced at all the worried faces around her. None of them deserved to die like that. They had to dump the cargo, but Emily expected no pirate wanted to give up their loot in an escape attempt when they weren't certain about being caught. How else was everyone going to be fed, paid, and remain complacent?

"Naught else can be done?" Price asked, paling in fear.

"The *Sea Lion* is a formidable foe against merchant ships. And I'd wager friendly competition against a sixth-rate frigate, but I commandeered her for speed, not her guns. If we fight a first-rate man-o'-war, we'll lose," Captain Lemoine said with finality.

Emily swallowed a thick lump. If they were only a day or so from Nassau. Hungry, unpaid, and desperate pirates should be content for one day. They wouldn't turn on the new recruits... They wouldn't discover things they shouldn't...

Those worries only mattered if they escaped the warship's chase.

The first cannon rang out across the surface, followed by a splash. Time was of the essence. The captain gave his instructions to Karl, and the bald boatswain dished out the orders to the men. The assigned crew flew up the rigging and ratlines, preparing for full speed ahead.

"Dump it," Price said with defeat. Emily didn't like that disappointment and edge to his tone, so her concerns over the crew were justified.

The captain gave out his next orders, and Boatswain Karl barked them to the next teams. "Jettison the hold!"

Men poured down the ladders to obey, and Karl turned to her and Fergus. "You two, bring up the sand." Karl brushed past them on his way to supervise the change of sails.

Emily cocked her head at Fergus for clarification.

"Follow me." Fergus moved down the levels below, and in a room opposite the hold, Fergus opened the door and hefted a pair of burlap bags over his shoulders. All the warmth drained from Emily's face. How was she going to carry those? "Can ye handle a bag?" Fergus gave her a sly smile.

The bags were probably heavier than the barrel of rum had been. A small nervous smile tilted her lips, and Fergus handed her one. Emily hugged it, straining, and her knees felt the weight.

"After th'first crew rushes up wi' th'stores, we'll make our way. Gaining speed right noo is more important than gripping th'deck."

Another cannon fired, and shortly thereafter, wood crunched on impact. Panicked shouts came from below deck, but Emily was so preoccupied with understanding her assignment, she didn't give any other thought to it. "What are we doing?"

"In battle, th'deck becomes mighty slippery. Sand gives a foothold."

Emily pictured clanging swords and gunshots ringing her eardrums. And since the waves weren't crashing over the rail, Fergus must've meant blood. Emily's stomach flipped. She inhaled several humid, musty breaths from the dank belly of the ship. When Fergus commanded, she rushed up behind him on the ladder, knees screaming with each step.

Other pirates were already shouting for them to move out of the way by the time they reached the main deck.

Fergus tore into his bag and sprinkled it around like ice melt on a Wisconsin sidewalk. Finally, something familiar.

Emily couldn't tear hers. "Can I get a hand?"

Fergus smiled and ripped a hole in her bag. They both shook gritty sand all over the deck while some of it fell between the planks.

"I have a little brother back home." Fergus smiled wistfully. Emily figured he was picturing his impending escape. "He dreams o' sailing th'seas. I tried tae change his mind, but according tae his correspondence, th'lad is firm. Mum and Da insist oan encouraging him. I haven't th'heart tae wreck his dreams wi' th'reality o' merchant sea life. Are ye ever going tae tell me where ye came from? Ye and th'lost woman, Angela?

This time, the cannon blast got her attention. Emily straightened with her half-empty bag and followed the trajectory of the massive ball as it soared through the sky. It aimed right at the bulwark in front of her. She stared like a deer in the headlights, unable to make her limbs react, unable to believe what she was seeing.

At the last second, before the iron ball blasted through the bulwark right at Emily, she was forcibly shoved down for cover, head hitting the planks. The sandbag spilled, throwing a cloud in her face. Spots danced in her vision. Emily coughed. Her ears rang a high-pitched whistle above the crunching of wood and shouts from the crew.

When her vision cleared, she stared at the brilliant blue sky with white puffs of clouds floating on by like a gentle parade. She remembered one of her picnics with Angela while camping. They'd brought out a large blanket to cover the grass, and her friend carried a basket with junk food and beer. They'd crack and chug a few cans, and after the buzz eased every muscle in Emily's body, she'd drop over onto the blanket and gaze at the shapes in the clouds. The last time they'd partaken in the biannual excursion, Angela had pointed and said, "Over there. It's a rabbit!"

Emily had squinted. "I only see Wile E. Coyote chasing the Road Runner. Did you know his middle initial stands for Ethelbert?" Emily had chuckled at her own observation. "You're just too drunk to see straight. Toss me some Cheetos."

Angela had sat up too quickly. "Whoa, Road Runner's doing circles." They'd both broken out in laughter, and Angela tried twice to get her hand into the basket. "Too bad Robin had a shift today. Why didn't Tyler want to join?"

"He's starting on the business. It's pretty time consuming."

"Well, I'm excited for you. What are you selling or what service are you offering? I'll be your first customer." Angela tore into a fun size bag of Cheetos.

Emily considered. In all their conversations, that never came up. "I don't know."

Emily blinked. The ACME anvil floated overhead.

The ringing subsided and sweaty men's heads dipped in and out of her vision. Their thundering boots rattled the wood beneath her head. The wind had been knocked from her lungs. She sucked in a breath and sat up, rubbing the back of her head and coughing on the sand dust. Other than the smack on the skull and serious bruising that would hurt tomorrow, she was okay.

The bulwark was splintered and a big hole remained where it had stopped by for a visit. How did she avoid any serious damage? Someone must've pushed her out of the way on time.

The crew was focused on moving the ship away. Through the cannonball hole, the navy ship sank further into the distance. They were outrunning it! With a smile of relief on her face, Price stood on the quarterdeck shouting orders. Why wasn't Captain Lemoine up there? Emily craned her neck around but couldn't see him or her friend anywhere. She rose on wobbly legs and hooked her hand around the first man's arm, who came close enough, stopping him in his tracks. "Where's Fergus?"

He shrugged out of her grip and said, "Infirmary."

Emily's empty stomach twisted like she was going to be sick. "Which deck is he on?"

The meaty, broad-shouldered pirate pointed to the ladder. "Orlop. Two down, swing aft. When you see the coil of messenger cable, you're in the right place." He marched away without another word, and Emily made her way down and paused with a hand supporting her woozy head. Her damage might not have been from the cannonball, but the fall had been nasty.

After regaining her composure, she fumbled down the next ladder on unsure footing. She swung herself around the post and found the floor tilting. Emily paused and pulled in several deep breaths to steady herself. If Fergus had sacrificed himself for her, how would she ever forgive herself? Twice now men have risked their lives for her sake, and they didn't even know her!

Finding the door ajar and a serious commotion inside, Emily panted from exertion and worry while she peered inside. It was worse than she thought.

Chapter 13

THE SMELL OF BLOOD. The hurried and hushed voices. The groans of pain. All by the flicker of candle lanterns. Emily couldn't figure out what was happening. She pushed her way through the activity in the suffocating room. A beat-up old plank was settled over a pair of barrels, upon which a man writhed in pain. Fergus stood by his side, head tipped low.

Emily shuffled over to her friend, and a spin of her head had her gripping Fergus for balance. The redhead was startled at first, but he looked at her and smiled. "How are ye feeling? Ye took a good knock tae th'head. I dinny want tae leave ye up there, but ye weren't bleeding. We're waiting on Meeks. He'll see ye next. Sit over here while ye wait." Fergus moved a crate full of supplies and brushed the surface of the barrel clean with his hand.

"Meeks? Who's Meeks?" Emily asked, sitting and pressing a hand against her forehead.

"Th'doctor. Ye must be hurting." His gentle eyes searched her body for wounds.

Emily dropped her hand, fully expecting a headache. "I'll live. What happened? Are you okay?"

"I'm fine. Th'captain shoved me over an' tackled ye. If he hadn't, ye'd be oan this table, an' I'd be sitting in yer seat. Emile." Fergus rested a hand on Emily's shoulder. "I dinny admit when I'm wrong much, because it disny happen often. The captain is a fine man. Yer instincts were right in signing."

Emily didn't sign because of the captain, but that wasn't worth spoiling his apology for. "Thanks, Fergus, but why the change of heart?"

A large muscle-bound man with a shiny dome on top of his head ducked into the small space. "Meeks is dead. The last shot hit him square in the middle."

"The doctor is dead?" Emily's pulse quickened with the emergency response she'd trained for. She stood and swayed on her unsteady feet.

Retail workers often tried to lift too much and pulled a muscle, or they dropped something on their foot, or fell off ladders—despite safety equipment. Sometimes customers ended up with blood sugar emergencies. Emily was a volunteer first responder for her store. Her training only went as far as first aid, CPR, proper AED use, and under which circumstances to call an ambulance. Modern medicine wasn't an option here.

"Captain, who should fill the role now?" the bald behemoth asked.

Captain? Where? A groan came from the makeshift table, and Emily recognized that voice. Her heart leaped into her throat, and fresh guilt tore into her like a cannonball. It should've been her. He'd already taken a whipping for her, and he hadn't healed from it yet.

"I'll do it." Emily feared her skills wouldn't be enough for the captain, but she absolutely couldn't do nothing.

Her friend cast her a worried stare. "Ye need the doctor yerself. Surely someone more qualified—"

"I might not know how to sail. I might not have the strength to keep up with you, and I might not fit in, but I can do this. I have to do this." Emily moved around Fergus and approached the captain apprehensively. It was different when the patient was someone...she cared about.

The captain groaned with his eyes squeezed shut. Emily was terrified he was going to die because of her. She wished she'd packed more pain meds. "I'm not a doctor, but I'm the best you got. Is there a medicine chest on board?" she asked the behemoth over her shoulder. "And bring me fresh water and a cup." The large man nodded, accepting his orders, and left.

Emily turned to Fergus. "Help him, and bring some clean rags, too." She needed any help she could get, and she wanted privacy.

Fergus reluctantly left, and Emily rolled the barrel seat over to the captain's side and settled the lantern near. She trembled with adrenaline coursing through her as she observed his bloodied tunic. Shards of wood peppered the captain's side. His hand moved to cover the tender site. Holding back her tears, she tried to move his hands to see the injuries clearer, but he resisted. She palmed his shaking hands. "Please," she begged. "Let me see."

The captain's faced was pinched, but he met her gaze and grunted. "I don't want you to see me like this."

"Then you shouldn't have gotten in the way."

Captain Lemoine closed his eyes. "A captain protects his men, and dying to save his men is an honor."

Tears shimmered in her vision. "Don't you dare give up on me. You deserve a better life than this filthy ship, and you deserve a death when you're old. Not like this. Not...like this. Not...for me."

The captain's hands moved away and settled on the plank beneath him. She gently lifted a corner of the fabric, careful not to agitate the wounds, but the captain sucked in breaths and his body tensed. She didn't get a good look, but this was far beyond her pay grade. There was no one else. The tears fell. "Why? Why did you do that?"

His breath hitched and released in spurts.

Scolding him wasn't productive. "Try not to move. I'm going to do everything I can, but you must do as I say."

The captain groaned.

The thunder of boots turned her head, and the beefy behemoth deposited an old wooden chest and a pail of water by her feet. Fergus appeared behind him, white as fresh winter's snow, and he handed her a cup and an armful of rags—not as clean as she'd prefer, but beggars and choosers and all that. They hovered. Emily wanted more alone time with the captain, and having these two lurking over her shoulder wasn't going to help steady her nerves at all. "Go fix the holes in the boat or something."

Both men left, and Emily appreciated them listening to her—as if she were an equal.

The captain managed a chuckle and then another groan. "Taking over my job, are we?"

Emily smiled. "Nope. It's still yours. I'm doing my best." She opened the chest and shifted the lantern. "You need better lighting in this place. This is ridiculous. Who can work like this?"

"Meeks."

"Stop talking. I don't want you to hurt yourself worse."

"Words don't hurt. It's everything else."

Emily gazed at him thoughtfully, but she couldn't waste time talking when she needed to stabilize him. Inside the chest were strips of soiled cloth, glass bottles of uneven size and color with indecipherable labels, and various rusty metal tools she wouldn't know what to do with. Oh, and a pouch of powder. Emily didn't want to know what that was.

Pain management became the top priority. Emily used the cup to scoop out water. Opening her tiny ibuprofen bottle from her pouch, she offered the captain four white pills and the cup. "Swallow these and use this to wash them down."

The captain opened his mouth for the pills, and she set them just inside his lips, trying not to focus too much on the feel of his lips.

And he'd made such a big deal over her trying to feed him chocolate.

Brushing aside a minor amusement, Emily supported his head while the captain drank. She set the cup down and exhaled a deep breath. Next step. Emily slipped the tiny scissors from her sewing kit onto her fingers and lifted the captain's tunic.

"What are...you doing?" He blocked her.

A little humor helped with stress and pain. "I've already seen you half naked. Don't be shy now." His hand didn't move, so Emily resorted to begging. "I can help, but I need to keep the site clear. I need to see what I'm doing. Please let me help."

The captain dropped his head back and removed his hand, fingers curling into fists at his sides.

Emily cut off his tunic and freed the sodden material from the punctures, exposing his strong and tanned chest with a dusting of dark hair. Emily blew out a quick breath and examined his skin. Alongside his ribs, a series of wood fragments from the impact pierced his flesh. The darkening of the skin meant severe bruising was on the way. He needed an operating room. But the combination of her first aid skills and her experience with a sewing needle would have to suffice. How much different could sewing flesh be?

Emily dug into her pouch again and removed a small sewing kit she'd brought along to fix any costume malfunctions. She'd also packed ointment to stave off infection in case of splinters from sudden rough waters or touching the tour ship's rail. She hadn't expected to use these things to save a man's life.

"You might have some broken ribs, and I need to keep cutting." Emily snipped along the side of his breeches, finding the material difficult to split with her tiny scissors meant for thread. The captain didn't stop her. After cutting down to his upper thigh, Emily pulled the flap of fabric back only as far as necessary, keeping his privacy intact. She found more blood from several gashes. Not a fatal amount, but he needed stitches.

She pulled out a needle and thread from her sewing kit. What could she sterilize it with?

Price's secret rum! Hopefully, there was some left. "I'll be right back. Don't move."

The captain opened one eye, and the corner of his lips lifted. "Here I'd planned on taking a turn about the deck for fresh air, and you just had to ruin it." He chuckled and his face pinched in pain.

Emily smiled for his sake. Seemed the ibuprofen was helping. "A sense of humor is good for you, but it I mean it—don't move."

"As you wish, captain."

Now was not the time for more Westley devotion. Emily bit back her smile and darted across the lower deck, thankful everyone—including her—had tucked away their hammocks. She ducked and hoped over obstacles and climbed the ladder to the mess hall. She found the last barrel the pirates had, and there was hardly a glisten at the bottom. Emily tilted it and scooped out what she could with a nearby discarded cup. Desperate for more, she checked every mug left behind and dumped all the remainders into her cup. She had half a cup to work with. It would have to do.

Returning to the captain's side at lightning speed, Emily set down the rum and sterilized a needle and thread with it. She paused. He'd need something to bite into. What did she have? Emily used her tiny scissors and cut away some of the hem of her tunic, and tearing when the scissors surrendered. She fastened a string of knots into it. "Bite this. It'll help." She placed the knots between his lips, and he bit down.

"Here it comes. Try not to move." Emily poured a ration of rum over the biggest shard at his hip.

The captain grunted in pain, squeezing down on the knots. With a rubber thimble on her forefinger, she gripped the hunk of wood embedded in his flesh and pulled it out with a smooth stroke. The captain tensed, face burning bright red, cords on his neck straining, and a long groan passed his lips. The sooner she could get through it, the better, for his sake and hers. She poured more rum over the open wound and began the arduous process of stitching the bleeding wound closed.

She spoke to him, not expecting answers, just to help him keep his mind off the pain. "Few men would dive in front of a cannonball for you. Duty or not, I don't understand why you did it."

Another groan passed between his lips. "For the same reason I accepted your punishment in your stead. I couldn't bear to see you harmed."

Emily paused, stunned by his words. She'd begged him not to take her punishment, but she never thanked him. "It wasn't just a captain's duty?"

Captain Lemoine opened his sincere brown eyes, but he didn't answer, and that was answer enough.

"Thank you. You saved my life." Emily's heart pounded in her chest, and her hands shook. She took a quick break to shake the adrenaline from her fingers and noticed what might be tweezers in the doctor's chest. She dunked them into the rum and meticulously pulled out each of the smaller slices of wood, dropping them into a pile by her feet.

He groaned and tilted his head back, squeezing his eyes closed. "How did you learn to doctor?"

Chatting was a distraction. "I like to sew clothing, and this isn't much different. I even made my own clothes."

The captain smiled through the pain. "Then you went to a strange school. I've never seen stitches like those."

"You've never seen stitches like the ones in your thigh, either."

The captain chuckled.

Emily watched his face as she wiped the tweezers clean, giving him a small break. She snipped a fresh length of thread.

"The men on the rigging crew patch up the sails when they tear, but you're not a sailor."

Emily thought a question rested in there. She worked methodically, starting with the next worst injury at his rib, holding it together and securing it closed with pretty stitches. His muscles shifted under her hand, and she wished she could take away all his pain.

The captain's eyes opened and squeezed shut once again. She trickled more rum over the finished product. Not bad for a dimly lit rocking ship in the middle of the Caribbean with a sewing kit.

"The worst is over now. Only a few smaller ones left. Stay with me." From her untrained eye, none of his injuries appeared to have punctured anything vital.

Emily moved on to the minor gashes and stitched them one by one. She slathered antibacterial ointment around each clean wound, taking great care in her touch. She hoped he didn't succumb to infection.

"The answer is no," he said.

"To what question?"

His chest rose and fell with short breaths. "It wasn't my duty."

Emily captured his gaze and froze with a roll of what could be called gauze in her hand.

"Emile Porter...I can't thank you enough for what you've done for me. At a tumultuous precipice in my career, you saved my life from a mutinous crew, you gave me the chance to earn back their confidence, and now you're saving my life again. I don't have such luck with non-sailor conscripts, but I daresay I'm grateful to have you on my ship."

She was under the impression she only mastered the art of screwing up. "I'm glad I was here for you." Emily's face burned hot, surprised at her own admission. She didn't belong here. She wasn't supposed to be here. She clearly didn't fit in, but Emily was thinking of nothing but him.

Chapter 14

"Help me sit up," the captain asked.

"That's a good idea. Then I can wrap you with this." Emily held out what appeared to be a roll of gauze and set it off to the side. She braced herself for getting very personal with the captain. On an exhale, Emily straddled the captain's lap carefully, keeping too much distance between their bodies. The captain's gaze was unmistakable—there was heat and lust hidden behind all the pain. Warmth flooded her cheeks and sweat broke out on her back. Emily leaned in by his face and scooped her arms under his. Her body trembled. She wanted to press him against her and kiss those smooth lips of his. Their faces were inches apart. All she'd have to do was move a little.

She couldn't.

He'd definitely discover two things that didn't belong, and maybe a few things that were missing.

"Gently now. I don't need you tearing your new stitches. On three." Emily counted down and eased the captain upright.

His handsome face pinched, but he maintained a seated position on his own. He swung his legs down over the edge of the plank and winced, sliced fabrics draping haphazardly. Captain Lemoine shucked the rest of his tunic scraps.

Emily uncurled the gauze, appreciating the view of his upper body and exposed thick thigh. But her heart broke all over again at the train tracks of stitches running over his side. Those should've been hers. "Arms up, if you can."

The captain held his arms away from his gorgeous torso, and Emily leaned in close again, wrapping him to support his ribs. His eyes followed her as she moved her arms around and around, pulling the material supportively taut. "How does that feel?"

"It's missing something."

"What's that?" Emily thought she'd thought of everything. Sure, some morphine would've been nice, but that wasn't an option—

The captain closed the distance between them, his lips finding hers. His fingers rested on the nape of her neck and moved down to her back.

Emily's brows lifted. Her hands slipped along that soft scruff of his beard and held him close as she repositioned their lips, unwilling to let him go. They were as soft as she'd imagined, and he moved with care, testing her, questioning her.

Asking permission to be there.

Their breaths mingled, and Emily fought every carnal desire to leap at him and take him here on this dirty plank. As if their thoughts were one, Captain Lemoine pulled her closer.

Emily pushed against his efforts and backed away. She needed an excuse. Thankfully, there were several to choose from. "That's against the rules."

"Some rules were meant to be broken." The fiery heat in the captain's eyes was alluring, and she agreed wholeheartedly.

But breaking the most grievous of offenses wouldn't be excused with a single punishment, and the captain could handle no more. Her face pinched in confusion.

"What is the matter?" Captain Lemoine asked, dark eyes of concern flickering under candlelight.

He'd said he wanted her to reject him, but this was just the opposite. "Why did you kiss me?"

"I've sailed these seas for five and twenty years with my eye focused on one goal. Along the way, I've commandeered ships, I've recruited men to the account and lost many on the way. I've always been sure of what my purpose was. But as we progress through seasons in our lives, sometimes the life we've always seen changes when we least expect it. I want to know everything about you. I want to spend every moment with you, and the distance between was too much to bear. I kissed you because I am simply weak—no longer able to resist your allure. Emile Porter, I understand this might be different for you, but I want you, and I want you to be comfortable about it."

A warmth blossomed in her chest. She'd never felt more wanted in her life, and the feeling was mutual. Emily desperately wanted to be with him and be by his side, but how? They were from different worlds. And if he discovered she wasn't a man, would the captain still want her? And at her deceit, would he turn her in for the just punishment? It was a risk she couldn't take. "As long as we're both on this ship, we can't."

The bald behemoth lumbered into the tiny room and lit up with the sight. "Captain! Good to see you upright."

"Cantu, what is the status on the man-o'-war?"

"She's found terrible winds, I'm afraid." Cantu, the enormous man, grinned. "Most unfortunate about our prizes."

"Most excellent. Tell the men I'll be up shortly and not to worry."

Cantu nodded and gleefully left.

"I hope you have a change of clothing," Emily said, admiring the view while it lasted.

The captain looked down at himself. "I do, in my quarters. Please accompany me."

Captain Eric Lemoine had always been sure of what he wanted, always prepared to do whatever necessary to get it. The kiss had been the only thing in the world needed to dull his pain, but it would be the only one he'd ever get. Lemoine would remain on this ship until that one goal was met, and he wanted Emile at his side, but he couldn't ask Emile to wait for him. The handsome man was the first person Lemoine had ever wanted, but he couldn't have him. Lemoine should not have broken his own request to remain at arm's length. Now Lemoine could never let go.

Still, he had to.

Emile helped him to his feet and wrapped an arm around him for support. Lemoine groaned as he straightened. He was in worse shape than he'd thought.

As Emile took small steps, they found a slow rhythm to make their way up, and the handsome man's face was so close to his own, it pained him to not kiss him again.

"I thought pirate captains were supposed to be ruthless, evil, devils of the sea, enemies of every nation," Emile said near his ear.

"That's mostly the tales."

Emile stopped and turned his face to his. The distance, so little but so far at the same time, pressed a knife in his chest.

"Absorbing damage costs the crew in more ways than one, so intimidating ships into surrendering is a much wiser strategy. But that effect is the result of a carefully grown reputation. Only on rare occasions are deaths necessary."

"You never answered why you shot Captain Sinclair when you already doomed to die."

Captain Lemoine didn't want to withhold the truth from Emile. He'd put his trust in him, and as much as Lemoine wanted to learn everything about the puzzling man, Lemoine wanted to be known, too. He wanted to matter to someone. But if Lemoine couldn't have Emile, what was the point in offering a tale that could tarnish his reputation if shared?

Lemoine turned the questioning back onto Emile, hitting a place he knew the man wouldn't answer. "You're a very strange man, Emile. I cannot place it, and I wish you'd help me understand."

Emile gazed into his face with a softness and a pain of his own. "Let's get you dressed."

As expected, he'd avoided. Lemoine nodded, and Emile led the way, but he struggled with the listing of the ship, and he used bulkheads and other handholds to make his way on his feet. Too many times the cut material in his breeches sent a cool breeze where it didn't belong. Lemoine tried to keep himself proper, but he wasn't always successful. He'd never felt more like an invalid, but next to Emile, he wasn't embarrassed. He was grateful. The man understood the lengths Lemoine had gone for him, the cause of this pain.

Despite the cavern between them, he'd do it all over again without a second's thought.

At the main deck, Emile helped him stand up, supporting him from the uninjured side, and he brought Lemoine across the deck.

"Captain's on his feet! Everyone, captain's back to bring us to glory!" A chorus of cheers sang across the decks, and suddenly the men were in higher spirits and working faster. The captain smiled and waved to the men to show his strength.

Jettisoning the hold to outrun the Royal Navy meant they had nothing to sell. After they restocked their lost supplies in Nassau, the men would be eager to return to the seas to fetch a prize. And Captain Lemoine would lead them to the glory he'd promised.

EMILY TOOK MUCH OF the captain's weight up the decks and across to his navigation room and into his cabin. Inside the humid hull, and under the blistering sun, Emily was sweating. She'd held him a little awkwardly to prevent a boob graze, too. And she was already long overdue for a shower. Emily carefully set him on the bed, and Captain Lemoine adjusted the loose flap of his breeches to cover himself more appropriately. Emily wished for a better view, and the captain had put the option on the table, but Emily couldn't.

"In my trunk."

Emily unlatched the intricate trunk and chose a tunic and a pair of breeches. Emily figured out he hadn't been wearing anything underneath his breeches, but that didn't mean he didn't have any. While carefully searching for drawers, Emily couldn't help but fawn over the materials, the stitching...the quality. Cosplayers would die for such authentic attire.

Emily was already fangirling.

"Is something the matter?" Captain Lemoine asked.

She'd lingered too long. Her face flushed, and she closed the trunk, standing with her arms full. "Can you put on your clothes, or do you need help?"

"I will speak the truth, but it shall not leave the confines of this room, understand?"

He had her full attention. "I understand."

"I need a grown man to help me dress. Thank you for your help."

Emily smiled. "It's okay." She reached for the hem of his tunic, and the captain flinched as he raised his arms. Emily quickly removed the destroyed tunic, and to irritate the wounds as little as possible, she slipped the fresh tunic straight on. She'd already seen his chest and abs, but she didn't skip a chance to get another eyeful.

Emily reached for the waistband of his mangled breeches. "Can you lift, and I'll tug?"

"I cannot," he said, with an embarrassed tone.

Emily had to keep his dignity intact. This was difficult for him, but it wasn't difficult for her. He was magnificent and beautiful, and she relished the opportunity to help. Emily fished out her sewing kit and slipped her tiny scissors into her fingers. She cut the air apologetically. "They're already sliced up. I don't see any other way."

"Proceed." The captain watched her intently with each snip.

Could she have cut them off with only the metal grazing his skin? Yes, of course. Did she? No, of course not. Safety first. Emily began where she'd left off, cutting near his injuries, with a finger carefully keeping his skin protected.

The captain's head fell back as if he, too, enjoyed her touch.

After finishing the already damaged side, she moved to his other side and cut all the way down, one snip at a time. Her fingers ached and cramped, but she didn't care. She dragged a hand along his healthy thigh, lifting the fabric for each cut.

The damaged fabric twitched, and knowing what the captain was thinking, Emily blew air up her face while her heart pounded ferociously in her chest.

She freed his feet from his boots and brought the breeches over. "Ready?"

The captain nodded.

Emily moved the fabric away, exposing him entirely. His thighs were as firm as she'd pictured, mounds of muscle gave him a nice shape. And he was well hung, judging by the half mast down below.

Emily bit back a smile, and sweat trickled down her back. She exhaled and kneeled at his feet. Emily slipped the fresh pair up to his knees. "You'll have to stand up to finish putting them on."

"When you're ready." His features pinched.

"The question is, are you ready?" Emily wished she'd checked her phone for the time, so she'd known when to give him another dose of painkillers. Without a functional network, she doubted the time would be right, anyway. Emily moved over to his good side and counted down to three. She lifted with all her might, arms trembling with the effort.

She bent and lifted his breeches. The captain eagerly tied them as the door opened, but her face was near his bulge. Quartermaster Price scowled.

"It's not what you think," Emily volunteered.

Price scrutinized her and turned to his captain. "Glad to see you on your feet, Lemoine. When you're ready, we'll set a new course for Nassau. Porter, we owe you a great debt."

"Please, no. It's no big deal." Earning praise from the man who wanted to whip her a few days ago felt so jarring, so superficial. She didn't believe his gratitude.

"We haven't assigned to you a position yet," Price added. "Since you have a doctor's skills, and we happen to be short one, you'll do just fine."

"Wait, what?" Emily barked out in surprise and looked at the captain for his rebuttal. She belonged assisting with the sails next to Fergus.

But Captain Lemoine only nodded. From one moment to the next, she had no idea where she ranked on the totem pole of the ship. From a welcomed recruit to a rule-breaking amateur in need of scolding and punishment, to a fair sailor. Now she was the doctor.

"And since the captain is in such terrible condition, you'll have to stay by his side during shore leave."

Emily's mouth fell open. Her eyes moved to the captain, whose fiery gaze was plain on his face. If she was glued to his side, how was she going to get a shower?

"I take it this isn't a problem?" Price asked.

Emily shook her head. "No, not at all. Sorry. I'm just surprised by the promotion."

"I'll leave you to it." Price pointedly glared at her and the captain's waist, where he'd just finished tying his breeches. He closed the door on his way out, without another word.

"Is it such a burden to assist me ashore?" The captain asked with a mischievous glint in his eye.

"You know I'm not a real doctor, right?"

The captain smiled. "Better than the carpenter." Carpenters, good with hand tools—namely saws—were frequently moved into the position when the skills were required. Emily wasn't sure if that was a compliment or not. Their bar was so low.

"Ready to set the course?" she asked playfully. Emily actually felt like she belonged, and it put a spring in her step.

"Let's get to it."

Emily gripped the captain and assisted his steps, pausing when his ribs or his thigh wound hurt too much. They didn't have to move too far. The navigation room was next door.

That meant any noises made inside the captain's quarters could be heard by any of the navigation crew. Something to be mindful of.

After she moved him into the next room, only then Emily realized she'd forgotten to retrieve her necklace from the shredded clothing.

Chapter 15

When the city of Nassau glided into view the next day, the crew cheered. Emily gripped an oar and helped paddle ashore on a longboat, carrying a dozen pirates and the injured captain, while other longboats formed a line behind. They disembarked by rank, and since she was assigned to the captain's recovery, that gave her a position of authority.

As a retail worker bee, Emily was passive-aggressively scolded for not picking up shifts on her day off, forced to work most holidays, frequently denied unpaid vacations, but as thanks, gift cards and pizza parties were dangled for motivation. It was weird to be held in esteem, to be respected and admired. Here everyone mattered, and anyone stepping out of line—even if it was the captain—was corrected and the work continued in mutual agreement. From nothing, the pirates had created their own society that treated everyone fairly.

And yet, the Crown had destroyed them all—both in reputation and in sentencing to death. The Crown feared losing its power, a common theme in her modern world.

But seeing land for the first time in what felt like too long, she sighed in relief at the approaching solid ground. With sadness, Emily realized her pining for the sea had its limits—like any vacation would. The call of home was strong. And when she returned home, Emily expected the historical research would no longer hold the glamour it once did. She would have to write her own firsthand account of life aboard a pirate ship, but then what? Move on to a new hobby? She wouldn't know where to start.

More importantly, would she miss the Caribbean, the *Sea Lion*, and...Captain Lemoine so much the pining would be worse?

Eventually, she'd get that answer.

As the longboat coasted up to the dock, a pair of sailors knotted lines, securing the boat to the pilings. The others climbed out, but the captain waited back. Emily reached under him, and he stood with a wince. Muscular Cantu tried to clap hands and assist his exit from the wobbling boat, but Captain Lemoine refused. "I want the doctor to help, lest I break more bones in the process."

"Of course, sir. Pardon me." The helpful Cantu instead stabilized the rocking boat, and when the captain's feet touched the solid dock, the sailor helped the next longboat unload. Emily held the captain still and upright while the men gathered and headed off. They needed to restock supplies—particularly the rum. Since they'd dumped the contents of the hold to escape the Royal Navy, Emily hoped they had enough coin on hand to purchase—not steal—those necessities.

Flushed from rowing and exhilarated to be on stable ground, Emily secured Captain Lemoine's arm around her shoulder and waited for the captain's pain to ease. He'd saved her life. The least she could do was be patient. "Are you ready?"

"As much as I can be. Now that you're here, what do you want to do?"

Emily didn't expect the captain to ask about her needs, but perhaps they could both get what they wanted. "Let's find somewhere to rest," Emily insisted. "And I would love a bath."

"The Golden Macaw it is," the captain said in her ear, sending a shiver down her sweaty back. "Just beyond the blacksmith. Marta shall provide us the usual room."

This was Nassau, a famous pirate haven, and likely everyone knew everyone else. Emily wondered what stories Marta must have, what stories this town harbored beneath the surface, the ones that never made the history books. Emily shuffled along through sand and stone paths, feet itching for a hot soak, but all she could do was absorb the history in front of her. Townspeople strolled around them, some carrying goods on their heads in baskets, and others emptyhanded. One walked a goat on a leash. Emily stared at its little tail swishing, and she laughed. It was so weirdly cute, but she refrained from stopping to pet it.

"What's amusing you this time?" Captain Lemoine asked with a hint of playfulness, despite his pain.

"I've never seen a goat in person before."

The captain smiled at her in disbelief. "And the puzzle grows."

"What?"

"How is it possible you've never seen a goat?"

"Me and my mother were too broke to afford any luxuries, and that meant no traveling to the zoo. No movies. No shopping for fun. For vacations, we went camping. And on the weekends, we picnicked and spent time at city parks."

And that was why Tyler's theft hurt so deeply. It wasn't just the money. Stealing from people was never about the money. Money could be lost. Money could be made. The importance was what that money represented, what sentimentality the object held. Stealing tore something away from a person, disrespected their time earning it, damaged their soul. That money was her future, because she'd never had a past. And Tyler stole it. Emily couldn't accept thievery on any scale.

So while pretending to be a man, signing pirate articles, and playing doctor to an injured pirate captain who'd saved her life were all things she'd never dreamed of experiencing, that goat brought a tear to her eye.

"You weren't raised in privilege?" Captain Lemoine asked, surprised.

"Not at all."

The handsome man captured her gaze and worry filled his brow. "Why the tears? What's wrong, Emile?"

Emily smiled. "My mother would've wanted to pet the goat."

"Where is she now?" he asked gently.

"She passed a few years back."

"I'm so very sorry for your loss." The captain winced with a misstep and stopped in place.

"Are you all right?" she asked.

"We're here."

Above them was a painted wood sign reading The Golden Macaw. Men entered and exited the front door, and Emily waited until she could bring them across the threshold with no one pushing them to move faster. Several of the patrons lifted brows at her and the captain's situation.

"Lemoine?" One man stopped in front of them. He appeared to be in his mid-forties, hair thinning and waist widening. He tilted his head and beamed in recognition of a long-lost friend. His hand jutted out in greeting. "How've you been, mate?"

The captain shook carefully, and the friend was gentle enough not to further injure the captain. "Wilcox. Good to see you."

"Are you staying a while this time?" Wilcox eyed Emily for a brief moment, but otherwise didn't seem interested in meeting her.

"Long enough to restock, I'm afraid. Then back out to sea."

Wilcox smiled. "Word is spreading like fleas. Don't expect to be the only ones there. If I were going to make that attempt, I'd bring extra guns."

The captain nodded his gratitude for the vague advice. "Pardon us now, Wilcox. I have healing to do."

"Good luck on your account." Wilcox nodded and walked off.

Emily saw an opportunity in the tavern's doorway, and she swept the captain inside and straight into a cloud of tobacco smoke. Emily coughed. Potted palms rested in the corners of the open space. To the left was a registration desk with a broad stairwell leading up to the open second-story balcony. At the opposite end of the lobby was a bar, and in between were round tables. Butter yellow and soft green paint was flaking off the walls and banisters, but Emily loved the atmosphere.

A voluptuous woman approached. Her long hair was curled and piled high on her head. She wore an extravagant dress that looked more like a colorful bridal gown, and Emily couldn't image how she'd gotten into it or how she used the bathroom. The woman's friendly smile meant she was familiar with the captain also, and Emily presumed she was the hostess of the establishment. Emily followed the woman's gaze to the captain, and he smiled back. Familiar old friends, it seemed.

The woman leaned in for a hug, but Emily didn't want to let go. Her skin hummed with just the proximity. Besides, she still supported the captain's weight and couldn't stabilize him quickly enough to trust letting go. The woman moved in too close and personal. Loose curls tickled her face, and Emily blew them away, wishing her breath blew the woman herself away. No such luck. The woman released her embrace and placed her hand on Captain Lemoine's upper arm as if clinging to him like a dog.

What had gotten into Emily? Actual jealousy over this strange woman was rolling through her like fire. It must've been too much sun and the after effects of a concussion.

"Lemoine! How nice to see you again. Right this way, and I'll have your room ready for you." She turned her head and shouted, "Sarah! Captain Lemoine's room now!"

A young demure woman across the lobby dipped her head, lifted her skirts, and brushed upstairs.

Marta returned her attention to the captain, but she still hadn't released him. "Oh, honey. I'm so glad you've returned. Brought the entire crew, didn't you?" A slender finger caressed his arm. "How long will you be staying?"

Emily's concussion-induced possessiveness spiked. "The captain is injured. As his caretaker, I'd appreciate you not touching him."

Marta's brows popped, and she assessed Emily up and down, as if seeing her for the first time. Her gaze flicked back and forth between the two of them. As a knowing smile lifted her lips almost imperceptibly, the wheels in her head turned. For some reason, Emily read condescension in her expression. So much for that respect and admiration.

The captain spoke up, "Marta, this is my doctor, Emile Porter. I expect his needs shall be met. Do I make myself clear?"

Emily didn't like the sound of that. Her eyes swept the place in a new light. This wasn't just a motel. "That's not...no. That's unnecessary."

"It's necessary. Trust me," the captain insisted.

"No, it's really not."

Marta's smile spread as she watched their banter. Emily wanted to tell her to butt out.

"Emile," the captain countered with a playful interest. "Isolation at sea affects a man. You need some relaxation away from the brain-scrambling swaying of the ship. If you have no experience, Marta's ladies know how to do it right." The captain met Marta's eyes, and she nodded in agreement.

"I don't need ladies. All I want is a hot bath and some privacy. That I will gladly accept."

The captain said, "You're going to draw a bath for yourself? Carry the buckets at the right temperature all the way up the stairs from the stove?"

Emily's mouth opened. That wasn't what she thought at all.

"Marta, have a hot bath drawn for us." The captain smiled with a tease. He'd been playing with her.

This place must've been a motel as she'd first thought, and there was nothing in Price's orders that said she had to share a room. "Us?" Emily repeated, eyes wide.

"We're sharing a room. Price's orders—you must stay by my side."

Emily's mouth opened.

Lemoine leaned into her ear. "Unless you have the funds for the room next door."

The few bucks Emily had brought to the festival would be worth absolutely nothing here. She gave him a tight smile. "Can you handle the stairs?"

Captain Lemoine chuckled. "Broken bones never hindered me before."

Emily didn't want to think about the Captain having suffered severe injuries previously. "We'll take one room."

Marta nodded with a sweet grin. Emily led them both to the foot of the stairs. To preserve his pride, Emily counted prior to lifting up each step, so the captain could brace himself. Step after painfully slow step, they climbed up to the second-story balcony. "Why couldn't we have a ground-floor room?"

The captain smiled through his pain and pointed to the room Sarah had brushed into. "This one."

Emily brought them inside and set him gently onto the mattress. He fell back onto layers of plush bedding, legs hanging off the end. Emily crouched down and unlaced his boots without thinking twice about it.

"What in the devil are you doing?" he asked, head lifting.

"Taking off your boots so you can rest."

The captain's head fell back. "This place is more public than my private quarters, and you surprised me, but thank you."

Sarah and another young woman knocked on the door, holding pails. Without waiting for an invitation, they swept into the room and dumped their pails of steaming water into a tub. Emily sighed, wishing to strip down and soak to wash away the saltwater.

"A change of clothing would be amazing," Emily said to herself, feeling the layers of modern polyester and salty leather clinging to her skin.

"Bring one set of slops and charge it to my room," the captain said.

"What? That's unnecessary. I couldn't ask that," Emily backpedaled.

"Take your bath," Captain Lemoine said. "Enjoy fresh clothing. We're here for a reason, and I'm not going anywhere."

Emily caught the women before they left. "Is there a privacy screen somewhere?"

Sarah returned to the tub without a word and drew forth a folding partition. With a simple nod, they two women left silently, as if to be seen and not heard.

"Men of the sea are not bashful," the captain said while staring at the ceiling. "You'll adjust, eventually."

Not likely, Emily thought.

One woman immediately returned, as if a closet was next to the door, and set a folded stack of clothes on a table just inside the room. While lying on the bed, the captain gestured his acknowledgment. Sarah left again, closing the door behind her.

"Go, enjoy yourself," the captain said.

"And you're going to stay right there?" Emily retrieved the stack of clothing.

"I have no intentions of escaping you."

Emily smiled and hid behind the partition. That wasn't what she'd meant.

"Can you satisfy me one question?" the captain called over from the bed.

Emily unlaced her jerkin and peeled off her sticky shirt. "Sure."

"Where are you from?"

She'd dodged the question last time, so she gave him the lie she told Captain Sinclair, calling over the partition, "An island off the coast of the colonies."

Emily unfastened her breeches and pulled them down, and trusting he wasn't near, she slipped out of her underwear and the tank top with molded cups. If Lemoine saw her like this—naked, exposed, clearly not a man, the betrayal would be irreparable. Memories of Tyler berating her because she couldn't be trusted only added to the weight on her shoulders. And since she'd signed the articles, she'd be sentenced to 'suffer death'. Emily didn't want to think of the different ways they'd carry out that sentence, or Price's face while doing it. Or Captain Lemoine's. He probably wouldn't want her anymore, knowing she didn't have the right 'equipment'.

Emily couldn't change what she'd already done; there was no point in dwelling on the 'what if's'. She could only move forward, and that began with cleaning herself.

Emily dipped into the tub with a gentle swish of water. A sensual groan escaped her lips as a soothing warmth massaged the sore aches and salty sweat. Her nerves melted away. The water wasn't super warm, but since she'd been sweating, it didn't matter. It was fresh water. Emily untied the red rag on her head and let down her blonde hair. She dunked her head under and surfaced, pushing the wet strands back.

"Which one?" the captain asked. He was still on the bed, judging by the carry in his voice.

Emily scrubbed her arms and legs, and hung her hand off the back of her neck, massaging the aching muscles from carrying a man's weight on one side. She pinched her face in thought. "One off the coast of Florida." His stubbornness in refusing to drop the subject was frustrating. She didn't know what to tell him that he'd believe, so there was no point in raising alarms. Emily just wanted to clean up in peace.

Chapter 16

Captain Eric Lemoine knew Emile was lying. Instead of angering him, Lemoine began to worry. Was Emile running from something? Hiding from someone? If he were in trouble, Lemoine had every intention of solving it. Soon he could solve anything. "I daresay your continued dance around the question is only intriguing me more."

As expected, Emile didn't answer.

Captain Lemoine pulled himself upright, against doctor's orders, he thought with a sly smile, and rose to his feet. Every muscle from his chest to his knees ached as if he'd taken the shot directly. If he had, he'd been wrapped and tossed into the sea like poor Meeks. Lemoine was grateful his injuries weren't worse. And he was…grateful to Emile, the beautiful, puzzling man with a heart of gold. Terrible sailor, but he was a quick learner.

Had Lemoine been too forward when he'd kissed Emile? His response to Lemoine's pouring of affections had been, 'As long as we're both on this ship, we can't.' Well, they were no longer on the ship, but Emile still wasn't opening up. Had it been an excuse to push him away without hurting him? On the contrary, granting that sliver of hope was cruel if it hadn't been true.

He risked tearing stitches to seek information that would settle his heart.

Did someone already have Emile's?

With one hand reaching uselessly in the air for support that wasn't there, Lemoine shuffled over to the privacy screen. "If you care not to share that detail, can you tell me who your companion, Miss Angela, is? Someone dear to you?"

Lemoine leaned against the screen, careful not to topple it, and gazed upon Emile in the bath. What he found both answered many questions, but also angered him. Emile's face was flushed from the warmth of the bath, so when his—or Lemoine should say 'her'—arms covered her chest, he couldn't tell just how shamed she was.

"I—I can explain..." Emile stuttered. "It's not what you think."

Wet strands of hair clung to her face and narrow shoulders. Her thin arms. Her smooth jaw. Her beautiful face. It all made sense. How could he have missed such a truth before him? Part of his anger was on himself. He should've known.

"It's not?" Captain Lemoine couldn't keep the curt tone from his voice. "Please explain why a woman infiltrated my ship and lied to everyone."

Emile—not likely her name at all—looked down, unable to meet his gaze. "You wouldn't believe me if I told you."

Fury raged through his shredded veins. Not just for the breaking of Lemoine's heart, but also for Emile's sake. The consequences were dire. "Is that what you meant? You'd said we couldn't be together so long as we were on the *Sea Lion*. This is why, isn't it? You wouldn't expose the truth to me. You didn't trust me."

Her face lifted, showing disbelief. "That's what you're angry about? That I didn't tell a *pirate* captain I was a woman, when I signed on the line acknowledging I'd be *killed* for it? I knew the consequences, so how I was supposed to trust you with that information? And for the record, you kissed me, and that's against the rules, too."

She had a point. "Why did you sign?"

"I needed to stay on that ship long enough to get my necklace back. If I hadn't, I wouldn't be sitting here right now."

Lemoine was sure she would be here, still hounding him for that jewel, only her life wouldn't be in his hands. He still couldn't reconcile every piece of the Emile puzzle. "And this Angela, was she your traveling chaperone?"

"Angela is my best friend, and she's missing," Emile said, and with a dry tone, she added, "I don't need a chaperone."

Lemoine couldn't even relish in the knowledge Emile's heart had not been taken. Emile broke rules everywhere she went, which led him to want to know where she was from even more, but he wouldn't get that answer. The captain shook his head in disbelief. "Two women traveling alone."

What was he going to do with their new doctor? Emile had value, but he was burdened with exposing her betrayal and having her punished. The punishment was worse than dire. It was death. But even after this grave revelation, Lemoine couldn't see Emile killed. Resigned, he said on a sigh, "I accepted your punishment in your stead, and I bore the brunt of the shot's blast to keep you safe. I couldn't bear to see you harmed then."

"But now that I'm a woman, you don't see me the same way?" Emile asked cautiously.

"I don't." Lemoine wanted her more than ever, but now he couldn't have her.

Emile's face paled, and if Lemoine hadn't known better, he'd almost believe Emile was...heartbroken. Lemoine added gently, "But I still can't see you harmed. You can't return to the ship."

Emile stood, panic on her face. Water ran down her smooth naked body, and Lemoine didn't know what to do. He just marveled at the sight while it lasted.

"But...I'm your doctor. I need to help you heal," Emile said with rising tones, realized the blunder of standing before him, and sank back into the water. Lemoine happened to enjoy the view.

But she had a point again. Lemoine had been injured in battle many times before, but not quite this seriously, and if he could have a doctor on his arm tending his every need, he'd be unwise to dismiss such benefit. But to bring her aboard meant he would now risk his life as well as hers. For Lemoine to entertain the idea of protecting her once again, at great risk and benefit to himself, he wanted more from her. "Why did you risk mutilation, desertion, and death for a single jewel? What about your home is worth all that?"

Lemoine hoped the answer rested in something he could fix. A man he could hunt down. Seeds he could purchase. Land he could recover. Lemoine was all too familiar with the need to bring home something valuable. Soon, Lemoine would have all he needed to solve any problem, even his own.

"It's my only way to get home."

Lemoine didn't know how to work with that, but Emile was nothing if not obtuse. A spike of pain had his face pinching. Lemoine leaned harder on the screen, and Emile stood, wrapped a towel around her chest to her knees, and rushed to his side.

Emile supported Lemoine and brought him back to the bed. He didn't fight her. She saw all his vulnerability already.

Emile sat next to him. "Here's how this is going to go. We're both getting back on that ship, and you'll give me my necklace. I promise to help you heal so long as you need me, but the moment you don't or issues with the crew become too dangerous, I'll disappear. Then you can lead your men to rescue the next merchant crew in distress."

"I can't do that," Lemoine said, staring at his scarred hands.

Chapter 17

Emily dragged a hand through her wet hair. Sitting in nothing but a towel next to the captain, she was keenly aware of how little was between them. But it didn't matter. The captain didn't feel the same about her now that she was a woman. Emily had expected it, but that didn't make it hurt less. She was thankful Lemoine didn't immediately call the crew over, strip her in front of them for proof, and have her tied up for whatever creative death Price could conjure. But she didn't understand which part of her plan he was rejecting.

"What do you mean?" she asked with an edge to her voice.

"I can't do that," he repeated, softly.

His withholding the necklace meant she couldn't go home, but it angered her more that she couldn't make that decision for herself. The sharpness in her tone returned. "You can't kill me for being a woman who broke the articles, or can't let me go home?"

"I've sailed these waters as a captain ten years now." Captain Lemoine stared at his palms, a sincerity evaporated her anger. "My crew turned over more than once in that time. Some accounts were more successful than others. This crew has been on the verge of mutiny for weeks, whispers of losing my wits to find the best prizes, and you saved me from that. Despite your undermining my authority." He sent her a small lift of his lips.

Intrigued at the captain opening up to her, she asked, "How did you pacify them before?"

"Promises. But my ledger of promises has been red for some time. And that night, I had no promises left to give. I cannot thank you enough." He turned to her with a wince, gentle and vulnerable, breaking her heart. "And I cannot continue to use them."

"I don't need your promise then, and I don't want you to risk your life for mine again, understood?" Emily asked, guilt pouring out of her. His words sounded like a refusal, and she couldn't give up her only way back on that ship. "Just like before. You go on believing I'm a man, and we move forward with the plan I just laid out."

"Why don't you want help? It's strange to me a woman in need would be so fiercely against it."

Emily exhaled, relieved to give the man some truth, and maybe he'd agree for pity's sake. "My father abandoned my mother when I was young. My mother spent all her time working to keep a roof over our heads. Independence was ingrained in me. When I was old enough to work myself, I put all my effort into earning money with the hopes of changing my life someday for both of us. Then I met a man not long ago who made me promises."

The captain said nothing, just held her eye contact, waiting for her to continue.

"I could see a life of comfort I'd never known. My mother could finally quit working. But it wasn't to be. She passed away, and Tyler stole all my money. I'm broke."

"Both the men in your life are imbeciles. What kind of man abandon's his child? His wife? His lover?" Captain Lemoine's hand touched her thigh, and her veins sizzled with heat. "I don't think I want to know where you're from after all. I may not stop myself from teaching them a lesson."

She wished so much he wasn't gay. She wanted to kiss him for just listening, and that possessiveness light a fire in her chest. It was a strange feeling, like he still cared. "It wasn't all Tyler's fault. I was blindly excited about the business venture, and he asked for the money—a little at first, and then more and more. When I wasn't comfortable handing over everything I had, he continued with the promises. A week after I drained my account for him, he came back for more. I said I didn't have any left, that I'd given it all to him. He said he couldn't trust me to do what the business needed when it needed it. All I wanted was a few dollars back to pay a bill."

Emily's lips lifted. "If he would've given it, I'd still be in that cycle of promises, more money handed over, and no business yet."

"You were very generous. It's not your fault a thief manipulated you."

"I thought I loved him. I thought he loved me, and that we were going to be partners. But I broke up with him instead. He still hasn't paid me."

"It's a fortunate end," the captain said, jaw tightening. "You deserve better."

His kindness melted her like the chocolate in her pouch. Seeing he needed a pick-me-up just as much as she did, she opened the pouch and unwrapped a bite size chocolate. "You need this more than I do. Take it, and no, it's not stolen."

His brow creased. "Then where did you get it?"

"Back home, and I'm offering you a piece." He didn't move, so Emily shook it for emphasis.

"I can see how my words hurt you deeply. I don't believe you're a thief at all," he said gravely, as if the guilt burdened him. "For the necklace or this chocolate."

"Thank you." Damn it. Why did he have to be so sweet?

"In my defense, it's less shocking that a *woman* carries chocolate and a necklace on her person." He smiled wryly and leaned toward her fingers, parting his lips. Emily's heart pounded as she placed the treat in his mouth, and his lips captured her fingers and slid them free.

Captain Lemoine stared at her wide eyed as he chewed. "It's amazing. Very sweet and smooth. With a pleasurable silky texture. I've never tasted anything like it. Thank you for sharing your little luxury with me."

Emily smiled proudly, lifted off the bed, and gently pushed him down onto the mattress. "You need to rest, and we can return to the ship together."

He allowed her to position him comfortably, and his body relaxed on the mattress. "Promises are meaningless to you, so I *don't* promise your secret is safe with me." Despite his pain, he smiled for her. "Don't leave, doctor."

"I won't," she said. Emily flipped up a sheet over his body and took a long look at the man who'd saved her twice—from a brutal merchant captain and a military cannonball—and now he promised to keep her secret to save her life and his position. She was almost home-free. Emily smiled and stepped out onto the balcony.

Emily leaned her forearms on the balcony railing. The crowd below bustled through the smokey haze of the bar restaurant below. A stomach-growling scent of grilled meat wafted up. Men drank and played cards. Coins rattled on the floor. Women in billowing gowns served them fresh drinks and mouth-watering plates with pleasant smiles. A shout below focused her attention on a table below. A small group of the crew gripped their mugs, enjoying the establishment's entertainment. She could hardly believe many of them wanted to toss the captain overboard. He was such a wonderful man.

"There ye are," Fergus climbed the remaining stairs and leaned against the railing next to her shoulder. "I've been looking fur ye. Crew's been wondering if ye dispatched th'weakened captain."

Emily scowled. "Of course not."

Fergus chuckled. "I think it was said in jest." He glanced down below, watching the spectacle of laughing men telling stories.

Emily remembered Fergus's eagerness to escape the crew. "Why are you here? The captain fulfilled his promise to give you safe passage to Nassau. You're free."

"I canny leave before trying tae bring ye tae yer senses. Now's yer chance tae escape these ruffians fur good."

While the captain slept, Emily didn't feel comfortable leaving him, and since she had nothing better to do, chatting with her friend was better than being alone. "And go where?"

"I'll arrange fur a position oan a plantation oan th'other side o' th'island, or if ye prefer, I could be a fisherman. It disny matter tae me which." He was serious.

Emily squinted at him. That wasn't casual planning. "Why are you talking like this?"

"What dae ye mean?"

"Like my opinion on your life counts."

Fergus leaned into her ear. "I know ye're a lassy."

Emily lips parted, and she covered her mouth with her hand. "How? Why haven't you...? How!" She had been so careful. Even the captain never suspected.

"A man traveling wi' a necklace would immediately declare it's a gift fur a woman. Ye never attempted tae lift a barrel of rum. Ye struggled wi' a single bag o' sand. Th'curve o' yer face is just a little too feminine tae be convincing. But I knew right away, which is why I was helping ye." His hand brushed against her jaw with affection, and Emily pulled back. "I have money. I can support us until I find employment. Come wi' me, and ye'll be safe."

"Fergus, you've been a good friend, and I appreciate the offer, but..." she trailed off when his demeanor shifted. He didn't like her answer.

"Ye're no' one o' them. This isn't ye," he pressed.

After Emily had placated the crew with the rum, earning their accolades, and ordered them to help with the captain's injuries, and they'd listened, she almost felt like she belonged. She'd had their respect. The crew trusted her with the captain's wellbeing. She kind of was...one of them.

Captain Lemoine had agreed to allow her back on the ship, even after knowing the truth. If he could accept her, could everyone else? That meant she had a chance to stay with the pirate crew, live the adventurous life of her silly dreams.

They weren't so silly anymore.

But could she truly be happy, knowing she could never be with the captain? It was just her luck the one man she believed was perfect happened to be gay.

Was Fergus's surprising offer the best she'd ever get? Or should she take her chances on the ship and retrieve her necklace?

Fergus leaned in close and flicked his head toward the room behind them. He whispered, "Does he know?"

If Emily told him the truth, Fergus could tell the whole crew, and she'd have to flee for her life, preventing her from stepping foot on the ship. Even worse, the captain's wasn't in a position to escape. His punishment would be severe. Emily had to lie. "He doesn't."

"Well, I should've suspected, as yer still standing here. In which case, it's no' too late." Fergus rose to his full height, and Emily tipped her face up to meet his gaze. "Emile,"—he paused, knowingly—"Due tae our unfortunate location, I canny retain th'approval o' my kin, and likewise, yers. But I'll stay here, a farmhand or fisherman, if it means I can have yer hand in marriage." Fergus held out his open palm, offering her a hammered metal ring with two hands holding a single heart.

A proposal? Emily had to remember marriages were more for business than love in these days, so she shouldn't have been surprised. But she still couldn't take Fergus seriously. Emily touched Fergus's forearm to let him down gently. "I can't stay here with you. My only way home is back on that ship. You must understand."

Fergus stared her down, a thin line forming his mouth. "Canny I make myself more plain? Staying wi' them means yer death. Staying wi' me is a humble an' honest life. Can ye really choose *them*?" He was flabbergasted, not heartbroken.

Emily removed her hand from his arm. Captain Lemoine was her only means to the end she sought. If she couldn't have him—she clearly couldn't—Emily needed to get home. Her friends would miss her, and she'd be fired soon. Then unpaid bills would pile up all over again. She didn't want to slide back into the vicious cycle of collection notices, garnishments, and eviction. It was incredibly difficult to break that cycle and begin to save for another attempt at changing her life. Emily must get home before the life she knew was over.

"I am going with them," Emily said softly.

Fergus's back stiffened. His upper lip curled. "Ye're choosing a motley group o' murderers an' thieves. All they search fur is treasure. All they want is money! I thought ye were better than that. I was wrong."

Emily frowned. That couldn't be right. Emily witnessed them taking cargo to help fund their operations—saving men from brutal merchant captains. To avoid capture or destruction by the Royal Navy, they'd dumped all the cargo. In that case, saving her and Fergus earned them nothing. Fergus should be grateful. Emily was. The pirates had been nothing like Fergus's Captain Sinclair.

"I don't believe you."

Fergus's eyes softened. "Ye're making a mistake, but if ye change yer mind before the *Sea Lion* sails, find me. I'll be waiting." With that, Fergus pocketed the ring, and he descended the stairs and walked straight out the front door.

Emily turned around and startled at the eavesdropper. Captain Lemoine stood in the doorway, one arm across his middle, supporting his broken ribs. Admiration curved his lips.

"It's rude to listen to other people's conversations, and you should be sleeping."

The captain hooked his finger at her, urging her near.

Concerned, Emily rushed to his side and lifted his arm over her shoulders. "Is everything okay? Are you bleeding? Hurting? I have a couple pills left if you need one."

"Assist me back inside."

Emily frowned and moved them both back into the room. "You shouldn't have stepped out on your own."

The captain shifted his footing and flinched.

"You need more pain relief." Emily attempted to hunt down her ibuprofen in her pouch one-handedly.

The captain captured her chin with his fingers, stopping her. "You chose us."

"Of course I did. We have a mutual agreement, and I don't break promises."

"Before we return to the ship, separated not geographically, but in all the ways that matter, I need you to kiss me," Captain Lemoine said softly. "Even if it's for the last time."

Emily tilted her head, completely puzzled. "What? I thought you... You know, preferred men."

Captain Lemoine smiled. His thumb brushed against her jaw. "I prefer you. And if I can only have you for a day, so be it. I'd always chose a lifetime of pining over losing you, instead of bearing the unrequited ache in my heart. Kiss me."

"Unrequited?" Emily asked softly. He thought she didn't feel that way about him.

"Kiss me, please. I'll beg you until the very last moment."

He didn't have to beg. Emily's lips found his, carefully, gently exploring without injuring the captain further. Her hands moved into his long hair, so silky, and she melted against his chest. Those thick arms she'd waited for wrapped around her, holding her close, desperate to never let go. The world fell away. He still wanted her, and Emily wanted him, too.

Hope filled her chest with warmth, and she gripped it like a lifeline.

Chapter 18

A POUNDING ON THE motel room door stirred Emily awake. The captain dozed peacefully next to her, the lines of his face soft, and Emily brushed a lock of wavy brown hair from his eyes. He'd told her everything she wanted to hear, and Emily couldn't wait to explore the new man in her life. Except they had an expiration date the minute they stepped foot onto the *Sea Lion*. The rapping continued.

"Just a minute." Emily swung her legs off the bed and checked her man-like appearance. She tucked her blonde hair back under her red kerchief, even though most of the men had longer hair than her.

Emily opened the door to find the muscle-bound Cantu frowning. That couldn't be good news.

"Can I help you?"

"Emile, we're all grateful you saved the captain."

Emily didn't believe the man knocked just to show appreciation, when he could be doing any number of activities conducive to arriving at port. Still, she smiled. "It was nothing. I couldn't have done it without your help."

"I beg to differ, sir. Your knowledgeable skills and quick action saved him. Don't know how we'd continue the account without him. He's the one with the amazing plan, and because of that, I've been sent on behalf of Quartermaster Price. Where is the captain?" Cantu leaned around her shoulder to check the bed.

Emily didn't move out of the way. "He's sleeping."

"Rouse the captain at once. We have a problem he must address."

Emily didn't want to. His stitches needed rest, but Cantu had a concerning look of worry on his face. "One moment."

While the beefy Cantu waited in the doorway, Emily woke the captain. His eyelids fluttered open, and he smiled. His palm lifted to cup her cheek, but Emily intercepted, gripping his hand in hers as if supporting him to stand. Before he could comment on her blocking move, she said, "Price needs you."

The lines on his face returned, and Captain Lemoine found Cantu in the doorway. He nodded his acknowledgement, and the messenger left. "I much prefer spending our only day with you in my bed, but duty calls, I'm afraid."

Emily helped him to his feet, and he groaned and flinched. On his feet, Captain Lemoine held out his arm, urging her closer. Emily melded to his side like a steel structure supporting a wind damaged skyscraper.

Captain Lemoine gazed at the open door and exhaled. "Ready, doctor?"

Emily shuffled him out of the room and down the stairs meticulously. At the round table where the crew had entertained themselves the night before, Price, Boatswain Karl, Cantu, and the other officers of the ship waited. Emily eased the captain onto the last empty chair and stood behind him.

THE ACHES IN HIS ribs always eased with Emile at his side, and Lemoine was floating on clouds that she'd felt the same way about him. Alas, their day had to be spoiled. Staring at the grave faces before him, the pain spiked.

Quartermaster Price said, "As you know, dumping our hold to evade the Royal Navy has cost us. With nothing to sell and dismal funds left, our spending needed to be wise. So, I ordered the crew to stock up on supplies."

"Then what problem has urged my rousing?" the captain asked, frustrated at the disturbance to his sleep for nothing.

Price leaned forward. "We can't afford enough provisions for the whole crew to sail to Florida and back. Foregoing either is not wise, as you know."

That was a problem. The crew knew of the prize they were after. Asking for volunteers to give up what amounted to riches was simply not going to be accepted. "What of our credit on the house?"

"Used."

Emile asked from behind his chair, "I don't understand what's wrong."

Price said, "We need a guaranteed prize of meat...and rum...on our journey, or we must cut the number of hands continuing this account."

Emile cleared her throat and asked, "I don't see how anyone should be removed from the ship. So, how can we guarantee a prize?"

Price patiently explained to the new recruit, "There's a rumor of a goat supply ship sailing this way in a few days' time. If we can reach it first and take it successfully, then we'll have no problem."

"That's a lot of speculation," Emile said. She was right, but the officers glared at her. "What?"

At that, his officers turned to him for the decision. Captain Lemoine made a non-promise to keep Emile by his side so he could return her necklace. That jewel was rightfully owed to the crew. Its sale would solve this problem entirely. Not only would Emile never forgive him for such a betrayal, but the crew would punish him for defrauding the company of such a prize, punishable by marooning. As Emile's secrets had risked her life, so had his own. Lemoine said to the officers, "We lay out the situation for the crew, let them decide whether to continue the account."

"What does that mean?" Emily asked.

"Vote," Price said. "We need a minimum number of hands to overtake a prize and sail after an expected number of injuries. But if too few men volunteer, I'll choose who goes."

"Emile, how are the captain's injuries healing?" Price asked.

Lemoine didn't appreciate the slight. "I am at liberty of answering about my own condition."

Price countered, "A sound judgment; however, sir, you are not a doctor."

"Emile," Lemoine said. "You found broken ribs?"

Emile nodded. "As best as I can figure without proper equipment. I didn't want to palpate and make things worse. It's best to assume so for better healing."

The strange woman, traveling alone with another woman who carried chocolate and a jewel of great value, clearly had a fantastic education. How could he reconcile her appearing to have a privileged upbringing with the tale of her father abandoning her to poverty? That was the missing piece of the Emile puzzle.

Lemoine added to Emile's assessment. "I deal with recurring spikes of pain, but mostly a dull ache. I can function with assistance."

"Excellent. We hold the vote at noon. Spread the word." Price collected his cocked hat and strolled out. The officers followed, and at the doorway, they split into pairs to track down the rest of the crew. No easy feat when the men were granted shore leave.

There was a gentle murmur of patrons filling the tables for lunch. The clatter of dishware came from nearby as the lovely ladies served the orders. The scent of food wafted over. Lemoine had dined on hardtack and diluted wine near the end there. They'd come too close on their provisions. He needed to order Emile a proper meal.

Emile took his hand in hers and leaned closer. "Now that they're gone, can you tell me how you really feel?"

Lemoine didn't want her to worry. "Having you at my side lessens the pain. I told the truth." He smiled reassuringly. "Now, you must be fatigued from so much exertion and only tack to fuel you. As I require your further assistance, I need you to be strong and healthy. So, let us partake in The Golden Macaw's finest offerings on the island."

Emile nodded, and Lemoine was proud to feed her. He ordered a meal for them, but when the dishes emerged, Emile tilted her head. "What is it?"

Lemoine couldn't wait for this. Everything Emile saw and heard brought more puzzle pieces to life.

"I recognize the wine and grapes, but I don't know what this is."

Lemoine smiled and pointed. "That is turtle and this is fish."

Emile smiled. "I'm always down for something new. Thank you so much. I'm starving."

"It's not a gesture worthy of merit." The captain minimized her appreciation. Seeing her satisfied was enough for him.

"To me it is. You understand I have no way of repaying you?"

That necklace in his possession... "Do not worry yourself over it."

Emile lifted a forkful of succulent turtle to her lips, and she closed her eyes over the tender meat. A murmur came from her throat. She grinned. "It's beefy. Is it always like this?"

"The method of preparation does differ from one establishment to another."

"I mean life here, scraping by for food. Not knowing if the people around you are trustworthy, and at any second everything you've built could come crashing down. Oh, and the Royal Navy always seeking your head. It seems like a very stressful life."

Where would Emile get an idea like that? "My head?"

"I just meant in general."

"What you describe might sound stressful, but it's better than the alternative." The captain swallowed a generous gulp of wine, taking the edge off the ache from his ribs to his thigh.

Emile popped a grape into her mouth. "What alternative is worse than a noose?"

"I could think of many things."

"Such as?"

Emile wasn't giving this up. Lemoine wasn't sure what the woman was after, but since they only had the day together, there was not much use to bleeding for her. "Not having a home to return to."

Emile's eyes fell to her plate. "Your home? Are you from somewhere around France?"

Captain Lemoine grinned. "Did my accent give it away or my stunning good looks?"

Emile laughed, a harmonious sound that brought a smile to his heart.

The captain wiped his mouth on a cloth napkin and gave her the story. "King Louis the fourteenth revoked the Edict of Nantes in 1685. I'm sure you've heard about it. My grandparents refused to convert their religion, and they brought my parents and me across the ocean. At ten years of age, I found a new life in the French colonies, but I do miss the French countryside."

"What brought you out here to Nassau?"

"It's a long story, but pursuing finer things steered me from the plantation to the sea, and now I'm here to rectify that mistake, no matter how long it takes."

And the necklace would've gotten Lemoine off the ship at once. But the crew would've hunted him down for turning his back on them. He had to push forward. He had to claim as much treasure as he could find before it was too late. And after discovering Emile's poor upbringing, he was thrilled she'd earn a share just for being by his side.

She deserved the finer things in life, too.

Chapter 19

Sweaty men, calmer after a night of release on shore, crowded on the main deck and around the rail, bringing the scent musky man with them. Instead of whatever debauchery they'd engaged in, they should've made time for a bath.

The blinding noon sun had Emily squinting at the quartermaster during his speech. Being from the frozen north, she'd never wished for cloudy days, but today, the endless reflective light of the Caribbean Sea had her wishing for sunglasses. Too bad none of the vendors the captain had showed her carried eyewear.

She did get to pet a goat, though.

Despite the rules of her and the captain pretending like there was nothing between them, she stayed by his side like a good doctor. Emily wasn't just supporting his weight. She leaned into him, relishing in the touch. So far, he'd kept his word to keep her secret...*their* secret, but the chaos of the impending vote meant Captain Lemoine hadn't returned her necklace yet. They had time.

"We have sufficient provisions for forty men, no more. Show of hands who wish to continue the account toward Florida." Hands raised in the air, and Price wrote on his clipboard.

Men discussed it among themselves, and one man asked, "Spain will be there for the recovery, no?"

"It is presumed, yes," Price said.

Several men whispered to each other, and left in pairs and threes. Emily picked up some mumbles about not enough prizes lately to take on that added risk.

Emily hadn't figured out what they were after in Florida. She imagined a series of barbarous merchant ships ripe for their crews to be freed, all conveniently docked together and loaded with goods to be confiscated and sold. The prospect of helping other new recruits adjust to their new freedom and life aboard a pirate ship excited her—more people she could almost relate to. "May I ask what the nature of this account is?"

Heads turned her way in surprise, as if she was dumb for not already knowing. Perhaps she was.

The quartermaster strolled over to her. He still wore a stick up his ass, but since he thanked her for her efforts and gave her a promotion, she softened against him. He had a tough job. Price focused on her, not at all annoyed by the interruption. "A Spanish treasure galleon awaits us off the coast of Florida. As word spread, several ships have set sail to claim a fortune for their crew. We must move quickly."

The remaining men cheered. Confused, Emily caught a glance at the captain, whose face was impassive. "Is that all?"

"Is that all?" the quartermaster repeated in disbelief. "A fortune, at the expense of an enemy nation, is not good enough, Porter? What a strange man you are."

The crew laughed.

Emily wasn't. "You're planning to steal money from a foreign government? I thought you people rescued merchant crews." Emily turned to the captain for an answer, but he only looked at her, unflinching, unapologetic. Had Fergus been right this whole time?

Quartermaster Price squinted into the sunlight at her. "I understand you're new on this crew, and somehow confused about seafaring life. We have no ownership paying us wages. As the captain had explained when you signed, we all work together for a fair share of the earnings."

"Earnings from what work? Because it sounds like you aren't in the business of rescuing sailors from nasty captains and compensating yourselves with their trade goods."

Price tilted his head in utter confusion. The corners of his lips lifted in amusement—the first time Emily had seen such humor on his otherwise attractive face. "The Crown steals from everyone. We only seek to even the playing field, but we aren't greedy. Once we're rich, we'll depart each other's company. None of us wants to hang at the gallows of Williamsburg."

Wanting to be rich *wasn't* greedy?

"Now, if I've explained the situation clear enough for you"—the crew chuckled, and Emily frowned—"then we'll commence the vote."

At Price's question, hands went up, but not Emily's. How could she join this pack of greedy thieves and murderers? She wasn't one of them—the signature she'd signed wasn't her name.

"Emile, raise your hand so the quartermaster can count you," the captain urged quietly.

"No," Emily hissed back. "I'm not joining you. I'm not like you, and I don't want to be part of this monstrous, barbaric...thing...you have here."

The crew closed in around her, not with the excitement for the announcement of rum, but the darkness of an insult. Captain Lemoine sent her a warning glare, but Emily didn't care. Fergus was right. These people were despicable, and it was about time someone made it clear to them. "You're all selfish bastards. What is wrong with you? Why can't you get regular jobs and stop stealing from people? How would you feel if everything you worked for was taken from you, just because an opportunist wanted it? Put yourself in their shoes. You'd hate it, just as I did."

The captain gripped her upper arm and said to the quartermaster, "He stays. Count him in."

Price nodded.

With restrained fury, Captain Lemoine pulled her through the crowd and into his private cabin, panting and gasping with pain. He locked the door behind them and leaned against it, sweating with the exertion. "You promised to help heal me."

Emily's anger kept pouring out. "And you shouldn't be moving like that. You're going to tear your stitches or crack your ribs worse, and I can't do anything for your ribs. Do you want a punctured lung? Because that's how you get a punctured lung." She didn't know if that was true or not, but it sounded good.

The captain approached her and shoved her to the bed. Beads of sweat trickled down his forehead. The captain's voice sounded like gravel with restrained anger. "There is much you need to learn before you end up causing both our deaths."

Emily reeled. In the spirit of the moment, the angering betrayal of the truth, she'd forgotten her outburst could lead directly to the crew murdering them both—and rightly so. "Then talk fast." Because she was five seconds from trashing this cabin, until she found her necklace, and leaving.

Captain Lemoine paced, despite the pain clear on his features. Emily wanted to comment, but she let him talk. "You don't know any of their stories, where they came from, why they chose this life—not even mine! Yet you presume to know them all and judge them to be unworthy."

He was right, Emily thought, anger deflating. But that didn't ease the pain she felt.

"If any of them had been born to a privilege of earning livable wages, we wouldn't be here."

A single word caught Emily's attention. "We?" Emily had remembered his words—pursuing finer things steered him from the plantation to the sea. Did a plantation not pay fair wages? Were those 'finer things' just greed, and Emily's heart had missed that meaning?

The captain paced the room with a hand on his stitched hip for support.

Emily pleaded, "Please sit down before you make the injuries worse." There was condescension in her voice, but with all the adrenaline coursing through her system, she couldn't help it, even though the words were sincere.

The captain sank onto his mattress next to her and swiped at his brow. "Half of those men are freed slaves."

Emily's brows popped. She had no idea.

"Another fifteen are from merchant ships with tyrant captains, like you."

That was familiar.

"And the rest followed the call of the sea when the land was disappointing."

"Which category do you fit in?" Emily asked softly.

"I can be categorized by two of those groups. After the religious unrest I told you about, our family boarded a slave ship headed for the French colony, Saint-Domingue, in Hispaniola. Have you heard of it?"

Emily nodded, the modern Haiti.

He continued, "All of us children worked on the sugar plantation, but the plantation owner's daughter caught my wandering eye. Our quick romps during the evenings led me to proposing a marriage of love, but her father denied the pairing, citing my station as unworthy of her."

Emily cringed. That was probably a word that stung him personally.

"After that, I watched her each day—so close, but so far away—and it pained me, until one day I took to the sea. I signed onto a merchant crew, transporting sugar. Unfortunately, I didn't understand how poor the wages were."

The urge to rest a hand on his thigh in comfort distracted her. What could she say to that? The man was a romantic at heart.

"You insist on understanding why I shot Captain Sinclair before burning and sinking his ship."

Emily nodded, afraid of interrupting, but encouraging him to continue.

"My merchant captain was an abusive man, an equal to Sinclair. You saw those scars exposed during my whipping?"

Emily did. They were alarming in their numbers and depth.

"My merchant captain punished me several times, because I attempted to right the wrongs on board."

"But why transfer the abuse onto another man?"

Captain Lemoine smiled and looked at the floor. "Not everyone believes as you and me. Donald Sinclair had been my equal aboard the sugar merchant ship. He'd always been a nasty fellow, supporting our captain's devious ways. Cheering his punishments and figuring inventive new ones. I'd always known Sinclair would turn out like him."

Emily's mouth opened. "I had no idea."

"Admitting you were abused by an equal isn't information you want freely floating around. For a pirate, it could mean a merchant wants retribution, and that's devastating to everyone."

Emily finally understood, even though she'd never seen a true fight.

"When our merchant ship was taken by a pirate ship, it was Captain Hornigold and the *Marianne* who granted us freedom. Last I'd heard, he's still capturing prizes around the Caribbean and adding to his flotilla."

Emily blinked and sucked in a breath. *The* legendary Captain Hornigold? Emily had to stop herself from asking if Lemoine had his autograph. A light feeling overcame her, and she inhaled deeply to center herself.

"Is something the matter? You look as if you've seen a ghost."

"I...I just might have." Emily shook out her hands and exhaled several deep breaths to calm herself, but it wasn't working. Actual, real history was here. All around her. So many people she could meet. So many hands she could shake. So many questions. The fangirling was back.

"Well then, Shall I dispatch these upsetting apparitions before we set sail?"

Emily chuckled. "Not necessary." She replayed the captain's words in her mind. "Pirate Captain Benjamin Hornigold had rescued your crew. What happened to your captain? Was he tied up, shot, and blown to pieces?" The specific punishment would make ironic sense.

"Captain Hornigold's first mate, Edward Teach, shot him before sinking the ship. I continued the tradition of freeing tormented crews while on the account."

Emily grinned. "Blackbeard? You're talking about Blackbeard?" She couldn't believe it.

"For not knowing anything of sea life, you appear well-versed in people." Captain Lemoine squinted at her in playful suspicion.

"I have one more question." Actually, a million, but that would only lead to more questions on the captain's side, and she still needed to avoid those. "What did the crew mean when they said you only gave them 'failure after failure'?"

Captain Lemoine shook his head. "Many of the sailors were upset about the prizes being lower than they had been. Too long at sea wears on a man. But if you mean Hooper—if he doesn't get a pint of rum every night, he deems the day's work a failure. Too many in a row makes him want to mutiny, and he riled up everyone else. Loud mouth, that one."

"If it's so common, why *doesn't* he mutiny?" Emily thought on her words. "No offense, or anything. I think you're a great captain."

Captain Lemoine grinned at her compliment. "Hooper knows he can't lead. But he's mighty good at complaining. Now that you understand our situation, will you come peacefully on the recovery mission?"

"Recovery?" Emily was confused all over again. "I thought you're going after a Spanish treasure ship, which sounds...unwise, honestly."

"A hurricane felled the treasure galleon. She rests under the sea, with gold spread all over. Since the Spaniards have not the resources to chase away all opportunity seekers, whoever brings up gold and escapes keeps it. I want every man on this crew to capture their share of nature's happenstance, and walk away to live their lives."

Less thieving and murdering, and more like finders keepers. In some situations, she could get behind that. And a wealthy foreign government that stole from indigenous cultures all along Central and South America was okay to her. Ideally, it would be returned, but that wasn't feasible. "I'll stay."

The captain beamed and moved to kiss her, but he stopped himself. "I've survived torture, abuse, starvation, the threat of mutiny—actual threat by prior crews, and never once have I endured something this difficult."

Emily apparently didn't have the whole story. "What's so difficult?"

"Keeping my hands off you. I'm beyond delighted you're here now."

The captain told her everything. Nothing more from him stood between them. He was just as amazing as she'd thought. Did Emily trust him enough to tell her secret? Would he accept it? If they weren't going to stay together, it didn't matter. But could they?

She'd have to stay here, and figure out new skills and live without all the creature comforts she'd always known. Or the captain joined her in the twenty-first century. How would that work? He didn't have papers. He couldn't get a job or manage finances. He could learn, just like her, but the curve was much steeper in her world. There was so much to think about, Emily didn't know where to start.

Or if any of it was possible at all.

Chapter 20

Emily and the captain returned to the deck while the vote continued. The crew shifted their weight, frowning and gesturing, and the occasional outburst of disagreement startled her. The vote wasn't going well. Too many men weren't willing to go.

The captain frowned at the sight.

Emily held tight to his side as they approached Price.

"What's the status?" Captain Lemoine asked.

"The crew has been reduced by many," Quartermaster Price said. "But not enough. I need to start choosing who goes. Officers are all staying, including you, Doctor Porter."

Doctor Porter sounded so weird. Emily brushed it away though.

"And we have provisions enough for the remainders?" Captain Lemoine asked.

"If I can get ten more volunteers to go, we'll be set to sail."

The extended crew renegotiations didn't need her or the captain. Price was fully competent. Emily wanted a minute to rest herself. "I'm going to have a seat. Join me?"

"I must stay here with Price. Go ahead." The captain swung his arm off her shoulders.

Emily stepped away, watching him for signs of distress. Satisfied with his composure, she stretched her aching neck and back and wove her way to the bulwark. Emily hopped up onto the rail, watching the remaining activities unfold. Through the crowd, a twiggy man approached, and

Emily stiffened. "Fergus, what are you doing here? You left. You're free, just like you wanted."

"Being free disny seem as important when th'one person I want is trapped here, surrounded by murderers an' thieves. Who else is going tae keep ye safe?"

Emily frowned and read between the lines. "You signed the articles for me? But that's against everything you believe in."

Fergus leaned in close. "Aye, an' it was difficult, as Price is trying tae cut sailors fur the account. I thought o' what ye said. Th'risk is oot there. Whether I be oan th'merchant side awaiting th'pirates or th'pirate side awaiting th'noose. Then th'choise was plain."

Emily whispered, "You can't tell anyone about me, or they'll kill me."

He whispered in her ear, "I know, but I'm here tae protect ye, not hurt ye."

Emily didn't like a stranger having her life in his figurative hands. Mouth hanging open, she watched Fergus sink back into the sea of bodies. A longboat full of volunteers waited to be lowered to the water.

"McNeel, Abbas, Hazelip, Kanumba, you're off," Quartermaster Price ordered. Groans and whines came from the crowd as the chosen men wove their way toward the waiting longboat. "And that's it. Anchor's up in two hours."

The quartermaster closed his book and retreated to his private room below deck. The crew dispersed to their stations. Apparently, it took that long to lift the anchor. Men fitted the capstan with their levers and heaved around the axis point, singing a merry shanty to coordinate the rhythm of their movements. Others below deck must be working the messenger cable, a tedious process of attaching and detaching a separate rope to help lift the anchor.

Emily didn't see which way Fergus went, and she hoped to avoid him entirely. Just the idea that he wanted to marry her gave her the worst creeps. She didn't even know the guy. Him keeping her secret the whole while and disappearing after the account was finished was a best-case scenario.

The captain limped over toward her, and Emily rushed to his side and gathered him into her arms, intercepting his attempt at independence. Together, under the shadow of the cabin, they watched the crew set sail, a practiced dance of teamwork, shouted commands, and the rustling of canvas and sliding of lines through pulleys. All she could think about was the captain, an all-consuming entity who was strapped to her side and quickly invading her heart. Now was the perfect time to ask for the necklace, but she didn't want to disturb this peace between them. Not yet.

"How are the stitches feeling?"

The captain shrugged. "Enough rum and nothing is bothersome."

Emily couldn't argue with that, but they'd already struggled with the rum quantity, and the last thing she needed was another riot on her hands. Speaking of which, "Do we have enough rum on board to keep the masses content?"

"I wager Price has that settled. I must be off to chart the course to Florida's coast. Check on my person whenever you see fit." The captain winked at her and retreated to the navigation room behind them.

Emily glanced around for witnesses, but everyone was preoccupied preparing the ship. Alone on the deck, Emily climbed up onto roped cargo to enjoy a beautiful view without worrying about the waves tossing her overboard. A beautiful land, a barbarous time, and instead of reading about it in the books, she was here now. If Tyler could see her, would he laugh and say it suits her or would he tell her to grow up...again? Emily brushed him out of her thoughts and inhaled the soft sea air. She hoped wherever her friends were sent, they were having a relaxing and safe vacation.

A group of men came out to the deck, and with nothing pressing to do, Emily watched them. Fergus was in the mix, but so far, he stayed busy.

A pair of the men leaned over the rail on the opposite side of the ship from her and called down. They hoisted up a longboat full of men and the last of the supplies. With a wooden crate in his hands, Fergus broke away from the group and approached her.

"Have ye retrieved yer necklace yet?" he asked.

"Not yet. Why?"

Fergus hopped up onto the cargo next to her and rested the crate in his lap. "I saw it. Th'captain took it oot o' his pocket an' closed it inside a box in the hold."

A surge of excitement tore through her. "You're certain?"

Fergus nodded with a smile.

"Which one? Where?"

Fergus chuckled. "I have a plan. Just stay close."

Emily was thrilled to have someone willing to help her out. She followed Fergus across the deck and down the ladder, but someone was blocking the entrance to the hold—a security guard. Hooper, the man who conspired against the captain over rum but without the guts to follow through.

"What business you have here?" Hooper demanded, arms crossing over his broad chest, hopped up on his new authority.

"Last o' th'supplies are here." Fergus lifted the crate to prove his story true. "Price sent us tae check on th'rum supply tae make sure we have enough before we set sail."

Emily believed it was a lie, but she would take any help she could get.

"Is that so?" Hooper scrutinized them both, including the crate in Fergus's arms. "Anchor's already up. Price wouldn't send anyone back now."

"It's th'truth o' it, an' Florida's a long way off," Fergus said, and Hooper stepped aside. Fergus rushed her through the door and closed it behind them, having only candlelight to work with.

"Which one is it?" Emily asked, scanning for the likeliest contender, but her eyes hadn't adjusted yet. Fergus set down the crate in his hands, and Emily added, "What did it look like?"

While squinting at the barrels and shifting around crates, now much more full than last time she'd dug through here, the door behind her swung back open. Fergus approached Hooper and talked to him quietly. A frown on the guard's face set Emily on edge. Whatever just happened wasn't good.

"Come with me now, Porter." Hooper reached for her.

Emily tilted back out of the larger man's grasp. "What's this about? Price sent us, right, Fergus?" All the friendliness was gone from her friend's face and at once, Emily knew she'd made a grave mistake.

"He forced me tae help him enter th'hold." Fergus pointed at Emily like a child proclaiming the guilty party. "I'm innocent in this conspiracy. Just ask Price; he'll know naught o' this. It's all Porter's doing."

Fergus's word vomit to Hooper had Emily's stomach churning, and her avalanche of questions would only make her sound guilty. Emily said nothing, allowing Hooper to haul her to the aft of the gun deck. "This isn't right," Emily tried explaining as he dragged her along. "I only want what's best for the crew. You know that."

They ducked and swerved through the tightly packed narrow pathways. "That's not my decision to make, now is it?"

Up on the gun deck, rectangles of light dotted the floorboards alongside each cannon through the open gun ports, airing out the ripe scent of unbathed men. Their footsteps creaked against the hardwood, and gulls cawed nearby. If it weren't for the inhabitants of the ship, this would be the best vacation she'd ever had. Instead, Hooper stopped them at the quartermaster's cabin and knocked.

Price verbalized their permission to enter, and Hooper's firm hand forced her inside and explained what he'd caught her doing, focusing solely on Fergus's side of the story. Price nodded with a grim set to his mouth, and Hooper shut the door behind her on his way out, preventing her escape. Alone with the quartermaster, Emily crossed her arms protectively over her chest.

The quartermaster stood and strolled around his desk. "The captain had already taken your punishment for the last attempt to pilfer from the hold. Seems I was right to set a guard upon the door. Because of your position, I'll allow you a chance to defend yourself."

There was so much wrong with that, but Emily crafted a fib to lean into Price's reasonable side. "I needed to be sure there were enough medical supplies before we left. No one wants to be caught in a battle without the proper equipment to fix wounds." The humid dampness gave her a chill.

"When the mouse was caught creeping into the grain, the reason of a meal was excused once and warned against. When the mouse failed to heed that warning, and the cat held the mouse's tail did the story change. So which is the truth? The mouse's story before or after pressure was applied? The reason mattered not. The story mattered not. Words were meaningless when they didn't match the actions. The mouse's decision to disobey orders demanded consequences."

That was an eloquent way of saying Emily wasn't get out of a punishment this time. The question was the magnitude of it. "I'm the mouse in this story?" Emily asked with disbelief, already knowing the answer. Fergus had planned this since he'd uncharacteristically decided to sign the articles. Why did her friend trick her?

"When the captain arrives, *he* shall serve your punishment." Price returned behind his desk with an air of finality.

A light knock on the door churned Emily's stomach. Price granted the visitor entrance, and when Emily met the captain's gaze, she silently pleaded for help and mercy.

"What's this all about?" the captain asked, limping closer, and shot Emily a fast glance of concern.

Hooper's smug smile at the door angered her, but it was closed on him once again.

Price said, "Porter was caught persuading another sailor to lie to the guard at the hold. What he sought, we don't know, but an attempt is still intent, and our doctor here was caught in the act. His theft is punishable by marooning."

The captain's features darkened with a contained rage that made Emily nervous. "This involves Fergus and Hooper, does it not? A man who incites protests with the intent to mutiny, and the other, who rejected the articles but returned, begging to be allowed aboard. I trust your judgment, Price, but how is that not suspicious?"

Emily was grateful the captain had her side...and saw reason. Yesterday she'd had their respect and admiration. Today they wanted to maroon her, leaving her to die. It was almost unbelievable how quickly their loyalties changed.

"Whether or not I believe them, the men wove their tale convincingly, and it will spread regardless of its truth," Price said calmly.

The captain tensed. "How can you trust those men over Porter?"

"The possibility of a thief among them is a direct threat to their trust, and right now, we need the crew united. The crew shall not stand for brushing another crime under the rug. So you see, my hands are tied."

The captain leaned on Price's desk, fury rolling off him. "I will not maroon our only doctor because of a story from Fergus and Hooper. This issue stays between us, and I'll warn Fergus and Hooper if their tongues wag once about this, they'll be the ones heaved over the starboard rail. Is that clear?"

The quartermaster's darkening features meant he didn't like his position challenged.

Emily piped in before things escalated beyond repair. "Price, you said yourself this crew owed me a debt. I want to cash it in to stay aboard the *Sea Lion*."

Price eyed her with a glimmer of respect, but his words were firm. "We do need a doctor, and it's too late to find another. We also need a competent captain moving into this account. Make no mistake—concessions shall not be given again. Don't worry about Fergus and Hooper. I'll take care of them. Get us to Florida."

The captain straightened, satisfied, and Emily followed him out the door. She shot a nasty glance at Hooper and tried to assist the captain's steps down the quiet gun deck, but he refused. Outside of earshot, Emily said, "What's wrong?"

Captain Lemoine didn't face her. Concerned, she reached out for his arm, but he tugged out of her grip.

"I have work to do," he snapped.

Emily stopped, dejected, and watched the captain limp up to the main deck. What had she done wrong this time?

Chapter 21

During their journey, the sky remained bright and clear, the waters calm. They had not encountered a goat supply ship, and Emily had overheard concerns the target had changed course, or some other ship got to her first. Either way, she was grateful only half the crew was on board, just so she didn't have to watch them fight to the death for the limited provisions they afforded.

Boatswain Karl assigned her to Fergus's side. Her friend had deliberately sabotaged her, and now there was an unspoken awkwardness between them, and every time he neared her, the hairs raised on her arms. She hated that a sliver of fear lingered. What had been Fergus's intent in nearly getting her marooned? It ate at her, but like the captain ordered, no tongues wagging about the ordeal.

Fergus showed her how to tie up the sails on the yardarm, and without any safety equipment, it was a harrowing but exhilarating experience. A fall to the deck or the water from that height would mean death after many broken bones. OSHA would have a field day on this ship.

For days, Emily watched the captain over her shoulder, catching glimpses here and there, but Captain Lemoine had refrained from glancing back, as if she'd hallucinated their whole forbidden relationship. No matter the legitimate concern she offered over his care, he'd refused her. The captain acted as if they'd never kissed or shared other very intimate moments, and that cut her deeply. If not for him, Emily had no reason to stay here. All day she secretly plotted her next attempt to find her necklace. She didn't believe it was left carelessly in the hold to be jettisoned the next time the Royal Navy appeared, or more likely, the Spanish Armada.

But first, the captain's diminished limp meant she needed to check his stitches, no matter his stubborn and likely inaccurate opinion of her. While cruising at a speed of about six knots and weather that allowed for more relaxed temperaments, Emily excused herself from Fergus and knocked on the navigation room door.

"Come in," Captain Lemoine called through the door. He'd been making adjustments to their course as the conditions changed, and in the middle of a calculation, he hadn't looked at his visitor.

He didn't want to hear any more from Price. Lemoine was already furious with himself, and throwing himself into his work was the only way to make things right. He had to get them to Florida swiftly and safely. The sooner they retrieved their gold, the sooner he could give Emile her just dues and bid her farewell with her necklace.

It was better that way, even if it hurt untold amounts.

The door closed, and Lemoine wrote down the final number. Satisfied, he looked up and frowned. Emile didn't belong in here, and her presence was risky. "I told you I don't need your aid any longer."

Emile stiffened, and Lemoine felt a pang of guilt. "I noticed your gait has improved. If you're healed, I need to remove your stitches."

Lemoine met her gaze and his anger softened. He wasn't upset with her. Only himself. He couldn't keep her safe. Any mistake from here on out would be her life, and likely his as well. But he could give up resistance for proper care. "Fair enough. This way."

Captain Lemoine stood and gestured for her to follow him into his cabin. When closed in together, remembering her naked in the bath, his breathing increased. Lemoine removed his tunic and untied his breeches slowly, trying to plead with himself this was only a medical visit to be over and done with.

It wasn't working well.

Emile approached cautiously, cheeks pinking with a beautiful flush. He liked that effect on her, and he loved that he caused it. Emile ducked, her fingers pressing gently around the area. "I don't feel any alarming heat, and the site is soft. Everything looks good here." Emile opened her pouch and removed a sewing kit. She slipped the mini scissors through her fingers. She leaned in close as she began the process of removing the stitches.

Something inside her pouch caught his eye. Lemoine pointed at her waist and asked, "What's that?"

"What's what?" Emile asked, focusing on her work.

"This." Unable to help his curiosity, Captain Lemoine slipped free the strange device and turned it over in his hands. It felt expensive, but he couldn't figure out why. The top of it was reflective, but not a mirror. And small holes on the sides were for inserting something, but Lemoine could never guess what. He'd never seen anything like it. "What does this do?"

Emile slipped it from his fingers as if it were fragile or dangerous. She looked at it, debating. "I'm afraid you wouldn't understand if I told you."

The captain made a snort of derision. Surely she didn't just insult him? "I've traveled the seas, Emile, for five and twenty years. Been to many countries the world over, and yet, you think me such a simpleton?"

Emile turned the black device over in her hands. "I can tell you, but this cannot change anything between us. For my safety and yours. Can we make that deal?"

Lemoine had many ideas of what could need such a disclaimer, and finally the last piece of the Emile puzzle was at hand. "Are you a spy? Is that why you're on the run? Is that why you won't tell me of your origins? Is that why you're so unfamiliar with our world out here at sea?"

Emile's lips lifted in mild humor. "Spy? No. My life isn't that exciting...wasn't...that exciting." She thought further and said slowly, "Remember when I said I came from an island off the coast of the colonies? It's not true. I couldn't explain—in a way you'd understand, in a way anyone from here would understand. See, even where I'm from, the explanation of my home makes little sense. Do you understand?"

The captain blinked, trying to make heads or tails of it. "I'm not sure."

"It's not that I don't trust you with the truth; it's just...I don't want to be...I..." Emile trailed off.

"You can tell me, Emile. Whatever it is. Please tell me." He needed this trust from her. He wanted it dearly. If she could find it in her heart to open up to him, he could see a future with her.

Emile sighed. "I'm afraid of how you'll react."

Her declaration truly baffled him. "How could you be afraid of me? I've done nothing to cause you such unease. And if I have, my deepest apologies."

Tears shimmered on her lids. "Perhaps you should honor our previous deal. Return my necklace first."

The idea of making good on his word settled like a rock in his gut. Far from land, she couldn't escape with it. But knowing she had the option panged him. He knew he had to let her go, beyond this ship, back to her confusing home. But not yet.

Captain Lemoine still held onto a glimmer of hope. "Is that what you truly want?" A tear spilled over, and Lemoine brushed it carefully from her cheek with his thumb. "Why such tears, Emile?"

"I'm trusting you with the truth. I'm trusting you with my life. Remember that." Emile focused on the device, and it lit up like magic.

Lemoine frowned. Her fingers moved and after a few seconds, she turned the lighted side of the device to him. His eyes widened at an image so real, he had to touch it to be sure. No brush strokes were visible at all. How was it possible? The image was Emile, dressed in the most outlandish clothing he could imagine, smiling with her blonde hair down. And the next was her in the clothing she wore now with another woman, and both stood next to something shiny, metallic, and monstrous. Captain Lemoine couldn't begin to understand it.

Emile touched something and the image before him—the image in color!—changed again.

Lemoine backed up a step and fell onto the mattress. His hand moved to his forehead. "What is that? What…? How…?"

"These are pictures—photographs—of me out with friends. Everyday stuff. But that one was me and Angela in front of her car. This was us at the Tall Ships festival, where I was before appearing on Captain Sinclair's merchant ship. I didn't stow away." As she'd explained, her fingers moved the images back and forth…like magic.

Captain Lemoine didn't know what to believe. "Magic transported you here. You're a witch?"

Emile waved her hands to brush those words away. "No, not at all, no. Witches don't exist, but apparently time travel does."

Captain Lemoine considered the concept hogwash. Looking at the proof before him, he had been a simpleton, and his respect and fear grew.

"I'm from Wisconsin, a state in the United States of America, which doesn't exist yet. I was at a festival enjoying the ships of the past with vendors selling beer, food, and crafts." Emile swiped the device again, showing him while explaining.

Captain Lemoine was frozen in terror and fascination.

"My friend and I bought necklaces at a vendor. When we boarded the tourist ship, a barque, by the way, the guide ordered us to take them off the ship. Angela and I opted to wear them instead, and when I put mine on, the next thing I knew, I was here in the past. I don't know what happened to Angela. I have no other explanation, but I assure you, this is the truth."

As much as he didn't understand it, he believed it. "You'd told me if you got your necklace back, you'd return home. That necklace is the only way," he said softly.

"It's only a theory, truthfully. For all I know, I'm stuck here. But if I put it on, over my head, it should take me home the same magical way it brought here me." Emile looked at the device again, fingers moving.

"This won't hurt you. It happened in my past—your future, okay? And I hope you take this in deeply, because my battery's almost dead." Emile sat next to him and held the device once again.

Captain Lemoine watched a man laughing and sloshing a red cup of liquid with his arm around...Emile, who also harbored a grin, but there was a sadness to her features.

"This was a party. We were celebrating Angela's birthday. That's Tyler."

Captain Lemoine stiffened. His mind blanked.

With a touch of Emile's magic finger, the moving pictures stopped. "I'm sorry, I just wanted to show you. This thing also makes phone calls to anyone in the world who also has one."

Lemoine shook his head and stood. He paced the room, ignoring the ache from his side. "Which would be no one."

"As long as I'm the only one from the future with a cell phone, that's true. Although, without cell towers, it doesn't matter, anyway."

Ignoring her nonsensical words, the captain continued pacing the cabin. The answers he sought made no sense, but at the same time made perfect sense. It explained why she understood nothing of their world, but yet marveled over ordinary people—Hornigold and Blackbeard. She knew who they were from stories. Lemoine noted she hadn't heard of him, and he didn't know whether to be concerned or not.

It also explained how she could appear to be privileged with her clothing, smooth hands, and straight white teeth, while claiming a childhood of poverty. His world, what he knew, wasn't her world.

Emile slipped the device back into her pouch and removed more chocolates. "Here." She offered him a few. "These aren't rare or expensive where I'm from. And they aren't stolen." She emphasized the final two words.

He stopped and looked at her open palm. Unable to take from her, he closed her fingers over the candies. "They're rare and expensive here. Savor them while you still have them."

Emile frowned. "While I still have them?"

Captain Lemoine offered her a hand. She accepted, and he lifted her to her feet. "Kiss me."

"But the articles?" Emile said.

"Tell me one last thing. What is your name?"

Emile smiled. "Emily. Emily Porter."

"I'm certain Emily Porter didn't sign the articles." Captain Lemoine said, a sadness tugged at his heart. She didn't belong here at all, and there was nothing he could offer that would satisfy her. Not even all the gold in the wreck would be good enough. But he had to try. He wanted her to have all of it and return home to the life of privilege she deserved.

Emily chuckled. "She didn't."

"So kiss me, Emily," he whispered.

Her lips found his, and his arms found their way around her, pressing her close for the first time. His body felt hers. The shapes of a woman. He wanted his hands on her breasts, his mouth at the cleft between her thighs. He wanted his cock to explore regions that would have her calling his name in ecstasy. But so long as they were on this ship, as she'd explained, they couldn't.

Tears pricked his eyes. Despite knowing she needed to go home, he knew it would destroy him.

THE KISS HAD FELT like goodbye, and Emily memorized every movement, every taste of his lips she could.

Until an urgent knocking on the captain's door had him pull apart from her too quickly and too soon. With gruff irritation, he barked, "What's the matter?"

"Captain, sir, the location is in sight, but we're not alone."

Captain Lemoine turned to her. "I must go at once. I suspect we shall encounter hostilities. I *don't* promise to keep you safe."

Emily forced a smile and the promise of the non-promise. Unable to speak, she only nodded, and the captain rushed out the door, limping far less than he usually would.

Emily was alone. The captain bid her goodbye. He knew she had to return home, but he hadn't returned her necklace yet. She tried not to read further into that. He simply hadn't had a chance to since they'd made the deal.

Was it possible for her to stay here? Emily certainly wouldn't be happy minding a house while Captain Lemoine traversed the oceans, finding adventure, freeing merchant sailors, and collecting what he needed to keep themselves fed.

He was a pirate. He was a thief. Today he was collecting gold that was lost without harming anyone.

And he was an amazing man who was justified in his actions.

But could she join him here at sea, be a real pirate? Assuming the crew somehow accepted her as herself. Emily's job in the future was hardly sufficient to pay the rent. She'd dumped her thieving, disrespectful, gaslighting ex-boyfriend. Angela having put on her necklace meant she was gone, too. Her mother had passed away. Her father had vanished. She had just about nothing tying her to home.

Emily had the best adventure of her life in the last few weeks. And with a misty gaze at the captain's door, she no longer wanted to go, but knew she must. The crew—Hooper and Price especially—would never accept her. And Fergus would throw her under the bus in a heartbeat, because she'd rejected his proposal.

The vacation excitement of her trip through time would wear off soon, and she'd be missing her chocolate, hot showers, restaurants, safety standards of the future, grocery stores, online ordering, and even menstrual cups. She had bills, an apartment, and plants to water. Home was where she belonged.

Emily composed herself, double checked all her future stuff was tucked away, and exited to the main deck, hoping beyond hope they weren't going to be under fire again.

The captain stood on the quarterdeck above her with a spyglass pointing to the sea. Emily lifted a hand to shield the sun and gazed at the horizon. Several ships. Were they Royal Navy? Spanish Armada? Other pirates? Merchants on a detour?

Whoever they were, wouldn't be friendly.

Chapter 22

SEVERAL SHIPS DOTTED THE coastline, dancing along the fair weather waves. Emily didn't see a single Spanish banner among them. But the *Sea Lion* approached the starboard side of the nearest ship—a three-masted sloop with English emblems on the sails. Their ship had communicated a willingness to converse, and Emily watched them closely at the rail. The Englishmen aboard the sloop leaned over the opposite rail, lifted their loot, and hauled full bags below deck like dutiful ants, one after the other. A man who appeared to be the captain of the sloop waved, and out of politeness, Emily waved back with a smile.

These weren't monsters, murders, or thieves. Just opportunists trying to change their stars without harming anyone. And Spain wasn't exactly innocent in how they'd commandeered this gold in the first place.

"Ahoy!" Captain Lemoine called over. "Seeking the lost gold, are you?"

"Aye!" the captain from the other side called back. "And we won't be giving any up! Find your own and be gone with you!"

Captain Lemoine gestured for the quartermaster to join him on the quarterdeck, and the men spoke in private. What syllables made their way over were blurred by the breeze. With a quick nod, Price moved through the crew, passing along the orders. All but the essential sailors dropped their current tasks and turned their attention to the sloop.

Emily had a sinking feeling something bad was about to happen, and her stomach knotted.

"This Spanish gold is free for the taking," Captain Lemoine called back. "If you'll not share either your loot or your successful location, then we shall stake our claim to this free territory!"

Emily accepted a recovery of lost gold, but this sounded like blatant thievery. How could he lie to her face? Emily glared at the back of the captain's head, wishing to see the hidden truth buried under his magnificent hair and fancy hat. But the *Sea Lion* crew, who were freeing pistols and cutlasses from their waistbands, drew her attention. Emily wasn't a fighter, and she didn't have arms. As the worry crossed her mind, a cutlass was pressed into her hand.

Fergus.

Emily frowned and tried to hand the weapon back. She didn't want his help, and she had no interest in touching something responsible for how many deaths already? "What are you doing? You already framed me for theft and almost got me marooned for it. I don't want to talk to you ever again."

"I didny ask ye tae say anything," Fergus smiled at this play on her words.

Emily only glared to make her point.

"But since ye mention it, I created that spectacle tae get ye removed from th'ship, so ye'd be safe from these people, from this"—he gestured to the sword in her hands. "But since ye were too stubborn tae accept th'way oot I offered, now ye must place yer fate in th'hands o' these ruffians an' murderers. As th'ship's de facto doctor, we'll defend ye as best we can, so get below deck fur yer own safety. I hope ye have a robust constitution."

Emily's anger deflated. He'd only tried to save her life in the only way he knew how. "Why didn't you just say something instead of tricking me?"

"Ye wouldn't have gone voluntarily."

No, no she supposed she wouldn't have. "And how would you have saved me from marooning? It's kind of a one-person punishment."

"I would've jumped in after ye."

A warm friendliness blossomed toward Fergus.

"Together we would've sailed away into the sunset, alive, safe, and free from men like these."

"Thank you." Whether for the sword or the attempt to save her life, she didn't know.

Fergus grinned and nodded. "When those men cross, I can only dae so much since our crew is half th'normal size. An' if ye fall, I am deeply sorry."

Fergus had far more experience with ship battles than she, so his flippant discussion around impending death startled her, as if it were expected. In all the times she'd gone camping, surrounded by bears, coyotes, foxes, raccoons, and other critters armed with teeth and claws, never once was she concerned for her life. In most places she camped, either she or her friends had spotty cell service at a minimum. Roads were easily traversable by city commuter car. The biggest risk to her life had been when she and Angela had rented a jet ski to drag an inflatable raft on the lake. Far from shore, Emily had jumped off the raft for a swim and Angela, after a few drinks, thought it'd be funny to drive away with it.

Emily was a great swimmer, but this impending battle was so much worse than anything she'd ever experienced. Emily was only a pirate in spirit. But instilling hope and building courage could have tremendous positive effects—neither of which Fergus had apparently heard of. "You're apologizing for my death when I'm not dead yet?"

Fergus double checked his pistol for shot and grasped it with a trembling hand. His grip on the cutlass was slightly firmer. "Aye. I fear it's an inevitability. I'm only a moderate swordsman myself. But if we both die, we die wi' honor in defending ourselves against th'worst scum o' the nation."

Emily didn't miss that irony. "And now you're one of them."

"Aye, it's true. Ye know how tae destroy a man's pride. Hold on tae yer britches, because here they come!"

Men swung over from the opposing ship with grunts and growls and frowns creasing their faces. Emily's heart perched itself in her throat as if seeking its own safety. She didn't have time to hide, but if she got caught deserting the crew in battle, that was punishable by marooning, too. No room for cowards on a pirate ship. Emily gripped the sword, sweaty hands trembling. She'd never killed anyone, as most civilized people hadn't, but she'd also never been cornered and fighting for her life. Despite her extensive camping experience, she'd never encountered a bear. And now she might not get to.

Swords clanged and crashed. Pistols fired. Clouds of gunpowder obscured the deck. The ship tilted with the waves, sending swords flying, missing their targets. Men shouted and grunted with their efforts, and Emily ducked and feebly swiped at nearby engaged foes while attempting to reach the ladder to the lower deck. She'd rather take her chances with bears and marooning. Or marooning with bears. This was suicide.

An English pirate stalked up to her with a grimace and a sword aimed to swipe, blocking her exit from the battle. Emily's hand trembled, and her grip tightened on the sword. She dug deep for an intimidating voice. "Back away. I don't want to hurt you." It most definitely wasn't scary at all.

The pirate closed in on her.

Emily's hands shook harder. "Please," she begged in a weak voice, tears threatening to spring free. Emily scanned for the captain, but she couldn't see him. What if he were already dead? Tears sprung to her eyes, but she blinked them away.

The enemy before her snorted with amusement. "What kind of pirate cries in battle? For your cowardice, you deserve death." The man spat and held his sword high for a devastating blow. But he stopped in his tracks, face slackening. The Englishman fell over like a tall sack of potatoes, and Fergus pulled his sword from the man's spine.

Her friend was smeared in blood, but he smiled in good spirits. "So far, we're alive."

Fear twisted Emily's face. How could he be so casual? Swords continued to clang and crash around them. Blood slicked the deck. With the captain's abrupt orders, they had no time to sand it. Bodies, some writhing in pain and others still as a stone, cluttered the slippery main deck. The fight spilled over onto the enemy ship. The men retrieving gold stopped to pick up a sword and defend their loot.

A pirate approached Fergus's back, and Emily pointed. "Watch out!"

Fergus turned with his sword ready to strike, but the enemy was quicker, splitting Fergus across the middle. Emily gasped. Her friend's face slackened, and he dropped to his knees and flopped onto his side. With a quick glance at his fatal wound, Emily knew there was nothing to be done. She stifled a scream. All Fergus ever wanted was to be free of this ship and take her with. He'd died for it, and it was her fault.

She'd known returning to the *Sea Lion* was a risk, but she never thought the threat could come from within. Lemoine ordered this attack, and now Fergus and many others were dead.

For money.

Wild-eyed and terrified, Emily held her cutlass up, wishing she'd taken a self-defense class. An English pirate swung his sword down, and Emily's crashed against his, the jolting impact almost making her drop it. He pressed harder, closer. She was no match for his strength, not by a long shot. He grinned with malicious pleasure as his sword brought her closer to the slippery and red-stained deck boards. If he hadn't been enjoying it so much, she would've been dead already.

Emily kneeled down to the floor, still holding the English pirate's sword at bay. He was playing with her, pressing only as hard as he needed to pin her down. What could she do before it was too late? Emily held her breath, struggling with the effort, on the verge of crying out to spare her life. The pirate kneeled over her and lifted his sword for a final blow.

Emily saw her window. She kicked up at his crotch and sent him folding over. She scurried backward over the downed bodies and slick blood, smearing bodily fluids all over her outfit. The pirate's blade glinted with a slash through the air, but Emily moved her foot at the last second. Her arms shook with the force exerted to survive the attacker, and now a second one approached. Emily stood, wanting to run, but in every direction were small skirmishes of pirates on pirates, and even if she found a way through, she'd be sliced up by accident. This English pirate closed the distance, and Emily's insides turned to liquid. Surviving one was luck. She knew her odds against another were nil.

Less than nil.

THE SECOND ENGLISH PIRATE snarled and lifted his sword to strike. Emily moved her sword to protect her face, but her attacker paused, arm mid-air, and his head fell back. Her second attacker fell to the deck, and just as Fergus had before him, Captain Lemoine extracted his cutlass from the pirate's neck. Her captain held out his hand to her, and Emily smiled with relief. She was still pissed, but grateful to be alive.

"Are you well?" he asked.

Emily glanced at her blood-stained clothes and her friend's body. She doubted he was still alive. The crew of the *Sea Lion* had been far outnumbered. Emily was losing what small strand of hope she'd held onto. "I'm breathing. That's all I can say right now."

The pirate Emily had kicked in the crotch had returned to his feet and approached them both. Captain Lemoine swung at him, shifting the man's attention to himself. The captain's sword met the opponent's with grunts from his broken rib and a few slices on his arms. Emily could hardly watch as the men circled one another, feral rage of wild animals on their faces.

"Stop!" Emily shouted. She couldn't bear it any longer. The captain's head turned to her, and the pirate took the opportunity. Emily processed the movements in slow motion—the pirate's snarl turning to a smirk, the sword shifting position, the flickers of his arm muscles as he adjusted trajectory.

"Duck!" Emily shouted before the pirate could strike her captain down.

Captain Lemoine lowered himself and spun. With a smooth motion, he sliced through the English pirate's middle. The aggressor fell over, clutching his middle which was spilling onto the deck. Emily exhaled for her stomach's sake.

Her captain regained his footing, and with a hand hovering over his injured rib, he reached out and pressed her to his chest. "Are you injured?"

For the first time in several hours, she felt safe. Emily shook her head against his taut chest, tears wetting her face, and emotion caught in her throat. The captain kissed her forehead in such a fast motion Emily wasn't sure it actually happened. He turned to the rail and shouted, "Enough! Truce!"

Under the protective wing of the captain's arm, Emily noticed the bodies covering the deck were more enemy than friendly. Somehow, someway, with fewer hands than the enemy, the *Sea Lion* prevailed. To spare more lives, Emily was grateful the captain offered the other ship a chance to recover, rather than attempt to take them over.

The other captain seceded at once. "Truce!"

At once the few remaining skirmishes ended—mutual respect for their captains' orders. The foreign crew crossed back to their ship, some limping, others carrying their dead, while respectfully taking turns with the *Sea Lion*'s crew returning likewise. The enemy pirates slipped the planks back onto their side. Emily approached Fergus and checked his throat for a pulse. She felt nothing, and with a heavy heart, she lowered Fergus's eyelids.

A hand rested on her shoulder, and Emily stood to meet the captain. She wiped tears away. "What a waste. All he wanted to do was keep me safe, get me away from here." Emily gestured to the field of bodies. "And he was right to do it."

The captain brushed her chunk of sticky hair from her face. "I desire to comfort you, and I wish to tell everyone about you, about us, but I cannot. I also cannot assure you the danger is over, but I find a personal guard for you."

All this effort. All these lives. Anger spewed the words from her mouth. "What's the point of a personal guard when half the men on the ship are dead? Can we even sail back to Nassau? Is Giles, the cook alive? Why did you order them to attack? Why not just search for treasure next to them? This was all pointless! I can't believe after everything you said, you are, in fact, willing to kill and steal for money—the most selfish and depraved a man could be."

The captain recoiled as if struck by her words, and his lips parted, but when he spoke, there was an icy rage, "There shall be enough pieces of eight for us to do as we please, wherever we please it."

Emily's features twisted, and anger roared through her veins. She was shocked by Tyler's greed, and now she knew better. She should've expected it from pirates, of all people. The anger was at herself, for believing these men to be different, for not believing Fergus, who was now dead. "You know money will not get me home. Is there not a single way you could earn a living besides"—she used Fergus's descriptors—"Murdering and thieving?"

The captain's features darkened as if he'd taken offense, and she wanted to slap him. "We banded together under an agreement to seek our fortunes off the backs of wealthy merchants, who cared nothing for their employees. We were starved, refused wages, punished for minor infractions and accidents, and lived in cramped, unsanitary sleeping quarters. We live by only the code we signed on for, and we stay together until every man has earned 1,000 pieces of eight. Here at the sunken galleon, we'll collect 1,000 each, courtesy of Spain."

Emily remembered that article, but she hadn't known what it meant at the time. The history books were right—pirates murdered for money. She'd deluded herself. And whatever this attempt at something meaningful between her and the stubborn pirate captain only wasted her time. When a man was fueled by greed, how could she ever trust him?

Emily stomped away to blow off steam. "If any of the injured need me, I'll be on the orlop deck. No thanks to you." At the ladder, Boatswain Karl waited for her in desperate need of tending to his leg. She asked, "Can you climb down to get it dressed? I cannot carry you."

Karl chuckled. "I expect not."

Emily climbed down ahead of him to ready her work space. She laid out an array of ancient unsterile tools and grimaced at her patient's injuries. Karl plopped onto a barrel next to her. He pinched an eye shut to protect it from blood smearing his vision. Emily swiped it away for him, finding no gashes underneath. Must've been the other man's blood.

"That was quite the speech there, doctor." Karl grunted and used his arms to move his injured thick leg.

Emily cleaned off the gash in his thigh and threaded her needle. "This is going to sting."

The boatswain chuckled, bouncing his round middle. "No more worse than my leg, I wager."

Emily dunked her threaded needle in a small cup of rum she'd secured ahead of time and smiled. "Be careful, gambling is against the rules."

Karl laughed, and Emily made the first stitch. "Is this a normal occurrence?" she asked absently, referring to the abrupt order by the captain to invade another ship, but she feared questioning his authority directly, especially in front of witnesses.

"A cut from a cutlass? Aye, normal as can be. For a doctor, you are small and delicate of hand."

Emily darted him a look. "My appearance has nothing to do with my abilities."

"Aye." He didn't sound convinced. Emily tore the slashed fabric wider and continued stitching the gash by the poor light. Other pirates below deck made their way to the main deck, for whatever the captain wanted them to do next, she didn't care. "And you survived the fight. That's the surprising part."

"Why?" Emily squinted at him. She knew she was helpless, but that didn't mean she appreciated others pointing it out.

"Two good men protected you, one with his life. I wager the outcome would've been different had they not bothered."

Emily poked the needle through his skin rougher than necessary.

"I see how the captain looks at you. Never guessed he fancied men."

Emily's hand jerked and rather than crying out, the boatswain chuckled again. "It's not for me to know. But so long as I have my vision, I miss nothing. Curious, why do you disapprove of the captain so heartily? We take what we wish—it's our bond—and we all want riches to escape the life before the noose catches us. The captain most of all."

"I noticed the captain, more than the rest of you, takes pleasure in hunting other people's money, thank you." Her tone was sharp and condescending, but since she was covered in the blood of men and stitching one who didn't know how to keep his trap shut, she determined her attitude wouldn't get her in trouble—at the moment.

Emily quietly growled in fury as blood leaked from the deck above and dripped onto her shoulder. The air was too hot and stunk like the fetid soup she'd used to mop the merchant ship's deck. The lack of windows made her small workplace even more claustrophobic. And this jerk wasn't helping any.

Boatswain Karl laughed. "You make no sense. A pirate, like the rest of us, agreed to go on the account together, and now you changed your mind?"

Emily finished the last stitch and cleaned her needle. "I don't know what I want right now. You're done, so get out of my area and send the next survivor over."

"Be careful," Karl said, repeating her warning, only his had a serious tone to it. "The captain has his reasons for what he's doing. He deserves our respect for the time he remains."

This got Emily attention. "What do you mean 'the time he remains'? Is he sick?"

Karl stood. "That stunt you pulled with the remaining rum barrel. Know why it landed you in a heap of trouble with the quartermaster?"

"I made him look like a liar?" Emily's tone was clipped, but she was happy to listen.

"Half the crew was unsettled from the paltry prizes we'd had lately, and you noticed the stirrings of a mutiny. After we recover this prize, Captain Lemoine plans to retire from the account—woeful news for most of us, but joyous news for the dissenters. Price had been squirreling that measly rum away for the celebration. You know how strongly men feel about their rum."

Emily put away her needle. "None of that is justification for slaughtering people for their money."

Boatswain Karl shifted his weight with a grunt. "And that, good lad, is why you'll never survive as a pirate. I wish you luck in repairing injuries. You're going to need it."

He had no idea.

Chapter 23

Since Emily had declined to use whatever the strange objects in the doctor's chest were, she'd emptied her personal spool of thread stitching the crew's injuries. One man suffered a mortal wound to the chest. His mates didn't object to her offering him copious rum. Emily could do nothing but hold the man's hand while he passed.

After collecting fresh air from the main deck and vomiting over the port side rail, Emily swiped a sweaty forearm across her face and leaned against the bulwark, exhausted. A few men groaned as they lined up bodies of their fallen while others retrieved the hammocks. One by one, they wrapped the bodies in their own hammocks and sewed them closed. The quartermaster announced the name of each man as a pair of survivors lifted and discarded the body overboard. The crew fell silent until the melancholy ceremony ended. McKee, the master gunner, led the crew to inventorying the weapons and ordering their servicing. Boatswain Karl collected some men to repair lines sliced during battle.

Half a dozen ships or more, each giving the others a wide berth, had dropped anchor along the coast. One flew the Spanish flag, but it never assaulted the opportunists, not like how the captain had. Emily recognized the location and information from her reading. This must've been the infamous Plate Fleet Wreck of 1715, when a hurricane had surprised the fleet of Spanish treasure ships on their routine route from Havana to Spain. Fifty-foot waves crashed many of them into coastal rocks and swallowed others whole. Only the frigate escort who'd set off ahead of the fleet to warn away any incoming ships had escaped the storm. The sunken gold had been overwhelmed by opportunists, so the Spanish salvaged what they could, rather than waste precious time chasing off thieves.

Seven million pieces of eight were lost, hundreds of crew drowned, and the few survivors constructed camps out of the wreckage only to succumb to injuries or dehydration. But the men around her were only after the gold. To Emily, it was grave robbing. Just because this was Captain's last account before retiring didn't excuse his actions on this day.

Around thirty men had survived on the *Sea Lion*. A handful cleaned the deck of spilled blood. Giles, the cook, brought water to those remaining. Since he'd survived, they wouldn't starve, not that stale crunchy biscuits and salted pork were all that appetizing, anyway. If the waters steadied, the cook might fire up the pit, frying a portion of meat to chase away the hangry. After a battle, Emily figured all the men needed a hearty meal. Her stomach was too shaken to consider food.

The men not tasked with cleaning copied the English, using a ballast rock to sink below the surface and retrieve their own loot, since the captain failed to steal their opponent's. Pirates carried handfuls of gold and silver to a barrel secured by a few of the crew holding serviced weapons. She stared holes in the back of the captain's head and folded her arms across her chest. If Captain Lemoine had sent men for their own loot in the first place, a full quarter of their men wouldn't have died.

Why she ever thought they could work was beyond her. Some stupid fantasy where she let her research and TV shows color the reality of living among thieves and murderers. Captain Lemoine was no different from Tyler, a man who cared more about money than people, who would do anything to get it. Perhaps Tyler wouldn't have killed people, but thankfully, she'd never find out firsthand. And here she was, watching the worst depraved thing she could ever see—dead bodies dumped overboard while greedy men smiled at their twinkling precious pieces of eight, swiped from watery graves.

From a history fanatic's viewpoint, Emily wanted to see what the handmade gold and silver coins looked like brand new, but showing interest in what they were doing was against all she believed good in the world.

Emily was close enough to Florida's coast to jump into the sea and make a swim for it—sharks or not—but how long would she survive with nothing but the clothes on her back, a waterlogged cell phone, melted chocolates, and a used up sewing kit? Making a swim to the shore meant she'd starve or die of dehydration, just like the hurricane survivors. But there was something else she could do. With all hands preoccupied, Emily climbed down the ladder to the hold, left unguarded since the battle, and slipped inside. She hadn't seen Hooper. Perhaps he was one of the dead.

Emily lit a candle. The ship had restocked at Nassau, but now she didn't feel the pressure of time. She didn't care if she got caught. She pushed aside small boxes, sifted through open-top crates of green glass bottles with onion-like shapes, and shook barrels, but none of them budged. Standing and stretching under the low ceiling, Emily looked around, outstretching the candle for better light. Where would a small valuable necklace be kept safe?

The door behind her opened with a squeak of the hinges. Emily gasped from being startled, not about being caught. Regardless of the why, she'd dropped the candle. Flames licked at the fluffy crate packaging, and the man who'd caught her shouted for help. The fire grew rapidly, and men rushed in carrying buckets of sea water. They heaved water at the rapidly spreading flames.

"Fire! There be a fire in the hold! More water!" The voices carried through the floors and more footsteps thundered above. A crushing weight settled over her. Emily had already lost everything once, because of Tyler, and now she was on the verge of losing everything again. This time instead of money, it was her future hanging in the balance. Not knowing what else to do and worried her necklace was going to sink with the ship, Emily removed her sodden jerkin and swatted at the base of the flames.

Buckets splashed around her, soaking her not-so-white-anymore tunic, but the flames kept spreading. Emily swatted again and again as smoke filled the hold. Men coughed. Emily's eyes stung from the thickening haze. More buckets came, and Emily folded onto her hands and knees, spreading the seawater and patting out the flames.

"Move faster!" Emily shouted. They had to turn the tables on the fire before it reached the flash point. Not only would the firefighters all be dead from the heat, but the ship would be a total loss—leaving the survivors stranded on the coast. If she survived the flash point explosion, she'd already made too many enemies to survive the punishment. With each heave of water and whack of flames, the battle slowly shifted into the crew's favor. And with each patch of snuffed flame, more smoke billowed into the small room. Emily lifted the front of her wet shirt to breathe through, and as the heat baked them all, sweat rolled down her body.

The crew around her fought just as hard as she did. No one quit. No one fled. And finally, she heard a hiss as she patted out the last of the flames. What felt like hours was merely minutes. Smoke poured from the hold. Men waved fabric to force it out faster. The watering in her eyes turned to actual tears. Their supplies were destroyed. Likely her necklace was melted, damaged, destroyed.

Hugging her jerkin to her chest, Emily sobbed. A firm hand gripped her shoulder and led her out of the hold. "Nothing more to be done here. Come."

Emily followed on heavy feet, waving the air in front of her face, wishing for a fresh breath. She climbed up to the main deck and fell to her knees still hugging her jerkin like a teddy bear. Any chance she had of returning home was over. The entire crew was going to hate her for destroying the hold. As Price had warned, she would get no second...or third...or whatever chance. She'd lost count. How were they going to eat now?

"What happened?" Captain Lemoine shouted at his men.

Many of them looked at the deck, unwilling to meet the captain's glare.

Emily sank back on her heels, wishing to be anywhere but here, and she let the tears of remorse fall.

"Fire in the hold. Porter set fire to the hold!" The voice was unfamiliar, but Emily didn't bother to see who the accuser was. Did it even matter? She felt the captain's glare, but Emily couldn't react. Her mind was a blanket of sadness suffocating her. Never again would she see home. Never again would she see her friends, greet her coworkers, water her plant. Tyler won. He never had to repay her, since she'd be reported as a missing person soon—by someone.

She didn't know for sure who would discover her missing and care enough to report it. Maybe her boss, but not because he cared, only because she'd missed a shift and he hated wasting his time trying to find people to cover for her.

No more bills. No more pizza delivery, Netflix, hot showers...all the things Emily considered her life were now lost forever. The mourning settled upon her soul like an anchor tied to her ankles and dropped into the cold depths of the sea, slowly darkening, slowly crushing, and lungs screaming at the last flickers of life. Tears wet her face as Emily involuntarily gasped for the fresh air that wouldn't come.

She wanted a hug. The only one who'd be willing stared daggers at her.

More men rattled off their anger. No matter how hard she'd tried to fit in, one mistake ripped the trust clean away. Emily sniffled and listened to another man's accusation. "The fire 'twas an accident, but Porter was stealing, I wager."

"A thief among us!" Another called.

"There're rules against stealing from your own men, captain. He needs punishment."

Shouts of agreement poured from angry pirates' mouths.

Their assumption wouldn't change the outcome, but regardless, they were right. She was trying to steal.

"I'll handle the punishment," the captain said, and the men stood around waiting for immediate rectification.

"Back to work. Bring up the gold."

Men climbed down the side of the ship and jumped into the water with a rock in hand. The quartermaster approached the captain, and Emily stared at the deck boards, where only hours ago, blood pooled like a lagoon. "We have enough provisions to survive the trip back to Nassau. Fourteen sets of slops. Two barrels of wine, and one crate of punch. The rest is a total loss."

The rest? It was true then. Her necklace was nothing more than melted metal and—what happened to gems when they overheated?—charred or melted amethyst. Emily stared at her open palms, coated in soot and sea water, sweat and blood...and tears.

"The cooper insisted Porter caused the fire. Can you confirm?" the captain asked his quartermaster.

"Several witnesses agree. He was in the hold and started the fire. As this affects everyone, we'll hold a vote for the punishment." Price's tone was just as sharp as the first time.

The crew didn't cheer. There was no celebrating this.

Price leaned into the captain's ear and whispered. The captain nodded. Price then spoke up again for all to hear, "And it won't be lenient or disregarded this time."

A chill shivered down her soaked spine, and Emily clutched the jerkin. It was sodden, and she didn't want to put it back on.

Price marched below deck, and the remaining crew resumed salvaging the Spanish gold. The captain closed the distance. She couldn't look at him.

"I didn't steal anything," Emily blurted, staring at his leather boots. They reminded her of her own handmade boots—so similar. According to these men, she was one of them, a pirate. A thief. But worse, because she screwed up at every turn. Emily couldn't follow the rules. "The fire was an accident."

"Come with me," the captain helped her to her feet and led her into his cabin. Emily sat on the edge of his bed and remembered the last time they'd been here. Happier, more naïve, times. Still, her mind flashed back to touching the captain and kissing him feverishly. Seemed like a lifetime ago.

The captain paced the cabin, showing no signs of his aching ribs. Adrenaline must've been coursing through him.

"The quartermaster learned the crew believes you are a woman."

"What? How?" Emily blurted and stood. She touched her middle and realized her jerkin was off—to fight the fire. And underneath, her thin white tunic showed her tank top and breast shape clearly. Emily wrapped her arms across herself, hiding her chest.

"You were in the hold, and I can imagine why. Accidents happen. But you signed the articles, and the crew shall not forgive a woman on board."

There was no use in jesting about signing as Emile. "What will they do to me?" Emily asked, absently. She remembered all the favorite pirate punishments—cat-o'-nine-tails, marooning, keelhauling, duel to the death, dunking, hanging, being sold into slavery, tying to the mast for an indeterminate amount of time until delirium set in. If she could avoid keelhauling or a duel, the rest she could survive. Maybe.

"The longer I can delay them, the better off you'll be since the gold will lift their spirits. The vote is on the morrow at dawn."

Emily stood with a frown and stuffed her arms through the holes of her jerkin, ignoring the ickiness of it, and fastened the buttons. "You're the captain. Don't you have the power to do anything but decide whether to engage in battle?" She was still upset with him, but all the fight drained out of her with those tears.

"Even if the crew accepts the fire as an accident, there is no chance I can ask them to overlook a woman on board, who'd been in the hold again. Fergus and Hooper may have told a single person about their lie, and that's all it would take for them to never believe you were innocent down there."

"Yet *you* allowed me on board." Blaming the captain for her actions was immature, but a fresh sting at the injustice of it all brought back the anger.

"I didn't know you were a woman when you signed," the captain answered calmly.

"Or what? You'd have stopped me?"

The captain met her eyes, but he stood firm, strong, straight. He didn't need her any longer. "Your skills are invaluable, and I'm grateful for the time we've had."

Tears waved in her vision. "That sounds an awful lot like 'goodbye'."

The captain walked to the cabin door and paused with a hand on the knob. He said quietly, "I may harbor many regrets in life, but I do not regret you."

Captain Lemoine left the room, and Emily fell back onto the bed. She had until morning to earn mercy from the crew.

EMILY HAD NOTHING TO offer them as a bribe. They wouldn't listen to reason, and they had every right to. She'd broken the rules the minute she signed. These men were exactly what history said they were: thieves and murderers. Emily was never, could never, hurt another person. She honestly didn't understand how Price could do his job, but that was neither here nor there.

That left thieving. Could she be like them—not just in spirit but in reality? Could she become like Tyler and Captain Lemoine? Hooper and Price? Even Giles and Karl? If she did this, Fergus would've died for nothing. All he wanted was to save her from these people, this life, and here she was, considering volunteering.

Since those men believed she was a pirate, granted an unwanted *woman* pirate, her actions to save her own life didn't matter to them. They wouldn't judge her helping to pay them in both reparations and forgiveness. But doing this would make her despicable, a real, true pirate. Whether or not she could live with it mattered not. She couldn't guarantee they'd accept her offering. But if she did nothing, they were going to kill her, anyway.

Emily sat up on the captain's bed and stuffed her red kerchief away for safekeeping. She looked at her pouch. Her things were no longer of value, but they were all she had left of the life she knew. Emily untied the pouch and set it on the bed. She stood, chin held high and left, her soul forever on the captain's bed.

Emily swallowed her stubborn pride and self-righteousness and approached the salvage crew. "Can I help?" she asked, wretchedness on her tongue.

Hyde, the night watchman who tried to rat her out to the captain, snarled at her. "No woman shall touch my gold. You be an untrustworthy bootless bugger and a thief. Go below deck and patch some wounds. Be useful while you still can."

A man next to him Emily hadn't met said with a slimy smirk, "Hyde, she can touch the gold. We'll take turns thoroughly searching her afterward." The chuckles from them both chilled her blood. "Besides, mate, if the sharks make a meal of 'er, then we don't have to waste time with a vote."

Emily peered over the edge of the rail, watching the divers going down and up. The water was about twenty feet deep, and a lot warmer and clearer than Lake Michigan waters. She could handle that. Emily inhaled deeply several times and gripped a ballast rock. She positioned herself with feet dangling over the clear blue water. The waves had settled a little, but the very bottom was obscured. She'd always said she'd rather take her chances with the sharks. Now she proved to herself she was strong enough for this.

If they killed her anyway, at least she could see firsthand what that handmade gold looked like. On that happy note, Emily launched herself headfirst into the salty sea. Having only swam in freshwater before, the Caribbean was more buoyant than she'd expected. While using the weight of the rock to help her reach the bottom, she fought to reach the bottom, legs thrashing.

Emily marveled, too briefly, at the coral reef before seeking out treasure galleon debris. Her free hand brushed at the sand, lifting a small cloud of sand and uncovering a glinting metal coin. Emily slipped it into her pocket and brushed again. Each handmade coin bore differing defects, and each had a unique stamp from its origin. They shimmered in the light—a bright, beautiful piece of history.

After finding a pocketful, she released the rock and swam up to the surface. Gasping for air, she climbed up the wooden grips and held out her pocketful of shiny pieces of eight.

Hyde accepted them with a grim set to his mouth. "This doesn't change anything."

One handful, maybe not. Emily collected another ballast rock and sank to the bottom of the sea.

Chapter 24

Handful after handful hadn't been enough to prevent the vote. Emily should've figured there was no satisfying a bunch of greedy pirates. Fergus, despite his misguided attempt to keep her safe, felt like her only ally, and now she had no one left at all. It was isolating and the feeling of dejection sank into her bones, while the cutting of tight ropes sank into her flesh. Bound to the mainmast, grimy and salty faces stared at her, and she swallowed a dry lump.

Because she wanted what was rightfully hers, she was hated. Because she tried to take it back, she would be killed. And because of her anatomy, the men wouldn't hear reason.

When Captain Donald Sinclair had her bound to his mast, she'd kissed the wood. This time, the pirates bound her facing them. The *Sea Lion* hadn't yet set a course to return to Nassau. The men continued hauling up what they could, but the divers admitted this spot was nearly cleared out. They would need to move along the coast.

Emily worked at the stinging ropes, cutting and burning her bleeding wrists. She'd take her chances swimming with the sharks to the Florida coast. Maybe the Spanish refugees would treat her better, despite the language barrier.

Price approached with a creased brow, but his hands held nothing but a clipboard. No cat for her…yet. "Emile Porter is accused of theft in the hold."

The men mumbled.

"Porter is also responsible for the fire that destroyed nearly all our belongings and supplies."

Angry grumbles and shouts came from the crowd, and Emily blinked back tears.

"Finally, Porter made a fool of us all. He is not a 'he' at all. Porter is a woman!" Now angry shouts and dirty remarks flew at her like heat-seeking missiles, and Emily learned firsthand what 'swearing like a sailor' meant. They were brutal, but thankfully, she didn't understand all of it.

"Will anyone come to *her* defense?" the quartermaster emphasized her gender pronoun as if it were a sour pill, and his tone dared anyone who spoke up.

While burying her tears, hurt and anger boiled within. How could these men, who'd treated her as one of their own, turn their backs on her the instant they learned she was born with boobs? What difference did it make? Emily searched the unkind crowd for the captain while another onslaught of slurs flew her way. Emily exhaled a shaky breath. Her fingers pulled at the restraints and so far, they wouldn't budge. If nothing else, they knew how to securely restrain a person.

No one was going to defend her, so she had to do it herself. If nothing else, her delay bought time to escape. "I am defending myself. I'm a competent doctor on this ship. I've helped patch many of your wounds, without which, you would've bled out. Some of you owe me your lives."

Quartermaster Price stepped up to her and spoke privately, "We can find a new doctor on nearly any prize we take. Seducing the captain is inexcusable, as is hiding your true nature. The number of transgressions you have accumulated in such a short time makes your presence on this vessel a greater liability than an asset, and as such, one way or another, we'll remove you."

Emily whispered back on a hiss, "Not that it's any of your business, but I never seduced the captain. I treated his wounds and saved his life.

I also retrieved a hefty pail's worth of gold for you. Does that not count either?"

Technically, the captain had seduced *her*, but that was unnecessary nuance.

"We all signed the articles, and breaking them has consequences. This is not a negotiation. The vote is final. The captain has accepted his own impending punishment with dignity. You could learn a thing or two from that."

Emily's lip lifted in a silent snarl. Price was the most brash and irritating man she'd ever met, but she understood how he had power over the crew. He was logical and reasonable—for his time.

The quartermaster continued louder for everyone to hear, "One vote per man. Porter is guilty. Your decision is to choose which punishment fits her crimes: selling her into slavery or marooning."

Emily's heart sank.

"For the first option, I estimate we'd receive thirty pounds for her skills in doctoring, provided she return to her status as a man. That sum shall be split according to your share of prizes. Show of hands for the first vote: selling her into slavery."

Cheers filled her ears. Emily couldn't do the conversion in her head, but she'd wager the pail of gold she'd brought up from the bottom of the sea and gladly handed over was worth far more. Somewhere deep inside, these pirates cared about something more than money. It was the principal. The show of power.

"Second vote," Price called. "Marooning! Standard agreement states she receives a pistol with shot and powder, one day's worth of water, and one biscuit. A merciful finish to one's endless transgressions."

More cheers erupted, but Emily couldn't count the difference in hands.

While Price tallied up his count on paper, Emily said, "I gave you more than thirty pounds in gold. Despite my *transgressions*, I'm more valuable to the *Sea Lion* crew than a thirty-pound sale."

Hyde spoke up, "Keep her doctoring skills until we find the right spit of land, a perfectly bald lump of sand, clear of any shade, just waiting for the tide to take her."

"Aye, aye!" More cheers, and Emily suddenly hated them all.

The quartermaster calmed them all down. "The hands are counted. Punishment is as follows: Porter is to continue her skills while clapped in irons to prevent any new transgressions. When we reach the aforementioned spit of land, as Hyde so eloquently proposed, Porter shall be marooned."

The rattle of chain sank Emily's stomach. Hyde, a waif of a man, brought forth the iron manacles. Men moved forward and cut her ropes just as the manacles closed over her wrists. Any chance of swimming to freedom was now gone.

Hyde dragged her below deck to sit where her doctor's equipment was—along with lingering smoke haze, dried blood smears, and a light so dim her eyes struggled to see. Hyde locked her chains around the mizzen mast and walked away without a word.

Emily leaned against the mast and cried. She'd give anything to be back home. Even Tyler had never treated her so terribly. He was right to ridicule her love of pirate history. The fascination of reading about the brutal men was nothing compared to living it. Pretending to be a pirate was the stupidest hobby, the biggest waste of time. What good had it done her? She'd failed to be one convincingly, and now she was chained below deck.

If the *Sea Lion* were attacked, she'd be helplessly killed or drowned with the ship. Otherwise, soon they'd drop her off on a patch of sand that may only offer a reprieve for a few hours before the tide washed away her footing, and the weight of the manacles drowned her. Emily had no way home after the fire that she'd caused. All hope was lost, so wishing to go home wasted brain power.

If she survived this, never again would a man use and discard her. And never again would she blink at a man who put his selfish greed over another human being's life.

Emily daydreamed of how things could've been different. If she'd told Captain Sinclair her gender, would he have brought her to a city, safe and sound? What if she told the pirates upon meeting them she was a skilled woman? Would they have allowed her onboard to use her skills, knowing she wasn't a liar?

If only she hadn't sneaked into the hold, she wouldn't be chained to a mast. She just might've been in the captain's quarters on the verge of breaking other rules instead. Images of the captain's smiling face and soft lips came to mind. For a short while, she thought they could figure out something to make their relationship work, but clearly, he'd only been taking advantage of her. Now the game was over, and he'd cast her aside. Captain Lemoine didn't bother to show up for the vote. He clearly didn't care about her...like she cared about him. That made her pathetic.

Glancing at the filthy floor and imagining it was her favorite pizza place, Emily wistfully smiled at an invisible slice of fat greasy pizza. She chuckled. If only her friends could see her, they'd never believe her. Were they back home now? Had they found a more pleasant adventure? Emily was finished with adventure after this. That wanderlust was officially cured.

Wooden steps of the nearby ladder creaked as a man climbed down, and Emily swallowed her anger, ready to treat the patient who was injured through no fault of his own. But that didn't mean she had to be gentle about it.

The captain entered her infirmary.

Emily stood, the rattle and weight of metal an all-consuming reminder of her misplaced trust. "Where were you?"

His features were somber as if he regretted the course her actions had taken her. So much for the big rescue, jerk.

Captain Lemoine closed the distance and glanced around for witnesses before embracing her. Emily's bound fists pounded against his chest in feeble frustration, rattling the cold metal shackles. Emily sniffed and blinked back tears of betrayal and rage.

"I've done all I can without losing the crew. When we dock at Nassau, you'll be delivered safely ashore, never to behold the *Sea Lion* again." The captain softened his grip on her.

Emily swiped her tears. She wasn't going to drown during high tide on a spit of abandoned sandbar. Somehow the captain had renegotiated on her behalf to be 'marooned' into society, a society she'd never survive. "It doesn't matter. Without my necklace, I can't go home."

The captain brushed a lock of hair away from her eyes, his fingertips grazing gently across her cheek. He swiped away tears with tenderness. "I cannot jeopardize my standing with the crew further. Without their trust, I cannot protect you. Consider Nassau a mercy." Captain Lemoine turned away, about to climb back up to his high post.

"I don't want mercy! I want to go home!" Emily shouted, not caring who heard.

Captain Lemoine paused with a foot resting on a rung and whispered, "So do I."

Taken aback, Emily quietly watched the captain climb out of sight and swiped the remaining tears from her cheeks. Her heavy manacles clanked. She sat down heavily on her barrel of shame, remembering Boatswain Karl claiming the captain wanted to retire. Well, good for him. What did that matter to her?

An injured man, scraped by the barnacles on the hull, needed tending to, and as the pirates continued their pursuits of the gold beneath the sea, a steady stream of minor injuries trickled through her dark and dank infirmary. None of them were friendly, and not one made small talk.

Tending to them with her wrists restrained was extra difficult, but having pride in her work had long since washed away.

Chapter 25

The pirates had taken all they could while still capable of surviving the journey back to Nassau. Meanwhile, Emily had been chained to the mizzenmast on the orlop deck until the injuries diminished. Then she'd been sitting with Giles, peeling potatoes he'd been preparing in the kitchen during the fire. Her wrists ached with the scratchy cold metal, her arms ached with the weight, and her hands were sliced, trying to use a knife to peel with a rocking ship underfoot. But finally, they'd returned to port, and she'd been allowed on the main deck. The fresh air and sunlight were a welcome reprieve from the ship's humid and dank belly that still lingered with the scent of burned wood.

With a scowl, Hyde released the shackles at her wrists. Instantly her arms sagged with relief, and she rubbed her aching shoulders.

"Should've been desolate. You don't deserve this, but Price said he'd made a deal in the crew's best interest." Hyde spat on the deck by her feet. "Fancy that."

Emily didn't respond. Nothing she could say would change anyone's mind. Sailors worked the pulleys to set up the longboat for her. Holding her chin high, Emily climbed aboard when authorized to do so, and men filled the seats around her. A pair lowered them to the water's surface.

The captain wasn't one of them, and once again his inaction confused her. His kisses and words said he cared, and the deal he'd made with Price to exchange a spit of land for Nassau said he cared. But his lack of appearance said otherwise.

The pirates rowed, delivering her to an outstretched dock in Nassau. She stood on wobbly sea legs and shuffled to the rocking boat's edge, sloppily climbing up and out. Not one of them said a word to her, nor assisted, and they tied the boat to the pilings and climbed out, leaving her to purchase new supplies with her ill-gotten gold. But their spirits weren't high for the brothel as she'd expected.

"What about a gun with shot, water and a biscuit? That was part of the terms." Emily had no money. She at least wanted food and water.

One of the pirates leaned close while passing her. "Terms of your punishment changed, or haven't you noticed?"

Shielding the sun from her eyes, she searched the ship's rail, seeking the captain, but he wasn't there. None of the men watched her departure, except two who were simply awaiting the longboat's return.

Emily faced Nassau, the pirate haven filled with miscreants and less than savory rules. She walked down the dock, uncertain where her feet carried her. With no chance of returning home, no food or money, Emily had only one choice: survive in the primitive pirate world. She'd left her pouch on the captain's bed. He hadn't returned it. Emily needed a job.

The city bustled with activity. Men carried lumber on their shoulders, the blacksmith's hammer fell with an ear-piercing ping, and a group of women strolled by, socializing. Strolling down the sand and stone path between tightly packed buildings, she narrowly avoided colliding with a pack of chickens and a few confused goats. She smiled at the goats, but sadness lingered. Her mother would've wanted to pet them as she had, and now Emily was never going to visit her mother's grave again. She couldn't think like that. Emily had to survive.

Emily stopped at The Golden Macaw to find a familiar face. Inside the bar-restaurant-motel, Emily sought out the woman in charge. The voluptuous woman with her curly updo—silver wig of the times, no doubt—was behind the counter, checking in a guest. Emily waited in line behind him, and when Marta was free, Emily stepped up.

"Hello!" Marta said with a friendly and bright tone, and suddenly whatever jealousy she'd felt toward the older woman was gone. "How are you, dear? Where's the captain?"

Ignoring that disappointing reminder, Emily said, "I'm looking for a job. Do you have anything available?"

Marta gave her the once over assessment and frowned. "Not like that, I don't. Come with me, deary."

"Wait," Emily said softly. "Did you know I was a woman?"

Marta smiled deviously and winked.

Emily shook her head with a smile, happy to know the events of the *Sea Lion* would not be repeated. Willing to get out of her salt-ridden and damaged handmade clothes, Emily eagerly followed the older woman around the desk. She handed her a folded stack of clothes, and Emily assumed they were the previous worker's uniform.

"What exactly do you have available?" Emily's open mind only went so far.

"A housekeeper. You'll clean rooms after they become vacant and serve the guests in the lounge."

"Is that all?"

The old woman cocked her head. "Is there something else you had in mind?"

"Nope, no." Emily shut that down. "This is great, thank you."

"When you make yourself presentable, come back for your first assignment." She turned to leave as if that was all the instruction a woman from three hundred years into the future needed.

"Where do I stay?" Emily called to her back. "I'm between homes at the moment."

She turned and smiled kindly. "Second floor just above the desk here. All my ladies who have the need, sleep there. I'm sure Daphne can make you a cot." With that, Marta left to attend her own duties, whatever they were.

In the homeless women's room, Emily changed her clothes and cringed in the mirror. Dresses so weren't her thing. Authentic, antique gowns of the eighteenth century were definitely not her thing. If they made her wear a powdered wig over her blonde hair, she'd be out the door and asking the blacksmith if he needed an apprentice.

At least she could wear pants.

A woman swooshed through the doorway on a mission, collecting linens from a cabinet. This was the staff quarters and stock room, it appeared. Her dark hair was pinned in soft waves over her shoulders, and she wore a layered dress with structure to it. The woman dropped a stack of bedding on a bare cot, startling Emily, and said, "This is yours whenever you need it. Ready to come along now?" Lines in her face and a ruggedness showed years of labor. Emily hadn't moved, so the woman stepped forward. "I'm Daphne. You are?"

"Emily." It felt great to tell someone her real name.

Daphne kept her face impassive as Emily would've expected for someone who routinely trained new housekeepers. "Pay is not free. Follow me." Her curt turn was rude, whether she was busy or not.

Emily frowned at her back but followed. Daphne handed her a stack of clean linens from a hall closet and led her into the room next door. Emily pulled up short and covered her eyes against the naked man, who decided the best article of clothing to put on first was a shirt.

"Don't be shy," Daphne told her. "Good afternoon, Walter. Sleep well today?" Emily's mentor stripped the bed in a quick fashion while Walter smiled at Emily.

"Who's the new girl?" he asked.

"Be nice," she said without pausing in her work. "Emily, take these."

Emily rushed to the woman's side and accepted the stack of dirty linens. She fought the urge to grimace at the smell.

"Emily," he repeated. "Where you from?"

What a loaded question. Emily chose the easiest answer. "The *Sea Lion*."

The switch of the man's face told her that was the wrong answer. "Captain Lemoine's crew? How did a *woman* get aboard a pirate crew?"

With a fake smile, she answered pleasantly, "The same way a man does."

Walter laughed. "I understand now. How is Lemoine these days?"

"Can you put on pants or something?" Emily glanced aside, frustrated the man was so uncaring about his privacy. For some stupid reason, Emily felt uncomfortable around a naked man who wasn't the captain.

"Pants?" he asked, genuinely confused.

"Breeches," she clarified. "Cover up, please."

Daphne flipped fresh sheets onto the bed and asked her with narrowed eyes, "You were a pirate?"

Before Emily could answer, Walter said, "It's a shame I missed that."

Emily picked up on that detail. Squishing the sheets into a smaller, less obnoxious ball, she said, "You were on Captain Lemoine's crew?"

Walter tied his tunic closed at the throat and reached for his breeches. "For a time."

"What happened?" Curiosity overtook her sense of propriety.

"Captain Lemoine won the vote over me, so I dropped the account at the next port. Eventually I found my way back here. Too risky to be gallivanting anywhere else. What's your story?"

Emily gave him the watered-down version, like he said, too risky. "Captain Lemoine rescued me from a merchant ship. I joined until I was no longer wanted."

"Because you're a woman?" he finished.

"They didn't know for the longest time, but yes," she bit out.

Walter's sly smile irritated her. He stuffed his legs into his breeches while Daphne handled the dirty bathwater. "And that's not the only reason I wager, is it?"

Emily hadn't asked about the pay, but it better be worth tolerating the guests' nosiness. "That's none of your business."

He laughed. "Ol' Lemoine's been after a woman for far too long. Surprises me none he clings to the first one he meets. And that poor sap won the vote over me? I was a better strategist than he, but the crew ate up his tales of a sunken treasure fleet. I thought it hogwash. Well…" Walter tied his breeches, and Emily glanced at Daphne, who surprisingly wasn't giving her the stink-eye for socializing instead of working.

Walter's tale meant they crew had tried to dethrone Captain Lemoine just prior to this account. She wondered if many of them didn't believe the tale. They likely regretted that now.

"I'm feeling fortunate you joined The Golden Macaw. I expect to see plenty of you." Walter's tone suggested he intended to figure out why the captain wanted her, but Emily wasn't so sure the captain did. Otherwise, why did he let her go?

Emily said the only dismissive thing that came to her, "I hope your stay at The Golden Macaw is pleasant."

Walter's chuckle annoyed her, so when Daphne gestured for her to follow her out of the room, Emily eagerly kept on her toes. On the balcony connecting the second-floor rooms, Emily asked, "Are all the guests like that?"

"Like Walter? A few. You adjust or quit like the others. It's best not to respond in a personal way. Put the soiled linens in this hatch here, and we'll make our way to the next room."

Emily shoved the stinky load into the laundry chute and closed the small hatch. She followed her mentor until her eye caught on the table below, where she'd spent a marvelous lunch with the captain dining on turtle and fruit. He'd seemed so genuine, and she'd thought there was a mutual attraction between them, but as Walter insinuated, she was likely the result of a lack of options. Daphne handed her another stack of clean linens while Emily pushed away the crushing thoughts.

She followed Daphne into the next room, currently empty but clearly being used, and she helped her strip the bed this time.

"How long have you been here?" Emily asked her.

"Since I was a young girl."

At least that was job security. Emily couldn't picture herself entertaining naked men and cleaning their rooms forever, but money was money.

Daphne must've seen a look on her face she didn't intend. The brunette added, "It's not so bad as that. Regular customers, regular pay, and a good boss can mean the difference between a comfortable life and one of struggle. I must admit, a woman pirate is intriguing. How did you become a pirate? I mean, what were you before?"

Emily lifted the corner of the mattress and helped Daphne fold and tuck the sheets underneath, setting it down smooth, as if they were a well-oiled machine.

"A merchant captain stole my necklace, my only way home, and before being punished, the pirate captain of the *Sea Lion* rescued me, but he took it for his crew. I was a fan of pirates, from what I'd read, and I'd never met one before that day. So I joined up to get it back."

"Did you?" Daphne asked, eyes wide, captivated by her tale.

"I'm here, aren't I?"

Daphne's face scrunched. "Those scoundrels—the lot of them!—always stealing from others and never bothering to consider the damage they inflict. If those thieves' ill-gotten coin didn't keep these doors open, I'd spit on them all."

Emily chuckled and an urge to justify the captain's actions came to her lips. "They aren't all bad. Just trying to make their living like any other."

"I'm surprised you defend them after they stole from you and turned your life on its head."

Emily made a noise of acknowledgment. The woman was right. But she couldn't get the captain out of her head.

Chapter 26

Weeks ticked by and Emily fell into a dreary routine of fending off frustrating comments by men while cleaning up after them. Oh, how she missed the modern world!—wash machines, dishwashers, hot showers, and most of all, the ability for a woman to put a man in his place without getting slapped.

She also missed something else. Emily brushed away tears. The loneliness was so painful. She had no one to talk to. No one who knew her or understood.

Captain Lemoine and his sweet lips never left her mind. She stewed over him all day long, every day. The longer they were apart, the worse the pain in her chest festered, as if she'd developed an infection of the heart. But Walter's words still polluted her mind. When the captain first showed he was into her, he'd believed Emily was a man, so Walter was wrong. Captain Lemoine didn't cling to the first woman he'd met, because Emily wasn't a woman at the time. The unbearable loss, worse than any she'd ever experienced before, proved Emily loved Captain Lemoine, but she was a fool for it. She allowed herself to love again, and she'd been abandoned...again.

While squirreling away her extra wages to find a home of her own, Emily had scavenged spare parts to build a sanctuary for her to visit—a small hut away from the city. She couldn't eat, sleep, and work at the same place every day for her own mental health.

Right on the edge of the beach, just under the palms, not a sound carried but the gulls cawing and waves gently lapping. A gentle breeze picked up, whisking the palm fronds together in a dance. She'd chosen this spot for the panoramic view of the coast. Emily was stuck here, so she had to find something about it to enjoy, and that was watching the comings and goings of ships at port, their broad sails, and cheers of teamwork.

Setting down a bartered hammer from the blacksmith, Emily brushed away tears from her lids, using her dirty handmade tunic sleeve. Exhausted and calloused, Emily lowered herself on a barrel she'd converted to a chair and drank from her canteen. She scanned the horizon, looking at the different shapes of sails. She told herself it was entirely out of fascination and curiosity, but every time a set flickered in the distance, her heart thumped wildly. So far, her captain's ship hadn't returned.

The withered old vendor had told her the amethyst granted true desires and protected against bad humors. Emily had told the old lady she wished to see tall ships, that was it. And, she supposed, that wish had been granted. But something was missing.

This life of back-breaking labor, bare essentials, filth, and the risk of dying every five minutes ate at her. In her previous life, she'd organized merchandise and entered override codes at the checkouts. Although not mentally stimulating, it was so much easier than this. She'd do her job, go home, and have a life. Since getting tossed off the *Sea Lion*, all Emily experienced was work, work, work, and when she was too tired to lift a hand, it was work some more or starve. If this didn't count as bad humors, Emily didn't know what did.

This wasn't what she wanted. This wasn't a life. She missed her friends. She missed her home, but mostly she missed... Emily sighed softly and gazed at the sea.

EMILY PORTER HATED HIM, but Captain Lemoine couldn't live with himself if he couldn't repair the hurt he'd caused. For weeks, he'd pictured Emily's beautiful face and thought about what to say to fill the chasm between them. And now he'd journeyed back to her, and in silence, he gazed upon her as if in a new light. All alone in this little corner of the island, living in less than what he'd considered a shack. Back in poverty once again. He was right in what he'd done, and he needed her to see his side.

Mostly, Captain Lemoine hoped Emily would grant him permission to explain.

Emily sucked in a breath and glanced at the pouch in his hand. She stood at once. Emily had left it on his bed, and he didn't know if it was a thoughtless gesture or if it meant something. He hoped it meant something. When her beautiful hazel eyes landed on his face, his chest squeezed. He thought he did everything right to create a balance between keeping the crew satisfied and keeping Emily safe.

But clearly it hadn't been good enough.

She slowly stood and looked at his feet sinking in the soft, uneven sand. "How long have you been here?"

"Not long enough." Captain Lemoine moved forward, closer, and his heart pounded in his chest. He should've been here much sooner, but he couldn't. He couldn't face her with nothing to offer.

Emily's hands trembled, and she fidgeted to hide it. Her gaze traveled his body as he slowly approached, watching his gait. "Your rib must've healed well."

"I found this. I believe it belongs to you," he said, ignoring her comment and handing over the pouch with the strange device inside.

She accepted it, but didn't look in it. "Thank you."

He paused, waiting for her to send him away while clinging to that last shred of hope he'd carried as if it were the most valuable treasure in the world.

Emily set the pouch on a chair and waited.

Captain Lemoine wouldn't waste his limited time now. "I owe you an explanation. After promises had been broken so many times in your past, they are meaningless to you, but we'd made a deal, and I don't break my promises."

Emily's head tilted, blonde hair fluttering in front of her face.

"I never returned your necklace as we agreed, but I had a reason for it." The captain paused, letting his words sink in. "I didn't return it, not because the crew was owed a share of its value. Not because it had been destroyed in the fire. I toed around returning it, because I couldn't allow you to leave."

Emily squinted, confused. "You wanted me to be a prisoner?"

The captain gestured for her to sit.

Emily balanced herself on the chair, and it sank softly into the sand. Regardless if there had been another chair, Lemoine kneeled by her feet. "As you know, I had been losing the crew. My heart wasn't in the hunt any longer." He softly chuckled. "It was never in the hunt. I only yearned for the opportunity to score the one prize that would allow me to leave the account for good. Do you know what I want?"

"I would've guessed money," Emily said, "But now I assume that's not why you're here."

Well, that was not what he wanted to hear, but he had to continue, anyway. This was his one and only chance, even if he could see the sharp crags ahead about to obliterate his ship. "I am a farmer at heart, a plantation worker, but I gave it up to find the money to be worthy of the woman I loved. I became a merchant sailor to earn the money she needed, but I quickly learned that wouldn't get me there, so when the account had been explained to me, I leaped. I've been seeking that money ever since."

"I remember the story," she said dryly.

He continued, "After a few years passed, my memories of her faded, but my goal didn't change, only my reasons. I planned to buy that plantation. Not out of spite, but for the principal of it. My family still worked there, and I wanted to free them. Unfortunately, much had changed in the five and twenty years I've sailed these seas. My family had passed on or moved away onto new things."

Emily blinked, listening intently. Captain Lemoine wanted to cup her hands in his, but he waited.

"But then I met you, and I knew what I wanted right away. And when I learned you worked your whole life to fight poverty, only for your lover to steal that life from you, I vowed to do whatever necessary to return to you the money you'd lost."

Emily's face twisted with anger. "He cheated me of my life's savings by being a manipulative asshole. I hate selfish greedy bastards like him. I excused your desire for the Spanish gold, because it was a recovery mission, but the minute you chose to attack a ship full of men only trying to do the same, you lost my respect."

The captain lowered his eyes. He'd suspected she didn't understand. "What do you think would've happened had we collected barrels of gold ourselves?"

"Pirates near pirates and ships filled with treasure...?" Emily said with an edge to her voice. The anger still rumbled beneath her surface. "They would've attacked the *Sea Lion*. Exactly what you did first."

"Against an inevitability, I ordered the attack first, while we were rested and fit to increase our odds of success. But I can see how my actions disgusted you, and there's nothing more for me to say to convince you otherwise." Captain Lemoine finished pouring his heart to her. He said everything he could to convince her otherwise, but he failed. His heart squeezed in his chest, cutting off his ability to breathe. He stood to his full height and looked down at her. This was goodbye—the real and final one. He'd never see her again.

Captain Lemoine opened his palm and held it out to her. "You'll be wanting this."

Sunlight reflected off the amethyst stone on a copper chain. Emily's eyes widened in disbelief and a smile brightened her face. He'd hoped to see that face on her when he appeared, but it was not to be so. She scooped it up and marveled at it.

Captain Lemoine couldn't watch. He didn't want to see the magic that brought her to him, and he certainly didn't want to see it whisk her away to foreign, terrifying lands. With an ache still permeating his ribs and thigh, he turned and headed down the beach. Beneath the shadows of his cocked hat, he brushed away tears.

A LIGHTNESS, AN EXCITEMENT filled her for the first time in weeks. The captain had given back what mattered most to her in the world—her life, her freedom, and her right to choose. Somewhere deep inside those pirates, they cared about something more than money. Well, most of them.

Emily looked up, but the captain had made his way down the beach.

Her fingers turned the gem, failing to believe she really had it. She could go home to everything and everyone she missed. No more laundering dirty men's bedding and smiling at their rude comments. No more struggling to find food and bartering for tools, wondering if any at moment if someone wanted something more from her than she was willing to give.

The captain sank further into the distance, and the lightness in her chest dissipated, leaving behind a hollow ache. There was something she needed answered, regardless of her choice.

"Wait!" Emily shouted, and he stopped, but he didn't turn around.

Emily closed the distance, beat up leather boots sinking into the soft sand as she fought to get closer, but she wasn't willing to give up yet. Emily asked to his back, "The crew already had their gold. Why didn't you leave the ship with me?"

The captain turned around, eyes red. "You were to be marooned on a spit of land, yet you were brought here."

Emily remember the mysterious punishment he'd accepted.

"I gave them my entire share of the gold to spare your life." His gaze locked on hers as if pleading for understanding, but she didn't.

If his reasons for needing the gold had all been lost, she didn't understand, if he cared, why he didn't join her? "We could've had a life together. Why did you leave me?"

"I stayed with the crew and returned to the Florida coast."

Emily frowned. "For more money?"

"I wanted to buy that plantation for you, Emily, a life of luxury you deserved but lost."

Emily stared. The generosity was so foreign, so unnecessary. She'd never felt more respected in her life. "I didn't need money, Captain."

Her captain smiled, but still the sadness lingered. "I'm retired. Call me Eric."

Emily opened her hand with the necklace and bounced it in her palm. "There's something I need to tell you."

Eric Lemoine simply waited, a surprisingly patient man. The breeze tousled the hair fastened at the nape of his neck, and the brim of his hat fluttered. But his dark, red-rimmed eyes were locked on hers.

"I put on my homemade pirate costume for the Tall Ships festival, intending to explore history and have fun with my friends. While I was there, a woman sold me this necklace. She'd claimed it granted true desires and protected against bad humors. I've struggled to understand what she meant, but I know now. You were my protection. You are my true desire. She brought me to you. I may not have my life's savings, but I'll take having my life saved instead. I love you, Eric."

The man she loved pulled her into a tight embrace, hands pressing her as if afraid she'd disappear. Emily's lips found his. It was not the slow kiss of exploration. It was the deep, quick shifting need of desperation, of love almost lost but found, and of freedom. She clasped her hands behind his neck while molding to his body. This was a man who trusted her, whom she trusted, and who was the best thing to happen to her. The warmth of protection in his embrace felt like a fuzzy blanket and a cup of hot chocolate on a cold, snowy morning. Emily felt as if they were one; she was finally whole.

A seagull cawed overhead, and waves lapped near their feet.

Emily withdrew from his embrace and stepped back with a smile. "You are my home." She wound up her arm and heaved the necklace into the water. With a small splash, it sank into the depths, never to be found again. Not that she'd ever be tempted.

"You care not to sell it?" Eric asked, puzzled.

Emily smiled and shook her head. "I wouldn't want to curse anyone with a trip to the future. It's not all that great, trust me."

"You must tell me about it someday." Eric's brilliant smile was contagious, and they held hands as they walked along the beach back to her hut. "This is your home?"

She scratched her head. "My best effort. It's not much, but it's an escape from The Golden Macaw."

"Collect your things, we're going home."

Excited, Emily ducked inside, picked up a rough bag, and filled it with her newfound tools and other worthy purchases, but the hut and her chair were left to wither away on their own. Emily slung the bag over her shoulder and ducked back out. Eric insisted on carrying it for her, so she allowed it, happy to hang onto his arm while they walked along the coast back to town.

"Where's home?" she asked.

"You'll see." He winked at her, and Emily was excited to begin the next chapter of her adventure.

Chapter 27

EMILY HAD IMAGINED SOMETHING like a cabin, in all honesty. But Eric Lemoine had twisted his words just a little. He hadn't *planned* to buy the plantation. He bought it. Eric had sent word to his remaining family members to return as owners for a life of comfort. Eric's younger brother returned at once and stepped up to manage the fields. Their reunion was testy for a while until the retired captain explained why he'd left.

Emily sipped wine from a silver cup while Eric finished his breakfast at the table. This was a level of luxury that made her uncomfortable, but unlike the shack by the beach, she could get used to hand-carved furniture and real silverware. Underfoot were hand-woven rugs—not that machine-made were an option yet—and a square footage that would scare anyone with a vacuum cleaner and a steam mop. The estate had its own cleaning crew. Emily didn't know what to do with her own staff. But since she had plenty of experience being bossed around at her retail job, she figured she could model some of those skills, although kinder.

Eric Lemoine rose from the table and dropped his embroidered napkin on the surface. At the sound of his chair scraping on the wood floor, a woman appeared. "What can I do for you, sir?" she asked politely.

"Give us a tune, Letty." Eric circled around to her, in a dashing outfit like English noblemen wore, and he held out a hand, inviting her to stand. Emily smiled and accepted. Eric had a woman with taste choose a wardrobe for her, and since the clothing fit her, and she had help explaining how and why the layers were worn, she started to like it. Her shirting was gold and the top bronze. Her corset was sage green with little gold and bronze florets. Her blonde hair had been curled and pinned back with a lock dangling behind an ear. She honestly felt like a princess.

Letty sat at the harpsichord in the corner of the room, and with music sheets in view, she began playing a song.

Emily's dress rustled as he moved them into an open space. At one of the patio doors overlooking the seaside front yard, a darkening cloud system at the horizon announced its approach with thunderous claps, carrying promises of a refreshing rain.

"Dance with me," Eric whispered, offering his hand formally.

Emily smiled at the unnecessary gesture, and he captured her in his embrace, turning her around the room in timing with the notes. He was a great lead, since Emily didn't know the steps, but she never fumbled once. After a quick spin, he dipped her and kissed her. "Marry me, Emily Porter."

"I would love to, Eric. On one condition."

Eric's brows lifted. "Name whatever your heart desires."

"Kiss me again," Emily said, biting back a playful grin.

"As the lady wishes." Eric's lips met hers once more. Emily wrapped her arms around his neck and held on for the throbbing heat accumulating down low. As if he were thinking the same thing, he scooped her up into his arms, ready to take her to bed. Bells clanged offshore, catching his attention. Eric gazed out at sea.

"Do you miss it?" she whispered into his ear.

His soft, dark eyes returned her gaze. "She calls to me, but the greatest prize I could ever imagine is standing before me now. I have no reason to answer it. Come to bed with me and we shall be wed at the earliest opportunity."

Her fiancé carried her to their bedroom. He set her on her feet and gazed into her eyes with a burning desire she'd never seen before. His fingers slipped along her jaw as he moved behind her and untied the corset, nimbly freeing the constrictive material from her body and tossing it aside. He untied the gown and freed the petticoat from her hips. Emily stepped out of them. The painstaking process was sensual. The anticipating building.

When Eric returned to her front, she took the opportunity to remove his coat and slide off his tunic, a silent, sexy movement. Her palms pressed against his chest and slid along the fine dusting of dark hair. His nipples hardened at her touch.

Eric groaned softly. He reached her for shift and slipped it up over her head. Emily went for his breeches, now tightened in the front, and she untied them, hands trembling with desire. The fabric fell to the floor, and Eric stepped free of it. His drawers were tented with his arousal. He picked her up and settled her on the bed, and as he covered her body with his, Eric's mouth found hers. Kisses moved along her mouth and throat.

Breaths came in short bursts.

His mouth moved along her body, licking and teasing each nipple, hands cupping her breasts. The muscles on his back flickered with his movements. The throbbing continued to grow, and she wanted him inside her. Eric's kisses moved along her belly, down below. He sucked at her clit and Emily arched back and moaned. His fingers found her opening while his tongue lapped at her clit. Eric found a rhythm, and he kept a slowly growing pace. Heat surged, collecting where he worked at her, urging her release, refusing to give up until he'd won.

The necklace had magic, but Eric did, too.

Emily arched again and fisted his hair in her hands, holding his face in position.

Eric didn't relent his pace. She admired his rigorous stamina. Her breaths became hitched, and finally, she climaxed.

Eric slowed while she rode the waves, and when she giggled at the tickles and pushed at him, he stopped, resting his chin on her belly and grinning. He wiped his face on the bedding and loomed over her, cock stiff and ready for use.

Emily gripped it in her palm and, for a flash, she remembered one of her favorite movies, modified for the moment, of course. Eric didn't have paper and pencil in hand. "Fuck me like one of your French girls."

Eric's brows lifted, and a stream of French came from his mouth. "*Comme vous le souhaitez, madame.*"

Emily groaned. She didn't understand what he'd said, but the sexy accent and the words made her wet all over again. Eric positioned himself, and Emily relented her grip. He moved inside her, slowly and carefully, and he leaned down. Eric wrapped his arms up under hers, and when he'd glided all the way inside, he groaned. Emily arched her back and closed her eyes.

Then he moved. Slowly at first, and quickly gaining speed. Emily wrapped her legs around him and kept the rhythm. She kissed his neck. Her fiancé lowered himself to kiss her mouth through the panting and the thrusts. Sweat beaded on his forehead. "Is this how you imagined it?" he whispered against her mouth.

Emily smiled through her panting. He was far more generous than she'd ever imagined. "It's better."

Eric groaned and stilled as he came. He lowered himself to her chest, and they rested, breathing, stroking each other's hair in a comfortable silence. She had so many more ways to explore his body, and now she had all the time in the world to do it.

Eric Lemoine was her home.

Epilogue

The ship groaned under the swelling of the waves while they anchored at Nassau. Bright sun burned the leathery skin of all hands on board. Lemoine had been a great strategist, but the sea was never in his heart. He'd only ever wanted to collect his prize and escape back to the land, and now he and Emily had what they wanted. She was a strong woman, quick, formidable, determined. Price admired that about her, and many times when the situation aboard had been complicated, he'd regretted having to mete out punishments. Now, Quartermaster Price had a difficult task ahead of him. He had to lead an election for a new captain, and he had no idea who could fill those shoes.

"We vote!" Quartermaster Price shouted to all the new sailors crowding around him. After returning to Nassau for Lemoine to disembark for the last time, Price needed to refill their ranks. When news of their successful haul of the Spanish gold spread, Price had to beat beggars off with a stick. Now fully manned with sailors eager for their own riches, all they needed was to assign duties before heading off. These men weren't all green, and a few trusted associates remained—Cantu, Boatswain Karl Dillon, Giles, their amazing cook, McKee the master gunner, and Hodgens, the capable helmsman.

"We must choose the next captain." Heads turned and whispered to each other, and Price gave them a minute. He'd warned them ahead of time, so they could decide among themselves who to nominate. "Do we have nominees?"

Sailor Noah Riley stepped forward. "I nominate you, Henry Price."

Cheers deafened him, and Price grinned with the honor. When the noise settled, he said, "I'm the quartermaster. I do not wish to be captain." Quartermaster Price knew his strengths were in organizing the ship and keeping men on task. He wasn't the most accomplished in battle; however, he'd survived many throughout his forty years of age.

"In this, you are the best," Noah Riley argued. "And I nominate Boatswain Karl Dillon to step up as quartermaster."

With this, Karl's smile spread across his face, but he shook his head. "No, no! I'm no quartermaster, ya bumbling fools. If left up to me, we'd all stay in Nassau drinking rum and buried in women! I nominate Henry Price as captain and Noah Riley as quartermaster."

More cheers echoed around them. A voice of a crewman hanging in the rigging shouted down, "Price and Riley! Together, we shall capture the world!"

The crew chanted Price's name as successor, and he puffed up his chest in a show of acceptance. If he turned them down, he'd lose their respect, so he had no choice now. "It's settled. I'll be your captain, and Riley—you are the quartermaster." The men cheered again. "Weigh anchor while I plot our course. Be prepared for great success at sea!"

The men rushed to their stations, eager to hunt down their first prize. Price watched them.

Captain Henry Price.

Captain.

He never would've seen this coming. He hoped to be half as successful as his predecessor. And he knew exactly where he needed to go. Collecting Spain's gold wasn't enough vengeance for him. And just maybe, Price would be lucky enough to walk away with his skull intact and a bold woman on his arm.

A man could only dream.

PIRATE'S TREASURE

STEPHANIE FLYNN

Small Fish Publishing
USA

Special Note

While the events of this novel are fiction, the quick-witted maneuver to escape the Spanish warship awaiting the tide to capture the crew was real, performed by Calico Jack Rackham during the Golden Age of Piracy.

Chapter 1

ANGELA FOXE LOVED HER job until the summer crawled back to Green Bay, Wisconsin. She swiped the sweat from her forehead and palmed the steering wheel of her electric forklift, buzzing through the warehouse. When loss prevention or human resources wandered through, Angela wondered just how green the grass was on the air-conditioned side of her company.

Heading through receiving, Angela spotted Marcos between the racks, waiting to cross. She pressed the brake pedal, and with a friendly smile, she waved to him as he walked by. Their shift was almost over, and Angela was on her way to dock and recharge.

When she was a teenager, her mother needed money to help with the rent, so Angela had picked up the first job she found. Turned out, she loved to drive; it was her lifeblood. She had no need for college. She never wanted to do anything else. All things gas powered, electric powered, and if she happened upon something wind powered, she'd itch for the chance to feel its power beneath her hands. For a short while, she'd considered long-haul trucking for the bigger paycheck, but her mother's mental health declined rapidly. During a period of lucidity, her mother had told her she'd been proud of her all these years, and that still meant the world to Angela. She wouldn't give this up for air conditioning, even if it came with free donuts on Fridays. Even if it came with her fiancé being proud of her.

Brandon Spindleton was from a different world. She adored him, but after plenty of reassurance about their mismatched upbringings, she'd noticed the quips about her job. Angela expected it would take him time to unwind the thoughts he'd been engrained with since childhood. At forty years old, Angela had seen almost everything, and fully assure of who she was, Angela didn't take crap from others anymore. But those years also instilled her with plenty of empathy.

And patience for the right person who deserved it.

At the charging station, Angela turned the forklift key to the off position and climbed out. She collected her things from her locker and headed for the punch clock.

"Hey Foxe, gonna get ready for your wedding before the ceremony, or after?" Marcos called over with his stuff in his hands. Marcos was a great work friend and almost as excited about her wedding. Angela could swear he was a little bummed he didn't get to help pick out her dress.

Angela fell in stride with him, tugging at the front of her polo to fan herself. "It's tomorrow. The Spindletons have it all handled. I don't need days to wash away my warehouse sweat."

Her future mother-in-law planned the whole thing—from the location to musicians, to flowers, the color motif, and everything in between. Even her dress. Angela only needed to show up clean for the hairstylist, makeup artist, and tailor to work their magic. She'd always pictured an intimate beach wedding, not an opulent affair at a grand estate, but this was one of many compromises Angela had made. Brandon took a while to ease off on his comments about their differences; Angela allowed the elder woman much more grace.

Sometimes sacrifices had to be made for the greater good. In this case, keeping mother-in-law happy. All Angela cared about was beginning her life with her future husband.

At the far wall by the exterior door, Marcos swiped his badge through the card reader, and the little machine beeped to end his shift. "Every bride I ever met needed several days to dress and several more to shout at people, but not you. Oh, no! Foxe can walk down the aisle covered in dust and still look radiant."

"Suck up." Angela's cheeks heated. She appreciated Marcos, one of the few people in her life who didn't raise brows at her and Brandon's mismatched relationship. Or outright assume she was a gold digger. Angela hated that.

Marcos cracked up laughing.

"But *gracias,*" Angela added.

"I'm surprised Mrs. Spindleton didn't lock you in a room of her estate to make sure you didn't run away."

The Spindleton estate rested on the top of a grassy knoll overlooking the whole small town not far from the city limits. Angela didn't have to be locked inside to assure she'd show. The home was stunning, and she loved Brandon. They'd been together long enough to know each other's faults and love each other despite them. And even with different upbringings, they agreed on many hot-button issues, which truthfully surprised her. Brandon was not what most people assumed. He was a good guy, loyal, handsome as hell, and most importantly, he loved her. And when she was with him, she felt like a princess.

"His mother trusts me. I'll see you tomorrow."

"You won't recognize me in a suit. That man better spoil you good," Marcos said.

Angela swiped her badge, too. She *was* spoiled a little. Brandon bought her small gifts; nothing too fancy, but certainly more than she needed. Mrs. Spindleton was tight with the trust fund, but Angela didn't care about his money. "I'm so spoiled, I'm rotten. I can't wait to see you."

Marcos pushed through the door to the parking lot of the warehouse, and Angela followed since they'd parked next to each other. They squinted into the sunlight, and Marcos beamed, his teeth shining bright white against his dirty skin. "Find me. I might not recognize you without all your dirt."

"Just look for the dress." Her future mother-in-law chose the dress to match the Spindleton legacy of elegance, grace, and luxury. Knowing the woman, Angela figured the elder chose a similar style gown for herself. "On second thought, I'll be in a white dress and a veil. Make sure you find the veil first."

"Will do." Marcos's friendly smile slid away.

Something was wrong. Angela had to ask. "Did you forget to have your socks pressed?"

"I heard things about Brandon." Marcos waved the air dismissively. "It's nothing. Everyone hears things about him. If there was any truth to the rumors, you'd have discovered them."

Oh, she'd heard that concern before. Emily Porter, her best friend, mentioned those same rumors. Her mother mentioned it too, but Angela explained how click-bait articles worked. But still, after enough people worrying, what were they seeing that she wasn't? Angela stopped at her car door. Marcos was right. If there was something suspicious about Brandon, she would've figured it out by now.

"You have nothing to worry about."

The smile returned. "I thought so. *Adiós*." Marcos waved as he opened his driver's side door.

Angela waved back and dropped into her own driver's seat. Good thing marriages were about the spouse and not the family. She cleaned her fingers with the front of her polo before pulling out her cell phone. She sent a text to Brandon, asking to spend time with him tonight.

His bachelor party was a few nights ago, so he didn't have an excuse tonight. Angela's had been last week, hosted by Mrs. Spindleton. Angela, her tween future sister-in-law, and teenage future cousin-in-law, shared tea and watched a movie. Admittedly, it was dull. At least Emily Porter and Robin Hall had taken her out for drinks at the local dive bar. It wasn't as fun as their camping trips, but any time with Emily and Robin was a good time.

Angela asked her other friends if they wanted to throw her a bachelorette, but they'd declined. Emily explained the women snubbed their noses at Angela for not inviting them to be her bridesmaids. Angela didn't get to pick her bridesmaids. Brandon dismissed her concerns, explaining everyone acted out of character during the stress of weddings. His reason made sense to her, but the cold-shoulder stung, nonetheless.

A reply came back from Brandon on her screen. '*Not tonight. Too busy getting ready for tomorrow. Get your beauty rest.*'

They'd been together for over a year, and she still hadn't met his friends outside of one appearance at a fine dining event at the estate. So Angela knew they existed, but she didn't know any of them. Angela pressed, '*After all this time, can't I join you for one night of drinks?*'

'*Guy time, sorry.*'

Angela gritted her teeth. She worked with men doing arguably a man's job. What about her wasn't appropriate for his friends? Even the local news wouldn't care if she went out with the guys for a night. And even if some rookie reporter didn't know better, they were the Spindletons! They were capable of stopping whatever bad press they wanted. It didn't make any sense. Every relationship had its flaws, and hers was no exception. If not for this one silly but frustrating flaw, Brandon Spindleton was a great guy, and she was lucky to have him.

Chapter 2
West Indies, 1715

CAPTAIN HENRY PRICE. CAPTAIN, he kept repeating to himself. The word was still foreign on his tongue. This crew of bilge rats actually chose him to lead. He supposed they'd appreciated his efforts as the quartermaster—being a stickler for the rules and keeping the captain's whims in line. But quartermaster was a different role from captain, opposing in fact. Now Price was the leader of the whims. Although he'd daydreamed of the possibilities of this position, they were simply that—musings of an angry man.

Musing as such, no sane man would've voted for.

A knocking on his cabin door pulled him from his planning. Price dragged a hand through his hair and replaced the cocked hat on his head. "Come in."

Price never trusted a skinny cook. How could the palate of a thin man know what was tasty and what wasn't? The experience was in his size, and Giles had decades of it. "Captain, as much as I love our quartermaster, I wanted to take this issue to you directly."

Price clasped his hands together as the ship beneath them glided across the sparkling sea. To Price's forty years, the new quartermaster, Noah Riley, was a boy at six and twenty. He'd earned his votes for his charisma and friendliness. But Price was concerned his age wouldn't suit, and now Giles's worries had him extra troubled. "What is it?"

"May I speak plainly?"

Captain Price gestured for him to continue.

"Sir, Captain Lemoine struggled to reign in his crew, because working men will never be amiable with hardtack and a dribble of rum."

"I agree, but that's no longer an issue. We can afford provisions."

Captain Eric Lemoine had secured riches from the sunken Spanish treasure galleon off the coast of Florida, and most of the crew retired. Even crusty Hyde and the frustrating Hooper. Price had more than a man's share himself, but when the current account wasn't sufficient, he gladly offered the gold out of his own funds to fill it. The money wasn't why he hunted these waters.

"We can, but the last prize was mostly tobacco. Unless we return to Nassau to sell it, or pay a visit to a nearby settlement soon, we shall find an agitated crew once again."

That wouldn't do. Price couldn't lose time returning home, but he couldn't continue with an unsettled crew. Not with the plans he had. "Show me."

It was sunny with strong winds, and yet the ocean toyed with them, reminding them of its fickle whims, not too unlike the crew itself. These men were made for the sea, understood it, communed with it, respected it. Price simply used it.

Captain Price followed his cook below deck of the *Sea Lion*, into the murky and oft-unpleasant smelling lower levels. Sunlight filtered down through the companionways and open portholes, but he and Giles carried candles. The hold was much darker—a secure room meant for keeping their most prized possessions, including food and water.

At the door to the hold, Giles braced himself against a swell, tossing the ship to starboard. Price leaned with the force and kept himself upright. Water splashed down from above, and Price cradled the candle flame so it wouldn't drown out. When he finished the task he'd been planning for months, he never wanted to see the ocean or feel the hollow swish of his stomach again.

He belonged on land, where his old friend currently retired to. Lemoine hadn't left because he'd been satisfied with his gold. No, he left because he'd found a woman—a strange woman, willing to deceive the crew to her own ends. She'd broken the rules, and Price had to punish her for it. Secretly, he admired her gumption and was relieved Lemoine offered to take her lashes. Price hadn't known she was a woman at the time, but looking back on it, he would've been sick flogging her. What kind of woman had the strength to take on a pirate crew and live to tell about it? Price smiled to himself. He'd never found someone who challenged him and interested him at the same time. Maybe there was someone out there for him.

If his brother could hear the thoughts in his head right now, he'd be laughed at and slapped for losing his senses. William Price was a wise man. Just as his musings over taking the captaincy had filled his daydreams then, a nonexistent woman filled his daydreams now. Such a waste of time! A certain Spaniard captain had to answer for his crimes, because murder could not go unanswered.

The ship groaned and tilted, as if agreeing, and the men braced themselves. "A mighty storm approaches from the east. Any port for restocking is preferable."

"I'll take your advisement under consideration," Price said, dryly.

As the ship returned to level, Giles wiped sweat from his brow. "See there, captain?" The cook pointed to the barrels in the corner of the hold, but their candlelight didn't penetrate far enough.

"What am I seeing, exactly?" Barrels and crates were neatly stacked. Nothing stood out to him as unacceptable.

Giles squeezed through and lifted a lid of a barrel to prove his concerns. Tobacco. Another lid—more tobacco from their latest prize. Price asked, "Is it all tobacco?"

"The French crew knew they were losing, so they dumped the food just to spite us. Money's great, but you can't eat it. Or at least, I haven't figured how to cook it. We should return home, sell our prize, restock, and we'll avoid this storm." Giles gave a wry smile.

Price had taught their captain a lesson that day, but lessons didn't fill empty stomachs either. Not a satisfied man could live off crumbs alone. The cook was right in his worry. "We shall restock in Cuba."

"Cuba? Captain, Nassau is closer, and I daresay, safer?"

True, an island roaming with lawless thieves was safer than a settled society. Hunters like them called Nassau home, a city on the free island of New Providence. Cuba was Spanish territory, a fearsome, well-funded enemy, especially to Captain Price.

"How many weeks of food do we have aboard?"

"Weeks? Oh, captain, two at most, and I have a few days' worth of potatoes, and then we're back on hardtack."

That was the perfect excuse Price needed. "A few days of potatoes isn't enough to return to Nassau, and safer doesn't matter if the crew squabbles among themselves. We'll restock in Cuba and ride out the storm."

"Can we sell the tobacco in Cuba?" Giles asked.

The cook's concern was worth noting. Enemies didn't barter with each other, but Price wasn't going to drop his course. "Reduce the rations enough to stretch it to three weeks."

"Yes, captain," Giles said, defeat in his tone, and he left for the galley, taking his candle with him, casting shadows along his unsteady path.

While Price was down here in the hold, and had the free moment, he wanted to prevent more issues like this before they landed at Cuba. Riley's job was to keep inventory, but the man was busy at the moment, and old habits were hard to correct. If Price had done the inventory himself after their last prize, he wouldn't be caught in this conundrum. Price pulled a pad of paper out of his fine coat pocket and closed the door to the hold behind him.

A wave rocked the *Sea Lion*, a formidable ship in the best weather and trustworthy in the worst. An angry storm, approaching to test the ship's strength, stood between him and his personal enemy on Cuba. Price headed straight into it, because sailing the long way around meant they'd run out of food, and turning around meant he'd lose his one chance.

Chapter 3

Wearing jeans and a scratchy polo most days, Angela Foxe appreciated a chance to dress up and feel cute, but this was way beyond her comfort zone. Angela sat on a hand-carved stool in front of a dainty vanity, while her future sister- and cousin-in-law doted on her makeup and hair. Mrs. Spindleton supervised behind them while putting out fires with the wedding planner through text. As thick locks fell into her face and a brush swiped at her cheeks, Angela closed her eyes against the foreign barrage of pampering.

"One long year and it's finally going to happen." Mrs. Spindleton said, wearing a sky-blue pencil skirt and matching blazer. Pearls draped around her lined neck. Frankly, Angela was surprised the lady of the house had chosen something so...appropriate. "And here we never thought Brandon would settle down. At least he found you."

Angela smiled with closed lips and pressed her arms against the cape protecting her dress—an intricately beaded blue and white gown. It reminded her of the flowers decorating the ceremony room—orchids and white lilies. They were scented, sweeter than a department store's perfume section. She focused on the scent, a safety net to guide her through this day. Soon the pomp and circumstance would be over, and then Angela could live her life with her husband.

"I'm glad we got that prenup situation settled," Mrs. Spindleton continued. "What a stressful time that was!"

When Angela was twelve years old, her mother cheated and her parents divorced. Angela had spent one week at her mother's and the next at her father's before bouncing back again. Neither house felt like home, and most of her life was stored in a duffel bag she carried back and forth. Each of her parents remarried shortly thereafter and started a new family of their own. Angela was an inconvenience, a burden to be brushed aside, until that relieving moment she turned eighteen and started her own life.

The Spindletons didn't mind her less-than-lofty background, but in order for Mrs. Spindleton to allow the engagement to commence, Angela had to sign away all rights to any of the Spindleton estate. Angela's mother, during a moment of clarity, had snubbed her nose at the publicized family, rambling on about trust and tightwads. She'd recall scandals she knew had happened, but the media buried it. Her father didn't offer an opinion either way, but she didn't get much out of him, regardless. He'd never outright said it to her face, but Angela suspected she reminded him too much of his cheating wife, and couldn't stand to see her. Angela had never been doted on by a loving father, so when the Spindletons opened their arms to her, she'd thought she'd won at life.

Truthfully, the Spindleton money made her nervous. She didn't want to be sued by her future mother-in-law for knocking over a vase in the hallway with her wedding gown. So she wasn't upset at the pre-nup, but she'd be lying if she wasn't hurt a little. Then she was handed another document to sign, something called a non-disclosure agreement, for whatever reason. Angela never fed the press anything, no matter how much they...pressed. Angela never had a loving family where she felt accepted, so when the Spindletons asked her to sign, Angela considered that a minor roadblock to finally having found love.

Powder fell onto her cheek from Charlotte's brush. The girl used a pinkie finger to dash it away. Angela practiced shallow breaths to prevent herself from sneezing.

"When is your last day at work?" Mrs. Spindleton asked. "We need to have a small celebration. Nothing like this, of course, something quieter."

Uh, that was news to her. "What do you mean?"

"Hold still," Charlotte asked politely.

The excitement drained from the lady's pale face. "Oh, dear. Brandon never mentioned it? Or the attorney? The documents you signed included a clause requiring you to resign. No Spindleton in this family works at—"

"I'm not quitting," Angela interrupted with a cocked brow. "And no one ever mentioned it." Angela had conceded nearly everything the woman demanded, but that was too far. Perhaps Brandon didn't mention it because her employer didn't bother him. A flush of warmth settled in her chest.

"Oh, I see," the elder Spindleton said gravely.

The girls exchanged looks and private smiles, while Mrs. Spindleton focused on her phone. The woman texted with a vengeance.

The family had always been strict with appearances, but Angela figured by allowing her to marry Brandon, they'd eased a little. Her assumption appeared to be wrong, and Angela worried if she'd just screwed up her only chance at happiness.

Angela's cell phone rang, but since she was busy 'holding still', she ignored the call.

At forty, the dating pool was shrinking fast, and Angela wasn't a pampered teenager, never had been. From lifting and carrying cases of merchandise and climbing in and out of the forklift, Angela was built stronger than most women her age. And she exercised and lifted weights at the gym on the regular. Her hands were calloused, and her arms were broad. If she was inclined to brag, she had calves of iron. Despite all the hard work involved in maintaining her shape, her favorite feature was her long brunette hair, which she cared for and pampered harder than the Spindleton's dog.

Except Katherine was burning it with the curling iron.

"Stop moving!" Charlotte squeaked. The girl's dream was to become a makeup artist, but her mother forbade it, since the Spindletons were above all menial service work, and apparently Angela's fit that category like a mole needing to be excised. Well, Angela happened to like her spots, and that one was staying. She'd have Brandon explain it to her.

"You need to move!" The teenage Katherine argued with her younger cousin while flipping wefts of Angela's hair around a heated barrel.

"I can't get anything done with your arms in my way," Charlotte countered. And the bickering resumed.

Angela chuckled and rubbed beads of her gown between her fingers. Such delicate fine work. So dainty, so detailed, so...expensive. Everything Angela wasn't.

"Girls, girls, enough," Mrs. Spindleton scolded, sliding the phone back into her handbag. "How is Angela supposed to be relaxed on the biggest day of her life, with you two arguing in her ear?"

"Sorry, mother," Charlotte said.

"Sorry, Mrs. Spindleton." Katherine released a curled lock.

Both girls were monotone in their apologies as if it were a common occurrence. Their instant obedience irked Angela. The girls hadn't done anything wrong. They were just kids—passionate kids whose interests should be nurtured, not smothered.

Angela's phone rang again inside the matching beaded purse resting on the vanity. With a frown, she lifted it out and found several missed calls and four texts. She sighed and swiped her screen with only minor protests from Charlotte and a stink-eye from the girl's mother. Since calling would interfere with her hair being styled, Angela opened the first text message and read. Then she scrutinized the tiny photograph included and reread, disbelief and confusion growing. She covered the screen with her hand, and she stood, despite the protests.

"I need a minute alone, okay?"

Mrs. Spindleton nodded. "Come, girls. Give the bride some air."

Katherine set down the curler and turned it off, and the girls left the room with the lady of the house.

Angela paced in her satin high heels. Organza danced, and the chiffon swished with her steps. Beads swirled and shimmered. Up until she'd woke her phone screen, she'd felt like a princess. Now Angela had a sinking feeling her precarious crown was about to shatter.

Angela stared wide-eyed at her phone.

'He did this behind my back,' the anonymous text read. *Just thought you should know before it's too late.'*

Angela tapped the image to download, and filling her smartphone screen was a nude image of Brandon with a woman she'd never met. First, Angela searched the surroundings. Where was this? She didn't recognize the room, but it was clearly a bedroom and not up to the Spindleton's standards. Then Angela looked at the clothes on the floor, but she couldn't make them out. She checked Brandon's haircut and facial hair. He hadn't worn that buzzed style with a trimmed beard in a while. This image couldn't have been recent. Angela calmed down. Just an ex jealous of her wedding, but something tickled in the back of her mind, and Angela indulged in the curiosity.

'When was this?' Angela texted back.

'Two years ago. We fought because he only wanted to spend time with his friends and not me.'

That sounded familiar.

'Then I found out why. He's a cheater who keeps proof instead of burying it. BS warned me if I questioned his actions, he'd share the image with everyone I knew, and tell them he was the victim of lies and Photoshop to destroy me. I wasn't the first. You won't be the last. You'll know he's

lying when he first claims he was single at the time this was taken. He most definitely wasn't, and if you argue, then he doubles down with image editing.'

Angela's heart thundered in her chest like stampeding horses. Her fiancé did have many relationships before her, according to the local tabloids, but this...this was so far out there, she couldn't believe it. *'If he's a cheater, why did he threaten you with blackmail?'*

'Since he went out with friends all the time with no accountability, I decided I could too, but he didn't like that. He didn't like his reputation tarnished publicly. His mother is scary.'

Angela understood that.

'He forbid me from having my own life. All BS cares about his having fun, and he knows no bounds if he believes anyone disobeys him. It's an obsession. I still get messages from him warning me to keep my mouth shut. Threatening me with defamation and legal fees.'

It was almost too wild to believe. Besides, if his mother was that scary, and he was that much of a control freak, Brandon would've said something about her menial job.

'I never heard this reported,' Angela texted. Small towns knew everything about everyone. No whispers resembling anything like this floated around the social scene.

'And you never will. We all signed NDAs. Just like you probably did. Sorry.'

NDA. Non-disclosure agreement. This was about keeping Angela a prisoner in her own life to bolster Brandon's reputation. He had the freedom to do whatever he wanted and cared nothing for the woman he supposedly loved. And he would threaten and lash out for years at those who'd made mistakes in his family's eyes.

A cheater being a cheater was doubtful, but this whole vengeance obsession was absolutely crazy, and nothing at all like the Brandon she knew. This had to be some weird jealousy thing from an ex. Angela had known the Spindletons were capable of stopping whatever bad press they wanted.

The doubt lingered.

ANGELA STARED AT THE screen, hands shaking. Right now, in a room down the wing, Brandon dressed in his tuxedo with all his groomsmen—whom she had never properly met. The final words repeated in her head. '*We all signed NDAs.*' Angela sure did. The attorneys covered Brandon's shenanigans over the years, and they knew enough to enforce an NDA ahead of time. But the women keep tabs on him, warning each new love of his life.

Angela couldn't believe she'd been so oblivious. The mystery woman's reason for their fight rang true. Brandon never invited her along with his friends. Like she was some toy he collected from the shelf, dusted off, and entertained himself with for a short while, before returning it to its place.

With the picture on her phone as proof, Angela opened the boudoir door and called down the hall, "Mrs. Spindleton, I need a word with you."

The old woman cruised around the corner with her daughter and niece in tow. "Good timing. The guests are seated, and the musician is ready to begin shortly. We must finish getting you presentable." Her sunken eyes raked her head to her hem, and the excitement waned. "You didn't get makeup on your dress, did you?"

Angela held out a hand, stopping the girls. "I need a minute alone, okay?"

The girls looked to the head of the house, who nodded, and they turned and walked away. Angela waved Mrs. Spindleton into the room.

"What's the matter?" she asked.

Angela held out the photo on her screen, and the woman gasped, hand covering her mouth as if the photo of her son's naked rear disturbed her delicate eyes.

"Where did you get that?"

"A woman sent it to me. She claims Brandon cheated on her. Do you know anything about this?"

Mrs. Spindleton bristled. "That's a lie, I tell you! She used the computer to alter that image."

Angela double checked the photo. "You're telling me this *isn't* Brandon? Someone glued his face on this picture just to upset me?"

Mrs. Spindleton's brow furrowed. "Those useless damned attorneys! What good are they? Who was it? I'm going to bury..." With a final angry gaze, Mrs. Spindleton rolled her eyes, as if further conversing with Angela was a waste of her time. The elder Spindleton fished out her cell phone and dialed. When the ringing stopped, she said, "I need Arnold on the line immediately."

It was true. It was all true.

While Mrs. Spindleton continued ranting at the useless attorney, Angela collected her purse off the vanity and left the room. The girls had already busied themselves somewhere else, and Angela was thankful to avoid that awkward conversation.

Down the hall, swishing along on the hand-woven Persian rugs, Angela stopped at the door to the groom's chambers, exhaled a deep breath, and barged into the room.

Brandon stood in front of a tri-folding floor-length mirror, while the groomsmen in their tuxes hovered around him, leaning to see his phone screen. The men held open bottles of beer, and laughter filled the room. A gray-haired man in a dress shirt and pants with a tape measure around his neck kneeled at the hem of Brandon's pants, making last-minute adjustments.

Brandon noticed her entrance and blocked his hands from his eyes like an immature child. "Whoa, honey. It's bad luck to see the bride in her gown before the ceremony. You know that."

Angela marched right up to him, splitting the groomsmen, whose laughter died, and she held the incriminating photo to his face. "Care to explain this?"

The groomsmen whispered to each other, and Brandon dropped the levity. Her fiancé leaned over and squinted at her screen. The tailor at his feet made a noise when Brandon shifted. Angela didn't care about how even the hem was.

Brandon's face drained of color. "How did you...?" His whispered tone of disbelief had Angela question herself. Had this woman set her up? She was too angry at all of it to turn her cheek now. She needed the truth, regardless of the consequences.

"The mysterious woman in this provocative pose"—Angela tilted her head, admiring the angle—"sent me a text this morning. Is it true?" She wanted to hear it from his mouth.

"Sir, I insist," the tailor urged, tugging at the hem.

"If he doesn't explain," Angela told the tailor, "then your efforts are a waste."

At her clear warning, Brandon bristled. "You're considering throwing away our future because some bimbo ex-girlfriend texted you a pic of us?"

"The bimbo ex-girlfriend, as you call her"—What would he call Angela?—"said this woman wasn't her. You cheated and used it against her. Is that true?"

Brandon's face pinched with fury. "I wasn't with Brooke when this was taken. She lied, and you're willing to trust her word over mine? I thought we were stronger than that."

"Are you telling me you were single when this photo was taken?" Angela deliberately used the catchphrase to see if this mystery Brooke was right.

"Exactly. I'm glad you could see reason." Brandon smiled and leaned in for a kiss, but Angela leaned away. Brandon shifted his weight, covering for the failed kiss. Didn't want to be embarrassed in front of his precious friends. He cleared his throat and added, "I knew you were always a smart cookie. Now get out of here before you jinx our wedding."

A rock filled Angela's chest, pressing harder and harder with each of Brandon's lies and excuses. In a flash, one of the groomsmen grabbed Brandon's phone and tossed it to her. The tailor kneeling at Brandon's feet blocked his attempt to take it back from her.

Angela lit up the screen to see just what they'd been sharing when she walked in. With Brandon's hair, necklace, and clothes, she recognized exactly when this was taken. Brandon was elbow-deep in another woman just a few days ago. "Who is she?"

"This stuff always happens at bachelor parties. It's almost the rules," Brandon said dismissively.

The groomsman who'd whispered to others now tugged on a couple of the men's tuxes to signal them to leave. Several of the groomsmen sent her a look of pity.

Tears filled her lids, and the rock crushed harder, making breathing difficult. All these men knew what Brandon was doing. She glared at each one as they walked out in shame.

Alone, Brandon shook off the grouchy tailor and closed his hands over hers. "You know me, Angela. This whole thing... Those women... They didn't mean anything. I didn't love any of them, but I love you. I would never do anything to hurt you."

Angela gave herself a minute to steady her voice. "You already did."

"No, no, honey. It was an innocent mistake. I promise it will never happen again. We'll walk down that aisle together and start fresh, a new beginning, just you and me." Brandon squeezed her hands tighter, crushing the phones against her skin. She would've cried out in pain if she weren't already hurting too much to feel it.

Angela wished she could throw the phones in the garbage and never see them again. She wished she never seen another phone again in her life. Remembering all the good times they'd shared, she wanted to believe him, but she just couldn't.

"You were going to use that photo against me as blackmail if I ever disobeyed, weren't you? And you'd fixate on my punishment for years. Why?"

Brandon released her hands, and the sweet act slid from his face. A smirk appeared, and Angela squeezed his phone, wishing it was his neck.

"When you're someone like me, people come from all walks of life to take advantage. This is my way of not only preventing that but also enjoying the process. A personal insurance plan, if you will. You should be proud. I didn't set up this photo until just before our wedding. There really was something special about you. Everyone else got theirs much earlier."

Was. She heard it straight from his mouth, not that she'd ever consider reconciling. Too disgusted for words, Angela hurled his phone at the tri-fold mirror, cracking the screen and the glass, and hopefully destroying both. The tailor ducked and covered his head. Angela turned on her expensive heels and marched toward the door.

"Don't tell anyone about this," Brandon called after her. "You already signed the NDA. Brook's in big trouble with Arnie, and you don't want to join her."

Angela slammed the heavy door behind her and rushed down the hallway. Tears filled her eyes, and the edge of her chiffon snagged on a decorative table. With a wet sniffle, Angela yanked on it, not caring if the fabric tore, but a vase probably worth more than her car tipped over and shattered.

Chapter 4

Months later, Angela Foxe didn't know what to expect, but silence wasn't it. A stiff dude in a suit had arrived and collected her dress. Otherwise, attorneys had buried the scandal once again. Brooke never responded to texts about what happened, as if she fell off the face of the earth. It was eerie. Angela thought she knew the man she loved and trusted. Sure, Brandon's family was stuffy and uptight, but she couldn't blame them. They had a legacy to protect and assets to hide. Still, no more prenups and uptight mothers-in-law for her. And no more expensive vases taunting her into bankruptcy.

Angela was free, watching out for *numero uno*.

That was what she'd told herself in between bouts of ice cream and candies, wallowing in the loss of yet another family—rejected by her parents, rejected by Brandon and his family. She couldn't help but wonder what was wrong with her. Why wasn't she anyone's *numero uno?* When her confidence returned, Angela attempted to date, but no one ever went anywhere. How could she trust her date wasn't the next Brandon in disguise? Her judgment, along with her heart, was irreparably broken.

Emily had told her, 'Don't dismiss the entire sea because of one rotten fish.' The woman was right, statistically speaking, but Angela was too old to play games, so casual fun was her hard line. Hot guys only and one night only were the rules.

Marcos had been disappointed he didn't get to see her dress, but when he'd delivered a boatload of candy and a bottle of wine to her door, he bashed the Spindletons long enough to get over it. Angela even laughed a few times.

Now life was good. Life was simple. She had no complaints until Emily was destroyed by that greedy ass Tyler. Now a broke history buff, Emily needed someone to fill his ticket at the Tall Ships festival, so it would go to waste. History wasn't Angela's thing. She was quite content to leave the past where it belonged. But when Emily promised to go anywhere of Angela's choosing next, she reluctantly murmured her consideration. And when Emily had said many hot guys would be at the festival, some dressed like Captain Jack Sparrow, Angela agreed, excited to find a perfectly skimpy outfit.

Angela picked out a pirate wench costume. It was ruffly and short in the front and reached her calves in the back. The neckline was off the shoulder, with a sexy brown corset on the outside to push the assets up. She curled and pinned her long brunette hair away from her face in a romantic half updo, and covered it with a lacy, black tricorn hat with a pinch of feathers. But the boots were the best part. Black, knee-height, and cuffed. Although, walking with the pointed heels in the grass wasn't as easy as she'd expected. But Angela looked hot, and she planned to find herself a captain for the evening.

None of the early festival visitors had caught her attention, but the next best distraction—outside of alcohol—was shopping, and a particular vendor table enthralled her. In the farthest row, away from the others, a hunched old woman sold the most beautiful, handcrafted jewelry. She offered them special necklaces from a locked chest—amethyst on a copper chain—for a ridiculously low sum of five bucks. Angela couldn't turn them down.

None of that was weird.

In fact, Angela was having a great time as Emily led her up the gangway and onto the first tour ship. Lines were strung all over the ship and wrapped around massive cleats. The sails were furled to prevent the ships from moving in the breeze. This might've been Emily's scene, but a silly smile lifted Angela's lips. Angela scanned the deck for the ship's wheel. Maybe the tour company would let her sail it for a little while. Or at least pretend?

"Ladies, packages are not allowed." A tour guide, wearing a clean-pressed plain uniform, approached from behind them. "There's a basket on land to store belongings." With his hands clasped behind his back and his chest puffed, the employee continued his patrol on deck.

That was a little weird.

Angela and Emily glanced over the rail. Just off the ship was a large crate guarded by a man with a bored look on his face.

"I'm not leaving this behind to get stolen!" Angela whispered. The necklace was cheap, but uniquely beautiful.

"Me neither. He didn't say we couldn't wear them." Emily shrugged.

"True." Angela and Emily dug their necklaces out of their shopping bags and slipped them over their heads.

But this, this was very weird. What the hell?

ANGELA HAD BOARDED A replica antique pirate ship for a cruise...for tourists, filled with men and women in clean, machine-stitched uniforms and modern hairstyles. In the blink of an eye, the ship workers had disappeared, and Angela found herself below deck in a suffocating room with only a porthole for light and a stench reminding her of the meat department's expired waste. A strong scent of tobacco hit her nose and then the faintest odor of charred wood. The ship rocked and groaned.

How did she get down here? And why was it rocking? It had been secured to the dock with calm waters.

Angela hadn't partaken in alcohol lately. Was she experiencing blackouts while sober? Blackouts...jumps in time...missing memories. Angela's stomach sank. Those were the first signs of her mother's illness. Angela was forty years old. She'd expected to inherit the detrimental gift, but not for many years yet. How could it be happening already with such a severe leap?

Voices. Men were in here talking. Angela ducked behind barrels, holding her breath like a trespasser about to get busted. Gulls outside cawed like an alarm. She didn't want to get in trouble for being in a restricted area and ruining Emily's good time. She pressed herself lower, trying to keep her hands off the floor. The balls of her feet ached.

The men talked about Cuba, or something. Must be their next stop when they finished with the Great Lakes. Angela could hardly hear over the noise of the birds, the waves sloshing the ship, and the pounding of the barrel lids and her heart.

A heavy man's footsteps faded. He left. Angela listened to see if she was alone, and she didn't hear anything. She poked her head up above the barrel. A man held a candle in his hands, flickering yellow light over his handsome features. Angela smiled at the defined and stubble-covered jaw, angled Cupid's bow, and strong brow. It glinted over the gold stud in his ear. Where else did he have jewelry? He was exactly what she'd been looking for, but the man's clothing was unusual. Emily had warned her ship workers and visitors alike could 'get into' the pirate lifestyle.

This striking man wore a dark coat with gold buttons and a white neckerchief dangling over an ivory vest. Angela couldn't be certain in the lighting, but she thought breeches covered his thighs. He appeared to be her age. In his hand was a pad of paper, and he scrawled on a sheet as he maneuvered around the room. He was taking inventory! A hot flash rocked her body. Was it from the inventory process or an incredibly attractive, distinguished man?

Angela took off her frilly hat and forced herself to stay hidden. The leather pack clipped around her waist, containing her credit cards, stayed secured. Watching him, Angela's heart pounded in her ears. Why was she hiding? She wasn't a shy woman, and this guy was going to be her next fun fling—if he was willing, of course. Before standing and introducing herself, another man hollered from the other side of the door. Her sexy pirate turned his head. His dark brown hair was layered and shoulder length, something she didn't often anymore, and it was sexy as hell.

"What's the matter, Karl?" His voice was lilted with an English accent, and Angela swooned so hard she thought her corset buttons were going to pop off.

The man stepped closer and closer, scratching on the paper, until he stopped on the other side of the barrel from her. Angela ducked lower, holding her breath to stay silent, but her pounding heart and swishing blood in her ears were going to get her caught.

The voice was muffled, and with a grunt of annoyance from her sexy pirate, he left, taking the candle with him. Darkness returned and Angela's eyes adjusted to a single flashlight's worth of daylight filtering in through a smudged porthole. She still hadn't seen Emily. With the crew out of sight, Angela whispered, "Em? Are you here?"

No answer. Of course not. If Emily was in here, she would've dived at the pirate and asked him history questions. Just as Angela would've dived at him and asked questions about sailing this ship, but she didn't. Angela lifted up on her knees, craning her head around to see where Emily hid.

"This isn't funny. Come out."

Still, Emily wouldn't answer. This wasn't funny at all. Only the groans of the ship and rocking from the lake's waves returned her plea. Angela rubbed her elbow on the porthole glass to clean it and peered out. Her face scrunched. Those were big waves for Lake Michigan. The color of the water was off, and no land was in sight. How was that possible? From any location on the lake, some land formations could be seen. She hadn't been on the ship long enough for the crew to have navigated out of Lake Michigan, and that wasn't part of the tour. More concerning were the angry clouds on the horizon. What the...?

Angela stood up with a frown. The ship bucked into a wave, and Angela grasped the hull for balance as water splashed the porthole and rained down on her from the decks above. With a grimace, she swiped away the water from her face, but it felt off—wrong.

Warm.

Sticky.

She tasted it before thinking of all the surfaces it had just passed through. Salty? The Great Lakes weren't salty.

Angela climbed her way through the stacks of barrels, trying her best to avoid knocking anything over with the swaying of the ship and poor lighting. "Em, this isn't funny anymore. Where are you? Something's not right." She searched every inch of the hold to make sure Emily wasn't knocked out by something loose. This ship was worse than an amusement park ride, and her stomach flipped with the foreign sensation.

Emily wasn't in here.

Well, Angela wasn't going to stay down here and wait for trouble to find her. She pushed through the door and, keeping her head ducked from the uncomfortably low ceiling, she found a ladder. The stink of garbage or sewage hit her nose harder over here. Her eyes watered. For a paying customer, this tour ship was disgusting. How did she let Emily talk her into this? If she found Emily above deck flirting with the captain, oh, Angela was going to need a lot of schmoozing to make it up to her.

Angela climbed up just high enough to poke her head out. Men pulled lines and climbed the rigging, while others conversed in small groups. Not a single one appeared to be an employee of the tour company. Salty sea air blew in her face, whipping her dampened locks over her shoulder. As a group closed the distance, she noted pistols at their waistbands and...swords? Dirty, nicked, and way too real. Angela's upper lip curled in disbelief.

These guys were hardcore pirate fans. When Emily emerged from wherever she hid, she was in for a treat. And then Angela was giving her a tongue lashing.

"You there! Oy! You! What are you doing 'ere?" A man from a small group pointed at her with a snarl on his dirt-streaked face—honest disgust she hadn't seen since...Brandon's hateful confession. He wore a bandanna around his head of shaggy hair, a striped tunic and...yep, those were breeches.

"I...I..." No other words filtering through her brain connected. He seemed excessively offended at her being in the restricted area. She didn't touch anything. It was only a simple mistake—a medical problem.

"Captain! Captain Price!" the shaggy-haired man hollered. "We have a stowaway!"

At that alarm, men rushed to the unsteady deck and swarmed around her. They gawked like she was either a piece of candy or a filthy criminal. A little excessive for a simple misunderstanding.

Two large hands reached under her arms and lifted her straight off the ladder. "Let me go, you filthy jerks!" Angela swung her legs to free herself, but the men held her just above the deck. "Put me down! I'm not a child."

One released her. The other said with scorn, "Filthy? I resent that, wench."

As she dangled in the air, the gawking men parted for the man in charge. Angela's mouth gaped open. Her sexy pirate taking the inventory was the captain! And in the bright daylight, he was even more handsome and refined. The breeze tousled his hair beneath his hat, and his eyes were a stunning blue like the water. Angela figured she could sweet-talk him out of trouble, and maybe into something else.

"Let her go, Liverman," the captain ordered. Angela swallowed back an audible sigh at his voice, both deep and commanding, but the lilt of the accent stole her breath. Her feet touched the deck, and the men released her arms. She rubbed them with a frown, both for the soreness and the grime.

"You were just below deck, captain," the first shaggy-haired man continued with an accusing tone. "How did you miss a woman below deck?"

The captain assessed her, focusing on her clothing, or what her clothing didn't cover, and amusement lifted his lips just slightly. "Berger, I can certainly assure you I did not miss a woman on board."

Yes, he did.

The captain's words were tough, but his gaze said something else entirely—curiosity and amusement. "Certainly not one dressed like that." The captain's head cocked to the side, his gaze raked over her in a different way—steamy and smoldering.

Angela exhaled slowly. The deck listed with a wave, and Angela struck her hands out for balance. The men around her seemed unaffected by the ship's movements, but they had to be used to it. The things she rode had four wheels.

Or two legs.

A man next to her pinched her polyester material with dirty hands. "What is this made of, and why is it so shiny?"

Another man rubbed at the ruffles in her costume. "I don't know, but I think I like it. Less layers to get to the goods underneath." He snickered, and the others whooped with catcalls that made Angela's skin prickle. She twisted, pulling the fabric from their grimy fingers.

When she'd set out to have a good time with Emily, this was not what she'd had in mind. Angela folded her arms in front of her defensively, but with this many animals, any effort to protect herself would be in vain. She craned her neck, trying to see where the dock was, and the deck tilted. A wave splashed and soaked everyone on the main deck. With the force, Angela lost her balance and fell right into the captain's wet arms.

Beyond the blowing salty sea air, a masculine spiciness tickled her nose, and in that instant, the rest of the ship and all her cares and worries melted away. Water dribbled off the rim of his hat. Up close, his eyes were beautiful. His chest was firm, strong against the listing, an anchor, exactly the kind of man she'd been hunting for. Someone with the strength to handle her.

Unfortunately, the scowl on his face meant he didn't reciprocate. "You have caused me quite the problem," the captain growled. "And your timing couldn't have been worse." The captain gripped her arms, stepped back, and released her at a short distance, after assuring himself she was stable on her feet.

"Karl!" the captain shouted. "Send your men up to furl the mizzens."

A barrel-chested man with a bald head nodded and gestured. Slender men rushed up the ratlines in obedience.

The shaggy cretin, Berger, if she remembered right, said, "Stowin' away is cause for marooning, captain. We shan't make exceptions."

Angela swiped dripping hair out of her face, wishing she'd taken her hat from the hold, and folded her arms over her chilled chest. "Marooning? Stowing away? You people can't be serious. I didn't sign up for a reenactment, but if that's the case, take me back to shore, and I'll be going home."

The captain studied her with the same confusion haunting her and the crew. Men around her glanced at each other. Some murmured. A couple lifted their hats and scratched their sweaty, unwashed heads.

"Reenactment?" one whispered to another. "Buckley, you heard of a reenactment?"

A lean man with a leathery face and black shoulder-length hair shrugged and said, "Nay. Where's this pretty creature from?"

Angela chuckled, amused but on the edge of frustration. "Okay, that's enough. I want to go home. Emily! Emily Porter!" she called for her missing friend. No response returned, of course. She faced the men. "It's not funny anymore! Take me home."

Another man, younger than many others, pushed through and said, "What's all the hubbub?" His eyes landed on her and face became bleak. "Oh."

The captain stood before her, white as a fresh winter's snow and speechless.

Chapter 5

THE BREWING STORM ROCKED the hull, and they were headed straight through it into enemy territory. Rather than focusing on the brutal task ahead, the men were fretting over the sudden appearance of a woman. They had questions, and he couldn't blame them. Because, despite the chaos, Captain Henry Price stared dumbfounded at her. She was like nothing he'd ever seen before, but two things were familiar. Her accent matched a woman he'd met recently, and he knew the name she called.

Where were these women from?

The quartermaster, Noah Riley, gripped his shoulder against the onslaught of the next wave. "Captain, we must find a port, any port, to shelter against the incoming squall. By Hodgens's calculations, Cuba is the nearest hard, but I think taking our chances against the storm is wiser."

Price only stared at the woman—her bountiful breasts and tantalizing hips. Her arms were thick with muscle and power—not a dainty flower to be damaged by the wind. He'd never been so transfixed, so distracted, in the face of grim danger.

Riley leaned in close, "What's gotten into you, captain? We don't have time to deal with this right now." He glanced at the stowaway and back. Riley was right. They didn't have the time, but Price couldn't ignore the situation either. He'd put out flames over and over when they'd last had a woman on board, and they hadn't known she was a woman at the time. This was so much worse and couldn't have come at a more terrible time.

Liverman, a new member of the rigging crew, leaned closer to her accusingly. "How'd you get aboard? Price, you checked the hold but didn't see her?"

The dark tone ripped Price from his perplexity. "I counted the inventory, and this woman was not there, I assure you." He would've remembered someone so...unusual, completely stunning. His eyes raked over her body and her indescribable outfit once more. Frustrated with himself and this new distraction, Price rubbed his face. He had a tight schedule, a plan, and this turn of events threatened everything he worked toward for months.

"Well then. A sneaky little mouse slipped by all of us and the captain. I wonder what other skills she has," Berger said with a devious glint in his eye.

The newest recruits—some far younger than Price's years—hadn't seen port in two weeks and a prize in longer. A woman in their midst meant belligerence was inevitable, and he needed cooperation to complete the mission at hand. But the rules were the rules.

"Berger, several barrels were unsealed, and this storm threatens our stores. Seal them, would you?" the captain ordered.

Berger grumbled to himself and headed off. That left Liverman, but the captain didn't have any repairs needed to the skeleton of the ship...yet.

"Rules state what happens to the wench, but I'm curious what the captain has in mind." Liverman folded his arms over his soaked chest. "Tell him, Riley."

The quartermaster sent a pleading look to the captain. Riley hadn't encountered such a thing before, and for the first time, the young man was silent.

"Rules?" the woman said with disbelief, interrupting Price's thoughts. "I don't know what's going on here, but I want to be left off this ship."

Her features twisted with honest confusion. She was his age, if he wasn't mistaken. "You people are insane. This isn't what I signed up for."

"You didn't sign, wench," Liverman said. "That's the problem."

"I'm not a wench. My name is Angela, and I just want to find my friend and go home." Anger and frustration boiled over her, and she spun, seeking a sympathetic ear among these bilge rats. Most of these men wouldn't budge on the rules. Hell, weeks ago, Price wouldn't have either.

Liverman cackled and pressed a hand on top of his hat to hedge against the gust of wind. "The woman picked her punishment. Marooning! That saves us time."

"Can you not talk about me like I'm not standing in front of you?" Angela asked, anger seething beneath her skin.

Liverman cocked a brow at her, seemingly not understanding the issue, and Price admired her strength to stand up to these men. Perhaps she simply wasn't aware of the level of danger they represented.

Vallo pushed forward. A short man with dark hair, he was quiet and easily ignored. Not seen. Price held him close in esteem, and when the man talked, Price listened. He knew things the crew held from the captain. "Women ain't allowed on this ship. We signed the rules. All of us, and she needs to go!"

Several of the crew cheered their accord. Price shot a dark look at Vallo for rousing the men further. But vocalizing his dissent only strengthened Vallo's position in the crew. Price needed Vallo to maintain their trust.

"We did sign," Price agreed. "But these are special circumstances, which warrant special attention, and since we're facing down a squall, the storm takes precedence."

"Special?" Liverman spat. "Are we tossing out rules when convenient? If that's the case, I know a few that can heave overboard." Liverman stared down the captain, a blatant threat. Oh, how Price hated that man.

"Stand down," Riley warned. "The captain makes the final decision. *That* is also in the rules."

Liverman pinched his face as if catching a whiff of the bilge water, and he folded his arms over his chest, silently waiting for the next declaration to argue.

"Final decision?" Angela blurted, quite ill-mannered. "I'm not a child. I have just as much bearing in this *decision* as you do. I didn't choose this. Bring me back to a nearby city, and I'll be out of your way." With a list of the ship, Angela gripped a line running overhead. It wasn't safe for her to remain out here.

The previous captain, Lemoine, had pulled Price aside and explained his plan to disembark at Nassau permanently and chase after the woman who'd stowed away. At the time, Price believed the captain to be suffering ill humors to drop everything, but when Lemoine explained where the woman came from, Price had worried for the mental state of his esteemed captain. A part of him had been grateful Lemoine retired, for the crew's sake as much as his own.

But now Price was trapped in a conundrum. Had the captain been telling the truth? He was certain no woman hid below deck, and considering her healthful condition, she couldn't have been pilfering provisions from the crew during the weeks since their last port of call. If this incredible magic were indeed real, for her own safety in this foreign world, Price could never allow her to chase after the missing friend all alone, but he also needed the woman off the *Sea Lion*.

His own conscience couldn't send her away nor keep her.

A wave breached the main deck, spraying the crew and soaking the woman again. Her mouth opened in a round shape, once again distracting Price.

Storm clouds closed the distance; the ocean warned them away. Navigating the squall would take all hands and all attention. He couldn't maroon her in this weather—not for the ship's safety or the rowing crew's. But the ship's crew crowded around her like she was a novelty toy.

His decision was made.

"Cantu, bring Angela to my chambers."

Cantu, a docile and dependable man of many talents, including his enormous strength, gripped the woman by the bare arm. Saltwater glistened against her smooth skin, which was the last thing Price needed to be noticing, no matter how long had passed since he felt the warmth of a woman's touch.

"This is an outrage!" Liverman protested.

Price really hated that man.

"I'm not your prisoner! What is this? Unhand me!" Angela struggled futilely in the broad man's grip.

"Captain!" Vallo added.

Price nodded to Cantu, and his trustworthy man ushered her across the deck to the navigation room and into his chamber door under an onslaught of angry protests. Price smiled at her feistiness, but his short-lived amusement was stolen by Liverman.

"Captain?" Liverman said. "We demand an explanation."

Price's patience for the insubordination was gone. They had a squall to best. "See yourself below deck and do your job, otherwise we'll all be at the bottom of the Caribbean Sea."

Cantu returned and gave a nod, indicating the order had been carried out. Price barked out the rest of his orders. "Buckley, batten down the hatches. Cantu, tar the leaks below deck. Vallo"—Price pointed skyward—"furl the lower courses. This storm is unavoidable now. No matter the circumstances, preserve the mainmast! All hands, man your positions!"

The crew sprang into action, and Price ran to the assistance of the helmsman, holding the rudder steady against the onslaught of the ocean's fury. Only a miracle would keep them alive with a ship-swallowing squall upon them, but his mind wandered into his private chamber.

Chapter 6

THE SHIP LISTED STARBOARD and port, the waves thrashing and fighting to sink the lumbering trespasser. Angela noticed the parallel. She was a trespasser to these prehistoric animals. Rather than return to the deck and demand her rights with waves attempting to wash them all overboard, Angela braced herself in the cabin. With the desk and bed frame mounted to the floor, the safest place was under the bed. She spread out for stability and gripped two frame legs with all her might.

Angry clouds darkened the skies, dimming the cabin around her. Books fell from the shelves. Silverware clattered to the floorboards and slid. Glass bottles tipped over and some shattered, sending shards bouncing. Cargo nets full of supplies thumped against the wall. Where the angry sea breached the cabin, water trickled from above, soaking the floor.

Soaking Angela.

When Angela had agreed to accompany Emily to the Tall Ships festival and board a tour cruise, she'd expected a romantic sail on the lake under the glittering sun while sidling up next to a handsome man.

This reenactment hadn't been explicitly described on the flier, and had she checked radar, she would've opted out. On a normal day, Angela loved to control heavy equipment, but even the roughest terrain of her favorite ATV trail had nothing on this old ship and an angry sea. Angela's stomach flipped and sloshed.

One thing was certain, when she returned to the festival grounds, she was going to find the manager and demand a refund—no matter how catty it sounded. And if he wasn't there? A firmly written letter should suffice. Perhaps a complaint on social media as well, but Angela preferred to avoid the tech space.

Her outfit was soaked and torn. Her phone was probably ruined. This was ridiculous.

A leather-bound book slid across the floor and stopped within reach. To give her fatigued arms a break, Angela scooted backward under the bed and braced her legs against the frame. She reached out for the book to keep her mind off her stomach. Maybe she could find a refund allowance, or a free parking pass, or something about the company she could use to alleviate her aggravation and inconvenience.

Angela flipped opened the cover and her lips parted. Loopy, angled handwriting—like something from a history museum—delicately penned on pale yellow pages. Fascinated, she deciphered the penmanship, what little of it she could. This was the captain's log.

They wouldn't put a prop in here, out of view of the paying public, would they?

Angela turned the moist page. In orderly columns, locations and dates detailed inventory on and off the ship. Several lines down, she read, "Goats and pigs. What in the world...?"

More paragraphs detailed weather events and ships encountered both at port and on the sea. Angela turned the page, unable to resist the book's allure. The crew's names and dollar amounts were listed—some were only ten and twenty bucks. Angela's face pulled into a frown. "Well, add that to my list of complaints. If the company paid better, they'd probably treat their guests better."

The groaning ship leveled, and Angela relaxed her legs and climbed out from under the bed. The cabin was a mess, and she was filthy. Testing the mattress and finding it soaked, Angela stayed on her feet while sweeping water and dirt off her arms and legs. Finally, this horrible chaos was over. Now she could disembark and fly home.

Shouts from the deck were muffled by the cabin. The ship stopped with an abrupt shudder, sending Angela careening over onto her knees. A loud crack—she was certain wasn't her own bones—turned her head. Angela frowned at the closed cabin door while standing up and brushing off yet again. Did they hit the dock at port? With the way those men treated her, she wouldn't doubt their ability to do their jobs.

Shouts permeated the wood. The water clinging to every surface of the cabin was warm enough to not worry her, but it was too cool for comfort. Gooseflesh rose on her arms.

Something was wrong.

The starboard side of the ship listed severely. The book slid along the floor, sticking against broken glass. Angela tumbled across the cabin and slammed into the wall with a sharp pain to her hip. Water poured in from all the seams in the walls. The ship wasn't righting itself, and instead of the water draining out to the lower decks, it was filling the cabin. Water reached her ankles and then knees way too fast.

Something was very wrong.

Angela climbed toward the door, pulled it open, and braced herself against the wall. Some sort of navigation room. Instruments clattered to the floor. The ship tilted further. No matter the captain's orders or the crew's baser desires, she had to get out of here. With the alarming angle, the door to the navigation room fell open and more seawater rushed in like a waterfall. Angela climbed toward the door, fighting the thigh-deep current throwing her back toward the captain's quarters—now nearly submerged.

Heart pounding her chest, Angela tried to swim toward the exit. Men were jumping over the rail. Others were splashing in the water as if they couldn't swim.

A hand reached into the doorframe, fingers splayed. The captain's head popped into view with panic on his handsome face. He braced himself. "The ship's going down! Give me your hand!"

Her rescuer was unstable too with the water pushing him, spraying around his body. If he lost his grip, they were both going to drown. Angela's breathing became shallow, and she fought to move her legs against the current, but she couldn't. She dove into the water to swim toward the captain's hand, but still the current was too strong, throwing her back against the wall. Angela considered herself a good swimmer, on an ordinary day, but being trapped in a small room rapidly filling with water deteriorated her self-confidence. Fear constricted her chest, and exertion burned her legs. If she didn't get out, she would die.

Another loud crack pierced her eardrum. The captain looked over his shoulder, eyes wide with concern.

"Now!" he shouted to her.

Using gaps between the wood boards of the wall, Angela climbed toward him, and when in reach, she grabbed his hand, her safety line. His grip was firm, sticky from the saltwater, and reassuring that he would bring them to safety. The captain gritted his teeth and with a grunting force, pulled her through the door just as the water overtook the opening. Suction pulled her back toward the door, but the captain held on.

Several feet of water covered the main deck. Rain pummeled the surface, blinding her. Thunder rumbled overhead. As the bow raised in the air, the stern beneath her feet sunk further, and Angela treaded water.

The captain's hand was torn from her. He hadn't surfaced.

Only a few men splashed in desperation around the ship. One clung to the top of the mainmast, still exposed to the storm's elements. Where was everyone else? Where was the captain?

Angela turned herself to find him, but a wave crashed overhead, pushing her down into the murky depths. She kicked and thrashed, fighting against the force of the ocean and the pull of the sinking ship.

As the wave rolled by, the suction lessened, and Angela's efforts inched her closer to the air.

Debris in the water clouded her vision—loose ropes, pieces of wood, and other objects she didn't recognize. A broken chunk of wood floated up next to her, and she grabbed it. The board helped her kick, propelling her upward. Her face broke the surface, and Angela gasped and coughed. She kept her chest pressed against the board like a life preserver.

Smaller waves blocked her view of the destruction around her. The ship had broken on a rocky outcropping, but the island cliff was too steep to climb. Angela kicked away from the rocks before getting tossed against them herself.

"Captain!" Angela shouted, but the departing storm muffled her voice. She kicked and paddled, hoping to find a suitable place to climb onto land. She rode the shorter waves, and a gasp nearby turned her head.

There! Captain Price's face breached the surface, and with a deep breath, he slipped below. Angela paddled over as quickly as possible, fighting the current trying to throw her into the rocks. She craned her neck, trying to find him. She was sure he was last right here.

He was gone.

Angela shoved a hand down and, fingers splayed, tried to reach him. Still nothing.

The man tried to keep her safe from his unruly crew. And if the storm was going to take her life, she didn't want to be alone at the end. Releasing the board, she dove under the surface.

The captain wasn't far away, but he was sinking. The man fought to remove the heavy garments pulling him down. With desperation, Angela reached him and helped remove his coat and boots. With all her might, she pushed him upward and kicked wildly to catch up to him.

His foot tangled on a sinking nest of ropes. Angela shifted the heavy hemp off his foot and continued to climb the water stroke after stroke.

Her mouth broke the surface, and she gasped. The captain breached next to her, gasping and coughing.

Through the pummeling rains, her life preserving board floated nearby. She paddled over to it and brought it back to him. The captain gripped it, panting.

"Good to know you can swim," he said, managing a smile.

Angela snorted. "Good to know you can sail." If Angela had been steering the ship—after getting lessons on how to do it—she was certain it wouldn't have crashed against the rocks.

The captain cocked his weary head at her in amusement.

"If we stay here, we're going to die of exhaustion trying to stay ahead of those rocks. Paddle with me."

The captain mirrored her on the board, elbow to elbow. They squinted into the torrential rains, and together they kicked through the angry water, keeping an eye out for other survivors.

"I don't see anyone else." Angela swiped ocean spray from her face, thankful the thunderous storm had moved on.

"Most of them can't swim." The captain cleared his face and coughed on water trapped in his lungs. "But I'm fortunate you can."

After rigorous thrashing, they made headway around a corner. The cove was dense forest with a strip of beach rimming it. Debris from the ship tickled the shore. A few men rested with the water licking at their soggy boots.

"Over there. Stop over by those men," Captain Price said.

Angela changed trajectory, and together they paddled until their toes touched sand, waters calmer by the protective cove. Rain pattered the trees.

The captain dragged the board on shore, and Angela fell into the sand herself, laying face up and panting. Working hard in the warehouse during the peak of summer, hitting three figures in temperature, was nothing compared to that, and it was something she never wanted to experience again.

Writing a letter to festival management seemed so...insufficient...now, and far too much work. The rain softened, and slowly the darker clouds floated away, dragging in white clouds. Angela blinked against the rainfall, but her body wouldn't move.

Every summer she'd spend weekends with Emily, drinking on the beach, watching the clouds drift by, picking out the shapes. They'd hammer the stakes and pitch their tent, cut firewood, and light it—with lighter fluid. They weren't Lewis and Clark reincarnated. Right now, Angela didn't have the energy for any of that. Right now, nature's cozy blanket or endless fury would decide how she spent the night.

She faded into a deep sleep with one question on her mind: where was Emily?

Chapter 7

SHE'D SAID, '*GOOD TO know you can sail.*' It should've been an insult, but with the friendly tone she'd used, Price could only chuckle at the irony. He was a fantastic sailor, but he'd replayed the events over and over, trying to determine if there was something that could've prevented such a catastrophe. Should he have ordered reefing sooner? Had they not heaved-to quickly enough? Had the drogue not been deployed on time?

During the night on the beach in soaked clothing with sand in places it didn't belong, Price decided his preoccupation with Angela had caused the ship's wreck. If he and the crew hadn't been distracted, they could've maneuvered safely through the squall. Instead, the ship had been dashed against a crag. His plan included having a ship, and not only had he suffered that loss, but now he didn't know how many of his crew remained. Angela remained, and she was still turning his life upside down. Price's sleep had been terrible, all because he'd kept an eye on her, sleeping soundly as a rock all night.

Daylight broke on the horizon, magnified by the ocean's reflection, beaming bright light into his eyes. Price groaned and rolled over onto his sore hip. Every muscle in his body ached. His fingers were stiff from gripping the helm with Hodgens and fighting to keep the *Sea Lion* afloat. All for naught, and time had never been a luxury to waste.

Price sighed and grunted as he stood, bare toes sinking into the sand. He looked down at the curious sensation. When he'd been descending beneath the ocean's surface, hope truly lost but before panic set in,

Angela had removed his boots and helped him shuck his coat. If not for her, he'd have drowned. Among his crew, less than a dozen could've done the same for him, and still, none did. Price would never forget an action so bold, so courageous and noble. He knew of only one person in his life worthy of such similar description—William Price—but the man had perished for his efforts. Captain Price couldn't let another meet that fate.

At low tide, the beach had grown significantly in size. Angela was still asleep, and his crew had already set to work. With so many questions invading his thoughts, Price left her, strolling along the beach, checking the flotsam for salvage or even a pair of boots. Along the way to the scene of the wreck, he collected an armful of spare lines and an empty barrel, but he dropped them with a gaped mouth at the *Sea Lion*'s condition. The damage before him twisted his insides. The vengeful sea had deposited the ship next to the rocky outcrop with a fatal gaping maw in her hull. Like visiting a gravesite, his ship was gone.

With stiff knees, Captain Price approached, and near the keel, a fallen sailor rocked in the softly lapping waves. Hayes. A fair man. Price considered whether the man's feet were of similar size before shaking his head at the loss and moving on.

Quartermaster Noah Riley ducked out of the hole and stretched. Upon sighting him, the younger man exclaimed, "Captain, you survived!" Riley embraced him with a pat on the back and obvious relief. Becoming captain was not a position to take lightly, and Riley wouldn't have wanted it thrust upon him.

Price pulled back with a grin. "I had help. I'm surprised to have found you upright and breathing. You swim as well as a line tied to an anchor. Remember when you fell overboard?"

Riley struggled to recount the tale, and the moment he did was evident on his face. "A gale heeled the ship, and I tumbled leeward over the rail. I floundered, but a rescue line luckily landed in my hands. I had different luck this time." Riley wiped his brow. "A tight stay can be the difference between sailing the seas and paying an eternal visit to the depths below."

The sound of lapping waves reminded him of the lost souls, and Price's levity left him on a breath. "What of the others? How many men do we have left?"

"About two dozen. In your absence, I had Giles set up a camp just inside the cove, hidden in the jungle, and I've rallied a few men to salvage what we can. McKee volunteered to collect, wrap, and record the bodies. I didn't argue, since we no longer have a doctor on board. Among the casualties are Miller and Cruz, and clearly Hayes. But a fair warning, Liverman, Vallo, and Berger survived. Berger clung to the mizzenmast not far from me. We have much damage to repair on the ship and families to recompense, I don't believe our reserve is sufficient."

Just when Price thought he'd received all the bad news, the men agitating the crew were going to continue their quarrel.

With no doctor, the duties fell to the carpenter, and without a carpenter, the remaining crew—and Price himself—would find themselves in yet worse dire straits. "What of the ship's repair? Where's Buckley?"

"Buckley is with Cantu in the hold, removing what cargo and personal effects of value remain, and determining the tools and supplies available for repair. Peter Gunner is assessing the guns and salvageable shot. Karl Dillon needs more hands to refit the lines on deck, but Liverman is up there helping. Berger is refilling our water barrels, what of them remains. But even if we can bring the *Sea Lion* to rights, I'm uncertain whether we have sufficient hands to sail her."

If that didn't burst his remaining bubble of positivity, he didn't know what would.

"You've done well, Riley."

"Captain, I don't know if you've noticed, but we're stranded on Cuba. If the enemy catches wind of our location and current state, we won't need to worry about having hands to sail," Riley said in confidence.

Price gritted his teeth. Unbeknownst to the crew, Price had planned to sail this way, but their landing here too soon was entirely accidental, and with their ship hobbled, not at all convenient. Before the crew voted Henry Price as quartermaster and, subsequently, captain, he and his older brother, William, were English Royal Navy, sailing with the HMS Bristol. Several years ago, pirate Ernest Wilcox of the *Sea Lion* captured the Bristol, a brazen move by any standards. But after being pressed, Henry and William accepted their freedom with open arms and relished in assisting other crews to their own freedoms—while filling their coffers in the process. Henry had sailed with William for years, and both of them planned to become captains of their own ships and sail together as a flotilla.

But it wasn't to be.

And the guilt Henry Price had carried festered, until it became rage—a silent, patient being, growing and maturing the perfect plan to exact that vengeance. But with every passing hour, the tide was returning to claim her prize. With every passing hour, the risk of being spotted by Spain increased tenfold. And Riley was right.

"I'm very aware of our location. Keep everyone quiet while we work. No shanties, no shouting. Are we clear?"

Riley nodded. "One last thing, captain. What of the woman?"

Seemed Riley couldn't forget her either, and at the thought of that special woman resting in the sand, Price bit back a smile. "She's sleeping in the cove."

Riley grinned. "I don't suppose, since we're no longer on the ship in a technical manner, the articles shall allow those of us wanting to take a turn?"

Images of the crew lined up, one by one, stealing her virtue while she helplessly screamed, fighting and failing to stop them, assaulted his brain. Price's sore hands curved into solid fists. Since she'd saved his life, he would protect her until she released him of the duty. It was the least he could do.

Through gritted teeth and a tense jaw, Price said, "Regardless of the status of our ship, we are still on the account, so the articles are still in force. She is not to be disturbed. If any men care to voice an opinion on the matter, send for me. Conveniently, we happen to be on shore to settle disputes."

Riley's smile slid away, but he stood firm in his position. "Your point is understood, and I shall direct opposition to you, but the articles also state any woman caught on board are to suffer death."

Price stepped forward. "If any of the crew insists on marooning her or any similar punishments while the ship remains a husk on the exposed sandbar, I wish to address them immediately. The woman is not their concern. We need the *Sea Lion* back on the water."

"Captain, she broke the articles. If you refuse them the rights in the articles, the crew will insist on reparations, and if the woman isn't from a wealthy family, they just might insist on receiving their payment in another form. And then we circle back to the original question."

If Riley pushed for using the woman one more time... "You have my answer. Go."

The quartermaster smiled in a friendly way, returning to the carefree young man Price knew so well. Riley swatted him on the shoulder. "I agree with you entirely. I only wanted to prepare you for the crew's opinion. I know how close Lemoine was to losing their trust, and I don't want to see this strange woman destroy everything you've built here."

"I appreciate the sentiment," Price said dryly, the hypothetical status of the conversation not having sunk in. Price climbed up to the tilted deck, not looking forward to Liverman's judgment. Only a few men were up here, including his boatswain, Karl Dillon. Liverman was busy on the other side, and Price joined a pair about to run the rigging through a replacement pulley.

Riley's words plagued him. Could one woman's presence dismantle everything Price had been planning?

"'Alo, captain, glad to see another set of hands." Peter Gunner twisted lines into an expert knot. He was a poorly named gunner's mate. The boy could repair weapons with the best of them, but his aim was something terrible. The kid had heart though. No surprise master gunner, McKee, had directed Peter onto the main deck. "Secure!"

"Pull!" Price yelled, and the men coordinated their efforts. "Pull!" Price repeated and gritted his teeth, heaving with all his might. The wood of the ship creaked in protest, threatening to snap, but it was a necessary risk.

"Steady!" Boatswain Karl Dillon yelled.

Price held firm with Peter at his side. The rigging was a snarled mess all over the deck and sand. How were they going to fix this by the return of the tide tonight?

While Price held steady with all his might, Karl lashed the ropes around the rocky outcrop and gestured for them to let go. "She's stable, but not for long."

The captain released his grip. "Good work, men! Let's get her capturing wind again."

The handful of men cheered quietly while they continued working. Most of his crew were agreeable—men he trusted to cooperate on their shared goal. Since they'd sacrificed so much just to reach this island, how would they react when they discovered his personal objective now?

Cantu approached down the beach, carrying a heavy log on his shoulder, and he gestured for the captain's attention. Price climbed down the outer hull, landing his bare feet in the sand.

"Captain, the woman's awake."

"Is she distressed in any way?"

Cantu shook his thick head. "More like a scared bilge rat. Reminds me of my little sister in a way, except for the unusual garments."

Price's lips pressed thin at the mention of her clothing. Why she had any effect on him at all was confusing. Their sole relationship was a favor for a favor—and she wasn't aware of the arrangement yet. "Never mind her dress. I'll handle the woman."

Chapter 8

Angela stared at the sand around her and absorbed its cool, damp touch. She turned her hands over and marveled at the white grains. With a finger, she pushed grains off, a swipe here and another swipe, and they sprinkled onto her lap.

Angela unzipped the pack at her waist and groaned. Her credit cards were full of sand. The ink on her club cards ran, and the paper disintegrated. Everything was ruined. She took out her cell phone, but even if for some reason a cell tower existed, her battery was dead. Or the saltwater ate it.

It felt real.

Wisconsin didn't have palm trees or oppressive humidity. There wasn't any minty colored saltwater. Wisconsin's beaches weren't white. She hadn't flown anywhere, and she was certain she didn't drive across the USA and wander without supplies into the jungle. She loved camping, but she wasn't reckless. Her skimpy pirate wench outfit, which she put on while standing in her apartment, was still on her body—now torn, crispy with the evaporated water, and scratchy with sand. But just as all this was clear, so was a sinking ship and saving the captain's life.

That felt real, but it couldn't be.

Years after Angela had been cast aside by both her families, Mom's replacement family struggled to deal with her new behaviors and begged Angela for help. Angela's mother had woven unbelievable tales of adventures she'd had during the night, and when Angela insisted they were just dreams, her mom lashed out. Then the sleep walking and blackouts started. The arguments over her safety morphed into fights.

After visits with specialists, Mom was diagnosed with dementia, and the blackouts and wild tales increased. Angela reluctantly toured skilled nursing facilities, dreading every step because Mom was too young for this. But her new family didn't have the emotional space or time to dedicate to her rapidly deteriorating condition. They couldn't keep her safe. Each facility was worse than the next, and Angela didn't have the heart to leave her mother in one. Angela offered to take Mom in, wanting to finally connect for the first time in years, to pick up where they'd left off and pretend the last two decades hadn't happened. A few days before she was ready to move in, Mom had an accident. And once again her mom had left her.

Please let this be real.

Angela could handle almost anything, but losing her mind scared her the most. Grains of sand glinted against the sunlight, and Angela shifted her legs just enough to catch the light and marvel at the sparkles.

The sparkles are real.

The sparkles are real.

The sparkles are real. Oh, please, be real.

DOWN IN THE COVE, Angela sat upright on the beach, right where he'd left her. After yesterday and last night, she must've been exhausted. As they all were, but they had a long day ahead of them. Extra long for Captain Price. With the crew moving along in their duties, but no imminent danger, they'd be calling for an answer. Price didn't have a satisfactory one to offer. As he closed the distance between them, Berger emerged from the jungle with an empty barrel and approached her.

Price broke into a jog on the soggy sand and reached her before anything serious happened.

"I knew it's bad luck to have a woman on board." Berger stood at her feet and spat on the sand. "Look at what you gone and done. You need to pay for all the damage you caused, woman."

Riley's assumption for the crew wanting Angela to work off her debts was dreadfully accurate. Price slowed his steps. "That's enough, Berger. Get back to work."

Berger spun on him. "And you, captain, steering us straight into Spain's territory like you have a wish for death. Liverman is right about you." With an angry glare, the shaggy-haired ingrate strolled down the beach with the barrel over a shoulder and spat into the water.

Price kept an eye on him until the man disappeared around the corner of the cove. Satisfied, Price sat on the sand next to her. "My apologies for him. The men aren't accustomed to women on board. In fact, it's against the rules."

Angela brushed sand off her hands, glassy eyes concentrating on her sandy legs, which Price found himself admiring. "Rules? A shipwreck and misogyny in my dreams. What'll I think up next?" Angela said with disbelief.

Price wasn't sure what that meant. "I owe you a great debt of gratitude, but at this moment, I find myself wondering the correct path I must take with you."

As if awakened from a daydream, Angela met his gaze and frowned. "What does that mean?"

"We have much more pressing concerns right now, but the crew is unsettled. They will want some satisfaction, and answering for a stowaway is how I can reunite the crew when I need them most focused."

"I'm not a stowaway. I don't know how I got on that ship."

Price believed her. "No boy or woman to be allowed amongst us. Any found are to suffer death," Price recited. "It's an agreement we all signed.

It prevents distractions and disgruntlement among the crew. And as you can see, your presence is causing precisely that. The quartermaster will have no choice but to ensure the rules are followed."

"Death?" Angela said with a pinch of disgust. "Isn't almost dying good enough punishment to them?"

"I'm afraid not." It was good enough for Price, though.

"Look at me!" Angela said, flinging her arms up in the air. "My cheap costume in a bag is shredded, my credit cards are full of sand and damaged by this sticky salty water. I still have my necklace, but it serves no purpose now. I need clothes, and I need to go home—with Emily. Where's Emily? Was she on that ship? Is she…dead?"

The wildness in her eyes and the rapid rise and fall of her ample chest made Price feel terrible for her state. He touched her hand and spoke softly, "I assure you, no such Emily went down with the ship."

"Then where is she?" Angela asked, terror in her beautiful brown eyes.

Price couldn't explain without risking everyone's safety, and right now he had a bigger problem—a broken ship on enemy territory. He craned his neck to keep watch for movement in the trees. Even if the crew managed to hide all the washed-up debris, the fresh markings on the sand would tell the locals they had company.

"I can help you, if you help me." It shamed him to make that offer, knowing a woman's hand should never have to do a man's labor, but he needed anyone able-bodied to help.

With a frown and a steely gaze, Angela said, "How?"

Price couldn't allow her to wander the hostile island alone—whether she searched for her friend or for a way home. Dealing with the inflexible and sometimes feral crew was still safer, as long as she stayed by Price's side. "That squall crippled our ship, and I lost many good men. If we cannot make repairs posthaste, we shall succumb to the enemy. I know how the crew will react over this. I blame them not; it's their nature. They might even challenge my captaincy, but I'm prepared to take that risk to protect you."

Her face twisted, and she shifted her body away from his. "Protect me? I don't need protection; I need a plane ticket. What is wrong with your company? I'm a customer, a *paying* customer. This reenactment stuff is...exhausting. I'm done. I've had enough. I need a shower. I need to get out of these ridiculous clothes. I have a shift on Monday, and I don't know if I can get home that fast. If I get fired over this..." Angela paused and studied his face. Some of the anger deflated. "You're serious. We're stranded here? Don't you have radios for the Coast Guard or something?"

"I don't understand." Just as he hadn't understood many of Emily Porter's actions and words.

"Explain to me why you can't call the head office for assistance," Angela said.

"If Spain discovers our presence in their territory, they will relish in seeing us swinging at the gallows. No company would move against the state, certainly not for us. There is no assistance out here. We help each other."

Angela snorted. "What company doesn't care about its employees? They have to maintain some liability insurance. You have a way with words that's so unusual. Did they teach you that in some acting school?"

Once again, her words baffled him. But if she questioned the crew in the same manner, she'd find herself with more attention than she'd prefer. Price had to remedy that risk. "It's not a school one learns to speak from. It's how one was raised."

"You were raised in England to speak like some lord duke guy?" Her brow lifted, a bit of amusement returned.

Price understood two of those descriptors. "Indeed...I wager?"

"Your family must be a hoot. I'm sorry." Angela sighed and looked up at the sky. "No reception out here in the middle of nowhere. And...no airports. Fine. What do you want from me?" Angela stood and her sharp heels sunk into the sand. Price attempted to assist her balance, but she crashed over too quickly and fell back onto the sand. Angela ripped off her boots and flung the curious things aside. She rose once again and brushed her dress and legs. "And if you say anything about me wearing less clothing or servicing or laying down or anything remotely like that—you can kiss my ass." Angela paused from her cleaning and looked Price in the eye. "But not literally. You know what I mean. Why can't I have normal dreams?"

Price climbed to his bare feet. Reception in a context that made no sense. Airports... Plane ticket... Reenactment... Radio... Words Price didn't understand. Captain Lemoine had told Price the unbelievable tale of the woman from the future who carried proof on her person. At the time, Price had worried about the mental state of his captain and brushed off such nonsense. But Angela was so different from anything familiar, except her stark similarity to Emily. And Angela's rants about things that couldn't be possible in his worldly travels only confirmed what he'd expected...and feared.

Angela Foxe was from the future, and she believed she was dreaming.

Suddenly curious of her life and everything the future had to offer, Price dared not scare her further. While he wanted to embrace her and reassure her everything would be fine, he couldn't. Price couldn't make that promise, and he didn't think she'd want his comfort. Instead, Price spoke honestly. "I understand how different this is for you, and I offer my apologies."

Angela's beautiful features softened. The urge to stroke her face and feel the softness of her skin under his fingertips was a powerful force he hadn't felt before. He wanted to touch those long dark waves cascading over her shoulders in wild loops.

"Apologies don't get us closer to home."

Something in her hair was curious. Price tilted his head and reached for it. "You seem to have some debris…what was this?" Price took the liberty of pulling a piece of metal from her hair—one side straight and the other lumpy. He pressed the blunt end into his fingertip. "I daresay, this is—"

"It's just a bobby pin." Angela snatched the curious thing from his hand and carelessly stuffed it back into her hair.

Price added that to the list of strange words. "If you help me get the *Sea Lion* back on the water, I promise you safe passage to whatever destination you choose."

"Fine. Time's ticking away, and I can't get fired." Angela marched down the beach, motivated by his promise. A small corner of his mind wished her motivation didn't come from the promise of leaving. But the idea of any other ending was preposterous. She was from a different world than him and keeping her alive would be a test like no other.

Price jogged to catch up, wanting to brace her for the site. McKee had been collecting bodies, and Price wasn't sure if the master gunner had collected Hayes yet. At the edge of the cove, he called, "Wait, I beg of you."

Angela stopped, facing the wreckage beyond the cove. She didn't move. She didn't speak.

Chapter 9

The ship, listed on its hull in the sand at low tide, was real as anything she'd seen. The storm, the sinking, that had to have been real. The tour ship with the reenactment crew was real. Angela believed none of that was a dream, but that only reinforced her concerns over her lucidity. Men worked tirelessly to untangle and repair the rigging and mend the sails. A hammer rhythmically pounded, slowly filling the giant hole in the hull. They used rugged hand tools. Salvaged materials. Angela frowned. What kind of modern company made their employees use old scraps for repairs? What company would abandon a ship full of employees? OSHA would have a field day with this.

The sunlight glinted on the water. Birds flew overhead. Just birds. Why hadn't a single plane flown by? Where were the motorboats? Container ships? Jet Skis? Judging by the palm-tree-shaped trees, they were somewhere tropical, which meant tourists should be noisy, littering, something.

A lump at the edge of the water, drifting with the gentle waves, caught her eye. Angela peered, squinting. It was human shaped with torn and stained clothing. It couldn't be... It wasn't... Was it?

"Is that a...?" Angela stepped closer. The pale drawn face with dead eyes made her jump back with a screech. "He's dead? Why hasn't anyone called the authorities? Where's EMS?" She gazed at the man's empty face. Where were the police?

Price stood at her shoulder and followed her gaze. He said softly, "This must be is confusing for you, because I know it is for me."

Angela gazed at him pointedly.

"I don't know what 'EMS' is."

How could he not know who the paramedics were? Angela studied the handsome man next to her. From bare toes and torn breeches to a hand sewn tunic and shaggy head of dark hair matted with sand. "What's the English version of EMS then? You know, paramedics."

Price only shook his head.

Could a poor sailor from England really never have heard of emergency medical services? He'd never seen or heard of a bobby pin either. How was it possible? "Cell phone? Jet Skis? Any of this ringing a bell?"

Price shook his head again.

Angela couldn't believe this. "You aren't from some isolated tribe in the middle of nowhere. You understand society. So how can you have no idea about technology?"

Price lit up. "I do have a few technological advancements." He faced his destroyed ship and his excitement fell. "I had...anyway."

Cautiously, Angela asked, "Like what?"

"Our last prize furnished us with a sextant. The men were ecstatic, as you can imagine. Navigation shall be so much more accurate now..." Price trailed off and looked at her face.

"Navigation? Like GPS?"

"I'm not familiar with that term."

"Global Positioning System. It uses satellites to track your position around the globe. Common for cars and boats to get where they need to go and not get lost." She felt like a jerk trying to school a grown man on basic foundations of society, but she couldn't believe his lack of knowledge.

Price just stared, completely dumbfounded.

There was no way this guy never heard of satellites. None of this made any sense. "So, you're telling me this whole lord duke guy captain persona and the penmanship in the captain's log are real? That ship *isn't* a tourist replica?" Asking the questions made her feel absolutely stupid, but she didn't know how else to bridge this disconnect between them.

"As you can touch me, I am authentic."

Angela knew she wasn't asleep. The lukewarm water and cool sand on her feet told her so. Her mom's hallucinations had always been grounded in reality. Angela's imagination was never this vivid or creative. Was she losing her mind? Or had something truly scientifically impossible occurred?

With a deep exhale, Angela steeled herself for the answer. Hesitantly, she reached out and pinched his fabric between her fingers. It felt real with every fiber of her being. She looked into his gorgeous blue eyes and pressed a palm to his heart. It beat rapidly, just like hers.

Captain Price pressed his hand over hers. Warmth penetrated her skin.

Death for simply being aboard. The men's outrage at her stowing away. No technology. The logbook. "Where am I?" she asked in a gentle whisper.

Price pressed his hand harder as if preparing her. "On the bank of Cuba in the Caribbean Sea."

There was a piece still missing, and she was crazy for asking. "When? What year is it?"

"The year of our lord, 1715."

Angela's knees gave out on her, and Price caught her with his strong grasp. He pulled her into a tight embrace, and she squeezed him back, face nestling at his collarbone. Angela's shoulders gently shook with quiet sobs of relief. None of this was a reenactment in real life or a dream from her uncreative mind.

Time travel was a farce, an impossible, with paradoxes preventing it from ever happening. It wasn't possible whatsoever. So, that meant

Angela had to be trapped in a sleep walking hallucination. She was losing her mind, just like her mom. No wonder her mom had been so adamant what she'd seen was real, because this was damned convincing.

It was real to her.

Angela closed her eyes, tightening her squeeze on his collar, relishing his touch, and Price's head rested against hers. He smelled of the sea and masculine sweat. And just as before, he felt like her anchor, like a flannel blanket wrapped snugly in front of a winter cabin's crackling fireplace, or a summer evening with butterflies dancing across the meadow, or an autumn breeze swirling red and yellow leaves across neighborhood lawns with pumpkin spice wafting through the air. He was comforting, relaxing.

After Brandon Spindleton tossed their relationship away like yesterday's news, she'd only wanted a commitment-free good time, never to be heartbroken again. Never to be rejected from her loved ones again. From what she'd seen of the captain, he was a gentleman, considerate and caring when he didn't have to be. The strong arms wrapped around her didn't feel like Brandon's. The soft sand under her feet didn't feel like the Persian rugs of his mother's estate. And yet, Angela pulled away from the captain's embrace, reluctantly, to double check the man before her was not Brandon and that she hadn't just hallucinated everything since the tragic wedding.

Angela rubbed her eyes and nose and looked at him again. Rough, rugged, tanned from hard labor in the sun. The opposite of Brandon. Could she have an affair with a hallucination?

With the way he looked...

Captain Price slipped something out of his pocket, and he held it out to her. "Does this help you?"

She accepted the shiny gold disk and turned it over. A coat of arms was stamped into the rudimentary coin. On the flip side were a series of letters and symbols. Nothing like anything she was familiar with. "It's not Lady Liberty."

"It's a Spanish piece of eight. This one was recovered from the treasure fleet that departed from this very island and wrecked near Florida a few weeks past."

Angela handed it back. She remembered Emily had mentioned something about a bunch of gold lost off the Florida coast, much of which had never been recovered. Angela was only half listening. History never interested her. She was paying attention now. This wasn't salvaged after centuries of sea water exposure. This was new. "You're certain that's the source of this coin?"

"Positively. I was there collecting it."

Angela blinked. She wasn't hallucinating either. She wasn't suffering from an early onset of her mom's disease. Then how the hell had she gone back in time? It simply wasn't possible. What was in the past didn't matter. The bigger concern was how was she going to get home? There were no cabs, no flights, no GPS, no phones....

On her wedding day, in head-to-toe exquisite chiffon and organza, Angela held her phone with an image that shattered her life. She remembered exactly what she'd thought at the time. Angela cackled.

"What is it?" Price asked gently.

"I wished I never saw another phone again in my life. When they say to be careful what you wish for, they mean it."

"Who's they?"

"I don't know." Angela studied his curious face. "Why didn't you ask me what a phone was, or GPS, or any of the other things I mentioned?"

Price shifted his weight and returned his attention to the ship, deflecting her question. "It matters not. We have a tide returning and a ship to fix. Are you up to the task?"

With terrible timing, Angela's stomach growled. She hadn't eaten since yesterday. Captain Price glanced at her, having heard it too, and he held out his arm like a gentleman. Angela embraced it, if for no other reason than she wanted to touch him, to keep herself grounded in this unbelievable reality. But instead of bringing her toward the ship, he brought her to the mouth of the cove. Just inside the dense vegetation, a hefty fellow had collected a circle of rocks, and above it, he'd whittled a spit.

Price dug in his pocket again and offered that same gold coin. "Giles, see if this will fetch a pig. Be discreet about it."

Giles the cook stood up and beamed, taking the coin. "Oh, this is plenty. Thank you, captain."

"Giles," the captain called after him, "see if you can find a set of clothing for the lady."

"And a set of boots for you both?"

Price nodded, and Giles headed out to shop.

"With that settled, we can get to work," Price said to her.

That piece, belonging in museum, was accepted currency, worth the cost of clothing and a pig at least. Angela had no concept of how valuable it really was. This world was fascinating, but as much as she loved to camp with Emily, Angela had her limits on the wildlife. She wanted to go home, and the longer they lingered, the longer it took. "What do you need me to do?"

The captain assessed the ship. "Can you wield a hammer?"

Angela smiled. "Finally, something I understand."

THE JAGGED HOLE IN the hull stood out like an eerie cavern warning them away. The scrawny man named Buckley, in desperate need of a barber, hammered mismatched pieces of wood into the gap, and Cantu, the size of a bulldozer, painted something black on the hull. Others were up in the ratlines, untangling and refastening the rigging, shouting orders to each other.

The quartermaster approached her and the captain with a broad smile, carrying a hammer. Angela figured him for the type of guy to be annoyingly happy in every circumstance, but considering where she stood, she'd take a little optimism.

"Status update, Riley? Where are we at?" Captain Price asked.

"Much of the hold is intact, but we lost all the tobacco and sugar, and we need a new cat."

"Cat?" Angela asked. Emily had said something about a cat being used to whip people as a punishment.

"Cantu says the little bugger scurried up the island shortly after the wreck. Damn resilient things, aren't they? But they're excellent mousers," Riley clarified.

Oh, he meant a real cat.

"If it were up to me, captain," the quartermaster continued, "we'd make all sign-ups and presses swim a quarter league. Our turnover rate would be much lower, I'd wager."

"Thank you for your council, Riley. I found us another hand to help." Price gestured at her.

Riley assessed Angela and frowned. She was used to working in a man-centric world, and she could handle what they threw at her, but she had to be careful in this barbarous world. If they threatened her, there was no police to come rescue her.

Quartermaster Riley shifted his body weight. "Captain, are you sure that's a wise idea?"

"We've discussed this already," Captain Price said.

"We have not discussed her joining our crew."

"She's only helping. There's nothing in the articles about helping."

"She's a woman," Riley said with a set jaw.

Seriously, this guy was insufferable. Being a woman didn't mean she was incapable. "I can help as well as any man."

The quartermaster's brows lifted. "Is that so?"

Angela nodded.

"Then you believe you can handle an angry pile of sailors?"

Concerned he meant what she was afraid he meant, Angela asked, "Handle them *how*?"

Riley leaned in close. "Prevent them from"—his eyes raked down her chest—"releasing...tension."

Angela snatched the hammer from his grip and leveled it on her shoulder like a baseball bat. She growled out, "Just try it. I dare you."

Riley backed up with palms open and brows lifted. "Message received." He turned to the captain. "I warned you. Whatever happens is your responsibility."

"Get back to work."

With a final glare, the quartermaster left.

"What did he warn you about?" she asked.

"It's been handled." The captain led her closer to the ship and shouted into the hull's hole, "Buckley!"

A general call of acknowledgment came from inside the hole.

Price added, "Need a hand?"

The lean man with a leathery face and black shoulder-length hair from the deck, who'd called her pretty, popped out of the hole. He grinned, displaying a missing tooth or two. "Anytime, captain."

"Excellent. Angela here will assist you in your repairs."

The smile fell from Buckley's face. "A woman? What is she going to do—knit me a scarf?"

Price sent her a knowing smile and backed up a step. "Not exactly."

Anger boiled beneath her skin. She didn't like her skills being questioned, and she despised feeling useless, but mostly she hated being treated inferior—as a plaything, a weakling to be dismissed. She pointed the hammer straight at Buckley and returned it to her shoulder in demonstration. "I can swing a hammer as well as any man."

Buckley howled with laughter. "All right then, lady. Climb aboard. Show me what's under that skirt."

Price touched her shoulder and whispered into her ear. "Thank you for doing this. Under ordinary circumstances, I wouldn't ask you to."

"I'm just as capable as them."

Price smiled. "In that case, Buckley is a hard worker and a critical asset on our ship, but be careful."

She didn't like that warning. "You aren't coming along?" Angela didn't want him to go. He was the only one she trusted.

"Riley and I will scout around to discover any nearby threats. You're in the hands of pirates who wouldn't cross me, but I do have a few agitators. Keep an eye out for Berger, Liverman, and Vallo." Price walked off after the quartermaster.

Did he say pirates? When Angela had first appeared in the hold, she'd thought the captain was a pirate re-enactor. Fake. For show to sell tickets. But Price had said no one would come to their assistance, because no one would move against the state, and if caught, they'd be swinging at the gallows.

They were pirates.

Buckley stuck his head out the hole and, with several nails between his lips, managed to say, "Lady, are you standing there or helping?" He leveled a rough-cut board into the hole. He struggled to press a nail to the board without it sliding.

To get off this island and find a way home, she had to help. They clearly needed it.

"Hold this here and clear your fingers," Buckley said.

Angela did as directed, and Buckley swung the hammer. He missed the nail several times.

"The captain seems like a nice guy." Angela fished for information. She had nothing better to do but occupy her thoughts.

"Nice? You'd call him 'nice'?" Buckley shrugged. "Such a bland word."

"Why do you say that?"

"I've known that man longer than any others on this ship, except for Lemoine, of course. But he's got himself a lady of his own and left us. Is that what you're planning to do? Steal our captain?"

"I want to go home." Somehow.

Buckley laughed. "Sure thing, lady." From a messy pile behind him, Buckley collected a board, checked its fit, returned it to the stack, and selected a different length. He seemed so...imprecise...to be a carpenter.

"Take your end, hold it snug there, and nail in your side."

"Where did you learn how to do this?"

"Do what?" Buckley hammered in his side, missing every third swing.

"Carpentry."

"Why do you ask?"

Angela's cheeks heated, but with the hole slowly filling, the lighting dimmed. "Just making conversation."

"Hmm. I was a carpenter's mate for years before my master died."

"Oh, I'm sorry. I didn't know."

"Ol' Gerow took a chain shot to the chest, but we captured a fancy prize that day." Angela stared at him, wide-eyed. "Then I stepped up to fill his shoes. Been doing it ever since."

"On the *Sea Lion*? This ship?"

"Of course! Where else would I be from? If I was pressed onto this ship, I would've gone off into those woods to escape once I touched land. No, lady, I'm here because I choose to be, and I won't leave this crew for anything. The sea is the life for me, and hunting is the freedom I need."

Angela cleared her throat, certain she heard wrong. "Excuse me, did you say 'hunting'?"

Buckley cackled. "You stowed away on a ship without checking the crew first? The *Sea Lion* is a vicious predator on the seas, taking what she wants and leaving behind a mess of destruction. Tales stretch from Boston to London and down to Barbados. Just between us, embellished tales only add to our cause. So, whatever you heard may or may not be true, but we never deny the story!"

Angela couldn't picture the captain as a vicious killer, a destroyer of ships and lives. It didn't match what she saw. "Tell me a story—a vicious story."

Buckley bent over the stack of boards and sifted through them. "We found a merchant ship owned by the Sea Trading Company. Overtook her with ease. Those guppies surrendered without a shot fired, which I admit is good for everyone involved. No one wants to careen for repairs when there're prizes to be hunted. Henry was the quartermaster then. We tied up their captain and captured all their remaining cargo. Captain Lemoine himself shot the captain and blew the ship to smithereens. That was more a tale of mercy. The merchant captain didn't suffer his wound for long."

"What about Captain Price? Any viciousness in his past?"

Buckley snorted and spat.

Angela fought a gag.

"If you consider his entire career, plenty. He followed the captain's orders, as we all did, but once he was voted into captaincy, Price has only one thing on his mind."

Curious beyond belief, Angela asked, "What is it?"

"William."

That was not what she expected. "Who's he?"

A shout from above stilled their hammers. The hole was half filled in, but daylight trickled in through many smaller cracks and breaks in the hull, and the stack of boards shrunk by the minute.

"Something's the matter. You best stay here."

In this darkened belly of a pirate ship with spit and who-knew-what-else rotting down here?

No way.

Chapter 10

ANGELA CLIMBED THE HULL, while carrying the hammer, following Buckley against his wishes. She would not be left behind if something happened, and being in the ship's bottom alone gave her the creeps.

Angela straddled the rail. The angled deck was asking her to tumble over and off the other side. With great care, she eased herself down and ducked out of sight. Price had warned her about the agitators, and after her last unpleasant encounter with them, she only wanted to find out if the wreck changed their opinions.

Several men crowded near the mainmast, shouting at each other with nasty scowls. She recognized Berger, Liverman, and Vallo, who, before the wreck, demanded her marooning, whatever that was.

This couldn't be good news.

"What's this about?" Buckley asked the men. "We're trying to work around here."

"The wench stole passage on this ship, but the captain wants her to join our crew like a man. What rubbish is that!" Liverman said.

Men murmured and nodded around him.

Join the crew? Angela only agreed to help fix the damage in exchange for safe passage. No way under any circumstances would she stay here—not with...*pirates.*

"She can hammer a board good as any man," Buckley said. "If you haven't noticed, we're in a bit of a pickle here. We've no time for blabbering."

A warmth of appreciation floated through her. Finally, someone got it.

"She deserves marooning," Berger said, and Liverman nodded smugly. "It's in the articles, *No woman aboard, and any caught are to suffer death.* But we can't maroon her until the ship is fixed. So, I say we pillage nearby towns top to bottom until all the recovered Spanish gold is ours. Spain took the time to recover it. Losing it a second time, at the hands of pirates, no less, shall sting so much worse."

"I'm with Buckley. Marooning her is a waste of breath if the ship's not repaired," McKee, the master gunner said.

"Don't you have more bodies to collect? I think Hayes is still floating down by the hull," Liverman countered. "If we don't abide the rules, we lose ourselves. What's the point of repairing the ship if we ain't a functional company any longer?"

Murmurs of agreement wove through the group.

Liverman continued, "For us to remain together and keep to the cause, I vote for marooning the wench. Row a longboat if we must! Unlike raiding a Spanish territory, Berger, dealing with the woman is both more amusing and less risk."

"I say we allow her to help repair the ship," their third cohort, Vallo said. "It was her cursed luck that caused the *Sea Lion* to kiss the rocks in the first place!"

"But as long as she stays in our presence, the worse our luck shall be!" Liverman countered. "We may as well blow the ship to smithereens then. At least we'd enjoy a show."

If ever there was an appropriate use for the phrase cutting off one's nose to spite their face, Liverman had it down. And since their opinions of her were both depressing and not going to change, Angela crept back toward the rail on silent bare feet.

"Until the captain and quartermaster return, I'm pulling rank here." Buckley said, squaring his shoulders. "That tide is licking our boots. Get back to work."

"Your rank?" Berger said, features darkening. "A scrawny old man? We follow Price and Riley because they can best us in a fight, and they made us promises. But those were broken when the woman was allowed to live. We don't take orders from you." Berger approached the carpenter with a menace on his face that made Angela flinch.

"There she is, the stowaway!" Vallo's finger pointed her out, turning the other angry heads in her direction.

Well, crap.

Buckley turned and frowned at her. The men stalked across the tilted deck like they'd just found their next meal. From Angela's camping experience, she knew the rules of safe wildlife encounters. Most animals were harmless. Squirrels and chipmunks tended to run up trees or down holes and squeak. Deer tended to freeze in fear and bolt away from danger if it approached. Others required more...finesse. In the case of territorial predators, their instincts to chase could be triggered if their prey ran.

Angela stood firm and kept her feet steady, channeling the deer's instincts to avoid a predatory chase.

Whether she'd listened to Buckley's orders to stay in the hull or not, the outcome wouldn't have changed. However, if she'd stayed, she could've run farther before they caught her. No sense dwelling on the past, but her future looked brighter if she had more of it.

"What's marooning?" Angela figured it was nothing good, but delay tactics were all she had.

"We row you out to a desolate spit of land with nary a lick of shade to protect you from exposure. You carry a pistol and shot, and we be generous in allowing three days' provisions," Berger said, encroaching too close.

"Then what?" Angela asked with a lump caught in her throat. She stepped back, on the verge of bolting herself.

"Then we row away." Berger motioned rowing in the air and laughed. Other men around her joined him in their fun.

Angela's mouth fell open. "You can't be serious."

"You broke the rules, you suffer the consequences, wench," Liverman said, closing in on her other side.

"I didn't stowaway!" Angela interrupted, furious at this insane treatment.

"You're off this ship, thief," Vallo said, taking her other side.

Angela stepped back again. A putrid stench reached her nose, reminding her of urine mixed with a mouth that hadn't seen a toothbrush in too many days. And here she thought children were filthy creatures.

"How about I pay for my ride?" Angela lifted the pendant around her neck from the Tall Ships vendor. Although it looked expensive, the amethyst jewel on a copper chain only set her back five bucks. "Take this in exchange for leaving me be."

"Is it valuable?" Vallo asked, eyeing it warily.

"Oh, very." Angela fibbed. "A family heirloom. But I'll give it to you *if* you leave me alone."

"If? Listen lady, if we want to take your valuables, we will, but a deal doesn't change the rules," Berger said.

"Taking valuables is an idea," Liverman said. "Maybe we sell her *and* that necklace instead of maroon her." The men turned to him in disbelief. "Don't go thinking I'm a fickle bastard. Just listen. If we sell her, then we all get a share of her. I know I want a piece."

"I want a share," Vallo said, stalking closer.

"Captain's not here to protect you," Liverman said, and his hungry eyes raked over her body.

Angela dropped the amethyst back against her chest, and she backed up until her butt bumped the rail. She smoothed her tattered skirt and squeezed the handle of the hammer.

Liverman smirked, oblivious to her stance. "She's not Puritan tail, lads, which is a shame, because I'd wager breaking her in would be—" Liverman paused, smirk sliding away.

Angela positioned the hammer over her shoulder, ready to swing. "Touch me, and you'll have a bad day."

Berger laughed in her face and spoke about her like she wasn't there. "She's just a woman. What harm can she do?"

Vallo stopped at her side. All three were within arm's reach, but she couldn't hit all of them at once.

"We have time to decide the desolate spit and fill the longboat with provisions. In the meantime, I'm claiming my share, too," Liverman said with a sinister grin. "We need to vote which man gets the first pump."

"That's enough!" Buckley shouted. "The sea is coming to claim this ship, and she don't care none who's on board. If we can't get her floating in a few hours, we'll be all stranded here another day with Spain lurking in that jungle. I've put up with a lot in my years, but never have my fellow sea dogs been so selfish. You've been hollering about rule breaking and demanding a just punishment, but you have no qualms about breaking your own: fornicating during the account is against the rules, too. Now get back to work, or I'm considering this an official quarrel to settle."

The three agitators turned on Buckley.

"One at a time," Buckley added, steadfast. "Duel to the death. The entire crew as witness."

Berger snarled and sized up the shorter man in a different light.

Buckley tilted his chin up. He was old, worn, and thin, but behind those experienced eyes, he had strength, quickness, and the skills—or at least the courage—to put his money where his mouth was.

"You're going to regret that, old man," Liverman said and pulled on Berger's arm. "Come on fellas. A ship is worthless with a hole in her side."

After darting her a nasty look, Vallo followed the other two. With the men diffused for now, Buckley returned to her side.

"One of these days I'm going to knock the bean off all those dirty dogs. In my days, you respected one another. We all agreed to the rules, but when situations changed, we adjusted. This rigidity they swear by is making them unruly, unfit for the sea." Buckley turned to her. "I don't believe in women on board either, but if one is useful, I take the help. Let's get back to work."

She was thankful someone cared enough to stand up to a group of men for her, and thankful the captain warned her of potential issues. Angela blinked back misty tears.

"Thank you."

"Eh, don't mention it." Buckley waved at the air dismissively.

Chapter 11

As much as Captain Price despised Berger, the man's venomous accusation had been accurate. *And you, captain, steering us straight into Spain's territory like you have a wish for death.* Whether he was brighter than Price believed or the man had questioned Hodgens didn't matter. Price had known the crew wouldn't accept the target he hunted. So, with a little luck from a squall, Price had brought them into Cuba.

Recently, a hurricane had brought down Spain's treasure fleet, and as word spread, pirates, privateers, and Spain herself scrambled to recover what they could.

"What exactly do you expect to find here, Price?" Riley asked as they pushed through the prickly nettles. Daylight would fade soon, but Price had to find it. He needed to know it was here.

"After the Florida wreck, Spain brought their recovered treasure back here, while they coordinated another attempt at a convoy across the Atlantic."

Riley stopped in his tracks. "You want to steal King Philip the fifth's gold right out from under his nose?" Riley approached him and whispered, "Have you lost your mind? Salvaging what we could from the sea is one thing, but sneaking into their territory to take it directly is something else entirely. The men would never agree to that."

Price smirked. "Good thing the squall brought us here."

"Convenient coincidence," Riley said dryly.

"If it's here, a guaranteed prize, they shall change their minds on the risk."

"We shall see," Riley said, and they continued their path through the jungle. Price winced at the prickles on his bare feet, wishing Hayes had worn bigger shoes.

Price needed a large enough prize and a solid win to convince the crew to follow him into a riskier venture, one which offered no compensation. A venture that had plagued Price for months. A venture so ingrained in his psyche, he couldn't quit the account until he'd completed it. Since the day Captain Lemoine resigned and the crew had chosen Price as their new leader, he'd thought of nothing else. The anticipation of seeing the man's shocked and fearful face as Price's cutlass pierced his flesh charged Price, drove his steps. That man deserved worse than a quick slaying, but Price was capable of mercy.

"And what of the woman?" Riley asked.

"What about her?"

"You want to take her along on a prize? See her get cut down by the enemy? Or leave her behind to fend for herself, unprotected?"

The fateful day Price had been given command of the *Sea Lion*, Lemoine had pulled him aside. Price eagerly awaited wisdom from the elder's vast experience on the ocean, but what he'd received softened the excited urges in his veins.

'The gold, silver, and gems make you believe there's this world out there where you can do anything and go anywhere, but after I met Emily, the real Emily, I learned everything I wanted was right before me. What good is enough silver to buy an estate? What good is enough gold to buy my own island? No jewels in all the world can buy the love, trust, and respect from a woman, and nothing else matters but her.'

'Congratulations, Eric. I wish you well,' Price had told him, a little disappointed.

'Thank you, my dear friend.'

Like Emily, Angela Foxe had magically appeared on the *Sea Lion*. Emily had changed Lemoine's life for the better. Price couldn't say the same for Angela. If she hadn't distracted him, they might not have wrecked at all. But if she *hadn't* been the cause of their wreck, Price would've died. Regardless, that beautiful and strange woman had saved his life. Was some force out there telling him to give up his perilous obligation? To see, as Lemoine had, what was right in front of him?

"She dropped out of the sky and saved my life like an angel." Regardless of her intentions, that was precisely what Angela was—an angel—and Price didn't believe in coincidence.

"She's an angel?" Riley asked with disbelief.

An angel in theory, not reality. Angela was a woman out of time and place, whose perfect arrival saved his life. Price tried to imagine leaving her alone in the camp, hoping locals or Spaniard scouts wouldn't discover her. Hoping she wouldn't go wandering, attempting to find Emily Porter or home by herself. Hoping she wouldn't hate him for making her stay behind, unprotected in this scary world. None of those possibilities, especially the last, could come to pass. "I have every intention of keeping her safe by my side."

"Then why isn't she here now?"

He had a point. "Scouting is dangerous. At this precise moment, she's safest with the crew."

Riley snorted.

"You disagree?" Price's insides swirled. Had he made a mistake? He trusted most of his crew. There were a few he certainly didn't, but he knew the others would keep those few in line.

Ignoring the worrisome thought, Riley asked, "What's that?"

Captain Price pushed aside a frond, revealing a beaten footpath. They were close. The hunt reignited the fire within his veins; excitement stirred afresh. Soon, very soon, that shocked and fearful face was coming.

A twig poked Price in the bare foot, and a shaking of his shoulder brought him from his thoughts.

"What was that? Did you hear it?" Riley asked.

Price was too busy daydreaming of what was to come. "Of what did it sound?"

"Voices and a rustling; men on the move."

Price leaned back on his haunches. Riley bent over his shoulder. Just ahead, two infantry soldiers of the Spanish Armada, wearing clean clothing and carrying muskets with bayonets, causally strolled together. They paced the beaten path for only one reason—they were guarding something, and the boredom on their faces meant they hadn't seen anyone of interest in a long while.

He and Riley retained the element of surprise.

"They aren't here to explore the sugar plantations. Should we take them down?" Riley asked in hushed tones.

"If they continue their course, they shall fall upon our camp and alert others. But if anyone finds their bodies, we shall be actively hunted."

Price trusted most of his men, heartily, to uphold their bond over the account, but if the enemy attacked, did he trust any of them to protect Angela? That was precisely why he wouldn't leave her behind. Suddenly, he wanted to return to camp and never leave her side again.

"So...is that a yea or nay?" Riley asked.

Price slipped a dagger out of its holster. Sometimes survival meant doing things he'd didn't much like. "On my count, we go."

Riley freed a dirk of his own.

As the Spaniard guards approached, Price gestured his countdown. On three, they rushed the men, clamped their hands over their unsuspecting mouths, and jabbed into the men's chests. When the fight drained from the guards, Price finished them off with a deep slice to the throats. Only gurgles and gasps remained. He and Riley dragged the men by their boots deeper into the underbrush and nettles to discourage discovery.

Price pulled a boot off the first man and tried it on. Way too big. He'd trip. Price cast it aside and removed one from the other man.

"What are you doing?" Riley asked.

"How would you like to traverse the jungle barefooted?"

Riley looked at Price's cut and bruised feet. "Do either of them fit?"

Price tossed aside the second boot. "That man has feet of an elephant, and these are too tight."

Riley held out a hand. "Give me the elephant sized boot and you try on mine. Then we'd both have loose boots. Better than you having none, and your vulnerability compromises our mission."

Price handed the quartermaster one of the castaway boots and Riley passed over his own. Price slipped it on, and it fit well enough. "Does it work for you?"

"I must have elephantine feet. I'll wear these." Riley bent and removed the other boot from the soldier.

Price accepted Riley's other and slipped it over his sore foot. He removed the muskets and handed one to his quartermaster while slinging the second over his shoulder. "Much better. Let us keep moving. We're getting close."

Despite being deep into enemy territory, Price continued to feel the pull of returning to Angela's side. Was she safe now? Had other scouts discovered their camp, regardless? The distraction was frustrating. "Riley? Do you have someone back home?"

"Me? No. I had a bride, but it never came to pass."

"What happened?" Price asked.

"Well"—Riley ducked under a swinging branch—"I suppose it depends upon who you ask. My betrothed might say I was the biggest mistake of her life. My father might say I was an imbecile."

Price chuckled.

"But no matter their opinions, her death still haunts me."

"I'm sorry for your loss, mate. I know how hard it is to lose someone you love." Price sighed.

"William?" Riley assumed.

The pain of losing William Price, his older brother, was so great, he'd locked the pain away in the deep fathoms of his heart, fearing its devastating return someday. Not even for Noah Riley would he go diving into those memories. Price had to stay focused on what mattered. "Yea."

The quartermaster must've picked up on his despairing tone, and he changed the subject. "What about you? Any beauty awaiting your arms back home?"

"There's no one for me. Never was." Angela's stunning face and the luck between Emily and Lemoine flashed before him. He swatted it away and kept his feet moving.

A skittering came from nearby. They stopped and listened. The light pattering paused and continued in a direction leading away. Not human. "Likely some critter."

The evening light faded until their eyes struggled to see.

"Why not?" Riley asked, continuing the riveting conversation Price didn't want to have. "You're a strapping captain of virile strength and age, and I'm sure any lady would be thrilled to share your bed."

Price grunted.

Riley waited.

Price sighed again. "When I became of age, I followed my brother into the Royal Navy. My only access to the fairer sex was at port, so I never allowed myself to get attached, and after what happened to William, I didn't have the desire to become attached to anyone again."

"What happened to your brother?"

Riley should know the story. Price needed someone sympathetic to their dangerous mission. "Spain happened."

After a beat, Riley said, "Cryptic as usual."

"You didn't allow me to finish."

"You're too slow, old man," Riley said in jest.

"Old? You're calling me 'old'? Have you no consideration that I'm you ten years in the future?" Price asked, playfully.

Riley beamed. "Precisely. Old."

Price groaned. "*Capitán* Delgado of the *Peibo del ler San Francisco* happened. In short, my brother sacrificed himself so we could escape. Quite genius how he did it, but still, it angers me greatly. So when the *Peibo del ler San Francisco* arrives to convoy the gold, I'll be personally delivering the Spaniards a message."

The quartermaster asked, "You're certain the *Peibo del*-something is headed this way?"

"I made sure of it."

"A convenient coincid—" Riley cut off again with Price's gesture.

A muted murmuring stilled Price's steps. Both men ducked low, and Price brushed aside prickly brambles. A trio of Spaniard guards sat around a table, playing cards by lantern. They spoke to each other. Behind them was a hut made of fronds with no light glowing.

"Do you understand them?" Riley whispered.

"No." Price didn't speak Spanish, and all attempts to learn were met with his steadfast grudge, a bitter pill he couldn't bring himself to choke down.

"How many do you think there are?"

"Appears to be just the three, unless more are sleeping in the hut."

"What are they guarding?"

"Something worth at least five men's lives." With only three left so far, Price liked those odds.

Price rose and, keeping low, gave a wide berth to the hut. A twig snapped and branches rustled behind him. Price turned and scowled at Riley, but the jungle canopy overhead shrouded his disapproval.

The trio of men paused their game and tilted their heads, listening.

"*¿Es una ardilla, no?*" the first guard asked the other two.

"*Probablemente,*" one man answered with boredom on his tongue.

"*¿Debemos ir a buscar?*" the first guard asked. He sounded nervous. Although Price didn't know what they were saying, he understood they heard Riley's noise and one wanted to investigate. Price leaned lower and waited.

"*No. Juguemos a las cartas. Es más divertido.*" The third guard responded.

Price understood 'no.' When the next player dropped a card on the table, Price crept forward. He waved behind him for Riley to follow. Step by step they circled around to the back of the hut and closed the distance. A small clearing opened the space, leaving their approach easier but also more vulnerable.

"Move quick. Any sound this close will get them moving."

Riley followed, and without disruption, they reached the hut's back wall. The windows were too high to peer inside.

Price knitted his fingers together into a foothold. "Step up."

Riley placed his foot in Price's clasped hands, and Price lifted with all his might—stifling a grunt. His arms shook as he held the man in place long enough for him to see the contents.

Price's hands burned from the strain. "Hurry, Riley."

The quartermaster bent at the knee and dropped himself down. Price brushed off his hands and panted. "What did you see?"

"Chests. Many chests. Only one is open, but it's full of gold coins."

A flutter of excitement tore through Price. "You're certain?"

"Completely."

"Let's return to camp. The crew shall be excited with the news."

As Price led their retreat, relief washed through him. After all these years, the perfect circumstances were within his grasp. All he had to do was lay out the perfect bribe.

Chapter 12

Despite her broken family and her mom's cognitive decline, Angela had been a glass-half-full kind of woman, who had plenty to look forward to. And even on bad days, she had no trouble finding the ray of light on a steaming pile of manure. But after the biggest embarrassing public shame of her life, Angela had realized she was forty years old, single, living in an apartment, and working a job she liked but received so much flak for she questioned her own judgment. Her optimism had taken the first bus out of town.

And ever since she'd appeared in this hostile world, she struggled hard to recapture that ray of light. Everywhere she turned was manure. Until now. The sea water had rinsed the putrid stench out of the hull. Angela's lips pulled into a soft smile. Her ray of light was returning...because of poop. And an embarrassingly low bar.

She had to start somewhere, right?

But she worried for Captain Price, who had been gone nearly all day. Was he wandering lost in the jungle? Was he held captive by locals? Was he injured and stuck somewhere? Price was the only barrier between her and the crew's filthy mitts. If they lost him, she lost herself. That wasn't the only reason she didn't want to see him hurt. Angela's judgment had always been crap, clearly, so she questioned it more thoroughly in regards to the captain. They'd shared a moment on the beach, her hand on his chest, and for just a second, she wondered if there could be something between them.

Footsteps creaked behind her. Buckley and Cantu carried the hefty final board down into the hull. With cold, sodden bare feet knee-deep in water, Angela held a candle for them, the only light permitted with Spain lurking about.

Buckley squatted down near the hole, where seawater gushed in, and he shifted the board over his head and into position with Cantu's help. "We had one last replacement board on the orlop deck. If we get this secured, we need to drop anchor. Otherwise she'll be adrift with no crew or supplies when the tide claims her. Hold here."

Cantu kneeled next to the carpenter, and Angela leaned to give them better light.

"If we don't get this blasted piece of—" Buckley trailed off in unintelligible grunts while the men pushed the board against the rushing water. After a day observing Buckley's carpentry skills, hammering nails in the best of circumstances was a challenge.

"Hold it there," Buckley said. "Light closer."

Angela reached the candle out further. The rigging wasn't fully functional yet, but they could escape as it was—assuming they had crew and supplies, of course. The hull had several smaller breaks and leaks in the boards, but Buckley had said the bilge pumps could keep up.

Angela was exhausted, sticky, and tired of being in the sun and eaten alive by bugs. Even when she'd camped with Emily, they'd had a bug-free tent and an air mattress. They'd rested on the beach under shade from massive trees.

There was no rest here.

Not with three men plotting against her. Or Buckley's inaccurate hammering. He swung and missed, spraying water in their faces. The candle flickered and hissed. The carpenter swore as nails dropped into the water. He blindly reached around in the water and made a noise of celebration while lifting two.

"Shall I hammer the board?" Cantu asked.

Buckley made a dismissive noise. "I've been doing this longer than you've been alive. Now, if you do yours, mine shall be easier. Press harder."

Cantu's brows furrowed, but from the shifting biceps in his massive arms, he did exactly that.

Angela's outstretched arm shook with exhaustion.

Buckley's words were punctuated by his hammering. "As I was saying, if we don't get this board into position, we're trapped here another day. It's too dangerous to sit here like ducks. We need to be minimally functional and get the hell out of here." The hammer swung again and again, leaving Angela wishing for painkillers. She tilted her ear against her shoulder and used her free hand to plug her eardrum. Angela closed her eyes and pictured what or where she would be happy...and immediately opened them.

She needed Price to return before they left, or she was going after him.

THE CAMPFIRE CRACKLED IN the woods, disguised by thick vegetation near the cove, and shrouded by supply crates. Giles turned a crispy pig on the spit, and it smelled like the finest all-you-can-eat buffet. Angela's stomach growled again. The other men broke into various smaller groups to socialize. Buckley stayed near Angela, rustling in the supply crates behind them, because the captain and quartermaster still hadn't returned yet.

The clothing Giles had brought her was certainly less itchy than the shredded polyester costume in a bag, but a shapeless cotton tunic and baggy breeches weren't high up on her list of comfort either. But, she was thankful for non-heeled boots.

"Tie this around you. Should help ya hold them up." Buckley gave her a small length of rope to help cinch her breeches where they belonged. It wasn't awesome, but it would do until she got home.

"Thanks."

"Time to eat. Pass the plates around." Giles held out a serving of steaming meat on a plate, and around the group it passed until the furthest man had his share. Around and around the meat went until finally, Angela had her ration. Ignoring where the plates had last been—in the galley with putrid water running down the decks—and if they'd ever been washed with soap, Angela's empty stomach overrode her brain's hesitation. Juice ran down her fingers and she licked them clean. The men around her softened their stories to murmurs, since they, too, were consumed with feasting.

Angela couldn't help but notice the strong cliques among the crew, not unlike high school—a rite of passage so long ago she'd rather completely forget. Her mother's cheating, and subsequent divorce, were the taboo subject at school. And she'd thought she'd escaped the gossip of her sleepy small town.

The three agitators, as Price had called them, with their ugly looks over their shoulders and the hushed whispering, only reminded her of those scarred years she'd buried ages ago. She was too tired to confront them, and with the captain still gone, she needed to be careful. These men were only on their best behavior because of Buckley and Cantu's respect for the captain.

What if Price never returned? Angela ate faster. She was not emotionally eating. Nope. She just hadn't eaten a meal in two days, so pigging out was completely normal. No emotional eating here.

After clearing her plate before any of the men, Angela was granted seconds. Giles filled her plate, and Angela thanked him profusely.

Cantu sat on the crate next to her. "Can't say I ever saw a woman eat so much."

"I'm starving. Haven't eaten since yesterday."

"Huh. The captain must find you quite agreeable. I'm not sure I see it myself…"

Angela glared at his gentle insult, and Cantu bit off a hunk of meat and chewed, glancing away as if avoiding the repercussions of that statement. A warmth rushed through her at the thought of the captain liking her, and immediately, she dashed those feelings away.

Price was a pirate, a thief, a scoundrel, someone with lower-than-average morals. And not only that—he led a whole crew of them! The last type of man she'd trust with her heart. After Brandon's public betrayal and her father's complete rejection of her, and numerous less-important boyfriends, Angela was just done with any commitment. And in fact, men altogether.

Cantu swallowed and said, "I only mean I don't see what caused the change of heart."

Despite her unreliable judgment, curiosity got the better of her. "Why do you say that?"

"The last time we had a woman on board, it was Price who insisted on marooning her. So I'm surprised he stood in your defense."

"*Why* did Price want her marooned?"

Cantu spoke with his mouth full. "For stowing away, of course. It's in the rules."

"Then why not me, too? Not that I'm volunteering or anything. I'm just wondering."

"That is the question on everyone's mind." Cantu said.

Did Price want something from her? Did he want to use her for something? A pawn against the agitators? Or was Cantu right—the captain just liked her?

Regardless of her own misplaced feelings, the last one was the hardest to believe. The sooner they fixed the ship, and Price brought her to safety as agreed, she was going home.

Somehow.

At a knock on his door, Marcos would fix her a fabulous martini, and join her and Emily in swapping man-bashing stories. Where was Emily? An empty hole in her heart ached at not knowing where her best friend was.

Chapter 13

A RUSTLING IN THE woods nearby quieted down the murmurs of conversations. Branches swayed and cracked. Twigs broke. Everyone turned, facing the sound, and set down their plates. As one, they placed their hands near their weapons. The pork in her stomach sloshed nervously.

Buckley rose from a crate and spoke up. "Arms raised if you want to live."

Buckley and Cantu, like the others, prepared for a fight. Angela set down her plate and wiped her mouth. She had a hammer. As long as the enemy hadn't brought pistols, she had a chance. Angela gripped the handle, oily fingers slipping. She ground her palms against her rough breeches to clean the grease off and find a better grip. With her heart thundering in her ears, Captain Price emerged from the bushes and raised his hands. Riley was just behind him.

"It's us, Buckley. Stand down."

Angela exhaled in relief. She set down the hammer and cleaned her face. Most of the crew smiled and softly cheered his return. The agitators, Berger, Liverman, and Vallo, frowned and turned back to themselves.

Angela's heart fluttered and beat faster, waiting for the captain to seek her out. Price and Riley shook hands with a few of the men and everyone resettled by the fire.

Finally, Price met Angela's gaze. She silently communicated her relief, and she could swear he had been worried for her, too. Angela rubbed her hands on her breeches again and stroked her unruly curls into place. Heat flustered her movements. She pictured herself tackling him and planting a needy kiss on his soft lips. More heat rushed through her. No need for a furnace tonight. Angela wanted to fan her tunic again, but that would make her state obvious.

Holding her fiery gaze, Price said, "Glad to see you in one piece, Angela. Did these old salts treat you well?"

Berger, Liverman, and Vallo cast her an ugly stare, but she wasn't going to let them push her around. She returned a grimace at them. "Most were great."

The three agitators mumbled to themselves, coming to some decision. Berger stood and approached the captain, fury on his furrowed brow. "This is an outrage!" He pointed at her. "She's a hypocrite!"

"How so?" Price asked calmly.

Angela was quite curious herself.

"She pretends to be one of us, keeping quiet on the goings on while you're away, but she stole passage from us. A woman on board is bad luck. She doesn't belong 'ere any longer, and we're overdue in giving 'er just punishment."

"Who else among you believes the same?" Price skimmed the group, but he avoided her gaze.

Vallo and Liverman joined Berger, no surprise there. Giles set down his servingware and stood. Angela's lips parted in horror. The cook treated her kindly! She never guessed his revulsion for her. Giles shifted his weight toward the captain, and Angela exhaled in relief.

"The young lady has done nothing wrong," Giles said. "Having a woman on board is a pleasant change of scenery."

At this visual vote, Cantu and Buckley joined the captain's side. Boatswain Karl Dillon, Hodgens the helmsman, and the master gunner McKee followed on their heels. Angela couldn't help a warmth of appreciation. These men, friends of the captain, not only treated her well, but cared enough to stick their necks out for her. She fought a mist at her eyes.

The rest of the crew, many she hadn't been introduced to, split evenly. A lump formed in her throat. Half the men wanted to harm her.

"Having a woman on board is dangerous for all of us! It divides us. It distracts us. It destroys us," Berger said. With the extra support behind him, his claims became bolder. "She's the cause of the ship sinking—a bad omen, a witch. What'll she do next?"

"What shall it take to make you agreeable, Berger? Liverman, you and Vallo, too?" the captain asked, scratching at his jaw.

"We stick to the rules," Liverman said. "Maroon the wench."

Vallo nodded.

The captain glared at the men supporting Berger. They exchanged wary glances, as if uncertain of their chosen position.

"Well," the captain chuckled. "Unless you see fit to row her to a desolate piece of land yourself, to entertain that idea requires her to join us once again upon the *Sea Lion*."

"Then we leave 'er 'ere," Berger said. "Spain shall dispatch 'er in no time."

Murmurs of agreement came from behind him.

"Is that your final answer, all of you? Leave her here to fend for herself against Spain?"

Vallo looked to the others before nodding. Liverman crossed his arms over his chest, and Berger stepped forward. "She takes provisions for one day, no pistol or shot, and walks. Never to return, and never to step foot on our ship."

Price and Riley exchanged looks, but Angela couldn't guess what was unspoken between them.

How was Angela going to survive on an island full of hostile people? These men spoke English, and they were hard enough to understand. She couldn't imagine Spanish from 1715 was any better. Her small weekend camping trips with Emily meant pop-up tents, groceries, cookware, a vehicle, and several changes of clothes. She wasn't some rugged survivalist, a doomsday prepper with years of supplies. And even if she could capture an animal—and stomached having to kill it—she didn't know how to clean it. And how would she cook it? Angela shivered.

Riley stepped forward. "If both parties cannot come to an agreement, then the rules state the dispute is settled with a dual. Are you both prepared for this?"

The captain stepped toward Berger, shoulders squared and chin up. Her life was literally in Captain Price's hands. She'd rather something else be in his hands, but clearly, not all wishes came true.

"Victor chooses the fate of the woman," the captain said, face drawn in silent fury.

"Victor is breaking the rules," Berger countered. "Then this dual is to the death, not first blood. Winner decides the fate of the woman and earns the captaincy."

"Agreed," Captain Price said.

Angela's mouth popped open. She had never felt more helpless in her life. If Price died, she would be crushed under the worst guilt imaginable. His death would be on her hands, and she could never forgive herself for it. To make this worse—she would be abandoned on this island to die herself, alone. The thought was so terrifying, she couldn't breathe. The only connection she had would be torn from her. As much as she wanted to trust Price's confidence, she had no idea of his capabilities in a fight. Angela leaned over and gripped the hammer. If she was going to be thrown away like yesterday's trash, she was going to fight on her way out. Her hands trembled.

The captain's eyes tracked her movements with the hammer. "Are you worried, my lady?"

Heat rose to her cheeks, both at his confidence and his term of endearment. "I prefer to be prepared. That's all."

Price grinned, easing the butterflies walloping each other in her stomach.

Berger snorted. "When I win, *my lady*," he mocked, "that hammer won't stop me or my men."

Vallo and Liverman snickered.

"Then all parties are in agreement with the terms," Riley said and sent a dark look at the captain before backing to a safe distance.

None of the crew on the captain's side spoke up. That wasn't reassuring.

The captain drew a sword and Berger copied, while the rest of the crew backed away, leaving ample space to avoid collateral damage. The fire crackled, and golden light flickered across the angry men's faces. Only one would survive the fight.

"On my count, begin." Riley counted down from three, and the swords crashed together with a sharp clang. Both cutlasses withdrew and crashed again and again. Angela flinched with each strike. Firelight glinted against the sharp blades. The captain dodged a swipe from Berger, stepped forward, and swung. His opponent leaped back, but a slice ripped open Berger's shirt. The swords locked, and the men's faces pulled close, straining in hate and fury.

Berger flung himself back and dodged the captain's strike again. The agitator rolled forward, kicking up sand. With an arc of his blade, he struck the captain, who tumbled backward to the ground, fist pressed to his chest.

Angela gasped and hugged the hammer. It wasn't over. It couldn't be over just like that.

The crew shouted at each other. The anger from both sides brought tears to her eyes. This was all her fault. The captain's impending death, the destruction of the crew, the destroyed ship and all the lives lost. If she hadn't come here, they would still be sailing the seas as one—focused, committed, and not distracted by her.

Angela wanted to run away, to save them from this horror, and to save herself the deep guilt of having caused it all. But the captain was on the ground, and Berger accepted congratulations from his side of the crew.

They considered it over. Angela squeezed the hammer. She should use the upper hand to her advantage and take out Berger. Maybe she'd earn enough respect to be left alone—to die in peace somewhere lost on this island. But she couldn't leave the man who'd saved her and treated her with utmost respect. She swiped away the tears blurring her vision. Wanting desperately to rush to his side, but not risking a deviation in Berger's attention.

Berger holstered his blade to pats on the back. One by one, Berger's half of the crew approached her with snarls of hate. Angela squeezed the hammer. In the storm, she knew she couldn't take on three men with her hammer. Now she certainly couldn't take on a dozen. Angela met Buckley and Cantu's eyes, silently pleading for help.

They gazed at the fire.

Price's half didn't come to stop them. The dual was final, and the terms were set in stone. She was to be left behind, but the looks on their faces meant they wouldn't leave her in peace.

The captain shifted on the ground. Angela only spared him a glance, so the others wouldn't be tipped off. And no one else paid him attention. It wasn't over.

"As much as your presence tore this crew apart," Berger said, now pulling ahead of his men as if he deserved dibs, "I have to thank you. I'm the captain now, and I'll take my congratulations the proper way."

The men behind him chuckled in a way that churned her gut.

Liverman shouted, "On your knees, wench!"

Another said, "I only want her mouth. You dirty dogs can have her other holes."

The chuckles returned.

"Buckley? Cantu?" she found her voice—softer and less commanding than she was used to.

"Rules are rules," Buckley said with the shrug, failing to look her in the eye. "Sorry, ma'am."

Riley said, "Captain's orders are followed. Berger won the duel, so his rule goes."

Angela couldn't believe they'd be this barbaric. Where was their humanity, and how the hell did Emily admire these bastards? "You can't be serious! I didn't do anything to you, and I certainly didn't ask for this." Angela swatted the filthy paws reaching out to her.

"It's what we all signed," Cantu added, turning away like he was unable to watch what happened next.

"Let it be known! As captain, I'm making changes. Our last rule, *no boy or woman to be allowed amongst them. If any man were found seducing any of the latter sex, and carried her to sea, disguised, she was to suffer death.* While *seducing* is still forbidden..." Berger trailed off to build suspense. The men paused, a little confused while waiting for the announcement. "All the sex you want is acceptable by all hands at any time unless in battle."

The men chuckled and hollered their appreciation, and when their short celebration was over, they approached like wolves to their prey. Playing deer would no longer work.

"Leave me alone!" Angela pleaded softly.

They didn't.

Chapter 14

Price's vision returned, fuzzy at first, and then clearer. Where was he? What happened? Searing heat stung across arms and sides. Warm liquid drizzled down his skin.

The fight.

Price moved his sword arm, still gripping his weapon firmly. The cuts were not fatal, but if he didn't breathe soon, it would matter naught. His lungs felt deflated, like a hefty weight pressed against his chest, and no matter his struggle to inhale, they would not cooperate.

His head pounded, and a spot on the back of his skull raged in pain. Price flinched and shifted, landing his wounded head on the soft sand. Minor relief.

The air wouldn't come.

His lungs felt afire. This was the end. He'd been bested by an opponent sure of foot and quick of eye, a fierce competitor. Price did not expect this outcome. He'd failed avenging his brother. He'd failed his crew. But most of all, he'd failed Angela. His promise to her was broken. What was the value of a man without trust in his word?

Half his sworn crew, bound by the articles, suddenly threw away all they'd agreed to, surrendering to their libidos. They intended to defile the woman in a way that made his blood curdle.

He'd gone from boy following his brother, to a man thrusting headfirst into the life he'd dreamed of, to a man broken by loss. Of all the things he could've imagined accomplishing, the one regret plaguing him at this moment was his failure to find a woman who loved him. He'd never know the loyalty, trust, and respect of a woman warm in his bed. Someone to share his dreams and fears, who wanted to be with him. Someone he could devote his life to. Someone like...Angela.

The revelation surprised him.

Anger at his failure, at Berger's threats on the other side of the campfire, and the cackles of the animals around her, lit a fire within. His lungs inflated with a deep gasp of air.

It wasn't too late for him to take back control, realign the crew, and rescue the woman he found himself dreaming of.

Even if he couldn't keep her.

From the tips of the toes to the hairs on his head, an energy surged through him like a hurricane's swell.

Angela needed saving. Angela needed him.

Price climbed to his feet and rubbed the back of his aching head while stalking closer to his usurper.

Berger pushed her closer to the fire. Heat scorched her skin. The other men untied their breeches, cackling like drunken frat guys and arguing over their position in line. Angela didn't know how to avoid the inevitable.

The captain's sword shifted in the air, and Price slowly climbed to his feet. He rubbed the back of his head and checked his bleeding chest wound. The crew was too busy with her to notice, and she declined to alert them. His presence was the only thing keeping her level-headed—she wasn't alone against all these animals.

Berger approached her, scowling, and he squeezed her arm.

"Let me go!" she shouted, twisting out of Berger's grip.

Another man locked on her arm in an instant, freezing her in place. A third man squeezed the nape of her neck.

Price moved closer, cracking his neck, sword positioned to strike.

Angela squeezed her hammer and swung at the man holding her arm. He took a bruising thump to the thigh and released her. Others backed up, except for the one clamped on her neck.

"Get off of me!" Angela swung the hammer behind her.

The cackling captor caught her wrist and squeezed. "On your knees, where you belong."

Angela dropped the hammer, yelping in pain.

Price stood behind Berger and leveled the sword at the back of the man's neck. "Next time you believe you're the victor, check your opponent, for it could cost your life."

The color drained from Berger's face. His lips parted, and his eyes widened. Lifting his hands in surrender, he turned to face the captain.

The half of the crew in support of Price smirked but didn't move to assist. Jerks. The other half released their predatory postures, and the man clamping on her neck released her.

"Be that as it may, the duel is not over." Berger parried the blade away from his throat and performed a duck and roll maneuver. Leaping back to his feet, he unsheathed his sword in challenge. "So let us finish this. I have more important business now."

With eyes on Berger, Angela discreetly collected her hammer with a firm grip. The captor behind her noticed her movement and fastened his hand on the nape of her neck again. Gritting her teeth, Angela swung hard at the man, impacting his abdomen. With a grunt, the captor folded and fell to his knees.

Another man grabbed her arm. "Try that again and you won't see daylight before each of us has a turn with you." He moved to take the weapon from her, but Angela swung it at his hand and quickly adjusted to swing at his head. The creep ducked, and Angela kicked him in the crotch.

The man folded and fell to the sand. Anger flashed across his beat red face, and Berger's other supporters surrounded her, ready to take their turn in subduing her, as if she'd challenged their manhood.

The captain and Berger circled and struck, blades swooping and crashing through the air. The captain couldn't help her now. But knowing he was on his feet empowered her. She wouldn't give up.

Angela lifted the hammer over her shoulder. Her stomach swirled with nerves, and her hands shook with the adrenaline, but pretending to be strong was a better choice than showing her fear. She had nothing else to lose. "Who's next?"

Three of the agitators cackled. Liverman said, "Did you hear that, fellas? The wench wants a fight!"

Price's supporters whispered to themselves, a quiet argument with hands moving.

"I'll take a fight with her. Sounds like a good time to me." A filthy miscreant grinned, missing half his teeth, giving her the impression the man didn't usually win those fights. Not that she was willing to place bets right now.

Quartermaster Riley led the group of Price's supporters, and they surrounded the agitators. "All of you, keep your hands off the woman or lose your fingers."

Several of the men turned to the threat with scowls twisting their features. Cantu towered over Liverman, and the instigator leaned around the bigger man to see the status between Berger and the captain. Both men suffered bleeding cuts and torn clothing. Both panted heavily, exhaustion haunting them. No matter the outcome, the fight was certain to end soon.

The crew opposing the captain shared glances and shrugs, an internal war waging over whether to comply or rebuff.

"We were a crew once," Cantu added. "A trustworthy crew bound by a single goal: claiming freedom for ourselves. And now we're split even, fighting each other, when never has there been a time when we need to stay together more. How can we trust you aboard the *Sea Lion*? But neither can we sail without you. Drop this crusade you're on now or we will find a new crew."

Liverman chuckled nervously. "You don't scare us."

"I'm only trying to delay you."

Liverman cocked his head in confusion.

A gargling groan came from behind them, followed by a thud. The statuesque Cantu smiled, and the divided crew turned to see the outcome. Angela's heart caught in her throat. She pushed through the men, still gripping the hammer, and stopped short.

Captain Price kneeled on the sand, head hung low, blood smeared all over him. Berger's body rested in the sand at the awkward angle he fell. The captain wiped his face with his forearm and climbed to his feet.

Price wiped his sword on Berger's body and sheathed it. Casually, he strolled around the fire and faced Angela. Heat rushed through her body as he stood only a foot from her. She wanted to embrace him, treat his wounds, care for him. Seeing him in pain hurt her. Tears pricked her eyes. Not only had he survived, but he'd suffered on her account, and now she would be saved a fate worse than death.

The captain cleared his throat.

STANDING SO CLOSE TO her, Price's heart thundered in his ears, but he regretted not a second of his decision to challenge Berger. Had he known he'd win? Berger had far more agility and immature confidence, but Price had cunning and patience. In essence, no, Price wasn't certain he'd win, but he had been certain he couldn't leave Angela in danger, and that had been the only solution.

"All those who dissented from my leadership, leave immediately," Price said, addressing half the crew while gazing into Angela's beautiful brown eyes. She was afraid, but there was relief and perhaps a dash of lush in there.

Desire and need flooded his veins, but he couldn't kiss her. Not like this. Not in front of the crew. He'd lose his authority in a flash—no matter what his triumph proved.

The men glanced at each other, as if unwilling to think for themselves, and no one moved.

Price gritted his teeth. Half this crew betrayed his leadership, and now that they'd lost, these men were too cowardly to uphold their position of dissent. "You'll be allowed safe exit from the area, and no one will hunt you down. Go. If you don't want to be on my crew, I don't want you either."

Buckley and Cantu stared down Liverman and Vallo, but still no one moved or spoke.

Price addressed his most frustrating men. "Liverman, Vallo? Anything to say on your own behalf?"

"If it pleases the captain, I shall stay on the crew," Liverman said, toeing the sand and keeping his eyes down.

It certainly didn't, but Price needed men to sail the ship, and there were no guarantees he would find suitable replacements on this island. "Agreed. Vallo?"

"I'll remain as well," Vallo said, as Price expected. The quiet man may have been one of the agitators in the crew, but that was his job, and Price was convinced of his loyalty.

"Anyone else want to speak up? We are all listening."

The murmurs began and when they cleared, all hands agreed to stay—both a relief and a stress. Now he'd have to watch his back until he replaced half the crew.

"Let me make this clear: if any of you attempt to harm Angela again, you'll all be marooned, even if I must sail this ship on a skeleton crew! Now, get some sleep."

The crew dispersed, but Angela remained next to him. He offered his hand. "Come with me."

Liverman scowled, but if the man had anything to say, his chance was over.

After a second's hesitation and a quick glance over her shoulder, she accepted. The captain took her soft hand and led her away from the crew, deeper into the woods, into the darkness.

Price needed privacy.

Leading her through the easiest, clearest path, he held branches out of her face and pointed out obstructions to step over. Behind a thick tree, he turned around.

"What is it? What's wrong?" Angela asked. "Are you seriously hurt? Are you going to be okay?"

Bluish light pierced the canopy overhead, shining an eerie but beautiful glisten on her features. He couldn't get the woman out of his mind: where she came from, where she planned to go. How was she going to reach her destination safely? Price didn't want to leave her side.

"I tried to keep an eye on you, but Berger's quick feet and an unfortunate stone in the sand distracted me. Did the crew harm you?" Price brushed a lock of long hair over her shoulder.

Angela touched his hand, not to stop him, but to hold him. "You almost died, and you're worried about me?"

Price remained silent, answering the question for her.

"Oh." Angela rubbed an arm. "They didn't. They tried, but no, they didn't hurt me. I think I might've hurt a few of them." She lifted the hammer. "This is my new friend."

"Keep it."

"These men don't seem to like you very much."

"We are business associates. As long as we agree on the goal, we are in accord, but if not, well, you've seen what can happen."

"Killing each other is a little extreme, isn't it?"

"Depends. In these trees lies outposts for the Spanish Crown, enemies of England. If they find us, or you, they shall have no qualms about killing us. They see us as less than men, as animals. They'll do much worse to you first, which is why I shall do anything it takes to keep you safe."

Angela shifted her weight and glanced off to her side before locking eyes with him again. Heat bloomed in his chest like the petals of a Mexican daisy opening for his sun.

"Why me? Why are you risking your life to help me?"

Price couldn't put to words exactly why he was so drawn to her, so he gave her a reasonable reply. "I promised you safe passage."

"Oh." The disappointment on her intelligent face caused the fire to roar through his body. She wanted more than safe passage. As did he.

"Kiss me," he whispered, hoping beyond everything she didn't reject him, hoping that he hadn't misread, hoping...for a possibility.

Angela moved her hands to his neck, thumbs stroking his jaw. His heart pounded in his chest. He heard nothing but the swish of his own blood and nearby critters. Angela leaned forward, pressing against his injured chest, but he swallowed back the gasp. This was too important. He needed this.

He needed her.

Angela's soft lips gently pressed his, and every worry and concern melted away. His arms wrapped around her, holding her tight, never wanting to let go. He shifted positions, tasting her, teasing her, losing himself entirely. She was more than he'd ever expected or hoped for.

He understood why Lemoine risked everything for Emily, because Price would do anything for Angela.

Slowly, she pulled back and studied his face as if questioning her actions. She smiled, wrinkling the corners of her eyes. That wasn't enough. He needed more.

Price buried his fingers into her tangled hair, ignoring the pokes of the bobby pins, and found her lips once again. He pressed harder, working her sweet lips, driving his desire wild. Their breath fought through their noses, and Angela panted, pressing herself against him and pushing them both against the tree.

He wanted all of her.

But that would make him no different from the other men, and if they were caught, he'd be back in the same position as before: challenged for the captaincy and Angela's life. Only this time, all the dissenters, and perhaps many of his supporters, would simply execute him. Reluctantly, Price slowed and released her.

Angela beamed under the moonlight, and she rubbed her arm. "Wow."

He had no idea what that breathy word meant. To think he failed to please her was worse than a sword to the chest. "Is that good?"

"Very."

Price's lips pulled wide, and she raked his unruly hair out of his face, tucking it behind his ears.

"I like your earring. I wonder if you have others elsewhere?" Angela asked with a teasing lilt.

"Someday you'll have to look for yourself."

She chuckled. "Thank you, by the way, for saving me from those men."

"You've already thanked me plenty."

Angela laughed, but a twig snapped behind them, silencing her. Price leaned around the tree, and a rustle of footsteps darted off into the filtered light.

"What was that?" she asked.

"Not a what, but a whom." Price squinted into the light to identify the man, but he wouldn't chase that fool's errand, leaving Angela alone. "I realize you aren't a sailor of the *Sea Lion*. You didn't read and agree to the rules, as I have. If any consequences become of this, I need you to know two things."

Angela waited patiently.

"The crew and its rules are my responsibility, and I shall take all the blame. And two, whatever the consequence, it was worth it."

"What are you talking about?"

"Women on board are forbidden, hence their insistence on a stiff punishment for stowing away, as are any relations between women and the crew."

"The rule Berger wanted to change."

"Right."

"I didn't hurt anyone. We didn't hurt anybody. Why does my presence matter at all?"

"Women are a distraction. The rule is to keep the crew agreeable and rational. Focused."

Angela frowned. "What about the gay men?"

Price didn't know what that had to do with anything. "Sometimes they are," he said slowly. "No one minds, as long as their activities don't interfere with the men's sleep."

"That's hardly fair, giving a pass to men but not women." She sighed. "If that witness says anything, what are they going to do this time?"

Price gently touched the woman's jaw. Judging by the direction of the mysterious man's retreat, he wasn't *Sea Lion* crew at all. "Come with me. We're going to find a new place to rest for the night."

Angela took his hand. He'd keep both eyes open the rest of the night if he had to.

Chapter 15

Angela opened her bleary eyes to check the time, but there was no alarm clock. No end table. No Serta. Her aching back and neck reminded her an air mattress was a necessary minimum when sleeping away from her supportive bed, but the aches quickly receded when she found who was next to her—the captain, sprawled on his back on a prickly bed of flattened plants. His head rested in his hands, elbows out, eyes closed. Hating these inches between them, she wanted to get closer. She wanted to cuddle up on his chest. Her excuse for not making a move? The gash in his skin. Angela didn't want to hurt him.

Angela closed her eyes against the brilliant oranges and purples of sunrise, remembering the kiss that swept her clear into a dream. An energy pulsed through her like an invisible force—just her and the captain together in their own private bubble of safety.

Nothing else would ever compare.

But even back home, she could never stay in bed all day, and coffee called. Angela rose and stretched the aches. As the morning sun penetrated through his off-white tunic, revealing his shape underneath, she gazed at his delicious form but frowned at the mar to his flesh. She leaned down to shake a shoulder and wake him, but his hand caught hers before she touched him.

"I'm already awake." Captain Price popped his eyes open, meeting her gaze.

Heat flushed her cheeks at being caught. He brought her hand to his mouth, and he kissed her knuckles. A deep flutter erased her need for coffee. She was wide awake now, and she noticed the dark rings under his eyes.

"Did you get any sleep?"

"I shall catch sleep when it's safe to do so."

Guilt nagged at her. He'd suffered on her account...again. One thing she learned since landing here in time: some pirates were true gentlemen. And now she wanted to know his story. How did he end up with these barbarians, and why hadn't he left?

The captain grunted sitting up. Angela held out a hand to help him to his feet. Captain Price stared at it, confused.

"Take my hand," she insisted.

"I don't understand why."

Angela snorted and grabbed his hand. She pulled him, and he stood with the assistance. "That's why."

"Where you're from must be a strange place." His hand pressed against his wound. "But, thank you."

He'd never believe her even if she tried to explain, so she had no intention of trying. "Do you need something for that?" She pointed at the blood-soaked material.

"It's more pride than injury. Let us return to camp. Giles should have breakfast shortly, and I need to return to repairing the ship. Do you still have your hammer?"

Angela bent down and lifted it. "It's right here."

"After the loss of Berger and the aggressions against you, I hope you'll continue to assist us. We need you."

There was something deeper to those words, something far beyond patching a hole in the hull. Angela didn't want to pry, so she said the first thing that came to mind—getting off this dangerous island. "I don't want to be stuck here any longer than you do."

"Excellent. I have a speech to give the crew while they break their fasts."

What could that possibly be? Angela was curious but not enough to prod. Hopefully, they would get off this island and then she had to figure out how to get home, but landing in US soil was a good start. A pang of sadness rolled through her.

The crew gathered around the fire as Giles dished out portions of the morning's pig. Although everyone passed the plates without a fuss, and ate quietly, the angry stares shivered her spine. Liverman and Vallo were still upset with her presence, and too many for comfort sat by them. It hurt. Those men meant nothing to her, but the hatred they displayed honestly hurt.

When she'd met Brandon Spindleton, and finally believed he was genuinely interested in her, Angela assumed his upbringing meant he'd be a perfect gentleman. From a childhood of rejection and poverty, she'd truly thought she'd caught her break, a real life Cinderella. But after months of replaying every memory, she believed Mrs. Spindleton wanted her son's hidden life under control to prevent a scandal, and she'd chosen Angela to control her, strip her of her rights, and bury her under legal documents. Despite the legacy needing protection, Angela couldn't figure out why she wasn't enough to rein in Brandon's wild ways. He had to be ashamed of her or he simply never cared at all. Thankfully, Angela got out of there before it was too late.

All she really wanted was to be accepted and loved. So why, with her newfound self-esteem did the pirate crew's rejection bother her so much?

Captain Price respected her, treated her like an equal—which was baffling in these times. He fought for her and saved her life. The man even stayed awake all night just to keep her safe. His lips were amazing, but beyond that lustful exterior, he dispatched one of his own for her.

Angela's eyes drifted to the captain, who ate with the rest of the crew, keeping an eye on her. Captain Price put her first. He wasn't ashamed of her—if he could understand what her job entailed, anyway—and he did care. If Angela allowed herself to open up to him fully, to fill that broken hole in her heart, with him from the past and her from the future, how would it work?

Captain Price set down his plate and brushed his hands clean. "We all know we're currently stranded on Cuba, surrounded by Spain, but I have a plan."

The *Sea Lion* crew closed in tight, elbow to elbow, and grease shined on their dirt-streaked faces. Sand snarled the hair on their heads and faces. Despite their repulsive self-care, their eyes were sharp.

"There's a settlement to the west and forts to the east. No warships are presently at anchor. The first priority is repairing the *Sea Lion*. To prepare for departure, a small group will join Giles in procuring provisions and additional fresh water. The locals offer everything we need to set sail, but we risk their betrayal to the Spaniards. At my authorization, Giles shall take a bribe with him. Giles, pick two men."

The cook named a pair who smiled and stood eager for their assignment. Captain Price handed the cook a pinch of gold coins and pointed for them to move out at once.

"With the expectation all hands maintain the repair schedule throughout the day, at nightfall, we shall break into two groups ready for action. Riley will lead one with Karl, in charge of heaving to immediately upon our return." The captain listed off the names he expected to follow the quartermaster. McKee and Hodgens were also chosen for ship duty. "The second group will join me. Last night, Riley and I discovered treasure recovered from the Spanish wreck hiding in a hut, guarded by a handful of men. We must raid the hut before the warship arrives to collect and transport it home."

"Wait," Angela said, confused. The men faced her, half of them fill with utter disgust. Swallowing back their glares, she said, "A warship...so, a ship full of healthy, well-rested, and fully armed men are coming to collect an extremely valuable state-own treasure. I have a hammer. Many of you have swords and a few have pistols. No offense, seriously, but what are you going to do against a small army?"

Angela hadn't met true undiluted scorn until now. If looks could kill...

"Of course the wench wouldn't understand..." Liverman cut in.

Captain Price smiled gently. "That's why we move quickly, quietly, and under the cover of darkness. An army would be impossible, but we can take on a handful."

Angela had no reply to that, and the murmurs from the promise of an easy hunt returned.

"Treasure without having to take a prize for it?" one man asked with growing excitement.

"Treasure without having to dive for it?" another asked, equally happy, since most men on ships apparently didn't know how to swim.

Price nodded at the growing excitement. "All the costs from the squall damage and lost life shall be covered in full with more money leftover than any one man could reasonably spend."

"We can live like kings? Take no orders? Hide from the Crown's noose forever?" the first man asked. Several others shared looks of bursting excitement.

Captain Price smiled hungrily. "Precisely."

The men exchanged laughs and beaming grins.

Angela couldn't help but be appalled at their greed, but their lives were different from what she was used to. Brandon Spindleton's estate wasn't altruistic, but as far as she was aware, the Spindletons weren't engaged in active piracy either.

Captain Price paused from his celebratory speech to glance her way, and at the look of disappointment, his smile faltered. While the men eagerly organized their assignments and plans, the captain approached her.

She stood to meet him. "You didn't say what my assignment is." As if she was important enough to consider. As if she was one of them...

"Come with me." Price took her by the hand, leading her away from the group planning.

"What a minute there!" Liverman shouted and stood.

The captain stopped, sighed, and turned around, but he declined to address the man. Captain Price only stared with hatred and warning.

"You won the duel, so you decide the woman's fate, but that doesn't give her rights to be on the ship, and it certainly doesn't allow the captain to have sex with her," Liverman said, gaining the attention of the rest of the crew. "If you get a turn, then we all get a turn, such is the way on this ship!"

Men murmured, and a couple let out shouts of agreement.

The captain addressed Liverman while still grasping her hand. "There is no sex aboard the *Sea Lion*, or among the crew while still on the account. I did sign the rules, as did you, and unlike you, I have never broken them. I am afraid, Liverman, the squall has knocked and tossed the wits from your head. But fear not! The lady and I shall go seek them out. Come, my lady."

Cantu and Riley snorted and covered their laughs. Buckley barked out unrestrained laughter while others simply smiled. Liverman frowned, blushed bright, and sat down.

Angela covered her own smile.

The captain pulled her through the dense Cuban jungle until far from earshot. Angela's heart raced in her ears, hoping for a chance to steal another kiss.

He stopped near a thick fern. "Now that Liverman and his mouth are out of our way, I've weighed both options thoroughly, and it's a risk either way, but I want you to accompany me on the raid."

Her? Captain Price wanted her to hunt down some treasure with him? How was this plan in any way ensuring her safety? Perhaps she misunderstood. "Ummm. What?"

"I split the crew to ensure the best possible outcome based on trust. Riley is my right-hand man, and I'm giving Riley the thorns in my side. I can't take them with me, because I don't trust them to not betray me to Spain. That means you must join me. With you by my side, I can protect you, but if you insist on staying with the ship, I cannot presume Riley's team shall restrain themselves, given the *enormous* temptation to give in to their baser desires." Captain Price pointedly raked her body with his hot eyes.

Heat rose in her cheeks, but something he said stood out. "You don't think much of your crew, do you?"

"Men with a goal in common can be a powerful force, but when those goals are disrupted, the men split, and nothing remains predictable. Trust is destroyed, chaos ensues, and the entire mission falls apart. I won the duel. It's my choice to leave you stranded on this island or take you with us. I should think my preference is clear. And since I cannot return you home safely at this moment, I need you to stay by my side."

Remembering what the captain said about a warship full of trained soldiers, Angela swallowed a thick lump in her throat. Fighting off a dozen filthy pigs with a hammer sounded easier. Instead, a dozen men headed into a fight against a possible hundred. Those odds were so much worse.

"I know what I am asking of you," Captain Price said, holding her arms in desperation. "But I believe you can do this. I will keep you safe. I promise you."

A flush of heat warmed her chest, a lightness, a foreign sensation of being important. She was *numero uno* to someone else, and she wanted nothing more than to stay by the captain's side. He was the only one she fully trusted.

"I'll go with you."

Price pulled her against him, and his lips found hers in a stolen secret moment, but it was over so fast, she wasn't sure it happened.

That would be a daydream to hold on to.

Chapter 16

THE MEN WORKED AS a tireless team all day. Karl's crew replaced the rigging with spares from below deck, but the extra set was a tangled mess, and shouts of frustration liberally flowed from him and the men assisting. That was not a job Price would ever care to do.

Cantu cut down and chopped up a tree for replacement planks, and even with an assistant sawing, producing viable boards would take a long time. Price had to urge Cantu to use the boards as they were, but the perfectionist fought, grumbling under his breath. Time was of the essence.

Buckley kept his group in line patching and tarring the smaller wounds in her side, and Price leaned back on a freshly filled barrel of water, giving his aching neck and spine a break. He mopped the sweat from his forehead and checked on the wound in his chest. He needed fresh bandages, but there were none left.

Watching the men work as a coordinated team, too busy for drama, brought a smile of nostalgia to his lips. Just like the good old days when men focused and cared about nothing but getting the job done. Mountains could be moved with enough hands willing. And that wasn't the best part. Last night, calms waters brought in a gentle tide and the *Sea Lion* lifted up. Their laborious efforts would succeed, and when the tide returned tonight, regardless of weather conditions, the anchor shall keep her in place until the time they needed to escape.

Everything was moving along according to plan.

Except one thing.

Angela tirelessly hammered in new boards all around the hull. Her laboring alongside his men pained him deeply, but she'd insisted. What world could a woman come from where work such as this was expected of them? Certainly no high society. In any case, Price had no choice but to accept her assistance. All able-bodied men were forbidden from idleness unless taking a needed break.

Including Price. With a final deep exhale, Price lifted off and headed back into the shade. He'd been assisting master gunner McKee with salvaging weapons from the hull for maintenance and repair for tonight. Typically, it wasn't a captain's job, but he was leading the raid on the treasure hut, and he wanted a firsthand count of their serviceable weapons. Price lowered himself across from McKee at a makeshift table—an empty barrel, too damaged to hold liquids.

McKee unscrewed and removed the lock assembly of a pistol, checking for saltwater corrosion, and inserted a plug in the vent hole. Price lifted the next pistol in line, inspected its condition, and filled and emptied the barrel to wash out the black-powder fouling.

"Having a skirt on board is bad luck," McKee said over the soft noises of metal clashing and clattering as they worked.

"You, too?" Price sighed. "I need men who can focus on the account, not on a woman."

The crew's backlash was not unexpected, but its continued presence was a meddlesome pest. Not one man on the crew could see reason above breasts. Although, if the situation were less dire, Price would gladly admire Angela's ample soft chest for hours on end. A leisure he hadn't sought in ages.

"We're on land. A woman can make use of herself easily. Why not send her away and remove the wedge in the crew?" McKee asked calmly, keeping his eyes on his cleaning.

"We lost too many good men in that squall. Navigating these waters is difficult enough with all hands."

"She can sail?" McKee lifted a brow.

"No, but she's helpful." Regardless of her capabilities, Price had promised himself he wouldn't allow another's noble efforts to cause their death. Not for him. Not again.

McKee uttered a noise of amusement. "I fear this is history repeating itself. Do you not fear Lemoine's end?"

Price's hands stilled in their cleaning. Captain Eric Lemoine, retired, resided in a seaside plantation with a woman, someone he tended to and someone who held him accountable. That was an enormous responsibility. After all his years of freedom, would Price want such a thing? His gaze traveled to the hull, where Angela hammered away on a patch. A glimmer of hope fluttered through his mind.

Price tried to picture it, but he couldn't reconcile their two worlds. Angela only wanted to go home—back to her family. Who was he to stand in her way? The stolen kiss had been unbecoming of a man, but he couldn't help himself at the time. Price already had his future carved out. After his business on this island was complete, he was retiring with his bountiful share on the mainland, where his feet could plant firmly on the ground. Where food was a short stroll away. Where the sea was quiet, the air was dry. Only after he found a man who'd guess an oar to be a strange shovel, then that was where he'd find his peace. If he survived at all.

"Lemoine's end shall not be mine."

"Of course not. You'll get yourself killed long before then," McKee said.

Price shot him a sharp look.

McKee poured black powder down the barrel. "Your crusade against Spain is not the secret you think it is, not for us who've been around.

Frankly, so long as my pockets are heavy, I care not who we fight." He paused, and Price returned his attention to his pistol.

"But life at sea is too short as it is, so if you feel your heart is screaming at you, listen to it. Don't waste a chance at happiness."

Price wouldn't waste it, he just couldn't see it.

"And if your gaying instrument is shouting in your ears, do us a favor and go box the Jesuit. Last thing Liverman and Vallo need is more fuel for their fire, and they'd be right. It's the rules, captain."

Taking advice from a younger man never settled well in Price's gut, but he couldn't deny the misplaced wisdom. "You need not concern yourself with my affairs. I retain control over my own body, unless angered enough, then I cannot say for sure what my trigger finger shall do."

McKee rammed the rod down the barrel harder than necessary, but without a reply, Price presumed his point was received. Unlike some of the baser animalistic crew, Price was a gentleman, capable of maintaining himself.

After cleaning the next pistol, he passed it to McKee for loading. There weren't enough pistols for each of the raiding crew, but if Price succeeded in his plan, no one would fire a single shot. Plans rarely went according to plan.

McKee placed a shot over the patch and pushed it into place carefully. "That's the last one."

"Get them dispensed to the men accompanying me tonight. Check on Peter Gunner. Make sure the guns are in working order and the munitions are ready. When you see us returning, likely at a swift pace, alert Riley to weigh anchor and get us underway immediately. I want you to have men at the guns prepared to return fire."

"And if the *Sea Lion*'s sails are not ready?"

"Make them ready." There was no alternative option. They must succeed or die trying.

"Can do, captain. Wish I was going with you."

Captain Price stood and sheathed a pistol for himself. "I'd prefer you at my side, but I need you here."

McKee smiled. "Get out of here and make history."

Price planned on it.

Chapter 17

Even out of the sunlight, Angela's itchy tunic clung to her sticky chest. She swiped her forehead, now understanding why the pirates wore bandannas. With the stifling air in the lower decks, Angela wished for a fan. Her arms were heavy from a long day hammering in patches and scraping barnacles off the hull so the mighty Cantu could tar the seams and leaks. The man was bigger than any bouncer she'd ever seen, and Angela was thrilled he was a decent person. The crew mostly left her be, almost like she was one of them—respected, but otherwise kept at a distance and asked for help when needed. Reminded her of working with Marcos, which was a familiar relief, but she couldn't help but wonder about the raid and the armed soldiers. Something far outside her comfort zone.

Every time her stomach fluttered with nerves, her thoughts drifted back to the captain's sweet lips. A smile tugged at her lips. If only they'd had some privacy, Angela could've had her one night with a captain. Would one night be enough?

Not a chance.

She needed at least two to fix her itch—the good kind.

The ship creaked as the tide slowly crawled back, but so far only a few trivial leaks remained. Angela lifted a small board, blotting out the cone of fading daylight, and pinched a nail against it. Her tired arms relentlessly swung until the nail was flush—also of note, she didn't miss.

None of this felt like reality. She couldn't believe she'd actually fallen through time. How did it happen? Recalling her exact steps, Angela had entered the festival grounds with Emily. They'd waited in line and bought tickets for the ship tour. While waiting for the tour ship to open, Angela had insisted on shopping at the vendor tables, and the only thing she'd purchased...

Angela leaned down for another board, and the copper chain around her neck touched her chin. She straightened, and with a frown, her hand touched the amethyst. Could it be? Could this necklace have sent her back?

If she removed it, would she return to her time? And if so, where would she land? Since she slipped it over her head while on Lake Michigan and ended up in the middle of the Caribbean Sea, would taking it off in Cuba drop her somewhere far from land, helpless to the unforgiving ocean, or on a less friendly ship—perhaps an aircraft carrier? Uncertainty released the jewel back against her chest.

Angela climbed to the main deck to restock her small pile of boards.

"Ah, Angela, just who I was looking for." Captain Price's voice.

Angela turned, relief rushing through her, and she grinned. He was still so amazingly beautiful. Heat flushed up her chest, neck, and cheeks. She fanned herself with a small board. "Why's that?"

The captain pressed a gun into her hand. "Take this. I want you to have extra protection tonight."

Angela fought a recoil at the weapon. Despite its stunning craftsmanship and reflective beauty, it was a means of killing. She didn't like guns. "I can't take this."

"I insist."

"I don't know how to use it."

Captain Price smiled. "It's already loaded. You simply aim and squeeze. After all you've done so far, I think this shall be the simplest task you'll encounter. You need one of these, too." Captain Price slipped a short dagger off his belt and held it out to her.

She hesitated.

"For your safety, I insist," he repeated.

Angela accepted, finding a blade more practical for survival than a gun, and slipped it into her belt. The weight of weapons at her waist was foreign and uncomfortable. Coupled with her pouch—why she still carried her fried cell phone, she didn't know—the weight at her hips was going to leave her back sore in the morning. Regardless, she was still bringing her hammer—that was her security blanket.

"Daylight is falling. The rest of the raiding party awaits us. Let us go at once."

Nerves sloshed her stomach as Angela followed Captain Price off the ship. The crew staying behind moved swiftly to load the ship with all the provisions and supplies as Captain Price directed, preparing to set sail upon their return.

She crossed the soft sandy beach and into the green palms and ferns, where a small group of men chattered to themselves. All of them carried cutlasses and daggers at their belts, but only a couple had guns. Liverman inspected her loaded belt and frowned. She had one, and he didn't.

Angela fidgeted, wanting to give the man her gun if he'd drop that glare of hatred. Vallo's belt was lacking a gun as well. In the fading light, she saw guns and blades on Cantu and Buckley. Angela had been given special treatment over some of the crew, only dividing them further.

"Stay close, stay silent, and follow me," Captain Price addressed the party. "The hut is a thousand paces northeast by east."

That sounded far.

As if sensing her uneasiness, Captain Price grabbed her hand. "You can do this."

Her stomach knotted and twisted. Her hands trembled, but she nodded. The only way home was forward. The safest way home was by Captain Price's side.

Angela placed one foot in front of the other, gripping the captain firmly. The men mumbled behind them, but right now, she didn't care what they were saying.

In the fading sunset, wayward branches were harder to see. Angela ducked seconds too late, earning herself scratches on her cheek and shoulder. Her hand covered the sting and rubbed. Marching through endless soft sand burned her calves. She panted with the exertion and caught glimpses of the captain next to her, who never let her hand go, and his stamina was apparently much better than hers.

What else did he have excellent stamina for? Angela turned her sweeping gaze away and bit back a smile. He couldn't see her in the dimness, but she didn't want reaction noticed.

The men behind them skulked through the underbrush, refraining from arguments, jokes, or running commentary, surprisingly.

Captain Price pulled back on her hand. Angela stopped immediately. He whispered, "Just up ahead. Look about."

From behind a palm tree, Angela leaned, watching. Four armed men in uniform argued in front of a sad hut made of palm fronds. She listened to their Spanish. The syntax was different from what she was used to, but they'd found two bodies nearby, their own men. Price had said if they'd found the bodies, the pirates would be up against many more than a few soldiers. Their odds would be slim.

Angela asked, "Are we leaving now?"

"Why would we leave?" Captain Price asked, confused.

She was just as perplexed. "They found the two bodies from earlier. The other guards." She pointed toward the men as if he didn't understand where she got the information from.

"You speak Spanish?" Captain Price asked with astonishment.

"Don't you?" Angela was just as confused now.

"A few phrases and numbers, but nothing substantial. What else are they saying?"

Angela focused on the angry men and listened. "Two of the soldiers want to sound the alarm and wake the rest of the guards to scour the cove. The other two want to wait until the *Peibo del ler San Francisco* arrives so they can still effectively guard the hut. I think that's the name of a ship. I can't tell which pair are winning their case."

"A Spanish first-rate man-o'-war," Cantu said.

A shiver danced down her spine. "Uh, I think we should go. Finish the repairs and get out of here. No money is worth your life."

"And that's where you're wrong, my lady," Price said with a dark voice.

Angela frowned. The captain actually had a dollar value on his life? The greed of these men knew no bounds.

"What's going on up there?" Buckley asked.

"Four soldiers. Prepare to disable them and keep it quiet," Price said.

The men dragged swords from their belts.

"You can't be serious!" Angela whisper-yelled.

"You shouldn't be here, wench," Liverman said. "Do as you're told and stay quiet before you get us all killed."

"Stay by my side but out of swinging reach. You're far too valuable to lose." Over his shoulder, Captain Price said, "Go now!"

The men silently lurked closer, and Angela waited for all the pirates and their shiny weapons to move far enough away. When the four soldiers were engaged with the crew, Captain Price and the others entered the hut. Angela left the cover of the tree and followed them inside.

Barrels, like those in *Sea Lion*'s hold, were stacked all over. A few chests were among them. The men pried open lids with fervor.

"Furs," one man said.

"Sugarcane," another said.

"Tobacco," a third announced.

"Where's the treasure, Price?" Liverman asked.

"I know what I saw. It's here. I'm sure of it." Captain Price stretched his hand for Angela's hammer. He pried open another lid, and metal rattled. "Light! Give me light!"

A lantern was lit, and men leaned over the barrel. Eyes brightened and widened.

"What is it?" Angela asked and tilted her head out of the door, watching out for incoming threats.

The men snickered and cackled. The noises of excitement grew to laughter—true belly laughter. The men shouted in celebration.

"Load it up!" Captain Price ordered and gave Angela her hammer back. "Take it all!"

The men cheered, and with smooth cooperation she hadn't so far seen, the crew coordinated their efforts to carry out as many barrels as possible. Several more trips were necessary to get it all, but she noted the captain ordered them to take the gold coins first.

Angela stepped down from the hut, staying by the captain and Cantu, who shared a heavy load. This was silly. If she took a barrel, they'd move that much faster. Angela jogged back into the hut and shoved on the barrels until she found a lighter one. The furs. Hefting it over her shoulder, she quickly caught up.

"What in the devil's name are you doing?" Captain Price grunted.

"I'm helping."

"A lady doesn't work like a man!"

Pfft. "A lady who wants to get off this island and go home does."

Captain Price darted her a look, but he kept quiet.

The men of this time thought of women differently. Well, she was going to show the captain she wasn't useless, since all her hammering hadn't made it obvious.

Chapter 18

The *Sea Lion*, bathed in eerie moonlight, floated at anchor ready to return to the seas. A longboat awaited just offshore with Hodgens and Riley set to receive, and the raiding crew one-by-one dropped their barrels of ill-gotten goods into the boat. Despite how lightweight the furs were, the barrel still ached on her shoulder. Angela waded into the saltwater and added her barrel. Her calves burned, and she rotated her shoulder to soothe it. What she wouldn't give for a bath, a fuzzy robe, a recliner, and a book.

Captain Price and Cantu heaved theirs over the low rail with metallic clinks of coins. She watched his backside as he exerted himself. Perhaps she'd skip everything after the bath if she could have a few hours with him. The warm fuzzies brought a smile to her face, but sharp arguing on the boat pulled her from the sweet daydream.

The captain was steaming angry, facing off against the quartermaster.

"We have enough treasure to split among us. We're on Spain's territory, on borrowed time. I insisted we must get underway," Riley said. His group lined the rail of the Sea Lion, awaiting orders from below. Couldn't these people ever get along?

"There's a hut full of goods unattended. We cannot just leave it. Never again shall we encounter such easy wealth," the captain said.

"We've lost too many men already. It's not worth the risk now. If we return to Nassau and add more men, we can succeed in taking the rest, after proper repairs are completed."

"The gold shall be gone by then. The *Peibo del ler San Francisco* is returning for it. It's now or never."

"I'm with the captain on this one," Liverman said, and everyone turned to him in surprise. "With double or treble the treasure, we shall never need to sail another day. Not one of us will ever find ourselves wanting for women, wine, or food ever again. It would be foolish to pass on it."

"I agree, too," Vallo piped up.

Buckley sighed. "I'm old. I have no need for more than we've already taken. But you young bucks deserve to live your lives like I never could. We go and we take it all. I just don't want to spend my final days in shackles or hanging from the gallows. I trust you, Captain, to make the right call for all of us, not just myself."

"I'm with the captain, too," Cantu said. "It's too easy to pass up. This could be our only chance. Instead of standing around arguing, we ought to return at once."

Quartermaster Riley folded his arms over his chest. "I don't like it, but I can't stop you. Take as much as you can carry. When you return, I'm setting sail, fully restored sails or not, even if that means I'm the new captain."

"Very brazen of you, Riley, but we shall be back. You keep this ship at the ready," Captain Price said.

Riley nodded and, together, he and Hodgens rowed their goods to the ship.

"We must hurry, men. Angela, since you can speak Spanish, I want you at my side again."

With the quartermaster at arms with the captain, she had even more reason to stay with Price. She'd never once thought of stopping the longboat for a ride to the *Sea Lion*.

The raiding crew made their way back into the cove, and Price and Angela moved slowly behind them, out of earshot. Price's jaw worked at some unknown stress. Was he worried Riley would take the partial treasure and leave without them?

Price had always been the level-headed leader, and seeing him in distress only caused her anxiety to boil over. Just like when she'd heard of her ailing mom's condition, Angela rushed into action.

"Hey," she said, gently touching his shoulder. "It's going to be okay."

Captain Price stopped and gazed into her eyes.

"Whatever happens next will be fine," she added. "You have a plan. We'll get through it, and when it's over, then decide the next steps."

He didn't reply, only studied her silently under the blue hue of the moon.

Angela repeated, "It's going to be okay."

Did she believe her own words? She'd spoken them so many times to her mom, mostly because the woman didn't remember Angela's previous attempts at comforting her, so for Angela, they were rote. True or not didn't matter; they weren't for her.

Worry lines creased the corners of his eyes. With a gentle finger, he tilted her chin up slightly. "No matter how grim the circumstances around you, no matter the threats to your life and safety or the strangeness of the world you landed in, you still offer to support me."

"I had practice," Angela said, dismissively.

Captain Price's features darkened. "You have a husband, and you never told me?"

Angela reached for his forearms and gripped him firmly. "I don't. My mom was sick. I cared for her."

Captain Price deflated. "My apologies for the err in judgment. I don't know much about the future, but if all women are as kind, skilled, and flexible as you, I welcome it's coming."

Angela squinted suspiciously. "What do you know of the future?"

The lines softened. "Enough to know that as much as I welcome your arrival, I fear constantly for you. A curse, if you will."

"I'm a curse?" Angela asked, taken aback. She released him. "I'm a burden to you?"

"Well, yea, technically."

Angela flinched at the stinging words.

He leaned closer. "You're a burden I would gladly accept a hundred times over on my worst day, through squalls, droughts, and fair winds. I owe you a great debt of gratitude, and couldn't imagine my life had I not met you. It truly might have ceased already."

Angela's heart thumped in her ears, and her chest warmed. Did he just say what she thought he said? Too much seawater was making her hear things.

Captain Price collected her hands and squeezed. "Angela, you are my angelfish. If I knew the men weren't peeping, I'd ask you to kiss me, but it's too risky right now, and my plan is falling apart before we can even finish repairs on the *Sea Lion*." Price headed toward the remaining raiders, and Angela kept stride, pushing brush out of their faces.

Angela thought he only wanted another trip or two's worth of gold from the hut and sail away to safety. "What plan is that?"

"That gold was only to appease the crew. I need them to assist me in a task I know they shall not volunteer for, but now I can't even get them to agree to want the rest of the gold."

"Why do they need to want the gold?"

"I made a promise to my brother."

Angela's eyes widened with interest. "For what?"

The captain shifted aside a frond and exhaled. "My brother and I enlisted in the Royal Navy, as our father had and his before him. The sea was all we knew. But the world isn't the same anymore. We suffered with insufficient and sometimes skipped rations, and little to no pay. If any of us spoke up, we were given lashes." He paused and shook his head. "Every time the cat came out of the bag, we all held our breaths and quelled our panic."

"Cat? Is this another real cat?" Angela recalled the feline's escape from the sinking ship.

"Cat-o'-nine-tails. A whip for punishment. It's something you never forget: the quick snap of the lines, the stinging heat of the tears in your flesh, and the warm trickle of your own blood. Cry out and the captain counts extra just for his own pleasure. So when Wilcox and the *Sea Lion* approached, hoisting the black, our captain's fear showed on his face, and we all silently rejoiced. The captain took his own lashings that day, and my brother and I joined the pirates. The promise of freedom was too great to resist, and the riches were a bonus."

"Sounds like becoming a pirate was good for you." Better than the alternative, anyway.

"I never intended to continue as long as I have. We were restocking near Port Royal when a Spanish man-o'-war anchored off shore, and my brother, the brazen dolt, offered his life so we could flee, and that day I made him a promise I cannot break."

The captain had saved her life many times—from the sinking ship to the overzealous crew, and she wanted to do this. "I want to help you keep your promise."

"And that, my lady, makes you the finest woman I've ever met." Price found her hand and held her tight.

No one else had treated her like such an equal, trusting her so fully. Brandon Spindleton, with his idiotic and immature blackmail scheme and a team of attorneys at the ready for vengeance, was not a man compared to Captain Henry Price. She'd finally found a man worth his salt.

Angela smiled. She wanted to feel his heat, to explore his body, and caress his skin. But there was never enough time or privacy. She ached to touch him, to climb aboard his sexy body and drive him like a forklift.

"Are you ready to translate for me?" Price asked.

Of all the things she'd done lately, that would be the easiest—but not the most fun. She'd forgotten to ask what the promise to his brother was exactly, but it didn't matter. Some things were meant to stay private.

"Let's do this."

Chapter 19

In sight of their target, Price gestured for his men to take refuge behind the trees and watch for an updated count on the guards. They likely had more men on alert, but Price brought more too. For a second, he worried how she would handle this. Being from the future of kind and caring people, he couldn't imagine Angela would keep herself level watching men fight to the death.

And this wouldn't be an honorable, fair fight.

He pulled Angela against his chest until her scent filled his nose. He closed his eyes and breathed her in deep, wishing he could do something else deeply. Upholding his promise to his brother would break his promise to Angela. Leading her into the fray deliberately put her in harm's way. Price's insides twisted. His resolve faltered, and his heart fluttered.

This was not a situation to take lightly. Price never did, but suddenly it felt tremendously heavier. He whispered, "I don't know what the outcome shall be, but I want you to know..." he trailed off, unable to voice his fears.

"What is it?" she whispered.

The skies through the canopy lightened just slightly, threatening the coming of dawn. The Sea Lion would part from this island soon. Time was almost up. "Stay close."

Price couldn't see anyone near the hut. He gestured for the crew to approach, and they all crept forward into the clearing, alert for an ambush. Price led Angela and a couple others inside the hut, while Vallo and the rest waited as lookouts.

Captain Price pushed barrels and chests until he found a light one. He offered it to Angela, still annoyed she strained herself on his account, but maybe her cooperation and effort shall earn her leniency with the crew. So if he failed to return to the *Sea Lion*, the crew might treat her with a shred of dignity.

He could only hope.

Price collected barrels and passed them along until everyone's arms were full. Satisfied with their take, he and Angela exited behind the others.

Instead of an orderly and efficient line of men rushing back to the ship, he found Liverman standing next to his barrel, and a pistol pointed at Price. The rest of the men stopped when they noticed. Several dropped their burdens and glanced at each other, wondering what to do. Angela wisely stayed behind him.

Fury surged within Price. "What's the meaning of this, Liverman?"

The smirking traitor said, "Since you trained your loyalties on the wench, we sit fit to dispatch you as captain. Anyone who disagrees, I shall duel them at once."

Cantu and Buckley stared in disbelief, and Vallo approached Liverman's shoulder. This is exactly what Price didn't need at this moment, but he trusted Vallo to make the right move.

"Is this your decision?" Vallo asked Liverman, slipping a pistol from his sash and holding at his side.

"With certainty, just as I expect your support, my friend." Liverman kept the pistol aimed at Price's chest. "Since none of you are short of wits enough to fight me, then I declare the treasure and the *Sea Lion* are now under my control."

No one made a move, not even Cantu or Hodgens, as expected. Most of the crew were content in their roles and preferred to ignore the politics of the sea, but Price shot a glare at Vallo. He'd expected the man to keep a closer eye on the agitator, not encourage him.

"You brought this upon yourself." Vallo leveled the pistol at Price too.

Price's lips parted, his brow furrow. Liverman's betrayal was expected, truthfully, but Vallo's, that was a devastating blow. They'd had a deal. Vallo was supposed to stay undercover with the agitators and feed information back to Price. He was also supposed to manipulate their traitorous speak and prevent exactly this.

It couldn't have come at a worse time.

With a smug smirk, Liverman loosened his guard. Vallo abruptly swung his arm at Liverman. Before the traitor responded, Vallo squeezed the trigger. A single blast rocked the sleepy island. Angela gasped and gripped the back of Price's tunic. Birds fluttered from the trees, and the men flinched from the noise. Liverman grasped his chest and collapsed, mouth gaped open like a fish.

Price blinked and smiled in relief. For a moment there, he was truly worried. "Thank you, friend."

Vallo nodded and returned the smile.

Price gently urged Angela out from behind him. "It's over now. The last of the thorns in my side has been vanquished. Let us return to the ship with our prize."

Angela shot him a look of disbelief. "You set this up from the beginning?"

"I must maintain relationships to protect my standing." Price labored too long and hard to give up everything for a couple of men with selfish ambitions.

"I... I can't believe this. A thief and a murderer? And here I thought Brandon was a piece of shi..." Angela met the eyes of the pirates around her and trailed off.

Price touched her arm. "I can explain better once we are safely aboard the ship. Spain is lurking in this jungle, and we are standing here with their treasure. I insist we move at once."

Candlelight flickered through the brush, just beyond the darkness, catching his attention. Price stiffened at the indecipherable voices. The soldiers were returning. They were way too close, and at this distance, the crew couldn't outrun them—with or without their arms full.

Angela turned to the captain. "They're here. There's someone here."

Regret was a funny thing. Sometimes it was there, teasing on the horizon. Other times it popped up unexpectedly, like a startled jackrabbit. Right now, the horizon soared toward him at unimaginable speeds. He only hoped the next few minutes didn't reveal the jackrabbit.

Cantu whispered, "Men incoming!"

Pistols would draw plenty of attention, but when those soldiers spotted the crew, they'd open fire. Vallo scrambled to reload. Another man picked up Liverman's unspent pistol. Cantu and McKee had theirs drawn and ready. Everyone added a sword to their empty hands.

Soldiers emerged from the brush into the clearing, surrounding them, but it was Vallo's weapon once again trained on Price that stilled Price's hand.

Boom. The startled jackrabbit popped up.

Chapter 20

When Angela was younger, she learned quickly to avoid social media. She had too many personal issues to deal with, and she didn't want to be inundated with useless epithets from people who didn't truly care about her struggles—not to mention the Spindleton's privacy requirements. She'd found the drama at times could be more harmful than supportive. Words were powerful—dangerous when used wrong and had the potential to kill.

But a pistol in someone's face made social media feel...insignificant. Artificial. Cowardly. Angela knew what the captain needed right now, and even with a pistol in the face of her only ally, Angela stepped forward, shoulder to shoulder at Price's side in solidarity. She was no longer the only one hated by the crew, but she didn't understand why they kept turning on the captain. All he wanted was to lead them toward the treasure they wanted while he upheld a promise to his brother. It made no sense.

"Captain, I cannot allow such nonsense to continue," Vallo said with a self-satisfied smirk and addressed everyone. "In this, I must apologize. In the essence of truth, you don't know of your captain's true objective, so hear me all. Price planned to destroy the *Peibo del ler San Francisco.*"

Amid the gasps, Angela faced the captain. He thought they could best a first-rate man-o'-war? The ship carrying a small army he'd already admitted would be impossible to defeat? All in the name of wealth and riches? Angela exhaled slowly to calm her fury. She still had to contend with an angry armed man and a handful of Spaniards with stern faces and bayonet blades attached to their muskets, clearly not understanding much.

Vallo continued, clearly enjoying this. "No one is arguing the hunter's merit of retrieving recovered Spanish gold, but using it as a bribe is beyond even your integrity. Sending the crew to slaughter a warship full of Spaniard soldiers is even worse. *Capitán* Delgado was only doing his job. If you had done yours, you wouldn't be in this mess."

Price tensed next to her.

"Why not ask the crew to jump overboard and drown? The end result ought to be the same. So I did what any well-meaning sailor would do to save his crew: I called upon Spain and disclosed your petty plan of vengeance. In exchange for your life, the crew shall be allowed their freedom."

The other crewmen murmured their shock and disbelief, and Angela's mouth gaped open. This whole ruse was for *revenge*? Angela's vision narrowed, and her chest ached. She pressed a fist against her heart as a flash of the betrayal from Brandon and his scheme loosened her knees.

Once again, she'd been used and betrayed.

After everything she'd shared with Captain Price, he'd withheld the devastating truth from her. He was using her to exact vengeance. The kisses were fake. The help he'd asked of her was for his own selfish gain—repair the *Sea Lion* to take on a warship, translate the Spanish for their upper hand.

Tears flooded her eyes as history repeated itself. She couldn't face Captain Price. Angela darted away into the jungle.

"*Recuperarla!*" a man barked orders to retrieve her.

"Angela!" Captain Price shouted, voice thick with panic.

Pain tore through her. Angela ran harder, slapping branches and slicing her hands on thick leaves. She sobbed and stumbled, landing on her knees and burying her hands in more sand. So much sand! She was tired of being filthy, sticky, sandy. Sand was in areas it didn't belong, irritating her skin and making her wish for a hot shower. With angry knees, Angela got up and dusted her hands off. She ran. Branches stung her face, but she couldn't stop.

Where could she go? The men on the ship all wanted her killed—or worse. Even if she pleaded her case for help, would they bother? It was a suicide mission! Would the *Sea Lion* even still be there?

Instead, Angela could head toward the interior of the island, pretend to be a lost local, and use Spanish as her first language again. But she was rusty, and the people here spoke differently from what she was used to. Why would they help her? She had no money or useful skills. It wasn't like she expected to find a ship repair shop and apply for a position.

Angela tripped again and rested on her hands and knees, panting. The necklace swung in front of her face, bumping her chin.

When she'd purchased her necklace at the Tall Ships festival, she remembered the old woman saying, '*These powerful gems have been known to grant your truest desire while protecting you from bad humors, so be careful how you use them.*'

If putting the necklace on brought her here, in theory, removing it would take her home. Brandon's destruction of her social life was nothing compared to being used by dozens of men or killed. In that case, she wished to return home. She had friends who meant more to her than anything, especially Emily. She had extended family she hadn't seen in a while, and a job she loved, and coworkers she adored.

Angela wished she were somewhere safe, warm, and happy. She wasn't going to find any of that here—except for the warm, but warm wasn't the same as hot, humid, and sticky.

Angela fisted the necklace and lifted it off her head. It snagged in her nest of hair. She pulled harder, tearing hair with it. She sniffled and looked around. Nothing changed. She didn't feel anything. Was she in Cuba but in her time or was she still in the past?

Angela stuffed the necklace into her pocket and stood, dusting off her knees. What she wouldn't give for a cheeseburger and a chocolate milkshake. She wiped her face, and a cold metal tube pressed against the back of her head.

She'd never been held at gunpoint, but Angela was certain that was a gun. Angela sucked in a breath and held out her hands in surrender. Either she was the unluckiest woman in the world, or she was still in the past. Did that also qualify for unluckiest?

"*No se mueva*," he'd ordered her to stay still. His hand retrieved the blade tucked into her rope belt. Then he tugged free her pistol, which she wouldn't have used, anyway. When she'd darted off into the woods, she'd forgotten about the hammer left by the hut. Now she had no means of defense.

"*Vamos*." He pushed the barrel into her head, sparking pain, forcing her to move one foot in front of the other.

"*Más rápido ahora, mujer*."

His annoyed tone was clear, but she had no reason to move faster. She was a coward, just like her father, abandoning people when they were needed most. The sooner she returned to the group, the sooner they'd kill her. But she wasn't one of them, only a tool to be used. Tears returned.

Angela walked back with a gun pressed to her skull. In the small clearing around the hut, the soldiers had trained guns on each of the *Sea Lion* crew. She didn't want to look at Captain Price, but also worried for him. The captain's pain was clear on his face. What had they done to him? She couldn't see any new injuries, but that didn't mean he wasn't hurt. Holding her chin high, Angela focused on the faces of her captors.

"*Llevamos a la mujer también*," the man behind her said in a gleeful tone. Soldiers cackled and smiled. The man gripped her arm and shoved her forward. Angela landed painfully on her knees in the sand. Didn't take a genius to figure what they had in mind.

Vallo watched with that same smirk on his stupid face. One of the soldiers approached the weasel, and together they spoke Spanish fluently. Vallo asked to keep some treasure for his efforts. The guards allowed him to take one barrel and leave, expecting messages of any new developments on the *Sea Lion*, like he was some hired spy.

Vallo nodded and said to the crew, "Good luck with Spain's noose. I hear it's quite disagreeable." He cackled and left, disappearing into greens with a barrel of gold in his arms.

"*Los llevamos todos*," another Spaniard soldier said. He waved his gun, urging all the crew to set off toward their fate, including Angela.

The purple and pinks in the sky shifted into yellows and oranges, lighting the worn path leading away from the hut. A pair of soldiers started off, leading the way, followed by one soldier per pirate. The one who'd chased her lifted her up and shoved her forward. She had no chance to steal her hammer back.

Marching through the scratchy undergrowth, Angela swatted at bugs and scratched at bites. Streaks of blood covered her hands. Her cheek still stung. But none of that mattered if they intended to hang her. After all their deep-throated chuckles, she figured they had other things in mind first. Angela ducked under a low-lying branch, and the soldier behind her shoved her shoulder. She couldn't believe this was reality.

As the captain, Price was somewhere near the front of the line. Angela couldn't see him. She didn't want to see him. All she'd ever wanted was a man who respected her, and treated her like an equal, and included her in his life, among his friends. She'd thought Captain Price met those desires.

He'd kept secrets from her—secrets that changed everything.

He'd kept her safe—only to use her in other ways.

And the crew hated her—wanted her dead or worse.

She had been wrong on all counts, and her necklace wouldn't get her out of here.

Angela swiped her forehead with her tunic, wishing for rain. After hiking for what felt like an hour, the jungle cleared to a beach and a shallow cove. Anchored just out of the cove, out of sight of the *Sea Lion*, was a massive warship with multiple decks of cannon ports, and directly behind it was a smaller ship—very different from theirs.

A lump settled in her throat while they were all forced into a longboat. Angela climbed in last. For the briefest second, she met Captain Price's eyes.

She thought real concern was there. For himself or for her and the crew?

The soldiers rowed them to the hull of the warship. Angela read the name painted on the back and shivered. *Peibo del ler San Francisco.* And a second, smaller ship was behind it, as if the warship didn't have enough power on its own, but she couldn't find the name.

Captain Price lived with the burden of regret for so long, he'd become accustomed to its heft on his shoulders, never imagining it could crush him entirely.

Then she appeared.

This angel had dropped onto his deck and saved his life. Keeping her secure against the crew was a challenge he hadn't planned on, but he persevered. She was his sign to give up the sea life and take her to the mainland to live out their lives in peace.

Just like his old friend Eric Lemoine.

Captain Price never wanted to fail at his promise to William Price, but when he did, he planned take his enemy with him—that was realistically where he'd find his peace. All the while, Price had primed Noah Riley to take over the ship, and Riley succeeded. The quartermaster followed the rules and kept the crew's focus toward the right goals. And as a show of strength, Riley had threatened to take ownership of the crew if they didn't return. Everything was set.

But over their short time together, Angela switched from burden to gift, and he'd made a grave mistake. Instead of turning his back on the men and embracing the gift, stubborn Price had to rally his cause. She was his hope the insurmountable plan could succeed at all, and he'd blindly rushed headfirst into it.

That hope was gone.

As they approached the warship, he realized now, far too late, avenging his brother's murder was a waste of his life. The dead no longer cared about their business. The dead only cared their loved ones lived full, happy lives. In that, Price had failed his brother, also.

As the longboat rowed them to their deaths, the most beautiful, strong, and courageous woman he'd ever met was going to die right along with him, all because he couldn't choose her first.

If he could give it all up, hold her in his arms, tell her how he felt, and beg her to stay with him, he'd do it. He'd do it without thinking twice. But she didn't want him. He saw the look of horror on her face, and that was after she'd declared she wanted to go home, and he promised her safe passage home. Now he couldn't keep that promise, either.

Once in a lifetime did a woman appear on a ship who saved a man's life, fixed his ship, and showed him life had more meaning than he could see. His thoughtless mission would cause her death. An innocent. A woman who deserved so much more. He was too blind to see it before it was too late.

Always too late.

Just like with William.

I'm sorry I failed you, brother.

I'm sorry I failed you, my angel.

Price would always be a failure.

Chapter 21

AT ANOTHER URGING FROM a gun barrel, Angela stood up inside the wobbly longboat and climbed the hull of the *Peibo del ler San Francisco*. On the main deck, about two dozen armed Spaniard soldiers stood around her with snarls on their clean faces and adorned muskets aimed at her. Angela's hands went up in surrender. The rest of the captured *Sea Lion* crew settled in around her, but they didn't raise their hands.

Cantu was stoic and standing tall, but Buckley's face was showing downright terror. Vallo was nowhere to be seen, not surprising.

Angela hoped Captain Price was behind her.

The guards who caught them climbed aboard and spoke to the others in Spanish, explaining the pirates had murdered the guards and stolen from King Philip V. One of the soldiers asked why a pirate crew had a woman and what they were going to do with her. Another man grinned and wagged his brows. Angela swallowed a thick lump caught in her throat. But he was quickly elbowed by the soldier next to him.

A gangly and weathered man in a fine uniform pushed through the gaggle of armed soldiers, clearly their leader. The soldiers addressed him as *Capitán* Delgado, who at once brushed by Angela and approached Captain Price with a confident swagger and a nasty smirk. Angela exhaled deeply knowing Captain Price was behind her, but nerves returned when a pair of soldiers fastened their grips on Captain Price's upper arms—restraining him. Based on Captain Price's set jaw and furrowed brow, restraint was needed.

Capitán Delgado's spoken English was heavily accented. "Henry Price, we meet again, and I see not under better circumstances."

Captain Price lifted his chin to the taller man, neck muscles tense. "*Captain* Henry Price, if you will."

Capitán Delgado snorted in derision. "You thought you could escape with gold belonging to King *Felipe*?" His condescending tone elicited chuckles in his ranks. "Not only shall you *not* escape my clutches again, but when the tide returns, *Peibo del ler San Francisco* will sink your little *Sea Lion* back to the bottom of the ocean where it belongs, and any pirates who fall with it are merely a bonus for the Crown."

Captain Price struggled in the guards' grips, and Delgado smirked and strolled along his other captives. Facing Angela he stopped. Dark pools of evil deviously raked over her body. Angela recoiled.

"Leave her out of this! She has nothing to do with our business!" Captain Price shouted with fear in his voice.

"Oh, it's far too late for that," Delgado said.

Captain Price struggled harder, true terror and fear on his fine features. "Angela! Listen to me, Angela! I'm beyond words of gratitude for all you have shown me. I'm an imbecile for choosing a past I can't change over a future I didn't know I wanted. I cannot properly convey how much despair these unfortunate circumstances have caused me. But it's not too late for you. Angela, you belong back home, in your own time."

Angela flinched. *He knew?* That was why he'd never questioned her strange costume in a bag or her mention of GPS or any other modern technology. He never questioned her sanity. In fact, when she was questioning her own, he was reassuring her everything was real. *He knew.* Regardless of her million new questions, the most important was clear: Captain Price cared about her. He pulled forward against his captors, trying to reach her, but it was no use. Tears pricked at her eyes. Angela stayed in place, hands raised in surrender, but she desperately wanted to rush to his side.

She wanted to tell him just how much she cared too.

Delgado watched with amusement as Price continued his plea, sounding more like a sorrowful goodbye filled with desperation. "I was blind! Blind by the desire to seek justice in the name of my brother. I know now how foolish I was, but it's too late for me. Spain shall have its ceremony. Go home. Save yourself."

His thoughtful apology was just what her heart needed to hear, but the goodbye ripped her to shreds. Angela stifled her sob and blinked back the tears flooding her eyes.

"Please, *Capitán* Delgado, I beg of you. Spare Angela. Set her free, and I promise full cooperation."

She didn't know how to go home, but she'd take her freedom.

"How charming," Delgado said, dismissively. "Ortega, retrieve the gallows at once. Spain shall not wait another day for justice against these uncivilized cretins."

The first mate rushed away. Now? They were going to hang Captain Price and the crew *now*? This could not be happening. No, no, please no. Angela had to do something. The Spaniard hadn't agreed to release her, and if he killed the whole *Sea Lion* crew, there was no hope for her.

"Let us go," Angela ordered in English with controlled emotion in her voice.

The warship soldiers remained stoic, ignoring her plea. *Capitán* Delgado rubbed his smooth jaw.

Without her captain, she had nothing left to lose. She'd do whatever it took to save his life...again.

"*Libéranos,*" Angela repeated herself in Spanish, more firmly this time, eliciting chuckles and mumbles from the soldiers.

Capitán Delgado lifted her hand and kissed her knuckles. "We have not formally met," he said in Spanish. "I am *Capitán* Delgado. I must know the name of the lovely face before me."

"Keep your hands off her, Delgado. This has nothing to do with her," Captain Price said, straining against the arms holding him.

Angela wrenched her hand free with a fake smile on her face. "You don't care about my name, and I don't care about yours. Let us go."

Delgado frowned at her flippant demand, but desperation had her saying things she'd never consider before, especially lying, especially to the authorities. She added, "*We* meant you no harm. The man responsible for the affront to the Spanish Crown was Vallo. As I understand, he worked for you."

Capitán Delgado straightened and smoothed his button-lined coat. "Not a simple woman, I see. I usually have a use for women, but that mouth of yours shall become a problem."

Jerk. But she could work with that. in Spanish, she said, "Then we agree, having me—us—out of your hair will prevent problems. Allow us to leave, and this burden on you will be no longer."

Delgado lifted his lips as if an idea sprang to mind. Ignoring her plea, he strolled back to Captain Price. "She means something to you, correct?" A vicious smile split his lips.

"Please, I beg of you, free her. I shall turn over all the gold taken and return for the punishment you see fit, but I beg you... Please." Captain Price's distraught eyes broke her heart. Price couldn't see a way out of this, and he was willing to give his life to preserve hers. For all the injustice, for all Price's suffering and fear, she wanted to attack Delgado in fury, but she couldn't. Her stomach knotted and her hands trembled. She hated to feel useless.

"Garcia," the enemy captain said, "show the woman our lovely accommodations below deck, while I spend some quality time with our prisoners."

Fury roared through her, but she didn't know how to stop any of this. The blade Captain Price had given her had been confiscated. The hammer had been left by the hut. She packed a mean punch when she needed to, but that wouldn't get her far with a deck full of armed soldiers.

Garcia's hands gripped her arms, and he shoved her forward to the ladder. With a last look at Captain Price, whose withdrawn face of despair crushed her, she wrenched her arms out of the man's grip and climbed down the ladder with her dignity.

Shafts of light from the sunrise through the portholes illuminated squares on the floor. Into the dank underbelly of the massive ship, Angela allowed her eyes to adjust, and the soldiers behind her forced her forward and down another ladder, and another. With each step lowering her further and further under the waterline, the light went out. A twinge of claustrophobia reared its head.

One man lit a lantern behind her and told her to turn left, and having no other choice, Angela obeyed. Where they were taking her couldn't be a bedroom.

Was that a relief or a bigger fear?

Angela stopped at a closed door. The soldier with the light unlocked it, and the door creaked open. He carried the light inside, and Garcia shoved her forward. Iron bars cut the stifling, stench-filled room in half. Chains were anchored to the walls and floors like marionette lines. One man in chains slumped over on the floor. Others leaned against the back wall, still like death. They may as well have been dead.

Sure didn't smell alive.

The first soldier unlocked the iron bars, and Garcia shoved her through. The doors screamed as they clanked shut behind her, and the soldier locked the door. "Stay in the brig until the captain is ready for you," Garcia told her in Spanish.

Angela held the sticky bars in her hands and blinked back tears from the strong urine stench.

Would she ever see Captain Price again?

Chapter 22

ORTEGA AND ANOTHER SOLDIER carried an armful of hangman's nooses and climbed the ratlines. One at a time, the men dropped them over the boom and secured them. Their faces glistened from the exertion. Price wished all the discomfort possible on these vile men. At gunpoint, his crew solemnly awaited the fate expected by all pirates.

But Angela didn't deserve this end.

She didn't deserve whatever was happening below deck. Picturing the enemy attacking her while she cried out in horror, fury sparked in his veins, powering the urge to fight, but even if he and the crew broke free from the Spaniards, the aimed guns would end their endeavor before they reached the companionway.

He was not leaving this ship without Angela.

Capitán Delgado settled at a small table, and a petty officer retrieved tea and paperwork for him. When the nooses were lashed around the boom, the soldiers lined up wood crates to finish the makeshift gallows. Satisfied, Delgado nodded to the men restraining Price, and he was released. The muskets remained, ready to fire.

Price flexed his shoulders and exchanged glances with his crew. Cantu kept his chin held high, while Buckley appeared distraught at his worst fear manifesting. He couldn't focus on his many regrets. Price couldn't see a way out of this, but he had to keep his eyes open, just in case. For Angela, he couldn't give up.

"First set of men, please." *Capitán* Delgado sipped from his teacup.

Price wanted to shove the porcelain through the captain's teeth. "Where is our trial? The Piracy Act of 1698 states we are entitled to a trial to determine guilt."

Delgado set down his cup and saucer and licked his lips. He spoke as if reciting from rote memory. "If delivering the accused to such a place for questioning about their piracies and robberies is too much trouble, acts of piracy can be examined, tried, and adjudged in any place at sea." He grinned deviously. "Even I read England's amended statue dated the year of our lord, 1700. Since you are English, I am following your laws rightfully, not that I must."

Price gritted his teeth. "The statue also states that a commissioner calls a court of admiralty consisting of at least seven people voting in said court."

Delgado tilted his head in contemplation. "If that is your wish, so be it. Men! Our pirate here requires a guilty verdict of his capital crimes before his conscience can accept his rightful death. All in favor of guilty, raise your hand!"

Every Spaniard soldier on deck lifted his hand. Bastards.

Price ran a hand down his face. He needed more time to think. "And of Angela? She is not a pirate. Let her go!"

The Spaniard captain sipped from his cup and uncorked his inkwell. "The woman in your crew, at a minimum, is guilty by assisting acts of piracy. She was witnessed with stolen goods in her hands."

"She was pressed. She's innocent," Price countered.

Ignoring the desperate plea, Delgado gestured for his soldiers to commence the hanging, while dipping his quill in the ink.

"Too late for begging and bargaining," *Capitán* Delgado said with boredom.

Obediently, soldiers stepped forward and threatened four of his crew to obey at gunpoint, including Buckley. The fear twisting the old man's face crushed Price. He was a good man, an experienced old salt, even if his eyesight failed him on occasion. Knowing the man would prefer instant death at the hands of his own crew rather than the enemy, Price couldn't do anything to save him from his worst nightmare.

This was all Price's fault.

Four men were stopped with their toes touching their own crates, just under the boom. All but Buckley stepped onto the crates before them. The carpenter refused, and his disobedience earned him a sharp jab in the back. Buckley stepped up, and the soldiers fastened his men's hands securely with rope.

No man deserved this humiliation. All their deaths would be on his conscience.

"You cannot use English law as an excuse to deal out your own vengeance," Price said, hoping to delay the captain's next orders with a plea for fairness.

"Your pathetic ship attempted to take the *Peibo del ler San Francisco* as a prize. My father's ship, my ship. You all should've been hanging at the gallows for it, but my father, rest his soul, was too kind for a captain. I have no such qualms. This punishment is long overdue. Be thankful for the extra time you had and didn't deserve."

"Most of this crew is new. They're innocent."

"No one's innocent the moment they step foot on that ship."

That was it. No more negotiating. Delgado wouldn't see reason and didn't understand mercy. Price shouldn't have been surprised.

The *Sea Lion*, with a stolen Spanish banner at her masthead, had been hunting a prize off the coast of Hispaniola. The *Peibo del ler San Francisco*, indeed, a first-rate man-o'-war, surprised them and hailed for communication. Too close to flee and vastly underpowered, the Sea Lion had no chance of survival.

Captain Lemoine had decided to send a man to distract the enemy. William Price had volunteered. William agreed the moment he cleared the rail, the *Sea Lion* was to immediately leave while he put on his best show, or his sacrifice would've been for naught. Price had argued with his brother, and the shouts heard around the ships. Spain became suspicious. Captain Lemoine had told William to go at once or their plan was wasted.

William went.

Unwilling to let such selflessness go and unable to part from his brother, Henry Price followed.

The *Sea Lion* had shifted forward, gliding, hoping to make range before further suspicions were raised. But the plan had been a failure.

"William Price and I tried to negotiate with you. We meant you no harm," Captain Price said, trying one last approach for mercy.

Delgado looked up from his writing. "Your brother claimed he had was hunting a pirate ship with stolen porcelain bound for England. And that such goods had left this very island."

"That's how I remember it, yea."

Delgado set down his quill. "Cuba never exported porcelain, and your banner was stolen. Spanish merchants and naval ships know the proper condition our banner must maintain, and yours was in near tatters. Such shame! Your brother lied, and I simply challenged his word. At that, he was afraid. A little mouse, so knowing nothing else, he attacked me in a panic. My father took leniency on you both, and accepted his deal to free you, knowing one captured pirate was more valuable than whatever stolen goods the *Sea Lion* truly had on board. When the tale of William Price's cowardice and surrender reached the *Boston News-Letter*, damaging the pirate reputation, the black banner would no longer instill terror on the seas."

Price stared at the Spaniard, dumbfounded. He'd never read the story.

Delgado retrieved his quill and dipped it. "I would've hanged you. Better late than never, as they say."

Price had leaped to the *Sea Lion* before it was out of range, believing his own skill had led to his escape. All these years, Captain Price had carried such guilt, plotted with all the spare energy he had, hoping for the opportunity to lay waste to this ship and everyone on board, because he was strong enough. He was capable. He was cunning. And he'd shouted over the rail a promise to avenge William Price's sacrifice.

His brother had simply made a deal.

Price moved to strike. If he couldn't prevent any of their deaths, he could take one of the enemies with him, and he knew just the man. A sharp pain struck the back of his knee, and Price fell to the deck. A cold metal barrel of a musket was pressed against his neck, and the glinting blade of the bayonet stretched just past his face.

Delgado scratched the pen on parchment. "The official documents shall list your death as...accidental. And such an untimely mishap prevented your crew from receiving their due justice."

The flippant use of 'due justice' only infuriated Price, but showing anger wouldn't help. "Is there anything I may offer in bargain for Angela's life? She is an innocent in all this. You've taken a deal once, do it again."

Delgado gestured to his men again, and the soldiers slipped nooses over the *Sea Lion*'s crewmen. Delgado set his pen down and approached Price with loose arms at his sides. "The only thing I want from you is your long overdue death."

In a flash, *Capitán* Delgado unsheathed a short blade from his backside and stabbed Price discreetly in the abdomen and slid the blade out clean.

Mouth gaped open in surprise, Price stumbled back and covered the wound. The blade was short enough to cause a higher chance of suffering than death, but the wound was unfortunate.

"On my count," Delgado ordered, "swing the boom starboard over the deck. Allow their bowels and bladders to empty into the sea as they hang to their deaths."

Price inhaled a shaky breath. If torturing him and his crew was of no consequence, what did *Capitán* Delgado have in mind for Angela?

Chapter 23

Cutting onions was like a gentle lake breeze compared to the vapors down here. And she thought the *Sea Lion* had been awful. Urine, feces, sweat, vomit, and who knew what else stung her eyes. Angela pulled at the sticky iron bars, but they didn't give. She reached for the lock, but it was welded to the cage, and there was no obvious latch. She was trapped in the guts of a warship during a time in history she should've only read about in a textbook.

Emily would've had a field day with this insanity. Angela? Not so much. She didn't belong here. Good thing Robin didn't show up on time. Robin would've struggled so much worse with all this lawlessness.

Groans and a rattle of chain turned her head. A filthy, stringy-haired man leaned against the bulwark. He tilted his face up to hers, and a shaggy beard covered most of his face. He looked to be in his forties, and far from prime health. Other men in similar condition were chained to the wall and floor nearby. Clearly Delgado didn't take care of his prisoners very well. Looking at the men made Angela ache for a shower, and the cheeseburger craving returned.

"A companion in the hold," the stringy-haired man said with awe. By his accent, he was English. "And a woman at that. How quaint. Never expected the Spaniards to be so generous. If this is the delusion of a dying man, I welcome it."

"You're not delusional, but if you try anything..." Angela trailed off her warning. The shackles made her warning useless.

The stringy-haired man chuckled. "You must be real. Come sit. Give a tired man's neck a break."

Angela sat on the floor near the man, but out of chain reach. Since she couldn't change the horrible events above them, conversation was a welcome distraction. "What did you do to land yourself in here?"

Her chatty fellow prisoner pushed hair out of his face. "I tried to do the right thing. The more interesting question plaguing me is what did *you* do?"

Angela reflected on the exact cause that brought her aboard and cringed. "I helped pirates steal Spanish gold."

His shaggy brows lifted, and he grinned. "Is that so? Then I'd say your rightful place is here by me. For the sake of my otherwise mundane endless hours in this cell, what great ship did you sail upon? It deserves recognition."

"The *Sea Lion*."

The prisoner blinked once then twice, silently staring.

"The *Sea Lion*," she repeated louder.

"I heard you. I just cannot believe you. The *Sea Lion* is outside this hull right now? Is that what you're telling me?"

"Not exactly. It's—" Angela pointed in the rough direction she thought it was "—somewhere over there. We're still repairing the storm damage. The rigging's a mess, last I saw."

Interesting that she referred to the crew as *we*.

"The *Sea Lion* is...is here?"

"Yes." Angela frowned. This guy's company was quickly becoming less enjoyable than she'd hoped.

"Who else is on this ship? Your mates? Who are they?" The eagerness in his voice was strange. He must know the crew.

"Cantu and Buckley are up there. A bunch of men too, but I don't know their names. And—"

A gleam of excitement lit his eyes. "What about the quartermaster?"

"Riley is on the *Sea Lion*. He was in charge of getting ready to escape. He's probably going to leave us behind now." That was a depressing thought, but that was the instruction. Leave before the *Sea Lion* was caught too.

"No, no no." His hand slashed at the air in frustration. "Price. Where is Price?"

This man did know the crew or maybe he was one of them...long ago. "Captain Price is up there. *Capitán* Delgado seems to have a bone to pick with him, though."

"Captain?" the shaggy brows lifted again. "I daresay..." A smile shifted his beard.

Figuring this stringy haired prisoner had intimate knowledge of the *Sea Lion*'s crew, Angela asked, "Who are you?"

"Price," he said, holding out a filthy hand, "William Price."

Angela stared at the hand, dumbfounded. "But you're dead."

"Not yet, and I suddenly feel much livelier. What is your name, my lady?"

"Angela Foxe." Angela leaned over and took his hand, but William Price collected her fingers and tilted her wrist to kiss her knuckles. The formality of the time sent a tickle of appreciation through her.

"It's not every day I find a worthy pirate woman. Such a pleasure to meet you."

Angela couldn't help a grin at the intended compliment. "For what it's worth, I don't think we'll be alive much longer, and I don't know what to do about it. They're going to hang Captain Price and the rest of the crew they have up there. Delgado asked for nooses. I—I wanted to do something, anything, but they grabbed me, and I just...I wish I could do something."

Tears misted her eyes. If she'd done things differently, could she have prevented this? "I wanted to fight, to stop them all. But there's just so many, and I don't have any weapons. I asked them to show mercy. I pleaded with them, but they laughed. It's unfair what they're going to do to him, and I can't stop it." Emotion caught in her throat. Angela didn't realize just how far her caring went.

"I've seen men beg for their lives. I've heard their cries—far more often than I'd rather remember. The begging and pleading is always the same—spare me, save me, please don't do that. I can offer whatever in exchange... There's a difference with you. Your pleas ring true, but without concern over your own life. No, you and I are in the same situation, awaiting death or worse, but yet you worry for someone else." William paused and studied her.

Angela swiped tears from her eyes. It was true. She did care for Captain Price, and she wanted more than anything to save him.

"Do you love my brother?"

Love? Did she *love* Captain Price? Her instinct was to deny the accusation, but yet, she couldn't utter the denial. Love a man she'd only just met? The idea was ludicrous. And yet, when she pictured him and remembered his lips filling her body with tingles and need, and when he stood up for her, defended her, protected her... He was her hero, and all it earned him was a noose. Angela sobbed. The first man who'd treated her right was ripped from her grasp before they'd had a real chance. Why? What had she done wrong for the universe to throw her a curve ball? Angela struck out. She always sucked at sports. Angela composed herself and dashed away the tears with the dirt-streaked back of her hand.

The other prisoners rustled, now watching the evening's entertainment. Angela didn't care what they thought.

Since words failed her, William said, "Don't confuse me for a sap, but my brother is a good man. With my disappearance, I'm certain he's become...misdirected. He's always been devoted to the people in his life. As long as you're willing to give him your love, there's always hope."

His words were beautiful, but Angela couldn't find the hope behind thick iron bars, when an enemy captain had every intention of hanging

Captain Price at any moment. For all she knew, he could already be dead. Angela's face twisted with her unrelenting tears.

William patted her shoulder in an attempt to console her while maintaining the respectful distance society demanded.

Screw society.

Angela fell into his arms, and he held her, gently patting her back and snagging his hands on her snarled hair.

"Oh, what is this?" William tugged on a tangle of strands.

"Leaves? Sand? Sticks?" For all she knew, Angela carried a family of chipmunks with her.

William tugged once more and freed something.

Angela leaned back and smiled. "It's a bobby pin. Supposed to hold my chaos in order. I think sticks would've worked better."

William inspected the small piece of metal and bent it. "Oh, no, sticks are far inferior compared to this. This... Do you know what this is?" Excitement once again lit his eyes.

Angela shook her head.

"My lady, this is hope. I think your wish is coming true. Do you have more of these?"

Angela sniffed and dug in her hair, dropping pin after pin on the floor.

"Take these to the others. We're getting out of here."

Angela scooped up her pins and roused each man who wasn't already enraptured with the drama in their cell and handed one to each. They accepted the pins and bent them like William did, and the prisoners quickly set to work on the locks holding their shackles closed. With Spain's numbers on deck, the *Sea Lion* crew had no chance, but with more men...

Angela remembered the captain's concern over the crew's numbers after the storm.

"If any of you are looking to join a pirate ship, the *Sea Lion* is hiring."

The tired men glanced at each other and mumbled. Some nodded.

William's shackles dropped free with a rattle of chains. He rubbed his wrists and ankles and stood, stretching his back and neck with a euphoric moan. "Far too long I've been stuck hunched over. A sweet kindness like none other. I'm in your debt, my lady Angela. How many soldiers are on deck?"

"Two dozen maybe. Enough."

More chains dropped, and the prisoners stood and approached the gate, but no one celebrated. They understood the gravity of what was to come. William worked at the tumbler standing between them and the warship full of soldiers.

"What's the plan?" Angela asked as William's tongue peeked between his lips.

The tumbler ticked and clicked until it thumped free. Prisoners gasped.

"Stay quiet. Overtake any man encountered and take his weapons. Make our way to the main deck. I need you all"—he nodded at the fellow prisoners—"to hold the soldiers on the main deck at gunpoint. I'm going after the captain."

"I'm going after Captain Price," Angela said. "Now let's get out of here."

William nodded with a smile, and he swung the iron gate open with an angry creak. One by one they filtered into the narrow gangway. The first soldier stood guard at the end of the hall, facing outward, as if more concerned about who was coming down rather than going up.

William covered the man's mouth to muffle an attempt at a warning shout and another prisoner behind him collected the knife at his belt. The prisoner stabbed the soldier, and softly he sunk to the floor.

As Angela passed him, the gurgles from his throat and drifting eyes made her queasy. The soldier was only doing his job, and he died for it. But if he didn't, none of them would survive the next twenty minutes.

Up the ladders they climbed through the decks, one after the other, on silent feet taking down oblivious soldiers and collecting a small arsenal to defend themselves with. Angela accepted a knife from William, hoping she didn't need to use it.

Chapter 24

AT THE FINAL LADDER to the main deck, William stopped to survey the scene, squinting into the daylight. His eyes weren't adjusted. How long had he been captive? Impatiently, Angela pushed her way up next to him. Four of the *Sea Lion*'s crew, including Buckley, stood on crates with nooses around their necks. The rest of the crew had soldiers holding them at gunpoint—at point-blank range.

Just away from the crew, Captain Price was buckled over on his knees with *Capitán* Delgado walking away from him and smirking. Price then fell over to the deck. Angela gasped. They were too late!

"Lift him up," *Capitán* Delgado said, sitting at a table…with tea? What the…? What kind of man could be so nonchalant about killing people? A monster. Delgado was a monster, who sipped from a teacup and said, "He must watch his men's deaths. On my count, remove the crates and let those feet swing free."

"No!" Angela whisper-yelled into William's ear. "Do something."

He hushed her. "We must coordinate our actions, or we are next."

William pointed at the prisoners waiting by his feet. "You fellows, go for the soldiers on the port side. Tell the men behind you to head starboard." The prisoners immediately conveyed the message while William turned to Angela. "Go for Price, but watch out for Delgado. He'll be desperate."

Angela gritted her teeth and gripped that knife. "He's never seen a woman scorned."

William's lips lazily lifted in a crooked smile. "Go!" he whispered, and they scrambled up the ladder, pouring through the narrow companionway. Angela booked across the deck with William at her side, heading straight for the one man who meant more to her than anything.

The soldiers paused and stared, dumbfounded with disbelief, and Angela and the prisoners used that to their advantage. She and William crossed the deck without any resistance, both carrying weapons at the ready and snarls on their faces.

Captain Price remained folded over.

Her insides swirled in fear of being too late.

The soldiers regained their wits and shouted, scrambling for defense. Swords were unsheathed. Guns were aimed and fired. Crew fell. Prisoners fell. The rapid pops around Angela shook her eardrums.

Prisoners reached the crew at the nooses and freed them, but not without consequences. Several prisoners dropped, and the freed crew took up their weapons. The surviving prisoners joined the crew in fighting back, but still they were far too outnumbered.

Angela turned away from the gruesome scene before she froze in panic and kept her legs moving across the deck. Perspiration dampened her already filthy clothing, and she startled when something or someone brushed against her foot, making her lose her balance, but Angela recovered and kept going. Through the chaos, Angela focused on Captain Price and tucking her knife into her rope belt. She didn't want to cut him accidentally.

Capitán Delgado's face pinched in fury at the sight of her. The gangly man launched to his feet, knife in hand. Right before the Delgado struck in rage, Angela ducked and William engaged the captain.

Angela slid to Captain Price. She held out her hands, wanting to touch him, but afraid of hurting him further, or of discovering she was too late.

"Captain Price?" she asked, voice shaky. "Captain Price, are you okay?"

A soft groan broke through his lips. Angela held her breath as her captain's head shifted. His shoulders tilted. Not believing her eyes, she brushed the hair out of his face.

Captain Price shuddered, and his face moved to meet her gaze. Surprise, worry, and relief flashed across his features. "Angela?"

Angela smiled. A flush of her own relief mixed with the heart-pounding adrenaline. Soon this would all be over, but whether they'd succeed was still up in the air. The sooner they got off this ship, the better their odds.

"I'm here."

"Call me Henry."

Angela smiled and inspected his hands for binds. "Henry, can you move?"

"I believe so." Henry's eyes lifted to Delgado, and they widened in fear. "Move!"

Angela looked up and ducked under a swinging blade, but it wasn't meant for her. William Price and Delgado were locked in a battle. Metal of meeting swords clanged in the air. The pistols, spent and too burdensome to reload, had been abandoned.

Buckley was ringed in uniformed bodies, but for an old fellow, he was shockingly skilled, holding back a handful of soldiers by himself. Angela's brows lifted. With him as an ally, she didn't need to worry about the others after all.

Cantu held his own also. A big lumbering giant, he had reach that the soldiers didn't.

A blade swooped through the air, and Angela rolled out of the way. Henry shuffled after her, folded with a hand pressed against his abdomen and a pinched face. Angela helped him to his feet, clear of the smaller skirmishes.

"Are you hurt?" she asked.

No longer the headstrong, determined man she'd met, now he was broken, in pain, lost. Henry pulled a bloody hand from his clothing.

"My need for vengeance clouded my judgment, but in all this time, I never truly believed I'd lose, and if I did, I was going to sacrifice myself to save those who bravely joined me." Henry lifted his eyes to the men fighting. Tears glistened on his lower lids. "I can't beat Delgado like this."

"We aren't trying to win. We're trying to survive. Escape. Get out of here while we still can."

"This is the end for me," Henry said, studying his bloody hand. "I've lived with many regrets in my life, but lately I've added so many more. I regret sailing into that storm, killing half my crew. I'd be sailing in depths with them if it weren't for you, my angel." Henry smiled, and his hand graced her jaw. "But I fear that effort was in vain. And I regret coming here, losing many more good men. Mostly I regret risking your life. I thought I lost you, and I was devastated."

Angela hated this goodbye speech. "Don't give up on me now. You have to live today and fight another day."

Henry shook his head. The defeat was crushing. "I won't give up my promise to you. Your safety is all that matters to me now, and I'm shocked you were able to escape, but somehow not surprised. You are strong, beautiful, and beyond anyone I deserve. I need you need to get out of here."

"We're both getting out of here now. All of us," Angela said. "I'm not that strong. It's only dumb luck that I escaped. You've been my protector all the while, and I need you. I need you to be strong, because you can't quit on me."

Henry's features twisted in surprise, looking over her shoulder, and before Angela reacted, Henry pushed her aside. Angela tumbled to the deck. There went her knee again. She flicked the nest of hair out of her face, and at the last second, Henry dodged an arcing blade from Delgado and William's fight.

Delgado disarmed William, who panted heavily. They were both bruised and bloodied, and their clothing torn. William had been in chains for so long, leaving him in this weakened state, how could he beat a healthier man?

Angela had to do something. The knife William had given her—Angela pulled it free from her belt and slid it across the deck. It stopped at William's bare foot. He bent and gripped it and rolled away from a strike.

Now she had no defense—not that she knew how to fight, anyway. More soldiers poured onto the deck from who knew where. They craned their necks, assessing the condition of their men. In moments, they would attack.

Henry rushed to her side and helped her to her feet. "Are you all right?"

"I will be when we're out of here. I need you, Henry. I need you to come with me. Your brother wouldn't want you to stay behind. Not like this." She spoke for the man, but she was certain she was right. She hoped her words got through to him, because they were almost out of time.

Chapter 25

ANGELA WANTED HIM SO dearly, could he choose to give up on her, too? It would break his heart to leave her when she needed him most. He'd already failed his brother, rest his soul, and now, wounded and bleeding, Price wouldn't fail Angela.

Besides, given the chance, his older brother would slap him upside the head for turning away from the chance at happiness right in front of him. He gripped Angela and held her close. With a confident smile on his face, "I won't quit on you. I shall not fail you. We must evacuate now."

Angry faces closed in and assessing them, Angela said, "Agreed."

"Abandon ship!" Henry roared and then winced at the ache in his gut. He really hated Delgado.

At the signal, the *Sea Lion* crew and the freed prisoners disengaged and rushed across the deck before throwing themselves over the rail. Delgado tracked one particular shaggy prisoner's retreat and roared, "This isn't over yet!"

The shaggy prisoner rushed to Angela, but Price didn't feel concerned over her safety. He had a feeling this man helped her escape. "We must go now. No delay!" The prisoner met Price's gaze for a flash as if to urge his escape, too.

Buckley and the others jumped from where they fought.

Only he and Angela remained, and the soldiers and vindictive captain closed the distance, holding swords aloft. No mercy remained on their bloodied faces.

Angela tugged on Henry's arm. "Can you swim?"

Henry had enough spirits in him to send her a small smile. "You first."

Angela nodded and climbed over the rail. Without hesitation, she jumped. He heard the splash and shifted to maneuver his legs over the rail. The enemy captain grabbed him by the shoulder, stopping him entirely.

"Henry! Captain Price!" she called from below, and the panic in her voice tore his heart.

She called again, "Henry!"

He couldn't answer. Calling back to her would only delay her escape, and there was nothing he could do from here. Price twisted free of Delgado's grip and stumbled over a downed man's outstretched arm. The victim was thin and woolly, wearing torn clothing. He appeared to be a prisoner. Freed from his burdens for only a minute to lose any hope forever. That could've been Price if Angela hadn't convinced him otherwise. A discarded body, waiting for disposal, never to be thought of again.

The grave injustice of Delgado's mere existence enraged Price, but the prisoner at his feet was barehanded.

"Mark my words," Delgado said in English, pointing a sword at Price's throat. "When the tide rolls a dawn tomorrow, the *Sea Lion* shall be volleyed into a cloud of smithereens, drifting quietly beneath the surface, and every last pirate on that wretched ship shall be hung under the gallows or making his peace with Davy Jones' Locker."

Price had learned his lesson, and thankfully, it appeared he wasn't too late after all...for Angela. Rather than engage the enemy he'd sworn to destroy, knowing it would be his useless end, Angela's words rolled through his mind, '*We aren't trying to win. We're trying to survive. You have to live today and fight another day*'. As always, she was right. He could heal up, regroup, and do it right for the last time.

Without further hesitation, Price cast his enemy a smirk and flung himself overboard. *Please forgive me, dear brother.* He hit the water with a heavy splash and swam up. With far less clothing, the task was much easier, but Price was never a great swimmer. Gasping for air at the surface, he sought Angela, but he didn't see her. Price swiped his face clear.

"Angela?" he called and swam away from the ship. "Angela!"

"Henry!"

Captain Price exhaled in relief at her voice. A lightness filled him as he paddled toward her. She'd been halfway to shore, but she turned around for him.

"Stay there. I'll come to you."

She didn't listen.

Price paddled harder, so she didn't return within range of the *Peibo del ler San Francisco,* and he caught up to her a safe distance from the enemy warship.

"Are you okay?" she asked, brow creased in worry.

"I'll be fine." But his abdominal wound now leaked rapidly in the water.

"There's something I need to tell you," Angela said.

"It can wait. Let's get out of the water." Price paddled toward shore, keeping a close eye on Angela to be sure she stayed at his side. He'd never expected to survive that ship a second time. He'd lost men, again, but at least he didn't have to lose someone he loved.

Last time it was William.

This time it would've been Angela.

He'd been spared that pain, and for that, he was eternally grateful. He touched sand and stood. Angela panted, marching out of the water. He held his hand out to her, and she took it. He assisted her through the soft sand underfoot.

They both needed a break, but Spain would destroy the *Sea Lion*, and Price couldn't let that happen. "We must return to the ship immediately."

Angela wiped water from her face. "Why?"

A flicker of movement caught Price's attention. A man revealed himself from the jungle, and Price turned, shoving Angela behind him. The filthy but soaked man was one of the prisoners. The one who'd fought *Capitán* Delgado.

"State your name, sir," Price called over.

Angela pushed around Price, refusing his protection. "He won't hurt me."

After all they'd survived, Price couldn't take that risk. "How do you know such things? Look at his condition. He was clearly a prisoner. What do you think he did to earn that spot?"

"What did I do?" Angela retorted.

She had a point. Price waited for the stranger to approach and speak. His clothing draped on his thin frame like rags. His disheveled hair and overgrown beard obscured his features, but despite all that, he walked with a familiar confidence. The gleam in his eye reminded him of...

Angela stepped back to give them space. A small smile lifted her lips.

It couldn't be. Could it? After all this time and complete certainty of the man's fate, was it possible? No, no, it couldn't be. The Spaniards—Delgado and his father—held the man surrounded by swords. Death had been imminent. Price had seen it with his own eyes! Delgado had claimed they made a deal—William had publicly admitted his crimes of piracy, turned himself over, and was hung for it. But Price had never heard the story. The pirate reputation had never been tarnished. There was no reasonable chance the man strolling across the sand was his William, but still his heart wanted to believe.

"Brother?" Price asked with a whisper.

"It's I, brother." William pulled Price into a hug.

Tears pricked his tired eyes. A crazed laugh rose from within, and Price burst in laughter, in relief, in true amazement. His chest swelled with appreciation and relief. They patted each other's backs and squeezed. Price never wanted to let go.

"I thought I'd lost you." A sob broke through his celebratory laughter.

William shifted back from his embrace. "The Spaniards busied themselves with other matters, so I was stashed away for future use. They never expected you to arrive and throw them into disarray. And they never expected a woman to set us free."

William gestured Angela to come closer. The beautiful woman had tears of joy in her eyes, and when she stepped forward, Price and his brother pulled her into a tight squeeze.

"I owe you my life in so many ways," Price told her. "I am forever in your debt."

"That's not necessary. I didn't do it for accolades," Angela said.

"Then why did you risk your life for me and William?"

Price and William loosened their grip on her. She sniffled and leaned back to look him in the eyes. "Because I love you."

The world around them dropped away. All Price saw was her. The kind soul who risked everything for him; she showed him real life—one free of a pact to destroy an enemy nation—was possible. A blossom of heat rose through his chest, unlocking tingles of need and desire he hadn't felt in so long. Being so near his brother, he shoved those feelings down for later.

But the buzz trembling through his brain was real, and he knew just what to say, "My dearest Angela, I've loved none other but you, and it's because of you that I breathe. You are an angel, and I shall cherish the ground you traverse for all of my days."

"I've never heard such sentiment from you, brother," William said with a chuckle. "I'm thrilled that heart of yours is capable of it, but Spain is sure to send soldiers ashore after us, and I'd hate for our little reunion to be dashed so soon. Let us set sail at once."

Price, now realizing William witnessed his whole declaration of love, blushed furiously, but his brother was right. And they had bigger problems than soldiers chasing them. "Delgado claimed he shall volley the *Sea Lion* at high tide. We must go now."

"Are you certain?" William asked.

"Delgado follows through on his threats. After we escaped his clutches twice, he won't stop until we're dead—orders from the Crown or not."

"Then we hurry. Where does she anchor?"

Price pointed to the entrance of the cove. "Southeast by south, around the cove entrance."

More filthy men appeared from the jungle, and Price turned on them in defense. After getting a miraculous second chance with the people he loved most, he'd never allow anyone to harm Angela or his brother.

William touched his shoulder in reassurance. "These are good men."

"I invited them," Angela said. "I thought after the wreck you were shorthanded. They can sail."

Price stared at her in surprise. "You invited them? Where did you find these filthy men?"

"The warship's prisoners. Most of them are English merchant sailors."

Just when he thought he'd seen all her surprises, Angela pulled yet another out of a labyrinthine bag. Price turned to the shy crowd, beaming with hope. "All who want to join the *Sea Lion*, follow us for a fair share and freedom. You are most welcome."

William led the way, and Price collected Angela's hand. They marched just inside the jungle, out of direct line of sight of the Spaniards, and a line of men followed behind. No matter the struggles before them, Price had never been happier.

Chapter 26

ANGELA CRUNCHED TWIGS AND short plants under her steps and ducked under low-hanging branches. She was exhausted and overdue for sleep, and her salty, damp clothing irritating, but Angela walked on soft clouds. A lightness lifted her, giving her the energy to float through the dense jungle behind William. Henry insisted on staying behind her to keep an eye on both her and his brother. Personally, she'd rather have Henry's round ass to marvel at while they walked, but considering what Henry went through, she humored his minor request.

Angela yawned.

"You best be staying awake there," a familiar voice said. Buckley popped out of the woods and joined them. Cantu was just behind them.

"Price," Buckley addressed one of the men. "And Price," he addressed the other.

The brothers both gestured their welcome. They were both tired, too.

Henry said, "You made it, Buck. Cantu, good to see you."

Cantu nodded.

"I didn't think we were going to survive," Buckley said. "But I'm glad I'm not a betting man. You did good back there, for a woman." Buckley fell in stride alongside her.

"Uh, thanks." Angela didn't have the energy to correct Buckley's quip, not that she alone could change his mind, so she accepted his compliment as he meant it.

"Is Delgado finally dead?" Buckley asked.

Henry spoke up, a harshness in his voice. "He lives."

Buckley's brows rose. "All that plotting, planning, and stewing, and you let him get away?"

Henry darted him a look of annoyance. "I know when I'm outmatched, and since I have what I wanted, I have no reason to further my campaign against him."

"Huh. Something sure has changed with you, and I don't think the elder Price was the reason," Buckley added and glanced at Angela.

At Henry's silence, Angela looked at him. She smiled, and he winked in return. With the top few buttons of his tunic torn off, the peeking chest hair sent tingles crawling down her aching body. What else lay beneath that fabric precariously clinging to his skin? More jewelry like his glinting ear? She wanted to peel it off and find out.

Tongues optional.

Waiting for a private moment for just the two of them left her heart thumping and her mind a swirling mess. She hadn't been with any man since Brandon, and those were memories she'd rather delete. Instead, she shifted her gaze to Henry, wishing to strip every layer of fabric off his body and explore every inch of skin. He was a beautiful man, and he'd do anything to keep her safe.

She'd never felt more important in her life.

Henry had been adamant about returning her home, but with her admission, would he change his mind? Angela wasn't certain on much, but she knew life aboard a ship wasn't for her. Would Henry's call for the sea keep him from her? Did he mean to keep his promise: *safe passage to whatever destination you choose?* He'd known she was from the future. She still never got a chance to ask how he knew that.

A branch struck her in the face.

"Ow!" Angela flinched and cradled her cheek. A greater force was sending her a message, but she had no idea what it meant.

"Are you injured?" Henry asked.

"It's just a scratch." Angela turned to show him, and the sight of blood on his tunic made her gasp. She stopped in her tracks. When she'd seen Henry curled up on the deck and the captain walking away, she'd assumed Delgado punched him in the abdomen or kicked him in a sensitive region. "What is that? Is that what Delgado did?"

Henry gestured at it and waved it off. "It's nothing. Do not worry yourself over me."

William stopped his lead and returned to them. "We're almost out of the cove. What's the commotion back here? Oh." William lifted the sticky shirt from Henry's abdomen and checked the wound over. "How deep did it go?"

"Five centimeters, give or take. It's nothing. We must reach the *Sea Lion* and set sail before the tide returns."

William frowned at it. "Does the vessel have a medic on board?"

"Meeks was struck down by a Royal Navy man-o'-war, and his replacement retired inland."

"So, that means no. Buckley?"

"I can fix the ship with my tools. I don't see much resemblance between a wooden beauty and"—Buckley eyed the captain pointedly—"a flesh and blood man, but I'll do my best."

"Buckley, your hands tremble like palm trees in a squall," Henry countered.

Like Henry's hesitation, Angela liked the old man, but not enough to allow him to fix the captain's wound. "I can do it, if you have supplies for me to work with."

"Excellent," William said. "Let's get to it."

"Riley would know if the doctor's chest survived the sinking." Henry collected Angela's hand and smiled in reassurance. It didn't work. If his brother was that concerned, she was doubly so. Her stomach knotted as he led her out of the safety of the jungle and down the beach, out of the cove.

The tide had crept in, and the *Sea Lion* was afloat. They'd left a longboat just in case, and the survivors and escapees climbed inside and rowed as the sunrise blinded them. After being locked in that eye-watering cell, the sea breeze was a welcomed fresh air.

Henry and William urged her up the hull first, and the brothers climbed up behind her. She felt special. She felt loved and protected. And she smiled as she clambered over the rail. Buckley and the other established crew, who'd survived, followed closely. The prisoners stayed behind in the longboat.

Moving over the rail, Henry winced, holding his abdomen. That was her priority.

"Riley!" Henry shouted.

The quartermaster popped out of the navigation room at once and approached while assessing their condition. "You made it out. Sort of. I guess that means I'm not the captain. Thankfully, I'm glad you're back." Riley smiled, but Henry didn't share his relief. "What happened?"

"Did Vallo return?" Henry asked.

"No. What's this about?"

"No time to explain. Is she sea ready?" Henry asked.

"I'm afraid not. All the holes have been patched in the hull to the best our supplies allowed, and I believe with fair weather, she'll make it to a safer port, but the rigging is still a mess. Karl said we need weeks to sort the tangled lines. Without them, we're at the sea's mercy."

"There's no way to move this ship before dusk?" Henry asked again.

"Not in our current position, captain. Maybe if we had more men." Riley scanned the deck, worry settling on his features. "No others survived? The few of you, that's all?"

"Not exactly," Angela said, and Riley sent her a confused glance.

"Bring up the new recruits," Henry told his brother.

Riley scrutinized their small group more closely. "New recruits? What happened? Who's that?" He nodded toward William.

William gestured over the rail for the prisoners to come aboard and moved aside. "We need hands. They need a vessel."

"Well," Riley said with a smile. "This is great! Who are you?"

William approached Riley. "William Price, former Royal Navy armorer, former *Sea Lion* armorer, and former *Peibo del ler San Francisco* prisoner."

Riley grinned. "Captain Price's brother has risen from the grave."

"Feels that way," William said, rubbing the nape of his neck.

The prisoners filtered onto the deck, and Riley greeted them. "Hope has been restored."

"Riley," Henry said, "You can thank Angela." Henry winked at her.

Heat of appreciation warmed her. Angela ached to scurry him to his cabin and inspect his wound. Inspect other things. She wanted to capture his lips, strip him naked, show her appreciation for a long, long time. She'd never wanted a man more than Henry at this very minute and the throbbing down below wouldn't let up.

The quartermaster approached her, wearing the features of a conflicted man. Angela swallowed. Lust fully extinguished. She'd forgotten for just a moment how much she wasn't welcome on this ship. "I owe you an apology. Woman or not, you have proved yourself worthy of a place on the *Sea Lion*. If any of the crew continues hostilities against you, send for me at once. Because of you, we have a chance to escape this enemy island. Thank you."

"You're welcome." Angela smiled.

Pirates or not, these were good men—well, mostly. Angela squeezed the edge of her tunic, wringing out excess water. Drops pattered to the wood floor, reminding her of Henry's wet wound. "Did the doctor's chest survive the wreck? We need it."

"Who's injured?" Riley asked.

"Price has a knife wound. It needs tending before all these efforts to destroy Delgado end with gangrene," William said.

"Buckley," Riley said, and the carpenter disengaged from the newcomers. "You remember where the chest is?"

"If they put it back where they found it, then I do."

"Will you assist Angela and Price below deck?" Riley asked.

"Consider it done. Come with me, you two," Buckley said.

"Which Price?" William asked with a naughty smirk.

Henry slapped his brother upside the back of the head playfully. "She's mine, and don't you ever forget it."

William chuckled and rubbed his head. "Feathery gull."

Angela didn't know what that meant, but she figured it was a friendly insult between brothers. She followed Buckley while holding Henry's hand, and on their way across the deck, several of the prisoners patted her on the back in thanks. A shiver of excitement filled her as she climbed down the ladder to find the medical supplies. She was respected, accepted.

Once the darkness enveloped her, that excitement waned. She needed to save Henry's life.

Again.

Chapter 27

HOLDING HENRY'S HAND AND trying to ignore the current his touch zipped through her, Angela stopped on the ladder before plowing into Buckley. He paused, and she squinted into the dim interior to see what the matter was. Shimmers of light...on the floor? She squinted harder.

"The bilge pumps ain't keeping up, but now that we have men, shouldn't be a problem." Buckley jumped off the ladder and landed knee deep in water. "The infirmary is back here. The chest maybe wet, but it was put back after the wreck."

Angela sighed before getting wet again, and Henry entered the water without hesitation. Thankfully, his wound stayed out of the water this time. Her tired legs fought the water tension, and she brushed aside floating debris.

Through the mess hall with wooden bowls floating in the corner, Buckley stopped inside a narrow doorway and swung his arm wide. "Here it is. Good luck. Hope you sew up well, captain."

Buckley left to return to work—or maybe catch some sleep.

Angela scanned the tight room half-filled with water. "Is there any light around here?"

"Even if I found a lantern, I have nothing dry to light a candle with," Henry said, releasing her hand and sitting on a barrel.

Angela groaned in frustration and struck out her hands, approaching a shelf. She knocked over something metal and left it. Round objects, conical objects, a small crate. A book! She handed that to Henry. "Hold on to this."

Her fingers kept searching blindly until she found a handle connected to a large box, but it was out of reach. "Can you help get this off the shelf?" She hated to ask, but if it was what she needed, then getting it was better than not.

Henry sloshed over. "Is there anything else down here you wish to use?"

"I don't know what most of this stuff is."

"I don't suppose a woman from the future would," Henry said gently.

At confirmation she hadn't heard him wrong before, Angela turned. Eyes adjusted, his features were outlined in a soft light. "How did you know? How could you possibly...?" She mumbled, brain misfiring. Too many questions and not enough time.

"Angela, you aren't the first."

Angela blinked several times while processing that statement. People regularly traveled to the past? Was it some government technology they kept secret? How could someone hundreds of years into the past understand a phenomenon known only as science fiction in the future? If others had been here before her, then there is a way home.

Angela reached again to help Price lower it off the shelf, and the old vendor's amethyst necklace in her pocket pressed against her thigh. Her smile waned. Since the moment she'd arrived, she'd been asking herself how she was going to get home. The act of placing it over her head brought her here. The act of taking it off had no effect. So Angela could only assume placing it back over her head would bring her home. But now with Henry's sweet smile fluttering through her like a bunch of drunk butterflies, obscuring her thoughts, testing that theory no longer seemed so important.

Price collected the chest off the shelf. "Let us get out of the water. You'll catch a chill."

"Right." Angela frowned and quickly searched the shelf, indecipherable objects puzzling her worn brain. "I don't think there's anything else useful, but I'm flying blind here."

Henry made an amused noise.

"I...I mean—"

"The concept of flying is intriguing, but I can surmise your meaning. Come then. We must be on our way. There's much to be done."

Angela pushed her way through the rising water and followed Henry, who shouldered the burden of the chest himself.

Guilt weighed on her. "Let me help you with that."

"A lady doesn't assist in a man's duty."

The brush off sparked frustration. "I don't care if you think you don't need help, give me a side before you make that injury worse."

Henry paused, but didn't relent.

"This stubborn pride of yours is going to lead to surgery, and there's no doctor out here. Unless you want Buckley rooting around your insides, let me help carry."

Henry sighed. "It's a habit I'm afraid shall take much time to break. Forgive me, but if anyone asks about your assistance, inform them that my wound is much worse than it is, especially William."

Angela snorted. "Didn't you hear Riley? He thanked me. I'm no longer a useless, cursed woman on their ship. They aren't going to think less of you for needing my help. And if any of them secretly thinks so, well, they can go fu—" Angela stopped abruptly. Getting Henry to see her side was one thing. With a ship full of men who'd just welcomed her, equality wasn't an argument worth bringing up right now.

"They can what?" Henry asked, amusement lurking on his lips.

Angela gripped a handle alongside his fingers and headed up the ladder first. "Never mind."

Henry stood firm, and the chest jerked in her hand. "I insist you tell me what you planned to say. No need to hide your curious thoughts on the matter."

"You really want to know?"

"I insist."

"I was going to say that where I'm from women are just as capable as men. We're not dainty flowers who need chaperones. I drive a forklift and carry heavy shipments of merchandise every day for work, just like my male peers. I can handle this chest, and I can handle a few sassy men. I'll admit, if they all came after me, they'd win, but if the situation were reversed—a bunch of women after one man, he'd lose, too. It's beyond frustrating to me to be treated like I'm less than. My skills make me no better or worse than any of this crew, if I were given the chance to learn how to sail."

"I agree with you—" Henry started.

Angela's frustrated speech continued, not registering his words. "And for that matter, I helped patch the hole below deck, and I can swing a hammer just as well as anyone. I can hit a nail better than Buckley. But it's a good thing we have Giles, because if you wanted the lady on the ship to cook..." Angela laughed. "We'd starve."

Henry reached out and touched her hand. "I said I agree with you."

"Then why are you being stubborn about carrying the chest?"

"Do you have its weight?"

Angela tilted her chin up. "I couldn't reach it, but I can carry it."

"You are not equal to the men on this ship." He paused and fury boiled within her. "You're better. But not all of them know you the way I do, and I need to maintain the appearance of strength even in the face of injury. The sooner I can be at my best, the sooner we can get out of here. I fear vulnerability in the eyes of the company."

Henry slowly released the handle she'd been holding, and Angela caught it. The chest was heavy, but no big deal.

Angela's heart softened for him. "I understand the important of keeping up appearances. Truly, I do. So long as we're in this together, I won't let anyone hurt you."

The captain snorted. "I should be the one professing my protection to you. Instead, I find myself desiring the touch of your lips."

Heat rushed through Angela's body, sparking energy she'd thought was all spent, quickly renewing her need to touch him. "Then kiss me."

"It's a risk with the crew nearby, and their favor of you is finally tilting in the right direction."

Angela released the chest on a half-submerged barrel. "Shut up and kiss me."

With desperation in his eyes, Henry closed the distance. Angela flung her arms around him, and her lips met his. The kiss wasn't satisfying. It only made her crave more. She wanted all of him. Angela shifted her lips against his smooth but wanting kiss, her hands clawing at his back, urging him closer. The pivotal fear popped back into her head, and tears wet her eyelids. Would he survive the injury? And if he did, could she leave him? Angela pulled away and brushed the tears aside.

"That's not the reaction I usually get." Henry's dark blue eyes filled with concern.

Angela couldn't hold his gaze. "Let's get you patched up."

"Are you all right?"

She was. He wasn't. Angela nodded and lifted the chest. She climbed the stairs, glancing over her shoulder for the captain's ascent. She watched his flinches with each of his steps, and worry settled on her shoulders.

THE CREW HAD BEEN too busy working on the ship's repairs to notice her and Henry on their way to his private chambers, or they didn't care. She'd dreaded returning to the room that almost drowned her and was responsible for the quartermaster's assumptions turning the crew against her. But as Henry sat on the now-dry mattress, and Angela opened the chest at the foot of the bed, suddenly the soft bedding and peace and quiet were very appealing. She was so tired her eyeballs hurt. Yep, that was a thing.

Henry lifted his tunic, and Angela took a beat to marvel at him. A pair of gold rings hung from his nipples and scars crisscrossed his rounded pecs. He was beautiful, experienced, hardened. She dragged her eyes to his wounds and inspected them with bated breath. Would he be okay? Judging by the condition of it, she assumed the stab had been a clean cut with no organ damage, but every time he shifted, the wound's edges popped apart. "Lift higher. Since I have you here, I want to see that slice from Berger."

Henry did. The sword gash was scabbed over and dirty. "There's nothing I can do for that. It should heal fine." She hated to see him in pain, much less be the cause of it, but Delgado's stab needed closing to heal. The daylight from the row of windows at the stern was enough to work with, but she needed something to sterilize the needle.

"Lie down for me please." Angela rifled through the chest and lit a candle. Speaking softly, she asked, "How did you know I'm from the future? Is it common around here?"

"I met another like you, but no, it's not common at all. I recommend you don't tell another where you came from."

Angela thoroughly heated the needle, and when she turned, the captain had removed his tunic entirely. His head rested on his arm as a pillow. Angela reached over, grabbed his actual pillow, and swapped them out for his comfort. He smiled. "Thank you."

"Hang on tight. This is going to hurt." Taking a deep breath, she poked his flesh.

Henry winced and pressed his lips thin as Angela tugged the line through. "What did you mean by another like me?"

The captain exhaled slowly. "Our previous captain, Lemoine, entrusted information to me that I believed to be the words of a madman. I'd feared for his well-being and insisted he sought help. I was not as gentle as I should've been. He was our leader, voted to be the best of us, and my concerns for his mental clarity in his position were valid. I urged him to keep his foolish ideas to himself and never speak of them again."

"What did he say?"

"Lemoine insisted our newest crewman was from the future. He'd claimed to have seen proof, but he could not share with me. I never believed his tale until I saw you. I checked the hold myself only minutes prior to your appearance. No man on the *Sea Lion* saw you either, at port nor after. Since you're not a mermaid, the only explanation is Lemoine told the truth. Imagine my relief in learning my best friend had not lost his mind. Is there such a device in the future which allows travel through time? I can only imagine the possibilities."

"Time travel is science fiction where I'm from. Well..." Angela trailed off. "It *was*. Now I'm not sure of anything anymore. Hold still." She inserted the needle one last time and knotted off the ends. The bleeding stopped. "That's the best I can do."

Henry inspected his fine, flat abdomen dusted with a sexy layer of dark hair. He was a gorgeous man and Angela almost sighed at the sight. Henry yawned and tried to sit up. "I thank you kindly for your services.

I'd rather stay here with you, but I must return to work. You can guard the supplies or come with me. I believe my crew shall treat you well."

Angela stopped him with a hand on his firm chest. He hardly resisted; a feather could've pushed him back. "No. As your doctor, I am ordering you to sleep. The men can work during the day, and you and I are getting rest. If you want to successfully evade Spain before dawn, we need to sleep."

"Under one condition." Henry's blinks slowed, eyelids heavy with the need for sleep and healing, and Angela yawned.

"What's that?"

"Join me."

She wanted to so damned desperately. "Is that a good idea? It didn't go well last time we were caught together."

"Much has changed since then."

Angela smiled and closed up the medicine chest. Henry splayed on the mattress, and Angela tucked alongside him, warm and comfortable. His chest rose and fell with soft even breaths within moments. Angela drifted off seconds later.

Chapter 28

For the first time since she'd arrived in the past, Angela woke without worrying about the state of her mental health. Her eyes fluttered open, and a grin pulled at her lips. Henry was still snoozing next to her. He hadn't moved the whole day. Night shrouded the cabin in darkness. Such an eerie feeling to have no source of light but the moon. Cities bled light into the skies. Satellites and airplanes showed signs of life moving around. Not here. Just a splinter of moonlight reflecting off the gentle waves of the sea.

Angela yawned and sat up to stretch. Henry shifted next to her. His hand moved to where she'd laid, and his eyes popped open at once. "Angela?"

"I'm right here." She took his hand. "How are you feeling?"

"Better. I needed that rest." His head swiveled toward the windows. "I don't sense any movement. Are we still anchored off Cuba?"

Angela laughed. "I forget to get a status update before you woke. Let's go find out."

"Right, right." Henry stood and together they left the cabin. The men were still working hard at repairs, exhaustion slowed their movements. Giles walked around handing out plates to the men where they stood, skipping dining in the mess all together. Angela caught a plate for her and Henry, who had bigger concerns at the moment.

"Riley!" Henry shouted.

The quartermaster turned from Karl and approached with a smile. "Glad to see you on your feet."

"Why haven't we set sail yet?" Henry asked with increasing urgency.

"Karl just informed me the *Sea Lion* should be in ship shape by tomorrow mid-afternoon."

"You're certain?"

"You can ask him yourself." Riley pointed to where Karl directed the prisoners. The newcomers pulled lines and others untangled them. Crew wove lines around cleats, knotting them taut. A smooth oiled machine, they worked well and efficiently. But from the sound of it, not efficient enough. Angela released her captain's hand and helped herself to the pork.

Henry rubbed his face from forehead to chin. "Never thought I'd say the words, but we must abandon ship."

Riley snorted. "Abandon ship? Are you mad? We're stranded on Spain's territory and loaded with treasure. If we don't get out of here soon, Delgado is bound to find us."

"It's too late," Henry said on an exhale as if defeated. "*Capitán* Delgado and the Spanish warship *Peibo del ler San Francisco* are just around the corner. He vowed to volley this ship when the tide permits them to maneuver into range at dawn. We won't escape."

"You're certain?" Paleness hollowed Riley's features.

"Completely," Henry said. "Load up the longboats with anything of value on board. We're taking a new ship."

Riley shook his head. "If you think we can take a Spanish warship as prize, you, dear sir, have lost your mind. I will not agree to it, and nor will they."

"We are taking the English schooner they captured. Only a half dozen or so Spaniard soldiers are guarding it. After all, who would be foolish enough to attempt such a thing with the warship anchored right next to it?" Price grinned deviously. "With our newest recruits and their dwindled numbers, overwhelming the schooner shall be easy, and when Spain appears around that headland at dawn, they shall be sorely disappointed to find us on the horizon, instead, sailing their prize."

Riley groaned. "I cannot argue your logic. I'll relay the message to the crew." The quartermaster turned and shouted, "Eat up and unload this ship!"

Angela stifled a laugh at the unexpectedly impromptu orders.

Before the quartermaster could run off, giving more orders, Henry recaptured his attention. And the excitement fell from the younger man's face. "Tell me you don't have more bad news."

"Only a question. We spent the day together in my cabin. Why didn't you accuse Angela and I of breaking the articles?"

"I trust you," Riley said. "Besides, the ship wasn't rocking, so I didn't bother knocking."

Angela's face heated. She'd needed the rest, but if Henry was capable of that, she wanted him. She wanted all of it.

Henry's brows lifted and his cheeks flushed. It was cute. "Why, thank you for assuming I have such prowess in bed."

Angela laughed. Riley grinned and patted him on the shoulder. "Don't let the words swell your skull!" Riley rushed off to coordinate the crew's efforts.

With a smile, Henry held out his hand as if expected her to accept it, but Angela handed him his plate.

"That's not what I wanted, but on second thought, my stomach is empty."

"I remember scraping by from one meal to the next, and I can't say I ever liked it."

"We try to avoid it. Keeps the crew content to have a belly full. If we can manage tonight, I don't think anyone will worry about their next meal." Price finished his plate, took her empty, and added them to Giles's stack. He brushed his fingers clean and asked, "Now where were we?"

"I don't know," Angela said, confused.

The devious grin returned, and Price gestured for her to follow him back into the cabin. Sparks of heat roared through her, picturing exactly what she wanted to do, but with his injury, she'd never attempt it. Perhaps there was something else they could to in the meantime...

Henry lifted the medicine chest.

Angela rushed over and took the weight of it. "Do you want to rip stitches? Because that's how you rip stitches."

"We all must do our best."

"Your best is leading, not lifting. Let go."

While deadlocked in a staring contest for power, William Price entered the cabin, holding his plate and chewing. "You two are quite the entertainment. Best listen to the lady, dear brother. You've made it this far. We'd hate to lose you to a petty cut from Delgado."

Henry broke eye contact to glare at his brother. "I'll be fine."

"Says every man ever injured and trying to do something stupid," Angela countered.

The brothers stared each other down.

"Don't be so stubborn. Angela can help the crew by lifting the precious cargo. You can help by leading this desperate folly. Unless...you'd prefer me to take over as captain."

Henry released the chest and asked, "Do you want to?"

Talking with his mouth full, William pointed his meaty rib at his own chest. "Me? Oh, brother, no. I'm not taking the blame for this. Even if you get us away from this island in one piece and the crew wished it, no."

Henry's lips thinned. "Dreams change?"

William chewed and cast Angela a knowing look. "Indeed." The captain's brother strolled out.

"What was that about?" Angela asked, holding the chest.

Henry raked a hand through his dark locks. "We were supposed to sail together as captains. Create our own flotilla, doubling our prowess on the seas under the black. But after his *presumed* death, it could never happen. I hated the sea, and I never wanted to step foot in saltwater again. As he confirmed, dreams change."

"I'm sorry things didn't turn out how you wanted." Angela's pork settled heavily. Price wanted to stay on the sea. His old dream had returned with his brother, but they wouldn't sail their own ships. Perhaps share one. Knowing she and Price wanted different things was hard to swallow, and the weight of the necklace in her pocket suddenly got much heavier.

Chapter 29

With their supplies safely on shore, a handful of oil lamps lit their meager supplies. "Load the vanguard with the best pistols and sharpest swords. We're going after the English schooner now. The rest of you stay on shore to guard the supplies and treasure. I don't suspect you'll be harassed, but be prepared." After they'd escaped from Delgado's ship, they'd added more men to their crew, but also pistols. It still wasn't enough for everyone.

Captain Price needed Angela, not because of her brilliant language skills, but because he loved her. This woman, who simply glowed in the soft light, marveling at the weapons before her, saved his life more than he could count. And now she was by his side, ready to save the crew. Captain Price wouldn't leave her behind with the crew in charge of the supplies. Not with Vallo out there somewhere. Not with Spain lurking. He didn't trust any of his crew to defend her as much as him.

Maybe Buckley, Cantu, and Riley. But he needed their skills on the vanguard.

Maybe William.

...eh, probably not.

Price selected a pair of pistols, one cutlass, and two daggers. He added a third at his ankle, checking each for integrity prior to equipping them.

Angela lifted a hammer. "I'll take this."

"Excellent choice," Henry said. "but take this, too." He held out a small dagger. "Strap it to your ankle like mine."

She stared at his open palm. "Is it necessary? I'm more comfortable with the hammer."

"It's better to have and not need then the other way around."

"Okay."

Figuring the foreign term to originate in the future, he determined it meant both acquiescence and a favorable state of being. The future sounded confusing. But the women, judging by the two he'd met, were far more open about their stances and opinions. They refused to bow to the rule of men, and they made themselves known. Something about that forwardness made Price visualize a woman in bed with a strong knowledge of what she wanted and how she wanted it. Remembering her warm lips grazing his sensitive skin sent a heat of desire roaring through his loins. He desperately wanted to test his hunch.

If he survived the night, of course.

With each what *if* and *but*, the odds of survival dwindled dramatically. He saw no other outcome but taking the schooner, and he'd do everything to secure Angela's safety, for he knew of someone she'd want to see.

Angela strapped the blade to her ankle, and Price focused on her backside, bending in his face. Just beyond her luscious shape, the shifting of his brother caught his eye. No matter how much his brother had endured, William needed to prepare, too. "Wait here. I'll return swiftly."

Angela nodded, and Price filled his hands with extra weapons. While the vanguard armed themselves by the light, William was busy relieving himself against a palm tree.

"Take these," Price insisted.

William, still holding himself, said, "My hands are busy. Care to wait?"

"At the rate of your watering, Spain will find us standing here and kill us all."

"Such a dramatist. You, my dearest brother, should write down your tales of embellishment. I care to absorb such words while emptying my bowels at the head."

Price held the weapons closer. "We have no time for games. I've spent ages waiting to hunt your killer only to discover not only were you alive, but apparently well enough to retain your sense of humor."

William shook himself clear of drips and a seriousness eliminated the jesting. "I regret the loss of your freedom of mind. I knew once Spain had accepted my offer, they'd deliver me wholly to the authorities for a spectacle at the gallows, and you'd waste the rest of your life avenging me. In my cell, wondering why the journey had been taking so long, I thought of nothing else except you biding your time for the right moment to pursue the enemy. Focusing on Delgado would've driven you mad with obsession. I regret what he's done to you. At the time, I could see no other way, but this isn't you. This wasn't us."

On the verge of battle, Price couldn't lose himself to emotions tearing him apart. Calmly, he said, "Take them. I cannot bear the thought of you being killed or recaptured. Take these, for my sake."

"You remember why we took to the seas?" William accepted the extra weapons and tucked them appropriately on his person. "We had nothing left for us back home, so we joined the Royal Navy together to fight Spain, but we endured punishment unfit for a dog. We gladly accepted the offer of freedom by Wilcox. Remember our first captain? Do you remember what he wanted?"

Price just stared. He knew, but he didn't want to say it.

"Wilcox wanted love, but to have it, he needed the money to be worthy. So he took the money he needed."

A story told a thousand times. "Certainly, but Wilcox was last seen at The Golden Macaw, stumbling around drunk. Lot of good it did him."

"I believe you. I also believe his gambling addiction bested him. But that is not my point here, brother. He wasted his life trying to get something, and he lost it. Then he wasted the rest of his life miserable. My point is you have that lovely lady over there. She's the reason why I'm here with you. Don't let her get away and don't let your obsession with vengeance destroy your future. That's over."

Frustrated with his brother's lack of understanding over the situation, Price said, "It's not me who keeps us apart. It's her need to return home." Price glanced over his shoulder at the woman glowing by the flickering light, seated on a log, inspecting the hammer she'd chosen. Why would an amazing woman like her want to give up everything for him? "It's my doubt—"

William uttered a dismissive grunt. "Then change her mind! Dear God, Henry, your head is a bag of cats. You're a predator on the water. You take what you want for sport. Do you want her? Then take her!"

Price sighed. His brother didn't understand. Some days he wished for that careless, worry-free sentiment. But Captain Price knew what was right there, but he wouldn't take her. He respected her too much to force her into something she didn't want. She had to choose him and his world.

"Thank you for the words of wisdom, as always," Price said with a hint of mockery, because William wasn't known for making wise choices. And his advice was terrible. Price returned to Angela's side.

She smiled sweetly at him. Would she give up her home for him? Would she consider staying for *him*? Would Price be as lucky as Lemoine? None of these questions mattered a lick if their attempt tonight ended unsuccessfully, but knowing the answer would propel him further toward success.

Price smiled back. "I must ask you something of great consequence. The answer is a difficult one, but I must know before our excursion for my own selfish reasons. Could you bear the question for me?"

Her face tilted with endearing confusion. "You can ask me whatever you want, and I'll do my best to give you an answer. Is that what you're asking?"

Price collected both her hands in his. Ignoring the crew's curious eyes, he asked her softly, "Will you consider, if we survive the night, which the outcome is not certain... Now, just for a moment, if you will, could you see the possibility of a home here, but not here, somewhere else, wherever you want. In essence... I'm... I'm failing to articulate my thoughts properly."

"You want me to do something. The rest is not so clear." Her soft smile calmed the nerves jolting like lightning through his body and subdued the turbulent ocean in his stomach.

Only a little.

Price squeezed her hands and focused, trying with great difficulty to ignore the scrutinizing gaze of the men and the haughty smirk of his brother. He closed his eyes and exhaled. "If we survive the capture of the schooner, if we survive escaping the *Peibo del ler San Francisco*'s volley, if we survive the crew's agitation over changing the articles—"

"That's a lot of 'ifs' there," Angela interrupted, smiling.

"Would you," he continued, ignoring the interruption for the sake of his thoughts and bravery. "Would you consider staying here with me?"

Some of the crew uttered teasing noises, but Price blocked them out. He'd deal with them later. All that mattered was Angela's answer.

"I...I..." she stuttered.

Price waited patiently, having experienced the weight of the words himself.

Her soft lips opened to speak again.

"We must go now!" Riley's voice interrupted her.

Damn that man! With a furrow on his brow, Price turned to his quartermaster. "Not now!"

"The warship is shifting position. If we are to succeed, we have no time to lose!"

Gritting his teeth, the captain shouted his orders, "Vanguard, to the longboats. We take our prize now!"

Such terrible timing, but the future was here—whether they saw tomorrow, and whether Angela would remain at his side.

Chapter 30

Smooth quiet oar strokes brought them closer to both the English schooner and the *Peibo del ler San Francisco*. Lanterns lit the warship, and Angela kept a fearful eye on the movements on deck. The moon hid behind cloud cover, giving the vanguard the needed head start. Angela sat next to William in the first longboat. Henry sat at the bow across from her.

The butterflies wrestling in her stomach weren't just about the ships or the impending attack. Henry's question had been so loaded her brain misfired attempting to answer. She'd given him mumbles, just like how he'd asked, which was endearingly sweet.

Captain Henry Price asked her to make a massive life-changing decision for him. She hadn't understood what he'd meant by 'crew's agitation over changing the articles' until after she'd thought about it. Not only did he want her to remain in the past, but he wanted her to stay with him *here*. On the *Sea Lion*. Even if he could get the crew to agree to change the articles for her, Angela was certain she didn't want to sail forever.

Or after this wild adventure, sail after next week.

Angela's palm cupped the necklace's bulge in her pocket. There was a strong chance the necklace was a one-way ticket, anyhow. No more movie nights with her friends. No more burgers and fries. No more camping with Emily—on an air mattress, natch. No more driving a forklift and slinging cases of merchandise with Marcos. No more visiting her mother's grave site.

Mostly, she missed Emily.

She would give anything to have that woman back in her life.

Could Angela give up hope of ever seeing her best friend again and forget returning home, in exchange for a man who treated her well, kept her safe, and drove her wild with sexual need she hadn't felt in so long—making her feel decades younger?

Henry made it possible for her to be one of them, among his crew, his friends, *almost* an equal. His brother appreciated her—or at least her bobby pins. Was all this possible?

Captain Henry Price was everything Brandon Spindleton was not. When Angela had boarded the tour ship, she wanted one night with a captain. The problem was—one night wasn't enough anymore.

Henry kept watch ahead, directing the rowers, and Angela noticed he'd avoided eye contact with her since he'd asked. Was he embarrassed for asking? Was he ashamed she couldn't answer him?

As they neared the warship, a flurry of activity on board churned in her stomach, and dread settled in her bones. Sails were shifting while men rotated the anchor's capstan, and the rest were doing who knew what.

The longboat oars sank below the surface and stroked as silently as the soft waves lapping on shore. Dwarfed by the warship, the English schooner moored peacefully behind its stern. It had ten gunports on her starboard side, so Angela assumed ten on the other, and mounted to the rail were six swivel guns. A handful of Spaniard guards stood sentry on her deck. The schooner was larger and more heavily armed than the *Sea Lion*, ignoring the repair work.

Henry held out a hand to stop the rowers. The second longboat eased alongside, and men from both boats grasped each other's rails to steady them.

The captain addressed the men in their boat, "We shall approach on the port side and climb as quietly as possible. Riley," he addressed the head of the second boat, "have your men climb starboard. When as many men as possible are ready, we'll slip over the rail together, taking her over on swift feet. Our silence is pivotal to our success. If Spain's warship catches a whisper of our activity, she shall train her guns on her own prize, and we shall be finished."

Riley nodded, and Henry gestured for the rowing to resume.

"Are you ready, brother?" Henry asked.

"I'm always ready for a fight, especially for one where we have the upper hand. Strategy is a luxury we shall not squander on this night."

"Are you ready, Angela?" Henry asked, finally meeting her gaze.

Angela's stomach churned like the angry sea from her arrival, and her head swam like when she dove off the *Peibo del ler San Francisco*. Her hands trembled, but the hammer squeezed in her grip stayed steady. Somewhere deep down, an electrifying rush pumped through her veins, preparing her for what was to come. It was adrenaline, and boy, was it welcome. "I'm ready."

Henry leaned close and captured her hands, in full view of the whole vanguard. "Excellent. When this is over, no matter your answer, I'm giving you a kiss."

Heat flourished at her cheeks and chest, and Angela refrained from fanning the front of her tunic. "Promise?" she teased.

William grinned sheepishly beside her. Other men snickered...quietly.

"Certainly, and I never break a promise."

Angela flustered, wanting to dive for him right there, but she refrained.

"Except to me, dear brother," William said.

Henry ignored his brother's jab, so she did too. "Then save some energy for me. You'll need it."

The vanguard cackled. William snorted and shoved Henry on the shoulder. Henry grinned, ignoring their reactions. He rubbed her hands with his thumbs and released her.

Angela darted William a look, and the other brother tilted his head away and scratched at the scruff covering his lower face as if he were innocent. The rowers also tilted their faces aside playfully as if pretending to have not heard the conversation either—almost like they were...friends.

Within reach of the schooner's bow, Henry held up his hand to stop the rowers once again. He reached for a handhold on the schooner's hull and gently eased them alongside.

William slipped the longboat's anchor below the surface and allowed the line to slide in his palm. When the lined stopped, he twisted it around a cleat on the rim of the longboat. The men climbed out, and Angela swallowed back bile as she gripped the ship's hull, waiting.

The second longboat, having delivered the pirates to the starboard side of the ship, reappeared at the stern and signaled them to charge. The longboat returned to position, so the last man could join.

Silently, they tipped themselves over the rail, one after the other, filling the deck from both sides. Clouds shifted, allowing the moon to shine rays on the deck. Blades of metal glinted in the blue light. Men dropped from stab wounds before they drew their own swords. Bodies thumped to the floor, and limp hands released their metal, clattering to the hardwood.

Whispers and grunts alerted other soldiers to the muted attack, and men rushed from below deck, swords drawn. The pirates took on the soldiers with metal clashing in the night. Angela's job was to protect the longboat on her side from soldiers attempting to escape or attempting to remove their chance of escape. She gripped the hammer like her life depended on it, and the shifting and swinging skirmishes around her kept her alert and skittish.

While scanning the deck for anyone attempting to rush her way, she found her attention drifting to Henry. His blade slashed through the air, clashing against his opponent. The urge to rush over and assist threatened to overpower her. Before she realized, Angela left her post and shouldered the hammer. Ducking and dodging the fights around her, and keeping her eyes alert for incoming threats, Angela approached the man fighting Henry and swung at his side.

The man arched his back in crippling pain and dropped his sword. He hugged his side and toppled over the rail, splashing into the waters below.

Henry's chest heaved with exertion, and he lowered the heavy weight in his hand. His soft eyes melted her. "Thank you, my angel." Henry leaned forward and kissed her on the forehead. A quick peck of appreciation and admiration.

Angela smiled. She'd walked through sword fights for him. She'd stolen treasure for him. She'd freed prisoners for him, and she would walk through fire for him, too. Captain Henry Price was the man for her. The answer was yes. Angela would stay here with him.

"Yes!" she blurted with a beaming grin.

"Yes, wha—?" Henry abruptly cut off, eyes widening.

Angela spun to see what caught his attention, and a wounded soldier's pistol aimed straight at them. Without another thought, Angela found herself pulled as the gunshot ripped through the air.

Angela fell and rolled with Henry, who tucked her against his side. His quick hands drew the weapon at his hip, and he aimed and fired at the soldier. The man's hand dropped the gun and hung limp.

Henry said, turning to her. "Are you injured? Have you been struck?"

Angela patted herself just to be sure. "I'm fine. He missed."

"Most excellent." Henry's neck craned around the deck, and he dropped his spent pistol. He fisted another and fired at a man engaged with William.

William swiped his forehead with his sleeve and panted from exertion. The men searched for more opponents, but no more came.

Henry climbed to his feet and held out his hand to help her up. Angela accepted, and as he lifted her, he said, "I'm going to feel that on the morrow."

"No kidding."

"You three," Henry ordered, "check for more below deck. Report back immediately."

Three of the prisoners who'd joined nodded and rushed below deck.

William stepped over bodies, checking them for signs of life. "Your plan worked. Didn't think it would, but I must hand it to you brother, job well done."

"They would've heard the gunshots. The cover of nightfall is our only protection, but since we're very close and they know where they left this ship, we need to weigh anchor at once."

At that, the three of them checked on *Peibo del ler San Francisco's* position. The warship, with weak winds, slowly approached their old ship. When day broke, they would be capable of aiming and firing. Their current position allowed them to volley both the schooner and the *Sea Lion*.

"And there's much to be done before we're safely underway. I want four men, each boat. Return to shore and collect our supplies and the treasure. The rest of you, put on the soldiers' coats, cravats, and cocked hats and dispose of the bodies. We need to look like them."

Clever. Gross, but clever. The men immediately set to work.

"Angela," Henry said, interrupting her hunt for the cleanest coat. "You owe me a kiss."

"You already stole one," she said teasing.

"That doesn't count." His lips fell upon hers with a deep hungry need, working at her lips like they were the only two people in the world. All the bloodshed and danger around her vanished. For that sweet-but-too-short moment, the only thing in her life was him, and all she wanted was him. All the pain of her past simply became petty. Why had she allowed the humiliation of a bunch of strangers to hurt so much? They wanted her to be someone she wasn't—a square peg in a round hole.

But here, with Henry Price, he was her square hole. An odd thought, but with his soft and sensual lips taking her over, his hands on her ass pulling her toward his stiffening cock, her brain hardly strung linear thoughts. But she believed with every fiber in her body, Captain Henry Price would never abandon her.

Angela pulled back and grinned. "I'm your *numero uno.*"

Henry opened his mouth to answer, but something thumped against the hull of the schooner, and that got his attention. Angela pulled away from Henry's sweet embrace. "What was that?"

It DIDN'T SOUND LIKE cannon fire to her, but Angela wasn't completely sure what it sounded like. Her only experience had been watching movies.

Henry pressed his lips thin and gazed across the deck. "The longboat returning too hastily. The imbecile ruined a perfectly good moment."

"No." Angela smiled, moving back into Henry's arms. "He just gave me a chance to tell you something."

Henry waited patiently, gazing into her eyes as if trying to read the answers on her retinas.

Unlike the nerves warning her away from her doomed wedding, Angela was calm—excited, but calm—and she lifted her arms and wrapped them around his neck. "I tried to tell you earlier—"

"What is it?" He stared at her like she was the only person in the world. Men climbed aboard with arms full of supplies, ignoring them.

Angela's heart swelled, and she swallowed back the emotion clogging her throat. "Yes. I tried to tell you my answer is yes. I will stay with you, Henry."

Her captain grinned for a joyous few seconds before planting another, deeper kiss on her lips. Any deeper and they were going to need a private room. He leaned his body into hers, but a few whistles broke them apart. Nose to nose, his gentle eyes met hers. He smiled and gave her yet another quick peck on the lips. "You have made me the happiest man on this ship."

Angela made a point to glance at the remaining bodies around them. She chuckled. "That doesn't mean much right now."

Henry looked at the bodies too. "I mean to say, you have made me the happiest living man on this ship."

Heckles from the moving crew broke them apart. Angela stood up straight and smoothed her clothing. The trio returned from below deck. "Sir, uh, captain sir," the first one said, trying hard to cover his grin. "The ship is all clear of enemy soldiers, sir."

"Excellent work. Assist with the provisions," Henry said.

Another longboat bumped the hull again, and the trio assisted hoisting the barrels up over the rail. Giles the cook climbed up with great effort, and Captain Price rushed over to give him a hand. Giles settled his feet sturdy on deck, face red with the effort. "This load is the last of our supplies. We can get underway when the boats are secured on board."

"Excellent news, Giles. Take inventory of the provisions below deck. We should have enough to reach our next destination."

"Aye, sir."

"McKee!" Henry called for his master gunner, who immediately approached, still stuffing his arms in a too-tight Spanish coat. "Collect Gunner and inspect the guns and our stock of shot. I want numbers."

The master gunner nodded and walked away, still struggling into a coat.

"Karl." Henry tapped the passing boatswain on the shoulder. "Set sail at once. With the *Peibo del ler San Francisco* encroaching upon the *Sea Lion*, we must get underway. I want the hard in the distance when she opens fire at dawn."

Karl nodded and shouted for hands to assist. Men climbed the ratlines and unfurled the sails from the stays while others raised the anchor.

"What about me?" Angela asked, feeling useless.

"I want you to stay by my side," the captain said with a proud smile. "I never want you out of my sight again."

Angela smiled, equally proud to stand at his side.

"But," he added, leading her toward the stern of the ship, "I remember you claiming if you'd have commanded the ship's helm, the *Sea Lion* wouldn't have wrecked against the outcrop. Care to prove your word?"

A rush of excitement flooded her limbs, and her lips spread wide in a beaming grin. "Oh, yes, I want to sail! Can I?" The idea of driving this behemoth ship made her turn to jelly with ridiculous excitement.

Henry stopped near a serious man, gripping the wheel. "Angela, this is our esteemed Hodgens. He will grant your wish. Hodgens, allow our special guest to take her to sea."

Hodgens pressed his lips thin but nodded once.

Henry said to her, "If you need me, I'll be nearby. Enjoy yourself."

Angela's smile stung her face, but she couldn't relax. Move over forklift. Holding a hundred tons of power in her hands was a thrill like nothing else. Angela bounced on her heels, ready to fly across the seas.

"Be mindful of what you're doing here, lady. It's not child's play. Now, keep your eye on the wind. Spain shall be after us the instant they notice their prize missing, so if those sails start flapping, we start slowing. Understood?"

Angela nodded.

"The vane will help you capture the wind. Adjust your trajectory as I order, and when you need a break, let me know before letting go."

Angela frowned. Way to put a damper on the fun. "I got it. What do I do?"

"When the sails fill, keep the bowsprit aimed where we want to go." Hodgens pointed to the horizon, away from nearby islands.

"Where *are* we going?"

"East to Hispaniola."

Angela steered as directed, squinting straight into the breaking dawn, giving the warship a wide berth. Up ahead, Spain opened the gunports on the starboard side and loaded cannons were pulled into position and aimed. The poor *Sea Lion* had no chance against that ship, and neither did Angela's ears. The thunderous booms of the full broadside echoed off the rocky cliff. One after another after another. Then two came and two more. Wood splintered and splashed. Angela tucked an ear against her shoulder and flinched at the pain, but she wouldn't release the wheel.

Devastating explosions of wood cracked in the air. The mast shattered and toppled. Sails collapsed and draped over the listing deck, and the seawater churned, swallowing the last of their old ship. Cannon smoke filled the area, allowing the English schooner to skirt on by.

Chapter 31

Captain Price found Riley busy in the navigation room, plotting their course out of danger. It was most fortunate for the crew the new three-masted ship was greater in size and strength than the *Sea Lion*, but because of the schooner's size, they'd lost speed and a shallower draft. Once they fully escaped Spain's reach, Riley should be most pleased. When Price closed the door behind him, the quartermaster looked up with a seriousness Price hadn't seen in the younger man. That shall serve him well.

"You sent for me?" Price asked.

Riley set down the quadrant and divider and folded his hands over the map—once Price's but now Riley's, a change that made him wistful. Watching the *Sea Lion*'s destruction had brought tears to his eyes, but he hid them from the others. It was a goodbye in more ways than one, but toward a future rife with a woman he adored.

Riley nodded for him to sit, so Price rested on a chair across from his desk.

"How is your wound?"

"Better every day." Price was grateful Angela had patched him up, and he'd healed without any difficulty. He credited her for saving his life too many times to count.

"Wonderful. You know, if your plan to raid the Spanish treasure failed, I declared I would be their captain, and I had their full support. But you returned one load successfully, and per the articles, we have more than enough to break up the account."

Price had been concerned the crew would disallow his request and maroon him for abandoning the account, but the news sounded favorable. "Not a soul on board contests my request?"

"The crew has accepted, and Hispaniola stands three days hence. But everyone currently aboard, aside from the obvious Angela, decided to continue the account without your leadership. We lost many great men but gained more I hope to see flourish upon these waters." Riley leaned back in his seat. "Only a short time ago I was a child, appreciated by the crew and voted to represent their needs against the captain. I must admit, these tumultuous times have aged me, and you were the best captain I've ever known. I'm going to miss you and certainly your objective"—Riley tilted his head and smiled—"*and* biased decisions in the interest of the crew."

Price blinked away the tears pricking his eyes. He'd never considered goodbye to be so difficult, but he wanted Riley to have the same secret Captain Lemoine had bestowed upon him, just in case. "Noah, there's something I need to tell you. It's about Angela. Do you remember Emily Porter?"

Riley nodded, pulling up chaotic memories. "I remember the captain taking lashes for a woman who'd disguised herself as a man. She was in front of our faces the whole time, and only Fergus knew, may he rest in peace."

"Emily and Angela were friends."

"I'm aware. It's all the other called for."

"They're from the same place."

Riley leaned forward again. "Just spit it out. What is so important about them?"

Price couldn't just spit it out. The man would laugh at him or kick him off the ship prematurely for such a tall tale. "Have you noticed their speech patterns and accent?"

"Yea." Riley frowned. "Never thought much about it."

"They're from the future. Their necklaces, those amethyst stones—they brought the women through time."

Riley stared.

He blinked and continued staring.

Still no response.

"Say something," Price insisted.

"You want me to believe magic necklaces bring women to the past?"

"It's happened twice. I want to warn you as Lemoine did for me. If another woman appears on this ship, understand she's lost, scared, and from a time completely foreign to us. Take care of her. You never know what may transpire."

Riley rubbed his face, clearly not believing him. "I'm the quartermaster. If anyone stows away on this ship—"

"She's not a stowaway!" Price interrupted. "I'm trying to explain to you she's not a stowaway. She simply...appears."

Riley sighed. "If the woman *appears*, I'll make sure the captain is agreeable to her presence and stop the crew from tearing itself to pieces over it."

Price nodded. "Thank you. Have you heard from Vallo at all?"

"No. He must've been lost on Cuba."

As long as Vallo stayed clear of Price's crew, he'd rest peacefully at night. "The man is a traitorous snake. I'm sure Cantu, Buckley, and Hodgens—well, maybe not Hodgens—have told you Vallo was an informant for Spain. Don't trust him."

"In that case, may the enemy be swift and just."

"Agreed," Price said. "There's one last favor I must ask of you."

"Name it," Riley said, "and it shall be done."

"Perform the naming ceremony to appease Poseidon. Have this schooner named Angelfish, after my dearest Angela."

Riley nodded, and a gentle smile lifted his lips. "You have my word, and it shall be my honor. You were a good captain, and we'll miss you. Or...most of us will."

Price stood and discreetly swiped his eyes. "If you need me or Angela, we'll be in my cabin."

Riley stood and stretched out a hand to shake. "Good luck to you both. You're a lucky man."

"I know it." Price shook firmly. Not every day a woman of the future fell into his hands. Certainly not one like her, and he wasn't going to waste a moment of it.

"Also, don't forget to take your share from the barrels left below deck. Not only did we pilfer Spain's recovered treasure and manage to bring it on board, but some poor nation just lost several barrels of gold and silver left on this schooner. Oh, and Price?"

Price stepped back, wishing to further hide his emotion.

"Don't rock the boat." Riley winked.

Price chuckled.

BORROWING THE CAPTAIN'S CABIN, Henry held the door open for Angela to walk through, but before she crossed, he said, "It's customary for the groom to carry his bride over the threshold."

Angela stopped and turned to him, brows knitting in confusion. Certainly Angela misheard. She couldn't forget such a momentous moment.

Henry continued, "But as this isn't our marital home, and I have not yet asked for your hand, I'm allowing you to walk on your own vocation."

Angela stared, breathless. He'd just told her he intended to ask her to marry him. Advance notice, so this time, she could answer him more swiftly. She supposed no one wanted to wait hours for the answer to a proposal.

Henry led her by the hand into the quarters and closed the door. With sunlight glittering through the bank of windows at the stern, he collected her hands in his. Bright ocean blue eyes met her gaze, and all the best things projected from his beautiful face. Henry was excited but serious and full of adoration, and she caught a hint of nervousness. Angela's breath caught, and her knees were weak. He was doing it now, she knew it.

"Before I met you, I was a jaded man on a mission surely to end in my demise. So long as my vengeance had been finished, I cared not what happened to me. With my brother presumed dead, I had no reason to live." Angela squeezed his hands in sympathy for his suffering. He rubbed her knuckles in return. "But you, my angel, you gave me a purpose, and now I fear losing you more than anything else. Angela, my lady, I love you, and I don't want to spend one more day on this earth without you. Will you do me the honor of becoming my *numero uno* forever?"

Tears flooded her eyelids, and she furiously blinked them away. Henry was a real man, bleeding his heart out for her with words that turned her to mush and reminded her that kindness and true love still existed. When she'd donned the magic necklace, her wish had been to never see another cell phone again, but deep down she wished to meet someone special. She had.

"Are you asking what I think you're asking?"

"Marry me," he said simply.

"Captain Henry Price," she began slowly, formally, trying to keep her emotions in check to finish her statement. "You are the best person I've ever met. You're kind, considerate, and more handsome than I ever hoped for, but—" she paused when Henry's wide smile of anticipation threatened to interrupt "—you're also a great leader and a strong fighter, and I feel safe with you. I love you more than I thought possible. I have your answer, and you were right to assume I needed time to decide."

Henry's smile waned a little, but he didn't interrupt.

"I never wanted to stay on a ship. The crew life isn't for me, but handling the helm has its perks, and for you, my Henry, my answer is yes. I'll stay with you forever, and I'm thrilled to marry you." Tears wavered her vision. She blinked them back to see his reaction. His features melted with happiness, and his arms opened to embrace her. "Absolutely, yes," Angela repeated, smiling, and swiped her tears.

Henry scooped her up into a tight embrace. The world could fall apart around them, but as long as she had her captain by her side, they could conquer anything—even a sinking ship, an angry crew, and a warship full of vengeful enemy soldiers. Henry shifted his hands to her throat and jawline. He took her lips with the gusto of a man ready to possess her in new ways. The articles forbade such acts on board, for the equality of the crew, so Angela stopped him when he motioned her toward the bed.

"We're so close to disembarking. I'd hate to cause a crisis with the crew now," Angela said. The wait had been its own kind of torture, but the building anticipation meant when the main event happened, it was going to be glorious. Angela felt something pressing against her, and ignoring the part that was clearly Henry's excitement, she dug in her pocket.

Henry groaned at her continued rejection. "You're right. Riley is just getting his feet wet; he doesn't need the crew rallying. Rules are rules."

Angela backed up with a frown and stuck her hand in her pocket.

"What is it?" Henry asked, concern taking over.

Angela palmed the amethyst on a copper chain.

"Your way home?" Henry asked.

"Not anymore." Angela moved to the captain's private head, lifted the lid, and with a deep breath, she dropped the necklace straight into the ocean. She returned to the captain's embrace. His strong arms circled her. "That never truly was home."

Chapter 32

The horses' hooves clopped against the dirt path leading away from the dock, pulling her and Henry in a tight covered carriage. Suspension was definitely not a thing yet. In the captain's quarters of the schooner, a chest had held various gowns, and Henry insisted she wear one. Despite the fluffy layers acting as cushion, her butt was getting sore. She adored the dress, even more so after wearing ill-fitting, sodden, salty, scratchy men's clothing. Even her sweat work polo wasn't as bad.

Her top was a ruffled ivory blouse, and the bottom was layers of gold. The boned corset had embroidered swirls in the gold, and she felt like a regal princess. Henry wore a black tunic with a similar patterned coat and black breeches, a gentleman on the outside like she knew he was on the inside.

At this distance up a hill, Angela could make out men refitting the new schooner, preparing to set sail once again. She was going to miss it. Well, parts of it, like Buckley and Cantu, and the beautiful sunrises and sunsets.

Not so much the jungle bugs, the hard night's sleep, Vallo and his tricks, and the Spanish threat. Whatever happened to Vallo? Ultimately, it didn't matter, she supposed.

When Henry had said Riley was just getting his feet wet, he'd meant Riley was taking temporary command until a new captain could be elected. Henry didn't want to remain on the sea, either. She would've done it for him, honestly, but she was glad they wanted the same thing.

Henry held her hand during the rocky ride, and dust kicked up behind them. This was their first moment of privacy, without the risk of death, since they'd met. Angela couldn't help her eyes from drifting to his peeking chest hair.

"Is something the matter, my lady?" Henry asked with a saucy tone.

Heat rushed to her cheeks and pooled lower, far lower, where she'd been aching for attention. "Can we take a detour? Somewhere private."

Clothing shifted in Price's lap. "Are you needing something at this moment?"

"Oh, yes. Very much."

"I think we have time for something." Henry held his hand out for her, and she took it without a second thought. He pulled her into his lap, and a firm length greeted her, bouncing with the uneven road under the carriage. Henry groaned.

Angela gasped. The throbbing between her legs, matching her increasing heartbeat, made her want to tear off every last shred of destroyed clothing on his body.

As her lips fell upon his, Angela slipped her hands up his tunic. She blindly explored the ridges of his chest, the rings dangling from his nipples, the softness of his skin, but she avoided his bandaged wounds. Henry was perfect, and now it was her turn to groan. "Are you sure we have enough time? I'm going to need a week."

Henry laughed and his thick hands gripped her butt and pressed her closer. His thick cock eagerly awaited her. "Let us enjoy one quick round. And I promise you many more to come."

She'd take what she could get. Angela was feeling downright feral by now. She lifted her layers of dress and Henry untied his breeches and loosened them enough. She dug at the ties on his underwear, releasing his length. Angela spit in her palm and lubed him up, which surprised him. But his reaction may have been for her touch, rather than her action. She wasn't going to stop and analyze proper lady bedroom etiquette in the back of a bumpy carriage ride.

Gripping his hard cock, Angela lowered herself onto him, and Henry moaned with pleasure, and she cried out.

At once she started to grind against him, and Henry captured her lips. He wouldn't let go, and she had no intention of leaving this carriage until she exploded from the built tension she'd carried since she first laid eyes on him. He was her anchor. She was his *number uno*.

Forever.

ANGELA SMOOTHED THE RAT'S nest of hair on her head and attempted to smooth her dress, which was nearly impossible in the carriage. Her face was flushed red from the exertion, and she couldn't stop smiling. Henry's own face was peaceful and relaxed while he tucked his tunic into his breeches. When this surprise was over, she needed at least two more rounds to be satisfied.

A vast seaside plantation appeared over the hill. The horses followed the long driveway and stopped with the carriage aligned with the fancy front door. Henry had promised her a surprise, but since he wanted to settle in the colonies on the mainland, she wasn't sure what this stately manor was about, and he refused to tell her.

The driver circled around and opened their door, offering a hand to Angela. His delicate treatment was so strange to her, but out of politeness, she accepted the assistance.

Henry climbed out behind them and, recollecting her hand and folding it around his arm, he led her up the short stairs and knocked. While waiting for the door to be answered, he asked, "Do you have a...phone...on you?"

Absently, Angela said, "Yeah, but the saltwater fried it. Plus, the battery's dead. I hate phones, anyway..." She trailed off and stared at him. "You know what a phone is?"

Henry only smiled with amusement, and the front door opened. A woman in a drab-colored dress folded her hands together and said, "Master Lemoine and Mistress Porter shall see you now. Right this way." She stepped back and waited for them to entered.

Angela's features twisted at the titles—master and mistress. She visualized many bedroom images. Her mind was already heavily focused on Henry, she didn't need more creative thoughts plaguing her while she needed to be a lady. She gripped Henry's forearm tighter.

Henry led them into a vast entryway with vases, flowers, and a delicate chandelier. Impressive.

The woman, Angela guessed a housekeeper, stopped and gestured toward a room.

Henry brought her over the threshold, where two people sat in antique upholstered chairs with intricate carvings. Their clothing was extravagant, considering the heat of the tropics, and Angela's excessive, but appreciated, dress fit right in. She uselessly smoothed her ratty hair, and when the lady of the house set down a teacup and rose to face her, Angela's hand stilled. She blinked several times and tilted her head, squinting at the familiar face in an unfamiliar world.

After all that time at sea, now she was hallucinating. "Em?"

The woman beamed with recognition and rushed toward her with fistfuls of cumbersome dress. Her arms opened wide, and Emily crashed against Angela.

"It's really you?" Angela asked, tears flooding her eyes. "You're really here?"

"Ange! I missed you so much. We have so much to talk about! I thought I lost you."

Angela sobbed and turned to Henry. His eyes were pink with his own emotion, and he smiled gently.

On the beach after the wreck, when Angela was worried for her mental health, Henry had told her he knew how different this was for her. Not difficult. *Different*. He knew where she was from. He knew all along, and that was the real reason he protected her...and brought her the greatest gift.

"You knew?" she asked him. "After all this time, you knew Emily was here? Why didn't you tell me?"

Henry said, "Is there a time you could've gotten here on your own?"

He had a point. Angela would've been distraught trying to find her way here, and she probably wouldn't have made it, not without Henry. She smiled at him in thanks.

Henry returned her smile, and he approached the man of the house, who also wore fancy threads. They shook hands and embraced, patting each other on the back, like long-lost friends.

Angela turned back to her friend. "I searched for you, but no one heard of you, except Henry. For a while, I thought I was going crazy."

"The necklaces were real magic. I still can't believe it myself. Still have yours?"

"Dropped it down the toilet. You?"

"Tossed it off the coast in Nassau."

Angela laughed and admired her friend's dress. "You hate dresses. What are you wearing?"

Emily chuckled. "It takes some getting used to. I tripped on these layers so many times. Good thing I tossed that necklace, or I would've been tempted to use it again to buy some jeans."

Angela laughed. "Good thing Robin never showed up. That girl doesn't do well without control."

"Could you picture her in this time? She'd go crazy."

Emily shook her head. "Come on, let me introduce you."

Angela took her friend's arm, and they crossed the room, approaching the men.

Henry and his friend pulled apart from their hug.

"Angela, this is my husband, Eric Lemoine. Eric, my best friend, Angela Foxe."

Lemoine took her hand, and on a bow, he kissed her knuckles. "The pleasure is all mine. I've heard of the missing Angela for so long, it's a relief to see you are well. And my friend, my old quartermaster, you've left the sea?"

Henry captured Angela's hand back from his friend. "I caught myself the best treasure a man could ask for. I have no use for the black any longer. I must tell you of our exploits in Cuba. Spain recovered barrels of gold from the treasure galleon's wreck. We found where they'd hid it, and we collected it first."

"Congratulations. I suspect you'll be wanting for nothing now," Lemoine said.

"No, and I have Angela here to thank for saving my brother's life."

Emily stared at her.

Lemoine's brows lifted in surprise. "You found William *alive*?"

Angela said, "Spain locked him in the hold of the *Peibo del ler San Francisco*, awaiting delivery for trial, but he escaped. Never underestimate the value of bobby pins."

Emily laughed. "Come. You must sit and share tea. It's not as good as the modern stuff, but you'll get used to it. Tell us all about what happened to you after you put on the necklace."

Angela took Henry's hand and together they sat and regaled their tales at sea. Emily told her tale as well, and Angela's life couldn't have been more perfect.

Chapter 33

THE CREW, OLD AND new, circled around Riley as he finished speaking the oath to Poseidon to remove all references of the schooner's given name from the Ledger of the Deep. He and Cantu poured a serving of champagne directly into His Majesty's sea. The men cheered, and Riley spoke the prayers to appease the gods of the four winds in the name of the *Angelfish*.

More champagne was dumped overboard, and upon the ceremony's completion, the crew eagerly guzzled down the remaining sparkling drink.

Buckley and his new carpenter's mate collected an armful of painting supplies to change the name emblazoned on the hull.

"Buckley, Watts, wait for a few moments more," Riley said, and addressed the officers. "We have Price, the armorer, returning to us. Hodgens shall continue to steer us. McKee shall lead the gun crew. Giles, our esteemed cook, we couldn't do this without you. Karl, you allow us to move along the sea. But we must vote for the captain and quartermaster to lead us on the new account."

"You're not staying with us?" Buckley asked.

"Much has transpired as of late, and I believe it is only fair that all voices are heard and agreed before we set sail on a new account. Now, in the matter of quartermaster, who are the nominees?"

McKee stepped forward. "I've been told you're going to vote for me, but I must assure all you fine men, I don't want it. Guns are my specialty and where I find I'm at my best. I vote for Karl Dillon."

Men cheered, and Boatswain Karl stepped forward with a placating gesture. "And I assure you all dirty rats, the quartermaster is not for me either. I must respectfully decline."

The men booed.

John Randall, a rescued prisoner, stepped forward next. "I was quartermaster under four captains on the Queen's Defiance over the course of several years, and although my crews trusted me fully, I understand that none of you know me. I offer myself as the nominee, because that is my best function."

The crew mumbled among themselves.

Riley thought it only a matter of formality that he'd step forward. Quartermaster was the position he'd been most comfortable with, but during an emergent situation, he felt empowered to handle the captaincy, and he'd allowed his dreams take hold. But that situation was no longer. "I nominate myself, in case you sea dogs have forgotten my many accomplishments for this crew."

The men laughed.

Riley added, "If no one else cares to step forward, we shall begin with the vote. All those in favor of Randall, say aye."

Many hands and ayes accompanied nods, which surprised Riley.

"And in favor of myself?"

No ayes. Dead silence. The wind was pulled from his chest, like an unexpected meaty fist to the gut. Riley's eyes settled on Cantu, whose enormous arms folded over his chest. Not even the gentle giant wanted Riley to retain his position.

The crew thought less of him than the newest recruit or the master gunner. How could that be? Steeling himself against the rejection, Riley exhaled quietly and said, "Then Randall is our new quartermaster. Let us pray your vast experience helps us greatly."

The men clapped and cheered the result while a crushing pain settled on Riley's shoulders. After all these years, from a young man to what he'd thought was leadership material, they'd shunned him. When the vote for captain was complete, he wasn't going to stay with the crew.

Riley still had his dignity. "Now for your captain. Nominees step forward."

The crew turned their heads back and forth like guilty children who didn't want to tattle on each other. Not a soul stepped forward. Not a soul spoke up.

"Anyone at all care to lead this crew?"

Cantu stepped forward, and Riley sighed in relief. He trusted the man, who'd proven time and again to have the crew's loyalty. "We only want *you* to lead us, Riley. We already decided unanimously. No need for the formal vote."

Riley cleared his throat and tried several times to swallow the lump forming. "You're certain? All of you...want me?"

"You showed great courage and strength facing Captain Price while on enemy territory. You handled a precarious position with a straight head and narrow focus, and we respected your actions. Despite your close relationship with the captain, you made decisions in everyone's best interests rather than trying to salvage your friendship. The mark of a great leader is in you. We trust you to lead us now into further victory."

"My age doesn't bother you?" Riley was six and twenty years of age, younger than most on the ship.

"Age is nothing but a number. It's the head on your shoulders that counts," Cantu said.

Captain Noah Riley? A voted captain, not one taken by force. *Captain...* The word repeated in his head, having never processed the title included before. These men wanted him to lead them to riches. He'd do whatever it took to show these men a grand time and riches beyond belief. For granting him his dignity and putting their full trust in him, he would reward them.

"Well, what are you waiting for?" Riley asked, slipping into his new role seamlessly. "Paint *Angelfish* on the hull at once. Swab the deck, and weigh anchor. We set sail at dawn, on the trail of riches."

Now that daydream could come true.

Epilogue

Vallo rubbed his eyes and climbed up to the main deck of the *Peibo del ler San Francisco*. He'd remained hidden while Spain had taken great losses last night, so what was one more? After Vallo had stashed his treasure on the English schooner, he sought safety aboard the warship until the perfect moment to commandeer the smaller vessel for his own use.

That time had come.

The sun blinded him. Holding his hand to shield his view, the seas were calm, both a blessing and a curse. The ship wasn't moving as quickly as he liked, but in light winds, the schooner would have an advantage. Vallo crossed amidships, and on the port side, the endless seas surrounded them.

Vallo frowned.

At the stern, figuring the smaller ship to stay in its place, Vallo still failed to find it. His heart thundered in his chest. All his treasure was on that ship. He rushed around the soldiers and knocked on the captain's door. Upon his approval to enter, Vallo rushed inside and closed the door.

Capitán Delgado sipped from a flute of champagne, and Vallo's throat was suddenly dry.

"What is the matter, Vallo?" the captain asked in Spanish.

"Where is the schooner?"

The captain leaned forward, face darkening with anger. "You tell me."

"I...I..." Vallo trailed off. He wouldn't tell the man what he'd planned. "What do you mean?"

"The prisoners from this ship broke free and stole my prize. Do you know anything about that?"

"Me? No. They were enemies. I gave them nothing. Are we heading in pursuit?"

"This warship was built for defense and destruction. There is no propulsion system known to man capable of bringing this ship within broadside distance of the schooner. Those pirates had stolen the schooner we captured and stolen Spain's treasure. By explaining their actions, I may find some level mercy, but the repercussions from the Crown to myself are expected to be of grave consequence."

Vallo fished out the meaning. "You're not pursuing the schooner or Price's crew?"

"I cannot."

Vallo gritted his teeth and left the cabin. He stalked over to the rail and searched the horizon for the sails of his enemies. Unlike Delgado, Vallo wouldn't allow the pirates to get the best of him. Spain had no idea Vallo had taken more of their treasure than he'd been allowed, and Spain wasn't going to help him retrieve it.

Vallo would never sleep until he had his treasure back, and he intended to slay every man on board that schooner to do it. Although...if he considered his plans more carefully, he needed a small crew just to sail her. So the ones most deserving of their lives and pledging the hardest shall be spared, only until he reached land and found a new crew of his own.

Price, Riley, and the rest of the *Sea Lion* crew and all the escaped prisoners, especially that woman, were all on his list to dispatch. First, they were going to experience the worst torture known to pirates at Vallo's own hand, and he would not sleep until his quest was complete.

They all needed to pay.

PIRATE'S PLUNDER

STEPHANIE FLYNN

Small Fish Publishing

Small Fish Publishing
USA

Special Note

While the events of this novel are fiction, the pirate raid on Gambia Castle was real, performed by Captain Howell Davis in 1718.

Chapter 1

Robin Hall spread her legs apart and leaned forward. Nerves tightened her stomach. It had been too long since she'd worked up the courage to do this. To be here. Focus. She gazed through the sight to her target. Aim for the heart. Aim for the kill. This man would not hesitate to take her out first. The rapid pops around her penetrated her hearing protection, but she didn't lose her focus.

Her index finger shifted into position. This time, she would prevail. Robin took up the trigger slack. Breathe in. Breathe out. Now or never. Tensing her arms, she squeezed off round after round in a rapid succession at her enemy. First at the heart. Then at the head. Between the eyes. No mistakes.

Pop, pop, pop.

Behind her eye protection, she blinked with each squeeze, but she focused like her life depended on it. Robin channeled her anger and pain at the target, ensuring he couldn't be a threat any longer.

Life wasn't fair—she'd been exposed to that lesson early on. Robin had tripped during a race and skinned her knee, causing her to lose. She was six years old at the time, but Robin wasn't capable of truly understanding. As a teenager, a devastating mistake had Robin questioning that lesson all over again. Her life had been torn from her, and through the pain and therapy, Robin tried to understand the 'why' of it. She never got any satisfying answers.

One by one, Robin unloaded the rounds. Her arms trembled with the recoil until the magazine emptied. Robin lowered the weapon and blew out a deep breath. She pressed the button alongside the partition to pull her target paper forward.

Direct hits to the head and chest. She counted the holes—no misses. There was nothing physically wrong with her aim. There was nothing wrong with her at all, but two people died because she froze up when it mattered most.

"Not bad for a rookie," Detective Todd Blenny said, reaching out for her target and tearing it off the hanger. He wore a suit, and he filled it out well. Too bad the insides didn't match the outsides.

"I'm not a rookie," Robin said sharply and removed her protective gear. Robin had dawdled in private security for years, strolling the properties of slumbering corporate assets, until she was finally accepted into the police academy a few months ago—her dream ever since that fatal mistake when she was a teenager.

But most of the city's police department treated her like she was still green. When she'd screwed up royally, and she'd been assigned to weeks of administrative leave for the investigation, she'd deserved their ridicule. Now she was back, and she just proved she was capable. No more mistakes. Robin couldn't live with another life lost on her account.

Blenny stuffed a finger through one of the holes. "I didn't think you could do this."

Robin had passed the academy's rigorous training. Of course she could. Without a rebuttal, Robin left the indoor shooting range, passing through the corridor of offices, but Blenny followed on her tail. If there was ever a proverbial 'wolf in sheep's clothing', Blenny's face would be under the definition.

"I meant to say welcome back," he called from behind her.

The words rang hollow. Blenny didn't want her on the force, none of her colleagues did. The unspoken truth was plain on their faces, and the snark and murmurs whispering through the office made their thoughts far more obvious. Even quiet Jessica, the front desk officer, cast her glares while making copies.

Several weeks ago, Robin had responded to an active shooter situation outside a bank, and when she needed to eliminate the hostile, she froze. Officer Clark Thompson took a round to the femoral and bled out, but *he* stopped the shooter. He was a hero.

Robin was the incompetent enemy still lurking among them. She'd needed that leave to recollect herself, reflect, and figure out where she'd gone wrong, and her colleagues needed even longer to rebuild that trust. But they didn't know Robin hadn't figured out where she'd gone wrong, and she'd convinced the department's shrink she had a handle on her mistake. Robin needed to redeem herself, so she'd lied.

Returning to the practice range today was the first step in figuring out why she'd failed to save Clark Thompson. It wasn't her aim.

Her response to Blenny was superficial and dry. "Thanks."

"So, can we make it a date? I'm free Friday night." Blenny held the door open for her.

Robin ducked under his thick arm with growing irritation at his tired request. "I already said no."

"I've heard of the mystical women who can subsist entirely on their man-eating thoughts, but I never saw one in person." He paused and quirked a sassy smile, attempting to provoke Robin into conversing with him.

Robin ignored him, passing by neat rows of desks with stacked files and humming computers. People moved around; always busy.

"Is this about the shooting? Look, you and me, we're okay. I wanted to take you out long before that, and it didn't change things for me."

It changed a lot of things for her. Blenny was the only cheerleader on her side, but for only one reason. Robin sat behind her desk and woke her screen. She asked dryly, "Would you like some pom-poms?"

The brute of a man leaned down into her personal space. "Come on. You gave Riggs and Angry Boston a chance. We both like food, right? I'll drive."

She had gone on a date with each of them once, before her incident, as the shrink called it, but neither of those dates ended well. The difference was she, Riggs, and Angry Boston had mutual interest. Robin could see through Blenny's crap, and she was never making the mistake of dating within the office again. "I'm busy."

Blenny laughed. "I don't buy that. You live alone, and you're an only child. Your mom passed away, and your dad is unknown. Your friends are those pathetic cretins at the Value SuperMart, probably working on a Friday night, whereas you and I aren't pathetic or working that night."

He rattled off her entire life's situation in a string of statements, each a verbal slap to the face. She knew her friends were all she had. Blenny didn't need to remind her.

Robin gripped the edge of her desk until her knuckles blanched, trying to hold back the reaction he fished for. "That information is none of your business, and you can't use departmental resources for your personal snooping."

After all that transpired in a short period of time, Robin wasn't going to stick around long enough to vest in her pension. She didn't want to let down her mom, but Robin couldn't stay here any longer.

"I'm messing with you, Hall. If you're truly busy on Friday, then I'll pick you up on Saturday," Blenny said softly.

Robin pressed her lips into a tight smile. "I'm busy all weekend. The answer is no. Now please allow me to do my job."

A detective in a navy blue suit pressed a file against Blenny's tie. "This one just came in. Lieutenant wants us to spearhead."

"Let's wrap this one up quick. I have plans this weekend." Blenny sent her what was probably a flirty smile and strutted away, matching stride with his partner on the case.

Robin exhaled in relief at the break. She'd wanted to move away to a small town, where no one knew her. A place where break-ins weren't commonplace. Where a murder didn't sit unsolved for years because of too little resources and too many dead ends. A place where bad memories wouldn't haunt her. After a festival this weekend with her favorite *pathetic cretins*, Robin was going to spend the rest of her spare-time job hunting. She didn't fit in as an officer.

She hoped Emily and Angela showed up this weekend. The outfit Angela had chosen for Robin made her skin crawl, but the woman assured her Robin would fit right in. That she could handle.

Robin didn't want Blenny seeing it, or anyone else on the force who already made up their minds about her.

Chapter 2
Nassau, New Providence Island, Bahamas, 1715

Captain Noah Riley sipped an indistinguishable liquid from his mug at the best tavern in town, the renowned Golden Macaw. Part ale, part punch, and a splash or several of rum—whatever it was, the liquor was hardly palatable. But he sipped the concoction slowly, so as not to raise concern amid the chorus of celebratory laughter.

Half his crew slammed empty mugs on thick oak tables, calling out for refills. The other half already buried themselves in the arms of the brothel next door. After their latest prize of Spanish gold from Cuba, the now-wealthy men deserved a shore leave—their first in weeks. The former *Sea Lion* and current *Angelfish* crew knew how to spend their money, and the funds dwindled with efficiency, which was fine.

A pirate's career was shorter than the average man's, so the captain's only goal was to find a prize to satisfy the crew and break up the account. Each day toiling at sea increased their risk of finding that short end: hanging by the neck until dead under King George's gibbet.

A risk Riley was comfortable taking.

Riley had never asked to become their leader, nor had he challenged the previous captain for the position, but as a dangerous situation unfolded with Spain on their last account, Riley had threatened to take the captaincy, should the foolish—but lucky—Captain Henry Price fail. It was a hollow threat; he'd never expected to follow through. But that was the precise moment he began to wonder. And now, at six-and-twenty years of age, Noah Riley was captain—elected unanimously.

As the *Angelfish* had hove to in the protected bay of Nassau to resupply, refit, and to give the crew its much-needed shore leave. Riley spent his time narrowing down his plan for the account, and Nassau's fort taunted him with its reinforced walls, range of artillery, and continuous defense by armed men.

He wouldn't dare raid the defenses of their pirate home, but as he'd studied it and picked the brains of sailors coming and going, Riley had decided on his target. This one would solve the crew's money problems for life and bring Riley back to his family. It was perfect.

Incredibly dangerous, but Riley didn't care. He swirled the liquid in his mug, avoiding its flavor.

"Captain, have another round with us. We're paying!" Buckley, the master carpenter, said, lifting a full mug and grinning with fewer teeth than customary. The old man brushed aside his black shoulder-length hair, the gray temples only appearing once in a while. The experienced man was dedicated to the sea, and although his aim with a hammer left everyone wanting, Buckley was dependable and willing to put the crew in their places should the need arise. He'd make a great quartermaster, but Buckley had always refused.

On their last account, Buckley had come within moments of the aforementioned gibbet. The carpenter had always said hanging by the throat was the worst way to die. Displaying a man's body in a spectacle was shameful in the worst way.

Riley figured once a man was dead, he no longer cared, so any shame was carried by the living. But Riley never voiced that opinion, lest the crew became suspicious.

A woman who'd appeared on their ship under Captain Price's leadership saved Buckley and many of the crew from that fate, including Captain Price himself. Riley still couldn't believe a woman had that much power and strength, but he hadn't been there.

"Come on, captain," Buckley pressed.

On an island full of ruffians and thieves, one could never be too careful with valuable information. As much as he trusted his crew, the drink tended to cause loose lips, and he'd kept his plans close to the chest for that reason. But apparently Riley had ignored his drink too long, and the crew noticed. "I haven't finished this one yet, but you go ahead. I insist."

Riley sipped to prove his word.

The carpenter patted him on the shoulder and gestured for his own refill. "Lighten up, captain. The day is young, and the rum is endless!"

Crew on the other side of him cheered the man's declaration, and Buckley chatted with them, leaving Riley alone.

But not for long.

Riley rubbed his thumb against the mug's handle, and the gangly William Price approached on sea legs, carrying his own sloshing drink. Riley smiled at the previous captain's brother, once presumed dead but rescued by that same woman. The only explanation Riley could swallow was witchcraft. How else could a woman perform such impossible feats?

If they were true at all.

Even with ample provisions since the rescue, William Price had never regained his healthful shape. Although Captain Henry Price retired from the sea with his impossible woman, William insisted on staying, claiming the domestic life wasn't for him, and with his history, Riley was happy to have him.

Price rested a hand on Riley's shoulder for balance and dropped onto a stool next to him. "I was chained in the hold of the *Peibo del ler San Francisco* for months. As much as I love the leisure time with the women, I want to see the open ocean again. What's the next move, captain? Any exciting leads?"

"Yea, we can't stay here forever," Cantu said, taking up the chair next to the armorer. The wood groaned under his heft of thick, corded muscle. Cantu was a highly regarded man on the crew. Trustworthy. Loyal to the articles. Strong as a tree and built like an elephant. A true asset to any crew, and he'd been with them since Riley first tasted the sea. "The musician is on the verge of pawning his violin soon, and I never saw a man drink as much as the boatswain. If Karl's not broke yet, he will be tomorrow."

"That man better slow down or he'll be begging for scraps," Buckley said, laughing. "Barkeep! Another fill!"

"Cantu has a point," Price said. "Some of us need another prize. Not that I'm ungrateful for our noteworthy luck thus far."

Riley couldn't keep their next target a secret forever, and since they were weighing anchor later this afternoon word couldn't spread fast enough to foil their plans, and since he needed full cooperation to pull off the incredible feat, Riley said, "Fort James."

"What about it?" Price smiled, crinkling the corners of his eyes, reminding Riley of the younger Price. As much as they'd fought in recent weeks, Riley missed his old captain, his friend.

Riley sipped from his mug and winced as he swallowed. "We're going to take it."

Price laughed. "I know I'm three sheets to the wind when I hear such preposterous words. What did you say?"

"What's preposterous?" Buckley asked, belching his approval of the rum-like concoction.

Riley had expected resistance. Pirates were thieves, but they weren't foolish. "We're going to raid the English fort on the Gambia River."

The men stared.

Price chugged down the rest of his mug and slammed the empty on the bar. "It may as well be called a fortified castle. Gun batteries line the perimeter. Soldiers number in the dozens, if not hundreds. If we're ambushed, the sheer cliffs on either side of the river mean we have no escape. There's no way we can succeed in taking her."

"Taking who?" John Randall, the new quartermaster, who'd also been rescued from the *San Francisco* by Price's woman, appeared on Riley's other side, thumbs hanging on his sash. He was well qualified for the job, but Riley didn't know where he sat with the man. All that mattered was the crew trusted him and voted for him.

"We're raiding a fort," Price answered for him, lifting his empty for a refill. "Going to need more rum for this one."

"A fort?" Randall asked. "That's a higher risk than we usually take on. What's the prize worth?"

Everything. "Enough for each man to say goodbye to the sea forever, if he chose."

Cantu shifted his weight, creaking the chair once again, and spoke in jovial celebration. "Why is it you want to retire us? Aren't we a good enough family?"

Riley hoped their excessive drinking and teasing would make them forget the question, but alas, they quieted down and waited for Riley to answer. On a sigh, he said, "I want you to have the freedom to choose."

"We love the sea," Cantu said. "She was made for us. Karl and Jack Watts would agree, too, if their arms weren't elbow deep in whore right now."

The men laughed, and drink sloshed over their mugs. Some rained down on Riley, and he frowned. Washing clothes was nigh impossible on the ship, but still plenty difficult on land, and these were his best garments.

In their stories, the crew mentioned a few others enjoying the brothel: Giles, the portly cook, which surprised everyone, and little Peter Gunner, which surprised no one. The men wanted to spoil the young man, as Riley had been at his age. Hodgens was apparently over there, too, but he refrained from participating, no matter how much Karl flaunted the flesh before him.

Randall's eyes glinted with greed, and he rose his voice to drown out the storytelling. "For one, I don't care why. My concern is, do we have the men for it?"

The crew quieted down, listening with growing interest. Price drank from his refilled mug. Cantu shook his head in the negative.

"I'm with Cantu on this one," McKee said, lifting his bald head above the others to be heard. Ale glistened on his scraggly beard, but no matter his rough appearance, the master gunner was a loyal man. "We need at least twenty more men. With the other crews roaming the island right now, finding enough free agents willing to sign is going to leave us scraping the bottom of the barrel."

Riley's men numbered a dozen from the original lot, and another dozen who were rescued and agreed to join the account. But to take a fortified castle, they did need more. "Randall, as quartermaster, I task you with recruiting. Make sure the hands are experienced."

"Consider it done," Randall said. "After I finish my next round. Barkeeper!"

Riley smiled and pushed his mug toward his quartermaster. "Take mine. I need air."

Buckley laughed. "Another round, men, then it's our turn at the brothel!"

The crew cheered.

Chapter 3

THIS WAS A MISTAKE. A huge mistake. One she would bury in the fathomless depths of her mind for all eternity. If anyone dared speak of it, she would vanish in embarrassment. Robin covered her thighs with her purse, attempting to shield herself against the gawkers—who were dressed as normal people. Why had she listened to Angela and Emily? They'd both said the festival-goers would be dressed in pirate-y wear. The few here and there were vastly outnumbered by people wearing pants.

Robin was not.

Angela Foxe told her which costume in a bag to buy—the exact same one as Angela's. Something about sexy twin pirates. Robin didn't know anything about this stuff. The ivory blouse was rimmed in ruffles, and the length of the dress was uneven—on purpose, Angela had said. The brown corset on the outside was restrictive, and there was nowhere in this outfit for her to conceal-carry, so she left her weapon at home.

Along with her dignity.

Where were Angela and Emily? They were supposed to meet her here, and as far as Robin was concerned, there was safety in numbers. Right now, she was the lone gazelle, and the cheetahs eyeing her like a tasty meal made her eye twitch. Robin pulled out her cell phone, pretending to be busy, and tried to hide her blushing hot face.

Robin sent them both a text. *'I'm here. Where are you?'*

A cell phone chimed nearby, and Robin turned her head in anticipation of joining her lost herd, but she didn't recognize the man eagerly checking his phone. Robin sighed and texted, '*I was at your store yesterday picking up a shoplifter, but you were both at lunch. Sorry I missed you.*'

She waited a beat and put away her phone.

Down the grassy hill, rows of tented vendors sold refreshments, gear, and trinkets for the enthusiasts. To the right, along the dock, was a single tall ship, about to set sail. And into the Bay of Green Bay—the large swath of water connected to Lake Michigan—another tall ship was returning to shore with tourists.

Knowing Emily's obsession with pirates, Robin's friends didn't wait once the ships were ready to sail, and they wouldn't have a cell signal way out there. Robin shielded her eyes from the sun and scanned the festival grounds, looking for something—someone—comforting.

Security. There had to be security on the grounds. She'd talk shop and network, and if the situation called for it, she'd assist while off-duty, especially with those ancient boats being the draw of the day. How sturdy were those old ships, anyway? Was the Coast Guard on standby in case one took on water and sunk? Robin didn't like boats at all. The last time she'd boarded a pleasure boat, it ended terribly, making her that much more fearful of boats in general, but especially ancient ones. Even though she could swim, she liked keeping her feet on dry ground.

Robin didn't see any security station or any uniformed officers roaming the festival. There had to be someone.

"Hall? Is that you?" Blenny's unwanted voice penetrated her eardrums, and a skitter of nerves ran through her. *Someone, anyone, but Officer Blenny, please.*

Robin turned her head, gritting her teeth. Blenny, in sensible cargo shorts and a dark polo, leaned into her view, and his eyes roamed her outfit, lingering on her bare legs. Robin's back stiffened. It didn't take a genius for Blenny to learn one of her best friends was a nut for pirates, so Robin would be here.

"Stalking is illegal in all fifty states," she said dryly.

"And I didn't know you memorized all the laws applicable to each state. Color me impressed."

That was not her intent. Robin returned her purse to the front of her thighs. When she wore her uniform, she stood her ground, held her chin high. But wearing this? She was a self-conscious piece of meat.

She hated it.

"Have fun then," Robin said dismissively, coldness in her voice.

"Oh, I'm going to have fun," he said, staring at her exposed cleavage and miles of bare skin. Her chest didn't fill it out entirely, not like Angela, but the frilly lace and layers of polyester filled in where she was lacking.

A few weeks ago, Emily shared her progress on her own outfit, perfectly home-made and masculine. Robin wasn't into this scene, and therefore, not motivated to make her own costume—whether she'd decided on breeches or a skirt—so she trusted Angela's judgment on which costume in a bag to purchase. She wouldn't make that mistake again.

"Hold still. I need a picture." Blenny slipped his cell phone out of his back pocket.

"Absolutely not!"

This could not happen. She survived the work day despised by everyone; she couldn't stand to be a laughingstock.

"I only need a few seconds. Hold still."

"Leave me alone." Robin walked away. Hopefully he didn't choose to record a video instead, but she wasn't going to turn around to find out.

With Blenny left behind in her dust, Robin intended to make something from this bust of a day—one circle in good faith to find her friends and get credit for showing up. Then she was going home to put on soft clothing that covered her body, make a cup of hot cocoa, and binge watch television. Alone. After her eyeballs stung with sappy daytime drama, she planned on filling out applications, so there was no point in rocking the boat by complaining to the captain about Blenny's behavior.

Blenny, with a look of frustration, popped into her view again, slowing her steps. The humor had left his features. "You know what your problem is?"

Robin stared him down and stopped. "You're in my way."

"You didn't let Riggs or Angry Boston inside your apartment. I'd like to find out why." Blenny paused, groping her with his eyes.

Robin couldn't believe what he'd admitted. She wanted to slap him, but that would only encourage him further. She uttered a noise of disgust. "They shared details? With you?"

A mischievous grin split his face. "Everyone got all the details, so I know you must be so...*frustrated*. That's your problem."

His outrageous accusation was not only unfounded, but incredibly insulting and callous. Robin's mouth dropped open.

Blenny smirked. "Oh, I'm on the right track."

Robin tipped her chin up and marched around him, fighting back tears of humiliation. Not only did they hate her as an officer, but they didn't respect her as a person, either.

All she wanted was a man who could take care of himself and would cover her back, which after many failed relationships, fellow police officers sounded appealing, but that was clearly a non-starter. Based on experience, the trifecta of independent, strong, and *respectful* was as attainable as a magical unicorn. Six-year-old Robin was disappointed in learning the truth. Thirty-five-year-old Robin was only...

Relieved.

She was done hunting for her unicorn, a simple decision.

A freeing decision.

And this afternoon, Robin would begin the job hunt. Soon enough, she wouldn't have to face any of them again. Robin smiled to herself.

Destiny called for her to become a crazy cat lady, and she would embrace it.

"I can fix your problem," Blenny called after her. "Think about it."

There's nothing about me that needs fixing.

Robin strolled by the vendors while scanning the festival grounds for her friends, or for anyone in need of assistance—any distraction from this craptastic day. Despite smiling about adopting a herd of cats, she would miss being an officer. Protecting people filled a need deep in her bones, and right now, that was all that kept her at this festival. With no security on staff and her friends incommunicado, Robin needed reassurance that everyone would remain safe. Although, if Blenny dropped over, clutching his chest, Robin *would* hesitate, wondering if he faked it for attention.

People conversed, laughed, and lounged on picnic tables with drinks in their hands. Others waited in line to buy food, which smelled like seared beef and oily fries. Other visitors took photos of themselves and some with strangers in costume. A few drank from bottles hidden in paper bags. Robin frowned at them, but since she was off duty, she let them be. With no real distractions here, Robin approached the vendor tables. The trinkets and food didn't interest her, but she stopped at a display of shiny swords. "Are these real?"

The vendor sitting behind the table wore a greasy stained apron around his thick waist. Lines on his face and cracks in his calloused hands suggested a lifetime of unparalleled craftmanship. The swords were real.

"Yes, ma'am. Handcrafted by the finest swordsmith this side of the snow belt. Be careful now; don't want to cut yourself, such a pretty thing like you." The gray-haired man smiled.

Robin pressed her lips together and walked away. She fished her phone out of her purse and checked the screen in case she'd left it muted or on vibrate.

No messages.

While walking, Robin texted them again. *'Guys, I'm by the vendors. Where are you? Still on a ship?'*

This time she waited a minute, but still neither replied. Robin had enough. She'd subjected herself to enough unwanted attention and embarrassment. Angela was going to hear about this, and Emily's sanity was going to be questioned.

Robin tucked her phone away and craned her neck to be sure Blenny wasn't behind her before she headed back his way toward the parking lot.

"Good morning, child." A woman's raspy voice stole Robin's attention.

She braced herself for more unwanted comments, but none came. Robin turned around and smiled politely. "Hi."

"See anything you like?" The withered woman stood up from a stool, her back hunched with age and pain, and she smiled with years of gravity pawing at her skin.

Pity brought Robin's eyes to the woman's wares, and her brows lifted at the stunning pieces of jewelry. "I need to get going, but your stuff is beautiful."

"Here. Hold on a moment. I have just the thing for you." The woman bent over, and Robin half expected to hear her spine crack.

"It's okay, really. I have to go."

The old woman rose and held out a necklace—a copper-colored chain holding an amethyst pendant. The stone shimmered a soft purple in the sunlight, a uniquely gorgeous piece, but with her job, jewelry wasn't practical. And when she wasn't at work? Jewelry was unnecessary. Where would she ever wear it?

"Five dollars and it's yours."

Seemed too good to be true.

With Robin's hesitation, the old woman added, "Amethyst has been known to grant your truest desire while protecting you from bad humors, so be careful how you use it." Her arm reached closer, urging her to accept the deal.

A gem would protect her? More like her nine-millimeter, which…she didn't bring. "Thank you, but no thanks."

"If you're in need of something you can't quite explain, you know where to go." The old lady returned the necklace under the table, but the smile never faltered.

With an awkward smile, Robin shimmied out of there, eyes glued to her phone. One last message, and she wouldn't feel guilty about abandoning the ship. She smiled at her silent pun. *'I'm leaving, guys. Sorry I missed you.'* She moved swiftly toward the hill where her car was parked.

The sounds of a man frantically panting pricked her ears. He shouted a word Robin didn't recognize. Her feet stopped. Something about it wasn't like Blenny playing games. It was real. Panic. Someone needed help. Robin tucked her phone into her purse, took the strap and slung it across her body to keep it out of her way, and turned, senses heightened for an emergency.

Her mouth dropped open at the shocking sight.

Chapter 4
Nassau, New Providence Island, Bahamas, 1715

RILEY COLLECTED HIS COCKED hat with the frilly feathers—the finest wear reserved only for shore leave—and meandered his way out onto the cobblestone street. He pushed his hat over his head to block out the blinding sun. Endless heat and humidity kept the sweat pouring under his layers of fine clothing: a long-tailed vest with carved buttons over a tunic, a lacy cravat, and a leather baldric currently sporting only a cutlass. The pistols were left on the ship to be cleaned, inventoried, and reloaded. The things misfired half the time and were terribly inaccurate the other half. Riley preferred swords and knives. His own skill was what he trusted when the time arose.

He headed down to the water where small waves shimmied the surface of the Caribbean Sea. A few sleepy boats rocked in the bay and sails dotted the horizon, but he recognized only a couple. A grove of palm trees shook with the breeze, and as Riley approached, sand entered his boots. Away from the noise of the town, the gulls kept him company.

Next to the water's edge, Riley sat on a homemade chair and leaned against an abandoned hut, resting in the shade, and used his hat to fan his face. He didn't know who crafted the small escape from town, but if they returned, he relinquish his seat.

The path to Fort James would send them through the *Peibo del ler San Francisco*'s territory, a hundred-gun, first-rate Spanish man-o'-war. A ship where both Price and Randall, among others, had been prisoners. The men understood the near-insurmountable risk ahead of them. And

William Price was right to be concerned over the cliffs of the Gambia River. If Spain, indeed, found them, the crew's English schooner was no match for the warship. Taking the English castle was the most dangerous plan imaginable, but if these men would dash into a guarded hut for a chance at gold, they would raid a castle for the untold sums hidden below. Frankly, he'd expected more resistance for his plan.

A glimmer in the sand caught Riley's eye. It wasn't the green of an onion bottle, nor the silver of a blade, nor the gold of a piece of eight. Curious, Riley leaned over and lifted it free. In his palm rested a necklace...one he'd seen before. The chain, a copper metal, and the amulet, a striking violet. Where had he seen such a gem before?

Riley bounced it in his hand, shaking off the loose sand, trying but failing to pull the images from memory. Either way, it was valuable, and he wouldn't let it go.

"Riley! I thought it was you!" The familiar voice stiffened Riley's spine. A short man in a clean dress approached with a smile behind deadly eyes.

Riley closed his fingers over the amulet and checked the man's hands for a pistol or a blade, but he found none. Still, Riley didn't relax. Standing to his full height, he said with a friendly but stilted tone, "Vallo. What brings you here?"

"I've been searching for you."

Not long ago, Vallo had been in close ties with Captain Henry Price to fish their own crew for traitors. After performing his duty, Vallo turned on the captain and almost killed him. Vallo had been secretly in league with Spain and *Capitán* Delgado of the *Peibo del ler San Francisco* the whole time. And he was rewarded handsomely for his efforts with a share of the loot the crew had taken. No one had seen the traitor since. At present, none of the sails in the bay or on the horizon displayed the red crosses of Spain.

"I can't imagine why," Riley said, keeping his distance and watching Vallo's movements closely.

"The *Angelfish* out there, that's yours now?"

"It is."

During their escape from the Spanish warship and under a blinding and deafening full broadside, Riley assisted Price in commandeering the English schooner, Spain's prize. Since renamed the *Angelfish*, Riley never saw or heard of a connection between Vallo and the schooner.

"I lost something of mine, and I think it was left on the schooner. Did your crew find anything on board?"

Vallo's presence was bad news, and the sooner he rid himself of the traitor, the better. A mockery of an offer should be sufficient. "Nothing out of the ordinary, unless you had personal chickens."

Vallo's face twisted with confusion. "You only found chickens?"

"If you want, I can drop by the bank and request a fair sum in exchange." It was a bluff to keep the peace. Riley had no intention of paying Vallo anything after what the man had done to the crew.

"I'm not sure I understand."

Riley continued, this time giving truth, "According to Giles, only the chicken count was beyond ordinary. If it's not chickens you're missing, what is it?"

With a frown, Vallo turned away and gestured to dismiss him.

Riley didn't like that slight. "I insist. I want to make this right. Many things have happened between us, and I want no one to harbor ill will."

Vallo stopped and turned. "I prefer to see the hold for myself. I'll let you know if I find what I'm looking for."

He didn't want that man anywhere near their ship. "As captain of the *Angelfish*—"

"Worry not, I shall take care of the problem myself. The crew knows me well enough to grant permission to board," Vallo said with a smirk.

Randall's new recruits would have never met Vallo, and half the current crew was oblivious to Vallo's treachery to keep Henry Price from looking weak. Only a handful of men knew the full extent of the traitor's crimes, and they wouldn't be enough to convince the crew to forbid a seasoned sailor's presence. Not when the promise of a fort's hold required more sailors. And Vallo would be smart enough to show up with a fabricated story, rather than outright demanding his treasure back. The pittance remaining in the hold would only enrage him. Since Vallo wasn't the direct type, Riley worried what he'd do in retaliation.

Riley's hands balled into fists of frustration. The necklace he'd forgotten about cut into his palm. Rather than drop it on the sand, he lifted the familiar amulet over his head. "As the captain of the *Angelfish*," he repeated, "I order you to stay away."

The traitor turned back over his shoulder and smirked.

The necklace fell around Riley's neck, and with a blink, the sand underfoot disappeared. The humid salty air vanished. The temperature dropped. Most concerning, Vallo was gone.

But where did the sand go?

"Vallo!" Riley shouted, turning in place. "Vallo!" The grass under his sandy boots was unlike any he'd seen since...England. The ships at the dock were familiar, yet unrecognizable. The people around him wore...what exactly? Women wore breeches of a material he couldn't guess. Men wore shirts on the outsides of their outfits, and not one man wore a cocked...

Riley sighed in relief. One man, in point of fact, wore a cocked hat. As the man strolled by, it was of a material Riley hadn't seen. The necklaces draped around the man's neck jingled with a sound he'd never heard, and the bright red and black stripes of his breeches weren't familiar either.

Riley's heart pounded in his chest. He was too hot. He spun in place, breaths pulling in and out of his chest.

"Vallo!"

The cool breeze dried his sweat, sending chills along his skin, but yet, he burned up.

Where was Riley?

Chapter 5

Instincts taking over, Robin rushed through the meandering crowd and stopped short. Up close was so much worse. The distressed man smelled like he'd rolled out of a dumpster. His costume was old, tattered, and clearly handmade—a blue coat with gold buttons over a black vest and an ivory tunic, which altogether was way too warm for this weather. His breeches were brown, and his boots were black leather. A black tricorn hat with silly feathers covered his dark hair pulled into a ponytail tied with a ribbon. His wild eyes were dilated with confusion, and the look of horror—and a crooked lift of his lips on his bearded face broke her heart. Had he been drugged? *And where is that smell coming from?*

Either way, this man needed help now.

With hands held out to prevent defensive aggression, Robin approached cautiously. "Sir? Sir, are you all right?"

The man looked at her, but his gaze was unfocused, searching. *What happened to this guy?*

"It's going to be okay now. Take a deep breath." She declined to state her disclaimer. Since Robin was off duty, there was no need to incite further panic from those uneasy around law enforcement. The scent of liquor wafted off him, and Robin relaxed. Likely a case of spiked drink. "I'm Robin. What's your name?"

"Riley. Noah Riley." The man returned to scanning the area. His mouth gaped open, and his arms hovered around his waist as if on the verge of wanting to shoot, but he carried no gun. He was afraid, and Robin sensed he was lost. With Halloween months away, where else would a man dressed as a pirate go than the Tall Ships festival? Robin herself looked ridiculous as well, and she pushed that image down deep. She had a job to do.

"I'm Robin Hall. Do you know where you are?"

Riley met her gaze and took in her ridiculous outfit. Heat flashed behind his eyes. His dark features were certainly handsome, although hidden behind a beard, tangled hair that had fallen out of the ponytail, and sweat glistening on his high cheekbones. And the silly costume. Now was not the time. Robin focused on getting the man help.

"This was sand a moment ago." Riley shifted his weight and lost his balance, falling over onto the grass. A long sword angled awkwardly from his hip. Based on what she saw at the vendor, his was real. Riley was a true enthusiast. He touched the trimmed blades as if feeling grass for the first time. "Seems the ale was mixed too strongly today."

Robin smiled, assuming ale was some sort of mixed alcoholic drink. "I thought I smelled it on you. Do you need medical attention? I can call you an ambulance."

"You can what?" He looked up at her, puzzled.

"I can call you an ambulance," she repeated, louder and clearer. Riley only stared at her in confusion. Whatever he was on was strong. Robin reached for the man's wrist and waited for him to accept her help. "I'd like to check your pulse."

Riley hesitated before reaching his arm out to her. His eyes tracked to her exposed cleavage.

Robin wasn't surprised, but she kept herself professional. This man was clearly nothing like Blenny. She admired his high cheekbones and curving lips. His steely gray eyes were captivating, and she guessed he was in his mid-twenties—too young for her. But that shaggy long hair on his head pulled back into a pony was so rare to see and...alluring. Heat rose on her cheeks at her wandering thoughts, so unlike her.

Man in distress. Focus.

Robin slipped his coat up his wrist and heat rushed through her fingers. Actual heat. Was he running a fever? Robin felt for his pulse, but she wasn't wearing a watch. She dug out her phone, tapped the clock app, and started a time counter. Setting the phone down on the grass, she watched the digits change and focused on the hot skin beneath her fingers.

Eyes locked on her smartphone with a crack on the screen, his face turned ashen. "What is that?"

Robin laughed sarcastically. "I know it's old, but it still works. The department pays for my office-issue, and I don't see the need to have two newer phones."

"Department?"

Oh, shit. He was going to flip out. Better to rip off that bandage. "I'm a police officer, but I'm not going to hurt you. I need a minute to check your pulse and see if you're okay." She met his terrified gaze hidden beneath all those layers of grime. If he wasn't homeless, something bad must've happened to him. Pity tore through her.

"Where am I?" he asked.

"The Tall Ships festival." Robin looked over his clothes again, and the corner of her lips lifted. Chatting about his interest would help him relax. Robin could channel her inner Emily. "This is kind of cheesy, huh? I swear I don't dress like this on normal days. I was told this outfit would blend right in, and I guess you understand that. Did you make your costume? It looks so...authentic. And, uh, not at all cheesy." She didn't want to offend the guy as he was cooperating.

Riley glanced down at himself as if looking for the first time. In the short span of silence, Robin felt the pumping of his radial artery. The pulse was even but firing rapidly, which made sense considering his confusion and panic, but it didn't make sense considering his recent imbibing. Riley wasn't drunk.

"I think we need to get you to a hospital."

Riley pulled his arm away. "I don't need a hospital. Where am I?"

Perhaps his confusion went deeper than the festival grounds. Whoever drugged and dumped him here needed to be behind bars. "Look, you're in Wisconsin, and I promise I'll keep you safe."

He gazed into her eyes, completely baffled.

"I know it sounds weird, but you can trust me. You're in good hands." He didn't seem afraid of her job title, which was a relief, but after she'd lost her mom and caused Officer Clark Thompson's death, she didn't take her promises lightly. This guy was in trouble, and Emily would insist a fellow pirate enthusiast be kept safe, and that was what Robin intended to do.

"Where's that...Wisconsin?"

Robin noticed his English accent. It sounded almost....elite. Was he royalty or someone important in Parliament? Judging by his disheveled appearance, he likely couldn't handle an American medical bill, and by his complete confusion about being here, he probably didn't purchase a health plan for travelers. Robin was going to have to help in a different way.

"How about something to eat? Are you hungry?"

"Quite famished."

Robin rose to her feet and held out a hand to assist him up. She didn't want him to fall again; then she would have to send him to the hospital, regardless of the consequences.

Riley looked at her hand like it was poison.

"Take it. Let me help you. Trust me, you don't want to injure yourself on this side of the pond." Her hand hung in the air, waiting.

With a frown, Riley pulled himself to his feet, and Robin let her hand drop. She chalked that up to cultural differences, not a sexist slight.

"What are you in the mood for? The festival has burgers, hot dogs, brats, fries, and a few beer-battered deep-fried things—generally involving cheese—which are excellent by the way."

Riley's upper lip twitched like it all churned his stomach. Well, there weren't any vegan options here, unless fries counted.

"We'll keep it simple with burgers, but you have to try the cheese curds. It's mandatory for all Wisconsin visitors. This way." Robin headed straight toward the food tent, which at this hour had no line.

Riley stayed by her side, neck craning around like he'd never seen a portable kitchen before. How did a person travel half-way across the world and not remember it? Or deliberately put on those clothes for this festival and not remember his destination? The best she could offer was helping him remember where home was and safely putting him back on that plane—after she was certain he was sober from whatever caused the confusion. At this point, it had to be a drug-spiked drink. No vendors sold alcohol, so he didn't get it here, which only brought up more questions.

Robin placed their order and paid with a credit card. Riley watched her intently, but she wasn't concerned that he'd mug her. There was a genuine innocence there, not a manipulative con game. Even if he tried, she could take him. Collecting the plastic baskets of food, she handed one over to Riley.

He stared at it.

Robin chuckled. "You've seen hamburgers before, right?"

Riley stared at her, his eyes roaming her outfit once again, and heat rushed through her body as if his hands glided along her skin. If any other man looked at her like that, she'd give him a piece of her mind and a particular finger thrust in the air. It was the accent. Had to be. What American woman could resist the charms of an English accent? The allure of a different life, a different world. An escape.

Robin cleared her throat. "There's an open picnic table over there."

Riley followed her to a table and mimicked her sitting and pushing aside the tissue paper in the basket. She fisted her burger, elbows resting on the table, and took a big bite.

Rather than lift his own burger to dig in, Riley continued staring.

"I bought you lunch. The least you could do is try it. Here. Start with this." Robin pinched a deep-fried cheese curd and offered it to him.

He stared at it, face blank of expression.

"Come on. My hands are clean..." she trailed off at her insensitive gaffe. Nice move, Hall. *Go ahead and insult the homeless English guy.* She glanced aside.

Noah Riley took the juicy cheese curd from her fingers and reluctantly placed it into his mouth. He chewed slowly as if exploring the texture for the first time.

"How is it?"

"Different."

He spoke! But not enough. "Different good or different bad? What's the food like where you're from?"

"What is this?" Riley lifted a cheese curd out of the basket and inspected it.

"It's cheese with a coating."

"It's more pleasant than it looks, I admit." Riley placed the bite into his mouth, chewed, and swallowed. "On a bountiful day with fully stocked provisions, we feast on salted pork or chicken, potatoes, biscuit and rum. When provisions run low and rations are thin, we subsist on biscuit and diluted rum."

"That sounds bland." And dreadful. And clearly not the diet of a high-society man. Who was this Noah Riley?

"Food is only a means of survival. We hope to have sufficient quantities for the account, and that it won't spoil before we take shore leave." Riley lifted his burger and bit down. He chewed, gagged once, and swallowed. He wiped tears from his eyes. "That's...uh...bold of flavor."

"You're a sailor?"

The corner of his lips lifted. "Captain, newly minted, in fact."

Robin's brows rose. Even more interesting, his memory was returning. "Military or commercial?"

Riley smirked. "I declined to enlist in the Royal Navy after hearing of their decrepit conditions." He reluctantly took another bite and this time, he paused mid-chew, suppressing a gag. He was being polite.

"The Navy can't be that bad. Cramped, sure, but decrepit? That's a little harsh."

"I find my word choice is not wanting."

"What ship do you captain?" Robin asked, drawn to his story and trying to link where he'd come from to appearing in Wisconsin.

"After turning my back on the Royal Navy, I took up the black. I am one of the few who have no shame in it." He studied her face, waiting for a reaction.

She expected an answer similar to *HMS Queen Elizabeth,* or something generic like a submarine, or even *I cannot disclose that information.* "What's *the black*? Is that a commercial vessel?"

Riley cleared his throat and drank a few swallows with a grimace. Astonishment lifted his brows, and he asked, "You've never heard of the black?"

"Black what?"

Riley puffed out his chest in pride. "The black banner, of course. A crew of men, devoted to their cause, enemies to all mankind, and free of the Crown. Your lands have never experienced the marauders of the sea?"

Robin's rude snort broke through, and her lips pulled into a smile. "I should've known you're talking about pirates. I guess you're in the right place."

Lips pressed firmly, Riley wasn't amused. "In what world are pirates a laughing matter? Do we not instill fear in your people here?"

Was he delusional or a method actor? Since Robin enjoyed the conversation, and the man needed food to help sober him up, she humored him. "Pirates are fiction for children's tales. Not sure why? None of the true stories are child-friendly." At Riley's serious demeanor, she dropped the levity. "All right, fine. If you want a serious answer, there are pirates on the other side of the world. In small motorboats, they grab and smash before the authorities can catch them. But no, they aren't a concern here."

Having finished his meal, Riley downed the rest of his water and sat upright. "If you remain under British rule, then this is an oppressed world where freedoms are nothing but a veil."

"We aren't ruled by the British."

"Spain?" Riley asked.

Robin cocked a brow, and her phone chimed with a text. "Finally!" She dug out her phone and lit up the screen, but it wasn't Emily or Angela. Robin's enthusiasm sunk. An organization was begging for a blood donation. She followed Riley's gaze to the dock. The next ship had already unloaded and reloaded, heading back out. And another two more were closing the distance.

"What is that device? You said a phone. What is it?" Riley said, leaning forward.

This disheveled Englishman with an elite accent, who appeared and smelled homeless, claimed to be a captain, but not of a military or commercial vessel. A pirate captain, who didn't know what a phone was. This had to be beyond method acting, but if it wasn't, he was damned convincing. More realistically, this handsome man with his striking features and broad shoulders suffered from a poorly managed mental illness.

"It's a phone. You've heard of a phone, right?"

Riley didn't like her answer, and Robin could read anger when she saw it. Just like Blenny, it roared whenever he didn't get what he wanted. Next was demanding, then backpedaling and apologizing, like clockwork.

Instead, Riley shocked her.

Chapter 6

Robin Hall was beyond vexing. What madness had he been thrown into? More importantly, why was this strange woman so gracious to him? A woman officer. A woman who was stunningly beautiful with bright pink lips, bold hazel eyes, and brilliant red hair cascading in curls down her back and chest. A woman with an impossible palate. Everything she said was so confusing, and yet genuine. The phone device was in her hands. He couldn't deny its existence. The growing confusion only angered him, but his sharp tone was aimed at himself rather than her.

"I'm sorry to have burdened you with my lack of comprehension. Where I'm from there are no phones. Those sizzling machines under the tents don't exist, and not minutes ago, I was standing on the sandy beach of Nassau, but now I'm in Wisconsin—next to familiar yet different ships. I cannot explain what transpired, so pardon me, I'm simply frustrated."

Robin frowned and tucked that strange thing away. "You're serious?"

"As serious as a trip to the gibbet," Riley said flippantly.

Before she responded, he thought deeper on his remark. This woman wanted to help; that much was clear. Although facing the Crown and accepting just punishment was Buckley's nightmare, Riley had only preferred to avoid it until the due time. One of two fates awaited all pirates. The preferred was death during the account and reuniting with all the crew he'd lost over the years—good men taken too soon. The alternative was death at the hands of the Crown, made into a public speckle on a gibbet.

After discovering Riley's mind had finally broken, there would be no honorable death a sea for him. Leaning forward in secrecy, he swallowed a lump caught in his throat. "You said you're an officer. Can you surrender me to the authorities?"

Robin rubbed her face and exhaled. "Yeah, you know what? This was fun and all, but I need to get you home. Authorities sounds good to me. What facility were you in? Summerset? Longview? Brown County?"

Riley didn't recognize any of those ships, but after the morning he had, he wasn't surprised. If he could find his ship, then he needn't succumb to the authorities at all, and he could save his crew from the danger they faced. He leaned forward in urgent secrecy. "*Angelfish*. I'm captain of the *Angelfish*. Have you heard of her?"

Robin twisted her lips and stood up. "Can't say that I have."

Riley glanced at the food and shifted his eyes to the strange objects surrounding him. Since he'd never heard of or seen these things before, they weren't trading with England. The goods never appeared on ships crossing the oceans. Robin and her unusual dress loomed over him. He'd seen it once before...on a strange woman...shortly before a squall sent the *Sea Lion* crashing against an outcrop off the coast of Cuba.

The stowaway who'd been lost and confused.

The magic woman Price had warned him about.

But this was wrong. Riley's hands trembled, and a sinking feeling crushed his chest. Impossible. All of this was impossible. It couldn't be, could it? Was traveling through time a regular occurrence here?

"What...what year is it?"

Robin chuckled. "Okay, now you need more help than I'm qualified for. You must've missed a dose of medication or something. We need to get you admitted, Captain Noah Riley. Is that your real name?" She held out her hand.

"What's the year?" he demanded harshly with a slam of his fist on the table. He needed to know the truth.

"I bought you lunch; you could be nicer."

Riley flinched. He had no right to take his frustrations out on her. She was only trying to help. "My apologies for scaring you. Please answer the question."

"What year do you think it is?" she asked carefully.

Riley rose to his full height, hand resting on the hilt of his cutlass. "Seventeen-fifteen."

Robin frowned. "Are you sure?"

Having lived on a ship packed with men since his teen years, Riley didn't have much experience with women, but he was certain her confusion was as genuine as his. The anger pumping through his veins softened, but his hands trembled harder.

"I captured an English schooner with my previous captain not weeks ago. We recovered a Spanish prize off the coast of Florida not months ago. I'm certain of the year."

"Well, I hate to break it to you, but you're off by about three hundred years. Let me call the station and see if there's an endangered missing person alert. Stay right here." Robin retrieved that phone from her coin purse again.

Three hundred years. Riley had fallen into…the future? His knees gave out, and Riley dropped onto the bench of the table. Robin rushed to his side, but seeing he was stable, she frowned and continued talking at the device.

Riley glanced at the tall ships docked, and his gaze tracked over the crowd in clothing both familiar and so foreign or scandalous he never would've imagined it. Robin was right. Riley was certainly missing…from his home centuries in the past.

He had no way of getting back, as he had no way of knowing how he'd gotten here. As soon as Robin handed him over to her authorities, his struggles would end, a fate he welcomed with open arms, because Riley would reunite with his family.

Riley missed his dear future-brother-in-law, and despite the circumstances, he missed his betrothed, too. Robin reminded him of her. Generous to a fault, blindly trusting, and admittedly stunning with lips that curved into shapes betraying her thoughts. It amused Riley to watch her mouth move against the phone. Her hazel eyes met his and shifted away. Again they came back, and...no, Robin was not like his betrothed. The young woman of his past was a burden he'd forever carry in his heart. Robin, though older than Riley, could never be a burden. She was simply...a bonny rescuer dropped into his path to guide his way off this mortal plane.

Robin tucked away her phone. "There's nothing the department is aware of. Let's get you down there and file a report. I've had enough of this place myself." She gestured for him to follow, and he stood on sea legs.

He'd sailed with the best men he'd ever known, and the worst scum with nary a flinch, knowing his end approached every day he sailed the seas. But facing down that reality was something else entirely. Robin watched Riley's unsteady knees, and she rushed to his side, supporting him, and holding his arm. But in his current state of confusion and resignation, he accepted the bonny rescuer.

"My car's this way."

Riley didn't know what that meant, but he allowed her to lead him up a small hill. His legs became stronger with each step, but people around them stared like they were animals. He deserved their scrutiny...and worse, but he carried no shame. He could not change the choices of his past, so he willfully accepted their disgust. If Robin knew all Riley's secrets, she'd join them in their prejudice.

Atop the hill, Riley froze in place. Bright shiny beasts lined up for the attack. One purred to life, and its eyes glowed in territorial fury. Riley had never seen such animals. His pulse raced, and instinctually, he pushed Robin behind him for her own safety. Unsheathing his cutlass he roared, "Back you beast! Back, or I shall slay you and dine on your entrails!"

Riley lifted his sword to strike, but he didn't know how the animal was going to attack—he'd never seen one before. Nevertheless, an end was still an end—via the Crown's gibbet or a beast. One was decidedly less drawn out and embarrassing. With a bellow, Riley charged, legs pumping full speed ahead. But after a step or two, he found himself knocked straight off his feet, and he landed on his back, immobile. His legs were weighed down. His arm pinned away. But how? The beast didn't move, and he never struck it. A magical beast from a magical world. "You haven't got the best of me yet! Unhand me and fight like the foul beast that you are!"

The weight pressing his chest was oddly warm. Peeling his furious glare from the beast, Riley glanced down, and to his surprise, Robin sprawled over his body, and her arms and legs tangled with his.

"Did you look that those models?" she scolded. "Do you have any idea the property damage you were facing? You can't do things like that here, understand?"

The beast had pinned her as well. Riley tried freeing her, but she wouldn't budge. "Are you injured, Lady Robin? Has the beast hurt you?"

Robin's lips twisted, and she shifted on his chest to meet him face to face. "Robin, just Robin. No lady. There is something wrong with you."

Impressed with her lack of fear, Riley said, "I feel no pain, and yet I cannot move. The magical beast has bested us both. I'm sorry I could not save you from it, and it's my fault for angering it. I beg of you to forgive me."

She only stared at him with disbelief.

"How bad is my injury?" he asked, still unable to move, hoping the end continues as swiftly and pain free.

"You're being serious," she said, gazing into his eyes. Worry framed her face. He didn't like that look.

Riley frowned. "I never laugh in the face of death. It's disrespectful."

"That's a car. I'm the one restraining you. If you calm down, I'll release you."

Riley shifted, trying to free himself, and indeed, feminine hands pinned him. How remarkable. Something else caught his eye entirely. As he shifted beneath her, friction developed against his body, and the most wonderful cleavage popped up to say hello. Heat rushed through Riley's body, pooling where he didn't want it. He looked at her chest again, helpless to look away.

"I saved you from a lawsuit." Robin sank back on her ankles, releasing him and taking the marvelous view with her. "What you say makes no sense at all, but a part of me wants to believe you. Let's get you cleaned up, and then I'll see what I can do, okay?" She offered her hand in assistance again, but being sturdy on his feet, he needed it not.

Riley rose on his own accord and followed her, reluctantly. He'd done many dangerous and wild things in his years, but never before had nerves affected him so. His legs were still loose but capable, his stomach gurgled, and the rapid fire of his heart made him feel like a young man alone with a woman for the first time. Nothing made sense to him, but he walked along in this strange world of the future, avoiding his sword nor his hand touching the shiny beasts, lest he stir them awake. The entire herd waited silently.

Bangs nearby turned his head, but Robin showed no concern.

Strange world indeed.

When Robin walked into another row of slumbering beasts, he couldn't do it. Riley's breaths became shallow. As she walked farther and farther from him, his chest squeezed. He tried focusing on her exposed backside as motivation to follow, but his body wouldn't move. One of the shiny beasts chirped and flashed nearby, and Riley startled in his skin.

Robin stopped and with a single bare hand, she peeled back the outer flesh of a beast, and it didn't protest. What sorcery was this?

"Sit right here. It won't hurt you."

She turned her head, and Riley still hadn't found his legs.

"Riley? It's okay. You have nothing to worry about." Robin returned to his side. With her hands gripping his arms, she pulled him toward the open flap of the beast.

He resisted, unable to coordinate his muscles, but somehow his legs moved, and Robin stopped him at the opening of the beast.

At one point, he'd stared down a Royal Navy man-o'-war opening its gunports on the verge of unleashing a full broadside without mercy. That had fueled Riley to spring into action. Another time, he'd stared down the barrel of a rifle during a standoff on shore. He'd hated to open fire on a fellow sailor, but the man left him no choice, and still, his hands and feet had reacted with expert timing. When the famed *Sea Lion* wrecked, Riley had gripped the mainmast. Because he'd never learned to swim, he watched in horror as he sank toward the abyss, but when the hull rested on the soft sand beneath and he remained above water, Riley leaped toward shore, knowing his own uncoordinated efforts were the difference between living and dying. Somehow, he'd made it to dry land, coughing and gasping, but he'd done it.

Riley stared at the shiny beast before him. Its flesh or wing hung open, daring him to climb inside, but he only stared. "You want me to what?"

"Sit on that seat." She pointed to a velvety shape, suspiciously shaped like a throne. "I'll close the door. It won't hurt you. I promise."

With shaky limbs, Riley folded, and Robin helped him lift his long legs inside the beast. His knees pressed against its firm insides, making his own stomach swirl with nausea. Robin shifted the seat, startling him, but leaving him more leg room.

"Watch your fingers. Here comes the door."

Riley gripped his thighs.

Robin closed the beast's wing and rushed around it, as if concerned for Riley's well-being. Riley only stared wide-eyed at all the gauges and buttons. Slipping into the seat abreast, she leaned over him, and Riley caught a whiff of her scent. Not of flowers or the salty sea, but a feminine fragrance of her own sweat. Quite pleasing.

A pleasant distraction.

Riley returned his eyes to the insides of the beast, and Robin's scent wasn't distracting enough. Finding a measure of comfort in her presence, his eyes followed her movements. "What are you doing?"

"Buckling in." Her arm brushed his chest, and Riley sucked in a breath. Heat rushed through his body and pooled in his lap. His palms squeezed his thighs harder.

A click startled him.

Robin sighed. "I'm going to move us now. If it's too much to bear, you can close your eyes. I won't judge."

She called him a coward. What nonsense! But since Riley's jaw clamped shut with tension, he couldn't dispute it.

Robin sent him a gentle smile, and her wrist twisted. The beast underneath roared with anger. Riley startled again and gasped. This was a mistake. He needed to get away from these monsters. He wasn't prepared to handle them. What weapons would work against such strong flesh? Not a cutlass, nor a dagger. He didn't believe a pistol capable either. A powder flask might do the job, of which he had none. His knuckles turned white, wishing for something to defend himself against these foreign creatures.

Robin pulled a lever, and the beast moved. "I know there's nothing I can say that will make this easier, but hang in there. You can do this."

Riley panted with his rapid heart rate.

"I should take you to the city campground to shower and then drop you off at the mental health crisis center. Not only would I not feel guilty about leaving you in the state you're in, but I would've fulfilled my sworn duty as an officer."

Robin didn't continue her statement, so Riley said, "I believe you had more to say."

A shy, feminine smile lifted her lovely lips. "I'm taking you to my place, where you can get real soap, hot water, and clean clothes. But I'm warning you, I know self-defense in case you've forgotten, and I'm good with weapons. If you try anything..." she trailed off, glancing at the shifted fabric in his lap.

Heat tore up his cheeks as he squeezed his thighs tighter. A forward woman. How novel. How distracting.

The beast left the area of the sleeping nest, and at once, many moved in a coordinated line. Riley sucked in a breath and released his painful grip on his thighs. Instead, he squeezed protrusions inside the beast. The cause of his discomfort would experience its own discomfort. Served it right. He didn't know what survival meant here, and every moment more of this world terrified him further.

At least it would end soon.

Chapter 7

Robin had dealt with mental illness cases before, but never anything like this. A mental patient with a foreign accent from the other side of the world on a spiked alcohol bender with a debilitating car phobia. Who also claimed to be a pirate captain from the year seventeen fifteen. None of this made sense. Public transportation was available, but Riley couldn't even handle *seeing* a car. The sooner she reached her Glock and spare mags and removed these hideous clothes, she'd feel safe and functional.

A quick clean up should help Riley sober. Once she got real answers, she could get him real help. Since no missing person report had been filed yet, perhaps a private nurse was about to clock in for her shift to find him gone. Or maybe the mental health facility hadn't done a head count on their padded rooms. Someone had to be looking for him.

Robin turned the wheel, guiding her car into her complex's parking lot while keeping the corner of her eye on this captain fellow with a wild imagination. She stopped the car in her assigned space, but Riley didn't move. Robin exited the vehicle, circled around, and opened the door for him. He still didn't move.

Riley's hands squeezed the arm rests, like a man terrified of flying who heard the notice for take-off.

"It's safe to come out now." She held out her hand.

Still nothing. Riley faced forward, body rigid with fear.

Robin leaned inside and unbuckled him. "Lift out your legs. It's okay. You can trust me."

He looked at her hand, and one leg at a time, he slowly climbed out of the car without taking it. She shut the door behind him, and he startled.

Robin shook her head and walked toward her brick two-story apartment building. Up the single step, she typed in the security code to the foyer. It beeped and flashed green, and Robin opened the door. There was no shadow of a man behind her. She turned.

Riley had moved away from the car, but he stared at the building. Now he was afraid of apartment complexes too? She didn't live in a dangerous area or anything. Letting the door close and relock, Robin scooped up Riley by the arm and dragged him to the door. He resisted, but only a little.

"This is your home?" he asked, perplexed.

Trying not to take offense to his confusion, her tone was clipped. "Second floor. Right this way." Robin pulled him through the main door, past the bank of mailboxes and the coin-op laundry machines, and up the stairs. At the rate he functioned, getting him cleaned and questioned would take all day.

Robin didn't have all day. She had applications to fill out so she could escape the hell that had become her job. Using a standard key, she unlocked her door and opened it. "This is me."

Robin walked in, never happier to be home, and she tossed her purse on the round kitchen table. She didn't hear the door close. Turning around, Robin found Riley standing at the threshold. "You're letting the air conditioning out."

Riley stared at her.

"You're not a vampire, are you?" she asked as a joke. "You can come in."

His eyes moved around her living room as if seeing a comfortable home for the first time. What kind of padded room did he stay in? The more time she spent with him, the more her pity grew and the less she wanted to return him to whatever those poor conditions must be.

With a patient sigh, Robin returned to the doorway and dragged the man inside and closed the door. "I have some menswear in my closet. Give me a minute to find it. It's been forever since anyone else's been in here."

Blenny had been right about that detail. She rarely brought men home, and never from her workplace. Along those same lines, she never had many visitors either. Well, none actually.

As Robin entered her bedroom, she averted her eyes from her mom's memorial on her end table. Heading straight to her small walk-in closet, she shuffled through stacks of folded clothes. Buried at the bottom was a pair of sweatpants and a plain T-shirt. She assessed the size and figured they'd fit well enough to get his outfit washed. She set the stack on her bedspread and returned to grab pants for herself. She peeked at Riley, who stood observing her home as before, and she closed the closet door. Robin changed her clothes, slipping into a comfortable T-shirt and tight jeans, excited to be free of the scratchy polyester. From the gun rack in her closet, she collected her Glock, checked the safety, and stuffed it into the back of her waistband until she was sure. Robin exhaled with a smile. Now she felt better.

Robin returned to the living room and dropped the folded stack onto the coffee table near Riley. She tracked his eyes to her beige carpet, empty white walls, and plain white appliances. It wasn't *that* interesting.

"It's so clean and spacious," he said in awe.

The evening sun made her apartment glow, casting long shadows across her floors, and her eyes strained. Robin flipped a light switch, and Riley looked up, lips parting slightly.

"Light in an instant? That's marvelous! What candles are these?"

Robin's turn to stare. Was he serious? Deadpan, she answered, "Bulbs. Not candles. Listen, the bathroom is right there. I have disposable razors in the top drawer and clean towels in the one below. Take a shower and clean up. I'll get your costume washed."

Riley looked down at himself. "I'm not wearing a costume."

Robin closed her eyes for a moment and gestured to him. "Your outfit. It needs washing."

Riley frowned. "A sprinkle of ale doesn't spoil my clothing."

Alcohol, nailed it. Robin chuckled. "I assure you; it needs to be washed."

Riley pressed his lips together and discreetly sniffed himself. With a nod, he went to the bathroom without the clean clothes. What was he planning on wearing instead? With a frown, Robin pulled out a jug of coffee grounds from an upper cabinet.

"Pardon me, ma'am," Riley said, leaning out of the bathroom. "Where do I find the water? The basin is fixed to its location."

Robin laughed. He was a master at keeping up this bizarre charade. Of all the things she could believe about this Captain Noah Riley, never having seen running water was not one of them. Robin pulled out two mugs and humored him. "Turn the knob, and I already told you to call me Robin."

Water gushed in the bathroom, and Riley laughed with the giddy joy of a child.

Robin shook her head with an infectious smile as she made them fresh coffee. His clothing landed on the floor with a heavy thump, and he closed the bathroom door. Robin retrieved his things.

He believed—what had he said?—the year was 1715. Well, he'd studied the period well. Robin lifted what amounted to rags to her. The stitching on his vest was something only Emily would admire. The breeches were tie-closed. No elastic. She was convinced every detail, down to his authentic cutlass, was meticulously period accurate.

Robin needed to introduce those two.

The bathroom door cracked open. "My apologies for my crude disposal of my clothes, but you insisted on their needing washing."

"Don't worry about it," Robin said from the living room.

If he were institutionalized his entire life, was it believable he'd never heard of cheese curds? Sure. But what institution would allow him an authentic sword? Riley must not be an escaped mental patient. So then what? His innocent interest in electricity and pure joy from running water seemed a little too authentic. Robin hadn't traveled to England ever, but were there villages without running water or cars, like an Amish society across the pond? She really had no idea. It was plausible, and more likely.

But then how did he get on a plane and not remember? Or get to the airport with a fear of cars?

Robin unsheathed part of his sword. It was dinged and scratched with use. Unbelievably real. Riley didn't need this here, as she didn't need her gun. Robin settled his things, removed her gun, and placed it into her purse. Just in case, she collected a few more mags from her gun closet and paused as a sweet melody came from the bathroom. The man sang beautifully. She smiled, hugging her mags.

What if he was from the past?

A glance at her mom's memorial had her sitting on the bedspread. "It's ridiculous, isn't it?" she asked her mom, but the photograph never responded. Sometimes she heard her mom's voice in her head, but as the years had gone by, her voice faded, almost like a punishment for failing to protect her. Robin missed her dearly. Her murder incessantly grated at her like a woodpecker's beak against a tree. Resolved. Determined. Unrelenting. Robin didn't know how to make it up to her, so she talked to her as if it never happened. "It almost makes sense. Do you think he's the captain of a pirate ship from 1715?"

Her mom's flowing waves and bright youthful smile never moved. She was laughing in this photo, taken by Robin's grandmother ten years before her mom's murder. Robin smiled back, wishing beyond everything she could've prevented that tragedy.

"I know, it is ridiculous. But what if the government discovered a method of time travel, and they kept it a secret? Considering they only admitted to having alien contact seventy years after the fact, it's plausible, isn't it?"

After giving her mom a chance to answer, which never came, Robin set the photo down with a sigh and returned to Riley's clothing. She sorted the washable from the non-washable. The leather looked hand-tanned and rough cut. Then dyed black, but the color wasn't perfectly even. This wasn't bought in a store.

The notes from his song, which she didn't recognize, lifted to a crescendo, and the water stopped.

What would it be like to travel through time? Scary, for one, especially going to the future. But going to the past and seeing what the history books described—probably a little fun. Maybe a lot fun if one could return home.

Like a vacation, of sorts. A temporary escape.

The door to the bathroom opened, billowing steam into her apartment, and breaking her wild thoughts.

"Pardon me, Miss Robin, but I seem to have forgotten the clothing you offered." Riley stepped out of the bathroom, holding a white fluffy towel around his waist. Loose wet hair and a pendant clung to his sculpted broad chest. Rounded muscles flickered with his small movements. Riley's clean-shaven face revealed bright teeth against sun-tanned skin, high cheekbones—she'd admired those before but were worth mentioning—and deep-set gray eyes. He smiled bashfully. He was simply gorgeous. Who knew something so beautiful could be hidden behind so many layers of grime and hair and...silly costume?

Robin exhaled. Twice.

Her face burned, and she collected the stack of clean clothing from the coffee table and brought it to him. Such a shame. She liked him better without clothes. Robin cleared her throat and cast her eyes aside, hiding her dopey smile behind her hand.

"Thank you, Miss Robin. What is that smell?"

"Coffee. That's, uh, coffee," Robin sputtered. Riley was incredibly attractive, and she needed to keep her head straight. He was in a vulnerable position, and that didn't give her free rein to lose herself. Speaking of reign, Robin needed to shake herself out of this unfamiliar and uncomfortable charge surging through her. "Who's the queen back home?"

"Queen?" Riley set the stack on the edge of the bathroom vanity, and yep, Robin still watched. His back muscles danced with his gentle movements. The vanity itself, after the man had shaved, was clean. Robin repeated her thought: *The man cleaned up after himself.* She was going to faint if she didn't sit.

Resting his hands against his hips, holding the towel in place, Riley said, "King George took up the throne last year, the Protestant bastard. But since I've renounced my loyalty to the Crown, they can have him."

He sounded so sure of his words. For the first time since she'd met him, he wasn't confused. Inferring from his statement, Robin asked, "You're Catholic?"

Riley made a dismissive noise. "Absolutely not, but the king isn't of royal blood. Strategic positioning rained good fortune upon him, handing him England, Ireland, and the Electorate of Hanover."

Curious about this strong opinion and incredible detail, she asked, "So you prefer only pureblood royals take the succession?"

"He manipulates people, winning himself vast wealth and the support of half a country. At the same time, everyone else is only trying to earn a living, and what do we get for it? Branded a traitor and threats of the noose. Then the newspapers deliver *eyewitness* accounts, who've never been on a ship in their lives, but the readers take their word as gospel. What makes *him* different from us? Why do the people accept his actions but not ours?"

He lost her again. "You're the captain of a pirate ship. Doesn't that mean you avoid all the politics? I don't follow your anger."

Riley glared at her for a second, as if unwinding the fury within. Whatever this issue was, he felt strongly over it. His features softened, and his eyes followed her snug clothing. Robin stared at his most pleasant shape, likely thinking the same thing he was. Having a naked man in her apartment was a bad idea.

Chapter 8

RILEY SHOULDN'T HAVE UNLOADED his restrained energy on her—it was very inappropriate, but so were her distracting clothes. The woman wore pants! The tight curves were scandalous and highly revealing, but he couldn't look away. Of all the unbelievable things he'd seen today, one thing was certain: Robin Hall was a stunning woman. And any woman who could pin him on the ground so effortlessly and disarm him, was fascinating...and distracting. He needed to change this dangerous course.

"When I was in the washroom, I heard you speaking to someone. Did I miss them?" Riley craned his neck around, seeking the hidden visitor. Dressed in only a damp towel, he was in no condition to meet anyone, but he needed an excuse to break this unspoken lust surging through him.

Robin blinked. "I was talking to myself."

Riley's brows lifted.

"Um, well, my mom," she corrected.

"Might I meet her?" Riley had some questions of his own, like how a woman became an officer and learned to overpower him. And how did she command the shiny beast? Such feats were beyond his comprehension. Her mom must be an amazing woman as well.

Robin's spirits visibly fell. He'd hurt her, but he didn't know why. She shook her head and disappeared into her bedroom. Holding the towel at his waist, he followed her, unwilling to allow his blunder to be brushed aside. She dropped onto the bouncy bed and lifted a frame from an end table. After a wistful smile crossed her lips, she turned its face for him to see.

Riley sat next to her. With the towel secured under and around him, he accepted the frame, but his brows knitted in horror. This was no painting. He tipped the frame around. "Is your mother trapped in this? How did she get in here?" The colorful image of the smiling woman baffled him. What was this witchcraft?

Robin took the frame from his frantic hands, and her brow furrowed. "It's a photo. She's not..." Robin scrutinized him with a keen eye.

Riley only watched. He was truly horrified by this tiny woman.

Robin pressed her palm to her forehead as if fending off a headache. "Your sincerity is admirable. I'm so confused."

As was he. "How do you talk to her in there?"

Robin rubbed her thumb on the corner of the frame. "When I was a teenager, my mom was busy in the kitchen while I completed my homework in the living room. As a man in a ski mask rushed through the front door, my mom came around yelling at me, because she thought I was letting in a friend. She wasn't angry; her hearing had declined severely, so we yelled back and forth. My mom wanted to make them tea." Robin chuckled softly and sniffled.

Riley's hand rested on her thigh. Robin stared at it, but he didn't remove it.

Allowing his touch, she continued, "When I yelled back that it wasn't a friend, my mom saw him and stopped short. She told me to get the gun. Since it was the two of us, we keep—kept—a handgun in the house at all times for situations like this. Never used it before, but I ran, grabbed the thing, and aimed from around the corner of the kitchen. And when she repeated her urgent cry, I had the burglar in my sights, but I couldn't do it. I couldn't pull that trigger. What if I hit him, and it only made him angrier? What if I missed? What if...? The burglar grumbled about the yelling, and he shot her."

Riley only understood the important parts. "I'm so sorry."

Robin gripped the frame in her hands and anger curved her lips. "It's my fault she's dead. Only because he didn't see me, I was spared. He tossed the living room and the bathroom and took off with some pills and cash. I hid until he left and called for an ambulance. I held my mom's hands, and I selfishly begged her to stay with me. I apologized for not stopping the burglar. I told her it was all my fault, but only a bead of blood dribbled from her mouth. The wet sounds coming from her..." Emotion clogged her throat, and she swallowed thickly, as if trying to hide the painful memories. Robin inhaled deeply and blinked away tears. "When she'd bought the gun, we both promised to keep each other safe with it, but I failed. I failed her, and now she's dead."

Riley continued to hold her thigh. If she needed more reassurance, he'd give it, but he didn't want to force anything she wasn't comfortable with.

"I became a police officer because I wanted to stop men like him. I wanted to protect the innocent. But I couldn't even do that."

"Your mother's death wasn't your fault. It was the burglar's," Riley reasoned.

"You weren't there." Robin closed down and returned the frame to the table.

Riley rubbed her thigh and sent her a crooked smile. "You protected me from those shiny beasts, which I'm surprised you did, considering I was the instigator trampling on their territory."

A wet chuckle greeted his light comment. "Shiny beasts," she repeated quietly. "They're cars. Why don't you call them cars?"

Another reminder that Riley didn't belong here. Wearing nothing but a towel draped over his lap, and Robin being caught in a vulnerable moment was a dangerous combination. He'd made many mistakes in his past, and he wasn't going to add another to his long list—not right before judgment by the authorities. "If you'll pardon me, I shall dress now."

As he rose, her yearning eyes trailed along his damp chest and stopped at the amulet he'd picked up on the beach. Her interested face tilted as she scrutinized it.

She sniffled, clearing away her story, and rose. "That looks familiar. Where did you get it?" Without her boots, Robin stood a few inches shorter than his five-ten height, and she dragged a finger along the chain hanging from his neck. Heat followed her touch like a burning torch. Riley closed his eyes to fight off the desire pumping through his body and shifting the towel.

Where did he get it? Focus. He needed to focus on the piece of jewelry, not her soft fingers dancing along his skin.

Focus! Necklace. Sand. Sweltering heat and blistering sun. Images of what happened before he arrived in this confusing place returned to his mind like moving pictures. His heart rate sped up, and his breathing quickened. Eyes pulling wide, Riley exclaimed, "Vallo!"

He grasped the amulet with both hands, dropping the towel.

Robin sucked in a breath and turned around, shielding her eyes. "I'm sorry! I didn't know *Vallo* meant you were going to get naked. Next time warn me with something more obvious."

Riley picked up the towel haphazardly, holding in front of himself one-handed. "I must return to my crew before Vallo destroys them."

"Whoa, slow down." Robin pinched the bridge of her nose and caught a glance at him to be sure he was covered. He liked that his appearance flustered her, but now was the worst time. "If—and I mean a big 'if' here, because I'm not crazy, but *if* you are from the past, how did you get here?"

After commandeering the English schooner, renamed the *Angelfish*, he'd had a conversation with his previous captain, Henry Price, who'd explained the unbelievable tale. Riley lifted the amulet over his head and held it out on his open palm, displaying the gem under the blindingly bright unexplainable indoor lights. "With this. I found it on the beach."

"I think I've seen that before." Robin tilted her face at it, studying its color.

"I thought it familiar as well, which is why I picked it up."

"How does it work?" Robin touched the gem, tilting it, and it reflected off the overhead lights. "You know, assuming this is real."

Riley exhaled. He hadn't thought about it before but remembering his experiences with women appearing on the crew and staying in the past, a sinking sensation in his gut pulled his excitement down. On a deep sigh, Riley said, "I know not, but from what I've seen, the necklace only works one way."

His crew was blind to the danger before them. Without Riley, they had to discover Vallo's past before the traitor got them all killed. And if they survived and intended to take Fort James on their own, they had to elect a new captain to lead them. Everything he knew was over.

Everything he was—his name, his accomplishments, his trustworthy friends—it was all over, caught in a land of shiny beasts and automatic lights. Facing this fascinating woman before him, six-and-twenty years was too short, but Riley didn't get to choose that. With an air of defeat, Riley said, "I think it's best if you deliver me to the authorities."

Robin squinted at him before her face relaxed. She stared at his magic necklace. "Oh, the police station? I... I don't know if they can help you."

Defeated once again, Riley dropped the necklace onto his hat and collected his personal effects. His sword slipped a few inches free of its sheath.

"Can I see it?" Robin asked with a spark of interest in her eye. "It seemed so authentic. I'm not a swordsmith myself, but I was impressed."

The sword was useless against the beasts of this world. Head hung low, he handed over his cutlass.

"It looks so real," she said, sliding a finger along the imperfect edge.

Sharpness permeated his tone. "Of course it's real. What else would it be?"

"A prop." Robin gave him a curious look and said, "Did you get it from the vendor at the festival? But it looks heavily used. Do you train with it?"

Riley tilted his chin up. "I keep my sword in serviceable condition, as required by the articles. It's both capable of severing a line on deck or slaying an enemy." At least, an enemy made of flesh.

"Okay, okay. I didn't mean to offend you. Look, you being here might feel strange and scary, but I'm as confused as you are. I know people really get into the reenactment stuff, but the only pirate swords I've seen before today were plastic."

"You said there were no pirates." In that case, he needed to keep his sword. He could only imagine how much more ruthless these pirates were. Riley held out his hands to take it back from her.

"Pretend. Costume. Halloween, you know? My outfit was pretend, too."

Riley's lips parted, and he took his sword back with a frown and hastily shoved it back into his bandolier. "You people *pretend* to be pirates? What insanity is this?"

Robin's hand rested on his forearm. "It's not insane to pretend. It is insane to believe."

"Pardon me, ma'am," Riley said coldly and returned to the washroom. He closed the door and stared at his unfamiliar face in the mirror. He had lost himself in more ways than he imagined.

"I'm going to wash your clothes. I'll be right back," Robin called through the door, and Riley stared at it, unwilling to answer her.

A different door closed, leaving him in silence.

With nothing better to do, Riley dressed in the outfit stacked on the vanity. Comfortable, stretchy, but a little snug in places. He raked a hand through his damp hair and pulled it back. Finding his ribbon on the floor, he tied his hair at the nape of his neck. He smelled like a bowl of fruit, but he looked clean for the first time in ages. That was one thing he could get used to.

Being treated like an imbecile was not.

Left alone with a deep curiosity, Riley browsed her living quarters. The strange 'photo' of Robin with her mom showed them both warm and radiating love—something missing in Robin now. A persistent sadness settled beneath the surface—easy to see when he knew it well.

Next to the photo was a small ceramic pot with a floral design painted with expert precision—a level Riley hadn't seen before. He lifted the lid and frowned. Ashes? Why would Robin keep ashes? He replaced the lid and lifted a locket next to it. His thick fingers fumbled with the clasp, but he opened it. Robin as a child and the same smiling mom.

No father.

No siblings.

There were no other photos in the room.

Was she as lonely as he?

Chapter 9

ROBIN PUSHED RILEY'S CLOTHES into the wash machine downstairs. She dropped in the coins and switched the knob over to the shortest delicate cycle. She'd hate to destroy his costume. The way he dressed meant he cared for it deeply, reminding her of Emily's enthusiasm for pirate history.

Everything he told her seemed like the ramblings of a delusional man, like he believed he was a real pirate. She wasn't enough of a historian to know if the facts checked out about King George, but considering his level of detail and passionate opinions, he'd likely memorized every historical text to back up his stories. Another clear sign of mental illness.

Or at least an unhealthy level of obsession, and Emily still functioned. And now this mentally ill patient was currently alone in her apartment. What made her trust him when she wouldn't allow her own colleagues inside?

When Riley had stepped out of the bathroom, dripping wet with a towel around his waist, showing off sculpted angles and sexy hair reaching a little beyond his collarbones, Robin hadn't wanted anyone more than him. And when the towel dropped, she had to hold herself back from his semi-erect state. She hadn't been that attracted to someone ever.

But he seemed mentally ill. Except his belongings wouldn't be allowed inside a facility. If someone stored his things for him, Riley would've gone back to that person. His sculpted physique wasn't possible while confined to a padded room. His passionate ramblings were coherent and reasonable—things she never saw in drug cases or mental patients. He absolutely didn't know what a car was, and his accent was as authentic as she could tell...as was his sword.

All signs pointed to him telling the truth.

But it wasn't possible.

So, Robin circled back around. She needed a straight answer out of him, so she could get him back where he belonged.

It was getting late, and Riley couldn't stay the night—not with him being so tempting. And she needed to check in with her friends. Robin was going owe Emily and Angela a girls' night out for bailing on them. Robin lifted her phone and checked the screen. Still no messages.

Weird.

When short gentle cycle finished, she lifted the outfit. The time spent handcrafting the clothing was impressive. He didn't use a machine. The stitches were uneven, handcrafted. Riley put love into crafting his outfit, so she wouldn't put it in the dryer. Plus, leather.

As depressing as reality could be, Riley, like her, had to face the real world.

RILEY KNEW WHAT LONELINESS felt like. He had his crew, many dedicated completely to him, but those sea dogs were no substitute for a family. With a fresh sadness weighing him down, Riley closed the locket and went to the kitchen to find a meal. He opened cabinets and found nothing familiar besides pots and pans. Even if he knew how to cook, he had no idea how to start a fire here.

Trusting that Robin wouldn't leave him alone with dangerous creatures, Riley pulled the handle on the large white thing. Cold air blasted him in the face. What a marvel! He recognized nothing inside, but he knew it was supposed to be food. Cooled food! Right inside the kitchen!

The front door opened, catching Riley in the act. He was giddy with his discovery. "I don't know what any of this is. How does it stay cold? It's amazing!"

He shut the wondrous creation, and Robin held his clothing hanging over her arm. "I didn't want to put leather in the dryer. It's still damp from the spin cycle, but it shouldn't take long to dry." She draped the clothing over the backrest of a chair. "Find anything good to eat?" That air of sadness still hung in her voice.

"Thank you kindly, ma'am."

"Robin," she said on a breath. "Just Robin. Look, it's getting late. I have a lot of work to do tomorrow that can't wait." She gestured to a sleek silver rectangle on the table, but Riley had no idea what that meant. "Can you tell me your name? Where you came from? As much fun as this has been, I need to return to real life. You should too."

What was this accusation? Anger furled in his stomach. "I've been truthful with you."

Robin sighed. "Well, if that's the position you insist on, you can't stay here. Get dressed in your own clothes, and I'll bring you to the station."

His anger melded into a rock, settling heavily on his chest. He'd known this end would come, but for the flicker of a few hours, he'd enjoyed himself for the first time in a long while. He hoped to explore the spark between him and Robin. Instead, he cast his gaze aside. "Understood."

"I need a shower. Feel free to use the living room here to change. I won't spy on you."

Riley turned his back on her and waited until she turned on the water in the bathroom. He dressed in his breeches, tunic, and leather vest. He strapped his bandolier belt around his waist and over his shoulder. He holstered the cutlass and stepped into his boots. Finally he shrugged into his coat. Although, the coat was a little warm, shore leave or not, but sometimes appearances caused discomfort. He pushed his cocked hat onto his head and the tinkle of metal remaining on the table turned his head. The amulet. Seeing as he had nothing left of value, maybe the authorities would think better of him decorated with an expensive gem. He set his hat down and collected the amulet.

Riley slipped the amulet back over his head.

Chapter 10

ROBIN HAD BROUGHT HER own clean clothes into the bathroom so Riley could change in private. She chose clean skinny jeans and a T-shirt to take Captain Noah Riley and his crazy story down to the station. Maybe when he saw how serious she was, he'd come clean with the truth, and she could simply change directions in the car. Robin squeezed her wet hair with a clean towel and opened the bathroom door. "Coming out. Let me know if you aren't ready."

He didn't respond.

Robin frowned and leaned around the door. "Riley?"

Still nothing. Where was he?

Robin crossed to her bedroom and peeked inside. Not there. She returned to the living room, nope, and swung around to the fridge. Her apartment wasn't that big. She moved to the patio and stepped outside, scanning the area for a man in a pirate costume on foot. In the dusk, she found no one matching his description.

"Riley!" she shouted. A resident in the parking lot looked at her like she was nuts. Her face heated, and Robin went back inside.

Where did he go so fast?

Robin turned around and found the borrowed clothing folded neatly. His costume was gone, but he'd left behind his frilly tricorne hat. Why would he leave it behind? Was he trying to tell her something? Did he remember where home was and left? Did he change his mind about going to the police station? So many questions and no answers.

Robin checked inside her purse, in case this ruse was an elaborate theft, but her Glock, spare mags, and wallet were intact. She stared at the hat of a man, so wild in his choices and passions, and a small smile lifted her lips. "You do whatever you want, whenever you want, and no one can force you to do anything you don't want to. I can admire that."

Her eyes returned to her patio doors, and the smile slid away. He had to be out there, now even more lost and confused. Scared. She'd promised herself she'd keep him safe, and the way he reacted to cars would mean he'd react dangerously to traffic. She could flick on the scanner and wait for the inevitable call about a man in a costume attacking cars with a sword.

If he didn't get hit first.

Robin grabbed her purse and jumped in her car. She closed the door behind her and stopped. "This is crazy. What am I doing? I'm going to go chasing after an ill man who ran away from me?" She gripped the steering wheel and gazed beyond the parking lot. But if she didn't go...

"I can't leave him all alone, lost in the throes of panic. I'll make a few passes around a couple blocks, up and down. He couldn't have gone far. I can do that, yeah. It's not crazy; it's my duty—the duty to safeguard lives and protect the innocent. Then at least I tried. Right? Tell me I'm not crazy."

There was nothing in her car capable of answering.

Robin groaned and started the engine. She turned on her headlights and pulled out of the parking lot. With the festival wrapping up for the evening on the other side of the city, traffic was light. She rolled down the roads as slow as she could get away with while searching for any and all pedestrians. More specifically, for a handsome face with a stunning body—miles of muscles, carved to perfection, slick with steam.

Robin couldn't have imagined a man's form more pleasing to the eye than Captain Noah Riley, whoever he was. Heat rushed up her face—both in the raging desire for him but also in shame. Riley was a vulnerable man, and she had no right to think of him that way.

But she could still be a respectable person who completed her job with dignity and ethics while still daydreaming about his perfectly sized, partially raised mast between his legs? Robin turned on the car's radio, needing a distraction.

At the corner of her next turn, a few people waited for the city bus, wearing jeans and T-shirts or shorts and hoodies. Still, she kept going while checking the clock on her dash. This was crazy, wasn't it? Driving around near-dark looking for a harmless innocent man who'd walked away from her, a man she didn't know, a man who, by all accounts, was mentally ill.

With a sigh, Robin turned around and went home. She changed into lightweight pajamas, and after a nice cup of hot cocoa, she distracted herself with television, but her eyes fell on Riley's tricorne hat every few minutes. And after darkness fell, she no longer glanced out her patio door. Instead, she turned down the volume on the television in case Riley shouted for her attention.

He didn't.

ROBIN BLINKED AS THE numbers on the alarm clock switched over. With a groan, she turned it off before it buzzed. How many cups of coffee would she need to get by with no sleep? Robin rolled out of bed and shuffled to the coffee pot, which was programmed to have a cup ready for her. Good ol' trusty coffee pot.

Robin poured a mug and turned around. He was real, wasn't he? She didn't dream she brought a complete stranger into her apartment, did she? Leaning against the counter, the tricorne hat stared at her.

Robin crossed to her patio and stepped out for fresh air. Crisp morning dew clung to her bare arms. Birds flew from maple tree to pine tree, singing and chirping. The sunrise bathed the landscape in pinks and purples, lighting the parking lot and front door of her complex. Maybe he came back and slept outside her door, uncertain how to buzz her apartment.

Riley was not there.

Robin sipped her coffee and went to her bedroom. On the end table, she rested her steaming mug next to Mom's smiling face. Riley had said her failure to pull the trigger wasn't her fault, and her mom's death wasn't her fault. "He was wrong; you know that."

Mom smiled.

She knew.

Robin dressed in the same T-shirt and skinny jeans from yesterday, because they weren't worn long enough to justify another round in the coin-op downstairs. Retrieving her mug, the gleaming laptop called to her. Robin sat at the table. Remembering Riley's bold assertions and strong passions—no matter how strange, Riley did what he wanted, when he wanted, and he wouldn't be forced to do anything he didn't want to—including taking off to avoid returning to his facility. He was free, and despite appearing lost, he was happy. Taking a page from his book, Robin refused to work with a bunch of men who'd created a hostile work environment. And right now, she wanted to end that chapter of her life.

With a smile on her face, Robin opened her laptop, chugged the rest of her cooled coffee, and typed up a resignation letter. After it printed, she signed it and smiled. This was her freedom. This was her saying no more, that she was in control of her life. To be honest with herself, two days ago she wouldn't have made this move. Likely, Robin would've typed it up, signed it, and tossed it. She had bills to pay, and no job lined up. It was irresponsible. It was rash. It was everything Robin wasn't. Instead, Robin grabbed her purse and keys, and Riley's fancy hat.

Pushing through the police department doors on a quiet Sunday morning, Robin's stomach twisted in knots. She could do this, no big deal. The corners of her eyes searched for judging eyeballs, but the office was thin. No one paid her attention. She strolled toward the officer in charge, hunched over a desk, and she stopped short. "Blenny? I thought you had the weekend off?"

The towering detective in a suit turned around and smiled. He leaned his bulk against the desk and folded his arms over his broad chest. "Riggs needed the day off, surprise family function. What can I do for you?"

"You can take this to the lieutenant when he comes in." Robin handed him her resignation letter folded in an unsealed envelope. "And these." She dug her badge and office-issue cell phone out of her purse and held them out to him.

Blenny's face was surprisingly disappointed as he collected the phone and badge from her hands. "You can't leave. You've only been here a couple months. Is it something I said? 'Cause you know I was joking, right?"

"Blenny. It wasn't what you said." *It was Riley*. Robin smiled. "Bye."

Robin turned on her heels and left while Blenny's mouth hung open, catching flies.

IN HER CAR, SHE checked her phone for messages from Emily or Angela, but she had none. That was worrisome. Maybe their phones fell overboard or somehow got damaged by water. Or they were too drunk and having too much fun to respond. That was more likely.

But to be safe, Robin pulled out of the department parking lot and crossed town to the festival. She motored up and down the rows and stopped at Angela's car. With her lips pressed thin, she pulled in alongside it. "Figures."

Taking Riley's hat with her, Robin got out of her car and cupped her hands around her eyes. She peered into Angela's driver side window. Empty.

Robin slung her purse over her shoulders, across body, and double checked her Glock and spare mags. She was no longer an active officer, but that wasn't going to stop her from coming to anyone's assistance. Robin walked to the festival grounds, scanning for familiar faces.

Who was she really looking for? Brushing that thought aside, Robin took in the sights. The tall ships slumbered dockside. The tents were erected but quiet. A few vendors were setting up for the day and the scent of cooking oil wafted over. A couple people were sleeping on picnic tables. Robin walked by each person, checking for her friends, but they weren't here.

Neither was Riley.

He'd left his hat as a message, she was sure of it, like he'd called to her to find him. But he would've come here. This was his home in a way, his comfort zone. Where was he?

Unless he gave up waiting.

Robin refused to believe that. She stroked the velvety trim.

Unless he remembered who he really was and went home.

No, he'd been far too adamant that he wasn't crazy. There was no way he'd voluntarily return to whatever home had suppressed him.

She kept moving, kept searching. Strolling by the vendor tables, a gravelly voice called to her, "If you're in need of something you can't quite explain, you returned to the right place."

It was the old woman, the seller of beautiful necklaces. Wait a minute. A delicious image came to mind: Wet Riley, naked, holding a towel precariously placed. A shiny amethyst pendant on a copper chain hung from his neck. Now she remembered why the necklace was familiar.

Robin stopped and smiled. "I *am* looking for something. You remember me, right? I was here yesterday, and you offered me a necklace for five dollars. Do you still have it?"

Or had Riley bought it?

The old woman's smile lifted her wrinkles. She bent at the waist and fished under the table while Robin scanned the people filtering in for the day. The old woman straightened, and her slender arm held the gem out to her. It glistened in the morning light, simply stunning. "It's yours."

Robin dug in her purse, unzipped her wallet, and flash a Lincoln.

The woman held out a palm to reject Robin's payment. "Don't worry about it. What am I going to do with it?"

Robin frowned. What kind of person didn't want money?

The old woman's thin arm bounced, insisting Robin take the necklace free of charge.

Robin checked the ground beside the woman's feet for a cash box. Why would she offer Robin a free necklace? There was no way the woman could've known Robin quit her job this morning. "I can't take it for nothing. Please, I insist." Robin held out the bill while accepting the necklace.

The stubborn and confusing woman wouldn't take it. Holding her hands clasped loosely in front of her, she nodded and smiled. "Good luck and safe journey."

Robin didn't know what to think. Such a strange thing to say, like a salute to someone leaving on a momentous occasion. Was Robin quitting her job that obvious on her face? With creepy suspicion, Robin set the bill on the woman's table anyway and nodded her thanks.

Walking away, Robin marveled at the gem, glinting off the morning's warm sun. It was the same one Riley wore, but he said he found his on a beach back home. He must've been delusional. She had no other explanation, but either way, Robin needed to get him out of her head. Just because she promised to keep him safe, didn't bind her to it forever. As much as the gesture held meaning, adults broke promises. Riley had left on his own accord, and she didn't own him.

Robin walked back to the parking lot, ready to fill out some job applications, because that was what responsible adults did after quitting on a whim. She frowned at Riley's hat. He would've wanted it back.

Robin placed her reminder of Riley over her head.

Chapter 11

In the blink of an eye, Noah Riley stood on the beach in Nassau, right were the last remembered being, sitting on a homemade chair, propped against a makeshift hut. Still in the shade, same sails dotting the horizon. He'd merely fallen asleep, but never before had he experienced a dream so real, but if he were to ask for one, a vision of the future with a beautiful woman was more than he deserved to experience. Dusting himself off, Riley reached up to adjust his hat.

It was gone.

Riley spun in place as if the wind had pulled it from his head, but he found nothing. He checked for nearby footprints from the thief, but the wind had already obscured them. Such a shame. He liked that hat.

How much time had he lost? Did Vallo sneak onto his *Angelfish* while he'd napped like a child? Riley crossed the soft sand and returned to The Golden Macaw. After allowing his eyes to adjust, he searched the room. Only a few patrons milled about quietly. His crew was gone. Many of the crew knew of his favorite resting location. Why didn't they rouse him before leaving?

Riley approached the owner who'd taken over behind the bar. She promptly turned and smiled broadly for him. Her voluptuous stature commanded attention, and her curls piled high were of the most distinguished taste. Everyone respected Marta, and since she had sharp ears when her bar was filled with loose lips, they also listened to her.

"Aye, my Riley. Where've you been?" She grinned while cleaning out a mug.

"I'm looking for my crew. Have you seen them?" Riley leaned against the bar and smiled to charm the information out of her.

Looking at her mug, she tilted her head. "I've been hearin' 'em. You lost two captains to women, the word says. Sounds like your crew is cursed, and you're next." She pointed at him with a rag.

Riley thought of his dream, but that was impossible. He knew where his end would be, and nothing could change that. "I don't believe in such things."

Marta set down the mug and tossed the rag on the bar. Her hand rested on her hip. "People pour through my doors like sand and glide out like the tide. I'm here to keep the mugs full, and they go about their business, renderin' me invisible. But I see you." She gestured for him to take a seat and then returned that hand to her hip.

No one defied the orders from the lady of the house. Riley sat on a stool across from her.

"For years you've been comin' here on shore leave," she continued. "When the haul's good, you've got an empty smile on your lips, but when its bad, the smile is the same. You're not after the prize."

He couldn't argue with that, but he was curious where she was going with this. "What's it matter?"

"If your heart's not in it, get out before the men learn your interests don't align. Some of them already been whispering."

Vallo intended to raise a ruckus on board, but Riley tensed at her usage of the plural. "Oh?"

"You don't want to be on that ship anymore, so quit. Stay here. Find yourself a woman and live the life you've been wantin'. Not such a bad way to go, endin' things like that. A woman on the arm is better than a noose around the neck."

Frustrated with the useless information, Riley said, "I'll take your advice into account, but I doubt its value."

"Well, I hate to see a good man flounder."

"Marta, where's my crew?" Riley's tone was sharper than he intended, and he stood, not wanting to waste more time.

The plump woman dipped her chin and raised her brow. "From the chatter I heard, they was headed to the ship. Mighty excited, they were."

Riley slapped the bar's surface. Finally, something he could use. "Thanks, ma'am."

She nodded with a grim set to her mouth.

Riley set off through town to the docks, sand slowing his every frustrated step. How could Marta suggest he walk away from the captaincy and stay here, a dull life on a despicable island of sand and sweat? That was worse than what he already had. Besides, what kind of woman would accept a pirate like him?

The only woman who piqued his interest and didn't despise him was merely a dream, an illusion. Miss Robin Hall. Riley didn't believe in curses, and he didn't need to yearn for something impossible. Allowing his hopes to soar only ended in a pain he refused to repeat.

Riley already had his plan, and his crew was in danger. All her warnings and useless advice were nothing but distractions.

At the dock, various men loaded and unloaded boats for the market, many of which participated willingly in the island's illicit trade, including Riley when the occasion called for it. Shielding his eyes from the harsh sun glaring off the water's surface, Riley identified ship after ship by the markings on the sails or the names scrawled on the hulls. None were enemies—that he was aware of—-and none were his. Still, he kept searching, squinting against the light. One single-masted sloop, a fishing vessel, sailed forward. The *Angelfish* anchored slightly beyond, bringing Riley's lips into a grin. He wasn't too late. Rushing down the dock, Riley found Cantu climbing aboard a longboat and two rowers with him.

"Good of you to continue working," Riley said to their backs. "Are we refitted and ready to cast off?"

Cantu turned and smiled. "Captain! We thought we lost you to the brothel. No one could find you!"

"How is the account coming along?"

"Ship's restocked for the voyage across the Atlantic. We recruited two dozen men willing to sail with us."

A total of four dozen. Probably not enough, but more than he'd expected. "Excellent."

"Come along, captain. This is the last boat over." Cantu gestured for him to join them.

With one last look at Nassau, Riley climbed in. Would he see this town again? Would he visit the bar and brothel again? How many of his crew would survive this perilous course? He'd do whatever it took to make his crew richer than they'd ever dreamed. Starting with keeping his crew in good spirits despite the odds stacked against them. Riley didn't need encouragement. He knew where his end would be found. Picturing his future-brother-in-law and his betrothed, Riley smiled.

Soon.

The row over to the *Angelfish* was efficient. As an English schooner, her draft was shallow, at a mere five feet. She could anchor much closer to shore than most ships of her size, an advantage during escapes, and although she was outfitted stronger than the *Sea Lion*, she wasn't a formidable opponent at sea. With their account chosen as a fort on an island in the middle of a broad river, that disadvantage was not a concern.

On the main deck of his ship, Riley breathed in deeply, relishing the familiar salty sea air, the humid breeze, and flapping of the sails unfurling. He was home, and after his wild dream against the shady hut, he was happier than he'd been in a while. Too bad it was only an illusion, but one which would carry his spirits until he no longer needed them.

Quartermaster John Randall approached with a status update. He read from his notes, "Fully stocked with chickens and salted pork. Giles is confident we have plenty of provisions to make the round-trip journey. Buckley and Watts say our lumber and fasteners are appropriate to manage repairs. McKee and Gunner inspected the guns. Ten serviceable guns with room for more." He chuckled at his own implication. "We currently have enough men to work the guns and satisfactory shot to concern any challenger. Price secured enough pistols and swords for every man on board. Boatswain Karl Dillon says the rigging is fit, and repair supplies and replacements are secured below deck in storage. Hodgens is ready for your coordinates, captain."

Riley was ready to get out of port. He smiled at Randall's optimism. *Any* challenger was an untruthful boast, but their odds of encountering a man-o'-war was slim. "Excellent work, Randall. Send word for William Price to meet me in the navigation room."

"At once, captain." Randall was an excellent quartermaster, as he'd claimed. Strong, sturdy, and thorough. But as Randall was not known long, and remembering Marta's warning, Riley chose his words with care and kept his distance.

Riley pushed through the navigation room door, where Hodgens made repairs to his own cocked hat. Riley glanced at it wistfully. He should've detoured for a replacement.

"Captain, a pleasure to see you've returned to us." Hodgens placed his hat on his head and stood. "I'm not sure what would've come over the hungry crew if you'd been left behind. Now that you're here, we need not concern ourselves with that. Give me your coordinates, and I shall get us underway."

Riley found the paper of calculations in his pocket, and it was damaged but legible, almost like the ink had gotten wet. Strange. Until he remembered ale rained on him in celebration in the bar. Riley gave it to the man.

"Most excellent, sir." The helmsman left with a nod as William Price entered.

"You called for me, captain?"

"Close the door."

William did and approached with an unusual seriousness to his features. Unlike his younger brother, the lanky Price was quite jovial, considering his imprisonment on *Peibo del ler San Francisco* for months.

"Have you heard from Vallo?" Riley asked.

The armorer scratched at his jaw in contemplation. "Below deck, sharpening the swords with little Peter Gunner. Well, I suppose after a trip to the brothel, he's not so little anymore." Price grinned with self-satisfaction.

Riley could only focus on the enemy lurking on board under their noses. He backed up a step and scowled. "And you allowed it?"

Price dropped his levity, as if offended. "I was younger than him when I had my first—"

"Not that," Riley interrupted. "Vallo. Why is he here?"

"I wasn't aware we had issue with the man."

Riley's anger grew. The one thing Henry Price had warned him about happened, and no one else seemed concerned in the slightest. "Buckley, Cantu, and Hodgens were part of the raiding party in Cuba. They witnessed Vallo's traitorous move. They said nothing?"

"Not to me, so I had no reason to suspect him. The orders were to fill the ranks."

"I recall." Riley slid a hand down his face, clearing away an insufficient amount of sweat from his brow. "All essential roles for navigation are to proceed as planned. Everyone else is to meet on the main deck for a vote."

"Consider it done." Price nodded and stepped out.

Riley fisted the first piece of paper he found and squeezed. He didn't need extra complications with a plan already too precarious for most to attempt.

As the *Angelfish* unfurled her sails for the open sea, Riley turned in place, addressing the crew with his hands clasped behind his back. "Many of you are new, some of you are seasoned." Riley glared at Vallo as he made his pass. "But it has come to my attention that one among you is a traitor. Because our plan hinges entirely on trust, we cannot allow his continued presence."

The men turned their heads, mumbling to each other in confusion.

"Vallo! Step forward," Riley ordered.

The stocky man emerged from the crowd, while the crew glanced between Riley and Vallo with surprise. The traitor casually held a sword, and a look of innocence and confusion sprung across his face.

Riley knew better. "This man colluded with the prior captain to ensure the smooth operation and cooperation of this ship," he began.

"Actually, captain, that was the *Sea Lion* you're referring to," Buckley said. "We didn't have the *Angelfish* then."

Riley pinched the bridge of his nose. "Right."

"Then what's the problem?" Kerr asked, one of the new recruits. How a man accustomed to the sea could manage to keep such heft on him baffled Riley. The portly Giles was the exception. The cook spent his time preparing and tasting food, usually seated, a position most respected. But Kerr claimed to be a seasoned sailor. A decade ago, perhaps.

"The moment Captain Henry Price needed him most, Vallo, who'd been considered a trusted mate, turned his weapon on Price. He'd sold the crew's location to the enemy for a handsome reward, directly resulting in Spain's swift arrest of the crew, an action that never would've happened if Vallo's own hand hadn't betrayed us. And we lost many good men that day."

Gasps and murmurs bubbled from the crowd, but Vallo stood in front of them all casually, still holding the sword as if displaying he'd been innocently interrupted.

The game had begun.

"Do I get to defend myself, captain?" His tone was dark, a warning, and by all rights Riley should heave the man overboard, but that wouldn't win him the respect of the newest members.

Riley nodded.

Vallo addressed the crew, mirroring Riley's pacing and inflections, "It's true. The captain asked me to betray my own friends for him, and without hesitation, I agreed. And I'd do it all again, because the captain told me my actions were in the best interest of the crew as a whole. I stayed by the captain's side as his fullest supporter, until he went too far. Henry Price's own actions led directly to the crew's arrest. I stand before you now grateful for the chance to assure everyone on this ship I will do anything to benefit this crew. If the captain needs me to do his bidding, I will agree." Vallo shot Riley a dark look. "Because I have the courage to do anything, so long as we all get rich in the end."

Murmurs of agreement, shoulders lifting in dismissive shrugs, and nods worried Riley. Eyes shifted to him for a rebuttal. He addressed Vallo, "We can trust actions, not words, and as you have already proven your word means nothing, we will vote now. *Aye* for the traitor to stay. *Nay* for him to be cast overboard." The ship was still within range of shore. Provided the man could swim, this result was merely a minor inconvenience. "All those in favor of him staying?"

The *ayes* rang loudly.

"And against?"

Not nearly enough.

Vallo smirked.

With frustration boiling, Riley asked the crew, "Can I ask why you prefer to keep a traitor among you?"

"Captain," Cantu said, stepping forward. "Most of these men saw nothing of his betrayal, and more than half only met him. Vallo is a competent sailor, and you said yourself this mission requires as many hands as possible."

With a defeated sigh, Riley gestured. "Back to work. Bring us to the African coast. Hodgens, you have your coordinates."

The helmsman nodded, and the men cheered, setting about their duties. Riley retired to his cabin and sprawled on the firm mattress of his narrow bed, surprisingly tired after his nap under the palms. He hoped peaceful sleep would drag him back to Robin Hall and her wild world. He missed her, and although Riley's mind wasn't in its best place, he was not troubled by his sudden need for an illusion. Riley drifted off to sleep with more hope than he'd held in a long while.

Chapter 12

Robin blinked and rubbed her eyes as they adjusted to the darkness surrounding her. The only light source was a small round window in the wall—a wooden, creaking wall. A stink, reminding her of a call she'd responded to for a medical waste dumpster fire, involving junkies, used needles, and cigarettes, filled her nose and watered her eyes.

Robin coughed on the fumes, and a loud groan of wood startled her. The floor listed heavily, tossing her off balance like a drunk. Robin jutted out her hands for stability and noticed the tricorne hat in her hand. Her face twisted in confusion as she shuffled to the window.

Rolling blue waters with no land in sight. Robin rubbed her eyes again, blinked, and checked again. Nope, same waves for miles. She was on a boat.

Someone must've dragged her onto the tour ship, but how could she forget walking from the festival grass to this pungent pile of wood? She hadn't drunk anything that could've been spiked. Her fingers pressed against the back of her head. She wasn't hit either. It made no sense. Her feet itched to run back to land, but only seeing water ahead of her, the odds of making that work were slim.

Robin hated boats, but it wasn't because of seasickness.

Years had passed since Robin had last been on a boat, which had been a slow pontoon and nothing like this ancient behemoth. Robin wouldn't have gone on this ship voluntarily—regardless of Emily's pleading, so this had to be a nightmare. She'd slept terribly last night—or not at all, actually, so she'd dozed off after driving home from the festival this morning. The theory made sense.

After Riley had left, she'd tossed and turned, thinking about him. Worrying? Yeah, she worried. So much so, she drove around half the night looking for him, and after a nap, she'd hunted the festival grounds for him. Had she dozed off *while* driving? For all she knew, Robin was comatose in a hospital after a car crash, and this nightmare-inducing ship was a trip to the unexplored gray matter of her temporal lobe, helped along by IV drugs.

Robin's brain, with nothing better to do, was testing her, but she glanced at Riley's hat in her hand. Perhaps not a test, but a tease. A taste of what Riley had described to her. A flash of his life.

That was all crap.

Emily must've dragged her on here, and complete terror had her blacking out the boarding process. Did Robin have the strength to survive this pungent ride on Lake Michigan and make it back to the festival?

Only one way to find out.

Robin used her hands for balance as she shuffled her way out of the nauseating room packed with barrels. Through the doorway, she found an open space where hammocks hung from the low ceiling. They swayed with the ship's movement. Lined up against the exterior walls were long, black tubes of some sort. She couldn't make them out. A beam of light shined on a staircase in the center of the strange room. Fighting the floor rocking under her feet, Robin rushed to the ladder and gripped it with one hand while hugging Riley's hat with the other. She stopped.

She held Riley's hat. The crazy pirate captain who'd appeared at the festival and vanished from her apartment. The sexy man who'd said her mom's death wasn't her fault.

Riley was never real.

Robin's grief conjured him to attempt to bring her absolution in her mom's murder. And as she stood here now, holding the imaginary Riley's hat, standing at the foot of a ladder with light shining down, on a terrifying boat, Robin had only one answer.

In complete exhaustion, chasing an imaginary being, she had crashed her car. This nightmare scene was her subconscious pushing her toward the light.

To find relief.

To escape her grief.

To escape.

But climbing toward the light meant dying, as she understood it, and like any healthy person, she didn't want to die. Robin glanced around herself. If this was some sort of in-between the living and the afterlife, where was her messenger? Wasn't someone supposed to give her guidance on which way to go? If climbing the ladder meant dying, how did she return to her body?

How did she fight back?

Releasing the ladder, Robin turned around and searched the darkened space. She approached one of the black tubes and pushed on the square outlined on the wall in front of it. A series of ropes and pulleys shifted. The square moved. Light showed her the tube was a...cannon? Two tidy rows of cast iron cannons hugged the exterior walls.

A dreadful thought popped into her mind. She wasn't religious in the slightest, but was this purgatory? Had the ancient texts been right? Was she going to hell next? She hadn't lived long enough to justify dying this young. She'd learned the painful lesson that life wasn't fair, but knowing that truth was easier than accepting it. What had she done that was so terrible?

She'd failed to save her mom from a burglar and she'd died.

She'd failed to save Clark Thompson from a robber and he'd died.

Why couldn't she go back and make it right?

With nerves tensing her stomach, Robin peered through the square trap door. More waves of water greeted her. This was definitely not a tease of Riley before her final destination; this was definitely a test.

Robin turned around, facing the light shining down on the ladder. There was no way out, no guardian, no last words of comfort or advice. There was only up.

The ship bucked under the waves, and a spray of water hit her on the back. With a cringe, Robin stood and repositioned her purse over her shoulder and hugged the hat. At least she had her Glock—a small comfort. The only comfort...

No, that wasn't right. Someone would be up there to greet her. Robin smiled, and a warmth of relief flooded her chest. Tears stung her eyes, and she swallowed back the pressing emotion. Dying wasn't all bad.

Holding her arm out for balance, she crossed to the ladder and gripped it tight. Wood creaked overhead. Footsteps thundered.

"I'm coming, Mom."

Robin climbed the ladder into the light.

Robin Hall's eyes widened as men scurried all around her, pulling and tying lines, while others climbed skyward—a flurry of activity she couldn't begin to understand. Where...where was her mom? The smile vanished. The tears dried up. The ship listed, tugging Robin to the side of the opening, and she gripped the rim of the damp deck with her hat-free hand, but she slipped. A prick of her finger had her pull away. Robin inspected her injury. A splinter, tiny and insignificant, but real enough.

She bled.

This wasn't the afterlife she'd expected. The test wasn't over. She needed to prove to herself she could escape her mind's game and return to her body, which based on the setting given to her, meant getting off this ship and returning to the festival—a metaphor her brain conjured because of Riley's wild stories. Survive this game. Return home. Face the consequences of the irresponsible crash she'd caused by being severely sleep deprived. She hoped no one else was hurt because of her.

"Stowaway!" a man yelled behind her.

Robin followed the voice, and a hand with several missing fingers pointed at her. A scowling face on an emaciated body accompanied it. He seemed so real. Frankly, Robin was surprised at her mind's creativity.

"I'm not a stowaway." Robin played along, digging in the pockets of her skinny jeans and finding nothing. She unzipped her purse and fished around for a ticket. She didn't have one. "Maybe I am. I don't know. I'm sorry. Is that the right answer?"

"Look at her clothes, Landry." Another man, hefty around the middle with a stained outfit straight from a historical movie, said to the first. He looked like the type of man Robin would request backup for, a man who wouldn't play nice or listen to authority.

"Don't need to, Kerr," Landry with the missing fingers said. "Rules demand stowaways go overboard."

Overboard? Why did her subconscious feel the need to punish herself further? The possibility she hurt or killed someone in the crash returned. Robin swallowed that terrible thought and repeated her plan: Survive first, beg forgiveness after, and serve out whatever sentence was handed to her last.

"I didn't mean to, I swear. Please take me to land, and I'll pay you whatever I owe, plus interest."

Robin met the gazes of each man around her. No one said anything. One folded his arms across his chest. Several raked their eyes along her body. Rough men, indeed. Precisely the men she wouldn't envision if this were a dream, confirming this was a test. With a voice pleading for a deal, she added, "And a tip? A big tip?"

"Overboard!" Another man shouted from the back.

"Hold on there," a short, stocky man pushed forward. His dark eyes met her gaze, and he reached out a hand. "The name's Vallo. How do you do, ma'am?"

Robin could play hardball with her own mind, and to show herself how much she hated this game, Robin left Vallo's hand hanging. One, it was filthy. Two, she didn't trust any of these men—imagined or not.

Vallo leaned down and took her hand, anyway. Before she could tug out of his grip, he flipped her hand over and kissed her knuckles. Robin recoiled from his touch and rubbed her knuckles clean on her jeans.

"I'll do better when I get home, I swear. You need to turn this ship around." She checked her knuckles to be sure the germs were gone.

Men laughed and murmured to each other.

Yeah, okay. She couldn't rub germs off.

Vallo's calculating eyes landed on Riley's hat in her hand, and a devious smile stretched his lips. "We need to consult the captain. Aye, we need him to see this."

"Captain takes all the fun out of it," Landry countered. "Lady, I hope you know how to swim." The smirking sneer on his gaunt face told her too much. She could swim, but glancing at the horizon in all directions, that skill was pointless. She hated boats, and now she couldn't escape. What kind of test would be impossible to complete?

That flash of nerves formed into a heavy rock.

"Wait, wait," another man in the front of the crowd said, holding out his hands in a placating gesture. He smiled at Robin, displaying yellowed and blackened teeth. Robin held back a cringe. Despite his revolting appearance, at least the man had some decency to defend her against these ridiculous requests. "We want her naked first."

Guess not.

Piggish laughter and a wave of agreement rolled through the crowd. On her own turf, Robin could handle herself well. Even on this listing imaginary ship, she could subdue a few of these men with no problem. But this many was definitely a problem. Despite Vallo standing up for her, briefly, she didn't think he'd raise a hand against his own colleagues.

Robin had brought her Glock, but these men didn't appear to be susceptible to intimidation. She was trained to shoot for the kill, since an injured suspect was still a dangerous one. If she caused the death of one of these men, none of the rest seemed likely to surrender. And shooting all of them would leave no one to sail the ship back to the festival.

This entire scenario rested on her ability to pull the trigger in the first place. If that wasn't an obvious test wrapped straight around the writhing pain in her heart, she didn't know what was. Even if that was the answer—stand up and fire—she couldn't. Not with this many men. No one on earth was that fast at shooting and reloading, and Robin hadn't brought enough mags.

Completion of the test had to be something else. Something more subtle.

A man pawed at the neckline of her T-shirt. Without thinking, Robin struck downward at his elbow, flinging his arm off her. At once, her pulse kicked into gear, ready to defend herself. The perpetrator's smiling face fell with surprise and concealed pain.

Another grabbed at her waist, and with a grunt, she kicked him in the knee. Her chest lifted and fell with rapid breaths, adrenaline surging at the unprovoked attack, and whatever remained to come next. On a barrel behind her, Robin set down Riley's hat, a symbol of her subconscious she wouldn't ignore. She raised her arms in a boxer's stance, and the men backed up a step.

"Seems we caught ourselves a slippery fish, mates." Kerr said with a devious grin. Clearly, he wasn't planning on challenging her next.

"What kind of game is this?" Robin asked, mostly to herself. Perhaps asking out loud would encourage her mind to respond directly through the mouths of these men. She held her arms at the ready, in case her brain didn't like that question.

The men exchanged confused looks.

Why would her brain be confused by her own question?

"What's going on over here?" A thin, black-haired older man pushed through the pungent crowd. This one was missing teeth too. His bushy brows lifted when he laid eyes on Robin, and a flash of recognition at Riley's hat on the barrel confused her. "I see. Green, Landry, Kerr, the rest of you scurvy dogs, get back to work!" he addressed the men, most of which listened. They scattered to their roles and resumed whatever they were told, but Kerr and Landry hung back.

"We have a woman stowaway on board, Buckley, and you want us to ignore her?" Kerr asked in disbelief.

"That's right. You heard my orders."

"Unbelievable," Landry said, anger burning on his face. "This ship lives up to its reputation. The prize better be worth it."

Kerr and Landry walked away, whispering to each other. Only this Buckley fellow remained. Assessing his strength and casual posture, she relaxed her fighting stance. He meant her no harm. Robin picked up Riley's hat, a security blanket of sorts. She wouldn't read too deeply into that.

"Another one of you, eh? The curse is real." Buckley shook his head in amusement. "You're lucky Cantu, I, and a couple others have been through this show before, otherwise those dirty dogs would've had their way with you, and I suppose a few dozen others."

Robin scowled.

"No worries, lady. You see that door over there?" Buckley pointed to the only door at the stern of the ship.

Robin nodded.

"Introduce yourself." Buckley, the old man of the ship, smiled slyly and turned away.

Robin pressed Riley's hat to her chest while she crossed the rocking ship. Angry eyes glared back at her from all sides and above. The masts must've reached a hundred feet in the air, and from way down here, she couldn't see any safety harnesses on the men. Despite her recent status as an unemployed police officer, public safety was her biggest priority, so her mind should've placed harnesses on them. Then again, her mind allowed her to crash her car while sleep deprived. She couldn't even trust herself.

Okay, subconscious, bring on the next section of the test.

At the creaking wood door, Robin lifted her fist and knocked.

Chapter 13

Captain Noah Riley groggily pulled himself to a seated position on his mattress, knocking a bottle of rum onto the floor. The heavy glass thumped and rolled to the wall with the sway of the ship. He pressed his fingertips to his throbbing temples and rubbed. After a quick glance around the room to judge its position, Riley determined the drink had worn off. Shame. He stretched his neck and shoulders with a soft groan and bent and retrieved the bottle. It was empty.

Bigger shame.

Riley sighed. They were weeks from Nassau and days from their target on the Gambia River. His private stash was now gone, and he couldn't take from the crew without dire consequences. Each day he'd checked in with Hodgens, and once he was satisfied with their coordinates and progress, Riley returned to his private cabin and indulged in the tart rum. He'd never been much of a drinker, since needing to keep his wits strong and alert were critical of a captain, but now he couldn't stay away from it.

Every day and every night he hoped for a chance to see Robin Hall again. She had brought him peace from the faces haunting his thoughts, and for that, he was eternally grateful. But no matter his efforts, the only place her gentle face existed was in his awake mind. As the days passed, he began to wonder if he could keep the details of her alive. Would the wisps of her dark hair go first or the tantalizing hem of her blouse? Could he hold on to the precise stitching of her tight breeches and the strange tangle of laces on her shoes?

Or her soft lips when they twisted in confusion?

Or her searing touch as she caressed the chain on his neck?

Oh, when that white fluffy towel was all that stood between him and her. How could he have imagined such an impossibly soft fabric? Wherever the inspiration came from, he couldn't let it go.

Riley tilted his head back. Aye, grateful for the new haunt.

A knocking on his door turned his head, but no one yelled in alarm, which meant no one was injured, dying, dead, or overboard, and they hadn't spotted sails on the horizon. Taking his time, Riley blew out a heavy breath and shrugged into his vest, tightening it over his tunic, and he checked his weapons in his bandolier. The last thing he needed was to be caught unarmed with an unstable crew. They'd already voted to keep the traitor on board, who knew what other foolish actions they were capable of.

The knocking repeated.

Riley mumbled frustrations to himself and dragged his heavy feet across the cabin. A list of the ship had him tilting off balance. He rubbed his eyes, wishing to return to sleep. Even snarling at the man interrupting him was too much effort. Riley opened the cabin door with a slack face.

He blinked twice and rubbed his eyes again. He looked over his shoulder at the empty bottle of rum and skimmed his eyes around the room. It wasn't spinning or tilting in any way out of the ordinary. Certainly he was sober. Well, sober enough to believe what his eyes showed him existed, right? Had his deep desire to hold on to her memory brought her forth from the caverns of his mind into his reality?

Looking over her shoulder, he checked the manners and behaviors of his nearby crew. No one glanced at or acknowledged her.

She stood here directly from his imagination, carrying that same look of confusion he knew so well. A t-shirt hugged her pleasant chest, and pants so tight he could see every curve on her body. He'd done it. The rum had granted his wish, and he had no intention of letting her go. Not knowing if his mind would direct her where he wanted her to go, he gestured for her to enter.

She did.

Riley closed the door behind her to prevent the crew from seeing him talking to himself. The last thing he needed was the crew more upset this close to their last prize.

She turned to face him, holding his lost hat. His favorite hat. At that thought, she held it out to him. He didn't want to take it. He feared reaching out would only confirm she was an apparition. He wanted to believe she was real.

"Riley?" Robin asked, confusion twisting her features as her arm continued to hang in the air. "Am I dead?"

What a dreadful thought. Was that the secret to her appearance? She'd chosen him to haunt for eternity. If that be the outcome, he was happy to see her. The corner of his lips lifted in a solemn smile. "I hope not."

Robin gently placed his hat on his mattress. Her fingers released the worn leather, and with bated breath, Riley stared at it, waiting for the crushing moment both the hat and Robin disappeared forever.

Robin approached him and tears pricked at his eyes, but he couldn't peel them away from the hat.

"Are you okay?" Robin leaned in close, scrutinizing his face with worry on her brow. "Your shave. How did it grow in so fast?"

As much as he relished this moment, he knew it could never last. He needed to rip out the splinter now before the pain overtook him at a terrible time—between a crew's argument, in the middle of a battle, or during the confrontation of the impending prize. He had to face the truth. Riley held up his palm.

"What are you doing?" Robin frowned.

"Humor me."

Robin mirrored with her palm in the air.

Riley dashed away tears warping his vision and reached forward slowly. Fighting against the desire to remain blind to the truth, he persisted; he had to know, even if his actions caused her to disappear forever. With a last-second shaky breath, his palm closed the distance. A solid and warm hand with soft skin pressed against his. Disbelief loosened his body, and Riley's fingers wrapped around her hand and pressed it against his chest. The weight against his body sent a wave of relief barreling against him, and he could hardly stand. He closed his eyes, pushing away the remaining tears.

"How? How is this possible?" he asked, meeting her worried gaze. "You're here. You've answered my call and come to me."

Robin's hand stayed firm, grounding him. "I don't understand. Is this...heaven?"

Most certainly not. A wet chuckle breached his throat. "The Atlantic Ocean, last I checked. By now, east of the Cabo Verde islands."

"So, not a test," she said absently. "A tease. Only a final tease." Tears formed on her lids, and Riley swiped them away with his thumb.

"It's my turn to bear the confusion."

"Last I remember, I was heading to my car. I'd been worried about you all night, so I didn't sleep much. I must've crashed, and now I'm dreaming I'm here in your world. I don't know if I'm destined to wake up and face the consequences of driving unsafely, or if this is my final goodbye. I must've called you into my subconscious to ease my crossing. But the details—the smell—are so real. It doesn't make any sense. I need to know, after you left my apartment, did you make it home safely?"

Riley opened his mouth to answer.

Robin slipped her hand free of his touch, and the warmth left his body. She gestured to stop him from answering, and she stepped away from him. "No, no don't tell me. I can't have that reassurance, or I'll be sent away. I want to believe where I'm going is the land of peace and love.

I need to know my mom's waiting for me." A wistful smile lifted her beautiful mouth. "But I can't go. Not yet. So don't give me that solace."

Riley replayed her words while recalling the framed image of a woman at Robin's bedside. He remembered the details of her mother's untimely passing. Robin's fraught rambling now made sense.

Robin thought she was dying.

Why would Riley's mind invent such a heartbreaking twist for a headstrong and beautiful woman who treated him like a man, rather than a dog? Her touch felt real. She wasn't visibly injured, only lost and confused, something he'd been intimately familiar with two weeks ago.

The truth of their situation dawned on him as details popped into his head. Prior to the previous captain stepping down, Henry Price had warned Riley about women traveling in time. Although Riley had met the unusual Emily Porter and Angela Foxe, he dismissed the idea as nonsense.

Was it possible that not only had Riley done it when he'd met Robin, but that she somehow followed him back here? There was one way to know for sure.

Riley closed the cold distance between them, heart pounding in his chest. He couldn't lose what he'd gotten back. "You're not dying."

Robin met his gaze and frowned. "What?"

To help ground her, he lifted his palm again. She reached for it quickly this time, and he gripped her tight. "There's a connection between us; we are linked together. As I was in your world, you are now in mine."

Robin tilted her head and scrunched her nose in thought.

"You're standing on the *Angelfish*," he added.

"How could I imagine...?" Robin trailed off as the thoughts in her head showed on her face, and Riley held her like a lifeline.

"You didn't. I'm not in your head, as you are not in mine. We are both real, and we're both here. I can prove it to you."

Robin looked at their clasped hands. "How?"

Riley gently cupped her neck and leaned down. He slowly brought his lips to hers, for if he was wrong, this would be the one and only kiss. Closing his eyes, he pressed against hers. Heat, like the incredible hot shower pouring over his body, once again rushed through his limbs, and pooled down low. His breeches tightened as their lips changed position, and he released her hand and pulled her against his body, against her lips, leaning into her. Desperation for her touch swallowed him whole. Desperation for this to be real kept him kissing her. He couldn't stop. He couldn't open his eyes and have all this torn from him again.

Robin's arms wrapped around his neck, demanding he stay close, and that was a wish he would grant over and over. Riley grasped Robin's hips and pressed her against his hard length, growing with the need to be inside her.

Something hard pressed back.

"Ow," he exclaimed unintentionally. He pulled back and looked down at Robin.

She followed his gaze to the sack between them. "It's my gun." Her chest lifted and fell, and she twisted the bag to her back. "Where were we?"

"You were deciding if I'm real."

Robin smiled deviously, sending heat surging through his body once again. "I haven't decided yet."

The cabin door flung wide with a screech, startling them both. Armorer William Price split the doorway with his lanky frame. "So it's true, Captain."

"Captain?" Robin whispered to herself, as if finally believing what he'd told her was the truth.

He couldn't help a prideful lift of his lips. As she was realizing the full gravity of the truth he'd given her, Riley was realizing Robin Hall was really here.

Price glanced at Robin. "You found our stowaway. How much longer are women going to keep infiltrating our ships? Like rats, they keep popping up no matter how many you dispatch."

Robin whispered, "Rats?"

With impatience, Riley asked, "What business do you have, Price?"

The armorer shook his head in bewilderment. "As you know, I have no interest in the trappings of the fairer sex—"

"Trappings?" Robin repeated on a whisper.

Riley didn't respond to her aggravation, primarily because she could handle herself, but also Riley understood Price's stance on women: He wanted nothing to do with them. And while Price was still a fair and trustworthy man, many sailors on this ship were not. Riley listened closely to his armorer's concerns.

"But the rumor of another skirt on deck has the crew in a fuss. The newest recruits aren't aware of our unusual history. If you want to keep her to yourself, you must assert your position."

Not a problem. "I shall address the crew. In the meantime, you'll do well to insist they have nothing to worry about."

"It's not their worries that concern me." Price shot a look at Robin.

More troublemakers. When Angela had appeared on the *Sea Lion*, Vallo, along with his best friends, Berger and Liverman, were the biggest noise on the ship, rallying the crew against Henry Price. The latter two were dead, but the former? The biggest thorn in Riley's side.

"Was Vallo one of the instigators?" Riley asked.

"No, sir. Haven't seen him."

If that wasn't surprising, Riley didn't know what would be.

"I saw Vallo," Robin said. "He introduced himself."

That would do it.

"Thank you for your council, Price," Riley said in dismissal.

The armorer closed the door, and Riley blew out a breath. No longer worried over the crew's opinions on his uncharacteristic imbibing, now he had someone special to take care of, a responsibility he both relished and feared. The biggest worry he could've imagined.

"You were calling his name at the festival," Robin added. "What's so alarming about this Vallo guy?"

"He's someone you'd do best to avoid." Riley took in the sight of her scandalous clothing and said, "As much as I enjoyed the *shapeliness* of your world, let's get you out of those clothes, they shall only add to their case here. And so you understand your predicament, only McKee, Giles, Price, Buckley, Cantu, Karl, and Hodgens are trustworthy."

"You expect me to remember all those names?"

"If any of them talk to you, ask their name. If it's familiar, they're likely safe," Riley said with a gentle smile.

"I recognize one. Buckley sent me in here."

Just like the old coot. "And as such, you're lucky. Your presence on this ship is forbidden, and by all rights you must answer to the crew."

"How?"

Riley saw no gain in lying to her. "The typical punishment is marooning. Since neither you nor I want that, a wise choice is for you to blend in. Convince the crew you are one of them, regardless of the status of your breast. Here in my trunk I have extra clothes. I'm sure something will be suitable." Riley leaned down and lifted his hat. "Thank you for returning it to me. It's my favorite hat."

Robin smiled in response and kneeled at his trunk. She picked through his spare clothes, lifting garments and looking at them closely. One was a fancy dress which she promptly returned.

Captain Riley couldn't believe she was here before him, now sharing his world as he shared hers, and she handled the change much better than he had. But his smile of gratitude at his good fortune slid away. Riley was leading the crew into a perilous raid, so perilous, in fact, he had no intention of surviving it. He wanted her nowhere near this prize, but he couldn't leave her behind on the ship either, when the majority of the crew wanted her dead.

Chapter 14

CLOUDY SKIES BROUGHT RELIEF to Robin's tired eyes. An ache of exhaustion tugged at her eyelids, but now was not the time for rest, because if she did anything wrong in the next few minutes, she'd be resting permanently at the bottom of the Atlantic.

In her short-lived career as a police officer, sometimes Robin had to take the stand as an expert to give testimony or as a material witness in a case. Within those parameters, a set of defined procedures to moving a person of interest through the legal process was...mostly clear. But here, where she was miraculously alive with Riley at her side, Robin felt like not only was she on a high-profile murder trial, but that the judge, jury, and executioner had a personal bone to pick with her.

Instead of wearing her department blues and holding her head high, or her street clothes and having a sense of self, Robin formally stood before the crew, but now her clothes were uncomfortable, ill-fitting, and yeah, they smelled like salty fish. For whatever reason, many of these men hated her.

Standing at her side, Riley sent her a sorrowful smile while the quartermaster paced around the interested crew. When she'd arrived on this nightmarish boat, she thought she was being tested by her subconscious to see if she had what it took to return to her body and make amends for whatever damage she'd caused in her car accident, but once she saw Riley, she knew it had to be a tease instead. One last reward before traveling over the rainbow bridge.

Then he kissed her...that was real.

Noah Riley wasn't an escaped mental patient from somewhere in England. Here he was no longer scared, lost, or rambling on about impossibilities. Everything he'd said about the Crown's unfairness, all his confusion about vehicles and food, all his excitement over a refrigerator, electricity, and running water were genuine. A man from a different time, who'd crossed not only once, but twice. And somehow, she'd followed him.

Riley had told her he was the captain of the *Angelfish*, but the way the quartermaster and the crew scowled at her and Riley, she wondered what power the captain had. And the flag flying on the masthead was an English symbol, not 'the black'. As he had been confused about her world, she was lost about his. She should've spent more time listening to Emily's tales of the past.

Robin hadn't crashed her car. She wasn't dying at all. She still believed this was a test, but an entirely different one. This wasn't to cleanse her subconscious of guilt. This was survival.

"Upon our decks, we have a stowaway," Quartermaster Randall said, holding his hands behind his back and pacing like a military officer. "Upon our hearts, we have the articles. An agreement we all signed to ensure the proper behavior and mutual agreement of all those on board. One among us did not sign, nor was granted permission to board. In fact, this person stole from us."

The crew murmured to each other, and the tone settled a pressure on Robin's shoulders.

When they quieted down, the quartermaster continued, "Our agreement is clear. Any stowaway is to be marooned. Any accusation of thievery is to be satisfied by a duel on shore."

This time the murmurs grew into excitement.

"There is one additional factor to consider. Our stowaway is a woman, and Captain Riley would like to say a few words before the decision is handed down."

Riley left her side and took up the center of attention. "Everyone, this is Robin Hall, my personal guest. My sincerest apologies for not announcing her presence sooner."

The scowls turned in her direction, and Robin hugged her arms.

"Where's she been hidin'?" a voice called out.

Riley turned to face the questioning man. "Does that matter?"

The man glowered.

"No one is to harm Robin. Anyone who attempts to lay a finger on her shall answer to me personally." Riley sent her a wink. His confidence, assertiveness, and public declaration defending her sent a rush of heat scorching her veins. As he strolled along the deck, addressing all the men, she pictured his naked form and wished she'd taken a better look. That visual softened the pressure from her shoulders. This sexy, strong man was going to save her from these pigs.

"This ship ain't that big, captain. How did she get past all our checks?"

This man's statement was more an observation than an accusation, and the captain smiled.

"It's the curse, don't you see?" another answered. "This ship is cursed!"

The crew mumbled its concern.

The man with the missing fingers, Landry, stepped forward. "What curse? I wasn't told nothing about no curse."

"Aye, a curse be an important factor in signing the articles," the hefty Kerr said, stepping up to Landry's side.

"If this ship's cursed, we want a bigger share, captain," a man with yellow and blackened teeth said, standing with his upset friends.

Riley faced the three of them. "What share do you deem fair, Green?"

The unsightly Green conferred with Kerr and Landry briefly. One of the men grinned in a way that sent shivers down Robin's back. Breaking their huddle, Green said, "If we're taking the risk of a woman on board, then what's fair is we all get a turn with 'er."

Most of the crew cheered. Buckley, who'd sent Robin to the captain, didn't. Neither did a very large man. A portly fellow with a stained apron also looked solemn, as did the helmsman. Five men against a crew of what...dozens?

Robin swallowed a dry lump in her throat.

Riley spun on his men, face flushing red, and his body clenched for action. The situation had escalated, and Riley intended to take them all on. For her. Worry gripped her chest as she remembered his attempt to fight a parked car. She had been able to subdue him easily.

"Randall, care to control your men?" Riley asked through gritted teeth.

The quartermaster smirked and motioned for the crew to settle down. When they quieted, Robin exhaled in relief.

"This isn't how we settle things on this ship," Randall said to the captain. "If one of us starts breaking the rules, then we all will, and then we no longer have an account. Agreeing to the articles is what keeps us whole and functional. As representative of this crew, by their vote I remind you, I cannot allow such disregard for the rules to stand, despite extenuating circumstances. We are two days at most from the mouth of the Gambia River. This is the worst time for you to spring such betrayal on us."

Riley tensed. "Be careful with your accusation, Randall. I did not stash a woman in my cabin for weeks. As you can see, she's clean and nourished. Giles, you never brought extra rations to my cabin?" Riley addressed the wide fellow with an apron, who promptly shook his head.

"And as I am still in a healthful shape," Riley added, "I have not shared my rations."

"You've been drinking a lot, captain. No need for extra rations if you've got rum for fuel," Landry said.

Riley spun with barely contained rage. "I'm telling the truth. If you believe her appearance to be the result of a curse of good fortune, then we are in agreement. But accusing me of betrayal is a serious offense. Robin is one of us. She will dine with us, assist the crew, and pull her own weight." Riley glanced at Robin with pity in his eyes. That was unnecessary. Robin could handle herself, and if climbing around this ship was all it took to keep these brutes pacified, so be it.

"Pretending to be an equal doesn't make her one," the quartermaster argued.

This guy didn't know a thing about Robin, but he assumed she was useless and helpless. What was wrong with these men?

"That's a fair statement," Riley said, and Robin shot him a look. Riley winked, indicating he had other plans, so Robin trusted him to stand up for her. "Since you have vitriol under your skin, for her safety, Robin will share my cabin."

The crew erupted with anger.

Robin stiffened, and Riley returned to her side and whispered in her ear, "They don't accept change well."

"Clearly. Now what? How are we going to argue against all of them?" Even if those few allies stood up against the rest of the crew, would they fight for her, or would they back down at the first threat? She didn't know any of these men.

"They need time."

Robin didn't understand. "You're the captain. Can't you order them to calm down? Can't you tell them to leave me alone?"

A flicker passed over his features. "The captain holds ultimate power during battle, and he leads the crew on the account. When it comes to matters of the crew, the quartermaster is their voice. A balance of power, if you will."

As the men raged, nothing looked balanced here.

Randall quieted the crew. "I need not remind you of my position. As the crew has come to an agreement by their voices, Robin will not share your cabin. If you disagree, we will find ourselves with a problem."

Riley's fists squeezed until his knuckles blanched. Robin wanted to stay by his side. If she couldn't, where was she going to go? What was the crew going to do with her? Too many 'what ifs' left her stomach unsettled.

"Sails!" a voice shouted from above.

THE AGREEMENT WITH RANDAL against Captain Riley persisted until the warning call repeated. The crew calmed down, and Riley crossed the deck to the rail and pressed a spyglass to his eye. With a grim set to his mouth, he said, "Spanish merchant ship."

Riley handed the spyglass to Randall. Seconds ago, they were at each other's throats, but now they worked together, and the rest of the crew ignored her.

Randall viewed through the spyglass. "Southeast by south. She's a couple hours away. Do we risk taking this prize?" Randall asked, deferring the power to Riley, as the captain had explained to her. He returned the spyglass to Riley, who took another look.

"She's armed. Likely has valuable cargo to warrant such guns. If we can add to our supply of weaponry, I think our odds will be that much better."

Odds for what?

Nerves swirled in Robin's gut. She hugged her purse against her chest. Merchant ship meant friendly, right?

Riley faced the quartermaster with a sly grin. "I say we find out what she's carrying."

Randall nodded as if Riley wanted his approval before announcing the plan to the crew. The captain faced his men and tucked away his spyglass. "Karl, get us under full sail! You heard me you dirty dogs, let out the reefs! Tighten the halyards! We're going to hunt a Spanish prize."

The men cheered and rushed to their posts. Others cleared the deck by collecting barrels and lines and stacking them away.

Robin stood still, hoping to avoid the chaos. When a man approached, she sidestepped a barrel to avoid a confrontation. These men acted like monsters around her, and if they prepared to 'hunt' a ship, whatever that meant, she didn't want the surging testosterone turned on her.

"Speed check, Gunner!" Riley ordered. Watching him take command of a ship, of dozens of men, made Robin flush with pride. He'd protected her from these men, and now they licked out of the palm of his hand. A whirlwind of activity had Robin shaking with nerves. What else had Riley explained to her that she'd dismissed as mental illness?

A lanky young man, no older than fifteen carried something tucked into his arm like a football and rushed to the rail. He and another man worked together. The man called out, "Ten knots."

"McKee," Riley said, and a bald man with a grizzly beard gestured before approaching.

"Aye, captain."

"Make sure everyone is armed. Get the gun crews below deck and ready to fire on my command," Riley said. "At our speed, we will overtake her in a couple hours, perhaps less."

The mast lined with sails overhead turned slowly, hauled by the hands of men. If the situation were different, she'd be impressed by the feat. The deck beneath her feet listed with a wave and the sun broke through the clouds.

"Sails comin' about!" A man far above their heads shouted down.

Riley faced the stern of the ship and gestured. "Raise the black!"

He'd mentioned that before. She didn't know what 'the black' was as he referred to it, but something about it rang in her memory. The English flag on the masthead was lowered in jerky movements. In its place, a black flag climbed skyward, and the wind pulled it open.

Emblazoned in the center was a white skull and crossed swords, and Robin gasped.

Pirates?

Real pirates?

"You've got to be kidding me!" Robin shouted. That was the missing piece. Captain Noah Riley commanded a *pirate* ship.

Men turned and scowled at her, but most ignored her entirely. Robin pressed a hand against her forehead and raked her fingers through her tangled locks. With her mouth hanging open and eyes wide, Robin stared at the captain with disbelief. From what she'd seen in movies and television shows, this wasn't going to be a battle—more like a slaughter—and she was stuck in the middle.

Riley approached. "Fear not, I shall keep you safe."

She pointed at the flag and remembered Riley's words at the festival, words she'd dismissed as delusions of a history fanatic. Anger and disgust charged her. "That's the black banner? You're really pirates? The real thing—enemies of all mankind, marauders of the sea, and you're going to kill all those people on that ship to steal from them?"

Riley's warmth slid away, but rather than lash out in angry defense, his shoulders slumped ever so slightly in defeat. She'd hurt him.

Good.

"The goal of the black is for them to surrender. I've been nothing but honest with you." Riley reached out for her arm.

Robin backed away from him, hand on her forehead. "This can't be happening. I can't believe this." She paced the deck, avoiding the commotion. Falling through time was hard enough to wrap her brain around, but landing on a pirate ship in the Atlantic Ocean was something else entirely. And now they prepared to kill those people because they happened to be in the area.

If Riley hadn't stood up for her, what would the crew have done to her? Took turns with her body and then tossed her overboard like spoiled meat when they bored with her? She didn't want to know what marooning was.

Her stomach churned with the movement of the water and the unease of everything around her. She hated boats. If land was in sight, she would've taken her chances with the sharks. And then what?

How would she get home?

How was she going to survive the next several hours?

She didn't know how to wield a sword...but she had her Glock.

"Robin," Riley said, catching up to her. "I know this is difficult to process. Believe me, I was there." A charming smile lit up his features. If he was trying to cheer her up, he failed. Robin wanted to punch him for it.

"Fearing a parked car is nothing like an impending battle to the death." Her tone was snarky and rude, but she didn't care.

"And that is how we differ. I'll take a battle any day."

Robin's features pinched with confusion, and she stared at him thoughtfully. His ridiculous choice actually made sense. This world wasn't scary to him, because it was all he knew, like her world wasn't scary to her. But that was no excuse for this, and she saw firsthand the rows of cannons below deck. "You're choosing to fight those men over there. *Your* decision. Why? Don't you own enough weapons?"

Riley rested a hand on her shoulder while busy men cast her ugly glares. Riley leaned to catch her eyes. "Never mind the crew. Listen to me, I will deal with them, but until then I need you to stay safe. Lock yourself in my cabin, and I'll come get you when it's over."

Like hell.

Chapter 15

Captain Riley had given her every detail she'd asked for, so her anger and hurt was unfounded. And that reaction, to him, was a direct punch to the heart, if such an action were possible. He'd hoped easing her into this would allow her to overcome the fears and prejudices a woman of the future held—a woman who laughed at the idea of pirates.

But things moved too fast.

Riley needed a level head to keep his men alive. They were already angry with him. Robin didn't understand how precarious their situation was, and he didn't have time to explain, if she'd even listen. Hate radiated off her like heat from a boiler. If the prize hadn't appeared when it had, Riley was certain the outcome for both her and him would've been different.

"You didn't answer me." Robin shrugged away from his touch.

"We don't have time for this."

Robin stepped forward in challenge. "Then make time."

Riley stared her down, but she refused to yield. The longer he persisted, the less time they had to prepare for battle. For her sake, whether she understood or not, Riley relaxed his stance and said calmly, "I told you the Crown took everything from us. We only take what we need to survive. Nothing more."

Robin paused to chew on his words. She asked, "Then what's all the talk about prizes?"

Riley shifted his weight, patience running dangerously thin. "Sometimes, to buy food and pay wages, we need a little more." Or a lot more, in the case of men who wished to retire from the sea and the whispers of a noose in their ears.

"You're thieves and murderers. In my city, you'd be arrested and imprisoned until your trial, which would end with your guilt and further imprisonment."

She did understand; she simply didn't approve. Riley couldn't blame her. He could hardly look at himself anymore.

"Your rules aren't much different from ours."

"Then why?" Robin's voice rose, and men glared her way. Her continued argument placed them all in further danger. "Why risk prison? Why not sail around him?"

"Her," Riley corrected. "Ships are female, and she's coming about, and we're responding. If that ship over there is aggressive in any way, we shall defend ourselves."

Robin pressed her lips thin, finally accepting.

Riley patted her shoulder. "Lock the door and don't come out for anything."

Robin nodded and wove her way to the cabin, once again earning scowls from the crew. This was the bed he'd made. Now he had to sleep in it. He waited until the sound of the lock clicked over.

She was as safe as possible...for now.

SUCH A STUBBORN, FRUSTRATING man. Robin couldn't bear to see him killed or captured and imprisoned. When she'd met him, she'd first thought he was an escaped mental patient, but after appearing in his world, for a brief while, she believed him of sound mind.

Until he ordered the attack of a nearby ship for no reason.

Now she knew he suffered from mental illness. Why else would a healthy man choose to charge headfirst into a bloody battle? More importantly, Robin couldn't stop him. She couldn't keep Riley safe from himself. Now all she could do was hope.

She wasn't good at hope.

With time to kill and her worries draining her dry, Robin paced around Riley's private quarters, looking at all the neat things of the past while her legs worked out their excess energy. She found a captain's log, which she paged through. The handwriting, although beautiful in its artistic penmanship, was hard to decipher. She found a manifest—same handwriting—and she determined he'd listed cargo and its value, and the individual crew member's accumulating balances, which were shockingly tiny. Robin didn't have an inflation calculator to determine a frame of reference for how much this stuff was worth in her dollars, but she learned they lived with very little.

Why though? Why did they choose to scrape by on the stomach-churning sea at the whimsy of the weather and the hope of finding what they needed either at landfall or by brute force? The risks seemed far too high to be worth it.

Sean Coulder, the man who'd robbed the bank. The man Robin had failed to shoot upon his exit, and her failure lead to Officer Clark Thompson's death. Like these men, Mr. Coulder risked his life for a few bucks. The result was prison for him, the death of her colleague, and mandatory therapy for her. What was the point? Why choose the more difficult path?

Her mom had chosen that path. When faced with the choice of struggling as a single mom or staying with a deadbeat boyfriend, she left. Robin hadn't understood at the time, and she remembered crying about leaving daddy, but sometimes one's values and beliefs had to drive their actions, regardless of what was easy. But in the end, her mom died, anyway. Almost like fate had stepped in.

Fate could kiss her ass.

With Riley's passionate speech about standing up against the injustices in his world, Robin could see that same drive in him. The thought of his drive ending the same as Mr. Coulder's or her mom's lingered in the back of her mind.

Resting next to a sealed inkpot, Robin found another book. It was small and narrow, almost diary sized. She lifted the lid and skimmed the text. Her eyes caught on words that stilled her heart.

My Dearest,

I have missed you for another long year. Many things have changed that you must know. Captain Lemoine retired from the sea when he met a woman. It shocked me so! The woman had been pretending to be a man for weeks, and no one caught it! She seemed lovely once we got to know her.

Lady Luck struck our ship once again, and Captain Price left us to be with his woman, a very surprising woman, a Miss Angela. Two stowaways, several weeks apart. And we have not figured out how they got on board. No one admitted to the action, so no one was properly punished.

If I see another woman brought on this ship, so help me! Only a dozen men are still on the crew since Lemoine's time. The perpetrator must be one of them, one of my trusted men. If I had known how accepting they would eventually be, I would've brought you along. I miss you dearly. I love you.

We will be together again, soon enough.

Your Captain Riley

Robin checked for a date on the page, but since she didn't know what year she'd landed in, it was useless information. What wasn't useless was knowing Riley had a woman waiting for him back home. A woman he loved.

A rock formed in her chest as tears pricked her eyes. Why was she surprised? Her luck with men was the worst, and something unexplainable brought Robin here, so how could she think falling into a man's life meant anything? Fate didn't kiss her ass. Fate slapped Robin in the face.

She should've known to keep her heart guarded when it came to the office. Sure these men shared hammocks and a mess hall instead of a copy machine, but the rules still applied. No more dating colleagues.

Robin closed the book and exhaustion pulled her eyelids. She felt like she'd been awake for more than a day, and Riley's lumpy mattress looked inviting, like a hot cup of coffee on a cold winter's night. She sat heavily, ignoring the bounce, and collapsed onto her back. With hours to spare, Robin drifted off as tears streamed down her cheeks.

Chapter 16

SOMETHING STARTLED ROBIN AWAKE way too soon. Coffee. Where was the coffee? Peeling her tired eyes open, wood beams overhead and a pungent smell reminded her the pirate ship was not a dream, unfortunately, but that meant Riley wasn't a dream either. She knew she was awake, and that the test to clear her subconscious hadn't been real. But there was an element that was: she needed to survive and find a way home.

That very real and very crushing letter reminded her of that goal. And since she quit her job, time was of the essence.

Shouts turned her head toward the locked cabin door, and a rapid fire of thumps and scrapes, like metal dragging on wood, left her with a sinking feeling. Robin approached the door and listened. Metal clanged and crashed, like swords. Gunshots went off. Robin pulled away with a gasp.

They were in battle.

She could stand here in the relative safety of the captain's private cabin, or she could go out there and see if she could help. Riley had said the plan was to take what the crew needed from the Spanish merchant ship with no resistance, but based on the sounds penetrating the thick door, a frightening level of resistance was happening. She'd made a promise to keep Riley safe, and finding out he wasn't available didn't change that, no matter how much it stung. Robin exhaled and flung the door wide.

Clouds of gunpowder obscured the main deck, but she could see the deadly dances of men taking turns parrying and attacking. Blood smeared their faces and pooled under their feet. Blades swiped through the air with the intent to kill. Men slipped and fell and had their throats cut. Gargles and screams of anger penetrated her ears.

With that rock tumbling in her stomach, Robin stepped forward into the light. She'd never experienced anything like this, not even a gang fight. These men, so brutal and cold, reminded her of several suspects she'd detained. She shivered at the memory of the threats the suspects spat in her face when she'd cuffed them, but this was worse. So much worse, because people didn't call the police before the fights happened, and by the time emergency services arrived, all Robin found was the aftermath. Watching it happen before her eyes was paralyzing. How could men do such things to each other?

With smoke-obscured air and rapid movements, she couldn't tell who was friendly and who was foe.

To her, they were all monsters.

One man with a red bandanna wrapped over his head stabbed another, and as the body dropped to the deck, his face lit up in victory. Seeking his next target, Bandanna's eye caught on Robin. With a filthy frown on his bloody face, he used his boot to pull his sword free and kick the defeated man over.

Robin wanted to vomit, but now was not the time. His lips curled back in a sneer, displaying rotten teeth. His face was lined with age and sun damage, and his hair draped over his shoulders in knotted lengths, not that his appearance changed Robin's disgusted reaction.

Bandanna tucked away his sword and stalked closer to her as if planning on something other than a quick death. "Look what we have here. I say we found ourselves a prize worth takin'."

"Me?" Robin backed up a step. "I'm not a prize."

Bandanna laughed. "Oh, and a feisty one at that. The men will love me for this, but you better watch that mouth of yours." His grimy hand reached out for her arm.

Robin ducked to the side and shoved the confused man forward. From behind him, she kicked the back of his left knee, and he crumpled over with a yelp. The scowling man turned on his knees.

"Why you little bi—" His angry declaration abruptly stopped, and the snicker twisting his lips slipped away, replaced by confusion.

Robin held the Glock pointed at his face, right between his ugly eyes.

"What in the bloody hell is that?"

Keeping the brute between her sights, her arms trembled. If she squeezed the trigger, a nine-millimeter bullet would fly through the man's forehead. Bandanna made no move. He'd already put away his weapon; he didn't intend to kill her. The gun shook in her hands, bouncing the sight in and out of aim.

"Some sort of toy?" Bandanna climbed to his feet and unsheathed his sword, positioning it for a strike. "I'm not afraid of toys."

Robin's vision blurred, and suddenly Mr. Coulder the bank robber appeared in her sights, aiming his gun and firing on Officer Clark Thompson. Gunshots rang in her mind, but they weren't hers. She'd only watched.

Robin flinched as her mom's panicked pleas filled her ears. The shooter had towered over her with his face shrouded in a stocking. He'd fired without a word, without a care, while Robin hid around the corner like a terrified coward with a gun in her hands, a gun loaded and ready to protect her mom. She'd broken her promise to keep mom safe.

Robin hadn't been able to take someone else's life even if it meant saving another. No wonder the force wanted her out. She couldn't handle the job. Robin's arms shook harder. Failure swept through her, and she dropped the gun with a clatter.

Bandanna's grin split wide. "As I thought. You're going to regret threatenin' me." With his sword hanging idly by his side, his meaty claw grabbed her by the nape of her neck.

Robin's lips parted in shock, and her chest squeezed in fear. There was no dispatch to radio. No partner to call on. She was on her own.

"No more funny business, or I might decide you're not a prize worth bothering for."

If she fought back, he'd kill her. If she didn't, he'd take her to his crew. Robin didn't need to guess what an angry crew capable of cold-blooded murder wanted with a woman. If those were her choices, it wasn't hard for her to lift her fists alongside her face in a boxer's stance.

If he wanted to take her, then he had to work for it.

Robin lifted her arms high and smashed his elbow downward, freeing herself. She spun away from his reach. Rolling back to her feet, she spun to find Bandanna standing still, face crumpled in pain, and Riley pulled his sword out of Bandanna's neck. Blood spurted, and his body tumbled after.

Robin collected her gun and put it back in her purse. What was the sense of keeping it if she couldn't use it against anyone? Still, it was a security blanket for her, the only normalcy in this crazy world.

"Are you injured?" Riley asked, worry creasing his brow. Stepping over the brute, Riley held out a hand, and she took it without hesitation. In the midst of all the pain and death, and no matter her opinion on his leadership decision, Riley was still her safe place until she returned home.

Riley pulled her in close and wrapped his arms around her. His warmth calmed her trembling. Over his shoulder, most of the fights were over. The deck quieted with soft groans while men picked through the carnage, checking for survivors. Since Riley was relaxed, she figured team *Angelfish* had triumphed. But she wouldn't underestimate a merchant ship again.

"I think I'm okay." Robin braced herself to be chewed out for disobeying his orders. She'd heard it all from her police captain after the Thompson shooting, from the department shrink—but in nicer words, and of course Blenny's endless reminders. All of it was unnecessary. Her nightmares were always fresh.

"This way. Let me look you over." The captain wrapped his arm around her shoulders and guided her back toward his private cabin.

Robin stared at him. "You're not mad?"

"Last I checked, I still possess all my wits," he said playfully.

Robin tilted her head in confusion.

The captain released her, sending her inside ahead of him. She expected him to close the door behind her, like a disobedient child who needed a time out, but Riley followed her, closing the door behind them both. He approached her with caution and worry.

"Are you hurt anywhere? Sometimes injuries can take time to process. I once saw a man who lost a finger and didn't realize for hours." Riley chuckled to lighten the air.

"How can you be so flippant about what happened? People died."

Dropping the levity, Riley motioned for her to sit on his bed. After she sunk into the mattress, he lifted her loose sleeves and checked her arms. "Dwelling on the darkness pulls you down farther, but when you have someone depending on you, it's easier to stay focused away from it."

He had someone depending on him, waiting on him, whoever he wrote that beautiful letter to. The woman he loved. Riley met Robin's gaze, but she looked away. Suddenly she didn't want to be this close. It was wrong. Riley lifted her pant leg next, and Robin pulled away.

"I'm fine." Changing the subject was the only way for her to pull herself from her own darkness of death, failure, and Riley's love for another. "What happened out there?"

Riley swiped his tousled hair back from his face. "The merchant ship turned out to be pirates in disguise. They hung their banner after we did.

Sneaky bastards, but at least they gave us a warning. Sometimes that's the difference between walking away and being tossed overboard."

"And your crew won?" Robin asked with a twist to her face. There was no winning on the battlefield.

"If you want to count heads, we did. Randall and Karl are checking the merchant hold now. Hopefully those bloody thieves left something for the taking."

Robin shot him a look, and Riley glanced away and added, "As soon as we take whatever we need and have room for, we'll be on our way." He reached for the lower hem of her tunic. "May I check?"

"I'm fine," Robin said, pushing his hand back. "Shaken, but intact."

Riley dropped his hands. "I understand. Is there anything I can do?"

Kiss me. Hold me. Tell me it's going to be okay.

"Water would be nice."

Riley smiled and patted her thigh as he rose to his full height. "I'll be right back."

WHEN HE LEFT, ROBIN stared at the diary. Why had she read it? With a groan of frustration, she fell back on the mattress. She'd sworn off men, and Riley wasn't available, so why was her heart tugging her around? This had to be some very lucid dream because time travel wasn't real.

It wasn't.

After a restless beat, Robin got off the bed. Waiting in his room within eyeshot of his diary was too much to bear. Pushing through the cabin door, Robin stared in surprise. As if the battle had never happened, the deck had been restored—cleaned, supplies at the ready, and men nonchalantly at task.

The only proof anything had happened was the merchant ship remained tied up alongside the *Angelfish*, and crew walked across a plank hauling barrels, lines, and tools on board. One man carried a small cage with chickens. Another man lifted the last dead body off the *Angelfish* deck and tossed him overboard. They weren't kidding when they'd threatened to do the same to her. Pirates were truly monsters.

Brushing that pointless opinion aside, Robin crossed the deck. While the ship was safe and the crew occupied, she might as well explore a little, distract herself. Heads turned, glaring at her, like when she'd walked the police department halls after her 'incident'.

"You don' belong here, skirt," Landry, the man with missing fingers said with a sneer.

"Aye," his partner, Kerr added. "You best be stayin' by the captain, lest something bad happens to you."

"Battle's over," Landry added. "Know what that means?"

Robin shook her head and said, "What?"

"Captain's not holding the power, so you best you be stayin' on the quartermaster's good side," Kerr said, twisting a line around a cleat.

"Gentlemen, gentlemen," a pleasant voice interrupted. Vallo approached with a smile. "Don't scare the poor thing. The captain favors her, so we should treat her with the respect a guest requires."

Robin smiled at him, grateful for the assistance.

Kerr and Landry scowled and returned to their work.

Vallo touched her arm. "With that settled, Giles is asking for you below deck."

"Thank you for your help. I don't understand why they're so upset with me."

Vallo walked her across the deck to the ladder like a bodyguard, returning hateful glances from each man they passed.

"All they know is a woman appeared on this ship, which is against the rules. They want someone to pay for the infraction. Since you wouldn't have enough money to satisfy them all, they insist on the debt being settled another way. I'm sure you can guess what that is."

Robin swallowed a thick lump. "I can."

"Fear not. If anyone's giving you grief, and the captain's not around—he's a busy man, after all—you can always come to me."

Robin smiled with appreciation blooming through her. Besides the captain, no one's been truly kind. "Thank you. I mean it."

He gestured at the ladder, and Robin waited for a turn between men carrying heavy loads. She climbed below deck with a last nod at Vallo. She didn't know why Riley warned her about him. He was great.

In the dim light, Giles the cook approached her. Riley had said he was one of the trustworthy men. She relaxed.

"There you are, Robin, is it?" Robin nodded, and he held out a mug to her. "Captain wanted me to bring you this."

"Where's Riley?" She accepted the mug and looked inside it. All she could tell in the insufficient lighting was it contained liquid.

"He's sorting a commotion in the hold. Do you peel potatoes? I could use a hand."

"Sure." Throat parched, Robin took a healthy swig and cringed. It was tart and bitter with a note of sweetness, but not nearly enough to make it palatable. She used her fist to cover her gag. After a short internal pep talk about manners and her body's need to have fluid, she swallowed and coughed. "What kind of water is this?"

"Water? We don't have water, but there's plenty of punch."

Great. Just great. Her faith in the cook's skills dramatically decreased after tasting his version of punch.

Giles gestured for her to follow him, and deeper into the belly of the ship they went. Near the stern of the ship, a stack of crates centered around a large metal pot, and a pile of raw potatoes rested on the floor. The galley. "Have a seat."

Robin lowered herself on an empty wood crate, and Giles sat next to her and resumed his peeling.

Robin picked up a potato. "Do you have an extra peeler?"

Giles cocked his round face at her. He glanced at her hands and smiled with understanding. "No knife on you? I daresay, I've got a spare somewhere." He dug in the crates behind him but came up empty. He patted his pockets and lit up when he found one. He offered her the dirty blade. "Here it is."

Had it been used to kill a guy not moments ago? Robin shivered and shook that thought away. She smiled, accepting it graciously, and set about peeling—the most normal thing she'd experienced since the festival.

"Where do you come from?" Giles asked.

"Far from here," Robin said, eyes on the spud.

Giles chuckled. "I've heard that before, like you've been coached to say it or too afraid to speak the truth. Either way, it's smart to hold back. Most of the men on this ship have never encountered a woman on board, and you can see the disruption it causes, which is why we have the rules in place. Why you chose this ship is beyond my comprehension—why any of you had, as a matter of fact. But fear not, some of us who have encountered this situation before will help you."

"What is *this* you refer to?"

She had a feeling whatever he was going to say was insulting. She braced herself.

"A woman popping out of the hold."

Well, that wasn't what she expected. "This ship is like a reverse Bermuda triangle, and I'm the next unfortunate person to take this crazy ride?"

Giles knitted his brows together in contemplation. He probably hadn't heard the concept, but he seemed to understand her point all the same. "Around these parts, you're the third so far. I don't believe in coincidence." He glanced at her with a twinkle in his eye and returned to his peeling. "I find the whole thing utterly fascinating, and I can't help but wonder if there's a young sprite out there for ol' Giles someday, but no use in wishing. I'm not the looker our previous captains have been, and I'm far from comparable to the alluring exterior of our current captain. Combine that with his big heart, and Riley's hard to resist."

Robin's brows lifted at the forward compliment.

Giles chuckled. "I daresay, I might prefer women in my bed, but I can still appreciate an attractive form when I see it, and your beauty is simply a treat to behold."

Robin's face burned with a flush of heat. "Uh, thank you."

"Pardon me, but the captain is an idiot."

Robin laughed at the unexpected statement. "What? Why would you say that?"

"Oh, that dear boy. He's been on this crew since he learned to wipe the snot off his own face. Picked 'im up fresh from a bar, straight away. He never wanted to be anything but a pirate, and although most of us never survive more than two years at sea, raiding ships, Riley's been around a long while. I've gotten to know him better than most." Giles paused.

Where was he going with this?

"He needs you."

Robin's heart skipped a beat or two. This conversation was so far removed from her expectations. "Why do you say that?"

"Has he told you about dear Gwyneth?"

Now he had her interest. "I've never heard of her. Who is she?" The woman in his diary, she'd guess. *I miss you dearly. I love you. We will be together again, soon enough.* A tight pang squeezed her chest while curiosity had her studying every movement on Giles face to glean any information possible.

"Ah. In that case. You should ask him."

Robin frowned and peeled her potato, slicing her thumb on the imperfect blade. That was like dangling a juicy bit of bacon and then eating it out of spite. It left her needing to know more.

She supposed that was the point.

Chapter 17

Robin had been understandably shaken from the battle and he wanted her to relax with a refreshment. Riley wanted to be here, comforting her. Instead, he was stuck down here in the hold, dealing with the crew again. He only needed to keep them cohesive for a short while longer. Riley's tenure on this ship was coming to an end.

"She can't stay here," Kerr said. The man made a stink bigger than any other. Considering his size, it was fitting. Typically, Riley would screen men before allowing them to join the crew, but he'd detailed how urgent the recruitment was, so Randall was given power to accept any man with a working pair of hands.

Except in Landry's case of fewer digits, he had decent sailing knowledge.

Kerr had threatened Robin earlier, but even before that, Riley didn't like this man. He and his small pocket of cronies were getting on Riley's nerves. They were trying to turn the crew against him, but he couldn't formally charge any of them with anything, and tossing them overboard on no grounds would only lead to mutiny. Then both he and Robin would be in serious trouble.

"We've gone over this," Riley said, hands on his hips.

"We were interrupted," Landry countered, setting down a barrel taken from the merchant ship and standing next to his friend. Landry was a string-thin man with more sense than fingers. How he worked so efficiently with so few digits amazed Riley, honestly. But like Kerr, Riley didn't like Landry either. Fortunately, one's opinion of another didn't preclude them from working together.

"The rules state marooning is the fit punishment for stowaways. Now I agree with everyone; she gets no exception no matter who she is, *but...*" Landry trailed off to capture the attention of those around him.

Riley was certainly listening.

"But the nearest suitable island is too far from our course. We'd lose too much time. Instead, I have a satisfactory substitute, and it's one you can't deny."

Substitute meant she'd be stranded somewhere else. Riley's jaw tightened.

"With an empty ship over the rail, we can send her over and cut her free. Problem solved," Landry said with a self-satisfied smirk.

Over Riley's dead body would he allow these animals to abandon Robin, leaving her to fend for herself on the empty merchant ship and die of dehydration or starvation, while these men sailed away to their own riches. "She's staying on *this* ship until I disembark myself. I expect coordinated thievery from you, but that's cruel and you know it."

"That's funny coming from you." Kerr leaned in close as if trying to intimidate Riley into submission.

Riley restrained himself from punching the man in his plump face. Instead, Riley leaned forward, meeting his challenge. "What's that supposed to mean?"

"Word buzzing around says you insisted on marooning the last woman on this ship. You yourself led the charge against her, but now you changed your tune. Imagine that."

Riley had been the voice of the crew under Captain Henry Price. Like the situation at hand, Riley's duty then had been to stand against the captain in the matters of Miss Angela. Personally, he didn't like a woman on board. She was too disruptive. Was then and continued to be now.

But Captain Price had found a way, and Riley would, too.

"Even better, I think the wench needs a companion on the empty ship," Green, another new man, added with a petulant tone and stared Riley in the eye. "Someone who understands her. Someone to rescue her from a slow suffering death."

Green implied Riley was going to join her on the merchant ship, so he could kill her, saving her from dying a miserable death like a pirate. The idea of Riley being forced into something so heinous angered him to no end, and he couldn't sail the ship with only one unexperienced sailor. Riley grit his teeth and squeezed his fists. Their escalation was getting out of control.

"Are you suggesting a mutiny?" Riley asked, body rigid for a fight.

"Now, now, men. We can discuss this calmly," Vallo said with a friendly tone, inserting himself between Riley and Green.

Riley sent Vallo a suspicious brow. He, of all men, was the least trusted. If Riley had it his way, the traitor would've been cast overboard with the bodies from the battle.

"The only thing keepin' us calm is following the rules," Kerr replied while glaring at Riley. "Until someone steps up and decides to lead based on our written agreement, I consider us in a pickle."

"Well, for one I agree with the captain," Vallo said, sending him a friendly smile. "Let the woman stay with us. She's not the first. Possibly not the last. What harm is there in allowing her to help? We're all strong men, capable of containing our whimsies, capable of *patience*. Our turn will come."

Riley didn't like that last statement, but for now he needed to ignore it. With a liked crew member in agreement with him, Riley sent an appreciative, if not apprehensive, glance at Vallo. Now was his chance to redirect the crew before things got too far out of hand to rein in. "Vallo's right. Do we have the guns and enough shot to make a noise at the fort?"

McKee, said, "Sufficient shot for all hands. Plenty of swords and pistols, too. I'll make sure they're cleaned and prepared, but in this matter, there is no concern."

"Good. Now if we're done here, I have things to do." Riley turned on his heels.

"Better not be with that skirt," Landry warned.

"By rights, we deserve our turn with her," Kerr added. Snickers bounced around the tight room. "I'm glad Randall ordered her to her sleep down below with the crew. Who knows what will happen?"

Riley couldn't believe what he heard. "Robin is not to be touched. End of discussion." Riley moved his hand to the hilt of his cutlass. "Anyone unclear?"

The men stayed silent, biding their time. When Riley decided on Fort James as the target, he'd planned on rewarding his crew with treasure beyond belief and with his own sacrifice, making sure the crew survived to spend it. A worthy end to a long piratical career. But their lack of appreciation for his efforts had him doubting his plan.

Riley met the angry gazes from several of the crew, but they dared not speak up. They were placated for the moment, but it wouldn't last. Riley had to do something more, but even if it worked, he could never trust these men.

Robin had claimed the future was safe, despite Riley's firsthand experience, and every moment on this ship was a risk to her life. These men were animals. Riley needed to get her home before it was too late.

With a warning glare, Riley took his leave and found his quartermaster on the upper deck discussing logistics with Boatswain Karl. The captain had no time to waste with the threats to Robin's life.

"Randall, might I have a word?"

"Excuse me a minute, Karl," the quartermaster said, and Karl left. Out of earshot, Randall asked, "What is it, captain?"

"Kerr and Landry are threatening to leave Robin on the merchant ship when we set sail. I need you to get them under control before we reach the Gambia. That river has no exit points. We're either all in or not at all, and there's no room for disagreements."

Randall crossed his arms over his chest. "You put me in a quandary of a position. You're asking those men to ignore a grievous disregard for the rules that holds this crew in one piece...in order for the crew to function as one piece? That doesn't make sense. The solution to your problem was already given. Relieve the crew of the woman or share her. I've sailed on many ships, and never has this been a point of contention."

Riley's hand squeezed the hilt at his side. "Two shares of the prize for each man. Three for the officers."

Randall's brows lifted. "A rate simply unheard of. If what you say about Fort James is accurate, that is a substantial offer. You must love that woman."

Riley flinched. Why would the quartermaster make such an assumption? He was only doing right by protecting an innocent woman. Ignoring the ridiculous accusation, Riley said, "Do we have an accord then?"

"This raid was your idea. What about your share?"

Where Riley was going, he didn't need anything. "None."

Randall backed up a step, lips parting.

"But I insist Robin receives a share in my stead." Just in case things didn't go as planned.

Randall's lips pressed for a moment. "I'll convey the offer and do my best to insist their acceptance."

"Thank you." Riley patted the man's shoulder and set off.

He'd dampened the fire on their intent to abandon Robin or steal her for their own amusement, but at any moment the crew could mutiny, leaving Riley's efforts void. And now Randall's words had him fretting. Since meeting Robin in the future, weeks of drunkenness proved he couldn't get her out of his head, but the recent threats to her life showed him something he hadn't felt in a long time.

He needed to protect her—not to clear his conscious before the final raid, but because he, in fact, loved her.

Chapter 18

DESPITE THE PRIMITIVE TOILET in the captain's private quarters opening directly into the ocean, the noise and stomach upset from sleeping in a swinging hammock with the crew, horrible food, and almost undrinkable...*punch*, Robin managed to crack a smile. She didn't know what had changed, but the men were ignoring her, rather than looking at her as an enemy or a piece of meat.

She sipped from her mug what Riley had said was ale, and her face pinched, reminding her of learning to acquire the taste for beer at twenty-three years old. The more she exposed herself to the tart flavor, the better it would get. At least, that was what she told herself with every swallow, and it was still better than the punch.

She'd once thought going back in time would be a fun vacation. That was the dumbest thought she'd ever had.

William Price, the lanky armorer, stood at the head of the mess hall and lifted a mug for a toast. He called out for everyone's attention, and he hiccupped. When the crew quieted down, he said, "Many of you never met Hyde, our night watch on the *Sea Lion*. The man never cracked a smile in all my years of knowing him. Except once."

Men who knew the story chuckled with their memories. Price nodded to them with a wide, knowing grin.

"We had taken the *Elizabeth,* and Hyde wanted only one prize. He darted for the captain's private stash, claiming he could sniff out top-shelf wine like a dog. While we inventoried the hold and cleared out everything of value, Hyde found the captain's stash all right."

More chuckles followed and Price grinned.

"While we watched, he drank down his prize as if proving his prowess, but not a second later he spit it out in a fit of disgust. Turned out the captain kept empty bottles around for the times he couldn't make it to the head." Price folded over in his own drunken laughter.

Fits erupted throughout the hall. Liquid splashed from mugs, and men began singing in the far corner, which rapidly spread through the hall. A violin joined the tempo. Robin couldn't help a smile at their cheerfulness, so different from what she'd seen before.

A hand settled on Robin's shoulder, and a whisper tickled her ear. "Do you want to get out of here?"

Robin's lips pulled into a smile, and she tilted her head to find Captain Riley, but the smile slid away. A hint of despair shadowed his handsome features. What could be wrong? She took his offered hand. "Yes, please."

The captain gripped her tightly as he led her away from the wild after-dinner noise. Robin caught disapproving looks from Kerr and Landry on the way, and a shiver of nerves tore through her. At least they didn't say anything.

Up the ladder, Robin stood with Riley under a blanket of stars. Gentle waves lapped at the hull, and a soft breeze fluttered her hair. The music wafted up from below deck, a spirited violin accompanied by happy voices.

With a note of seriousness on his brow, Riley turned to her and said, "After all you've been through, you deserve far better from me, from all this." He waved his arms around to indicate the ship.

Robin frowned. Where was he going with this?

"Please hear me out. I have a favor to ask of you, and I want you to consider it carefully. But I'll give you my disclaimer first, I don't want you do to it."

Robin's lips lifted, disbelieving the severity of this mysterious request. "You can't give me all that lead up and not tell me what it is."

Riley ran a hand down his face, distraught.

Okay, now Robin was getting nervous. What did the captain want her to do that he didn't want her to? With the looks she'd received on her way up from below deck, she imagined the worst.

"Does…does this have to do with the crew's hate for me? Do you need me to"—she could hardly finish the sentence—"*placate* Kerr, Landry, and Green?"

"No, oh, no, not at all. Never. Don't ever think you would have to do something like that. I would never allow it." Riley collected her hands in his. "I sent a letter ahead to Commander Mitchell of Fort James, requesting an audience to discuss business. He regretfully declined, so I needed something more persuasive. I replied with an insistence my wife wanted to see the protection the commander offered the English Crown, and that she was especially impressed with the guns I'd told her about and the vast supply of soldiers."

The part of his story that stuck in her mind and replayed like a broken record was 'my wife'. The beautiful letter in the diary was to his *wife*. Robin couldn't believe after all this the man was actually taken, confirming what she'd dreaded. Robin didn't know whether to be insulted at his flirtatious behavior or hate herself for allowing herself to care so much.

"The commander accepted. You see my problem?"

What did any of this have to do with her? She looked at his hands holding hers. "Your wife's not here."

"Precisely. I need you to pose as my wife."

"What if I wasn't here?"

"Then I'd be putting a wig and dress on Buckley. Our odds would be ever slimmer." Captain attempted a humorous smile, but it didn't touch his eyes.

Riley needed her to pretend for this commander guy, but he didn't *want* her to do it. Did Robin remind Riley of his wife too much? Was she a temporary substitute until they got back together?

Not days ago, he kissed her like it was his last time. The vibes from him were clear that he had feelings for her, but this simple act of pretend was too much for him? Did he think of Gwyneth when he'd kissed Robin? She checked her anger and asked evenly, "Why don't you want me to do it?"

Riley exhaled. "It's dangerous."

"You said you handled the crew."

"Nothing is a guarantee, but it's not that."

"I don't understand." Robin freed her hands and folded her arms over her chest, hugging herself. "What did you do that being close to you is so dangerous?"

Riley flinched as if her words stung. "It's not what I've done, but what I will do."

"And that is?"

Riley sat on the rail and stuffed a hand through his hair. There was so much he wasn't telling her.

"What's already been set in motion cannot be undone. For that, I am sorry. Your cooperation, I believe, will help us succeed in my plan for the crew, but having you join me puts your life at great risk. One that pained me greatly to ask of you."

Robin stared, still waiting for him to give her something to understand.

After a pause, Riley's burdened face met hers. "If I leave you behind with the crew, our odds of success are far too slim, and I've told you about the narrow string keeping the crew in line. So you see, I must leave you behind, but yet I cannot. The risk is yours to decide. Pretend to be my wife when we pose as merchants at Fort James or stay on the ship with the crew. Kerr, Landry, and Green will be remaining on the ship during the meeting."

Since the crew still harbored resentment toward her, the answer was easy. Robin approached him. "I'll go with you to the fort, but I don't see how it's dangerous."

"Then I have failed to properly convey the situation. Fort James rests on a spit of land in the center of a river with cliffs, impassable mangroves, and sand dunes on either side. It has reinforced stone walls, harbors dozens of trained and armed soldiers at the ready with access to an endless armory, all led by an esteemed English commander. It is nigh impenetrable, and escape depends on...luck."

"Wait." Robin held up one hand while pressing the other against her forehead. "You want to stroll in there acting as merchants and overpower all the soldiers inside?"

"That is precisely correct."

"Why?" Robin could guess, since they were pirates and all, but she wanted him to say it.

"What do you think all that protects?"

"The English Crown?" she repeated his phrase.

"A vault of immeasurable wealth."

Figures. Robin couldn't even be upset about it, but the risk was beginning to settle into her mind, along with doubt.

"You think this crew can outmatch trained soldiers with weapons...and all their fingers?"

"I must be transparent with you before you confirm your decision."

Robin sat on the rail next to him, her thighs touching his.

"I hadn't planned on leaving the fort," he said softly, like it was a secret confession.

"What do you mean, like taking it over as commander?"

Since the crew had been on the verge of mutiny, that didn't seem like a bad plan.

"No." Riley stared at the deck, too ashamed to look her in the eye.

Not leaving the fort, but not taking over... He didn't mean, no, he couldn't choose something so selfish as that. Realization sunk in like a rock headed straight to her gut. Riley had nearly begged her to take him to the authorities. He didn't need to atone for a crime committed, no. Guilt of some sort drove him to want to end his suffering.

Robin appreciated he admitted his troubles to her, but she was furious he'd concoct a plan like that in the first place. It wasn't her place to be angry at him, but she couldn't stop it from punctuating her words. She hopped down off the rail and faced him. "This wasn't about *risk*. You wanted the crew to steal their riches, and you were going to sacrifice yourself so they could escape."

Riley nodded, confirming her theory. He still wouldn't meet her eye.

How could he do that? It was so selfish she wanted to slap him. "You *wanted* to kill yourself."

A glimmer of light reflected off the tears on his cheeks. Robin's heart broke for him. He was hurting still, and the anger drained away.

"Please don't think lesser of me. If I could go back and dash this plan from my head, I would. But it's too late now." He lifted his face her.

Robin reached out and wiped his tears away.

Riley pulled back.

Robin reached out again and closed her hands over his. Regardless of what his wife would think, Robin was going through with the plan to make sure Riley made it home to her. Gwyneth would have to forgive Riley's faults, or she wouldn't get him back at all. "If we are to pretend to be married, we need to be comfortable with one another. Let me do what I do best."

"What's that?"

"I'll cover your back, as long as you have mine." Good thing she brought her Glock.

Fresh tears glistening, Riley's lips pulled into a small smile. "I want to celebrate your agreement, but I admit I'm afraid. For tonight, dance with me." Riley hopped off the rail and framed his arms in invitation.

Robin glanced over her shoulders. "Does the crew know about this?"

Riley chuckled. "Their ire remains, but their disagreement has been settled. Join me."

"But that was for me to stay here, alive, not this—"

Riley pressed a finger against her lips and hushed her.

With a smile, Robin stepped into his arms, and his hands enveloped her. He moved them around the deck, slower than the melody commanded and careful to avoid obstacles in their path. A man overhead in the crow's nest sang a tune accompanying the music from below deck. Riley and Robin looked up and laughed.

And at once, Riley sang along.

Robin lost herself in his beautiful baritone melody, not listening to the words, but absorbing the fluid sounds comforting her. He carried them around the deck, avoiding obstacles, her and him, the sea, and the moon. And the beautiful music. And her heart sang. Despite knowing better, despite her history with getting involved with those too close to her, Robin's heart lifted with the melody.

Riley pressed against her and whispered into her ear, "You shouldn't have come here, but I'm grateful you did. Kiss me."

Before Robin could consider how she'd ended up in the past, his request brought their previous kiss to mind, and Robin wanted nothing else.

Riley leaned down, giving her easy reach to his lips, and he stopped their dance.

Robin gripped him tight. Heat surged through her body, pooling and throbbing down low, and she brought her lips to his. They were warm, soft, with little scratches of his grown-in beard. He pressed into her harder, and while they changed positions, she focused on his hips. To feel if he wanted her as much as she wanted him. She was going to keep kissing him until she felt him.

She hadn't forgiven his decision to take on the merchant ship, but to her, the captain had been kind and generous. He was a fabulous dancer with the voice of an angel. He was absolutely nothing like Blenny, or Angry Boston, or Riggs.

A strike of jealousy rushed through her.

Forgive us, Gwyneth.

RILEY HATED SHOWING HIS tears to her, but she moved him in ways he didn't know possible. He gripped the stunning woman from the future tightly, like his life depended on it, because it did. He didn't want to let her go, but he had to...eventually. That was a painful thought for another time.

He was a selfish bastard for asking her to take a chance for his unruly crew and his meaningless existence, but she agreed anyway—knowing full well the circumstances and risk involved. Now that she'd made her choice, it was up to him to keep her safely at his side, because he couldn't live with himself if something happened to her. The thin connection between them was the only thing keeping Riley's head level. He made many mistakes in his years on the sea, including taking the pirate ship disguised as Spanish merchants, but finding Robin might've been one right thing.

If they survived.

Captain Riley released her lips and hugged her tight, rocking with the music. Bauer, up in the mast, continued a gentle tune for them. The violin below deck quieted as the crew crashed for the night. Such as they must. Tomorrow they'd disembark and meet their fate. Tonight was too short.

Pulling back, he said, "Join me in my cabin tonight."

Robin's plumped lips parted. "We can't do that. The crew—"

"The crew is going to be wired and anxious over tomorrow's raid. You won't get any rest next to them."

Her lips twisted into a half-smile. "Who says I'd get any rest sharing your bed?"

Riley's head fell back, and he groaned at her forwardness. How did he get so lucky to meet a woman like her?

Robin's hands reached around his neck and pulled him back down to this new, amazing reality. "Let's go."

Riley grasped her hand in his and led her to his cabin. They slipped behind the door. Only the night watchman would've seen, but since Bauer offered the serenade, he mustn't mind.

Robin stopped in the middle of the dimly lit room. Moonlight bathed the floor in an aqua color, and Riley lit a candle. He wanted to see her. All of her.

He removed his bandolier with weapons and stalked up to her. Her eyes were hot, waiting for him. Not one to leave a lady wanting, his lips came down on hers once again, and he reached for her hips, sliding her dress up and exposing her smooth middle. She wore modern undergarments, and they were...quite pleasing.

His cock strained his breeches, and Robin panted, heaving her chest in the most alluring way.

She backed up a step, arms moving to wrap around her exposed middle. "This feels like some fairytale, but it's real. This is real, isn't it?"

"As real as my touch."

Thoughts wrestling in her mind displayed on her face. Robin sighed and frowned. She backed up another step and gestured to his bed. "I can't do this. You know I can't. I'm sorry. I thought I could." She picked up the dress.

With desperation and frustration coursing through him, he reminded himself he might not be a gentleman, but Robin was a lady. "Pardon my forwardness. It was not my intention to offend."

Robin pushed the dress over her head and wouldn't meet his eyes. "I have to go. Yeah, I have to. Goodnight."

And just like that, she vanished.

What the hell did he do wrong?

Chapter 19

Robin awoke in the swaying hammock with a headache and a dull pain in her shoulder. Carrying the weight of her gun and spare mags in her purse for so long was draining, and once again, she didn't catch enough sleep. The snores were one thing, pretending to be Riley's wife while he was already happily married was another. Robin needed to go home, she wanted to, so why was the pretend situation so upsetting?

With a groan, Robin fumbled her legs free of the loose fabric and sat up. The hammocks around her were empty, but an extra-large shadow of a man stood over her. Robin gasped.

"As payment for your passage, I have a need for you to satisfy. It's lodged somewhere here in my breeches." Kerr gripped her arm and forced her hand on his crotch.

Suddenly wide awake and completely disgusted, Robin twisted out of his grip and rolled backward across the hammock and up to her feet.

"What the…?" Kerr said with a growl. "Get back here."

"Keep your hands off me," she demanded. Knowing how precarious her presence was, provoking the man was a bad idea, but after that move, she felt it necessary. "You pig."

Kerr growled and shifted his weight to grab her, but Robin rushed through the gun deck filled with swaying hammocks, and climbed to the main deck. The crew was huddled around the captain's door. By the angry tones, something was wrong. Had something happened to Riley?

Heart pounding, Robin found a path to weave her way through the crowd while listening, hoping for safety in numbers and a distraction keeping her safe from Kerr.

"We never agreed to this. If you get a woman in your bed, then we all do."

Hollers of agreement startled Robin.

She checked her purse, verifying her Glock was still there, before slinging it in front of her body for easy access. Robin approached the captain's doorway, and through the stench, she found Riley filling the space, shirtless and terribly distracting. But alive.

"Now we get to tell her to her face," Landry said with a sneer.

Robin turned to face the missing-fingered man, and Riley shot her a quick look of apology before addressing the brute.

"Landry, have you spoken to the night watchman?" Riley shot a glare at Randall, who stood by the angry crew and wasn't doing his job of controlling them. "He can corroborate the amount of time Robin and I spent together. It's been a while since you were my age, but I assure you, I need more than a few moments with a woman."

A few men chuckled. The rest stared at him like they wanted him dead. If all these men had the quartermaster looking out for their own interests, who protected Riley?

Kerr approached from the back and glared at Robin. "We acquiesced to leavin' her on this ship and keepin' our hands off her for a hefty price. A price based on promises that have yet to be fulfilled. Her warmin' your bed wasn't part of the deal. She has to warm ours, too."

More angry hollers of agreement. A tingle of nerves skittered along her flesh, and the hairs on her arms lifted.

Muscles rippled beneath Riley's skin as anger erupted in his own sharp voice. "She is the only person on this ship that can guarantee your prize. Listen up, everyone. I did promise you double the normal share on this account, but for you to get that share, we need Robin, and you need me.

From this point forward, Robin is to be treated, not as a woman, not as a lesser, not as an object, but as one of the crew. And until we reach the shore of Gambia Island, she will share my bed, and *only* my bed. If anyone has a problem with that, challenge me now."

Robin gaped at him. If he wanted to incite a mutiny, she figured that was an efficient way.

"Any settling of disagreements is done on land, captain," Randall said evenly. "That's also in the articles."

Riley leaned into the older man's face. "This time I'm breaking the rules on purpose, so the men can return to what's important. Doesn't seem like anyone wants to focus on our account here."

"Randall," Kerr said, touching the man's arm with a light air of confidence. "The winner takes over as captain until the next vote. I think my skills would be a perfect fit."

Riley tensed. "Are you directly challenging me, Kerr?"

The man stood a few inches taller than Riley, but he tilted his thick chin up to make his point. "You heard me."

This couldn't be happening. Taken or not, Robin couldn't let Gwyneth become a widow when Robin could do something about it. She tugged on Riley's forearm, pulling him back a step, and she shifted her body in front of him as a shield. Robin two-handed her Glock and aimed at the angry crowd. "Back off. As the captain said, we have more important things to focus on."

The men exchanged glances of confusion and a couple chuckled.

Kerr belly laughed. "What are you going to do with that? Bop me on the head with it?"

The crew roared with laughter.

Robin's finger moved to the trigger. Demanding a favor in exchange for payment owed hardly justified a man's death no matter how depraved the favor to Robin was. Robin unwittingly broke their rules. They were right to be upset. Her vision slipped into a blur. Her hands trembled, bouncing her sight all over. Robin couldn't do it. She couldn't pull the trigger to defend herself. What was wrong with her? How was she going to protect Riley if she couldn't protect herself against a pig who deserved it? Robin's pulse pounded in her ears, and her chest rose and fell with growing panic.

Blenny had been right. Something was wrong with her.

Captain Riley's hand gently pushed the barrel down. He whispered into her ears, softening the pounding panic. "I have to do this."

"They're going to kill you," she whispered back, remembering his suicidal ideations. "I won't let that happen."

Riley's lips lifted in amusement. "Have you so little faith in my skills?"

Robin's mouth opened and closed, unable to answer that. She hadn't seen him fight, besides his wild attempt on a car bumper, but he'd also told her he wanted to end it all. Did she trust his word that he'd changed his mind? He seemed too quick to accept a mortal fight.

"Main deck in ten minutes," Riley said to his challenger. His voice rose, "Clear the deck. Prepare for a duel."

Kerr nodded and set off to prepare. Men dispersed to move barrels, lines, and stray supplies aside. Riley gestured with his head to invite her inside. She swept in quickly, and Riley closed the cabin door behind them. Without addressing the situation, he shifted through the clothes on the floor for his tunic.

"Are you crazy?" Robin spun on him.

Riley lifted a tunic and pulled it over his head. "If you would've asked me a few weeks ago, I would've said yes."

His nonchalance for the situation frustrated her. "They mean to kill you."

He tucked the tunic into his breeches. "It's a rare thing to have a captain unchallenged. It takes a great feat of bravery to do it in front of everyone. The crew needs a leader. They need someone to tell them what to do and in exchange, they're rewarded for it. Kerr is not a follower, and he's forward enough to vocalize it. The only unexpected part of this is the unfortunate timing. Rather than waiting until landfall, which is customary, we must settle this now. Where we're going, there won't be time for a duel."

Robin frowned, hating that a fight to the death was so commonplace and not in the least troubling to him. "Tell me you aren't going to lose."

Captain Riley's hands stilled, and he met her gaze. Riley laced his fingers through hers, and at the warm sensation, she closed her eyes, steeling herself for the answer she didn't want.

"I don't know what happened last night between us. We must speak of it later. But since you are comfortable with my touch, we'll have no trouble taking the fort."

Robin held his eyes again. "And if we never reach the fort?"

Riley shook his head with a smile. "Use that strange weapon you keep aiming. It does something effective, does it not?"

Robin frowned.

"I only jest," Riley said with a small lift of his lips. "I've sailed the seas for nearly a decade. I've been in this same situation plenty of times."

"You were challenged for the captaincy before?"

Riley released her hands and lifted his weapon belt. He wrapped around his waist and hung it over a shoulder. "I've taken men's lives with a blade several times before."

Robin dropped her eyes. Self-defense was one thing, and Robin believed in second chances, but *several*? Deadpan, she said, "You're a pirate. I shouldn't have expected anything different. Both of you can go slaughter a man who doesn't agree with you. See what that solves."

She turned to leave, but Riley's hand rested on her shoulder. With a sigh, she faced him.

Desperation filled his face. "Please be assured it was never without reason. Most of us don't want to take lives, but sometimes an amicable solution cannot be found otherwise. Kerr instigated this, and if I decline to follow through, they'll take the ship, and you and I..." he trailed off, voice breaking. Taking a moment to compose himself, he added, "They don't take kindly to cowardice."

Robin pulled away, hating the situation. "They mean to kill you."

"I didn't expect anyone to call my bluff this close to a historic raid, but for your sake, I cannot ignore the challenge. So long as you remain aboard, I cannot allow them to take control. The choice is no longer in my hands." He leaned in close, breath warming her face. "Unless that black thing you wave around is some magic force from the future, my sword is all that stands between them and you."

He was right. The crew had backed him into a corner on this. Riley had to fight. His steely gray eyes met her worried gaze, and his lips came down to hers. Her arms wrapped around his upper back and his hands pressed her lower back closer. She could never get close enough. She kissed him like it was a goodbye kiss, because as much as she wanted to believe his words, Robin wasn't so sure a large, angry man with dozens of supporters could defeat a resigned one.

As their lips shifted, Robin realized he could be thinking of his wife Gwyneth. If so, Robin could grant a man that last wish. Robin couldn't heed her own rule about dating colleagues, so her heart would be crushed, regardless. Perhaps his could be healed still.

The captain pulled away too soon and hesitated at the door. "I have full confidence in my abilities, but if for some unbelievable reason I don't win, I want you to know I'm sorry."

"For what?" Robin gripped the strap of her purse, fearing the answer.

The corner of Riley's lips lifted in a sad smile, and he left, swallowed by the crowd pumped full of anticipation.

Robin didn't want to wait here, while he was out there, defending them. But she couldn't face his death. The strap of her purse slipped, and Robin repositioned it. She had her Glock.

Chapter 20

THE CROWD WATCHED INTENTLY as Captain Riley and his challenger circled, swords in hand. Riley's feet were sure and steady, his hands tight and ready. Kerr was a bigger man with a longer reach, but he was also older. Riley had years of experience, youth, and quickness on his side. Riley also had something Kerr didn't: A woman who cared.

And she happened to be watching.

Riley wasn't trying to impress her with his swordsmanship. He only wanted to dispatch the challenger and return to the plan, with Robin safely by his side. If the outcome should be unfavorable, the crew would destroy her self-worth, abuse her in ways he couldn't stomach, and rip her to pieces for spite. Riley skimmed the crew, searching for her, but she no longer stood where she had been. Riley tore his eyes back to his competitor. Whatever might've been happening to her now was nothing compared to what would happen if Riley fell to the sword.

"Gonna circle all afternoon, captain?" Kerr taunted.

Riley had been waiting for Kerr to make the first move. At the larger man's insistence, Riley struck.

Kerr parried easily.

Another strike and parry combination. Then Riley waited, wanting Kerr to begin his attack.

"Come on, captain. I don't have all day. There's a woman waiting for me." Kerr sneered.

Gritting his jaw, Riley swiped fast and dodged a return swing, anger driving his movements. With another strike, he sliced the man on the forearm, but it wasn't enough.

Kerr touched the wound and laughed. "Little man makes little cuts."

A few observers chortled softly. The rest were too enthralled in the fight to react to Kerr's baseless insult. Kerr had never seen Riley fight. It was brave but stupid to challenge an unknown opponent with such high stakes. Some lessons were only learned once.

Riley gestured to strike again, but he held back, forcing Kerr to move. Riley countered his opponent's shift and struck him on the hip.

Kerr wasn't laughing any longer.

The crowd murmured. No one braved to cheer. Showing loyalties to either meant instant problems for the victor. Riley was fine with that. The fewer distractions, the better. His eyes returned to the crew, seeking Robin.

With his eyes averted from the fight, Riley had no time to parry a striking blade. He leaned back as the blade pierced his shoulder.

Kerr laughed.

Riley stumbled backward and leaned against the cabin wall. He touched the searing wound, and blood soaked his fingers. His lips parted. He couldn't lose. He had no intention of losing. But the slickness on his fingers and poor range of motion didn't bode well.

Worry lines formed on Riley's brow as his fingers pulled back with blood. Robin gasped, straining on her tippytoes. How bad was the wound? Could he still fight? Fury roared deep in her chest. These monsters stood around watching like this was some sport, but too chicken to stop them. Too unreasonable to accept a calm discussion. Too barbaric.

All of them were monsters.

Except Riley.

Robin wasn't going to watch him get killed because she somehow appeared on his ship. Robin gripped the Glock firmly in her hand and wove through the crowd, fighting their bulk and unreasonable stench. When she found the man with a raised sword about to kill Riley, Robin palmed her weapon with both hands. Her finger shifted to the trigger. She lined up her shot. Kerr's head was angled and protected by his arms. She shifted the barrel to the man's chest.

Shoot him.

Do it now!

Her vision blurred. Her hands shook. Not again! She simply needed to squeeze, take his life, the life of a man who hadn't done anything wrong besides argue about some frivolous rules they'd all agreed to and made her touch him. She didn't know Kerr personally. Was he a terrible man? Had he done awful things? Most importantly, was he right to insist on following the rules they'd agreed to?

Robin tried to steady her arms and focus the shaky sight. With the added rocking of the ship and her unsteady balance, she couldn't line up the shot. Her hands wouldn't let her take a man's life, even if that meant saving another.

What the hell was wrong with her?

Kerr's blade came down, and Robin screamed with her eyes closed and squeezed the trigger. A stupid, stupid move, but it was too late to do it over.

Her chest rose and fell, but she dared not look at what she'd done. Someone grabbed her shoulder and shook. Robin tucked the gun into her purse and covered her face in her hands. The men would be very angry with her. For interfering. For killing a man—one of their men.

"Robin," a man's voice said.

On a sigh, she moved aside her trembling hands. The cook stood before her, lips pressed firmly. The other men around her had moved away, giving her and Giles space.

"What have I done?" she whispered, knees shaking. "I'm sorry. I couldn't stand by and do nothing."

"Go help the captain." Giles said gently.

Robin tilted her head in misunderstanding, and the cook moved aside. Both combatants sprawled on the deck, blood spilled.

Tears shimmied her vision, and she stumbled over, knees giving way. She watched the rise and fall of Riley's chest. Shallow. The captain's hand moved, and with great effort he sat upright, breathing hard with pain. His eyes locked on hers.

"Are you okay? Stupid question. So stupid. I'm sorry."

Riley chuckled and grunted from the effort. The sound was wet. "That's to be determined."

"What did I do?" Robin glanced at the fallen opponent, still lifeless.

"You startled everyone. That's what you did." Riley sent her a crooked smile and closed one eye against the blood running down his forehead. "That magic weapon of yours sure has a kick."

Robin gripped the captain around the waist and helped him to his feet. "Am I in trouble? Are they going to...?" she trailed off, afraid of the consequences.

"Don't concern yourself. I think they're puzzled by that gun of yours. It's not a toy after all."

A pair of men rushed to Kerr's body and rolled him over. With morbid curiosity, she scanned his body for evidence of a bullet hole, but there wasn't one. "Didn't I hit him?"

Riley glanced over his injured shoulder with a wince and said, "Not unless you struck him with a steel blade."

"I didn't kill him?" Robin asked pointlessly, voice raised in relief.

"No." Riley turned to the spectators and said, "Get back to work, men. We have a fort to raid."

Men moved into action, keeping quiet. Three men hoisted Kerr off the deck and tipped him overboard.

Robin gasped. "Are they throwing him over?"

"If he were a respected man of honor, he'd be wrapped in his hammock and given a proper ceremony. Since he isn't, what else are we going to do with him?" Riley leaned in close to her ear and whispered, "You don't eat people in the future do you? I thought your food tasted strange."

Robin stared at him, mouth gaped in complete disbelief. Riley winked at her, but she couldn't process that he'd made a joke.

"Let's go to my cabin. I need clean clothes," Riley said, lifting the hem of his shredded and bloody shirt.

Robin assisted his steps. One man, on his hands and knees, scrubbed the puddle off the deck. With a cringe, Robin brought Riley into the captain's private cabin and closed the door. She released him on the mattress and kneeled at his trunk of clothes. "You bandolier should have leather straps on both shoulders. Would've saved you some damage."

Riley didn't answer. He slowly peeled off his weapon holster.

Robin shifted through his private belongings. Deep under the layers, where she hadn't ventured during the hunt for her own attire, she found a small sketch of a young couple. Robin squinted at it. The man had a striking resemblance to Riley, who winced removing his tunic. And the woman...that must be Gwyneth. Pressure squeezed her chest. A lucky woman was waiting for him. Jealousy ripped through her. She wanted Riley. For once in her life, she wanted a man, but he was taken. Politely, she said, "She's beautiful."

Riley dropped his tunic on the floor. "Yes."

"Gwyneth is a lucky woman," Robin said wistfully. It wasn't entirely appropriate, but she had to say what she felt. If he hated her forward implication, she'd apologize, but she didn't want to.

Riley raked a hand through his disheveled and tangled hair, fingers catching. He blew out a deep sigh of pain. "Word always gets around. The men on this ship gossip like a group of women at tea. What did they tell you?"

"They didn't tell me anything." Robin took in his chiseled bare chest smeared with dirt and blood. Heat rose in her cheeks. Underneath the grime, which she'd had the pleasure of seeing in her apartment, he was a beautiful man. With the grime, his strength was plain sexy.

And that only made her feel worse.

Riley stared at her with disbelief on his features. "After what they did to you, I'm surprised you're protecting them."

"I'm not," Robin insisted. "Giles told me her name. Nothing more." After a short pause, Robin had to know more. She pressed, "Is she waiting for you back home?"

Riley lifted himself off the mattress high enough to pull his breeches down. With his injured shoulder, he only used one arm. Robin should've helped, but she didn't want to push too far into his comfort zone. She should've looked away but forget it. He wasn't bashful, and neither was she.

"My father insisted I accept a marriage proposal from the neighboring landowner. It was a good match for our poor family. Of all the available suitors, I have no idea why I was chosen."

"I could guess," Robin interrupted with a shy smile.

Riley shot her a confused look, but continued while sitting back down, "I agreed before I met her. When she arrived down from her home in her carriage, sporting an ocean's worth of material in her dress, and her nose pinched in the air against our farm smells, I knew life would never be the same."

Riley shook the breeches off his feet, leaving him in socks and some antique form of underwear in a beige color. It wasn't flattering, but he could've been wearing a windbreaker from the nineteen-nineties and still been hot.

"Do you want a hand with that?" she asked.

"I've had worse." Riley shook a long lock out of his face and winced. The corner of his lips lifted as if hiding how much pain he was suffering. "Shortly after the agreement had been settled, my father passed away. I didn't want to stay, and it took little to convince Gwyneth to make a new life in the colonies away from the filth. Her brother sailed with us across the Atlantic on a slaver." He stopped abruptly, before his voice cracked.

The story was upsetting him, and it was none of her business, anyway. "I'm sorry for pushing."

Riley collected her hands and motioned for her to sit next to him, so she did, carefully.

"During the voyage, they both caught the fevers. With her last breaths, Gwyneth cursed me and my father and regretted the trip. She wished she'd never met me." Riley's head fell in shame.

Robin squeezed his hands. "Their deaths were not your fault."

Riley lifted a brow. "Easier said than believed, am I correct?"

Robin's face burned hot. Without a word, she nodded.

Riley continued his story. "When I arrived at port, I buried them both. With nothing left to live for, I took to the seas, raiding and pillaging ships, hoping for the glory of the win and the finality of the end. That's the truth, and now you know the real me. And if you hate the animal I've become, I understand."

Robin glanced at the floor and rubbed her thumbs on his knuckles. "I don't think you're an animal at all. You're the kindest man I've ever met, believe it or not. And I'm so sorry for your losses. Do you have any family to lean on?"

Riley faced her, eyes rimmed with pain. "I have no one left."

"I know what that's like." When she didn't have plans with Angela or Emily, Robin was alone.

"What about a father? Siblings?" Riley asked. "Or anyone else?"

Robin shook her head. "I was never lucky enough to meet the right one, and I'm an only child."

"Love has nothing to do with luck, and sometimes you must take a few wounds for it too. Love takes work."

Sometimes less work than she'd imagined. Robin snorted, remembering all the awful dates over the years. That counted as work. "You're right. It does."

"A woman like you must have friends waiting back home," he said with a hint of hopefulness.

"Yeah, I do." Robin dug in her purse and retrieved her phone. She hunched in disappointment as the glowing screen confirmed her fears.

"What is it?"

"No signal. I really am in the past."

"Just as I was really in the future. With you."

Robin swiped to bring up her photos. The battery was almost completely dead. "Here's me with Angela and Emily." She tilted the screen to his face, and pure wonder opened his eyes wide.

Robin chuckled. "I'm sorry for snarking at you about my phone at the festival. And it's not just a phone. It's camera too. I suppose you don't know what that is either. It, uh, captures a moment in time to save for later. I wonder what these two knuckleheads would say about this whole trip. Especially Emily. She would die for a chance to be on a pirate ship. That girl has a screw loose—" Robin cut herself off and glanced at Riley. "Sorry, I didn't mean..." she trailed off, wanting to change the subject.

Riley squinted.

"Sorry. I'm sorry. Sometimes it's easy to forget. Take a pic with me." She held the phone out and navigated to the camera mode. "Say cheese."

Robin pressed the button and looked at the captured image. Riley's face of shock and fear made her laugh. She showed him the image. "Now I'll always have a piece of you."

Riley smiled.

"Or at least until the battery dies."

"How can you preserve its life?"

She'd never heard someone think of it like that. "Without electricity and the proper charging cable, I can't."

"Sounds complicated."

"Lots of things are." Robin's gaze fell on the blood at his shoulder. "But this isn't. Your shoulder wound is still bleeding. Do you have a first aid kit so I can bandage it?"

"Bandages? Buckley knows where the doctor chest is."

Robin's features twisted. "The carpenter?"

"Who else? We haven't found a doctor willing to join the crew, and we haven't had luck finding one to press. We make do with what we have."

Robin checked his exposed skin for more injuries. He had a youthful glow on his firm skin, and his frame was wrapped in layers of muscle from the strenuous work of sailing a ship. He was younger than her by several years and simply beautiful.

Filthy.

But that was easily rectified.

She recalled again the glorious memory of Riley standing in her bathroom doorway, covered in a sheen of steam, holding nothing but her fluffy towel—an image she'd never forget—and then he'd dropped it. She wouldn't forget that either. Heat rushed up her cheeks. She needed to restore him to that glory, because it was her fault he was battered, bruised, and bleeding.

And he was single.

A KNOCK AT THE door had Robin moving across the room to answer it. Opening it a crack, she found Buckley had delivered a heavy chest. "I figured the captain was in need of medical attention, and that you'd prefer your privacy while attending him."

"Oh, thank you." Robin moved to take the chest from the carpenter, but he walked around her.

"Captain," he said, lowering the chest at Riley's feet. "You've made your case and proven your point. As much as the crew isn't happy about the situation, Robin should be safe now."

"Much obliged, Buckley," Riley said, dismissing him.

Buckley understood. He nodded at Robin and took his leave. Just before he crossed the threshold, he winked at her. Robin smiled in appreciation and closed the door.

"That was convenient," Robin said, kneeling at the chest and opening it.

"Buckley is a bit of a softy. How he tolerates such a crude living puzzles me, but he seems content."

Robin removed bandages that had seen better days, and a small bottle she sniffed and guessed was alcohol. It wasn't enough to sterilize the wounds, from what she remembered during her first aid training, but it was better than nothing.

She collected the torn, discarded tunic from the floor and bunched it up. Pressing it against the wound to staunch the flow, Robin said, "This shouldn't have happened."

"What?" Riley asked, gazing into her eyes.

"You getting hurt on my account."

"This?" Riley glanced at the fabric pressed on his wound. "This is nothing. A small cut is nothing against what would've happened had I lost."

Reading between the lines, Robin squinted and asked slowly, "You said you had full confidence."

Riley chuckled. "Did you see the size of him? His reach is longer than mine."

Robin's jaw dropped.

"Don't worry about it any longer. Being quick is usually better than being bigger."

"Usually," Robin mumbled, irritated that he'd gone into a fight so precarious and lied to her about it, so she wouldn't worry. And now she felt like an idiot. He protected her in more ways than one. For being a pirate, he was a gentleman. Robin's heart fluttered.

She pulled the fabric away, and the bleeding had slowed. She bandaged him up tightly. "How does that feel?"

"Better." He moved his arm around, testing its strength.

"Don't do that. You'll pull it open. You need as much rest as possible before this raid. How are you going to swing a sword now?" If Robin had it her way, he'd be on strict bed rest for weeks, but they didn't have that kind of time.

Riley collected the fresh tunic she'd pulled from the chest. She assisted him placing it over his head, allowing her fingertips to graze his skin.

"The same way I always do."

"And that is?"

"By knowing my life depended on it."

She hated when he spoke like that, like every minute could be his last. Due to weather, mutiny, a raid, or who knew what else, living on a ship during... "What year is it?"

"Seventeen-fifteen." He gestured for his belt, and Robin picked it up off the floor and wiped it down before handing it to him.

"I can't believe everything you told me was true." Robin fell back on the mattress next to him.

From what little of the past she'd experienced, it was the most dangerous time in history. The captain was injured. She was ill-prepared. And together they were heading into a guarded fort to steal their treasure. And still, she didn't know how many of the crew she could trust.

If they survived, she still had to go home.

Somehow.

Chapter 21

THE SHIP HUGGED THE river's bend, and Fort James closed in ahead, a sentry on the broad African river. As Riley had warned, cliffs on either riverbank meant no exit except on this ship, and the fort had a line of black cannons along the battlements. If the soldiers inside sniffed out Riley's intentions, the *Angelfish* wouldn't stand a chance against it.

And they would have nowhere to go.

Robin stood on the main deck at the rail, among the chosen few to accompany Riley into the fort. She was understandably jittery with nerves, waiting for Riley to return from his cabin. She didn't trust these men. Would they have their backs inside?

The raiding party had dressed in the best clothing they had, but only Riley and Robin wore jewelry. Riley also had feathers in his fancy hat, which no longer seemed silly, but quite fitting. Robin wore a gown from Riley's trunk, and it was foreign, uncomfortable, and way too hard to figure out how to put on. Her purse didn't match, but she refused to go anywhere without her pistol. On the bright side, the pretty layers made her feel like a princess at a ball. If she believed in fairytales.

She was starting to believe in unicorns.

With heat rushing her cheeks, Riley returned from his cabin, holding a small box, a jewelry box. "I have something for you."

"What is it?" Robin asked on a soft whisper of anticipation.

Riley opened the lid. A shiny ring with a stunning pattern carved in the gold. A wedding band. Robin's breath caught.

"I know what this looks like, but since we're pretending, we need to be as believable as possible. I've been saving this for years. I thought it was a shield, reminding me of what I lost to prevent that heartbreak from repeating. But... Instead, I think somewhere deep down, locked deep inside here I kept it out of hope." He touched his fist to his heart.

"Hope that somewhere, some*time*..." He paused, and his lips lifted in amusement. "A woman would unlock my heart, drag me from the abyss, and show me life was still worth living."

Robin smiled, wishing all that could be true for him.

"Robin, my dear, you're the one. You hold the key, and you showed me the light. You own my heart and soul from this day forth until my last breath. Will you be my wife?"

If only he didn't remind her of the pretend portion of their deal, it would've been much more swoony, but still Robin blinked away tears as if his words were real. She nodded and smiled, waiting until the clog of emotion in her throat cleared. It was almost too hard to accept on false pretenses, but this was what Riley said was needed to convince the commander. "Yes, I will."

With a warm smile of his own, Riley placed the ring on her finger. It was a little snug, but then she knew it would never be lost. She wanted a hug, a kiss, and a celebration of the joy between two people in love, but as the crew was watching and the proposal wasn't real, Riley returned to his duty.

"Raise the English ensign," Riley ordered in preparation for their arrival. "Let out the sheets and furl those sails."

Men staying behind sprung into action.

If things went wrong in there, the looming cannons weren't the only worry. Long before the commander would order the sinking of the *Angelfish*, she and Riley would be arrested for piracy, and all of them hung.

Riley shot her a smile as if calming her unspoken fears. His strong arm hugged her shoulder, keeping her on her feet. Facing a shooter on a public street with vehicles to take safety behind, a team at your back, and wearing armor was already stressful, but this was on a whole other level.

She was almost helpless. A few words were the difference between riches and gruesome death.

The men prepared a longboat for launch and a pair of oarsmen climbed inside, waiting to take them to shore.

Riley stepped forward and brought her knuckles to his lips. "You're next, my lovely wife."

Heat rushed up her cheeks, and her chest swelled. William Price chuckled behind them, ruining the moment by reminding her she was only pretending. She scowled at the towering, lanky man.

Riley held her hips while she crossed the open air to the swaying boat dangling by pulleys. Yet another boat—a smaller, weaker, less stable boat. Just great. She couldn't wait to plant her feet on solid ground again.

"Careful now. Wouldn't want to fall into the water. That dress is heavy." Riley said with a strange edge of worry in his voice.

"Of all things you need to concern yourself over, my ability to swim shouldn't even rank." Robin's movements shifted the weight of the boat, and it swayed drunkenly in the air. She lost her balance as she maneuvered and smacked her hip on the edge of her seat. "Ow."

Riley climbed in after and sat next to her, followed by the four accompanying them. He'd insisted they must be seen with servants from the household to be believable. Buckley the carpenter, Price the armorer, McKee the master gunner, and Cantu the behemoth joined them as escorts. Riley insisted he trusted these four with his life.

Vallo, who'd stood up for her, chose to stay on the ship with the quartermaster and all the men who'd showed her outright hatred. She'd made the right choice coming along.

"Lower us away," Buckley ordered after everyone was seated.

Her hands trembled as she gripped the rail of the boat. *Focus on land. Solid ground. Sand and dirt. Grass and stone.* The boat jerked and bounced as it neared the surface. The pair of rowers placed the oars in position and began stroking through the calm water. Riley held her hand.

"How certain are you this is going to work?" Buckley asked, hand resting on the hilt of his sword.

Riley cast her a side glance and squeezed her hand. "Sure enough to try."

Robin pressed her lips thin. "That's not very reassuring." And it was too late to go back. The crew would have their heads if they voluntarily returned to the ship without trying. As Riley said, cowards weren't tolerated.

"Where did you say you were from?" William Price asked. "There's something familiar about the way you speak."

Riley sent him a glare of death daggers, warning him to shut up. Price only smirked. The armorer seemed like the defiant type, so she wasn't surprised at his curiosity. Robin didn't know how to answer. Likely any mention of her visiting from the future would make them all laugh at her. They didn't need a distraction right now. Understanding Riley's warning look, she said, "I'm not from around here."

"Indeed," Price said. "I think you're being obtuse on purpose. Not so long ago, I met a woman—"

"Enough," Riley interrupted. "We are walking into enemy territory in disguise. We need to focus."

"Some of us are perfectly capable of holding a conversation while battle looms ahead," Price said.

"Battle?" Robin asked.

"He speaks figuratively," Riley said, brow darkening. "And dangerously."

"I beg your pardon," Price said casually. "You're too tightly wound, captain. You remind me of my brother Henry, and it's not a good look on anyone. Only a few weeks ago you were as laid back about this plan as I am now. Something's changed."

Riley stiffened at her side.

"Leave the captain alone," Cantu said.

McKee rolled his eyes. "Price is right." Turning to the captain, he added, "Relax, captain. It's the only way this half-cocked plan is going to work. A wealthy merchant is dauntless and confident. Right now, you're shaking like a leaf."

Robin focused on the captain's hand. He was not shaking. These men were teasing him, but why?

"You're both right," Buckley said and glanced at McKee. "Riley, you need to loosen your nerves and lighten up, but we all need to take this situation seriously. There's a lot of soldiers in there and only a few of us. This is a battle of words, and the odds are not in our favor."

Robin frowned. "What do you mean?"

Riley squeezed her hand quickly but glared at the others in the boat. "The plan is perfect, but it takes men acting responsibly to pull it off."

"It takes a man acting married." Buckley winked.

Heat rushed up Robin's cheeks, and Riley cleared his throat.

The other men chuckled at their discomfort. Jerks.

"It's the curse," one of the rowers said. The laughter stopped, and the men focused on the rower. He added, "Our crew is cursed. Ever since Lemoine became captain of the *Sea Lion*, we've been cursed. You should've warned the new recruits what they're in for."

"What curse?" Robin asked, a disbeliever in the occult until she'd fallen through time. The men had whispered about a curse, but no one explained what it meant.

"It's making our captains go soft," the other rower said grimly.

Taking offense, Riley shot him a nasty glare.

McKee laughed. "There's nothing wrong with choosing a warm woman in your bed over a ship full of unwashed bilge rats."

"Because there's a time you'd choose a cold woman?" Cantu asked.

"If I must have a woman at all, a cold, aloof woman between dawn and dusk is preferable," Price said, glib. "But as McKee said, I'd prefer a warm woman in my bed, too, as long as she understood to leave in the morning."

Robin scowled at Price's disregard for women. Clearly he'd had a few bad experiences. The men laughed, and she glared at Riley, who covered his amusement. In reality, their teasing was mild compared to what she'd heard on a daily basis at the police station.

The boat slid to a stop on shore and immediately the nerves returned, but her feet couldn't wait to reach the sand.

"I hate to ask this, captain, but is there a signal or point in time you want us to turn back for the *Angelfish*?" one of the rowers asked slowly.

"If you hear yelling or gunshots, return to the ship. Notify Randall. It is his decision to proceed or abandon the raid," Riley said smoothly, as if that had always been his plan.

"Wait. If we need help, they're going to leave?" Robin asked. The true stakes of this endeavor hadn't been revealed to her.

Riley gripped her hands. "If the captain is lost, the quartermaster is in charge until a new one is chosen. I cannot fault the men for leaving us, but if they do, they're stupid. Buckley is a fine carpenter and the best the crew has. Cantu has great power and loyalty. McKee leads the gun crew, and Price..." the captain trailed off. While Riley searched the thin man's weathered face with a relaxed posture, the other men's chests puffed with pride. "Price is a special guy who's great at keeping things sharp."

"You are correct on all points, captain," Price said. "But you're forgetting one thing."

"What's that?" McKee asked.

"Randall is new to the crew. As much as we all elected him our leader, how much can we trust him? Landry is still there. And I heard all the stories about Vallo. I don't know why he's been so agreeable lately," Price said.

"I don't trust them either," Riley said. "Which is why they aren't here. I don't need either one of them messing up our plans. Besides, the dozens of men on board can keep them in line."

"Let's hope you're right," McKee said.

The men climbed out of the boat, and Riley assisted her careful steps. Feet firmly planting on solid land, Robin didn't feel as good as she thought she would. The fort neared like an unpredictable, dangerous hive.

Taking a few deep breaths to unwind her twisted stomach, she smoothed the layers of her dress and hooked her arm under Riley's. Together they marched with their servants behind them to poke the nest.

Chapter 22

Before the woman on his arm appeared in his life, Riley was sure, steady, and confident in the upcoming steps necessary to meet the ends he'd planned—riches for the crew, but the return to Gwyneth, her brother, and Riley's father for him.

Now leading Robin toward an unknown fate, Riley returned her worried smile to comfort her. For the first time, he no longer pined for the relationship he now understood he wore blinders for. The real thing was right before him, and that was the problem. The risk to Robin's life, coupled with the crew's teasing had him worried more than her. Riley had chosen his men well, but if the uncharacteristic teasing slipped during the meeting, their entire operation would be compromised.

Servants didn't jest with their masters.

And then Riley would never get to tell Robin what he wanted to say during his pretend proposal.

The guards at the gate were heavily armed and well-nourished. With one last look over his shoulder at the *Angelfish* anchored in the middle of the river, Riley approached. Using the heavy English accent from his childhood, he said, "Captain Riley, merchant. Here for an appointment with Commander Mitchell, if you please."

The guards exchanged glances, and the first one nodded. He turned and shouted to open the gate. The creaking heavy doors spread wide like the hungry mouth of the kraken, ready to devour its next morsel.

Just inside the monstrous door, a man in fine clothing held his hands folded in front of him, waiting for their entry. "Right this way." He turned to lead them into the belly of the fort.

Riley held Robin tightly to his side, and his men followed on their heels. The courtyard was larger than it looked from the outside, and as hoped, they'd arrived in time for lunch. The soldiers were not on the perimeter battlement. According to his information, close to a hundred soldiers were stationed here.

The crew was ushered into a spacious room with a long table and plenty of light. Two soldiers stood guard at the door. The commander, wearing an extraordinary hat and many decorations of service, waited with his hands clasped together.

The raiding party, finally taking on the role of servants, spread out, as if ready to spring to Riley's every need. They kept their eyes on the floor and their mouths closed.

The commander offered his hand to shake, and Riley took it.

"I received your letter. This must be your curious wife. She's lovely."

Heat rushed up Riley's cheeks. If only she would be... "You're too kind, sir."

"Well, I'll admit I was skeptical at first, but you've convinced me to hear you out. Please have a seat. As for your servants of highest regard, I imagine they haven't eaten properly in weeks. If it pleases you, Captain, I'll invite them to the table with us."

Riley suppressed his surprise. The man was beyond reasonable, or he had very high expectations and wanted to impress Riley. Either way, he had to be careful.

"It does," Riley said. "Your extraordinary kindness is noted."

The commander nodded and everyone took a place at the table. Riley never released Robin's hand, and he never intended to until they were out of the building.

At once, a cart was pushed into the room. As Riley's crew watched the goings on, the commander said, "Sweetmeat, seasoned potatoes, and tea are on the menu. I hope it shall suffice."

The crew hid their smiles of approval. Soon the commander wouldn't be as generous.

"It shall," Riley said, pretending to not be impressed by the spread.

Real servants set out food around the table, a setting for each person.

The commander tucked a napkin over his cravat and lifted his fine silverware. "Your request said you wish to enslave natives. Is that correct?"

Riley shifted his fingers to spin the ring around Robin's finger. Hopefully she understood this conversation wasn't real. "How many can you have available for me by this time next week?"

The commander chuckled merrily. "In a hurry, I see."

Buckley, McKee, and Price attacked their plates with the hunger of sailors caught for weeks becalmed at sea. Cantu was more reserved, carefully observing before tasting. Robin didn't touch hers. Riley leaned down to her ear and whispered, "Go ahead. It'll be the best meal you've had for a while."

"Pardon?" the commander asked.

Riley smiled politely, "I was telling the missus there's no need to be shy."

Commander Mitchell spoke with his mouth full, "We are hearty men. Dig in, my lady. Enjoy the fruits of everyone else's labors." He swallowed and laughed.

Cantu lifted a forkful of meat to his lips.

Robin cringed at the food. As he'd struggled to swallow the 'burger' from the future, she stared at the dish before her. There was nothing more he could say to encourage her without giving himself away.

Reluctantly, Riley released her hand and finally tasted the offering himself. It was most excellent. The finest in sweetmeat, seasoned to perfection, and buttered bread with sweetened tea. Not able to help himself, Riley inhaled his food as his crew did.

"Let me hear this proposal of yours." The commander belched into his napkin.

And everyone believed pirates had no manners.

Pausing from his most hearty meal, Riley said, "My hold is vast enough to carry thirty slaves. I'm seeking strong men and a few boys to work my plantation. If we can reach an accord, I shall return in three months' time for another thirty. I'm paying top dollar for the best you can find."

"A sugar merchant?"

"That is correct."

"Why did you bring your wife to a man's business deal?" the commander asked.

Robin's face darkened, but she refrained from objecting, and Riley didn't like that note of suspicion. Off the top of his head, he expanded on the fib given in his letter. "She wanted to see more of the world, and she has a fondness for the Crown's forts. Isn't that right, my lady? And I can never turn down my lady's wishes." He gazed into her eyes and smiled warmly. For that he didn't have to act. Robin smiled back, but she was nervous. He'd expected that.

William Price's comment had been correct. Before Robin had become part of this plan, Riley had been confident and at ease about it. Now he was nervous, too.

Buckley smiled with a mouthful like an old coot. Price snorted, and when the commander darted him a look, Price said, "My apologies, commander. My digestive tract is articulating its appreciation for such a fine spread."

The commander nodded, accepting the apology.

Cantu was impassive. He still ate, but slowly and carefully. McKee finished his plate on time. Riley's trusty master gunner stood at once. "If you'll excuse my own digestive tract, I must attend the toilet. Please direct me accordingly and pardon my untimely interruption. It was not my intention."

The commander pointed to the door. "Between my men there and to the left. Ignore the rowdy soldiers in the Great Hall. We don't have visitors frequently enough to polish their manners."

McKee bowed properly and left.

Excellent.

Price and Cantu finished their plates much quicker now. Robin ate what she could stomach, and Riley didn't mind her pickiness. He'd hardly kept down the 'burger'. What an odd food that was.

"How were the winds on your journey?" the commander asked.

"Full and expedient." Now it was Riley's turn to ask questions. "A marvelous fort you have here. How many men do you keep in these high walls?"

"Forty, give or take. A good third of them are in training. Whipping these boys into any form of moldable man is quite the task."

That was also excellent. "My lady here is fascinated. She wants to know how you can defend the fort with so few hands."

"The parapets are high and the walls thick," Commander Mitchell answered Riley without looking at Robin. "Getting inside the reinforced iron door is nigh impossible. So long as the enemy stays out there, we're safe in here, as I'm sure your lady is happy to hear."

Robin smiled politely and nodded, accepting the commander's slight as she set her napkin near her plate. Riley was sure she raged beneath her calm exterior, but he was impressed with her performance. The commander was about to receive a few knocks to his bloated ego.

Riley finished his meal, and McKee returned from the toilet and nodded.

Time to make the move.

With a careful eye on the pair of soldiers, Riley pulled his pistol from his bandolier and aimed at their host. The soldiers motioned for their own weapons. "Commander, please order your men to stand down."

Next to him Robin gasped. Riley hadn't given her the details of the plan, because he didn't want her to stop him, and he needed her reaction to be authentic. If they lost their attempt to take the fort, she could be spared. A long shot, but the chance was worth the deception.

The crew drew their weapons, and the commander visibly shook with shock and anger. After a long glare of indecision, which would set their fate's course, the commander said, "Do as our guest orders."

Riley smiled, but no one relaxed. "I knew you were a smart man. Now, the location of the hold, if you will."

The commander's mouth gaped open. "When the rest of my soldiers discover what you've done, they'll hang you."

"They're busy," McKee said. "You're on your own."

"But..." the commander trailed off, confused.

"The Great Hall has a great lock," McKee said with a self-satisfied grin.

Riley said, "Commander, tell us the whereabouts of the hold and allow us to leave in peace and no one shall be hurt."

"You're...you're..." He looked from one face to the next genuinely hurt. As he took in their appearance more closely and studied their weapons, Commander Mitchell's features twisted. "Pirates?"

"The hold, commander." Riley stood and waved his pistol to urge his tongue. The other pirates rose. "I recommend not giving your life for King George's pocket change."

The commander lifted his hands in surrender and sweat beaded on his forehead. "I'll lead you."

Chapter 23

THE CAPTAIN KEPT STRIDE with the commander, keeping the gun visible as if the man needed a reminder to behave. Robin followed Riley closely, hand in her purse gripping her Glock. The commander's steps were stilted as if he warred with the decision to comply with the pirates' demands.

For a moment, she wished the jerk would make a wrong move, but his rudeness abruptly vanished once a gun was trained on his head. Under duress, people sometimes reacted in unexpected ways, and she was glad the commander turned to jelly rather than take the offensive.

Robin realized she'd been jelly, freezing during her home invasion, leading to her mom's death, freezing during a bank shootout, causing her colleague's death, and Robin had choked again when Riley fought to the death with his challenger, Kerr.

Robin was not jelly anymore.

Men rattled the Great Hall's doors, shouting in confusion and worry.

The commander stared at the door and slowed his steps as they approached.

"It's in your best interest to keep moving, Commander Mitchell," Riley said with a dark tone. He pressed the barrel of his pistol in the commander's side.

The commander wiped sweat from his brow and nodded, resuming his steps. The crew followed, working as a practiced unit—watching each other's backs, keeping an eye out for soldiers above, and aiming at every open passage. Their coordination was impressive. They'd make a great tactical unit if they were on the other side of the law.

The commander led them down a spiral stairwell into the dank and dim underbelly of the fort. At the bottom, the commander stopped. The mossy scent had Robin concerned over ventilation and air quality down here. Hopefully they weren't staying long. Ahead of the commander stood a heavy door with a barred window in the center. Beyond the door was a corridor of iron gates, and from what she could see, shelves full of wood crates. If she ever pictured a castle's dungeon, this was it.

"Through this door is the hold. The keys are hanging there." Mitchell pointed to a rusty ring mounted into the wall.

Riley smiled. "You made the right choice here. Men!"

Buckley collected the keys and unlocked the door, while Cantu and McKee gripped the commander firmly under the arms.

Price sidled up next to Robin. "You're doing fine. Keep it together a little longer."

Robin frowned at Price. "I don't need a pep talk."

"Suit yourself. I only wanted to stop you from waving that strange weapon of yours. The sound would be unfortunate."

Robin frowned and pulled her arm out of her purse. It wasn't like she was reckless with the thing. She had only tried to help.

"You can't do this! I did everything you asked. Let me go, I beg of you!" The commander whined and panted with fear, but he didn't put up much of a struggle.

Ignoring the pleas, the crew passed through the hold's main door, and ushered the commander to the first cell. Buckley unlocked the gate.

"No, please, no. Anything. I'll do anything you ask, but not this. Please don't do this!"

Cantu and McKee shoved the commander in. He promptly lost his footing and landed on his knees. Buckley locked him in place, and the commander rushed back to the bars and held them like he was going to continue begging. He didn't. Only the withdrawn look of fear twisted his features.

Robin's stomach swirled. Pirates in action, hurting people for their own gain. She didn't like it, but she didn't stop them either. Her only focus was making sure Riley got out of this fort alive.

The carpenter rattled the keys with a grin. "Let's see this immeasurable wealth waiting for us."

Price held up a metal pin with disappointment on his face. A pin Robin recognized, and confusion knitted her brows.

"And here I brought this bobby pin to pick the lock, marvelous thing, but I didn't need it. Such a shame." He dropped it into his pocket and closed in around the gate with the others.

Buckley unlocked the next gate, and it swung open on squeaky hinges. The men rushed to the crates, ripping them open with bare hands. Price found a metal bar nearby, and he pried the trickier lids. Metal coins rattled, and Price giggled with pure joy.

Genuine happiness.

A sound so foreign to Robin.

Burlap flew in the air and more of the men laughed.

It was contagious. Robin's lips spread wide, happy for them.

"Take what you can carry but don't injure yourself. We'll need several trips. Congratulations, men," Riley said.

The crew nodded to Riley with beaming grins as they walked out with arms full. Robin picked up a sack and flung it over her shoulder.

Riley's smile slid away. "What are you doing?"

"I'm helping. The sooner we get out of here, the better."

Riley considered for a long moment. "If we're caught, plead with them. Explain that I forced you. Can you do that for me?"

He was asking her to sacrifice him to save herself. After all she'd been through, not a chance. But since the stakes were precarious right now, Robin said, "Deal."

Satisfied, Riley picked up a crate, and they ascended the stairs together. Through the corridors, across the courtyard, and beyond the Great Hall with angry shouts and rhythmic pounding on the doors, Riley and Robin reached the shore. Arms full, Robin set down the sack on the sand. She shielded her eyes against the fading sun. Riley set down the crate.

The longboat was gone, but the *Angelfish* was still at anchor.

"They are coming back, right?" Robin asked.

"The load they carried was only a tease. The soldiers are locked down, and the doors to the vault are wide open. They'd never sail away from such an easy target."

Robin was grateful for a moment's privacy. "I've been meaning to ask you something."

"Go ahead." Riley turned to gaze into her eyes, ignoring the ship entirely.

"How did you get to the future?"

Riley's face displayed his confusion as he searched his memories. "All I remember is picking up a shiny necklace out of the sand in Nassau, confronting a traitor, and...that's it."

Riley went both ways. The secret had to be with him somewhere. "What about how you returned here?"

"Let's see. I was dressing in your home. I put on my cocked hat." Riley paused, considering. "No, I took off my hat and put on the..." he trailed off.

"The necklace," she finished for him, excitement growing in her voice as she worked through her own path. "I bought one from a vendor, and when I was walking in the grass, I put it on. That's how I ended up here. How is it possible two magic necklaces are floating around? Did that vendor know what she was selling? I remember she said to me, 'Amethyst has been known to grant your truest desire while protecting you from bad humors, so be careful how you use it.' I dismissed it as occult superstition, but she was telling the truth."

"What was your truest desire?" Riley asked with heat behind his eyes.

Robin dug through her thoughts at the time and snorted a laugh. "A unicorn. I wanted a unicorn, which I didn't believe existed."

She believed now.

Riley tilted his head, completely lost, while he dug through the layers of his fine clothing and showed his pendant on a chain. "I'm not sure I follow."

Robin copied, showing her matching pendant to his, and laughed. "I'm not crazy. They're identical; they're magic. And since you went both ways..." Robin trailed off as the excitement drifted away.

"You can go home," Riley finished for her.

She glanced at the gold ring on her finger. It was a little too snug, but it felt right like it belonged. "I can't."

Riley faced her, eyes flashing between excitement and worry. "The raid is a success, if not yet complete. The crew is satisfied, so there's no reason for you to risk your life in my world any longer. I must insist you return home to your own life, to what you know."

Riley's plea to leave him stung, and she fought back tears. His promise might've been fulfilled to the crew, but she wasn't finished yet. Robin smiled softly. "There's a reason I can't."

Riley peered into her eyes, waiting patiently.

Robin glanced away to compose herself. Whether he wanted her in his life for real, that didn't change her resolve. "I made you a promise, and I won't break it. There's a traitor on that ship, and I'm not leaving until I know you're safe. There's nothing you can say to change my mind."

Riley sighed and closed his eyes in defeat. "Promise me this. Promise me when I'm safe, you'll go home."

Swallowing a lump of emotion, Robin said, "I promise."

A crushing weight settled in her chest. Would that be the one promise she made with the intention of breaking? Only if the stubborn man wanted her as much as she wanted him!

At least she bought herself more time to convince him they could make this work.

Chapter 24

THE LONGBOAT HAD RETURNED several times over, and with wide open gates, extra pirates joined to speed the collection of the treasure. Robin made trips in and out of the hold, piling the sand high with crates and burlap sacks for the men to load up, not willing to leave Riley's side.

All this weight and all those crates...trip after trip. There had to be hundreds if not a thousand pounds of silver. Robin had never seen so much, and during their hunt for the last of the cache, they'd found a stash of wine. The pirates confiscated all of it, and several bottles were guzzled at once in a sea of laughter while the rest were squirreled away on the longboats for later. Before departing the fort for good, the crew fired off the guns on the perimeter battlements in celebration.

At least, in their merry state of drunkenness, they didn't hit the ship. Sometimes luck came in weird ways.

At the end of the day, the *Angelfish* drifted back down river, loaded with a lifetime's worth of treasure, and most of the men on board were completely smashed, but the rigging crew abstained until their shift was over. Someone still had to sail the ship out of the precarious river. As much as she hated boats, she much preferred the *Angelfish* to taking her chances with a fort full of angry soldiers, who still rattled the Great Hall doors as they left.

Robin gripped the edge of the table in the mess hall below deck to steady herself. Unlike the crew, she still wasn't used to the movement.

Several men she hadn't met shared the table, but Riley sat next to her, and Cantu and McKee were across from her.

"What a mighty fine plunder we found, captain! A most successful raid. I didn't think it possible," McKee said and chugged down his mug of wine.

"I'll admit, the drink on this ship has improved," Cantu said, smiling.

That Robin could agree with. She sipped from her mug, stomach sloshing from the movement, and although she wished for water, the wine was better than ale, punch, or rum.

"Are you well?" Riley asked her. "You've been quiet."

"I hate boats, mix my stomach with wine, and I'm a little unsettled. No more wine for me."

"Why on earth do you hate boats?" McKee asked, brows raised in astonishment.

"I was on one a few years ago. Everyone was drinking." She pointedly looked at those around her.

"Sounds like a good time," Cantu said. He and McKee banged mugs and drank.

"They drank too much," Robin added, and the others listened. "A small fight rocked the boat, and everyone tried to break them up. One thing led to another, and most of us went overboard."

"That's no good," McKee said.

"It was dark. I was a good swimmer, and a few of my friends, too, but a few of us never made it back to the surface. Alcohol and water never mix well."

Riley rested his hand on her lap. "I had no idea."

"It didn't seem like a relevant point to bring up." She didn't need to give Riley another reason to insist she went home, so she'd kept it to herself.

"It's a good thing this ship is strong and study. No one's going in the water unless they want to," McKee said. "Or we make them."

She hoped that was true.

"Honestly, captain, I didn't think you were going to pull it off," Bauer said from the end of the table. Robin hadn't heard him speak before, but his fluid voice matched that of his beautiful singing voice.

Still didn't compare to Riley's. His voice in the shower was captivating.

"Me neither. But I'm damned glad you did!" Gunner, the scrawny teenager said and laughed.

Riley smiled and nodded. Others laughed.

"To endless wealth," Watts said, raising his mug. Cantu, McKee, Karl, and Price joined him. "And endless women and booze."

Robin frowned.

The men clinked mugs and drank, spilling wine down their faces. Nothing could ruin the crew's mood, and for once, Robin felt perfectly safe around them, Glock or not. She smiled and clasped her hands around the mug.

Buckley curled into a seat at the table on Robin's other side. "I'll drink to that every day. Maybe you're not the curse we thought. Perhaps this time, you're a good luck charm."

Riley stared at Buckley with that same death gaze. Robin's curiosity drew her in. "What do you mean by 'this time'?"

"You're not the first woman on board," Buckley said. "Not even the second."

That was what Giles meant when he'd said, '*A woman popping out of the hold.*' If others had been here before her, their surprise, fury, and insult at her appearance was unfounded...and infuriating. "And yet you treated me like some thief stealing passage."

"Men don't change easily," Cantu said. "Especially when you have new crew members." He darted a look at Vallo, Green, and Landry who shared a different table with the quartermaster.

"He's right," Riley said. "These men before you are familiar with the phenomenon. Those aren't. And a divide of the crew is difficult to manage. It always leads to conflicts and unwanted skirmishes."

Remembering her own random appearance on the ship, perhaps these men knew more about this mystical occurrence than she did. Maybe she'd find out what happened to those women. "What do you know about the curse?"

"It's witchcraft," McKee said. "As long as it keeps us in women, I'm bound to get one eventually, so I have no qualms."

Giles had told her the same sentiment. Men laughed.

"Every time a new captain has been voted in, a woman appears on board. The captain leaves us for her. Once was unfortunate. Twice a coincidence." Cantu sipped from his mug and stared her down. His eyes flicked to Riley for a second. "I no longer believe in coincidence."

Riley said nothing.

"Why are you looking at me like that?" Robin sipped from her mug to hide her face.

"You know why."

They assumed she was going to steal Riley from them and do what? She didn't live here. Riley's home was this ship, and there was no way she'd consider this pile of boards to be home. How crazy of an idea was that? How preposterous? How...? Robin was done drinking. More wine would only loosen her up more. The last thing she needed was to lose control.

"Well, I think I've had enough drink for the night. Robin, care to join me?" Riley held out his palm.

Several of the crew smiled knowingly. A couple cackled.

Robin took his hand, and he led her up to and across the main deck. Guess there'd be no dancing tonight. The idea bummed her out.

"Tonight," Riley said, stopping at his cabin door, "you're staying with me the whole night."

Robin relished the idea, but… "But what about the crew?"

"They're fed, drunk, and buried in so much silver they can't think straight. We'll be left alone."

"If you think so." The last thing she wanted was to be caught in bed. Rules were rules, regardless of riches. At least, that was the crew's whole problem with her. "You're a rich man now, captain. So what do you plan to do with all your plunder?"

Riley cast her a knowing grin and gestured for her to follow him inside. Robin did. Closed into together, he stalked up to her with hunger and desperation in his eyes. He brought his face close to hers, and his hands reached for her throat, thumbs skimming her jaw. "The only plunder I want is right in front of me." He paused, and demanded quietly, "Kiss me."

He didn't have to ask twice.

Robin's lips found his, and she pressed her body against the firm muscles beneath his layers of clothing. One by one, she stripped off the pieces covering his fine torso and released them. Riley reached around her and worked the buttons of her ill-fitting dress, while she ran her bare palms up the curves of his chest, from the rigid abs flexing with his movements to his pectorals, flickering from the effort. She kissed his throat in a teasing line, and Riley paused for a moment to groan.

Robin smiled from her prowess affecting him so.

The dress tore free and fell to the floor.

She wore her modern underwear, and Riley took a long look at her. The corners of his lips lifted. "Simply beautiful."

With a soft laugh, she said, "Shut up and get over here."

Riley scooped her up in his arms and settled her on the mattress. Looming over her and gazing at her with the hunger of a starved man, Riley worked at the ties fastening his breeches. Robin assisted. Once the knot worked free, she pushed the material down. Riley leaned upright on his knees and shrugged out of his drawers.

She drank in his beautiful, towel-free body, and it was simply divine.

Robin lifted her hips and slipped off her underwear. "Come here before I get cold."

A sly smile touched his lips. "Unlike Price, I only want a warm woman in my life, even if that means I have to work you all night to keep you hot."

Robin grabbed his neck and pulled him down. "Time's a-wastin'," she sang deviously.

Riley growled and positioned himself. His mouth found her body, and he paid attention to every heightened nerve on her skin, making her sing for him.

Captain Riley didn't quit until he sated the delicious throbbing pooling between her legs, and even though Robin begged him to deliver the thrusts faster, to climb that pleasure mountain quicker, Riley kept her quiet by capturing her lips as the explosive orgasm contracted every muscle in her body.

Sex was forbidden on this ship, but Robin couldn't have waited any longer. She loved him, and she could never let him go.

A POUNDING ON THE cabin door pulled Robin upright. The sheet fell away, exposing her breasts. Riley sat up, bleary-eyed, but he perked up when he caught an eyeful.

"You're the most beautiful and appreciated morning view I've ever had."

Robin smiled.

The pounding repeated.

"Something's going on out there," Robin said. "And they don't sound happy."

Riley climbed out of bed and dressed.

Unable to waste time on the excessive buttons, Robin found her previous dress from Riley's trunk and slipped it over her head. They dressed quickly together, chuckling softly like busted teens.

"What do you suppose it is?" she asked, balling up the fancy dress and dropping it into the chest. Hoping Riley had been right about their nighttime escapades being overlooked.

"Not sure." Riley tied his breeches while glancing out the cabin's windows and squinted in the rising dawn. "By now we should be leaving the mouth of the river, so from here out we should have smooth sailing back to Nassau for a couple weeks. Doesn't look like the weather is a concern." Riley fastened his weapons belt and slipped into his boots.

After a quick glance over his shoulder to make sure Robin was covered, he nodded, and stepped out.

Robin only needed an extra minute before she followed. On the main deck, the men gathered near his door. This time, Landry led the charge.

"A duel wasn't enough to scare the captain straight," Landry said, addressing the crew while snarling at the captain. "Silver and wine aren't enough to bribe me. Clearly the captain's got his head in the wrong place, and we need to do something about it."

Not again. Didn't Riley's success over Kerr and the raid on the fort mean anything to these monsters?

"Ah, there she is," Landry said, spotting her in the crowd. "The object of Riley's distraction. Last chance, captain. Either she accompanies me to my hammock this moment, or I officially call a duel. You and me or her and me. The choice is yours."

Robin wanted to know how Landry could confidently wield a sword with so many fingers missing, but if the man was brave enough to publicly challenge Riley, he had a reason to expect he'd win. As worried as Robin was about the treasure having no impact on the crew's view of her, she was morbidly curious.

"I don't think so," Vallo said, pushing his way through the gathered crowd.

Landry stared at the short man with hatred. "What did you say to me?"

"You're not challenging the captain. He's done a great job with this account. Regardless of the status of his...breeches...he's a remarkable captain."

Riley stared at him, completely baffled. Although Robin had experienced Vallo's support, this was a higher level than she'd expected considering Riley didn't trust the man.

"Oh, and what are you going to do about it?" Landry sneered.

With a quick movement no one saw coming, Vallo unsheathed his sword and buried it deep into Landry's scrawny neck. Robin flinched in surprise, as did half the crew. Riley's eyes widened.

A calm smile crossed Vallo's lips, and he pulled his sword free. Landry fell to the deck with a wet thump.

"Now, can we continue the celebrations?" Vallo asked.

The crew whispered to each other, deciding what to do next.

Green pushed his way through and scowled at his downed friend, displaying the revolting teeth in his mouth. "I say we hold an election this instant."

Robin's spirits sunk. Riley had told her the only thing standing between the crew and her was his sword, but if he lost the captaincy, the new captain's rules were fair game. She trusted Riley, but she didn't believe he could dispatch every man who insisted on taking her to bed.

"Now—" Riley started.

"A new quartermaster," Bauer, the night watch crooner interrupted and winked at Riley. "Some of us feel Vallo fits the position better. He knows what's best for the crew, and he's willing to act on it. So I say cheers! All those in favor?"

More whispers followed before the cumulative "Ayes" filled the air.

Vallo smiled and bowed. "Thank you all kindly."

Randall pushed his way through, a nasty scowl filling his features. "What did I hear?"

Vallo said with a smug smile, "You're out. I'm the quartermaster now."

Randall opened his mouth to object when a man high above in the rigging shouted, "Sails!"

Heads turned up, looking for the direction. At once the celebrations of the successful raid and the change in vote ended. Soberness took over as if they hadn't spent the night enjoying the bottom of many, many wine bottles.

Something was wrong.

Chapter 25

Head reeling with confusion and alarm from the abrupt change of quartermaster to a known traitor, Riley relished the day watchman's interruption. Just outside the mouth of the river, with bluffs all along the coast, a ship was closing in from somewhere. Riley concentrated, squinting into the night, and there... She was there. His eyes widened as he scrambled for the spyglass. He pressed it to his eye and sucked in a breath. The faintest glow of the coming dawn outlined her.

Peibo del ler San Francisco.

But how?

Riley gave his orders for a full sail with urgency. Their two advantages were draft and speed. They had to outrun her. They had no other choice.

"What is it? Who are they, uh, she?" Robin asked, approaching the rail at Riley's side.

Riley turned to her. The moonlight bathed her worried face. "An old enemy. That ship has no reason to head this way. Someone must've disclosed our course ahead of time."

He had only one guess who it was, but after Vallo's uncharacteristic friendliness to the crew, Riley couldn't accuse him otherwise. If the crew survived this encounter, Riley would see the traitor's punishment meted out with his own hands.

"Are they pirates too?" Robin asked, confused.

If only.

"*Peibo del ler San Francisco,* a Spanish warship captained by a man who has a history with our crew and a thorn in his side, a one *Capitán* Delgado. He's ruthless, he's angry, and he's been embarrassed. We're tacking along the coast. With the shallow draft of the schooner, it's our best chance to stay out of range."

But they were heavily weighed down with treasure from the fort.

"And if they enter the range needed?" Robin asked, voice shaking.

Riley didn't want to lie to her. "God help us."

Robin hugged Riley's middle and watched with him as the enemy sails became clearer to see. The *Peibo del ler San Francisco* followed their course precisely. The *Angelfish* had been spotted.

Riley hated that Robin stood here on this deck with battle looming once again, but this time their odds of survival were lower than slim.

A dull ache pressed against his chest, making breathing difficult. He had to issue the order at the cost of his own happiness. Riley choked back emotion until he could speak. He gathered her hands in his. "Robin, listen to me closely. Our schooner is severely outgunned. That's a warship. If we are forced to fight, we will lose." He pushed her to arm's reach and stared into her eyes. "Do you understand me?"

"I get it, but there must be some way out of this." She craned her neck, searching for an answer, but one side was open ocean with a warship and the other side was nothing but sheer bluffs. He saw no other answer.

Riley blinked rapidly. He'd risked her life too many times already. This wasn't a risk; this was certain death. "I want you to leave. Understand me? I need to know you're safe. Take off the necklace, and put it back on."

"I...I can't leave you like this. I promised, and I won't go back on it now." Robin pulled out of his grip.

Heart breaking, he begged, "If you stay, you'll die, and I can't live with myself knowing I did this to you. Please return to the safety of your home. I want you to live. That's enough for me."

"My decision to stay is not your fault. And why are you so doom-and-gloom? Your own crew said you have more experience on a pirate ship than any man here. Fight back, escape, do whatever it is you always do to win." Tears leaked down her cheeks.

A cannon fired, the boom echoing against the cliff. Robin covered her ears, and the splintering bang and screams hollowed Riley. He couldn't stand this. He wouldn't allow this. He reached for her throat and lifted the necklace over her head. Robin dove for his hand in a panic.

"Gun crews at the ready!" Captain ordered, and McKee carried the words to his men, who scrambled.

Another boom followed the first, and the chain shot severed a mast. Splinters flew. Wood cracked and creaked. The mainmast, tangled in lines, groaned as it toppled.

Their ship was a dead stick in the water.

"Open fire!" Riley ordered.

McKee took command of his gun crew, and guns exploded in retaliation, the booms deafening. While Riley was distracted with the orders, Robin stole the necklace from his hand.

Riley returned to face her. "We lost the main, and the hull is next. You need to go or we all drown."

Robin sniffled with the necklace in her fist. "I said I'm not leaving. If you want to use yours to escape, I'll go with you. Until then, I'm staying here by your side." Staring him in the eye, she threw the necklace overboard.

Riley fastened his palms against her cheeks as booms of guns fired both ways. Wood crunched and splinters flew. Injured men screamed. "Stupid. That was stupid, Robin. Can't you see? We won't survive this."

Her hands wrapped over his, and she sobbed. "I'm not leaving you."

The ship listed. Men cried out. Candles snuffed out from the splashing water.

The ship was going down. Hopefully so close to shore, the water wasn't too deep.

Riley couldn't swim.

She was stupid, but she was stupidly and stubbornly going to save Riley. The ship tilted severely. Robin lost her balance and tumbled. Riley gripped a rail and continued shouting his orders over the deafening noise. Keeping her Glock around her body like a lifeline, Robin caught onto the opposite rail and gripped it with all her strength. A cannon ball blew a hole in the rail near her, but she didn't get hit with any splinters. She still yelped in surprise.

The ship's tilt meant their port cannons pointed toward the water, useless to fire. The ones on the other side of the deck rolled uncontrollably backward, aiming in the wrong direction. They were useless, too. Water climbed the deck. Men rushed up from below with weapons tucked into their sashes and belts.

"There's nothing more we can do, captain," Cantu said. "She's going down. The *Angelfish* is lost."

Robin climbed away from the rising waters toward Riley, but the slickness of the ocean spray and lack of handholds left her sliding. Robin climbed on all fours, knees catching on her dress. Around her, men fell into the water. Some splashed, shouting for help. Others sank quietly.

Robin reached Riley's side. "Stay on the ship as long as possible."

"Aye," Riley said. His tone carried defeat.

Smoke from the gunpowder obscured the growing dawn's light, and slowly the cannon fire stopped. As the water filled the hull, the ship's angle straightened out and water rushed over their feet.

"It's going to suck us down if we don't get away now," Riley said evenly. All fear and anger had left him. He was resigned to their fate. She wasn't. The water reached her waist.

"Where do we go?" Robin asked.

Riley pushed wet hair away from his face. "I don't know. We're a league from the fort."

Could Robin swim upstream for three miles? The deck fell away from her feet. Robin dove to the side, off where the rail had been, swimming away from the deck to safety from the suction. She wouldn't have a choice now. Robin surfaced, turned around, and treaded water. Riley wasn't behind her.

"Riley!"

She spun, searching for him, fighting the weight of her purse and awkward clothes. "Riley!"

He was gone.

Robin dove under the water and opened her eyes. The coming dawn sprayed light, illuminating the clear waters below. The *Angelfish* had stopped sinking. It sat in about fifteen feet of water, the keel forcing the ship to tilt severely onto the sand bed beneath. Silt billowed slowly around it, but Robin found Riley, gripping a mast angled about seven feet below the surface. He was trying to climb to the surface.

Robin swam over to him. She grabbed his arm and pulled, kicking with all her might. He was like dead weight, but she moved her burning legs, because she had no other choice. Breaking the surface, she gasped. Riley took a breath before they were pulled back down. His clothing was too heavy. She maneuvered to his boots and removed them. Then she pulled his fancy coat off. With that, he was buoyant enough for her to keep him above the water.

Riley gasped again and then started sinking.

He couldn't swim.

And she couldn't keep bringing him back up for breaths. Her strength would only hold out for so long, certainly not for three miles of this, regardless of the dozens of soldiers waiting to arrest them. She had to swim to the warship and hope for mercy.

She dragged him. His arms paddled, helping.

"Kick your feet. One after the other. Keep air in your lungs. You can do this," Robin said between waves splashing at her face. Waves that fought to throw them back against the sheer cliffs.

Panting hard, Robin kicked and pulled, fighting to keep her head above water with the weight of Riley dragging her. She would not quit. Up and down the waves, she fought, closing in on the warship.

With each stroke, she spent more time paddling below the surface than above. The weight was dragging her down too much, but they were so close.

"Hang in there. We're almost there."

Relying on her feet to propel her, she used her arm to reach for the ship's ladder. Farther and farther she pushed, and finally her hand gripped the slick wood.

"Grab it. Take it," she ordered, pulling him within range and panting.

Riley gripped the wood and pulled himself free of the water. He coughed and gasped and dashed water from his face. "Why did you bring us here?"

"Where else was there?" she asked.

Riley offered his hand and pulled her onto the ladder next to him. "I don't know, but we can't stay here."

"*Usted!*" an angry voice from above shouted down.

Riley and Robin craned their heads.

"Do you speak Spanish?" Riley asked.

"A little."

"*Sube aquí de inmediato, o disparamos.*" The soldier pointed down at them.

"I didn't understand any of that, but I have a feeling he wants us to climb," Riley said.

"Climb or they'll shoot," Robin said.

"Thank you," Riley said breathlessly, too dramatic for the simple translation. His brows tilted with appreciation, but the lack of worry concerned her most. "Thank you for saving me in more ways than you can imagine."

"Oh, no, you don't," Robin said, reading between the lines. "This isn't goodbye. We'll figure out something."

His hand cupped her jaw. "I admire your optimism, but I'm afraid it's misplaced." His lips found hers and desperation poured through him. A kiss goodbye.

Emotion squeezed her throat, and her lips shifted with sobs. Robin pulled back. "This isn't goodbye. I won't allow it."

"¡Último aviso! Cinco...cuatro...tres," the voice said.

"That I recognize. It's a countdown," Riley said, standing and climbing. "Follow me."

Robin climbed the wet ledges behind Riley. Splashes behind her turned her head. More men were swimming to the warship. At least they weren't alone.

Falling over the rail with a mixture of relief and fear, Robin was circled by soldiers in uniform with muskets outfitted with bayonets at the ready. Robin lifted her palms in surrender. Riley did the same.

Through a break in the soldiers, a man dressed in a higher fashion than the remaining men approached. *Capitán* Delgado, she expected.

More men clambered over the rail behind her and Riley. First Buckley, then Cantu and McKee. Two more men she hadn't met appeared next, but she'd seen them working in the rigging.

All their hands reached skyward too.

Capitán Delgado stopped, hands casually fastening in front of him. His eyes tracked over the newcomers with unreadable features on his thin, lined face. His English was heavily accented. "I know not who you are, but I know that ship. That was my prize stolen by Captain Henry Price. Is he among you?"

"No," Riley said, taking the lead for his remaining men.

Another man dropped over the rail. William Price. He lifted his hands in surrender.

A smug smile lifted Delgado's lips at the news. "He is perished then?"

"No," Riley repeated.

Delgado's features darkened. "We misunderstand. Captain Henry Price is dead?"

William stepped forward. "He might as well be. He's married."

Delgado frowned and stepped closer to Price. "Your attitude is familiar. We've met, have we not?"

"I'm sure I would remember such an ugly mug, like the ass end of a dog."

Delgado visibly shook with contained rage. "I insist a miscommunication between us, correct?"

Price shrugged.

"Which among you is the leader?" Delgado said.

Riley stepped forward, but not without Robin's grip holding him tightly.

Capitán Delgado sized up Riley. "How did you come to own my prize?"

Robin checked the crew around her. Each moved hands to the hits of their weapons. She stuck her hand in her purse. The accuracy rate of those primitive Spanish weapons was not great, but at this range, they wouldn't need to be. Question was, did the antique pistols of the crew work after being submerged?

Her Glock did, and she'd rather fight and die than stand here, waiting to be slaughtered.

Delgado's keen eyes tracked their movements. He stepped back at once. "Stop now, or you'll all be killed."

The pirates exchanged glances, and Riley gestured to stop them.

With a smirk, Delgado said, "To the hold. All of them. *A la bodega, todos ellos.*"

The muskets were lowered, and the survivors were collected with tight grips on their upper arms. A firm grip wrenched Robin's hand from Riley's. He faced her with a look of sorrow that broke her heart. One by one, they were forced below deck.

This ship, although larger, wasn't much nicer than the *Angelfish*. While her eyes were adjusting, Robin tripped on debris strewn on the floor. Her hands landed on a board, and she tried to rub the musk of rotten fish and urine off her scratched palms, but no luck. At the end of the open deck, they were led into a narrow corridor that opened wide. Iron bars crossed the space. The brig. A jail.

Swallowing a thick lump in her throat, Robin, Riley, and the crew were shoved inside, and the gate screamed as it was dragged shut.

The soldiers left them alone.

Robin rushed to Riley's side, and he embraced her.

"Well, what a bugger to be back in here," William Price said, sitting down with his back against the bulwark.

"At least they didn't chain us to the wall," Buckley said, joining him.

"True," Price said. "I admit, the company is more agreeable this time around."

"There's not much we can do now," McKee said. "This warship is crawling with armed soldiers. We have a dozen useless pistols and half a dozen cutlasses between us."

That answered that question. Their pistols were paperweights.

"And we're locked behind bars," Cantu said, sitting on the other side of Price.

"Even if we escaped this ship, where are we going to go? The fort won't welcome us," Hodgens said, joining them.

"I daresay Hodgens is right," Giles added.

"And most of the crew is lost," Cantu said solemnly. "Randall, Vallo, Green, Watts, Gunner, Bauer…"

"I can't shed a tear for Vallo or Green, but you're right, Cantu. This is hopeless. We shouldn't have come for the treasure," Karl said. "Even if the tide rolls out, and we somehow patch the damage to the ship, we lost the mast. There's no coming back from that."

"Assuming we can escape," Giles said solemnly.

"A stupid gamble," Buckley said, sitting against the wall and leaning back. "And after all we survived, Spain's noose will be the end of us. A damned shame. A horrible nightmare. We pressed our luck one too many times. I just hope it's fast, and they do right by our bodies."

Captain Riley pulled away from her embrace. He gazed into her eyes to emphasize his seriousness. "You heard them. You must go."

The remaining crew all lined up on the floor like prisoners awaiting death row. Resigned. The fight had left, but they stared at her with curiosity.

"I can't. I threw my necklace," she said.

Riley reached behind the layers of his wet clothing and pulled the necklace off his head. He placed it in the palm of her hand. "Go."

Tears sprung to her eyes. How could he ask this of her? Leaving now meant he would die. She couldn't live with herself if she couldn't save him. Robin shook her head.

"Go now, I insist. We cannot survive this. I can't let you die when you don't have to." Riley's eyes shimmered with pain, and he sniffled.

"I…I can't go. You're still not safe."

Riley shook her shoulders, anger and tears sending the painful words pouring from his desperate lips. "Your mother's death wasn't your fault, and your colleague's wasn't either. None of this is your fault. You can't save everyone. Understand? You can't. And certainly not us."

Robin sobbed and looked at the amethyst in her palm. Slipping it over her head meant she could go home. What did she have back home for her to return to? Her mom had been murdered. Her father had never been in her life. She'd quit her job. Her apartment was cold and quiet. All she had were Emily Porter and Angela Foxe, but they loved each other, and although they would miss her, they would cry, and eventually they'd move on.

All she wanted was here—Captain Noah Riley. She wouldn't leave him. Not like this. Gripping the necklace tight she flung it away.

But Riley caught it before it went through the bars. In a flash, he opened the chain and pushed it over her head.

Chapter 26

Riley sniffled with relief. Robin was finally safe. He was going to miss her terribly, but the bright side was his pain wouldn't last long. Delgado's hatred ran deep, and his patience had been thin for a long time. Riley dashed the flowing tears from his eyes, no longer concerned over his crew's judgment. Buckley and McKee approached and patted him on the back in support.

"If it's any consolation, I think getting married is a terrible idea," William Price said casually.

The three of them glared at Price.

"What? Think of it—one woman for the rest of your days? One who is always there. Takes up half your sheets. Nags about the laundry. What's so bloody wonderful about that?"

"Says the man whose only experience with women came with a menu," McKee said. "Those negative factors are not negatives at all once you know what married life is like."

"Were you married?" Price asked, skeptical.

"My brother is," McKee said, "and he says it's the greatest thing ever."

"Was his wife nearby when he said it?" Price asked.

McKee paused, thoughts visible on his face. "Well, yea."

Price smiled in self-satisfaction. "Then that means he would've hidden his honesty. Getting in trouble with the missus, I have experience with, and a man will do anything to avoid it."

"Are you telling us Henry is miserable? Your own brother?" Cantu asked.

Price shrugged. "The man has a record for doing foolish things. His case is not a valid point."

Buckley chuckled. "Marrying is not for me either. I love my freedom, but if this was how my life was going to end, in a prison cell with you lot, I think I'd take a warm bed and a naked woman instead, even if she complains about the laundry."

"I'm married," Hodgens said quietly.

Everyone's brows rose.

"You never mentioned her," McKee said.

"No one asked."

That explained why he declined to partake at the brothel.

"What about you, Riley? You're awfully quiet over there," Price said with a sly grin.

Riley raked a hand through his sticky locks. A wistful smile tugged at his lips. "Pretending to be married was both the hardest and easier thing I've ever done. Easiest because Robin was simply perfection. The dawn of my morning, the ray of sunshine in my day, the sensual radiance of my nights. But having to say goodbye, having the swallow the fact that it was fake... I don't know if I'll recover."

"Regular poet over here." Price scoffed, but with a tone of playfulness.

McKee and Cantu made noises of happiness, and heat rose on Riley's throat and cheeks.

Footsteps approached, and all heads turned. More crew were brought down and shoved into the cell. Riley acknowledged each man and watched the soldiers retreat. The *Angelfish* survivors numbered a dozen—fifteen—survivors. A grim total which mattered not at all, since in turn, they'd all be hung.

Captain Riley greeted each man—each man who knew how to swim.

More footsteps approached. If they could get their numbers high enough, there was a chance to fight back. Hopeful, Riley maneuvered through his growing crowd and gripped the iron bars.

Vallo.

And he was unaccompanied.

Riley squeezed the cold iron until his knuckles blanched. "Why am I not surprised?"

The rest of the crew filled in around him. The murmurs began as they realized they'd elected a traitor as the quartermaster.

Vallo smirked. "I outright showed you who I was, but you gave me the benefit of the doubt. For that you are either too trusting or simply foolish. Since you pulled off the raid on Fort James, I've been leaning toward the former. And now that mistake will cost you and your crew a trip to gallows, where you belong," Vallo added.

Riley gritted his teeth. "Let me out and fight me. A proper challenge. A duel of swords. Then we'll see who belongs where."

Vallo laughed. "Unlike you cretins, I don't follow any rules or codes. I do what I must, a pure survival instinct, which clearly you lack."

Riley shook the bars and roared uselessly. Men around him drew their swords as a visual threat.

Vallo stepped back, a broad grin splitting his face. The traitor turned away and said over his shoulder, "Next time I see you, I'll wave to your swinging body."

Riley hit the bars with his open palm, frustration on the verge of breaking him. "If only we could get out of here. I don't care if we can't take them all. I want Vallo. Let me kill Vallo, that traitorous snake."

The previous captain, Henry Price, had warned Riley about Vallo. Although he took the man's warnings seriously, the traitor hadn't shown any sign he'd returned to his devious ways once on board, and Riley had been desperate for knowledgeable hands on deck.

Now he and the crew were paying for it.

"If only we could escape." William Price rubbed at his jaw. "I did get out of here once. Why not again?"

Everyone watched the armorer pull a pin from his pocket. "A woman gave me this handy tool, and since it worked last time, I was inclined to hold on to it. Surely she's forgiven my thievery by now." He climbed to his feet and pushed the pin into the lock, working the tumblers with the tip of his tongue sticking out. One by one, he lined them up, and the gate swung free with a loud squeak.

"They would've heard that," Riley said. "We must be swift. Single file, swords and pistols at the ready, but don't count on your shot working if it's still wet. When we get to the main deck, spread out. I'm going for Vallo first."

"I want Delgado," Price said darkly.

"Everyone else is fair game," Riley added. "It's been an honor sailing with you fine men. Just know whatever happens, I have no regrets."

Especially not about Robin. He wanted to be with her more than anything, but he couldn't stomach her joining him in this fight—one he knew was lost before it began.

ROBIN BLINKED. TWICE. THREE times. Something was wrong with her eyes. She turned in place. The festival. She was at the Tall Ships festival, surrounded by people enjoying themselves. Under her feet was grass. Robin sunk to her knees and touched the green blades. It was real, wasn't it? This was real?

"Hey, lady, nice outfit. Where'd you get it?"

Robin looked up and shielded her eyes from the sun. A man with admiring eyes wearing a polyester bagged costume and an imitation hat stood before her, holding a disposable soft drink. He carefully admired her worn—authentic—dress.

She really had been in the past. It was all real. The sexy captain, the magic necklace, the fort's raid of silver and wine, the sinking *Angelfish*, their capture by the Spanish captain.

But now she was here. Alone.

"Lady?"

Robin stood and dusted off her knees. "I...I made it."

The stranger smiled. "Awesome work. Looks real."

"Thanks."

He sipped from the straw and walked off.

Where were Emily and Angela? Robin dug in her purse and checked her phone. The screen was black. Saltwater fried it—before or after the battery died? Didn't matter. She dropped it back in and scanned the grounds for familiar faces. None. Her friends weren't here.

Robin dug back into the crusty layers of her ruined purse and fisted her keys. She climbed the small hill to the parking lot, desperate for a shower. Her fob didn't work. With a sigh, Robin manually unlocked her car, started it up, and drove home with shaky hands.

Dropping her purse on the coffee table, Robin stripped away the salty rough layers as she walked to the bathroom. She removed the necklace and set it on the sink vanity. In the mirror, her face was drawn with worry. Lines creased the corners of her eyes. Dirt smudged her face. She looked like she got lost camping for weeks. Felt like it, too.

Robin turned on the water, waited for the heat to reach her fingers, and fired up the shower head. She ducked inside and groaned with hot water gliding down her sore body. For several minutes she stood there, water washing away all evidence of...Captain Noah Riley.

The man, who'd appeared on the festival grounds as a disheveled homeless man in the throes of a mental breakdown, turned out to be a man who'd traveled three hundred years into the future. Robin's lips lifted at the memory. If that happened to her, she'd panic just the same.

But she went to the past. Where the panicked homeless man was a leader of a crew of thieves who respected none other than their captain and quartermaster and the rules they agreed to live by. And yet, Riley was still sweet, thoughtful, and more capable of having a heart than most men she'd met.

And they were two worlds apart.

Robin lathered up and paused. Around her finger was Riley's gold ring. His fake proposal for his fake marriage. Tears filled her eyes, but in the privacy of her shower, she didn't care. Sobbing, Robin washed her hair and body.

After turning off the water, drying herself, and getting dressed—in a fresh pair of skinny jeans and a clean T-shirt, she stopped at her mom's photo. She missed her mom. Robin touched the frame, and the gold ring around her finger glinted.

Riley's words returned to her mind. *Your mother's death wasn't your fault.* Robin smiled. He was right. He helped her through the painful truth, to see what she'd been afraid to see. The burglar was to blame for her mom's death, and the bank shooter killed Officer Clark Thompson. Robin wasn't the one hurting people, regardless of her ability to act.

Riley was amazing.

With a sad smile, Robin lifted the frame and sat on the bed. "Hi, Mom. I'm sorry I couldn't save you." She sniffled and sighed, pushing the words out with all her might. "I was young and scared, but it wasn't me who hurt you. A stupid, selfish act by a complete stranger took you from me. You motivated me to do better, to be better. I am who I am because of you, even if it took the encouragement of a...pirate to help me see it." Robin's lips lifted gently. "You'll always live on in my heart, but I have to let you go. I love you."

She set the frame back on her end table and rubbed her thumb along the tiny urn. All goodbyes, no matter how late they were, still hurt.

Robin stood and collected a clean purse from her closet and took another handful of spare magazines. From the crusty purse, she tossed her useless phone away and inspected her Glock. Damp, but still fully functional. Extra magazines intact. She transferred her useful weapons into her clean purse.

In the bathroom, she took a spare roll of toilet paper and her menstrual cup and crammed them in next. With a smirk to herself in the mirror, she gripped the magic necklace.

Riley was right about everything.

Except she was going to save him, because her test wasn't complete, and she loved that stubborn man with an amazing tongue.

Robin slipped the necklace over her head.

Chapter 27

Riley rose high enough on the final ladder of the warship to see what awaited grim scene they were headed into. He held his fist in the air, ready to signal the fateful charge.

He counted approximately two dozen on the deck performing various duties. A pair of soldiers were setting up what was meant to be a gallows over the boom. Captain Price had told Riley the details of their previous battle with Delgado. It appeared the Spaniard captain intended to finish the task he'd begun all that time ago.

Vallo sat in a chair, the enemy captain's pet, watching the construction and assembly of the gallows.

Captain Riley gritted his teeth.

Capitán Delgado was issuing orders to a man with a pad of papers. The soldiers appeared busy, distracted, and now was their best chance. Riley whispered to himself, picturing Robin's radiant smile, "Someday, in another life, we shall be together again. I will be waiting."

Riley signaled.

He went first, as silent as possible to give all his men the best chance to fight back before the slaughter began. When the soldiers turned their attention, he yelled a startling battle charge. The rest of the crew chimed in, attempting to distract and disorient the soldiers further.

Delgado shouted his own orders and swords clashed. Pistols fired. Clouds of gunpowder obscured the deck.

Riley headed straight to Vallo, whose face turned a shade of ashen. The man stood, drew his own sword and parried Riley's vicious downward swing. Vallo gritted his teeth under the strain, and Riley gritted his teeth against the agony of his injured shoulder.

"You think you're so witty," Vallo said.

"Not witty. Determined to seek justice."

At once, Vallo fell backward and rolled, and Riley stumbled forward from the surprising loss of resistance. The traitor leaped to his feet, smirked, and circled.

Vallo wasn't going to be an easy opponent.

IN THE BLINK OF an eye, Robin returned to the *Peibo del ler San Francisco,* exactly where she'd left: inside the prison cell bars.

But the cell was empty, and the gate stood open.

Had they already been taken for hanging?

How much time had passed?

Robin rushed across the deck, retracing her previous steps when the soldier had brought her down here. She was only going to sneak a look above deck. If at any point the crew was gone and the soldiers were around, she'd use the necklace's power one final time, and somehow survive in a world without Riley.

Choking back that terrible thought, Robin gripped the ladder leading to the main deck. She exhaled a deep breath to prepare herself for what could be her worst nightmare. Gunshots and clashing swords pulled her from the gruesome visual. Robin popped her head up to find the gruesome visual was real.

Pirates were down.

Too many.

The *Angelfish* crew was going to lose, but where was Riley?

Robin climbed up and retrieved her loaded Glock. Men fought all around her, so distracted and busy, none bothered her—if they noticed at all. Robin leveled her Glock, cupping it with both hands. Her hands shook while she searched the carnage for Riley.

Near the stern, Riley was engaged with one of his own crew. Both men were sliced and bleeding. They panted heavily. Vallo—she remembered, who'd been nice to her—stepped forward with his sword raised. Riley stepped back and tripped on a body. He went down. Vallo was going to kill Riley.

Why hadn't Robin been able to squeeze the trigger before? She couldn't choose to end a person's life during a deep spiral, a cry for help. In her mind, she'd always justified the bad guys' behavior, pitied them even. As if a lightbulb flicked on in her mind, Robin figured out the secret. Who needed a department shrink when you had a pirate captain whose life was always hanging in the balance?

As Riley had explained, her mom's and her colleague's deaths weren't her fault. The home invader and Mr. Sean Coulder were at fault. Their actions directly led to their own deaths, and they weren't to be pitied. Their actions weren't to be justified.

Instead of focusing on whether she could be judge, jury, or executioner, she needed to focus on the innocent. Robin would do whatever it took to save those she cared about...to save the man she loved. Because Robin could not live in a world without Captain Noah Riley.

This time, failure was not an option. Robin was not jelly.

Robin aimed her Glock, hands calming down. She moved the barrel until the traitor was between her sights. Robin took up the trigger slack. Breathe in. Breathe out. Now or never. This wasn't a judgment call on a stranger; she was protecting the man she loved. Tensing her arms, she squeezed off a round right between his eyes.

Vallo fell like a wet sponge. Robin rushed over to Riley, who searched the area with surprise.

She kneeled beside him. "Are you okay?"

Riley locked eyes with her. "What are you doing here? I sent you away. For your own good I need you to live."

Robin smiled. "Likewise."

"What killed Vallo?"

Robin waved her Glock.

"That thing works?" Riley asked.

"It does. Do you want me to help the crew or sit here and chat?"

"Do what you can, because otherwise, we're going to lose." Riley climbed to his feet and shook out his shoulders.

Whatever wounds Riley had needed to wait. "Stay here for a minute. Please?" she begged.

Riley still panted from his fight. He nodded, likely happy for a moment's rest before engaging again.

Robin lifted the gun and repeated her relaxing mantra. Breathe in. Breathe out. Now or never. This time, she only pictured Riley's smiling face. She did this for him.

Aiming at each enemy attacking her allies, she squeezed off round after round. Between the eyes. Center of the chest. A couple she had to aim for a thigh but injured was better than not.

Out of ammo. Robin ejected the mag and reloaded. *Pop, pop, pop.* Again and again until she emptied another. And another. Empty mags rattled to the deck.

Robin swiveled her sight, dropping every enemy soldier on the deck.

She paused at the Spaniard captain, whose wide, worried eyes scanned the deck.

Pirates panted, relaxed their swords, and stared at her with wild eyes.

"I'd like one of those," Riley said, gesturing to her gun. "The accuracy is impressive."

Robin pressed her lips together and said dryly, "Yes, the weapon has precision aiming. Do you want me to take out that guy, too?"

Capitán Delgado raised his hands. He was the only Spaniard left standing. A couple injured men groaned on the deck. Bodies littered the surface from both sides.

Riley gently pressed her barrel down. "Let me handle him."

Robin nodded, and Riley crossed the deck. He paused halfway and took something off a man and put it in his mouth. A whistle. He blew long and hard, signaling the battle had ended. Was he telling the other pirates the ship was safe?

Riley reached the enemy captain. Robin trained her Glock on him, just in case.

An injured man nearby climbed to his feet and rushed Riley.

Chapter 28

Riley couldn't believe Robin was able to beat an entire company of Spaniard soldiers single-handedly. If he hadn't seen it with his own eyes, he'd never believe it. Only now did he believe Henry Price's story about Angela's feats.

Riley owed Robin endless praise and appreciation. First, for too long *Capitán* Delgado had plagued Riley's crew, and after all this time, Riley was going to end it.

"Courtesy of one happily retired Captain Henry Price," Riley said, and reeled his arm back for the fatal strike.

Delgado curled up on the deck, covering his head in fear, but a hand blocked Riley's attack.

"I've been fighting this weasel since the battle began. I'm not giving up now," William Price said, wiping blood from his mouth and breathing heavily.

Riley nodded. "If you should fail, fear not. Robin will level him as she did all the other enemies on board."

Price looked around, as if seeing the battle's end for the first time. His eyes opened wide. "She did this?"

"Yea."

Delgado, unarmed, glanced between them as they conversed, as if deciding who the fatal attack would come from, but with no soldiers to back him up, he was too afraid to make a move.

Price lowered a hand on Riley's undamaged shoulder. "This once, I suppose I retract my statement of marriage. She's as fearless and strong as any other pirate. If I had to choose a woman, one like her would satisfy my whims. Don't let that one get away."

"Or what? You'll scoop her up from under me?"

William Price snorted a laugh. "Now don't be ridiculous. I gave you words of encouragement; I'm firm on my bachelorhood remaining intact." Price crossed himself in prayer.

"I thought you didn't believe," Riley said, amused at his movements from head to heart and shoulder to shoulder.

"When serious matters threaten one's livelihood, one can never be too careful."

Riley laughed and glanced over his shoulder at Robin, who helped survivors to their feet. Warmth filled his chest. He hoped she'd stay this time.

Price picked up a sword, and Delgado cried out, "Allow me to defend myself in a fair fight."

"You held me prisoner in that hold for months, and you had the gall to try it a second time. There will be no third, and you don't deserve the honor of fairness." Price plunged the sword into the Spaniard's chest, piercing just below the ribcage.

Delgado's mouth dropped open, and his face pinched in pain. He crumpled over, dragging in shallow breaths.

Price threw the sword away and pulled Riley into a hug. Emotion clogged his voice. "It's over. It's finally over."

"Henry would be proud," Riley said, and Price sobbed in his shoulder.

Riley held the broken armorer and caught another glance at Robin. She helped Hodgens to his feet, and the helmsman gestures of rejecting further assistance, assuring her he was fine. She helped Cantu stand next, and the large man pulled Robin into a bear hug. Their appreciation brought tears to Riley's eyes.

More pirates dropped over the rail to the deck and started assisting those who'd fallen.

Where was Buckley?

Riley pulled back from his friend. "He can't harm anyone again. Let's help the others."

William Price nodded and swiped away tears.

ROBIN NO LONGER NEEDED her Glock, which was great, because she only had a couple shots left. She'd found a man moaning nearby, and her instincts to save people reignited. Grateful for her jeans and T-shirt, she nimbly searched the deck for pirates, helping them to their feet, and for those who were too injured to stand, she tore off bits of their clothes to tie knots over bleeding wounds.

In her element, she canvassed the deck, triaging and assisting the downed men. Several who'd been hurt but were still lucid enough to watch the battle unfold offered their thanks for her most unusual weapon. One asked if she was a spy. She assured him she was not, but Robin had a feeling he didn't believe her.

One man lifted a hand for assistance, and Robin kneeled at his side.

Buckley.

"It's over. Anything hurt?" she asked.

He was bleeding all over, and one eye was swollen shut, but with her question, Buckley chuckled. The sound was thick and wet. "Noah Riley christened our new ship the *Angelfish*. I didn't realize an angel would be sent in reward."

His functional eye swept over her modern clothes. "Thank you, angel. Regardless of where that power comes from, thank you so much. I get to say goodbye after an honorable fight to the end, rather than a shameful hanging by the enemy."

A syrupy gasp made Robin wince, and tears stung her eyes.

"And I want you...to tell Riley...he's the best captain a pirate could ask for. Tell Price...to find himself a woman; it's not a terrible way to live. And for you, my dear, thank you for returning to us and saving the crew. I'll never see the future, but I have hope for you all."

Tears flooded Robin's eyelids and slid down her cheeks.

"And Robin?" he added.

She gripped his hand in comfort and he gasped again.

"Marry that man...for real this time."

Robin smiled, and a sob escaped her lips. Buckley gasped again, and his clear eye closed. His chest stilled.

A hand landed on her shoulder, and Robin looked up to see Riley. She set Buckley's hand down on his chest and stood. She fell into Riley's arms, and he hugged her tightly.

"Buckley's gone," she said, sobbing.

Riley didn't answer. He held her until she composed herself. She leaned back and sniffled. "He said you're the best captain he had, and that Price needs to find a woman."

Riley chuckled and sniffled. "Did he say anything else?"

Robin couldn't bring herself to push the captain into something he didn't want. She'd served her purpose. She'd posed as his wife to capture a treasure and saved the crew from the consequences. She didn't fail. Her work was done. Now Riley could tell her to go home to safety, and she had no logical reason to refuse.

"No, he didn't."

"He's a good man, but he's happy now. All he wanted was an end in glory. We're all happy for him."

"What about the *Angelfish*?" Robin asked, pulling out of his arms, and searching the water's shimmering surface.

"It's lost."

Seeing all the bodies pooled on the deck, anger surged through her. "You can't leave that treasure. Too many people died for it. You can't let it sit there and go to waste."

"It's over," he said, holding her hands. "It's finally over."

When she thought of her future, all she could picture was her secure in Riley's arms, but as he said, it was over. She'd fulfilled all but one promise. She'd promised to return home after Riley was safe.

With a shaky deep breath, Robin tugged his ring off her finger. "You can have this back then."

Riley stared at it.

Behind them, bright daylight showed the survivors cleaning up the deck and removing bodies by tossing them over. Blood coated the slick surface. Robin trembled with her receding adrenaline. Only about twenty men survived the sinking and the battle.

"I want you to keep it," Riley said, closing her fingers around it.

"I can't keep your family's ring," Robin said, urging him to take it.

"My wife wears my ring."

Robin stared at him. His eyes glistened with tears, and his lips pulled into a tender smile.

Her mouth opened, but before she could answer, Riley added, "For years I couldn't see a future. I was reckless, foolish, hoping a captain followed a dangerous hunt for the chance to end my life honorably, so I could return to my betrothed—only because I didn't know real happiness. Now I look into the future, and all I see is you. In the same breath you can save my life and kill my enemy. You helped my men when they didn't deserve it. And you returned to me. From the safety of your home, you came back to me. I want you to be my wife."

"I...I..." Robin couldn't catch her breath.

"I love you," Riley said. "I love you so much I can't live without you. Marry me."

Robin removed the magic amethyst from around her neck. She fisted it while Riley watched with worry on his brow. Shades of purple reflected the sunlight, a beautiful gem, simply stunning. Robin sighed. Such a waste. On a deep breath, she heaved the necklace over the rail. It soared and splashed, never to be found again.

Hope reached his eyes, and Robin smiled. "Yes, of course, I'll marry you. For real this time. I love you, Captain Riley."

He took the gold ring from her. With careful hands, he replaced the ring back where it belonged. "It's Noah. You've earned that right, my love, my Robin." Riley beamed and broke into a joyful song and held her hand up as if to begin a dance.

The cleanup crew paused to watch their mini celebration, smiles on their faces, and a few added their voices to the choir.

Riley spun Robin on the deck and dipped her low. "I already got my plunder, and I'm not sharing, but these sea dogs need their money." He winked and straightened her upright. Turning over his shoulder, he hollered, "Let's get that treasure, men!"

Robin laughed, and the crew cheered. Robin was home.

Chapter 29

The warship, now renamed the *Neptune*, sailed as close to the *Angelfish* wreck as the draft would allow. The warship's broadside volley had punched massive holes in the hull of their old ship, leaving easy access to the hold. All the survivors on board could swim, except Noah. Most of them took turns collecting a ballast rock, sinking to the treasure chests, and hauling up a handful.

In the meantime, Noah plotted a course, and Giles made dinner. The cook was ecstatic over the Spanish Royalty's galley. And Jack Watts, the new carpenter's mate and Buckley's next in line, managed to survive the sinking. He'd never bothered to climb aboard the warship. Now he fixed the minor holes in *Neptune*'s hull. Surprisingly, the warship was well-stocked with provisions.

Standing before the crew, Captain Noah Riley said, "With recent events, I have decided to step down as your captain. We will head to Hispaniola to allow myself and my wife-to-be to disembark. At which point, you'll need to elect yourselves a new leader. Hodgens, you have your coordinates. Weigh anchor, you sea dogs!" The men scattered to their orders, and Noah added, "Oh, one more thing."

They respectfully stopped to listen.

"If this cabin door is closed, don't open it."

The men laughed and made insinuating calls. Since Robin had saved the crew, all of them accepted her presence.

Wind filled the sails, and the ship moved through the water.

Noah approached her with an open hand. "Come with me."

Robin accepted it and followed him into the cabin, which was much fancier than the *Angelfish*'s. He closed the door behind them and turned to face her. She searched his hungry eyes. Before she could lay a hand on him, his lips stole hers.

Robin caught her breath as they changed positions, and her hands quickly undressed him.

Noah fought with her skinny jeans. Robin chuckled against his lips. "I'll help."

"What blasted material is this? Chastity clothing to keep men away? It certainly works."

Noah watched hungrily as she unbuttoned and unzipped the tight jeans. She wriggled her hips to slide out of the fabric, and Noah pounced on her lips again as if afraid to ever be apart again. She blindly fussed with his tunic, flipping it over his head, and flinging to the floorboards.

Noah's broad hands palmed her torso as he slid her T-shirt up. His fingers paused at her bra. He pulled away from her lips and inspected the lingerie with a sigh. "I say, I like the detail here, but I'd like it even better on the floor."

Robin laughed. "Isn't this easier than corsets or whatever women of this day wore?"

He pulled off her shirt and circled her, assessing her bra. "Indeed. I don't think we need a handmaiden to dress and undress you. I must say I find this smaller undergarment is quite...fetching."

"Quit talking and take it off."

Noah's eyes lit up. "Yes, ma'am. You don't need to ask twice."

He unfastened the hooks at the back, exposing her completely. While he stared, Robin untied his breeches and dropped them to the floor. He stiff cock, along with the rest of her, was happy to see her.

Noah scooped her up and set her on his new bed. "Do you want it fast or slow?"

Robin smiled slyly. "How long until Hispaniola?"
Noah groaned.

Weeks later the Neptune crossed the Atlantic and arrived at a port in Hispaniola. Robin disembarked with Noah Riley at her side, waving goodbye to Boatswain Karl, Giles, Hodgens, Cantu, McKee, Watts, and Price, and many others she hadn't personally met.

After several days, they'd managed to recover two thousand pounds of silver and a few bottles of wine, and since all the troublemakers had perished, Noah asked if the crew wanted to redistribute the silver equally. The survivors agreed unanimously, and no one complained about Noah and Robin each getting a share.

To her, it didn't seem like much, but Noah assured her it was a lifetime's worth of money. After a stop at a bank to deposit their shares, she and Noah took a carriage up a dirt road outside of town.

Besides ample provisions, the warship also had very fine clothing. Robin had dressed in a white and gold lacy top and a glossy-sheened full skirt with decorative green satin, which complemented her red hair perfectly.

Noah had dressed in an ivory tunic, a matching green vest, and to top it off, he wore a gold coat with tails. Brown breeches and an ivory cravat finished the look. He tied his hair back with a gold ribbon. Robin left her locks tumbling over her shoulders and down her back. They looked like royalty. And Robin felt like it.

At the top of a hill overlooking the ocean was a fancy two-story plantation with a sprawling front lawn. It was beautiful.

"Who lives here?" Robin asked, holding his hand. They followed the curving driveway and climbed the porch steps.

"Someone I want you to meet. I sent a message ahead. We won't be the only visitors."

Dinner party with Noah's friends? Robin was excited but very nervous. She didn't know he had any.

Noah knocked on the door, and they were promptly greeted by a woman in a dress, apron, and bonnet. She politely led them inside. The air was the same temperature as outside—hot and humid. Plants were artfully placed around the lobby, and a sparkly candle chandelier hung from the ceiling.

Noah continued bringing her deeper inside like he'd been here before. Through a door to the left, two men sat in fancy upholstered chairs with a detailed carving, facing a fireplace. Noah released her arm and walked toward the two men, who promptly stood with smiles on their faces. Noah hugged each man and faced her, beaming with joy.

Robin didn't recognize them.

Noah gestured for her to come closer. "Robin, I want you to meet Eric and Henry, my two good friends."

Robin smiled and approached. She held out her hand to shake, but each man kissed her knuckles. Sweet, but something she would have to get used to.

Movement out of the corner of her eye caught her attention. Two women in extravagant gowns stood with smiles of their own. Robin squinted. The faces didn't match the clothing.

"Robin!" Angela called.

"You're here!" Emily said, holding out her arms.

Robin stared dumbfounded. She said the first thing that popped into her head, "Neither of you answered my texts."

Her friends laughed and gestured for her to come closer. Robin was embraced by the warmth of her best friends, and she dashed away her tears. Noah was her home, but with her friends, she was whole.

"How did you get here?" Robin asked. "I mean, I know how, but like, how?"

Emily chuckled. "The necklace brought me to the *Sea Lion*, where I met Eric." Catching his name, Eric smiled, bowed, and said a phrase in French. "He thought I was a man most of the time he knew me, but we worked it out." Emily winked at him.

"*Sea Lion* for me too," Angela said, "until it sank, but the new ship had been renamed the *Angelfish* after we left. We were stranded in Cuba for a while. Camping took on a whole new meaning, and I'm perfectly happy to never step foot in sand again."

"Seems like the ship was named after you," Robin noted.

"It was," Henry said, catching his name next. "No one else deserved the honor." Henry gazed lovingly at Angela before returning to the men's conversation.

"What's your story, Robin?" Emily asked.

"I landed on the *Angelfish* and we raided a fort in Africa."

The men's conversation stopped so they could listen.

"We would've got away unscathed had Vallo not told *Capitán* Delgado where we were going."

"That blasted imbecile!" Henry shouted in frustration. "I warned you about Vallo, Riley. I warned you. What damage did the traitor do this time?"

"You did warn me, but he's dead now. So is Delgado. In fact, your dear brother killed Delgado."

"Good for him," Henry said gruffly. "My brother deserved that chance. I presume he lives? What of the soldiers, and the ship?"

"William Price is wealthy, well, and as we speak on his way with the crew back to Nassau, where I expect he will find the bottom of several bottles and a few whores."

Henry made a noise of derision. "That man needs to grow up."

"He's rich now. He can do whatever pleases him," Noah countered. "The crew now owns the *Peibo del ler San Francisco* to continue the account or sell it and break up. I wasn't part of their goings on, and I don't know who they voted to lead next. As much as I care for my fellow men, I have everything I need here." With a wistful smile of pride, Noah added, "Robin killed almost all the soldiers on board." He exchanged a glance with her, and heat rushed up her cheeks at the praise.

"How?" Eric Lemoine asked, brows raised.

"You brought your Glock, didn't you?" Angela answered for her.

Robin slipped it out of her purse. "I have three rounds left, maybe. It's pretty much useless."

Eric and Henry approached and stared at her gun like it was some zoo animal. They made noises of amazement.

"This took down the entire ship of soldiers?" Henry asked, pointing in wonder.

"Just about," Robin said, taking his appreciation as a compliment of her skills and not the weapon itself.

"Well then, it deserves a place of honor. Mount it above the fireplace," Henry said.

"It's not a trophy," Robin said, putting it back in her purse.

"It is. It truly is," Eric said and sat down with a hand pressed against his forehead.

"The warship is now the *Neptune*, in case you should come across that name," Noah said.

"Who has fallen?" Henry asked, joining his friend in an adjacent chair. Both men appeared overwhelmed with the news.

Robin's friends sat on a couch, dresses splayed around them. Eric gestured for Noah and Robin to sit and join them, and Noah took her hand. They sat on the couch next to each other.

"From the original crew, we lost Buckley. He went down swinging and died a happy man," Noah said.

"Good for him," Eric said. "He found peace."

As did Robin. Peace in knowing a unicorn existed, that there was happiness out there for her, and sometimes things had a way of working out okay. Robin squeezed Noah's hand.

The woman who'd greeted them at the door brought in tea and biscuits. Robin thanked her profusely before her friends educated her on proper etiquette. Getting used to the food would take time, but clearly her friends handled it fine. The clothing was another obstacle altogether. Noah's wild world was foreign to her, but if the only way she could have him was to survive it, she would. She'd do anything for him.

Catching up took hours and promises of regular visits were made on all sides. And Robin intended to keep every one of them. They waved goodbye to their friends, and Robin stopped Noah on the driveway.

She whispered into his ear, "Thank you. You've given me the world, and I love you so much."

Noah beamed with pride. "And if I hadn't met you, I wouldn't be here, so you've given me a reason to live. Let's get out of here."

After a very passionate kiss in full view of the house, they organized a wedding on Hispaniola for their friends to attend. They married, and Robin slept soundly, knowing those she loved were safe and happy.

Epilogue

As the Tall Ships festival wound down on a late Sunday evening, customers scattered from the vendor tables. Vendors packed up and took down their tents. The ships were preparing for a voyage to their next port of call, and a cleaning crew picked up the strewn litter.

Chaos strolled the lawn, taking in the sights. Every place he stopped still interested him, even after all these millennia. How humanity changed from one decade to the next was remarkable. How it changed through the centuries was shocking, but still, over the thousands of years, the changes entertained him greatly.

But he lived for it. He was Chaos.

If for no other reason than humanity would suffer worse at the hands of his brother, Order. That was some dystopian dysfunction. The two of them never saw eye-to-eye. So long as Chaos retained his preternatural form, he'd continue the fight to keep humans enjoying the life they chose, and there was no better way than making these silly humans fall in love.

Order hated that.

And Chaos loved it. And when humanity debated the concept of free will, Chaos pulled up a chair and grabbed popcorn.

He arrived at this particular time for a reason. Chaos stopped at a special vendor's table and watched Esther Brumley gather her wares before interrupting. He'd recruited her about ninety years ago. Without him, she would've passed from cancer. Instead, she lived a long life matchmaking couples through time. She appreciated it, because she'd called upon him each year and gifted him a fruit basket. What more could say 'thank you' than that?

"Are we all set then, kid?" Chaos asked his love curator.

Esther's thin, saggy arms dropped to her sides as she looked up and smiled. "Hi, boss. I'm still packing. I need a little more time before I'll be ready for my next assignment."

Chaos checked his watch. "Actually, that's perfect. I need to jump over to Milwaukee, nineteen-eighty-something."

"Recruiting another agent?"

"Kiko Takai. Had her heart torn out. She's going to need, oh...about a hundred years to heal the damage."

"Poor girl."

"Yeah, and she's much younger than I usually prefer, so this meeting could take a while. Good thing you won't notice."

Esther rolled her eyes. "Time jokes never end, do they?"

Chaos chuckled at her criticism and her pun. She was clever. "I'll be back when you're ready."

Esther nodded her understanding, and Chaos disappeared on a blink to find his next agent, currently shuffling through life in despair and cradling a knife in fear.

Chaos was the only one who could help.

He'd seen it.

Amended Special Note:

While the events of this novel are fiction, the pirate raid
on Gambia Castle, *where 2,000 pounds of silver and all the
alcohol were taken without a shot fired,* was real, performed
by Captain Howell Davis in 1718.
Also, the *San Francisco* was a real Spanish warship that had
been captured by pirates and renamed *Neptune* by Dutch
pirate Laurens de Graaf.

Dear Reader,

THAT'S THE END OF the Pirates in Time series. I hope you loved the
swashbuckling adventure as much as I do! Looking for similar but
without the pirates? Check out my Matchmaker in Time series. How
about vampires? I've got the Immortal Protector series, too. Find them
and more at StephanieFlynn.com.

As an indie author, I'm thrilled you decided to share your time with
me, exploring the crazy worlds residing in my head and keeping me up at
night. Your reviews are very important to me, so if you enjoyed this book,
please consider leaving some stars for **The Pirates in Time Complete
Trilogy!**

If you found any typos or errors, I blame my cat. Rat her out at:
support@stephanieflynn.com.

Thank you for your support!

Also By Stephanie Flynn

Find my catalog at StephanieFlynn.com

Immortal Protector series

0.5 Vampire's Distraction

1 Vampire's Deception

2 Vampire's Secret

3 Vampire's Promise

3.5 Elf Bound

4 Vampire's Demand

5 Vampire's Destruction

6 Vampire's Conquest

Immortal Protector Side Tales

Deer Holiday

Love Claws

Depths of the Heart

Matchmaker in Time series

0.5 Minutes to Live

1 Seconds to Act

2 Hours to Arrive

3 Days to Hide

4 Years to Savor

Pirates in Time series

1 Pirate's Prize

2 Pirate's Treasure

3 Pirate's Plunder

Time Travel Romance Shorts

Fateful Time

One Crazy Time

If you like your urban fantasy without the romance, too, check out Stephanie Flynn's other name, Marie Flynn!

About Stephanie Flynn

Stephanie Flynn writes action-packed paranormal romance filled with adventure, suspense, and danger. She lives in Michigan, USA, with her husband and kids, and she spends her writing time surrounded by a herd of normal cats who bat everything off her desk, including her coffee. Check out her website for more books: StephanieFlynn.com